Titles in the Garrett, P.I., Series

GARRETT TAKES THE CASE

•Old Tin Sorrows•

•Dread Brass Shadows•

•Red Iron Nights•

GLEN COOK

A ROC BOOK

ROC
Published by New American Library, a division of
Penguin Group (USA) Inc., 375 Hudson Street,
New York, New York 10014, USA
Penguin Group (Canada), 90 Eglinton Avenue East, Suite 700, Toronto,
Ontario M4P 2Y3, Canada (a division of Pearson Penguin Canada Inc.)
Penguin Books Ltd., 80 Strand, London WC2R 0RL, England
Penguin Ireland, 25 St. Stephen's Green, Dublin 2,
Ireland (a division of Penguin Books Ltd.)
Penguin Group (Australia), 250 Camberwell Road, Camberwell, Victoria 3124,
Australia (a division of Pearson Australia Group Pty. Ltd.)
Penguin Books India Pvt. Ltd., 11 Community Centre, Panchsheel Park,
New Delhi - 110 017, India
Penguin Group (NZ), 67 Apollo Drive, Rosedale, Auckland 0632,
New Zealand (a division of Pearson New Zealand Ltd.)
Penguin Books (South Africa) (Pty.) Ltd., 24 Sturdee Avenue,
Rosebank, Johannesburg 2196, South Africa

Penguin Books Ltd., Registered Offices:
80 Strand, London WC2R 0RL, England

Published by Roc, an imprint of New American Library, a division of Penguin Group (USA) Inc. *Old Tin Sorrows*,
Dread Brass Shadows, and *Red Iron Nights* were previously published individually in Roc editions.

First Roc Trade Paperback Printing, February 2012

Old Tin Sorrows copyright © Glen Cook, 1989
Dread Brass Shadows copyright © Glen Cook, 1990
Red Iron Nights copyright © Glen Cook, 1991
All rights reserved

Set in Minion
Designed by Ginger Legato

GARRETT TAKES THE CASE

•••Old Tin Sorrows

Just when you think you have it all scoped out and you're riding high, old Fate will stampede right over you and not even stop to say I'm sorry. Happens every time if your name is Garrett. You can make book on it.

I'm Garrett. Sitting pretty in my early thirties, over six feet, brown hair, two hundred pounds plus—maybe threatening to shoot up because my favorite food is beer. I have a disposition variously described as sulky, sour, sarky, or cynical. Anything with a sibilant. Sneaky and snaky, my enemies claim. But, hell, I'm a sweetheart. Really. Just a big, old, cuddly bear with a nice smile and soulful eyes.

Don't believe everything you hear. I'm just a realist who suffers from a recurrent tumor of romantic pragmatism. Once upon a time I was a lot more romantic. Then I did my five in the Fleet Marines. That almost snuffed the spark.

Keep that in mind, that time in the Corps. If I hadn't been there, none of this would have happened.

Bone-lazy, Morley would call me, but that's a base canard from a character without the moral fiber to sit still more than five minutes. I'm not lazy; I'd just rather not work if I don't need money. When I do, I operate as a confidential agent. Which means I spend a lot of time in the middle, between people you wouldn't invite to dinner. Kidnappers. Blackmailers. Thugs and thieves and killers.

My, the things kids grow up to be.

It isn't a great life. It won't get me into any history books. But it does let me be my own boss, set my own hours, pick my jobs. It lets me off a lot of hooks. I don't have to make a lot of compromises with my conscience.

Trying not to work when I don't need money means looking through the peephole first when someone knocks on the door of my place on Macunado Street. If whoever is there looks like a prospective client, I simply don't answer.

It was a false spring day early in the year. It was supposed to be winter out there but somebody was nodding. The snow had melted. After six days of unnatural warmth the trees had conned themselves into budding. They'd be sorry.

I hadn't been out since the thaw. I was at my desk reckoning accounts on a couple of minor jobs I'd subcontracted, thinking about taking a walk before cabin fever got me. Then somebody knocked.

It was Dean's day off. I had to do the legwork myself. I went to the door. I peeked. And I was startled. And, brother, was I fooled.

Whenever the big troubles came, the harbinger always wore a skirt and looked like something you couldn't find anywhere but in your dreams. In case that's too subtle, it's like this: I've got a weakness for ripe tomatoes. But I'm learning. Give me about a thousand years and . . .

This wasn't any tomato. This was a guy I'd known a long time ago and never expected to see again. One I hadn't ever wanted to see again when we'd parted. And he just looked uncomfortable out there, not like he was in trouble. So I opened the door.

That was my first mistake.

"Sarge! What're you doing here? How the hell are you?" I shoved a hand at him, something I wouldn't have dared do when I saw him last.

He was twenty years older than me, the same height, twenty pounds lighter. He had skin the color of tanned doeskin, big ears that stuck straight out, wrinkles, small black eyes, black hair with a lot of gray that hadn't been there before. No way to pin down exactly why, but he was one of the ugliest men I'd ever known. He looked damned fit, but he was the kind that would look that way if he lived forever. He stood there like he had a board nailed to his spine.

"I'm fine," he said, and took my hand in a sincere shake. Those beady little eyes went over me like they could see right through me. He'd always had that knack. "You've put on a few pounds."

"On in the middle, off at the top." I tapped my hair. It wasn't noticeable to anyone but me yet. "Come in. What're you doing in TunFaire?"

"I'm retired now. Out of the Corps. I've been hearing a lot about you.

Into some exciting things. I was in the neighborhood. Thought I'd drop in. If you're not busy."

"I'm not. Beer? Come on back to the kitchen." I led the way into Dean's fiefdom. The old boy wasn't there to defend it. "When did you get out?"

"Been out three years, Garrett."

"Yeah? I figured you'd die in harness at a hundred fifty."

His name was Blake Peters. The guys in the company called him Black Pete. He'd been our leading sergeant and the nearest thing to a god or devil any of us had known, the kind of professional soldier that gives an outfit its spine. I couldn't imagine him as a civilian. Three years out? He looked like a Marine sergeant in disguise.

"We all change. I started thinking too much instead of just doing what I was told. The beer isn't bad."

It was damned good. Weider, who owns the brewery, had sent a keg of his special reserve to let me know he appreciated past favors— and to remind me I was still on retainer. I hadn't been around for a while. He was afraid his employees might go into freelance sales again.

"So, what're you doing now?" I was a little uncomfortable. I never had the experience myself—my father died in battle in the Cantard when I was four—but guys have told me they'd felt ill at ease dealing with their fathers man to man when that first happened. Black Pete hadn't ever been a friend; he'd been the sergeant. He wasn't anymore but I didn't know him any other way.

"I'm working for General Stantnor. I was on his staff. When he retired he asked me to go with him. I did it."

I grunted. Stantnor had been a colonel when I was in. He'd been boss of all the Marines operating out of Full Harbor, about two thousand men. I'd never met him, but I'd had plenty to say about him during my stint. Not much of it was complimentary. About the time I'd gotten out he'd become commandant of the whole Corps and had moved to Leifmold, where the Karentine Navy and Marines have their headquarters.

"Job's about the same as it was, but the pay's better," Peters said. "You look like you're doing all right. Own your own place, I hear."

About then I started getting suspicious. It was just a niggling little worm, a whisper. He'd done some homework before he came, which meant he wasn't just stopping in for old time's sake.

"I don't go hungry," I admitted. "But I do worry about tomorrow. About how long the reflexes will last and the mind will stay sharp. The legs aren't what they used to be."

"You need more exercise. You haven't been keeping yourself up. It shows."

I snorted. Another Morley Dotes? "Don't start with the green leafies and red meat. I've already got a fairy godfather to pester me about that."

He looked puzzled, which was some sight on that phiz.

"Sorry. Private joke, sort of. So you're just sort of taking it easy these days, eh?" I hadn't heard Stantnor's name much since he'd retired. I knew he'd come home to TunFaire, to the family estate south of the city, but that was it. He'd become a recluse, ignoring politics and business, the usual pursuits of ranking survivors of the endless Cantard War.

"We haven't had much choice." He sounded sour and looked troubled for a moment. "He planned to go into material contracting, but he took sick. Maybe something he picked up in the islands. Took the fire out of him. He's bedridden most of the time."

Pity. On the plus side of Stantnor's ledger had been the fact that he hadn't sat in an office in Full Harbor spending his troops like markers on a game board. When the big shitstorms hit he was out in the weather with the rest of us.

A pity, and I said so.

"Maybe worse than a pity, Garrett. He's taken a turn for the worse. I think he's dying. And I think somebody is helping him along."

Suspicion became certainty. "You didn't just happen to be in the neighborhood."

He was direct. "No. I'm here to collect."

He didn't have to explain.

There was a time when we'd gotten caught with our pants down on one of the islands. A surprise Venageti invasion nearly wiped us out. We survivors had fled into the swamps and had lived on whatever didn't eat us first while we harrassed the Venageti. Sergeant Peters had brought us through that. I owed him for that.

But I owed him more. He'd carried me away when I'd been injured during a raid. He hadn't had to do it. I couldn't have done anything but lie there waiting for the Venageti to kill me.

He said, "That old man means a lot to me, Garrett. He's the only family I've got. Somebody's killing him slowly, but I can't figure out who or how. I can't stop it. I've never felt this helpless and out of control. So I come to a man who has a reputation for handling the unhandleable."

I didn't want a client. But Garrett pays his debts.

I took a long drink, a deep breath, cursed under my breath. "Tell me about it."

Peters shook his head. "I don't want to fill you up with ideas that didn't work for me."

"Damnit, Sarge . . ."

"Garrett!" He still had the whipcrack voice that got your attention without being raised.

"I'm listening."

"He's got other problems. I've sold him on hiring a specialist to handle them. I've sold him your reputation and my memories of you from the Corps. He'll interview you tomorrow morning. If you remember to knock the horse apples off your shoes before you go in the house, he'll hire you. Do the job he wants done. But while you're at it, do the real job. Got me?"

I nodded. It was screwy but clients are that way. They always want to sneak up on things.

"To everyone else you'll be a hired hand, job unknown, antecedents mostly unknown. You should use another name. You have a certain level of notoriety. The name Garrett might ring a bell."

I sighed. "You make it sound like I might spend a lot of time there."

"I want you to stay till the job is done. I'll need the name you're going to use before I leave or you won't get past the front door."

"Mike Sexton." I plucked it off the top of my head, but it had to be divine inspiration. If a little dangerous.

Mike Sexton had been our company's chief scout. He hadn't come back from that island. Peters had sent him out before a night strike and we'd never seen him again. He'd been Black Pete's main man, his only friend.

Peters's face went hard and cold. His eyes narrowed dangerously. He started to say something. But Black Pete never shot his mouth off without thinking.

He grunted. "It'll work. People have heard me mention the name. I'll explain how we know each other. I don't think I told anybody he's gone."

He wouldn't. He wouldn't brag about his mistakes, even to himself. I'd bet part of him was still waiting for Sexton to report.

"That's the way I figured it."

He downed the last of his beer. "You'll do it?"

"You knew I would before you pounded on the door. I didn't have any choice."

He smiled. It looked out of place on that ugly mug. "I wasn't a hundred percent sure. You were always a stubborn bastard." He took out a worn canvas purse, the same one he'd had back when, fatter than it had been before. He counted out fifty marks. In silver. Which was a statement of sorts.

The price of silver has been shooting up since Glory Mooncalled double-crossed everybody and declared the whole Cantard an independent republic with no welcome for Karentines, Venageti, or what have you.

Silver is the fuel that makes sorcery go. Both Karenta and Venageta sway to the whims of cabals of sorcerers. The biggest, most productive silver mines in the world lie in the Cantard, which is why the ruling gangs have been at war there since my grandfather was a pup. Till the mercenary Glory Mooncalled pulled his stunt.

He's made it stick so far. But I'll be amazed if he keeps it up. He's got everybody pissed and he's right in the middle.

It won't be long before it's war as usual down there.

I opened my mouth to tell Peters he didn't need to pay me. I owed him. But I realized he *did* need to. He was calling in an obligation but not for free. He didn't expect me to work for nothing; he just wanted me to work. And maybe he was paying off something to the General by footing the bill.

"Eight a day and expenses," I told him. "Discount for a friend. I'll kick back if this comes out too much or I'll bill you if I need more." I took the fifty into the Dead Man's room for safekeeping. The Dead Man was hard at what he does best: snoozing. All four hundred plus pounds of him. He'd been at it so long I'd begun to miss his company.

With that thought I decided it *was* time I took a job. Missing the Dead Man's company was like missing the company of an inquisitor.

Peters was ready to go when I got back. "See you in the morning?" he asked. There was a whisper of desperation behind his words.

"I'll be there. Guaranteed."

t was eleven in the morning. They'd roofed the sky with planks of lead. I walked, though the General's hovel was four miles beyond South Gate. Me and horses don't get along.

I wished I'd taken the chance. My pins were letting me know I spend too much time planted on the back of my lap. Then fat raindrops started making coin-sized splats on the road. I wished some more. I was going to get wet if the old man and I didn't hit it off.

I shifted my duffel bag to my other shoulder and tried to hurry. That did all the good it ever does.

I'd bathed and shaved and combed my hair. I had on my best "meet the rich folks" outfit. I figured they'd give me credit for trying and not run me off before they asked my name. I hoped Black Pete was on the level and had left that at the door.

The Stantnor place wasn't exactly a squatter's shanty. I figured maybe a million marks' worth of brick and stone and timber. The grounds wouldn't have had any trouble gobbling the Lost Battalion.

I didn't need a map to find the house but I was lucky. The General had put out a paved private road for me to follow.

The shack was four stories high at the wings and five in the center, in the style called frame half-timber, and it spread out wide enough that I couldn't throw a rock from one corner to the other of the front. I tried. It was a good throw but the stone fell way short.

A fat raindrop got me in the back of the neck. I scampered up a dozen marble steps to the porch. I took a minute to arrange my face so I wouldn't look impressed when somebody answered the door. You want to deal with the rich, you've got to overcome the intimidation factor of wealth.

The door—which would have done a castle proud as a drawbridge—swung in without a sound, maybe a foot. A man looked out. All I could see was his face. I almost asked him what the grease bill was for silencing those monster hinges.

"Yes?"

"Mike Sexton. I'm expected."

"Yes." The face puckered up. Where did he get lemons this time of year?

Maybe he wasn't thrilled to see me, but he did open up and let me into a hallway where you could park a couple of woolly mammoths, if you didn't want to leave them out in the rain. He said, "I'll inform the General that you've arrived, sir." He walked away like they'd shoved a javelin up his back in boot camp, marching to drums only he could hear. Obviously another old Marine like Black Pete.

He was gone awhile. I entertained myself by drifting along the hallway, introducing myself to the Stantnor ancestors, a dozen of whom scowled at me from portraits on the walls. The artists had been selected for their ability to capture their subject's private misery. Every one of those old boys was constipated.

I inventoried three beards, three mustaches, and six clean-shaven. The Stantnor blood was strong. They looked like brothers instead of generations going back to the foundation of the Karentine state. Only their uniforms dated them.

All of them were in uniform or armor. Stantnors had been professional soldiers, sailors, Marines—forever. It was a birthright. Or maybe an obligation, like it or not, which might explain the universal dyspepsia.

The last portrait on the left was the General himself, as commandant of the Corps. He wore a huge, ferocious white mustache and had a faraway look in his eyes, as if he were standing on the poop of a troopship staring at something beyond the horizon. His was the only portrait that hadn't been painted so its subject's eyes followed you when you moved. It was disconcerting, having all those angry old men glaring down. Maybe the portraits were supposed to intimidate upstarts like me.

Opposite the General hung the only portrait of a young man, the General's son, a Marine lieutenant who hadn't developed the family scowl. I didn't recall his name, but did remember him getting killed in the islands while I was in. He'd been the old man's only male offspring. There wouldn't be any more portraits to put up on those dark-paneled walls.

The hall ended in a wall of leaded glass that rose to the hallway's two-story height, a mosaic of scenes from myth and legend, all bloodthirstily executed: heroes slaying dragons, felling giants, posturing atop heaps of elvish corpses while awaiting another charge. All stuff of antiquity, when we humans didn't get along with the other races.

The doors through that partition were normal size, also filled with glass artwork from the same school. The butler, or whatever he was, had left them ajar. I took that as an invitation.

The hall beyond could have been swiped from a cathedral. It was as big as a parade ground and four stories high, all stone, mostly swirly browns from butterscotch to rust folded into cream. The walls were decorated with trophies presumably won by Stantnors in battle. There were enough weapons and banners to outfit a battalion.

The floor was a checkerboard of white marble and green serpentine. In its middle stood a fountain, a hero on a rearing stallion sticking a lance into the heart of a ferocious dragon that looked suspiciously like one of the bigger flying thunder-lizards. Both of them looked like they'd rather be somewhere else. Couldn't say I blamed them. Neither one was going to get out alive. The hero was about one second short of sliding off the horse's behind right into the dragon's claws. The sculptor had said a lot that, undoubtedly, no one understood. I told them, "You two want to scrap over a virgin, you should work a deal."

I headed for the fountain, heels clicking, the walls throwing back echoes. I turned around a few times, taking in the sights. Hallways ran off into the wings. Stairs went up to balconies in front of each of the upper floors. There were lots of polished round brown pillars and legions of echoes. The place couldn't be a home. Only thing I'd ever seen like it was a museum. You had to wonder what went on inside the head of a guy who would want to build a place like that to live.

It was damned near as cold in there as it was outside. I shivered, checked out the fountain up close. It wasn't going, or at least I'd have had its chuckles for company. Seemed a pity. The sound would have improved the atmosphere. Maybe they only turned it on when they were entertaining.

I've always had a soft spot in my heart for the idea of being rich. I guess most people do. But if this was the way the rich had to live, I thought maybe I could settle for less.

My trade has taken me into any number of large homes and every one seemed to have a certain coldness at its heart. The nicest I'd hit belonged to Chodo Contague, TunFaire's emperor of the underworld. He's a grotesque, a real blackheart, but his place at least fakes the life and warmth. And his decorator has his priorities straight. Once when I was there the house was littered with naked lovelies. That's what I call home furnishings! That's a lot more cheerful than a bargeload of instruments of war.

I dropped my duffel bag, put a foot up on the fountain surround, and rested my elbows on my knee. "You boys go ahead with what you're doing. I'll try not to disturb." Hero and dragon were both too preoccupied to notice.

I looked around. Where the hell was everybody? A place that size ought to have a battalion for staff. I'd seen livelier museums at midnight. Well . . .

All was not lost. In fact, things had started to look up.

I'd spotted a face. It was looking at me around a pillar supporting the balconies to my left. The west wing. It was female and gorgeous and too far away to tell much else, but that was all I needed to get my blood moving again. The woman attached was as timid as a dryad. She ducked out of sight an instant after our eyes met.

The part of me that is weak wondered if I'd see more of her. I hoped so. I could get lost in a face like that.

She did a little flit into the nearest hallway. I got just a glimpse but wanted her to come back. She was worth a second look, and maybe a third and a fourth, a long-haired, slim blonde in something white and gauzy, gathered at the waist by a red girdle. Around twenty, give or take a few, and sleek enough to put a big, goofy grin on my face.

I'd keep an eye out for that one.

Unless she was a ghost. She'd gone without making a sound. Whatever, she was going to haunt me till I got a closer look.

Was the place haunted? It was spooky enough, in its cold way . . . I realized it was me. Might not bother someone else. I looked around and heard the dash of steel and the moans of those who had died to furnish all those emblems of Stantnor glory. I was packing my own haunts in and letting the place become a mirror.

I tried to shake a darkening mood. A place like that turns you somber.

The guy from the front door marched in after the girl disappeared, his heels clicking. He came to a perfect military halt six feet away. I gave him the once-over. He stood five foot eight, maybe a hundred seventy pounds, in his fifties but looking younger. His hair was wavy black, slicked with some kind of grease that couldn't beat the curl. If he had any gray, he hid it well, and he still had all the hair he'd had when he was twenty. His eyes were cold little beads. You could get ice burns there. He'd kill you and not even wonder if he was making orphans.

"The General will see you now, sir." He turned and marched away.

I followed. I caught myself marching in step, skipped to get out. In a minute I was back in step. I gave it up. They'd pounded it in good. The flesh remembered and couldn't hear the rebellion in the mind.

"You have a name?" I asked.

"Dellwood, sir."

"What were you before you got out?"

"I was attached to the General's staff, sir."

Which meant absolutely nothing. "Lifer?" Dumb question, Garrett. I could bet the family farm I was the only nonlifer in the place, excepting the girl—maybe. The General wouldn't surround himself with the lesser breeds called civilians.

"Thirty-two years, sir." He asked no questions himself. Not into small talk and chitchat? No. He didn't care. I was one of *them*.

"Maybe I should have come to the tradesman's entrance."

He grunted.

"Tough." The General had my respect for what he'd accomplished, not for who he'd been born.

Dellwood had twenty years on me but I was the guy doing the puffing when we hit the fourth floor. About six wise remarks ran through my alleged brain but I didn't have wind enough to share them. Dellwood gave me an unreadable look, probably veiled contempt for soft civilians. I puffed awhile, then to distract him said, "I saw a woman while I was waiting. Watching me. Timid as a mouse."

"That would be Miss Jennifer, sir. The General's daughter." He looked like he thought he'd made a mistake volunteering that much. He didn't say anything else. One of those guys who wouldn't tell you what he thought you didn't need to know if you burned his toes off. Was the whole staff struck from the same dies? Then why did Peters need me? They could handle anything.

Dellwood marched to an oaken door that spanned half the corridor on the top floor of the west wing. He pushed the door inward, announced, "Mr. Mike Sexton, sir."

A wall of heat smacked me as I pushed past Dellwood.

I'd come with no preconceptions but I was still surprised. General Stantnor preferred spartan surroundings. Other than the room's size, there was nothing to hint that he was hip deep in geld.

There were no carpets, a few straightbacked wooden chairs, the ubiquitous military hardware, two writing desks nose to nose, the bigger one presumably for the General and the other for whoever actually wrote. The place was almost a mausoleum. The heat came off a bonfire raging in a fireplace designed for roasting oxen. Another gink without joints in his spine was tossing in logs from a nearby mountain. He looked at me, looked at the old man behind the big desk. The old man nodded. The fireman marched out, maybe to kill time practicing close order drill with Dellwood.

Having surveyed the setting I zeroed in on its centerpiece.

I could see why Black Pete was suspicious. There wasn't much left of General Stantnor. He didn't look anything like the guy in the picture downstairs. He looked like he might weigh about as much as a mummy, though most of him was buried under comforters. Ten years ago he'd been my height and thirty pounds heavier.

His skin had a yellowish cast and was mildly translucent. His pupils were milky with cataracts. His hair had fallen out in clumps. Only a few patches remained, not just gray or white but with a bluish hue of death. He had liver spots but those had faded, too. His lips had no color left but a poisonous gray-blue.

I don't know how well he could see through those cataracts, but his gaze was strong and steady. He didn't shake.

"Mike Sexton, sir. Sergeant Peters asked me to see you."

"Grab a chair. Pull it up there facing me. I don't like to look up when I talk to someone." There was power in his voice, though I don't know where he found the energy. I'd figured him for a grave robber's whisper. I settled opposite him. He said, "For the moment I'm confident we're not being overheard, Mr. Garrett. Yes. I know who you are. Peters provided me with a full report before I approved bringing you in." He kept staring as though he could overcome those cataracts through sheer will. "But we'll pursue the Mike Sexton fiction in future. Assuming we come to terms now."

I was close enough to smell him, and it wasn't a good smell. I was surprised the whole room didn't reek. They must have brought him in from somewhere else. "Peters didn't say what you needed, sir. He just called in an old marker to get me out here." I glanced at the fireplace. They would be baking bread in here soon.

"It takes a great deal of heat to keep me going, Mr. Garrett. My apologies for your discomfort. I'll try to keep this brief. I'm a little like a thunder-lizard. I generate no heat of my own."

I waited for him to continue. And sweated a lot.

"I have Peters's word that you were a good Marine." No doubt that counted for a lot around here. "He vouches for your character then. But men change. What have you become?"

"A freelance thug instead of a drafted one, General. Which you need or I wouldn't be here."

He made a noise that might have been laughter. "Ah. I'd heard you have a sharp tongue, Mr. Garrett. I should be the impatient one, not you. I have so little time left. Yes. Peters vouches for you today, as well. And you do get mentioned in some circles as being reliable, though headstrong and inclined to carry out your assignments according to your own lights. They say you have a sentimental streak. That shouldn't trouble us here. They say you have a weakness for women. I think you'll find my daughter more trouble than she's worth. They say you tend to be judgmental of the vices and peccadillos of my class."

I wondered if he knew how often I change my underwear. Why did he need an investigator? Let him use whoever had investigated me.

Again that sorry laugh. "I can guess what you're thinking. Everything I know is public knowledge. Your reputation runs before you." Something that might have been a smile in better times. "You've managed to do a fair amount of good over the years, Mr. Garrett. But you stepped on a lot of toes doing it."

"I'm just a clumsy kid, General. I'll grow out of it."

"I doubt it. You don't seem intimidated by me."

"I'm not." I wasn't. I'd met too many guys who really *were* intimidating. I had calluses on that organ.

"You would have been ten years ago."

"Different circumstances."

"Indeed. Good. I need a man who won't be intimidated. Especially by me. Because I fear that if you do your job right, you may uncover truths I won't want to face. Truths so brutal I may tell you to back off. You won't do that?"

He had me baffled. "I'm confused."

"The normal state of the world, Mr. Garrett. I mean, when I hire you, if I hire you, and if you agree to take this job, your commitment will be to follow it through to the end. Disregarding anything I tell you later. I'll see that you're paid up front so you aren't tempted to bend in order to collect your fee."

"I still don't get it."

"I pride myself on my ability to meet the truth head-on. In this case I want to arrange it so I have no choice, however much I squirm and ache. Can you understand that?"

"Yes." Only in the most literal sense. I didn't understand why. We all spend a lot of time fooling ourselves, and his class were masters at that— though he'd always had a reputation for having both feet firmly planted in reality. He'd disobeyed or refused orders more than once because they had originated in wishful thinking by superiors who hadn't come within five hundred miles of the fighting. Each time events had saved him embarrassment by proving him right.

He didn't have a lot of friends.

"Before I make any commitment, I have to know what I'm supposed to do."

"There is a thief in my house, Mr. Garrett."

He stopped because of some kind of spasm. I thought he was having a heart attack. I jumped up and headed for the door.

"Wait," he croaked. "It will pass."

I paused midway between my chair and the door, saw the spasm fade, and in a moment he was back to normal. I perched myself on my chair again.

"A thief in my house. Yet there is no one here I haven't known for thirty years, no one I haven't trusted with my life many times."

That had to be a weird feeling, knowing you could trust guys with your life but not with your things.

I got a glimmer of why he needed an outsider. A bad apple amongst old comrades. They might cover up, refuse to see the truth, or . . . Who knows? Marines don't think like people.

"I follow. Go ahead."

"My infirmity came upon me soon after I returned home. It's a progressive consumption, apparently. But slow. I seldom get out of my quarters now. But I've noticed, this past year, that some things, some of which have been in the family for centuries, have disappeared. Never large, flashy things that would be obvious to any eye. Just trinkets, sometimes more valuable as mementos than intrinsically. Yet the sum should add to a fair amount by now."

"I see." I glanced at the fire. It was time to turn me over so I wouldn't be underdone on one side.

"Bear with me a few minutes more, Mr. Garrett."

"Yes sir. Any strangers in the house recently? Any regular visitors?"

"A handful. People off the Hill. Not the sort who would pilfer."

I didn't say so but in my thinking the worst of all criminals come off the Hill. Our nobility would steal the coppers off dead men's eyes. But the General had a point. They wouldn't steal with their own hands. They'd have somebody do it for them.

"You have an inventory of what's missing?"

"Would that be useful?"

"Maybe. Somebody steals something, they want to sell it to get money. Right? I know some of the retailers whose wholesalers are people with sticky fingers. Do you want the stuff back or do you just want to know who's kyping it?"

"The latter step first, Mr. Garrett. Then we'll consider recovery." Sudden as a lightning bolt he suffered another spasm. I felt helpless, unable to do anything for him. That was not a good sensation.

He came back but this time he was weaker.

"I'll have to close this out quickly, Mr. Garrett. I'll need to rest. Or the next attack may be the last." He smiled. There were teeth missing behind the smile. "Another reason to make sure you get your fee up front. My heirs might not see fit to pay you."

I wanted to say something reassuring, like he'd outlive me, but that seemed too cynically a load of manure. I kept my mouth shut. I can do that sometimes, though usually at the wrong time.

"I'd like to get to know you better, Mr. Garrett, but nature has its own priorities. I'll hire you if you'll have me for a client. Will you find me my thief? On the terms I stated?"

"No punches pulled? No backing off?"

"Exactly."

"Yes sir." I had to force it out. I really was getting lazy. "I'm on it now."

"Good. Good. Dellwood should be outside. Tell him I want Peters."

I got up. "Will do, General." I backed toward the door. Even in his present state the old man retained some of the magnetism that had made him a charismatic commander. I didn't want to pity him. I really wanted to help him. I wanted to find the villain Black Pete said was trying to kill him.

●●●**3**

T he cool in the hallway felt like high winter in the Arctic. For a second I worried about frostbite.

The General was right about Dellwood. He was there, waiting. The way he did it suggested he'd been scrupulous about not getting so close he might overhear anything. Though I doubted explosions could be heard through that door. I decided I could like the guy in spite of the stick up his spine.

"The General says he wants to see Peters."

"Very good, sir. I'd better attend to that. If you'll return to the fountain and wait?"

"Sure. But hold on. What's wrong with him? He had a couple of pretty fierce attacks while I was in there."

That stopped him dead. He looked at me, emotion leaking through for once. He loved that old man and he was worried. "Bad spasms, sir?"

"They looked that way to me. But I'm no doc. He cut the interview short because he was afraid another one would be too much for him."

"I'd better check on him before I do anything else."

"What's wrong with him?" I asked again.

"I don't know, sir. We've tried bringing physicians in, but he throws them out when he finds out what they are. He has a morbid fear of doctors. From what they've said, I understand that a physician's care might not do any good. They haven't done anything but scratch their heads and say they don't understand it."

"Good to see you can talk, Dellwood."

"I believe the General brought you on board, sir. You're one of the household now."

I liked that attitude. Most people I meet either stay clammed or tell lies. "I'd like to talk to you some more when you get the time."

"Yes sir." He pushed through the General's door.

I found my way to the fountain. Wasn't that hard. But I'd become one of the company scouts after Sexton disappeared. I was a highly trained finder of the way. Peters often reminded me how much the Crown had invested in me.

I'd left my bag leaning against the fountain for lack of desire to lug it around before I decided if I was hired. It had seemed safe enough, still as the place was. I mean, I'd visited livelier ruins.

Someone was digging through it when I reached that temple to overstated militarism.

She had her back to me and a mighty fine backside it was. She was tall and slim and brunette. She wore a simple tan shift in imitation peasant style. It probably set somebody back more money than a peasant saw in five years. Her behind wiggled deliciously as she dug. It looked like she'd only gotten started.

I moved out on scout's tippytoes, stopped four feet behind her, gave her fanny an approving nod, said, "Find anything interesting?"

She whirled.

I started. The face was the same as the one I'd seen earlier but this time it wasn't timid at all. This face had more lines in it. It was more worldly. That other face had had the placidity, behind timidity, that you see in nuns.

Her eyes flashed. "Who are you?" she demanded, unrepentant. I like my ladies unrepentant about some things, but not about snooping in my stuff.

"Sexton. Who are you? Why are you going through my stuff?"

"How come you're carrying a portable arsenal?"

"I need it in my work. I answered a couple. Your turn."

She looked me up and down, raised an eyebrow, looked like she didn't know if she approved or not. Wound me to the core! Then she snorted and walked away. I'm not the handsomest guy in town but the lovelies don't usually respond that way. Had to be part of a plan.

I watched her go. She moved well. She exaggerated it a little, knowing she had an audience. She disappeared into the shadows under the west balcony.

"Going to be some strange ones here," I muttered. I checked my bag.

She'd stirred it up but nothing was missing. I'd arrived in time to keep her out of the little padded box with the bottles inside. I double-checked, though, opening it.

There were three bottles: royal blue, emerald green, ruby red. Each weighed about two ounces. They were plunder from a past case. Their contents had been whipped up by a sorcerer. They could get real handy in tight situations. I hoped I didn't have to use them.

I'd brought along more tight-situation stuff than clothing. Clothing washes.

I prowled the hall while I waited for Dellwood. That was like visiting a museum alone. None of the stuff there meant anything to me. Richly storied, all of it, no doubt, but I've never been a guy to get excited about history for its own sake.

Dellwood took his time. After half an hour I started eyeballing an old bugle, wondering what would happen if I gave it a couple of toots. Then I spotted the blonde again, watching me from about as far away as she could get and still be in that hall with me. I waved. I'm a friendly kind of guy.

She ducked out of sight. A mouse, this one.

Dellwood finally showed. I asked, "The General all right?"

"He's resting, sir. He'll be fine." He didn't sound convinced. "Sergeant Peters will handle the requests you made." Now he sounded puzzled. "I'm curious, sir. What are you doing here?"

"The General sent for me."

He looked at me a moment, said, "If you'll come with me, I'll show you your quarters." After we'd climbed to the fourth-floor east wing and he had me puffing again, he tried another tack. "Will you be staying long?"

"I don't know." I hoped not. The place was getting to me already. It was too much a tomb. In the other wing the master was dying and the place seemed to be dying with him. As Dellwood opened a door, I asked, "What will you do after the General passes on?"

"I haven't given that much thought, sir. I don't expect him to go soon. He'll beat this. His ancestors all lived into their eighties and nineties."

Whistling in the dark. He had no future he could see. The world didn't have much room for lifers with their best years used up.

Which made me wonder again why anyone in that house would want Stantnor to check out early. Black Pete's suspicions were improbable, logically.

But logic doesn't usually come into play when people start thinking about killing other people.

I hadn't looked at the thing yet. I'd keep an open mind till I'd done some poking and prying and just plain listening.

"What's the word on meals, Dellwood? I'm not equipped for formal dining."

"We haven't dressed since the General took ill, sir. Breakfast is at six, lunch at eleven, in the kitchen. Supper is at five in the dining room, but informally. Guests and staff sit down together, if that presents any problems."

"Not to me. I'm an egalitarian kind of guy. I think I'm just as good as you are. I missed lunch, eh?" I wasn't going to be happy here if I had to conform to the native schedule. I see six in the morning only when I haven't gotten to bed yet. The trouble with morning is that it comes so damned early in the morning.

"I'm sure something can be arranged, this once. I'll tell Cook we have a newly arrived guest."

"Thanks. I'll take a minute to settle in, then get down there."

"Very well, sir. If anything is not satisfactory, let me know. I'll see that any problems are corrected."

He would, too. "Sure. Thanks." I watched him step out and close the door.

could not imagine things going awry, considering some scenes I've endured. Dellwood had installed me in a suite bigger than the ground floor of my house. The room where I stood boasted rosewood wainscoting, mahogany ceiling beams, a wall of bookshelves loaded down, and furniture for entertaining a platoon. A dining table with seats for four. A writing table. Various chairs. Leaded and plain glass windows unfortunately facing north. A carpet some old lady had spent the last twenty years of her life weaving, maybe three hundred years ago. Lamps enough to do my whole house. A chandelier overhead loaded with a gaggle of candles, unlighted at the moment.

This was how the other half lived.

Two doors opened off the big room. I made a guess and pushed through one. What a genius. Hit the bedroom first time.

It was of a piece with the rest. I'd never met a bed so big and soft.

I looked around for hiding places, squirreled some of my equipment good, some so it could be found easily and the rest maybe overlooked. I kept the most important stuff on my person. I figured I'd better hit the kitchen while the staff were still understanding. After I stoked the bodily fires I could wander around like an old ghost.

In better times the kitchen probably boasted a staff of a dozen, with full-time specialists like bakers and pastry cooks. When I dropped in, there was only one person present, an ancient-breed woman whose nonhuman half appeared to be troll. Wrinkled, shrunken, stooped, she was still a foot taller than me and a hundred pounds heavier. Even at her age she could probably break me over her knee—if I stood still and let her lay hands on me.

"You the new one?" she growled when I walked in.

"That's me. Name's Sexton. Mike Sexton."

"Name's mud you don't show on time after this, young'un. Sit." She pointed. I didn't argue. I sat at a table three-quarters buried in used utensils and stoneware. Plunk! She slammed something down in front of me.

"You served with the General, too?"

"Smartass, eh? You want to eat? Eat. Don't try to be a comedian."

"Right. Just making conversation." I looked at my plate. All kinds of chunks of something I didn't recognize mixed up in slimy sauce, piled on rice. I approached it with the trepidation I usually reserve for the stuff they serve at my friend Morley's place, the city's only vegetarian restaurant open to a mixed clientele.

"If I want conversation, I'll ask for it. Look around here. It look like I got time to waste jacking my jaw? Been trying to carry it on my own since they threw Candy out on his ass. I keep telling the old skinflint, I need another pair of hands. Think he'll listen? Hell, no! All he sees is he's saving a couple marks a week."

I took a bite here, a bite there. There seemed to be mussels and mushrooms and a couple things I couldn't identify, and all damned good. "This is excellent," I said.

"Where you been eating? It's slop. I got no helper, I don't got time to fix anything right." She started tossing pots at a sink, sending sprays of water flying. "Barely got time to get ready for the next feeding. These hogs, you think they know the difference? Feed them hot sawdust mush, they wouldn't know it."

Maybe not. But I'd had old Dean cooking for me for a while and I knew good food when I bit it. "How many do you have to take care of?"

"Eighteen. Counting myself. Bloody army. What do you care, Mr. Nineteen and straw that broke the camel's back?"

"That many? The place is like a haunted house. I've seen the General, Dellwood, and you, and some old boy who was stoking the fireplace in the General's study."

"Kaid."

"And two women. Where are the rest? On maneuvers?"

"Wise ass, eh? Where did you see two women? That ass Harcourt sneaking one of his floozies in here again? Hell. I hope he is. I just hope he is. I'll have the old man put him on KP for a year. Get this cesspool cleaned out.

What the hell you doing here, anyway? We ain't had nobody new here for two years. No honest-to-goodness guests in a year and a half, just in and outs from uptown, their noses in the air like they don't squat to shit like everybody else."

Whew! "To tell the truth, Miss . . . ?" She didn't take the hook. "To tell the truth, I'm not quite sure. The General sent for me. Said he wanted to hire me. But he had some kind of attack before . . ."

She melted. The vinegar drained out in two seconds. "How bad is it? Maybe I'd better go see."

"Dellwood's taken care of it. Says he just needs to rest. He got himself overwrought. This fellow Harcourt. He has a habit of bringing girlfriends home?"

"Not since a couple years back. What the hell you asking all the questions for? Ain't none of your damned business what we do or who we do it with."

She had a thought. She stopped dead still, stepped away from the sink, turned, laid a first-class glower on me. "Or is it your business?"

I didn't say. I tried to slide around it by offering her my empty plate. "Wouldn't be a little more of that, would there? Just to fill a couple empty spots?"

"It is your business. The old man has another fantasy. Thinks somebody's out to get him. Or somebody's robbing him." She shook her head. "You're wasting your time. Or maybe not. Long as he's paying you, it don't matter if you find something, does it? Hell. Probably better if you don't. You can rob him yourself, taking money for nothing. Till the fantasy wears off."

I was confused, but covered it. "Somebody's been robbing the General?"

"Nobody's robbing him. The old boy ain't got a pot to pee in, not counting this damned stone barn. And it's too damned big to carry off. Anyway, if somebody *was* robbing him I wouldn't tell you word one. Not no outsider. I don't never say nothing to no outsiders. They're all a bunch of con artists."

"Commendable attitude." I wiggled my plate suggestively.

"I got my hands in dishwater up to my elbows and you don't look like you got no broken legs. Get it yourself."

"Be happy to if I knew where."

She made an exasperated noise, made allowance for the fact that I was new. "On the damned stove. Rice in the steel pot, stew in the iron kettle. I worry about the old boy. These fancies . . . More and more all the time. Must be the sickness. Touching him. Though he always did think somebody was trying to do him out of something."

Wouldn't say a word to an outsider. I was proud of her. "It isn't possible somebody might actually *be* robbing him? Like they say, even paranoids get persecuted."

"Who? You tell me that, Mr. Smartass Snooper. Ain't nobody in this whole damned place wouldn't wrestle thunder-lizards for him. Half of them would take the disease for him if they could."

I didn't make the point, but people work kinky deals with their consciences. I had no trouble imagining a man willing to die for the General being equally willing to steal from him. The very willingness to serve could set off a chain of justifications making theft sound completely reasonable.

She'd figured me out in fifteen minutes. How long would it be before word spread? "You ever have a problem with pixies or brownies?" The countryside suffered periodic infestations, like termites or mice. The little people are fond of baubles and have no respect for property.

"We had any around here, I'd put them to work."

I figured she would. "Dellwood hinted that the General has a prejudice against doctors. In his condition I'd think he'd be ready to try anything."

"You don't know that boy. He's got a stubborn streak a yard wide. He by damned made up his mind when the missus died, he wasn't never going to trust no quack again. And he stuck."

"Uhm?"

She wouldn't talk to no outsider. Not her, no siree! "See, he loved that girl, Miss Tiffany. Such a lovely child she was. Broke all our hearts when it happened. They laughed at him, he was so much older than her. But he was her heart's slave, him that never loved a thing before. Then Miss Jennifer came. She was in labor so long. He couldn't stand to see her in pain. He brought in doctors from the city. After Miss Jennifer finally came, one damned fool gave Miss Tiffany a damned anticoagulant infusion. Thought he was giving her a sleeping potion."

A big mistake and an especially stupid one, sounded like. "She bled to death?"

"She did. Might have anyway. She was a frail, pale thing, but you couldn't never convince him."

Mistakes that cost lives aren't easy to understand or forgive, but they happen. Despite what they want us mortals to believe, doctors are human. And where there are human beings, there's human error. It's inevitable.

When doctors make mistakes, people hurt.

Easy for me to be understanding. I hadn't known and loved the General's wife.

"Changed his whole life, that did. Went off and spent the rest of it in the Cantard, taking out his grief on the Venageti." And when generals make mistakes, lots of people hurt. "You going to hang out here all day, youngster, you better roll up your sleeves and get washing. Round here we don't got no place for drones."

I was tempted. She had plenty to say. Still . . . "Maybe later. If it looks like I'm wasting my time, I might as well wash dishes."

She snorted. "Thought that would get rid of you. Never knowed a man yet with balls enough to wade into a mountain of dirty dishes of his own free will."

"The lunch was great. Thank you, Miss . . . ?"

Didn't work this time, either.

5

That fountain in the great hall was a good hub from which to launch exploratory forays. I perched on the surround, digesting Cook's remarks. I had a premonition. I would get intimate with dishwater before I exhausted that vein of stubborn silence.

I had that creepy feeling you get when you sense somebody watching you. I looked around casually.

There she was. The blonde again, drifting in the shadows, bold enough now to be on the same floor with me. I pretended not to notice. I gave it a minute, got up, stretched. She ducked out of sight. I moved her way pretending I had no idea she was there.

She lit out like a scared pheasant. I bolted after her. "Jennifer!"

I ducked between pillars . . . Where did she go? I didn't see anywhere she could run. But she wasn't there.

Spooky!

"Hey! Mike. What are you doing?"

I jumped about five feet. "Peters. Don't sneak up like that. This place has got me believing in spooks already. Where the hell is everybody?"

Peters looked puzzled. "Everybody? Working."

That made sense. You could lose a lot more than eighteen people in that barn and on those grounds. "You'd think I'd run into somebody once in a while."

"It does get lonely at times." He smiled. That made two times in two days. A record. "Thought you might want a tour."

"I can find my way. I was a scout in the Marines, you know."

His smile vanished. He looked at me like the old Black Pete. Like I wasn't bright enough to tie my own shoes. He jerked his head toward the back of the hall, the north end, which was a wall of leaded glass with fifty furious combats going. There was a door back there.

Hey. Mom Garrett didn't raise many idiots. I got it. "I could use a look at the grounds, though, and somebody to tell me what I'm seeing."

He relaxed some, did a slick about-face and marched. I hup-two-threed behind him. I didn't feel a bit of nostalgia for the bad old days.

Peters didn't say anything till we were out of earshot of the house, clear of the formal garden behind it, away from cover where eavesdroppers might lurk. "You saw the old man. What do you think?"

"He's in bad shape."

"You know any poisons that could do that to him?"

I gave it an honest think. "No. But I'm no expert. I know a guy who is. But he'd have to see the General." Morley Dotes knows whatever there is to know about doing in your fellow man. Or elf, him being a breed with more dark-elfin than human blood.

"I don't think I could swing that. One outsider here has the place in an uproar already."

"Yeah. It's a regular busted-up beehive." Our walk to isolation hadn't shown me a single body in motion. "It was just a suggestion. You want to know something, you get the answer from somebody who knows."

"I'll give it a shot."

"The business about the thefts. Is it real? The cook thinks it's all in the General's imagination."

"It's not. She'd think that. Back when we first came here he did have a spell when he imagined things. She doesn't get out of the kitchen much and she has a few loose threads herself. Most of the time she doesn't know what year it is."

"She tried to draft me as kitchen help."

"She would. Gods! I remember your cooking."

"I remember what I had to work with. Muskrats and cattail roots. And bugs for garnish."

He grunted, almost smiled again.

"Don't tell me. You can't have fond memories of those days."

"No, Garrett. Even lifers aren't that crazy. I don't miss that part." He shuddered.

"Eh? What?"

"Bad rumor. They may call up the veterans to run Glory Mooncalled down."

I laughed.

"What's so damned funny?"

"Best joke I've heard in weeks. You know how many people that takes in? Every human male in the population over twenty-five. You think *any* of them would go without a fuss? A call-up like that would start a revolution."

"Maybe. You think it *could* be poison?"

"I suppose. Assume it is. Speculate."

"I don't know anything about poisons. How could it be given to him?"

I'm not an expert, but I have a professional interest and keep my ears open when such things are discussed. "It could be in his food or drink. It could be dusted into his bed so it would seep through his skin. It could even be in the air he breathes. Looking for 'how' can be a dead end unless you know 'what.' Better to look at the people. Who has access?"

"Everybody, one way or another."

"Take it a step further. Who'd profit? If somebody's killing him, that somebody has to have a reason. Right?"

He grunted. "Obviously whoever's doing it believes he has. I've been trying to figure that out from the beginning. And I can't come up with one."

I didn't have any trouble. "What's the estate worth? Who does it go to?"

"Doesn't make sense. Jennifer gets half. The other half gets divided amongst the rest of us."

"Give me a value in gold marks. Just a guess. Then ask yourself what some people might do for a share of that."

"Three million for the house?" He shrugged. "A million for the contents. Two or three million for the real estate. He was offered three for the two north sections last year. He was tempted because he's strapped for cash and he wants to set Jennifer up so she's fixed for life, no matter what she does."

"Three million for just part of the property?"

"Somebody wanted the land near the city. But the offer was withdrawn because he dithered. They bought a tract from the Hillmans instead. For less money."

"No bad feelings?"

"Not that I heard."

I did some rough division in my head. I came up with around a hundred thousand marks each for the minority heirs. I knew guys who'd cut a hundred thousand throats for that kind of money. So there was a motive—assuming somebody was in a hurry to get his share.

"Everybody know they're in the will?"

"Sure. The old man used to make a big deal of it. How if you didn't toe the mark you blew your share."

Ha! "Cook mentioned a Candy . . ."

"Not him. He's long gone. He wouldn't have the balls, either. He wasn't even human. Wasn't in the will, either. Wasn't one of the guys the old man brought home with him. He was one of the crew who managed the place while the General was in the Cantard."

"She mentioned a Harcourt who got in trouble for bringing girlfriends home."

"Harcourt?" He frowned. "I guess he got fed up with what he thought were chickenshit rules. He just took off about six months back. The old man cut him out. He'd know that. So there's nothing for him to gain. Let alone we'd see him around here."

"We may have to back off and go at this from another angle, Sarge."

"Eh?"

"What have I got to go on? Your feelings. But every time I ask you a question you make it sound more like there's nobody who'd want him dead. And nobody who'd profit from it since everybody's getting a cut anyway. We can't hang up a solid motive. And means and opportunity are limited."

"You're sneaking up on something."

"I'm wondering if maybe he isn't just dying of stomach cancer. Wondering if maybe you shouldn't hire a doctor instead of me till you know what's killing him."

He didn't answer for a few minutes. I was talked out. We walked. He brooded and I studied the grounds. Somebody had farmed the fields last summer. There was nobody in them now. I glanced at the sky. They'd thrown on a few more slabs of lead and added icicles to the breeze. Winter was coming back.

"I tried, Garrett. Two months ago. Somebody leaked it to the old man. The doc never got through the front door."

The way he said "somebody" I guessed he knew who. I asked.

He didn't want to say. "Who, Sarge? We can't pick and choose our suspects."

"Jennifer. She was in on the plot but she defected. She's a strange girl. Her big goal in life is to win some gesture of love and approval. And the old man doesn't know how. He's scared of her. She grew up while he was away. It doesn't help that she looks a lot like her mother. Her mother died—"

"Cook told me that story."

"She would. That old hag knows everything and tells anyone who'll listen. You ought to move into the kitchen."

We walked some more, headed south now, circling the house.

Peters said, "Maybe we have a communication problem. The deeper you get in the more you'll think the mess is imaginary. The old man has crazy spells. He *does* think people are out to get him when they're not. That's what makes this diabolical. Unless somebody sticks a knife in him in front of everybody, nobody's going to believe he's in danger."

I grunted. I'd had a friend, Pokey Pigotta, in the same line as me. He's dead now. But once he'd had a case that worked that way. A crazy old woman with a lot of money, always down with imaginary illnesses and besieged by imaginary enemies. Pokey discounted her fears. Her son did her in. Pokey was haunted by that one. "I'll keep an open mind."

"That's all I ask. Stick with it. Don't let it get to you."

"Sure. But we could shortcut everything if we could get a few experts in."

"I said I'd try. Don't hold your breath. It was hard enough selling you."

We continued our circuit of the grounds. At one point we passed near a graveyard. "Family plot?" I asked.

"For three hundred years."

I glanced at the house. It brooded down on us from that point. "It doesn't look that old."

"It isn't. There was an earlier house. Check the outbuildings in back. You can still see some of its foundations. They tore it down for materials to build the outbuildings after the new house went up."

I supposed I'd have to give them the once-over. You have to go through all the motions. You have to leave no stone unturned, though already, intuitively, I was inclined to think the answer lay inside the big house—if there was an answer.

Peters read my mind. "If I'm fooling myself and we've just got an old man dying, I want to know that, too. Check?"

"Check."

"I've spent more time with you than I should. I'd better get back to work."

"Where do I find you if I need you?"

He chuckled. "I'm like horse apples. I'm everywhere. Catch as catch can.

A problem you'll have with everybody, especially during poacher season. Cook's the only one who stays in one place."

We walked toward the house, passing through a small orchard of unidentifiable fruit trees with a white gazebo at its center, climbed a slope, went up the steps to the front door. Peters went inside. I paused to survey the Stantnor domains. The cold wind gnawed my cheeks. The overcast sky left the land colorless and doleful, like old tin. I wondered if it was losing life with its master.

But there would be a spring for the land. I doubted there would be for the old man.

Unless I found me a poisoner.

6

I heard Black Pete's footsteps fading as I stepped into the great hall. The light was dimming there. The place seemed more deserted and gloomy than ever. I went to the fountain, watched our hero work out on his dragon, thought about what to do next. Explore the house? Hell. I was cold already. Why not look at those outbuildings and be done with it?

I felt eyes on me as I moved. Already habituated, I checked the nearest shadows. The blonde wasn't there. Nobody was, anywhere. Then I glanced up.

I caught a flicker on the third floor balcony, east side. Somebody ducking out of sight. Who? One of the majority I hadn't yet met? Why they wouldn't want to be seen was a puzzle. I'd see everyone sooner or later.

I took myself out the back door.

Immediately behind the house lay a formal garden sort of thing that I'd paid no heed before. Peters had wanted to get away where we could talk. I gave it a look now.

There was a lot of fancy stonework, statues, fountains, pools that had been drained because at that time of year water tends to freeze. Ice would break the pool walls. There were hedges, shaped trees, beds for spring and summer plantings. It could be impressive in season. Right then it just seemed abandoned and haunted by old sorrows.

I paused at the hedge bounding the north end of the garden, looked back. The vista seemed a ghost of another time.

At least one someone was watching me from a third-floor window in the west wing.

Keep that in mind, Garrett. Whatever you do, wherever you go, somebody is going to be watching.

Twenty feet behind the hedge was a line of poplars. They were there to mask the outbuildings, so the practical side of life wouldn't offend the eyes of those who lived in the house. The rich are that way. They don't want to be reminded that their comfort requires sweaty drudge labor.

There were half a dozen outbuildings of various shapes and sizes. Stone was the main structural material, though it wasn't stone that matched that in the big house. The stable was obvious. Somebody was at work there. I heard a hammer pounding. There was a second structure for livestock, presumably cattle, maybe dairy cattle. It was nearest me and had that smell. The rest of the buildings, including a greenhouse off to my right, had the look of protracted neglect. Way to the left was a long, low building that looked like a barracks. It also looked like nobody had used it for years. I decided to start with the greenhouse.

Not much to see there except that someone had spent a fortune on glass and then hadn't bothered to keep the place up. A few panes were broken. The framework that had been white once needed paint desperately. The door stood open a foot and sagged on its hinges. I had trouble pushing it back enough to get inside.

No one had been in there for a long time. The place had gone to weeds. The only animal life I saw was a scroungy, orange, feral cat. She headed for cover when she saw me.

The building next on the left was small, solid, and very much in use. It turned out to be a wellhouse, which explained why it looked like it handled a lot of traffic. A place this size would consume a lot of water—though I'd have thought they'd pipe it in from a reservoir.

The stable was the next building over. I gave it a skip. I'd talk to whoever was there after I finished snooping. Next over was a smaller building filled with a jungle of tools and farm implements with an air of long neglect. There was another cat in there, a lot of mice, and from the smell, a regiment of bats. There's nothing like the stink of lots of bats.

Next up was the barn and, yes, that's what it was. Bottom level for the animals, dairy and beef. Top level for hay, straw, and feed. Nobody around but the cows and a few more cats. I figured there must be owls, too, because

I didn't smell bats. The place needed maintenance. The cows weren't friendly, unfriendly, or even curious.

The day was getting on. The gloom was getting thick. I figured I'd better get on with it and save the detail work for later. Supper would be coming up soon.

The building I'd thought looked like a barracks was probably for seasonal help. It was about eighty yards long, had maybe fifteen doors. The first I looked behind showed me a large, dusty bunkroom. The next opened on smaller quarters divided into three rooms, a bigger one immediately inside and two half its size behind it. The next several doors opened on identical arrangements. I guessed these were apartments for workers with families. Trouble was, there was a lot of waste space between doors, space unaccounted for.

The far end of the barracks had a kitchen the size of the bunkroom. Its door was on the other side of the building. Glancing along that face, I saw more doors, which explained the missing space. The apartments faced alternate directions. I stepped into the kitchen, a windowless, cheerless place that would have been depressing at the best of times. I left the door propped open for light.

There was little to see but dust and cobwebs and cooking utensils that hadn't been touched in years. Another place nobody had visited in a long time. I was surprised the stuff was still lying around. TunFaire and its environs have no shortage of thieves. All this stuff had some market value.

A gold mine that hadn't been discovered?

The door slammed shut.

"Damned wind," I muttered, and edged my way through the darkness, trying to remember what was lying in ambush between it and me.

I heard somebody secure the rusty hasp.

Not the wind. Somebody who didn't want to be my friend.

Not a good situation, Garrett. This place was far from where anybody had any business. The walls were thick stone. I could do a lot of yelling and nobody would hear. The door was the only way out and the only source of light.

I found the door, ran my hands over it, pushed gently, snorted. I stepped back a few feet and kicked hard.

The hasp ripped out of the dry, ancient wood. I charged through with a ready knife, saw nobody. I roared around the end of the barracks. And still saw nobody.

Damn! I leaned against the building and gave it a think. Something was going on, even if it wasn't what Black Pete thought.

Once I settled down, I went back to the kitchen door and looked for tracks. There were signs that somebody had been around, but the light was so poor, I couldn't do anything with them.

So. Nothing to do about it now. Might as well go to dinner and see who was surprised to see me.

was late. I should have explored the house. I didn't know where we'd eat so I went to the kitchen. I waited there till Cook turned up. She gave me a high-power glower. "What you doing in here?"

"Waiting to find out where we eat?"

"Fool." She loaded up. "Grab an armful and come on."

I did both. She shoved through swinging doors into a big pantry, marched through that and out another swinging door.

The dining room was a dining room. The kind where a guy can entertain three hundred of his closest friends. Most of it was dark. Everybody was seated at one corner table. The decor was standard for the house, armor and edged steel.

"There," Cook said. I presumed she meant the empty place. I settled my load on an unused part of the table, sat.

Wasn't much of a crowd. Dellwood and Peters and the brunette I'd caught rifling my duffel bag, plus three guys I hadn't met. And Cook, who planted herself across from me. The General couldn't make it, apparently. There weren't any other places set.

The girl and guys I hadn't met looked me over. The men looked like retired Marines. Surprise, surprise. The girl looked good. She'd changed into her vamping clothes.

Garrett, you dog . . . The thought fled. This one gave off something sour. She was radiating the come-and-get-it and my reaction was to back off. Here

was trouble on the hoof. What was it Morley said? Don't ever fool around
with a woman who's crazier than you are?

Maybe I was growing up.

Sure. And tomorrow morning pigs would be swooping around like swallows.

I didn't plan to outgrow *that* for about another six hundred years.

Peters said, "This is Mike Sexton. He was with me in the islands about
ten years back. Mike, Cook." He indicated the troll-breed woman.

"We've met."

"Miss Jennifer, the General's daughter."

"We've also met." I rose and reached across, offering my hand. "Didn't
get the chance before. You had both of yours in my duffel bag."

Cook chuckled. Jennifer looked at me like she wondered if I'd taste better roasted or fried.

"You've met Dellwood. Next to him is Cutter Hawkes."

Hawkes was too far off to shake. I nodded. He nodded. He was a lean rail
of a character with hard gray eyes and a lantern jaw, middle fifties, tough.
He looked more like a fire-and-brimstone prophet than an old soldier. Like
a guy with the sense of humor of a rock.

"Art Chain." The next guy nodded. He had a monster black mustache
going gray, not much hair on top, and was thirty pounds over his best
weight. His eyes were beads of obsidian. Another character who was allergic
to laughter. He didn't bother to nod. He was so happy to see me he could
just shit.

"Freidel Kaid." Kaid was older than the General, maybe into his seventies. Lean, slow, one glass eye and the other one that didn't work too good.
His stare was disconcerting because the glass eye didn't track. But he didn't
look like a man who had spent his whole life trying not to smile. In fact, he
put one on for me when Peters said his name. He was the guy I'd seen stoking the fire in the General's quarters.

"Pleased to meet you, Mr. Sexton."

"Likewise, Mr. Kaid." See? I can be a gentleman. Rumors to the contrary
are sour grapes and envy.

Jennifer didn't give me a chance to start eating. "What are you doing
here?"

"The General sent for me." Everybody was interested in me. Nice to be
the center of attention sometimes. I have to set the Dead Man on fire just to
get him to listen.

"Why?"

"Ask him. If he wants you to know, he'll tell you."

Her mouth pruned up. Her eyes shot sparks. They were interesting eyes, hungry eyes, but eyes that had been brushed by a darkness. I couldn't tell if they were green or not. The light wasn't good enough. An odd one. Maybe unique. A one in a million beauty and not the least attractive.

"What sort of work do you do, Mr. Sexton?" old Kaid asked.

"You could call me a diplomat."

"A diplomat?" Surprised.

"Sure. I straighten things out. I get people to change their minds. Kind of like the Corps, only on a small scale. Personal service."

Peters shot me a warning look.

I said, "I enjoy good conversation as much as the next guy. But I'm hungry. And you folks got a jump on me. How about you let me catch up?"

They all looked at me oddly. Cook more so than the others. She was wondering if maybe she'd missed the mark with her earlier guess.

I stoked the fires some, then asked, "Where's everybody else, Sarge?"

Peters frowned. "We're all here. Except Tyler and Wayne. They have the night off."

Kaid said, "Snake."

"Oh. Right. Snake Bradon. But he never comes in the house. Hell. He may not be around anymore. I haven't seen him lately. Anybody seen Snake?"

Heads shook.

Cook said, "He come for supplies day before yesterday."

I didn't want to ask too many questions too soon so I let Snake Bradon slide. I'd get Black Pete alone sometime and get a rundown on everybody. I said, "That doesn't add up. I heard there were eighteen in the house besides me."

Everybody looked puzzled except Cook. Chain said, "Ain't been that many people around here in years. You got us guys, Cook, Tyler, Wayne, and Snake trying to keep this barn from falling apart."

I ate some. I don't know what it was. As good as lunch but less identifiable. Cook was fond of stuff she could do in a pot.

After a while the silence got to me. I had a feeling it wasn't just for my benefit. These people wouldn't talk much more without me there. "What about the blond girl? Who's she?"

That got them looking perplexed. Peters asked, "What blonde?"

I looked at him for about ten seconds. Maybe he wasn't yanking my leg. "About twenty, gorgeous. As tall as Jennifer, even slimmer, hair almost white that hangs to her waist. Blue eyes, I think. Timid as a mouse. Dressed in white. I caught her watching me several times today." A recollection. "Dellwood. I saw her when you were there. You told me she was Jennifer."

Dellwood made a face. "Yes sir. But I didn't see her. I assumed it was Miss Jennifer."

"I didn't wear white today," Jennifer said. "What kind of dress was it?"

I tried my best, which isn't bad. The Dead Man's big accomplishment is that he's taught me to observe and recollect.

Jennifer said, "I don't have anything like that," trying to sound bored and failing. They all exchanged glances. I took it none of them knew who I was talking about.

I asked, "Who's taking care of the General? If you're all here?"

"He's sleeping, sir," Dellwood said. "Cook and I will wake him for supper after we're finished."

"Nobody with him?"

"He doesn't want to be coddled, sir."

"You sure as hell ask a lot of questions," Chain said.

"A habit I've got. I'm working on it. There any beer around the place? I could use some dessert."

Dellwood explained. "The General doesn't approve of drink, sir. He doesn't permit it on the property."

No wonder they were such a cheerful bunch. I looked at Peters hard. "You didn't mention that." If he'd done his homework, he would have known I liked my beer. He smiled and winked. The son of a bitch.

"Not a bad meal, Cook. Whatever it was. You need a hand clearing away?"

The others looked at me like I was crazy. She said, "You ask for trouble, you get it. Grab a load and follow me."

I did. And by the time I got back for a second load, the rats had scattered.

I was going to have to ask Peters about the disparity between Cook's head count and everyone else's.

8

After supper I wandered up to my quarters. As I approached the door, digging for the key Dellwood had left in the primitive lock, I noticed the door was a quarter inch ajar. So.

I wasn't surprised. Not after Jennifer's bold peek into my duffel bag and the trick at the old workers' barracks.

I paused. Go ahead like the cavalry? Or exercise a little caution? Caution didn't go with the image I wanted to project. But it did contribute to an extended life. And nobody was looking.

I dropped to my knees by the doorframe, examined the lock. There were a few fine scratches on the old brass plate surrounding the keyhole. As I said, a primitive piece of hardware, pickable by anyone with patience. I leaned forward to see what I could glim through the keyhole.

Nothing. It was dark in there. I'd left a lamp burning. Trap?

If so, a dumb one. Especially not getting the door all the way shut. These old boys weren't pros but I didn't see them making that basic a mistake. And if not a trap, but just a search, I doubted they'd snuff the lamp. That was a dead giveaway.

The word *disinformation* trotted through my mind. From the spy game. Provide not just false information but more information than necessary, most of it untrustworthy, so that all information received came under the shadow of doubt.

I backed off, leaned against a wall, nodded to myself. Yeah. That felt like a good intuition. I was going to be allowed to find out all kinds of things, most of which were untrue, useless, or misleading. Hard to put a puzzle together when you've got three times too many pieces.

Which still left me faced with a decision what to do right now. It was still possible there was some clumsy idiot hiding in the dark waiting to whack me.

So why not play the game right back?

The hall was a good twelve feet wide, oversize like everything else in that house, and cluttered up with the usual hardware. Not twenty feet from me was a suit of armor. I got it and lugged it over in front of the door, pushed it up close, backed off, snuffed the nearest hall lamps so whoever was inside wouldn't see anything but a silhouette. Then I got behind the tin suit, gave the door a nudge, walked the armor ahead a couple of feet, stopped like I was startled.

Nothing happened. I backed out and got one of the hall lamps and took it inside.

Nobody there but me and my decoy. I checked the closets and bedroom and dressing room. Nobody there and nothing obviously disturbed. If the place had been tossed, it had been done by an expert so good he'd noticed and replaced the little giveaways I'd rigged.

So what did we have here? Somebody had gone to the trouble of picking the lock just to snuff a lamp?

I closed the door, patted the armor's shoulder. "Somebody's playing games, old buddy. I think I'll let you stick around."

I lugged it over and shoved it into a cloak closet just big enough to contain it, lighted my lamps, took the hall lamp back, lighted the lamps there, went inside, locked up, sat down at the writing table to let my dinner digest.

Didn't work too well. I need a beer or two to get the most out of those occasions. I had to do something about the shortage. In fact, it might be a good idea to vanish for a while and consult some experts.

There was ink and paper and whatnot in the drawer under the table. I got it out and started making notes. I put down the names of everyone I'd met and hadn't, and a mystery woman to the side. Peters, Dellwood, the General, Cook, Jennifer. Hawkes, Chain, and Kaid. Tyler and Wayne, who had the night off, and somebody named Snake Bradon, who was antisocial and wouldn't come in the house. Somebody named Candy who, theoretically, didn't count because he'd been fired long ago. And Harcourt, who used to sneak his girlfriends in, but who had left six months ago.

Eighteen people here, according to Cook. By my count, eleven, plus the mystery blonde. We had us what the Marines call a manpower shortfall.

Someone tapped on the door. "Yeah?"

"Peters, Mike."

I let him in. "What's up?"

"I brought you a list of the missing stuff. Can't guarantee it's complete. Not the kind of stuff you see every day and notice is gone right away." He handed me a wad of papers. I sat down and looked it over.

"This is a lot of stuff." And all small. Each item had a guessed value noted. Stuff like gold medals, old jewelry belonging to Stantnor women long dead, silver serviceware disdained by rough, tough ex-Marines, decorative weapons.

"If you want, I can go through the house room by room and get a better count. Trouble is, it's hard to tell what's gone because there isn't anybody who knows what all belongs."

"Doesn't seem worth the trouble. Unless you could find out about something that could be traced." Little on the list fit that description. The thief had shown restraint.

Even so, he'd gotten enough so the bottom line made my eyes bug. "Twenty-two thousand marks?"

"Based on my best guess at the intrinsic value of metal and gems. I assume there'd be a big knockdown at a fence."

"There would be, partly offset by artistic value. A lot of this don't look like the junk that gets melted down."

"Maybe."

"Are we committed to finding the thief?" I was, that being the commission I'd accepted from the General. I was fishing for Black Pete's feelings.

"Yes. The old man may not have long. I don't want him going off burdened by knowing somebody got away with betraying him."

"Right. Then what I'll do is subcontract a search for the fence. Sometimes it helps to come back at a thief from the other end. Work me up a description of four or five outstanding items and I'll have somebody try to find them."

"You'll have to pay for that?"

"Yes. You going to squeeze the General's coppers?"

He smiled. "I shouldn't. But I'm not used to not having to watch every one. Anything you need?"

"I need to know more about the people here." I looked at my list. "Counting three guys I haven't met and not counting my ghost lady, I come up with eleven names. Cook tells me eighteen. Where're the other seven?"

"I told you she has some loose threads. She's been here since they built the first place—literally—and she never quite knows what year it is. When we first came here from the Cantard there were eighteen people, counting her and Jennifer. More before the old man finished dismissing the old staff. Now eleven is right."

"Where did the others go?"

"Sam and Tark just up and died on us. Wollack got on the wrong end of a bull when we were breeding cows and got himself gored and trampled. The others just drifted away. They got fed up, I guess, hung around less and less, then just didn't come back."

I leaned forward, got a fresh sheet of paper, divided five million by two and gave two and a half mil to Jennifer, then divided two and a half by sixteen and came up with a hundred fifty-six thousand marks and change.

Not bad. And I never knew anybody who would walk on a hundred fifty thousand, gold or silver.

I did some more math. Nine into two and a half million came out two hundred seventy-seven thousand and change. Damned near double your money.

Was there something else going on here?

I didn't mention it. It was something to keep in mind, though.

"You onto something?" Peters asked.

"I doubt it."

Time for some footwork. "Having a little trouble making sense of things. There any way we can find out where those four men are now? Also, I'm going to need to know more about the General's bequeathal arrangements."

He frowned. "Why?"

"It's a large estate. You said he used his bequests as a hammer. Maybe he ran those guys off. Maybe one of them might be trying to get even, either by doing the stealing or slipping him poison."

"You've got me there." He looked it.

"Two things, then. A copy of the will. And find out if there was a clash between the General and any of those four."

"You don't really think they'd be sneaking back?"

I didn't, no. I thought they were dead. With my confidence in human decency aroused, I was sure somebody was playing a game of last one left— and doing such a damned good job, nobody else was suspicious. But . . . If somebody was, then that somebody was innocent of trying to murder the old man. That somebody would want to keep the General healthy while the field was narrowed. That somebody might even bring in an outside specialist . . . presuming he had a genuine cause for concern.

"Anyone have a spare key or master key for my room?"

That caught him from the blind side. "Dellwood. Why?"

"Somebody picked the lock and got in between the time I left for supper and the time I came back here."

"Why would . . . ?"

"Hey. That's a petty one compared to why would somebody want to kill the General. If that somebody exists he might be real nervous about me. What did you all do when you split up after supper?" I was going to play logical puzzle. Eliminate me and Cook because I didn't do it and she was with me. Take Dellwood off the hook because he didn't need to pick locks. Peters because he knew about me already. Eliminate anybody who was with them the whole time. . . .

"Dellwood would have gone to get the General up and ready for dinner. I assume Jennifer went with him. She usually does. She stays till Cook brings his food and helps him eat if he can't manage himself. I was in my quarters writing up the list from notes."

"Uhm." I thought a minute. "I do have one problem with this, Sarge. And that's a reason for being here. I need to ask questions. I need to find loose strings I can pull on. Kind of hard to do that when I don't have a good excuse. Cook's already told me I'm too nosy."

"I suppose. I had hopes but I didn't really think you could manage without giving yourself away."

"How many people know about the missing trinkets? As opposed to how many know you think somebody's trying to kill the General? Why not tell the truth? Say the old man hired me to find out who's stealing from him. They might even find it amusing if they think he's imagining it. And the would-be assassin should relax. The others might open up after I convince them somebody *is* stealing from the old man. Right?"

"I suppose." He didn't like it, though.

"Figure out a way to let it get out. So everybody knows but it seems like I don't know they know. Maybe joke about the General having another fantasy."

"All right. Anything else?"

"No. I'm going to turn in. I'm going to roll out early and make a run into the city to put somebody on the track of the stolen goodies."

"Is that a hint?"

It was. "I didn't think of it that way. But I guess it is."

"I'll see you in the morning, then." He went out.

I locked the door behind him, returned to the writing table.

Seemed to me there might be three puzzles here: who was stealing from the General, who was trying to kill him, and who was eliminating his heirs. It seemed reasonable to suppose that each thing—if any were fact—would be going on independent of the others, since the thefts were petty compared to murder and killing the General wouldn't be in the interest of whoever was trying to enlarge his share of the estate.

I could be up to my neck in villains.

I did hit the sack right away. I doubt Peters believed I would, because he knew the hours I keep. But I did need sleep and I had plans for the wee hours of the morning.

9

At home I usually control my internal clock. Go to sleep when I want, wake up when I want, give or take ten minutes. I didn't leave the clock behind. I woke right on time.

And was aware of a presence before I opened my eyes. I don't know how. Some sound so soft I didn't catch it consciously. Some subtle scent. Maybe just a sixth sense. Whatever, I knew somebody was there.

I was on my left side, facing the wall opposite the door, sunk so deep in eiderdown, I couldn't move fast if you branded me. I tried sneaky, faking a slow rollover in my sleep.

I didn't fool anybody. All I saw was the tail end of the blonde sliding out the bedroom door. "Hey! Hang on. I want to talk to you."

She bolted.

I climbed up out of that bed, tangled myself in the covers, fell on my face, said colorful things. That's Garrett. Light on his feet. A real gymnast. Has moves like a cat. When I hit the sitting room she was gone and there wasn't a sign she'd been there. The door was locked.

I lighted a few lamps and surveyed the big room. I hadn't heard the door. I hadn't heard a key in the lock. I didn't like that.

Damned spooky old house was the kind that might come equipped with secret passages and hidden panels and all that stuff, maybe with secret dungeons below the root cellar and bones buried behind false foundations.

I was going to have a nice time here, I was, I was. All I needed to make it a real vacation were ghosts and monsters. I went to the window. The sky was clear. A nail paring of moon was headed west.

"Come on. You're not trying. We need some rain and lightning. Or at least some fog on the moor and something howling in the night."

Back for a circuit of the room. I didn't find any secret entrances.

I'd deal with that later, when there was time to measure walls and whatnot. Right now I had to prowl, while at least some of the denizens of the place weren't keeping track.

I dragged my tin suit friend out of the closet, into the bedroom. I detached him from the support that held him upright, put him in bed. Better than using pillows to make it look like somebody was home. Looked perfect once I pulled a sheet over his helmet. "Rest easy, buddy."

I didn't like the way things were going. Somebody here might be less than friendly. I collected my favorite head-knocker, an oak nightstick with a pound of lead in the business end, then slipped into the hall. I was alone out there. One lamp burned. Presumably Dellwood had been around to snuff the others to save oil. He was the only guy I'd seen working, other than Cook.

I'd have to find out what everybody did. Should've asked Peters while I had him.

I went to the east end of the hall where a small window looked out on the grounds. Nothing out there but darkness and stars. The werewolves and vampires were taking the night off. I retreated to the first door on the left.

I seemed to be the only inhabitant of that floor in the wing so I didn't try for quiet. I picked the lock and marched in, lamp in front in my left hand, head-knocker in my right. I needn't have bothered. The room was a warehouse for cobwebs. Nobody had been in there in a decade.

I did a cursory inspection, went to the room across the hall. Same story.

Every suite on the floor was the same, except the last, which showed signs that someone had visited recently. In that room I noted circles on the mantel where the dust was thinner. Like something had been removed. Candlesticks or small doodads. I tried to get something from the marks left by the visitor's feet. There's always hope you'll find something unique, like maybe feet the size of pumpernickels or only two toes if they run barefoot. It didn't pay off this time. The intruder had shuffled, probably not intentionally. Not the sort of thing your average thief thinks of.

The search was taking longer than I'd expected. I decided to take a quick tour and leave detail work for later. At least I'd know my way around.

There was a partial floor above mine, reached via an enclosed stair. I went up. That floor was one vast dark room over the great hall. It was stuffed with junk, mostly as dusty as the rooms below. But there was a path beaten from the stairhead across to a stair down to the fourth floor of the west wing. A shortcut.

The alternative was to descend to the second floor and cut across on a narrow balcony above the back door, placed there so somebody could address a crowd.

Might as well go across, work my way down the west wing, come back on the ground floor, and work my way up.

The west wing was inhabited. I didn't enter any rooms. Maybe tomorrow night. Maybe while I was in town I could have a locksmith check my key to see if he could create a skeleton key for its type of lock.

Fourth-floor hall and a stroll on the balcony there. Nothing. Likewise the third floor and its balcony. The design differed from my wing. The halls were shorter, ending at the doors of the suites of the masters of the estate. Two doors on the third floor showed light underneath. Either somebody was up late or somebody was scared of the dark.

Second floor had only five large suites, probably for honored guests like dukes and counts, firelords and stormwardens, and others a ranking commander might entertain.

The ground floor boasted rooms meant for other purposes. The west wing was where, in times past, the businesses of the estate and its masters had been conducted. The doors to several rooms were open. I invited myself in. I didn't find anything.

From the west wing I walked across to the east, where I knew I'd be into the kitchen, pantries, dining hall, and whatnot. I'd been through some of that but hadn't had a chance to pry.

As I passed the brave champion still stubbornly skewering his dragon, I got that creepy sensation. I looked around, saw no one. My blond admirer? I was beginning to think she was a spook.

Not literally. The place was creepy at high noon. It had fallen from a ghost story, but I didn't entertain the notion that it was haunted. The world is filled with the strange, the magical, the supernatural, but I didn't figure I'd need haunts to explain anything here. Any schemes here had been set in motion by the root of all evil amongst the living.

A closer examination of the dining room proved it to be what I'd figured, big, with decorations fitting the theme of the house. I wondered how many battles the Stantnors had fought.

The room had a high ceiling, which suggested that part of the second floor east didn't exist. True. I found out when I explored the pantry.

A door there opened on stairs. One set went up, another down. It was as dark as a vampire's heart in there. I went up. The way led to storerooms filled with housekeeping goodies, some of which looked like they'd been laid in before the turn of the century. Some dead Stantnor had saved by buying wholesale.

Nobody swept or dusted but the place was orderly. It was inhabited by moths who found my lamp irresistible.

Why so much room for storage?

I came on stacks of four-inch-thick oak things, bound in iron, each with a number chalked onto the black iron. Curious, I looked closer.

They were covers for the windows, to seal them if the house was besieged. They had to be as old as the house itself. Had they ever been used? Not in the past century, I was sure.

I found a strong room in the southeast corner. The door was latched but not locked. It was an armory. Inside were weapons enough for a company—as though there weren't enough around the house already. Everything steel was covered with grease, everything wood coated with paraffin. Might be interesting to find out what the climate was like when the house was built. Troubled times, apparently.

I spent too much time there. When I descended it was too late. Cook was banging around in the kitchen. I slipped out before she tripped over me.

As I hit the fourth floor I caught a glimpse of white across the way. My lovely mystery lady. I blew her a kiss.

'd had another visitor. This one had left in a hurry. He'd left a key in the lock with the door standing open. I saw why when I went into the bedroom.

My visitor had murdered the suit of armor. He'd walked in, wound up with an antique battle-ax, and had let the poor boy have it. The ax was still there.

I laughed. Bet he drizzled down his leg, thinking he'd walked into a trap.

I sobered quickly. That was twice. Next time more care might go into the attempt. I was way out on a limb here. I had to take steps.

I locked up, pocketed the key—which wasn't identical to mine, so might be a skeleton key. I got the tin man out of bed and the ax out of him. "Sorry about that. But we'll get our revenge." I used the ax to rig a booby trap. Anybody who walked through the bedroom door was in for a rude welcome.

Then I took an hour nap.

I was early for breakfast, first to arrive. Cook was up to her ears in work setting platters ready. "Need a hand?"

"I need ten. I don't know what you're up to, boy, sucking up to me, but you better believe I'll use you. Get over to the oven and see how them rolls are coming."

I did. "Maybe a minute more."

"What you know about baking?"

I explained the arrangement at my house, where old Dean handles the drudgery and cooking. He's a good cook. He taught me. I can put together a decent meal when I want. Like when I give him time off because I want him out while I entertain.

"Don't know if you're lying or not. Probably are. I never seen a man yet who could cook."

I didn't tell her Dean thought the only good cooks were men. "I should get you together. To watch the sparks fly."

"Huh. Time's up. Get them rolls out. Drag that pot of butter over."

I glanced at the butter. "Fresh?"

"Snake just brung it in."

"He going to join us?"

She laughed. "Not Snake. He don't have nothing to do with nobody. Just grabbed him some food and lit out. Not sociable, Snake."

"What's his problem?"

"Head got scrambled in the Cantard. He was down there twenty years, never got a scratch. On the outside." She shook her head, started piling sausages and bacon on a platter. "Sad. I knew him when he was a pup. Cute kid, he was. Too delicate and sensitive for a Marine. But he thought he had to try. So here he is, an old man with his head in knots. Used to draw the prettiest pictures, that boy. Coulda been a great painter. Had him a magic eye. Could see right inside things and drawed what he saw. Any damn fool can draw the outside of things, the way they want we should see them. Takes a genius to see the truth. That boy saw. You going to stand there jawing till lunchtime? Or you going to eat?"

I fixed myself a plate without mentioning the fact that I couldn't get a word in edgewise because I couldn't get a word in edgewise. She rolled right along. "I told the General then—he was just commissioned—it was a raging shame to waste the boy down there. And I told him again when he come back. And the General, he told me, 'You were right, Cook. It was a sin against humanity, taking him.' But, you know, he couldn't have stopped the boy if he'd wanted. Had that damnfool stubborn streak and thought it was his duty to go with the lord to war."

The rush came while she chattered. There were two new faces, presumably Tyler and Wayne. They looked like they hadn't slept. The whole crowd took their platters to the dining room.

I asked Cook, "That Tyler and Wayne?"

"How'd you guess?"

"Lucky stab. Anybody else I haven't met?"

"Who else could there be?"

"I don't know. Yesterday you said there were eighteen people here. I've seen ten, plus this Snake that's shy and a blonde that only I can see. Comes up short of eighteen."

"Ain't eighteen."

"You said eighteen."

"Boy, I'm four hundred years old. 'Less I concentrate, I don't remember where I am in time. I just cook and set table and wash and don't pay no attention to nothing else. Just sort of drift. Don't see nothing, don't say nothing. Last time I looked up they was eighteen, counting me. Must've been a while. Hell. Maybe that's why there's so many leftovers. Been cooking too much."

"I didn't notice too many places set at the table."

She paused. "You're right. Part of me must keep track."

"Been with the Stantnors a long time?"

"Came to them with my momma when I was a kit. Long time back, when the humans hereabouts still had emperors. 'Fore they ever moved out here and built the first house. This one's only maybe two hundred. Was a sight when she was new, she was."

"You must've seen some sights in your time."

"Seen some," she agreed. "Served every king and stormwarden and firelord right there in that dining room." She headed that way. That ended our conversation.

I stuck my head in. Nobody showed any special disappointment. Nobody turned handsprings, either. They were a depressing bunch.

These guys had spent their whole lives together. You'd think they could make conversation—unless they'd said everything there was to say. I feel that way with some people, sometimes before anything gets said at all.

Tyler and Wayne were cut from Marine lifer cloth. Whatever the physical differences between men, they gain a certain uniformity in service. Tyler was a lean, narrow-faced character with hard brown eyes, salt-and-pepper hair, and a thin, speckled beard trimmed within a half-inch of his skin. Wayne was my size, maybe twenty pounds heavier, not fat. He looked like he could throw cows around if the passion took him. He was six inches taller than Tyler and blond, with icy blue eyes, yet you felt the sameness in them. You even felt the identity with Chain, who had gone to seed.

I'd spent five years in the company of men like them. Any one of them would be capable of murder if he took a mind. Human life wasn't anything special to them. They'd seen too much death.

Which did present one puzzle.

Marines are straightforward kinds of guys. If one wanted the General dead, chances were he'd just do it. Unless there was some overpowering motive to make it a lingering death.

Like, say, hanging on to a share of the old man's estate?

Worrying about it was pointless. You can't force these things. They have to unfold.

I helped Cook clear away, then put on my traveling shoes.

••• **11**

I hadn't been to Morley's place in months. It wasn't that we'd had a falling-out or anything; I just hadn't had a need, nor any urge to graze on the cattle food that comes out of his kitchen. I arrived about nine. He's closed to business then. He's open from eleven to six in the morning, catering to every sentient species there is, all so warped they try to subsist on vegetables.

It takes all kinds. Some of my best friends eat there. I've done so myself. Without enthusiasm.

So. Nine o'clock. The place was locked up. I went to the back door and gave the secret knock, which means I hammered and howled till Morley's man Wedge brought a four-foot piece of lead pipe and offered to move my face to my belly button region.

"This's business, Wedge."

"I didn't figure you was in heat for some bean curd. You don't come around unless you want something."

"I pay for what I get."

He snorted. He didn't think it was right, me using Morley just because Morley had taken advantage of me, at deadly risk and without my consent, to get out of some heavy gambling debts.

"Cash money, Wedge. And he don't have to get off his butt. He just needs to have somebody do some legwork."

That didn't cheer him up. He's one of the guys who does Morley's leg-work. But he didn't slam the door.

"Come." He eased me in and barred the door, led me through kitchens where cooks were butchering cabbages and broccoli, parked me at the serving bar, drew me a mug of apple juice. "Wait." He went upstairs.

The public room was naked and forlorn, almost painfully quiet. The way it ought to be all the time, instead of overcrowded.

Morley Dotes is a headhunter. A kneebreaker and a lifetaker. Most of the guys who work for him help. Morley is a deadly symbiote feeding on society's dark underside. He's the best at what he does, barring maybe a couple of guys who work for Chodo Contague.

Adding up the account, Morley Dotes is everything I don't like. He's the kind of guy I wanted to take down when I decided to put on my good-guy hat. But I like him.

Sometimes you can't help yourself.

Wedge came down shaking his head. "What's up?" I asked.

"He's taking this health stuff too far."

"You're telling me? He's like born again, trying to save everybody else." The world's only vegetarian lifetaker. Wants to save the world from the perils of red meat—before he cuts its throat. I don't know. Maybe there's no conflict but it sounds like one to me. "He's added to the list?"

"Been a few months, right?"

"Last time I was here he'd sworn off gambling and was making it stick. He tried women but couldn't hold out."

"He forgot that crock. Say that for him. The thing now is early to bed, early to rise. He's up. Now. Up and dressed and fed and doing his morning workout. A year ago you wouldn't have caught him dead out of bed this time of day."

You could have if there was enough money in it. "Wonders never cease, do they?"

"He said come up. You want a refill?"

"Why not? Fruit juice is the only thing here I can handle."

He winked. He wasn't one of Morley's converts. He topped off my mug. I took it up to Morley's office, which is the barbican to his personal quarters. I'm about as close to a friend as he has, but I've never been past the office. My hair is too short and I don't wear enough makeup.

Dotes was doing sit-ups, chunking them out like a machine. My stomach hurt just watching.

"You're in pretty good shape for a guy your age," I told him. I wasn't sure what that was. It could be substantial. He's part dark-elf. Elves can last a long time.

"I take it you're working again." He said it while popping up and down. Like there was no strain to what he was doing.

I told myself I had to start doing a few exercises. At my age, when you lose it, it's hard to get back. "Why do you assume—"

"You don't come down here unless you want something."

"Not true. I used to bring Maya in all the time." That was before she and I had gone our own ways.

"You lost a gem there, Garrett." He rolled over, started doing push-ups.

His dark-elf blood doesn't scream out. He looks like a short, slim, dark-haired man in good shape. He's quick on his feet. There's an air of the dangerous about him, but not one of menace. Maybe that's why women find him irresistible.

"Maybe. I do miss her, some. She was a good kid."

"Pretty, too. So you going on with Tinnie?"

My friend Tinnie Tate, professional high-tempered redhead. Ours is an unpredictable relationship. "I see her. When she doesn't think I deserve to be punished by not seeing her."

"Only smart thing you've done since I've known you is not tell her about Maya." He completed fifty fast ones, jumped up. He wasn't swearing. I felt like kicking his behind. "What's up?"

"You heard of General Stantnor?"

"Used to be Marine commandant?"

"The same."

"What about him?"

"A guy who works for him, my old company sergeant, called in a debt. He got me to do a job for the old boy."

"Don't you ever work just to be working? I never saw anyone like you."

"I know. I'm a dog. You never see a dog do anything when he's not hungry. If I'm not hungry, why work?"

"What about the General? I do work when I'm not hungry. And I've got plenty of that here."

"The old boy is trying to die. My old sergeant thinks somebody is trying to kill him. Slowly, so it looks like a wasting disease."

"Is somebody?"

"I don't know. He's been doing it a long time. You know a way to do that?"

"What's his color like?"

"His color?"

"Sure. There are poisons you could use in cumulative dosages. The color is the giveaway."

"He's kind of a sickly yellow. His hair is falling out in clumps. And his skin has a translucent quality."

Morley frowned. "Not blue or gray?"

"Yellow. Like pale butterscotch."

He shook his head. "Can't tell you based on that."

"He has seizures, too."

"Crazies?"

"Like heart tremors, or something."

"Doesn't sound familiar. Maybe if I saw him."

"I'd like that. I don't know if I can arrange it. They're all paranoid about strangers." I gave him a rundown on the players.

"Sounds like a bughouse."

"Could be. All of them, except Jennifer and Cook, spent at least thirty years in the Marines, mostly in the Cantard."

He grinned. "I'm not going to say it."

"Good for you. We all make the world a little holier when we resist temptation. One more thing. The old man thinks he hired me to find out who's stealing the silver and his old war trophies." I produced the list. Morley started reading. "I'll pay legwork fees for somebody to make the rounds and see if any of that is moving through the usual channels."

"Saucerhead needs work."

Saucerhead Tharpe is a friend, of sorts, in a line somewhere between Morley's and mine. He has more scruples than Dotes and more ambition than me, but he's as big as a house and looks half as smart. People can't take him seriously. He never gets the best jobs.

"All right. I'll pay his standard rate. Bonus if he recovers any of the articles. Bonus if he gets a description of the thief."

"On the cuff?" That was a hint.

I gave him advance money. He said, "I thank you and Saucerhead thanks you. I know you're doing an old buddy a favor but it seems damned tame. Especially if the old guy is just dying."

"There's something going on. Somebody tried to off me," I told him.

He laughed. "I wish I could have seen the guy's face when he swung that ax and you bonged like a bell. You've still got the luck."

"Maybe."

"Why are they after you?"

"I don't know. Money? That's the one angle that makes this interesting. The old boy is worth about five million marks. His son is dead. His wife died twenty years ago. His daughter, Jennifer, gets half the estate and the other half goes to his Marine cronies. Three years ago he had seventeen heirs. Since then, two died supposedly natural deaths, one got killed by a mad bull, and four disappeared. A little basic math shows that nearly doubles the take for the survivors."

Morley sat down behind his desk, put his feet up, cleaned his pearly white teeth with a six-inch steel toothpick. I didn't interrupt his thoughts.

"There's potential for foul play in that setup, Garrett."

"Human nature being what it is."

"If I was a betting man I'd give odds that somebody is fattening his share."

"Human nature being what it is."

"Nobody walks out on that kind of money. Not you, not me, not a saint. So maybe you have something interesting after all."

"Maybe. Thing is, I don't see any way to tie it up in a package. If I find out who's stealing—which makes no sense considering the payoff down the road—I'm not likely to find out who's killing the old man. That doesn't make sense for whoever is cutting down the number of heirs. He'd want the old man to hang on."

"What happens if the daughter checks out before he does?"

"Damn!" A critical point and it hadn't occurred to me. If everything went to the boys she'd really be on the spot. "The odd thing is, none of them act like they know what's going on. They seem to get along. They don't watch each other over their shoulders. I did, and I was only there one night."

"A marvelous aspect of your species is that most of you see only what you want."

"What's that mean?"

"Maybe those guys are old buddies and only one of them realizes that throat-cutting can be profitable. Maybe nobody is suspicious because they all know their old buddies wouldn't do something like that after all they've been through together."

Could be. I'd kind of had that problem myself. I couldn't picture me turning on anybody I'd been running with that long. "And the whole thing could be what they say it is. Three dead by explainable cause and four who couldn't handle the lifestyle and walked because money didn't mean anything."

"And the moon could be mouse bait."

"You have a dark outlook."

"Supported every day in the street. The other night a thirty-six-year-old man knifed his mom and dad because they wouldn't give him money for a bottle of wine. That's the real world, Garrett. We're our own worst night-mares." He chuckled. "You're lucky this time. You don't have anything weird. No vampires, no werewolves, no witches, no sorcerers, no dead gods trying to come back to life. None of the stuff you usually stumble into."

I snorted. Those things aren't on every street corner, but they're part of the world. Everybody brushes against them eventually. They didn't impress me, though I was happy not to deal with them.

I said, "I could have seen a ghost."

"A what?"

"A ghost. I keep seeing a woman that nobody admits is there. That no-body else sees. Unless they're pulling my leg. Which they probably are."

"Or you're crazy. She's a gorgeous blonde, right?"

"A blonde. Not bad."

"You're daydreaming out loud in your eyes. Your wishful thinking has gotten to you."

"Maybe. I'll know before I'm done. There was something else I wanted but it escapes me now."

"Must not have been important."

"Probably not. I'd better get back out there."

"You take some equipment? Hate to think of you up to your ears in kill-ers with nothing but your teeth and toenails."

"I've got a trick or two."

He grunted. "You always do. Don't turn your back on anybody."

"I won't."

As I started to close the door, he asked, "What's the daughter look like?"

"Early twenties. A looker but not a talker. Spoiled rotten, probably."

He looked thoughtful, then shrugged, got up, dropped down and started doing more push-ups. I shut the door. I can't stand seeing a man abuse himself.

●●●**12**

headed south feeling smug. I knew my Morley Dotes. Curiosity would
get him. He'd push his end beyond what I'd hired him to do. He'd go
fishing amongst his contacts. If there was something going on involving
the Stantnors, he'd find out.

The smugness disappeared after I walked out South Gate.

That's when the drizzle started. That's when I started cussing myself for
my distrust of horses. Hell, if I couldn't ride, I could hire a coach. I had a
client. I could charge it to expenses. Expenses are wonderfully flexible—
especially if the client fails the attitude test.

I got some wet before I reached my destination.

Odd. Most of those big country places have names. The Maples. Wind-
ward. Sometimes something that doesn't make any sense, like Brittany
Stone. But this one could have been a squatter's hut. The Stantnor place.
Ancient family seat and museum but not enough of a home for anybody to
give it a name.

I was still a quarter mile off when Jennifer Stantnor flew out the front
door, headed toward me. She hadn't put a wrap on. Peters came after her,
gaining but not looking like he was trying to catch her.

They reached me at the same time. Jennifer looked irked that Peters had
come. Peters looked exasperated at her. I did my best to look puzzled, which
isn't hard. That's where I am most of the time. I raised an eyebrow way up.
It's one of my best tricks. Jennifer just stood there, panting. Peters, less

winded despite being almost three times her age, said, "There's been a hunting accident."

I kept a straight face. "Oh?"

"Let's get in out of the rain."

I looked at the girl. I think she wanted to talk. Grimly, she said, "I don't think it was an accident."

It probably wasn't, if someone had gotten killed. But I didn't say that. I just grunted.

Peters talked while we walked. "We've had trouble with poachers. There are deer on the grounds. A fair herd."

Jennifer interjected, "We put out feed. We don't take many."

"Three all last year," Peters said. "Peasants . . . The animals make easy targets. They're not so wary here. The past month we've had six intrusions. That we know of."

Jennifer said, "Dad gets more upset about the trespassing than the poaching. He has a thing about boundaries. Like they're lines of steel."

"After the last incident," Peters said, as we climbed the steps to the house, "the General ordered regular patrols. He wanted someone caught and an example made. Today Kaid, Hawkes, Tyler, and Snake had the duty. Hawkes apparently caught somebody in the act. He sounded his hunting horn."

Jennifer said, "When the others got there, he was on the ground with an arrow in him. A gutted deer was hanging in a tree fifty feet away."

"Interesting. And sad. But why tell me? Sounds like something you people can handle."

Jennifer looked puzzled. Peters said, "This is going to sound silly. You're the only scout around here. All these lifers and none of them can follow a trail."

"Oh." Maybe. "It's been years. And I wasn't that good." I recalled my stumbling around during a few recent cases.

"Mediocre is better than what the rest of us are." Peters looked at Chain, who was headed our way. "How is he?"

"I don't think he'll make it. He needs a surgeon."

"You know the old man. No doctors in the house."

"We can't move him without killing him."

Jennifer snapped, "Get a doctor! My father doesn't have to know. He never comes out of his room."

"Dellwood will tell him."

"I'll handle Dellwood."

"Go," Peters told Chain, and Chain got his carcass moving.

I said, "I take it Hawkes is still alive."

"He's fighting."

"Can I talk to him?"

"He's out. Way out. Not much chance he'll come around unless Chain gets a cutter in time."

"Show me where it happened before the rain wipes out the sign."

I got to ride. Lucky me. The horse was hospitable all the way out, but I knew it had heard of me through the grapevine those monsters have. It grinned when it heard my name. It was waiting for a chance.

It was a good ride out. The Stantnors had a lot of land. We didn't talk much. I took in the countryside, getting the lay, the landmarks. I might need to know them.

I'd developed the habit young. It was my apparent knack for knowing my way around that got me volunteered as a scout when the real Sexton vanished.

"Looks like Snake came back out," Peters said as we crossed a rise and came to the scene.

I saw a man under an oak near a hanging animal carcass. "Sarge, I never knew any of these guys when I was in. Did any of them know Sexton?"

He looked at me funny. "I don't think so."

I dismounted, tied the reins to an oak sapling. My mount got a forlorn look. "Thought I'd just drop them and you'd scurry when I turned my back, didn't you?"

"What?" Peters asked.

"Talking to the horse. I talk to horses. They make more sense than people."

"Snake, this is Mike Sexton. Scouted for me in the islands. You probably heard he's here."

Snake grunted. He looked me over. I returned the favor.

If Chain had gone to seed, this one had gone a step beyond. His hair hadn't been cut since he'd gotten out. His beard was a bramble patch. He didn't change clothes or bathe very often. His pants were covered with curious colored stains. He said, "I heard."

"You found anything?"

Snake grunted. It sounded negative.

I looked at the carcass. Wasn't much to it. "Kind of puny, isn't it?"

"Fawn," Snake said. "Just lost its spots."

Yes. A little rusty, Garrett. Why would a poacher take a fawn? If he was after the meat and the herd wasn't spooky, he'd go for a bigger kill. I gave the carcass a closer look.

It was ten years since I'd done my own butchering, but this job looked amateurish. Like it had been done by someone who'd seen animals butchered but who hadn't ever done it himself.

"This patrol this morning. Was there a set plan? Specific assignments?"

Peters said, "We had a routine, if that's what you mean. Routes we'd figured so four men could cover everything."

Not exactly what I wanted to know. I couldn't be more specific without giving away more than I wanted. "Where was Hawke when he was hit?"

"Up here."

I followed Peters. The spot was obvious once you got there. Hawkes had thrashed around after he'd fallen. He'd lost enough blood to draw flies too stupid to go for the bonanza in the tree. The spot was fifty feet from the deer. A blind archer could have made the shot.

I picked out what I thought was Hawkes's back trail. I followed it, found a place where he'd stopped. "I'd guess this is where he sounded the horn. Then he went down and stopped again there."

"And the poacher let him have it."

Somebody did. "What time did it happen?"

"About nine."

"Uhm." That fawn had been dead a lot longer than that.

I walked back down. Snake still stood staring at the carcass. I asked, "You look around some?"

He grunted. "Why'd anybody want to do that to a little fawn?" An old buddy getting an arrow through the brisket didn't bother him. The fawn did.

I took another look at the carcass. I couldn't find its death wound. "Was there an arrow in it?"

"No."

Snake wasn't going to be much good for anything.

The tree where the fawn hung was a loner ten yards from the edge of a wood that followed a creek. That wood was only a hundred yards across. I headed downhill, swinging back and forth, looking for the poacher's trail.

I found it. Somebody in a big hurry had charged straight through the underbrush. Understandable, if you've just plinked some guy and you know he has friends coming.

Peters followed me. I asked, "Was there a set pattern to who rode where on these patrols?"

No way to keep him from wondering why I asked. He frowned. "No. We mixed it up so we wouldn't see the same ground every time."

Then the sniper hadn't been after somebody in particular, just somebody. Assuming the arrow hadn't come from the bow of a panicky poacher but someone who had laid a trap.

I was sure that when Hawkes stopped the second time, he'd seen whoever let him have it. That he'd been startled into halting. Otherwise, he'd have kept moving.

How much of that was Peters figuring out? The man wasn't stupid.

"How do you get along with your neighbors?"

"We ignore them. They ignore us. Most of them are scared of us."

I'd be scared if I had neighbors like them.

The sniper had become less panicky after fifty yards of flight. He'd turned onto an old game trail. There were too many leaves down for the ground to take good tracks but I could tell which way he had gone by the way they were disturbed. "Got any dogs? Or know where we could get some?"

"To track with? No."

The game trail went down to the creek, split. One fork crossed over, the other ran along the bank. My quarry had taken the latter.

A hundred fifty yards along, that path dipped into a wide, shallow, sandy-bottomed section of creek. And didn't come out the other side. I looked around. "I've lost it."

"God damn it, look again."

I looked, satisfied that he hadn't noticed the horse apples in the shallow water. Whoever had come down here had ridden away, down the streambed. No big deal, since the water was never more than a foot deep.

How many peasants forced to poach deer could afford to keep a horse?

"Sorry. There's nothing."

"Then I'll find some damned dogs."

As we walked back uphill I asked, "Who takes care of the stables here?"

"Mostly Snake, with help from Hawkes and Tyler. I don't get Snake. Takes care of the animals. Likes to. But you can't get him on a horse to save his life."

That made sense to me, though it was a little extreme.

I asked questions that got me curious looks but no answers. Unless they were liars and fast to boot—or in cahoots—none of the men on patrol could have dropped Hawkes. And Hawkes didn't do it to himself. That narrowed the field of suspects, but not enough. I wanted rid of Snake and Peters so I could prowl down that creek to wherever the sniper had left it.

"Shit!" Black Pete exploded. "We've got our heads up our asses."

"What?"

"What did we do every time we hit the Venageti on the damned island? What did I pound into you guys every damned day we were there?"

He'd gotten it. "Yeah. You don't leave tracks on water." Before a raid we'd always made sure we had an escape route crossed by a lot of water.

"The bastard walked down the creek. That's why you couldn't find anything."

"Yeah."

"Let's go."

"I'll check it out. No need you taking any more time off."

He looked at me hard, checked to see where Snake was. "What're you thinking, Garrett? I've seen you like this before. I haven't forgotten the stuff you pulled."

"I'm doing my job the best way I know. Nothing personal, but everybody's a suspect till I prove otherwise. No matter how well I think I know them."

He started getting angry.

"Can it. You wanted me to find out who's killing the old man, right? Which one of you guys would do that? None of you. Right? But one of you is. Till I nail it down you get treated like everybody else. If only because I'm supposedly looking for a thief. Get me?"

"You want to play a lone hand. You're the professional. I'll put up with it. For a while."

"Good. You don't have a choice, anyway. And that's nothing to get mad about."

He got mad anyway. They always do. They all think they ought to be the exception to the rule.

He rode off in a huff.

I didn't care, so long as he rode off.

13

My horse looked forlorn. I got it and led it down along the edge of the wood, looking for tracks. If I didn't find anything before I reached the property line, I'd work my way back up the far side of the woods.

Our villain had cunning in limited amounts. The stunt would have been sufficient if there'd been no cause for suspicion. But there was.

I found where a horseman had come out of the wood barely far enough away to be out of sight of the place where Hawkes had gotten it. The spacing of hoofmarks said he'd been in no real hurry once he'd gotten away from the woods. Meaning he hadn't been worried about explaining his presence.

That put Tyler and Chain back on the suspect list. They wouldn't have been questioned because they belonged out here.

I'd have to question the survivors, find out who said and did what before they set out. Might be some subtle indicator there.

Whoever the killer was, he'd been bold. He'd ridden around behind the rise you crossed to reach the ambush, then had headed home. At least, I presumed that was what he'd done while the poacher-hunters were fussing over Hawkes. I lost the trail.

I circled and circled, quartered this way and that, and couldn't find it again. The drizzle and the chill breeze overcame my devotion to my craft. I headed for the house.

I was stomping through that museum of a central hall, headed for a change of clothes, when Jennifer fluttered out of nowhere. She looked more feminine and frail and vulnerable than she had. She was flustered and frightened. I waited, though I had no urge to see her.

"Sergeant Hawkes died," she blurted. "Right there in front of me. He just shook all over and made this funny sound and he wasn't alive anymore."

"When?"

"Just a few minutes ago. I was looking for Dellwood when I saw you. I need somebody to tell me what to do."

If she was looking for comfort she'd come to the wrong man. I didn't feel like comforting anybody. Not even a gorgeous brunette who had all the right stuff in all the right places, put together to make a dead bishop howl. My late night and early morning had me feeling like I was carrying an extra fifty pounds. Worse, I'd missed lunch.

I'd already determined that Cook was immune to my golden tongue. She didn't even know what was happening. It went right past her. "Dellwood would be the best man to tell you. And speak of the devil."

Here he came, moving without the usual sedate deliberation. "Miss Jennifer, you were supposed to stay with Hawkes."

"He doesn't need me anymore."

Dellwood's eyes got big. "He . . . He . . ."

"Yes. What do we do now?"

I said, "Dellwood, I need to see the General. At his earliest convenience. I'll be in my quarters."

I was going to take a nap. I expected I'd have another long night. I'd better rest while I could.

I glanced back at Jennifer and Dellwood. Maybe they were good actors. Maybe they were genuinely frazzled and upset. Whatever, they had exaggerated just that little bit that told me they wanted me to see them in a favorable light.

I didn't care if they cried or danced with joy. As far as I was concerned there was only one good guy in the house and his name was Garrett.

woke up in time for dinner. I didn't feel rested. The floor of my dressing room wasn't that comfy. But it was safer than the bed. That tin man's wounds proved that.

I decided I'd set up camp in one of the vacant suites. Make them hunt for me to murder me in my sleep.

Had Hawkes died because of me? I'd fallen asleep wondering. Had my presence nudged somebody into pushing his murder schedule? Things like that, that I can't control, nag me.

I walked to the end of the hall, surveyed the central chamber. Jennifer was seated by the fountain, leaning against one of the dragon's wings. Chain and Kaid walked past without acknowledging her. They were headed for dinner.

As I started moving I spotted the blonde on the third-floor balcony opposite, in shadow, looking down. "There goes a theory shot to hell." She glanced up. I waved.

Black Pete stepped out of the hall across the way. He caught my wave, frowned, returned it. I pointed down. He leaned over the rail.

Too late. She'd caught my gesture and drifted into deeper shadow.

I descended the stairs beginning to consider, if only half-seriously, the notion of a resident haunt.

I'd thought the blonde was Jennifer in a wig, making quick clothing changes. Their builds were similar, their faces much alike. My romantic streak made the blonde prettier, barely. I'd never seen them both at once. All I'd needed was some screwy motive on Jennifer's part to tie the knot.

Sometimes you guess right and sometimes you don't. I don't a lot more than I do.

When I hit the ground floor, I'd convinced myself I should've known better. The blonde really was prettier. Moreover, she had a lonely, ethereal quality Jennifer couldn't mimic.

Not that I knew much about Jennifer, I'd been on the job a day and hadn't gotten close to anybody but Cook, and her not close enough. Chances were I wasn't going to get close to anybody. These weren't the kind of people who would let you.

The case looked stranger by the minute. At least it was more low-key than the bloody whirlwinds that had swept me up lately.

Peters met me at the foot of the stairs. "You wanted something?"

"The wave? I wasn't waving at you. The blonde was on the balcony under you. She ducked out when I pointed."

He looked at me like he wondered if he'd brought in the wrong man. I figured I'd better distract him. "I have a question for you. Completely hypothetical. If you were to kill somebody here and wanted to get rid of the body, where would be the best place on the property?"

His look got stranger. "Garrett . . . You're getting weird. Or maybe you got weird since you left the Marines. What do you want to know something like that for?"

"Just tell me. Asking questions is what I do. They don't have to make sense to you. Hell, they don't always make sense to me. But they're the tools I use."

"Can you give me a hint? If I was going to bury somebody . . ." A little light went on inside. He thought I was looking for a place somebody might cache the General's goodies. "It would depend on the circumstances. How much time I had. How good a job I wanted to do. Hell, if I had time, I'd put the body ten feet down where nobody would have any reason to dig. If I was in a big hurry I wouldn't do it here at all. I'd take it up the road to the marsh, tie it to a couple of rocks, and throw it in."

"What marsh?"

"On down the road, the other side of the rise out front. Look out the front door, past the cemetery. You can see the tops of the trees. It's about a hundred-acre swamp. There's been talk about draining it because of the smell. Old Melchior, who owns the land, won't hear of it. Take a look sometime. It'll bring back memories."

"I will. Let's feed our faces before Cook forgets us."

She was delivering the final load when Peters and I arrived. She looked at me like I'd betrayed her by not showing up to help. Some people. Whatever you do, they expect you to do it forever.

It was a meal like last night's. No conversation except grumbles about how they might find the poacher and what they could do with him afterward. Nobody seemed suspicious of the circumstances.

Could that be? Somebody was picking them off and they didn't realize it?

Maybe it was their background, all those years in the war zone. When my company went in, there were two hundred of us, officers, sergeants, and men, who had trained together and been hammered into a single unit. Two years later there were eighteen originals left. Guys went down. After a while you accepted that. After a while you accepted the fact that your turn was coming. You went on and stayed alive as long as you could. You became completely fatalistic.

I asked, "Who took care of the stables today?"

They all looked at me like they'd just noticed me.

Peters said, "Nobody. Snake was on patrol." He wanted to ask why I wanted to know. So did the others. But they just looked at me.

My glance crossed Jennifer's. She was thawing. She smiled faintly. With promise.

Dellwood said, "I spoke to the General. He'll see you after we eat."

"Good. Thanks. I was wondering if you'd remembered."

All those eyes turned on me again. They wondered what business I had with the old man. I wondered what their theories were about my presence. It was obvious Peters hadn't spread the word.

I asked, "What do you guys do for entertainment? This place is pretty bleak." I'd forgotten to smuggle in some beer. Maybe tomorrow.

Chain growled, "Got no time for entertainment. Too much work to do. And the General won't hire anybody on. Which reminds me, troops. We got to cover for Hawkes. Which means we have to let something else go to hell."

Wayne said, "The whole place is falling apart. Even with us hopping like the one-legged whore the day the fleet pulled in. Dellwood, you got to try to get through to him."

"I'll try." Dellwood didn't sound optimistic.

They went on; now the ball was rolling. I learned more than I wanted to know about how and where the place was falling apart, what had been allowed to slide too long and what had to be done right now to stave off disaster.

Tyler said, "I say we worry about that damned poacher in our spare time. And say the hell with trying to catch the others. The General don't come out no more. How's he going to know we're not wasting time looking for them? They want a few deer, I say let them have them. We need to keep this place from falling apart."

That debate raged a while.

Jennifer contributed not a word. She seemed more interested in me. My fatal charm. My curse. Or maybe she just wondered how I'd gotten those old boys so animated.

•••15

helped Cook clear away. Dellwood helped me help. He didn't seem inclined to let me out of his sight. Cook was as tight-lipped as she claimed with a third party present.

Dellwood wanted to talk. He started as soon as we left the kitchen. "I hope you have some progress to report. It would be a good time to give the General an emotional lift."

"How come?"

"He had a good day today. He's been alert. His mind has had a keen edge. He managed to eat his lunch without help. Your presence seems to have motivated him. It would be nice if you could give him something to keep him feeling positive."

"I don't know." What I had to tell the General wasn't positive. "I'll try not to bring him down."

We were watched going up. This time I wasn't wrong about it being Jennifer. A strange woman. Pity. She was gorgeous.

I didn't get it. When was the last time a woman like that left me cold? I couldn't recall. Female is my favorite sport. Wasn't anything obviously wrong with her, either. Maybe it was bad chemistry. The opposite of lust at first sight.

"Who raised Jennifer?"

"Cook, mostly. And the staff."

"Oh. What became of them?"

"The General released them to make room for us. We should've been able to manage the place, putting the cropland out for rent. Hasn't worked out, though."

"He kept Cook. Why her?"

"She's a fixture. Been here forever. Raised him, too. And his father before him, and his father, too. He has his sentimental streak."

"That's nice." He hadn't been sentimental when he'd been my supreme commander. Of course, I hadn't gotten to know him.

"He takes care of his own." Dellwood opened the General's door, seated me in the room where I'd met the old man before. Old Kaid was stoking the fire. "Wait here. I'll have him out in a few minutes." The temperature was obscene.

"Sure. Thanks."

It was more than a few minutes but the old man was worth seeing when he came out. He had a smile on. His cheeks had gained some color. He waited till Dellwood and Kaid departed. "Good evening, Mr. Garrett. I take it you've made progress?"

"Progress, General, but I don't have any good news." Had his health improved because the poisoner had backed off with me around?

"Good news, bad news, better get on with it."

"I went into the city this morning. I put some acquaintances to work tracing the missing items through those people who deal in articles that stray from home. They're competent. If the thief disposed of anything through those channels, they'll find out and get a description of the seller. I do need instructions. Should they recover the articles? If they've been sold, you could be at the mercy of the new owners."

"Very good, sir. Very good. Yes. By all means. I want to recover whatever I can. I expect you'll have problems getting them back from someone who's taken a fancy to them." He smiled.

"You seem in good spirits, sir."

"I am. I am indeed. I haven't felt this well in months. Maybe years. Not your doing but it did start after your arrival. You're good luck. If I keep improving at this rate, I'll be dancing within the month."

"I hope so, sir. Sir, that brings me to the bad news. But first a confession. I didn't come out here just to unmask a thief."

"Ah?" There was a sparkle in his eye.

"Yes sir. Sergeant Peters believes someone is poisoning you slowly. He wanted me to find out who. If it's being done at all."

"And? You've found something?" He seemed troubled now.

"No sir. Nothing like that."

That pleased him.

"On the other hand, there's no negative evidence. And one has to wonder about your recovery. It pleases me but I'm suspicious by nature."

"And this is your bad news?"

"No sir. That's nastier. More pervasive, if you will."

"Go on. I'm not one to slay the bearer of ill tidings or to ignore them because they aren't what I want to hear."

"Let me preface this by saying I'd like to read your will."

He frowned. "Peters asked for a copy. Was that your doing?"

"Yes."

"Go on."

"I'm afraid it may be written so as to encourage villainy." I was starting to sound pompous. But it was hard to be one of the boys with General Stantnor. "If the number of heirs decreases, does the take for the survivors increase?"

He gave me the fish eye.

"I gather half goes to Jennifer and the rest to everyone else. Sixteen people originally. After this morning, only eight. Meaning the take for survivors has doubled."

He looked at me hard. I thought he might throw me out, earlier protests to the contrary. "Support your suspicions, Mr. Garrett."

"I don't think the four men who left you could have. One, maybe. Two at the most. But people aren't built to walk away from so much money. Four?"

"I can see that. Maybe. What else?"

"Whoever put the arrow into Hawkes set it up ahead of time. The deer was too long dead to be a fresh kill. The sniper rode away on a horse. Would a peasant who has to poach have a horse? And the horseman headed this way after the ambuscade. Though that's circumstantial. I lost the trail partway here."

He was quiet for a long time. His color deserted him. I pitied him then.

"On a more personal level, two attempts have been made on my life since I've been here. I don't know by who."

He looked at me but didn't say anything.

"Unearthing that wasn't part of my brief. But I thought you should know what I think is happening. Should I pursue it?"

"Yes!" He paused. "It doesn't add up. Theft that's almost petty. Someone possibly trying to poison me. Someone trying to kill everyone else."

"That's true. I can't make it add up."

"I don't want to believe you, Mr. Garrett. I know those men better than that . . . Two attempts on your life?"

I told him about them.

He nodded. "I don't suppose you . . . No. I believe you. Get Dellwood."

I rose. "A question first, General?"

"Go ahead."

"Could an outsider be responsible? Do you have enemies vicious enough to try to set your house against itself?"

"I have enemies. A man my age, who's been what I've been? Of course I have enemies. But I don't think any of them would try for the pain in something like this. . . . There'd still have to be an inside man, wouldn't there?"

I nodded, opened the door. Dellwood was in the hall a decorous distance away. "The boss wants you."

'll say this for that old man: He took the bull by the horns. I didn't think he was doing the smart thing, but it was his house, his life, his sanity, and his choice to take the risk.

He had Dellwood bring everybody in and get them seated. He had me stand beside him, facing them. They looked at him and me and wondered while Peters and Chain looked for Snake. Kaid tossed logs on the bonfire. I sweated.

Nobody said a word.

Then Jennifer tried. She barely got her mouth open. The General said, "Wait." One word, softly, that stung like a whip's bite.

Snake ambled in with Chain and Peters. He'd tried to clean himself up. He hadn't done a great job but passed inspection well enough to be given a seat. Stantnor said, "Close the door, Peters. Lock it. Thank you. Hand me the key, please."

Peters did so. The others watched with varying expressions, mostly in the frown range.

"Thank you for coming." As if they'd had any choice. "We have a problem." He reached out. I put his will in his hand. He'd let me read it while we waited. It was an invitation to mayhem, incredibly naive.

"My will. You know the details. I've hit you over the head with them often enough. They seem to have created the problem. Therefore."

A candle sat on the table before him. He shoved the end of the will into the flame, held it till it caught, laid it on the table, and let it burn.

I watched them watch it. They were shocked. They may have been disappointed or outraged. But they didn't move, didn't protest, didn't fall down and confess.

"That instrument has been a murder weapon, sure as any blade. But I won't make a speech. There's the fact. Motive has been eliminated. The will has been abrogated. I'll write a new one in a few days."

He looked them in the eye, one by one. Nobody shied away. Everybody looked baffled and dismayed.

Dellwood said, "Sir, I don't understand."

"I certainly hope you don't. Those of you who don't, be patient, it will become clear. First, though, I want to introduce the man next to me. His name is Garrett. Mr. Garrett is an investigative specialist, amongst other talents. I employed Mr. Garret to find out who's been stealing from me. His efforts have been quite to my satisfaction so far."

The old boy was a chess player.

"Mr. Garrett found evidence of more heinous crimes. He's convinced me that some of you have been killing your comrades to gain a larger share of my legacy."

"Sir!" Dellwood protested. The others stirred, looked at each other.

"Mr. Garrett *was a* scout during his service, Dellwood. He tracked today's poacher back to our stable."

He wasn't maundering or speaking imprecisely. He wanted them to think I'd done just that, not lost the trail in the fields. He wanted somebody to feel pressed.

"Mr. Garrett has an excellent reputation for handling these things. I've asked him to find the killer. He's agreed. I have every confidence in his ability. I tell you all this by way of letting you know where you stand. If you're innocent, I want you to cooperate with him. The sooner it's wrapped up the better. If you're guilty, maybe you ought to put on your running shoes. Be advised that I shall hunt you as implacably as the hounds of hell. You've betrayed my trust. You have done me a hurt I can't forgive. I'm going to have your head and heart when I find you."

I didn't look at him, though it was hard not to. The old devil had gone further than I'd expected.

By burning the will he'd eliminated the threat to the innocent. Nobody stood to gain now. If he died intestate, the estate could go to the Crown, which meant everyone lost. Even the poisoner ought to want to keep him alive till he wrote a new will.

A clever man, General Stantnor. But he'd left me swinging in the breeze.

"You understand your positions," he said. "Mr. Garrett. Ask what questions you like."

Chain said, "Sir—"

"No, Sergeant Chain. Mr. Garrett will ask. You're not to speak unless spoken to. We'll stay here till Mr. Garrett is satisfied."

I said, "Mr. Garrett doesn't think he can stay awake that long."

I'm not the kind of guy who can pull all the suspects together and expose a villain by weaving a web of clever questions. My style is bull in the china shop. It's jump in the pond and thrash till the frogs start jumping. I wished I had the Dead Man handy. One of his more useful talents is an ability to read minds. He could settle this in minutes.

I still entertained the possibility of an outside force with motives unfathomable. The arguments against these people being involved had to be answered before I could discard that possibility.

They looked at me, waiting. The General turned his gaze on me as though to say, *Show us the old Garrett razzle-dazzle, boy.*

"Anybody want to confess? Save us time and let us get to bed?"

Nobody volunteered. Surprise, surprise. "I was afraid you'd be that way."

Chain cracked, "I swiped a piece of rock candy from my sister when I was nine."

"There's a start. A criminal mastermind in the budding, I don't think we need to go back quite that far, though. Let's confine ourselves to this morning. What did you do today, Sergeant Chain? Account for your time and movements. Tell us who you saw doing what, and who saw you doing what you were doing." This would get tedious before we finished nine stories. But it might do the job. Each story would add a color to the portrait of the morning. Every tale told true would leave our villain less room to hide.

Chain got pissed. But before he could do more than grumble, Stantnor said, "I demand cooperation, Chain. Do exactly as Mr. Garrett says. Answer his questions without reservation. Or get off the estate. Followed by the knowledge that you've made yourself the prime suspect."

Chain swallowed his protests. He didn't look at me like a guy who wanted to become my drinking buddy.

I said, "Try to attach times to the major events of your day."

"I don't pay no attention to what time it is. I'm too busy doing what I got to do. I mean, I do as much as I can. Ain't possible to get done everything that needs doing."

"Thanks to our killer, who keeps taking away pairs of hands. Estimates will do. Once we've heard from everybody, it should be pretty clear who did what where and when. Go ahead. Just ramble along. Take all the time you need. You can't go into too much detail."

Clever, clever Garrett sets himself up for an excruciating night. It took Chain forty-five minutes to tell me he hadn't done anything interesting and that, between breakfast and lunch, he'd seen only five other members of the household. Excepting Dellwood and Peters, those had been on the patrol.

"Anybody disagree?" I asked. "Anybody want to call him a liar?"

Nobody volunteered.

"All right. Snake. You're uncomfortable here. How about we get you off the hook? Go ahead."

Snake's story wasn't any more interesting than Chain's. He'd seen nobody in anything but innocent circumstances. Dellwood before they'd ridden out. The other hunters during the hunt. Peters when he'd come out with me. Then he'd gone back to his stables to get away. "I don't like people that much anymore," he confessed. "I ain't comfortable around them. Can I go now, General?"

The old man had begun to doze, apparently. But he was alert enough. "You aren't concerned about what somebody might say if you're not here?"

"No sir. I ain't got nothing to hide. And I'm getting awful uncomfortable." He looked like he was about to suffer a panic attack.

The General looked at me. I shrugged.

Stantnor handed me the key. "Up to you."

I unlocked the door, held it for Snake. "Good night."

As he passed me he whispered, "You come out when you're done. Maybe I can guess who done Hawkes."

It didn't seem a good time to get hardassed. I just added him to a lengthening list of things to do while everybody slept. I closed the door, turned, glanced around, wondered if anyone had overheard. Their faces revealed nothing. But it had been a loud whisper.

I took Wayne next. He was a bust. Cook would've talked all night and next day if I hadn't gotten her to edit some. She'd seen everybody and they'd seen her.

Four down. Three hours gone. Five to go. A pattern had begun to develop. A trivial one, but a pattern. Dellwood had been seen too often to have had time for a ride in the country.

I hadn't thought him much likelier than Cook, anyway.

I had Peters go next. He resented having to be a suspect but he did what he had to do. The General seemed to be dozing again, but that meant nothing.

Peters didn't tell me anything I didn't already know.

He'd barely finished when Jennifer came to life. "Mr. Garrett. If that isn't a false name, too. How about me next? This's really wearing me down."

"Welcome to the club. Go ahead."

She hadn't done a damned thing all morning. She'd sat in her room knitting. Dellwood could attest to that. He'd found her there when he'd brought the news about Hawkes.

Fine.

"Can I go? I'm tired and I have a splitting headache."

I could empathize. I was developing one myself. It was part of an oncoming cold that seemed to be a legacy of the weather. "Not yet. Bear with me. I'll try to hurry it along. Anyone want to go next?"

No volunteers. I picked Tyler. He didn't bother to conceal his resentment as he described the events of his morning. They were dull. They dovetailed. They didn't point a finger. He added another Dellwood sighting to the list.

"Kaid?" I said. "How about you?"

Another dull tale, mostly to do with the patrol.

The idea wasn't working out. Only Dellwood and Cook—ninety percent—were out of the noose. "Dellwood, it's probably a waste of time but go ahead."

His report was only slightly less detailed than Cook's. He didn't put me on anybody's trail. Most everyone had had time to go do it to Hawkes.

Well, you can't leave the stones unturned.

"Thank you all for your patience and cooperation. I'll talk to you again, for as long as it takes. No killer is invulnerable. If you think of anything, let me know. I'll hold your name in confidence. You can go."

They headed for the door in a pack, forgetting that I had the key. Jennifer remembered first. She hollered for it, as ladylike as a wolverine in a bad temper. I tossed it to her. "One thing, folks. I've seen another woman around the house." I described her. "I want to know who she is. Secret or not."

Mostly they gave me baffled looks. A couple looked like they wondered about my sanity. They all went out except for Dellwood, who brought the key to the writing table. "I'll put the General to bed now, sir. If you don't mind."

"I don't if he doesn't."

"Go, Garrett," the old man said, proving he hadn't been asleep. "I'm not alert enough to continue. See me after breakfast."

"Yes sir." I got up and went out.

It was after midnight. I was tired. Should I grab a few hours? Sleeping would be a real problem now that the old man had made me a target.

No. Snake first. The way things were going, he probably didn't have anything I could use. On the other hand, he might. If he did I might not have to worry about getting the ax in my sleep anymore.

I headed down the hall. And got distracted immediately.

I spotted that woman again. She was on the balcony across from the head of the General's hall. My balcony. I froze, watched her just sort of drift along in a daydream. She didn't notice me. I darted to the stairs leading to the fifth floor, stole to the east wing, crept down to the balcony below.

All for nothing. She was gone.

I'd have to trap her if I wanted to talk to her.

I wanted to.

The mind plays games. She was getting a grip on that part of me inexplicably immune to Jennifer's fetching charms.

···**17**

As long as my room was just down the hall, I figured it would be wise to stop for some extra equipment. A sap and a sheath knife might not be enough if tonight's party got somebody excited.

The bit of paper between the door and the doorframe was the way I'd left it. But it was a decoy, meant to flutter down and catch the eye. The real telltale was a hair I'd left leaning against the door two inches in from the handle-side frame. It couldn't be replaced by somebody who stayed inside.

The hair was out of place.

Go on in? Or just walk away? I presumed somebody was waiting. There hadn't been time for a comprehensive search since the adjournment.

I considered getting comfortable and waiting them out. But every minute I wasted was a minute longer before I heard from Snake.

How about we just surprise the surprise party?

I got a shield off the wall, a mace, dug my key out, turned it in the lock, kicked the door in hard enough to mash anybody waiting behind it, went in with the shield up to take the blow of somebody against the wall on the other side.

Nobody. And it was dark in there. Someone had snuffed the lamp again.

I backed into the hall fast, not wanting to stand there in silhouette. A man with a crossbow could fix me up good.

Someone came toward the doorway, just far enough to be seen. "It's me." Morley Dotes.

I glanced along the hall. Nobody. I went inside. "What the hell are you doing here?" I shucked the shield and felt around for a lamp.

"Curiosity. Thought I'd see what was happening."

I got the lamp going and the door shut. "You just walked in?"

"Anybody could. They don't lock the doors."

"How'd you find my suite?"

He tapped his nose. "Followed my honker. We elves have a good sense of smell. Your suite is so heavy with the stink of meat eater, it's easy to pick out."

He was putting me on. "You're here. What do I do with you?"

"Any developments?"

"Yeah. There's another dead one. While I was in town this morning. So tonight the old man calls a meeting, tells everybody who I am and says I'm going to nail hides to the wall. Meantime, he burns his will. Anything from town?"

"Saucerhead made some rounds. Didn't find much. Some of those medals, you know how many they handed out? Every hock shop in town has a bucket full. The only ones worth anything are the silver ones. People on the Hill are worried about their silver supply."

The Hill is TunFaire's heart. All the biggies live there, including a gaggle of witches and wizards and whatnot who have to have their silver if they want to stay in business. Silver is to sorcery as wood is to fire. Since Glory Mooncalled whipped up on everybody in the Cantard, prices have soared.

But that was of no concern now. "What about the candlesticks and stuff?"

"He found a couple of things. Maybe. The people who had them didn't remember where they got them. Literally. You know Saucerhead. He can be convincing."

Like a landslide. You didn't talk when he said talk, chances were you would real quick. "Great. There's a dead end."

"He's going to try again tomorrow. Pity your thief didn't take something special so somebody would remember him."

"Thoughtless of him. Look. I've got an appointment with a man who says he knows the killer. Maybe. I'd like to see him before he changes his mind about talking."

"Lead on, noble knight." Morley rags me about being romantic and sentimental. He has his moments himself—like turning up here. He'd never admit he was concerned about me swimming in a school of sharks. He'd just claim he was curious.

"This is a real haunted house," he muttered as we stole downstairs. "How can they stand it?"

"Maybe they're right when they say there's no place like home. Maybe you don't notice after a while."

"Who's the brunette I spotted when everybody charged out of the hall across the way?"

"That's the daughter, Jennifer. A dead loss, near as I can tell."

"Maybe you don't have what it takes."

"Maybe not. But I think it's bad chemistry." We hit the bottom of the stairs. Nobody was around. We headed for the back door. There was a sliver of moon out, just enough to keep me from stumbling over things. Morley had no trouble. His kind can see inside a coffin.

"At least it's straightforward. No dead gods. No vampires. No killer ogres. Just greedy people."

I thought about the woman in white and hoped she wasn't supernatural. I didn't know how to deal with spooks.

Morley grabbed me. "Somebody moving over there."

I didn't see anything.

Somebody tripped over something.

"Heard us," Morley said. He took off.

I went to the stable, called, "Snake? Where you at? It's Garrett."

No answer. I stuck my head inside. I didn't see anything. The horses were restless, muttering in their sleep. I decided to circle around outside before I risked the inside.

Wavering light spilled between boards on the north end, near the west corner. It was feeble, like the light of a single guttering candle. There was a narrow door. I'd found Snake's hideout. "Snake? You there? It's Garrett."

Snake didn't answer.

I opened the door.

Snake wouldn't be answering anybody in this world again. Somebody had stuck a knife in him.

It wasn't a good job. The thrust had gone in on the wrong side of his breastbone, piercing a lung. The tip of the dagger had lodged in his spine.

Morley materialized. "Lost him." He looked at Snake. "Amateur work." Always a student, Morley. And always a critic.

"Pros make mistakes if they're in a hurry with somebody tough. This guy was a commando, way I hear. Be hard to take him clean."

"Maybe." Dotes dropped to his haunches, toyed with a cord twisted around Snake's neck. The killer had finished it the hard way. "Interesting."

I'd started looking for physical evidence. A killer in a hurry could have dropped something. "What's that?"

"This is a Kef sidhe strangler's cord."

"A what?" I squatted beside him.

"Kef sidhe. They have strict religious injunctions against spilling blood. They think if you spill blood, the murdered man's spirit can't pass on till he's been avenged. So they kill without spilling blood because murder is part of their religion, too. Using a cord is an art with them."

I looked at the cord. It wasn't a piece of rope.

Morley said, "The master assassin makes his own cords. Making your own cord is the final rite of passage to master status. Look. The knot is like a hangman's knot, except the noose is round so it can be drawn with the hands pulling apart. These knots in the cord aren't really knots; they're braided over cork cones. They work like barbs on an arrowhead. The cord can be pulled through the knot in only one direction."

It only took a second to see how that worked—with an example right there. I felt one of the tapered bulges in the cord. Morley said, "The cork crushes down going through the knot, expanding again on the other side."

"How do you get your cord off?"

"They don't. They use it only once, then it's tainted. I've only ever seen one before. Cut off his own throat by a man I knew years ago. Excepting you, he was the luckiest guy I've ever known."

I looked around, less interested in Snake than he was. If our killer wasn't good he was lucky. There wasn't a spot of physical evidence. "Kind of sad," I said.

"Death usually is." Which was a surprise, considering the source. But Morley has been full of surprises as long as I've known him.

"I mean the way he lived." I gestured at our surroundings. He'd lived like his horses. He'd slept on straw. His only piece of furniture was a paint-stained table. "This was a professional soldier. Twenty years in, mostly spent in the Cantard. Combat pay. Prize money. A man careful enough to stay alive that long would be careful about his money. But he lived in a barn, like an animal. Didn't even have a change of clothes."

Morley grunted. "Happens. Want to bet he came out of the worst slum? Or off a dirt farm where they never saw two coppers the same month?"

"No bet." I'd seen it. Raised poor, they can get pathological about squir-reling it away for a rainy day—and death comes before the deluge. Sad way to live. I touched Snake's shoulder. His muscles were still knotted. He hadn't relaxed when he'd died. Curious.

I recalled what Cook had told me about him. "Put it on his tombstone, he was a good Marine." I rolled him over in case there was something under him. There wasn't, that I could see.

"Morley. It takes a while to strangle. Maybe whoever killed him tried that first, then stuck him. Instead of the other way around."

He glanced at the damage, which wasn't all that obvious considering the state of the place. "Could be."

"You ever try to strangle somebody?"

He gave me a look. He didn't answer questions like that.

"Sorry. I have. I was supposed to take out this sentry during a raid. I practiced before we went in."

"That doesn't sound like you."

"That was me then. I don't like killing and I didn't like it then, but I figured if I had to do it and wanted to get out, I'd better do it right."

He grunted again. He was giving Snake's former downside the once-over.

"I did it by the book. The guy was half-asleep when I got him. But I blew it. He threw me around like a rag doll. He beat the shit out of me. And all the time I was hanging on to that damned rope. Only good I did was keep him from yelling till somebody could stick a knife in him."

"The point?"

"If you don't snap a guy's neck, he's going to fight you. And if he breaks loose, even with that Kef sidhe thing around his neck, he sees you and you got to make sure of him any way you can."

"What you're sneaking up on is this Snake guy was stronger than whoever hit him. Like that Venageti soldier."

I hadn't said the Venageti was stronger than me, but it was true. "Yes."

"Somebody in the house probably has bumps and bruises. If someone from the house did this."

"Maybe. Damn! Why couldn't I have had some luck this once?"

"What do you mean?" He thinks my luck is outrageously good.

"Why couldn't the killer leave something? A scrap of cloth. A tuft of hair. Anything."

"Why not just wish for a confession?" Morley shook his head. "You're so slick, you slide right past yourself. He left you a dagger and a Kef sidhe strangler's cord. How exotic do you want to get? I told you how rare the cord is. How many daggers have you seen like this one?"

It had a fourteen-inch polished steel blade, which was unusual, but the hilt made it especially interesting. It was black jade, plain except for being jade. But at its widest point, where the middle finger of the hand would rest, there was a small silver medallion struck with a two-headed Venageti military eagle.

"A war souvenir?" Morley suggested.

"An unusual one. Venageti. Nobody lower than a light colonel would carry it. A battalion commander in their elite forces or a regimental commander or his second in the regulars."

"Couldn't be a lot of those around, could there?"

"True." It was a lead. Tenuous, but a lead. I looked down at Snake. "Man, why didn't you blurt it out when you had the chance?"

"Garrett."

I knew that tone. Morley's special cautionary tone he saves for when he suspects I'm getting involved. Getting unprofessional, he'd call it. Getting bullheaded and careless, too.

"I have it under control. I just feel for the guy. I know what his life was like. It shouldn't have ended like this."

"It's time to go, Garrett."

"Yes."

It was time. Before I got more involved emotionally.

I walked away thinking the old saw, *There but for the grace of the gods . . .* Over and over.

orley wanted a crack at tracking whomever we'd heard fleeing. I gave him his head. He didn't accomplish anything.

"It's not right, Garrett."

"What?"

"I'm getting a bad feeling. Not quite an intuition. Something beyond that. Like an unfounded conviction that things are going to turn real bad."

Just so I couldn't ever call him a liar, somebody screamed inside the house. It wasn't a scream of pain and not quite one of fear, though there was fear in it. It sent those dread chills stampeding around my back. It sounded like a woman, but I couldn't be sure. I'd heard men scream like that in the islands.

"Stay out of sight," I told Morley, and took off.

The screams went on and on. I blew inside. They came from the west-side, third-floor balcony. I hit the stairs running. Two flights up I slowed down. I didn't want to charge into something.

The stair steps were spotted with water drops and green stuff in bits and gobs. Under one lamp lay what looked like a dead slug. I poked it. It wiggled and I recognized it. It was a leech. I'd become closely acquainted with its relatives on that one swampy island.

There was an awful smell in the air. I knew it from that island, too.

What the hell?

There was all kinds of racket up there now. Men yelled. Peters shouted, "Get one of those spears and shove it back down."

Dellwood, with a squeak higher than the screaming, asked, "What the hell is it?"

I moved upward carefully. I saw men against the head of the stairs, a couple with spears jabbing at something heaving on the stairs. There wasn't enough light to show it clearly.

I had a suspicion.

Draug.

I got a lamp.

I didn't want to see what I saw. That thing on the stair was something nobody ever wants to see, and whoever made it least of all.

It was a corpse. One that had been immersed in a swamp. What folklore called a draug, a murdered man who could not rest in death while his killer went unpunished. There are a million stories about draugs' vengeance but I'd never expected to be a player in such a tale. They're apochryphal, not concrete. Nobody ever *really* saw one.

Funny how the mind works. The thoughts you'd expect didn't come to me. All I could think was: Why me? This shot hell out of my simple case.

Peters yelled, "What do we do, Garrett?"

Besides puke? "I don't know." You can't kill a draug. It's dead already. It would just keep coming till it wore them out. "Try to cut it up."

Dellwood did upchuck. Chain shoved him aside, flailed away with the ax part of a halberd. A couple of fingers came wriggling down where I stood. They didn't lose their animation.

"Hold it there. I'll come around the long way." I backed down to the balcony.

As I retreated to the stairs to the first floor, I spied the woman in white watching from the top balcony east, from a spot where she wouldn't be seen by the bunch above me. She looked more interested and animated than usual. Like she was enjoying herself. I tried to sneak up on her but she wasn't there when I got there.

I wasn't surprised.

I crossed through the loft, went down. The guys were hard at work, poking and hacking and stumbling over each other. Peters said, "This is getting old, Garrett."

"I'll buy that. Who's it after?"

"How the hell should I know?"

"Who did the screaming?"

"Jennifer. She ran into it down there somewhere. It followed her up here."

"Where is she now?"

"In her suite."

"Hang in there. You're doing a great job." I started down the hall. Then came back. Kaid and Chain cursed me. I asked, "Who was it when it was alive?"

Peters bellowed, "How the hell should I know?" He needed to work on his vocabulary. He was in a rut.

"Catch you in a minute." I headed for Jennifer's suite, which was identical to her father's, apparently, one floor below. I tried the door at the end of the hall. Locked and barred. I pounded. "Jennifer. It's Garrett."

I heard vague movement sounds. They stopped. She didn't open up.

I wondered if I'd have the nerve, considering all the tricks the stories say draugs and haunts try.

I tried again. She wasn't receiving callers. I rejoined the boys. They were hanging in there. Chunks of corrupt, stinking flesh were everywhere. And the draug kept coming. Stubborn cuss. I found a spot from which I could kibitz. "Figure out who it was yet, Peters?"

"Yeah. Spencer Quick. Disappeared two months ago. The clothes. Nobody dressed like Quick. Lots of black leather. Thought it made the women swoon. You bastard. You just going to stand there?"

I rounded up a five-foot broadsword, the kind they'd used in knighthood days to bash each other into scrap metal. I tested its edge. Not bad, considering. I took up position out of the way, behind where the thing would emerge onto the balcony. "Let it come."

"You're crazy," Kaid told me.

Maybe. "Go ahead. Back off."

"Do it," Peters said, trusting me way too much.

They skipped away.

The dead man came in a cloud of stench, dragging what was left of him, lurching into the wall. "What're you waiting for?" Wayne shrieked at me.

I was waiting for the draug to jump its murderer, that's what. But it didn't. Of course.

They all panicked, grabbed axes and swords, and started swinging. Six of them in a crowd like that, it was a miracle they didn't kill each other.

I stood back and watched to see if anybody took advantage of the confusion to eliminate another heir.

Now that they had room, they carved the draug into little frisky pieces. Didn't take them long, either. They were motivated. Wayne, Tyler, and Dellwood kept hacking away long after that was necessary.

They backed off finally, panting. Everybody looked at me like they thought I ought to be next. I got the impression they weren't satisfied with my level of participation.

"Well, then. That takes care of that. Be smart to collect up the pieces and burn them. Peters, you want to fill me in on this Quick? Who was he and how did he happen to go away without anybody thinking that was strange?"

Chain exploded. Before he could get out a coherent sentence, I said, "Chain, I want you to come with me and Peters and Tyler. We're going to backtrack that thing."

"Say what?" Chain gulped air. "Backtrack it?"

"Yes. I want to see where it came from. Might tell us something useful."

"Shit," he said, and started shaking. "I want to tell you, I'm scared. I don't mind admitting it. All my years in the Cantard I wasn't scared like I am now."

"You never ran into anything like this. Not to worry. It's done."

Peters said, "We have some other men missing, Garrett. Suppose more of those things turn up?"

"Doesn't seem likely. Draugs don't run in packs. Usually." I recalled a couple of stories. There was the Wild Hunt, a whole band of dead riders who hunted the living. "You saw how slow it was. Stay alert. You can outmaneuver them. The thing to remember is, don't get excited. We might have wrapped this mess up if we'd let the draug go after whoever killed it."

"Shit!" Chain swore. "It didn't care. It just wanted to get somebody. Anybody."

"Maybe. So let's hit the trail." I tried to sound perky. "Another glorious night in the Corps." I didn't feel perky, not even a little. I was scared stiff. "Arm up if that makes you feel better. And get lanterns."

Peters grumbled, "I hope you know what you're doing, Garrett."

I didn't have the faintest. I was just rattling around, hoping something would shake loose.

19

"Tyler, move out to the left about ten yards. Chain, you go to the right. I don't see much of a trail. Keep an eye out." I disposed myself and Peters between them so we spanned thirty yards. We started from the base of the front steps. "Let's go."

Peters said, "It was walking when it came. Wouldn't leave much of a trail."

"Probably not. You going to tell me who Quick was before we carved him up?"

"We?" Chain bellowed. "Will you listen to that shit?"

"Calm down," Peters told him. "I know what he was doing. He was right. You should have told us, Garrett."

"And warn the villain?"

"He's pretty well warned now."

"Safe, too. Oh. Add a name to the victim list. Somebody did it to Snake."

Peters stopped, held his lantern overhead, glared at me. "You aren't kidding. Snake? Why the hell Snake?"

I tried to recall who'd been sitting where when I'd let Snake out that door. Hell. Anybody with good ears could have heard. He'd used a stage whisper. Maybe he'd wanted the killer to know. Maybe he'd had something planned and it had turned in his hand. I wouldn't let a known killer get close enough to put a noose around my neck.

"Here," Chain said. We moved over. A strip of rotten leather hung on a bush. We redeployed.

I said, "You going to tell me about Quick?"

"I can't," Peters said. "I didn't know him. He was almost as spooky as Snake. Stayed to himself, mostly. You had to use a pry bar to get three words out of him. He did fancy himself a lover. You want to find out about him, talk to the gals at the Black Shark. All I can tell you is he was somebody the General knew and thought he owed. Like all of us."

I'd passed the Black Shark on the way to the Stantnor place. It was an evil-looking dive. I'd been considering taste testing the house brew. Now I had business reasons to visit.

"Chain. You know anything about him?"

"Not me. Hell, sour as he was, I wasn't surprised when he walked. Him and the old man feuded all the time. He never gave a shit about the money, far as I know. He just didn't have nowhere else to go."

"Tyler?"

"I didn't know him, except he played a big role at the Black Shark. Guy was a werewolf, the way he changed personality when a woman was in sight. I figured he found somewhere he wanted to be more than he wanted to stay here."

Great. The live ones were weird and the dead ones weirder.

We were spread out just enough. We kept finding another trace just before we lost the trail. We adjusted and kept on. It was slow going.

"Who do you think is doing it, Garrett?" Peters asked.

"I don't have a clue."

Chain said, "He'll pass the word when there's only one of us left."

"That would work," I admitted.

Tyler kicked in, "I'd have put money on Snake. He was kill-crazy in the islands. He'd go hunting alone if he went too long without action."

I'd known a few like that, guys who got hooked on the killing. They hadn't made it through. Death has a way of devouring its acolytes.

"Here," Peters said. He'd found a place in tall grass where the draug had stopped. The trail was easy now. The grass was trampled down.

The trail pointed toward the swamp Peters had mentioned.

I asked, "You ever heard of Kef sidhe?"

"Kef she? What?"

"Sidhe. As in the race sidhe. Kef sidhe are professional killers. Religious assassins."

"No. Hell. The nearest sidhe are a couple thousand miles from here. I've never seen one."

Neither had I. "They're something like elves."

"What about them?"

"Snake was strangled with a Kef sidhe strangler's cord. Not exactly a common item in these parts."

Peters just looked baffled, near as I could tell by lantern light. Damn, he was ugly.

"How about a Venageti colonel's dress dagger? Were there any souvenirs around?"

"Black-handled thing with a silver medallion? Long blade?"

"Yes."

"Can I ask why?"

"You can. I won't tell you till I know more about the knife."

"Snake had one he took off a Venageti colonel that he snuffed during one of his private excursions," Chain said.

"Damn!"

"What's the matter?"

"Somebody stuck it in him when the strangler's cord didn't work fast enough." Wouldn't you know it? Stuck with his own sticker. Hell, next thing I knew I'd find out he committed suicide.

Our villain was probably more lucky than clever, full of tricks that were working out by accident.

Chain said, "Holy shit," in a soft voice. "We got trouble."

"What?" Peters demanded.

"Look at this."

We joined him. He held his lantern as high as he could.

Now there were two trails through the grass, one a yard to the side of the other. Peters and I exchanged glances, then looked at Chain. "Tyler! Get over here."

Tyler hadn't come. His lantern hung about two feet off the ground as he knelt to study something. "Wait a second."

I asked, "What have you got?"

"Looks like . . ."

Dark movement behind him. "Look out!"

The draug grabbed Tyler by the throat and hoisted him into the air. His neck snapped. He made a sound like a rabbit's scream; his lantern fell and broke. Fire splashed the draug's feet. It lifted Tyler overhead, heaved him into the darkness, turned on the rest of us.

"Spread out," I said.

"You damn well better do more than watch this time," Chain told me.

The fire blazed till the lantern's fuel was gone. The grass didn't catch. Neither did the draug. Both were too wet.

"We'll cut it up," I said. "Like the other one."

Chain said, "Let's don't talk, let's do."

I didn't want to. But this draug wasn't particular about whom it stalked. It hated life. If it had been after Tyler specifically, it would have fallen down, done, revenge complete. But it wanted the rest of us, too.

It didn't have much chance against three of us. We were faster and armed. But it kept coming. And coming. And coming. It's hard to cut a body up when it's chasing you.

The horror and fear subsided after a few minutes. I got my head working. "Either one of you know who this was?"

"Crumpet," Chain said. He concentrated like a clockmaker, making every move and stroke count.

"Crumpet? What kind of name is that?"

"Nickname," Peters said. "Real name was Simon Riverway. He didn't like it. Crumpet was all right. The ladies hung it on him in Full Harbor. Said he was a sweet bun."

Weird. I unleashed a roundhouse cut at the draug's neck. It got a hand in the way. My stroke sheered halfway through its wrist, one bone's worth. The thing kept turning toward me while I was off balance, grabbing with its other hand.

It grabbed hold of my sleeve. I thought I was a goner. Chain came in with a two-handed, overhead stroke, all his weight behind it. It hit the thing's shoulder hard enough to shake its hold. "I owe you one, Chain." I danced back a few yards, decided I'd follow Chain's example, and set my lantern down.

The draug kept after me—which was fine with Peters and Chain. Peters jumped in behind and took a wild cut at its right Achilles tendon, hamstrung it on his backstroke.

And it kept coming, though not as fast as it had.

It seemed to take forever, but we wore it down. It fell and couldn't get up. We carved it up good to make sure, spending a lot of fear energy. Once we were finished, I recovered my lantern, said, "I think we'd better hole up till dawn. If there were two of them there might be more. We can explore later."

"You said they don't run in packs," Peters said.

"Maybe I was wrong. I don't want to find out the hard way. Let's get out of here."

"First smart thing I've heard you say," Chain said. He examined Tyler. "Dead as a wedge. You think he's the one that killed them?"

"I don't know. I wouldn't bet on it. That one didn't care who it killed. It just wanted to kill somebody."

"Like the old joke about the hungry buzzard? Let's go. Before Tyler gets up and comes after us, too. I couldn't take that."

I didn't argue. Draugs are supposed to be dead a few months before they get up, but I wasn't ready to field-test the folklore.

···20

As soon as we reached the house I went to check on Dellwood, Kaid, and Wayne. They were out back. They'd gotten a roaring bonfire going and were feeding it pieces of the first draug. I told them, "Throw it all in and get inside."

"Sir?" Dellwood asked. He had his color back.

"There may be more of them out. We ran into one who used to be called Crumpet. It killed Tyler. Let's not find out what else is waiting in the dark."

They didn't fool around. They didn't ask questions. They pitched the draug in the fire and headed for the house. I glanced around as I followed, wondering what had become of Morley.

The survivors gathered at the fountain. They were chattering about Snake and Tyler when I joined them. Wayne and Kaid held the opinion that the second draug had gotten the right man.

I told them, "I'm not so sure. It just wanted to kill. It wasn't satisfied with Tyler. Dellwood, check the doors. Peters, are there other ways to get in?"

"Several."

"Take Chain and Kaid and check them out. We stay in threes till the sun comes up."

"How come?" Chain asked.

"I think the killer is working alone. If we're stuck with him, we'll outnumber him two to one."

"Oh."

Peters said, "Ask these guys about that sidhe thing."

Right. "Dellwood. Wayne. Kaid. You know anything about Kef sidhe? Especially a Kef sidhe strangler's cord?"

They frowned. Dellwood, puffing from his hasty trip to the doors, asked, "What's that?"

I described the thing I'd found around Snake's neck.

"The General had something like that in his study."

Peters brightened. "Yes! I remember it. It was with a whole bunch of junk, whips and stuff, in the corner by the fireplace."

I recalled the whips. I hadn't paid much attention. "Dellwood, next time you're up there, see if it's gone. Ask the General where it came from. And where it went if it's not there."

Dellwood nodded. I hated to turn loose but I couldn't keep him on my suspect list. He just didn't seem capable. If I discounted Peters, who'd have to be crazy to hire me if he was guilty, I didn't have many suspects left.

The others were thinking the same way. Chain, Kaid, and Wayne started giving each other plenty of room.

Peters started to go.

"Wait," I said. "There's one question I should've asked before. I've been too busy with murder to worry about theft. Does anybody have a drug habit? Or gamble? Or keep a woman on the outside?" All of those might explain the thievery.

Everybody shook their heads.

"Not even Hawkes or Snake or Tyler?" Three in one day. The old man wasn't going to be happy about the job I was doing, though he hadn't exactly hired me to keep people alive.

"No," Peters said. "You don't stay alive in the Cantard if you're the slave of your vices."

True. Though vice had been rampant in places like Full Harbor, where we'd taken our rare leaves and liberties. A hellhole for a kid, Full Harbor. But you learned what life was like there. You had no illusions when you left.

Karenta hadn't yet evacuated Full Harbor, though Glory Mooncalled said they had to go. His deadline had passed. Something would happen down there soon. A really big explosion. And Glory Mooncalled wouldn't have his usual advantages. You can't outrun, outmaneuver, or even sneak up on a fortified city waiting for you. I doubted he had friends inside the walls. His enemies there would include Karenta's top sorcerers, against whom he had no defense.

I didn't think he could take Full Harbor. But he had to try. He'd shot off his mouth one time too many. He was committed.

The fate of Full Harbor meant nothing now, of course. We had our own siege here, a siege of horror.

Peters's group split to make sure the house hadn't been penetrated. The rest of us stayed at the fountain, in reserve. After a while, I asked, "Dellwood, what do you figure on doing after the General passes?"

He looked at me funny. "I never really thought about it, Mr. Garrett."

That was hard to believe. I said so.

Wayne chuckled. "Believe it, Garrett. This guy isn't real. He ain't here for the money. He's here to take care of the old man."

"Really? And why are you here?"

"Three things. The money. I got nowhere else to go. And Jennifer."

I lifted an eyebrow. I hadn't gotten much chance to show off my favorite trick lately. "The General's daughter?"

"The same. I want her."

Pretty blunt, this one. "What's the General think?"

"I don't know. I never brought it up. I don't intend to before he goes."

"What do you plan to do with your share of the money?"

"Nothing. Let it sit. I won't need it if I have Jenny, will I?"

No, he wouldn't.

"Which is why I ain't your killer, Mister. I don't have to skrag anybody to get half the estate."

A point. "What's Jennifer think about this?" She hadn't shown any interest in Wayne.

"Straight? She ain't exactly swept away. But she ain't got no other offers and she ain't likely to get none. When the time comes, she'll come around."

What an attitude. He sounded like a guy who could work his way up a hit list fast.

"What do you think about that, Dellwood?"

"Not much, sir. But Miss Jennifer will need somebody."

"How about you?"

"No sir. I haven't the force of personality to deal with her. Not to mention the fact that she isn't a very pleasant person."

"Really?" I was about to probe that when Wayne jumped up and pointed.

There was a vague shape at the back door, not clearly visible through the glass. It rattled the door. I figured it was Morley. I walked toward the door slowly. Make him wait.

Halfway there a face pressed against the glass. I was able to make out decomposed features. I stopped.

"Another one. Don't panic. I don't think it can get in. If it does, stay out of its way." I returned to the fountain, settled, disturbed but not afraid. The draugs weren't particularly dangerous when you were ready for them.

One in a night was unpleasant enough, but not that unreasonable—except for the assault on reason. In this world almost anything can happen and it does, but I'd never seen the dead get up and walk before. I'd never known anybody who'd seen it—unless you counted vampires. But they're a whole different story. They're victims of a disease. And they never really die, they just slip into a kind of limbo between life and death.

Once was unpleasant, twice was doubly unpleasant, but three times was just too much to have been animated by hatred and hunger for revenge alone. Not all in the same night.

Mass risings of the dead, in story and legend, were initiated from outside, by necromancers. By sorcerers.

"Hey, uh, Dellwood. Anybody around here a trained sorcerer? Or even an amateur?"

"No sir." He frowned. "Why?"

I lied. "I thought we could use a little help laying some restless spirits."

"Snake," Wayne said. "He could do some spooky stuff. Picked it up from a necromancer. He was her chief bodyguard for a while. He painted her picture and she taught him some tricks." He snickered. Must have been a variety of tricks. "He wasn't much good at it."

"And he's dead."

"Yeah. That's how you get off the hook around here."

But . . . "Suppose he could think like a sorcerer?"

"What do you mean?"

"What I . . . ? Let me reach. I was supposed to meet him. He was going to tell me who the killer was. He seemed sure he knew. He'd be wary. But somebody got to him despite his training and precautions. Suppose he knew that might happen? Suppose that, if he had a mind to, he could turn himself into a booby trap."

"Somebody's a booby."

"Flatterer. Look, it's in stories all the time. The curse that gets you after you kill a sorcerer. Suppose he fixed it so that, if he got killed, everybody else the killer killed would get up and go after him?"

Wayne grunted. "Maybe. Knowing that spooky, paranoid bastard, he'd rig it so they'd get up and go after everybody."

That fit, too. Sometimes I'm so brilliant I blind myself.

So what? Suppose that was true? It explained the draugs but didn't settle anything. There was a killer on the loose—if that hadn't been Tyler. No way to know unless he struck again.

If he had an ounce of brains, he'd retire while he had the chance to get out free.

I have such confidence in human nature. "Gents, I'm bone tired. I'm going to bed."

"Sir!" Dellwood protested.

"That thing isn't going to get in." It was still trying. And getting nowhere. "Our killer, if he's still alive, has got a great out now. He can let Tyler take the rap."

What you call planting a seed for the slow of wit.

I was so tired, my eyes wouldn't stay open. I needed to set myself up with some safe time. "Good night, all."

Morley was in my sitting room when I arrived. He had his feet up on my writing table. "You're getting old, Garrett. You can't take one long night anymore."

"Huh?" I was right on top of things. We investigator types have minds like steel traps. We're always ready with a snappy comeback.

"Heard your speech to the troops, shucking them so you can make with the snores."

"My second long night in a row. How'd you get in? Thought we had the place buttoned up."

"You might. Trick is, walk in before the buttoning starts. You went off chasing the walking dead. I just strolled around front and let myself in. Poked around the house some, came up here when the troll woman started rattling pots and pans."

"Oh." I got the feeling my repartee lacked something tonight. Or this morning. The first ghost light of dawn tickled the windows.

"I looked through the kitchen. The things you people eat. The sacrifices I make."

I didn't ask. Cook favored basic country cooking, heavy stuff, meat and gravy and biscuits. Lots of grease. Though Morley might have liked what she'd had for lunch my first meal here.

He was saying he planned to stay around. He went a little further. "I figure you can use a ghost to balance off theirs."

"Huh?" I wasn't making a comeback.

"I'll haunt the place. Roam around where they're not looking, doing things you'd do if you weren't busy keeping them calmed down."

That made sense. I had a list of a hundred things I wanted to do, like look for hidden passageways and sneak into people's rooms to snoop. I hadn't had time for them and probably wouldn't because somebody would be in my pocket constantly.

"Thanks, Morley. I owe you one."

"Not yet. Not quite. But we're getting up close to even."

He meant for a couple of tricks he'd pulled on me back when. The worst was having me help carry a coffin with a vampire in it he'd given a guy he didn't like. He hadn't warned me for the good reason that, if I'd known, I wouldn't have helped. I hadn't known till the vampire jumped up.

I'd been a little put out.

He'd been paying me back with little favors ever since.

He said, "Fill me in so I won't go reinventing the wheel."

I got myself a handkerchief first. "This cold feels like it'll turn bad. My head's starting to feel like the proverbial wool pack."

"Diet," he told me. "You eat right, you don't get colds. Look at me. Never had a cold in my life."

"Maybe." Elves don't get colds. I gave him the full account as I would've given it to the Dead Man. I kept an eye on him, watching for giveaways. He finds ways to profit when he weasels his way in to help me. I'd watched him enough to recognize that moment when he grabs onto something.

The obvious way here would be to recruit a gang to loot the place. That would be easy. Not so easy would be eluding an excited and bloodthirsty upper class afterward. Not that that would intimidate him much.

They might not have much use for General Stantnor, but as a class they couldn't tolerate the precedent. Every stormwarden, firelord, sorcerer, necromancer, whatnot would join in to pass out the exemplary torments.

"We have three separate things going, then," Morley said. "Thievery. Slow murder, maybe. Mass murder. You have the wheels turning on the thievery. So forget that. The General . . . The thing to do is let me and a doctor look at him. On the other killer, the only thing you can do is keep talking to people. Eliminating suspects."

"Go teach grandma to suck eggs, Morley. This is my business."

"I know. Don't be so touchy. I'm just thinking out loud."

"You agree Dellwood and Peters look unlikely?"

"Sure. They all do. The old man is bedridden and probably couldn't be fixed up with a motive anyway."

I hadn't considered the General.

"The Kaid character is too old for the pace and not strong enough to shove these other guys around."

"Maybe. Sneakiness is the killer's trademark, though. An old man would be sneaky."

"Sure. Then there's the Wayne character, who plans to marry money. So who does that leave if everybody else is honest?"

"Chain." Obnoxious, argumentive, overweight Chain, to whom I'd taken an instant dislike.

"And the daughter. And the outside possibility. Not to mention maybe somebody who went away but didn't disappear because he'd been murdered."

"Wait. Wait. Wait. What's that?"

"You have four men who rode off into the sunset, right? Snake Bradon's presumptive necromancy recalled three. Where's the other one? Which one was he? What were the will provisions regarding those men?"

I didn't recall. One had gotten cut out, I'd heard that. But if somebody was good for a share even if he wasn't around, and everybody thought he was gone, or dead now, he'd be in great shape to do dirty deeds, then turn up for the reading of the will.

"Whoever got Hawkes headed for the house here."

"You lost the trail."

True. "If it was somebody who isn't on the inside, he wouldn't know about the General burning the will."

"Yes. He might keep on keeping on."

True again. "Somebody tried giving me the ax."

"There's that. But it could be related to your other problems."

"Morley, trying to puzzle it out will drive me crazy. I don't want to bother."

He gave me a look something short of a sneer. "Good thinking. You're goofy enough now."

I said, "Look, at this point what I do is just bull around and try to make things happen. When the bad boys get nervous, they do something to give themselves away."

Morley chuckled. "You have style, Garrett. Like a water buffalo. What good will bulling around do if your villain was Tyler?"

"Not much," I admitted.

"What about the cook? If she's been around four hundred years, she might think the family owes her a fatter chunk than the old man was going to give her."

I'd considered that in light of the fact that the nonhuman races don't think like us and trolls are pretty basic. Somebody gets in a troll's way, the troll flattens him.

"Cook's time is accounted for when Hawkes got it. Not to mention, if she was on a horse and her weight didn't kill it, it would leave tracks a foot deep."

"It was an idea. How's she look for poisoning the old man?"

I shrugged. "She's got means and opportunity but I come up short on motive. She raised him from a pup. I'd think there'd be some love of a sort."

He snorted. "You're right. We're not going to reason it out. Sleep on it. I'll go haunt."

"Don't walk into the bedroom," I warned him. "I have an ax rigged to carve sneaky visitors." I'd decided to go back to the featherbed. The floor in the dressing room was too hard. Maybe I'd move later, like I'd been thinking.

Morley nodded. Then he flashed a grin. "Wish there was your usual complement of honeys in this one. That would make it a lot more interesting."

I couldn't argue with that.

It seemed I'd just drifted off when somebody started pounding on the door—though the light through the window said otherwise. I cursed whomever and rolled over. I'm not at my best when wakened prematurely.

In the process of rolling I cracked my eyes. What I saw didn't register. It was impossible. I wriggled into the down, the old hound searching for perfect comfort.

I sat up like I'd gotten a pin in the sitter.

The blonde smiled faintly as she drifted out my bedroom door. I didn't even yell, I just gaped.

She'd been sitting on the edge of the bed looking at me. She'd gotten in without getting carved up. I checked the booby trap. It sat there looking back, loaded and ready to splash blood over half a county if some villain should cooperate and trip it. Just sitting here waiting, boss.

And the door was open.

It hadn't worked.

That gave me the spine chills. Suppose it hadn't been my lovely midnight admirer? Suppose it had been somebody with a special gift? I imagined being stuck to the bed like a bug with a pin through him.

By the time I got through the supposes and lumbered out of the bedroom, the blonde was gone. Without having used the hall door, where some obnoxious fellow was pounding away, trying to get my attention. He'd gotten my goat already.

I collected my head-knocker and went to see who wanted me up at such an unreasonable hour—whatever hour it was.

"Dellwood. What's happened now?"

"Sir? Oh. Nothing's happened. You were supposed to see the General this morning, sir."

"Yeah. Sorry. I was too busy snoring to remember. Missed breakfast, didn't I? Hell. I needed to diet anyway. Give me ten minutes to get presentable."

He looked at me like he thought it might take me a year longer than that. "Yes sir. I'll meet you there, sir."

"Great."

I'm getting old. It took more than ten minutes. It was twenty before I started hoofing it across the loft to the old man's wing. I wondered about the blonde. I wondered about Morley. I wondered why I didn't just go home. These people were nuts. Whatever I did, I wasn't going to strike any blow for truth and justice. Ought to fade away and come back in a year, see how things stood then.

I was in a great mood.

Dellwood was waiting in the hallway outside the General's door. He let me in. The preliminaries followed routine. Dellwood went out. Kaid followed after making sure the fire was the size and heat of the one that's going to end the world. I sweated. The General suggested, "Sit down."

I sat. "Did Dellwood bring you up to date?"

"The events of the night? He did. Do you have any idea what happened? Or why?"

"Yes. Surprisingly." I told him about Snake's whisper, our date, how I'd found him. "Dellwood suggested the cord might have come from this room."

"Kef sidhe? Yes. I have one. Inherited from my grandfather. He collided with the cult around the turn of the century, when he was a young lieutenant sent to battle the crime rings on the waterfront. They were bad back then. One of the nonhuman crime lords had imported some sidhe killers. The cord should be there with the whips and such."

I checked. "Not here now." I wasn't racked with amazement. Neither was he. "Who could have gotten it?"

"Anyone. Anytime. I haven't paid attention to it in years."

"Who knew what it was?"

"Everybody's heard me maunder on about my grandfather's adventures. And about the adventures of every other Stantnor who ever was. Since my son's death there's been no future to look to. So I relive the glories of the past."

"I understand, sir. He was a good officer."

He brightened. "You served under him?"

Careful, Garrett. Or you'll spend your stay having the old boy bend your ear. "No sir. But I knew men who did. They spoke well of him. That says plenty." Considering how enlisted men discuss their officers.

"Indeed." He knew. He drifted off to another time, when everyone was happier—or at least he remembered them being happier. The mind is a great instrument for redesigning history.

He came back suddenly. Apparently the past wasn't all roses either. "A disastrous night. Talk to me about those dead men."

I gave him my theory about Snake having raised them.

"Possible," he said. "Entirely possible. Invisible Black was the sort of bitch who'd think it an amusing practical joke to arm an untutored Marine with the weapons to accomplish something like that."

The name meant nothing to me except that another sorceress had adopted a ridiculous handle. Her real name was probably Henrietta Sledge.

"Have you nothing positive to report, Mr. Garrett?"

"Not yet."

"Any suspects?"

"No sir. Everybody. I'm having trouble making sense of the situation. I don't know the people well enough yet."

He looked at me like he was thinking I should be living up to one of those Corps mottos like "The difficult we do immediately; the impossible takes a minute longer." "What will you do now?"

"Poke around. Talk to people till I get hold of something. Shake it. I had one thought during the night. The man who's been picking the rest off could be one who apparently left you—if he thought he could turn up for the reading of your will."

"No sir. Each man executed an agreement when he joined me in retirement. To remain eligible he'd have to remain here."

I lost some respect for him there. He'd bribed them and indentured them so he wouldn't be alone. He was no philanthropist. His motives were completely selfish.

General Stantnor was a mask. Behind it was someone who wasn't very nice.

I wouldn't call it an epiphany but it was an intuition that felt true. This was a mean-spirited old man in a carefully crafted disguise.

I examined him more closely. His color wasn't good this morning. His respite was over. He was on the road to hell again.

I reminded myself it wasn't my place to judge.

Then I reminded myself that when I remind myself, what I'm doing is looking for justification.

Someone knocked. That saved me confusion and stole the General's opportunity to get righteous.

I'd sensed that coming.

"Enter."

Dellwood opened the door. "There's a Mr. Tharpe to see Mr. Garrett."

The General looked at me. I told him. "That's the man I had trying to trace certain items."

"Bring him up, Dellwood."

Dellwood closed the door. I asked, "Here?"

"Is he likely to report something you don't want me to hear?"

"No. It just seemed an inconvenience to you."

"Not at all."

Hell. He was fishing for entertainment again. He didn't care what Saucerhead had to tell me, much. He just didn't want to be alone.

"Mr. Garrett, could I impose on you to build the fire a little?"

Damn. I was hoping he wouldn't notice it was down to a volcanic level. I wondered if Kaid had a full-time job just hauling in fuel.

Saucerhead arrived lugging a bag. In his paw it seemed small. He hulks like a cave bear. Dellwood seemed a little intimidated. The old man was impressed. He cracked, "Cook sees him, she'll fall in love." That was the first I'd heard him try for humor. "That'll be all, Dellwood." Dellwood got out.

Saucerhead wiped his brow and said, "Why don't you open a goddamned window? Who's the old prune, Garrett?"

"The principal. Be nice."

"Right."

"What's up?" I was surprised he'd make a trip out, considering what he was getting paid.

"I maybe found some of the stuff." He dumped the sack on the writing table. Silver candlesticks. They wouldn't have been remarkable if silver hadn't become important lately.

"General?" I asked. "This your stuff?"

"Look on their bases. If they belong to the family, there'll be a seahorse chop beside the smith's."

I looked. Little sea critters. "We have a lead, looks like. What's the story, Saucerhead?"

Saucerhead has a kind of pipsqueak voice when he's just making conversation. Doesn't go with his size at all. He said, "I was jawing with some guys at Morley's last night, bitching about the job. Looked like it wasn't going anywhere. Talking about this and that, you know how it is. Then this one guy asks did I think there might be a reward for the stuff. I didn't know, you never told Morley if there was or not, so I said maybe and did he know something?"

"To make a long story short?"

"He knew some fences I didn't. Outside guys. So this morning I go to check them. First one I hit, he has the sticks. We talk a little, I threaten a little, he blusters a little, I make mention of how I know he don't have a connection with the kingpin and I happen to know Chodo personal, would he like me to arrange an introduction? All of a sudden he's eager to help. He loans me the sticks. I promise to bring them back."

Which meant he would and, if the General tried to grab them, Saucerhead would walk through him and the rest of the house. He keeps his promises.

"Got you. Can the fence finger the thief?"

"He don't know squat. Bought the stuff wholesale from somebody out in the country. He'll sell the wholesaler's name."

"Did you follow that, General?"

"I believe so. This dealer in stolen goods bought the candlesticks from another dealer closer to home, here. For a price he'll sell the man out."

"That's it."

"Go beat it out of him."

"It doesn't work that way, General. He offered a straight deal. We should follow through on those terms."

"Deal with criminals as though they were honorable men?"

"You have all your life, with those bandits off the Hill. But let's not argue. We have a lead. We could settle the theft problem today. Saucerhead. How much does he want?"

I was thinking long-term now. An unconnected fence? He'd need friends. He could be nurtured and stroked on the head and maybe become a good source someday. If he stayed alive. People aren't scared of fences the way they're scared of Morley Dotes or Chodo Contague.

Saucerhead named a price that was pleasantly low. "It's a bargain, General. Go with it. How much more are you willing to lose to avoid spending a few marks?"

"Collect from Dellwood. He handles the household monies."

That sounded like a cue for me to get away from a place where I was uncomfortable. "I'll take care of this, sir."

Maybe Stantnor sensed my discomfort. He didn't protest. But there was a glimmer of hurt in his eyes.

I'd never seen it in an old person before, but I'm not around them much. I'd seen it in children, the pain when an adult doesn't have time to be bothered with them.

That hit me in the spot where I think of myself as one of the good guys. Guilt. Its lack is something I envy Morley. Morley never feels guilty. Morley does what he wants or has to do and is puzzled by the behavior of those of us who had mothers. Where does it come from, that niggling little nasty?

23

Saucerhead said, "That old boy didn't look good, Garrett. What's he got?"

"I don't know. You're going to help me find out."

"Say what?"

"Dellwood, the General said give my friend enough to cover some upcoming expenses. How much do you need, Saucerhead?" Hand him a chance to make his trip worth the trouble.

He didn't bite. Not very big. "Twenty. The guy tries to jack me up, I'll pull his ears off." He would. And wrap them with a bow.

"Get the name, then get the guy. Right? But find a doctor somewhere and bring him out here, too."

"A doctor? You lost me somewhere, Garrett. What you want a doctor for?"

"To look at the old man. He's got a thing about croakers. Only way to get one close is fool him. So you do that. All right?"

"You're paying the freight."

"Hurry all you can."

"Right." He was supposed to be too simple for sarcasm but I smelled a load there.

Dellwood gave him twenty marks. He left. I went to the front door, watched him head out in a buggy he'd probably rented from Sweetheart, a mutual friend. I grumbled about his expenses. The old man had given me a nice advance but I hadn't counted on quite so many expenses.

Dellwood joined me. "May I ask what that was all about, sir?"

"You can ask. Don't mean I'll tell you. Part of the job. You going to tell the General I'm sneaking a doctor in on him?"

He gave it a think. "No sir. It's appropriate. Except for yesterday he's been sinking fast. He's pretending to bear up today, but last night is gnawing at him, too. If there's a way . . . Let me know if I can aid in the deception."

"I will. I have a lot to do today." Like what? Not that much specific. "I'll let you know before Tharpe gets back."

"Very well, sir."

We parted. I went upstairs to see if Morley was in the suite. He'd have a part to play. As I reached the top balcony I spied my friend in white across the way. I waved. She surprised me by waving back.

Morley wasn't there. Just like him, not to be handy when I needed him. Thoughtless of him. I grabbed my coat and headed out.

The blonde was still there. She wasn't watching for me. I decided to take one more crack at sneaking up on her. Slipped up to the loft, across, went down.

Ha! Still there!

Only . . . My imagination had run away with me. This wasn't my blonde. This was Jennifer wearing white and not the same white the blonde wore. She smiled kind of sadly as I approached her. "What's the matter?" I asked.

"Life." She leaned her elbows on the rail. I joined her, leaving a few feet between us. Below, our hero remained locked in mortal combat with the dragon. Chain passed without giving them a glance. I knew how the knight felt. Us heroes like to be applauded for our efforts.

I answered Jennifer with one of those "Uhm?" noises that mean you'll listen if your companion wants to share her troubles.

"Am I ugly, Garrett?"

I glanced at her. No. She wasn't. "Not hardly." I've known several equally gorgeous women who were more insecure about their looks than your less-than-average-looking ladies. "The guy who didn't notice would have to be dead."

"Thanks." Trace of a smile, trace of warmth. She moved maybe three inches closer. "That helps." Half a minute. "But nobody does notice. Even that I'm female."

How do you tell a woman it isn't her looks, it's her inside? That, nice as she looks, she feels like a black widow spider?

You don't. You fib a little to avoid the cruelty and hate.

Even standing close, with her radiating a need to be wanted, I couldn't find any interest inside me.

I began to worry about me.

"You don't notice me."

"I notice you plenty." Only somebody with very skewed standards, like maybe a ratman, would call her hard on the eyes. "But I'm taken." That's always an out.

"Oh." That infinite sorrow again. That's what it was. Sorrow. Sorrow that stretched back to the dawn of her days. An abyss that could gobble the world. "What's her name?"

"Tinnie. Tinnie Tate."

"Is she attractive?"

"Yes." The redhead is in the same class as Jennifer. That is, the howl-at-the-moon class. But we have our problems, one of which is that we aren't going anywhere. Sort of a can't-live-with-and-can't-live-without arrangement, neither of us with enough confidence to risk commitment.

I might have, with Maya . . . Or maybe she just said she was going to marry me so often that I accepted the possibility. I wondered what she was doing. Wondered if I was supposed to track her down. Wondered if she'd ever be back.

"You're awful thoughtful, Garrett."

"Tinnie does that to me. And this place . . . This house . . ."

"Don't be apologetic. I live here. I know. It's a sad place. A ghost town all by itself, haunted by might-have-beens. Some of us live in the past and the rest live for a future that'll never come. And Cook, who lives in another world, is the rock that holds us together."

She wasn't so much talking to me as putting feelings into words.

"There's a road down front, Garrett. Less than half a mile away. Its other end is TunFaire, Karenta, the world. I haven't been past the front gate since I was fourteen."

"How old are you now?"

"Twenty-two."

"Who's holding you here?"

"Nobody but me. I'm afraid. Everything I imagine I want is out there. And I'm afraid to go see it. When I was fourteen, Cook took me to the city for the summer fair. I wanted so badly to go. It's the only time I've ever been off the estate. It terrified me."

Odd. Most beautiful women don't have much trouble coping because they've had attention all their lives.

"I know my future. And it frightens me, too."

I looked at her, thinking she meant Wayne. I'd be disturbed, too, if I were the object of such plans.

"I'll stay here, in the heart of my fortress, and turn into a crazy old woman while the house crumbles around me and Cook. I'll never find nerve enough to hire the workmen to put it right. Strangers scare me."

"It doesn't have to be that way."

"It has to. My destiny was laid down the week I was born. If my mother had survived . . . But she probably wouldn't have changed things. She was a strange woman herself, from what I hear. Daughter of a firelord and a storm-warden, raised in an environment almost as cold as mine, betrothed to my father by arrangement between his parents and hers. They never met before their wedding day. My father loved her, though. What happened really hurt him. He never mentions her. He won't talk about her. But he has her picture in his bedroom. Sometimes he just lies there and stares at it for hours."

What do you say when somebody tells you something like that? You can't kiss it and make it better. Not much you can do. Or say. I said, "I'm going to take a walk. Why don't you get a wrap and come along?"

"How cold is it?"

"Not too bad." Winter was just blustering and fussing, bluffing, too cowardly to jump in there and bully the world. Which was fine with me. Winter isn't my favorite season.

"All right." She pushed away from the rail and walked to the stairs, down, headed for her own suite. I tagged along, which was fine till we neared her door. Then she got nervous. She didn't want me inside.

Fine. For now her fortress would remain inviolate. I retreated halfway down the hall.

If I'd had doubts about her lack of social skills, they disappeared when she returned in less than a minute. I've never known a woman who didn't spend half an hour changing her shoes. She'd done that and had donned a very sensible, military-type winter coat that, surprisingly, was flattering because it centered attention on her face. And that face made me wince because such beauty was shut up here, wasted. Such beauty, like a great painting, should be out for all to appreciate.

We went downstairs and through that hall between the Stantnor forebears, all of whom noted our passing with grave disapproval. So did Wayne, who maybe thought I was trying to beat his time.

It wasn't as mild as I'd promised. The wind had picked up since Saucerhead's departure. It had a good bite but Jennifer didn't notice. We descended the steps. I set course along the path that Chain, Peters, Tyler, and I had taken last night.

I asked, "Would you like to see the city? If you could do it without too much discomfort?" I had in mind turning Saucerhead loose on her. He has a knack for making women comfortable—though his taste runs to gals about five feet short.

"It's too late. If you're trying to save me."

I didn't say anything to that. My attention was on last night's trail.

"I saw something strange today," Jennifer said, shifting subject radically. "A man I don't know. I went up where you found me looking for him, but he wasn't there anymore."

Morley. Had to be. "Maybe my blonde's boyfriend."

She glanced at me sharply, the first time she'd looked up since we'd left the house. "Are you making fun of me?"

"No. Of a situation, maybe. I see a woman, over and over. Nobody else sees her. At least, nobody admits she's there. But now you're seeing ghosts, too."

"I saw him, Garrett."

"I didn't say you didn't."

"But you don't believe me."

"I don't believe or disbelieve. The first rule of my business is keep an open mind." The second is remember that everybody lies to you.

That seemed to satisfy her. She didn't speak again for a while.

We came to the place where Tyler died. Tyler wasn't there. Neither was the draug. I walked around trying to discover what had happened. I couldn't. I hoped Peters and the others had collected them. I'd have to find out.

The wind was biting, the grass was brown, the sky was gray, and the brooding Stantnor place loomed like a thunderhead of despair. I glanced at the orchard, all those bare arms reaching for the sky. Spring would come for the trees but not for the Stantnors.

"Do you dance?" I asked. Maybe we could force gaiety into the place at swords' points.

She managed a joke. "I don't know. I've never tried."

"Hey! We're making headway. Next thing you'll be smiling."

She didn't respond for half a minute, then bushwhacked me again. "I'm a virgin, Garrett."

Not exactly a surprise. It figured. But why tell me?

"The other day when you caught me in your stuff, I thought you were the man who would change that. But you aren't, are you?"

"I don't think so."

"Peters warned me—"

"That I have a reputation? Maybe. But the way this is, it wouldn't be right. It has to be right, Jennifer." Carefully, carefully, Garrett. Hell hath no fury, and all that. "You shouldn't want to do it just because you don't want to be a virgin. You should do it because that's what you want to do. Because you're with someone special and you want to share something special."

"I can get preached at by Cook."

"Sorry, just trying to tell you how I think. You're a lovely woman. One of the most beautiful I've ever met. The kind men like me only dream about. I'd take you up on it in a second, if I was a guy who could just use a woman and discard her like a gnawed bone, and not care how much she hurts."

That seemed to help.

Believe me, all that analysis and nimble-footing had me real nervous, prancing around a lot of mixed feelings.

"I think I understand. It's actually kind of nice."

"That's me. Mr. Nice Guy. Talk myself out of the winner's circle every time."

She gave me a look.

"Sorry. You're not used to my brand of wit."

I was following the backtrails of the draugs slowly now, climbing a gentle slope toward the family cemetery. Jennifer seemed too preoccupied to notice. After we'd walked another fifty yards, she stopped. "Would you do one thing for me?"

"Sure. Even what we were talking about, if it ever becomes right."

Strained little smile. "Touch me."

"Huh?" I was back into my trick bag of brilliant repartee.

"Touch me."

What the hell? I reached out, touched her shoulder. She raised her hand, grabbed mine, moved it to her cheek. I rested my fingers there gently. She had the silkiest skin I'd ever touched.

She started shaking. I mean shaking bad. Tears filled her eyes. She turned away, embarrassed or frightened. After a while she turned back and we started walking again. As we reached the low rail fence around the cemetery, she said, "That was almost as much."

"What?"

"Nobody ever touched me before. Ever. Not since I was old enough to remember. Cook did, I guess, when I had to be changed and burped and all those things you do with babies."

I stopped dead, faced that grim old mansion. No wonder it was so god-damned bleak. I faced her. "Come here."

"What?"

"Just come here." When she stepped closer, I pulled her into a hug. She went as rigid as an iron post. I held her a moment, then turned loose. "Maybe it's not too late to start. Everybody's got to touch sometime. You're not human if you don't." I understand what she wanted when she wanted to stop being a virgin. Sex had nothing to do with it. She might not realize it consciously but she thought sex was the price she had to pay for what she needed.

How many times has Morley told me I'm a sucker for cripples and strays? More than I like to remember. And he's right—if you call wanting to ease pain being a sucker.

I stepped over the cemetery fence, held her hand as she followed. She caught the hem of her dress, which wasn't exactly designed for a stroll in the country. She cursed softly. I helped her keep her balance while she worked it loose, looking around as she did so. My gaze fell on a tombstone less aged than most, as simple a marker as there was there. Just a small slab of granite with a name: Eleanor Stantnor. Not even a date.

Jennifer stepped over to it. "My mother."

That was all? That was the resting place of the woman whose death had warped so many lives and turned the Stantnor place into the house of gray-dom? I would've thought he'd built her a temple . . . Of course. The house had become her mausoleum, her memorial. The house of broken dreams.

Jennifer shuddered and moved closer. I put my arm around her. We had a biting cold wind, a gray day, and a graveyard. I needed to be close to somebody, too.

I said, "I've reconsidered. Somewhat. Spend the night with me tonight." I didn't explain. I didn't say anything more. She didn't say anything, either, neither in protest, shock, or accusation. She stiffened just the slightest, the only sign she'd heard me.

It was an impulse, almost, kicked up by that part of me that hates to see people hurting.

Maybe there's such a thing as karma. Our good deeds get their reward. A small thing, but if I'd overcome that impulse, I'd probably be dead.

24

We stood looking at the tombstone. I asked, "Do you know much about your mother?"

"Only what I told you, which is all Cook ever told me. Father won't say anything. He fired everybody after she died, except Cook. There wasn't anyone else to tell me."

"What about your grandparents?"

"I don't know anything about them. My grandfather Stantnor died when I was a baby. My grandmother Stantnor went when my father was a boy. I don't know who they were on my mother's side except that they were a stormwarden and a firelord. Cook won't tell me who they were. I think something bad happened to them and she doesn't want me to know."

Ting! A little bell rang inside my head.

A favorite pastime of our ruling class is plotting to snatch the throne. Though we haven't lately, sometimes we go through periods when we change kings like underwear. We had three in one year, once.

There'd been a big brouhaha when I was eight, maybe seven. About the time Jennifer had been born. An assassination attempt had gone awry and had been so blackhearted at its core that the would-be victim had gotten so righteously pissed off, he'd made a clean sweep. Not a bit of forgive-and-forget. Necks got stretched. Heads and bodies went their separate ways. Arms and legs got hauled around the kingdom and buried individually beneath crossroads. Great estates got confiscated. It hadn't been a good time to be related to the conspirators, however remotely.

From my neighborhood it had been great fun, watching the ruling class chase its tail and get it caught in a door. Or some such mixed metaphor. When those things come up, everybody on the outside hopes that crowd will wipe themselves out. But they never do. They just select out the least competent schemers.

Shouldn't be hard to find out who her grandparents had been. "Would you want to know?" I asked. "Is it important to you?"

"It's not important. It wouldn't change my life. I don't know if I care anymore." After some silence, "I used to dream about them when I was little. They were going to come take me home to their palace. I was really a princess. They'd sent me and my mother here to hide us from their enemies, only something happened. Maybe they'd forgotten where they'd hidden us. I don't know. I never figured out why they never came. I just pretended that they would, someday."

A common childhood mind game. But, "It could be true, Jennifer. Things were unsettled politically in those days. It's possible the marriage was arranged to put your mother out of harm's way. With your grandparents dead, your father might have been the only one left who knew who your mother was."

"You're kidding."

"No. I was young but I remember those days. Some people tried to kill the King. They blew it. He went crazy. A lot of people died, including some who had nothing to do with the plot." Sometimes you tell the white lie. Wouldn't hurt to leave her the option of believing her grandparents had been innocents caught in the storm.

She laughed without humor. "Wouldn't that be something? If my kid's daydreams were true?"

"Do you still not care?" I could find out about her grandparents without doing much but poke through some old records. Worth the effort if it would brighten her life.

"I think I do care."

"I'll find out, then." I started moving again. She followed, caught up in her thoughts, paying no attention, while I got back onto the trail of the draugs. We were almost to the road before she realized we were still headed away from the house. She might not have noticed then if we hadn't gotten into some cockleburs.

"Where are you going?" She sounded almost panicky. There was a touch of wildness in her eyes. She looked around like she'd suddenly wakened in enemy territory. Only the peaks of the house were visible above the hummock where the cemetery lay. Once we reached the road, those would be out of sight.

"I'm backtracking the thing that came to the house last night." I was backtracking all three, really. There were three trails smashed through the weeds. But there were no return trails. That left me a little uneasy. We'd only disposed of two. "I think it came from the swamp that's supposed to be up ahead there."

"No. I want to go back." She looked around like she expected something to jump out at us. And maybe something could. Those draugs hadn't behaved like story draugs. Who was to say they weren't immune to daylight? And I wasn't equipped to handle them. It hadn't occurred to me to bring any heavy weaponry.

Still, I wasn't particularly nervous. Without the dark to mask them, they couldn't sneak up on us.

"Nothing to worry about. We'll be all right."

"I'm going back. If you want to go out there . . ." She said "out there" like I was headed for another world. "If you want, you go ahead."

"You win. You seen one swamp, you've seen them all. And I got a plenty good look in the islands."

She'd already started walking. I had to trot to catch up. She looked relieved. "It's almost lunchtime, anyway."

It was. And I still had to find Morley and rehearse him for Saucerhead's return. "I should thank you. I've missed so many meals, I'm light-headed."

We went straight to the kitchen. We ate. The others eyed us curiously. Everyone knew we'd gone for a walk. Each invested that with his own special significance. Nobody mentioned it, though Wayne looked like he had a few words he wanted to say.

As Peters was about to leave I asked, "Where can I catch you later?"

"The stable. I'm trying to catch up for Snake." He didn't look pleased. That kind of work wouldn't thrill me, either.

"I'll be out. Need to ask you something."

He nodded and went his way. I ingratiated myself by helping Cook for a while. She didn't say much with Jennifer there, fumbling around. Cook never said much with a third party present. Made me wonder.

I hoped Jennifer wasn't going to attach herself permanently. But it did seem that way.

I'd just been kind to a stray. But pups run to where the kindness is. My own fault. A sucker, as Morley says.

I had to see him soon or adjust my scheme for the afternoon. I told Cook I'd be back to help later, then headed upstairs, hoping Morley would be in my suite. Jennifer tagged along till it was obvious where I was headed. Then she chickened out. Afraid of a guy with my reputation.

I said good-bye and kept a straight face till I'd let myself in.

No Morley. No sign of Morley. Curious.

It made me uneasy. Morley is an odd bird but he'd make an effort to stay in touch.

I had a bad moment imagining him dead in some hidden place, ambushed. Not a pleasant thought, a friend getting offed for helping with something that wasn't his concern. But Morley was too much a pro to get taken that way. The mistakes he makes aren't those kind. When he buys it, it will be because an irate husband appears unexpectedly while he's in no position to react.

I took a quick guess at how long it would be till Saucerhead returned, decided I'd have to manage without Morley. Black Pete would have to carry the load.

I shrugged into my coat and headed for the stable, making sure my telltales were in position.

I kept an eye out for my blond sweetheart, but the only person I saw was Kaid on the fourth-floor balcony west scoping out how to haunt the place after his own death.

Kaid was close to the old man. I ought to spend some time with him. He might give me a lead on who might want the General out.

shoved my head into the stables, didn't spot Peters. A couple of horses grinned at me like they thought their hour had come. "Think what you want," I told them. "Plot and plan and scheme. I've got an arrangement. The General can pay me in horseflesh. Horses that aggravate me are going to end up at the tannery."

I don't know why I said that. Pure bull, of course. They wouldn't believe it, anyway. Wish I understood why horses bring out the silliness in me.

"Peters? You here?" Not seeing him right away worried me. I'd had enough guys turn up dead.

"Here." From the far end.

It was dark in there. I moved warily, even assuming Peters wasn't one of the villains.

I found him at the nether end, all right, hard at it with a pitchfork. He grumbled, "That damned Snake must have been playing with his paint set all the time. He hadn't cleaned out in months. Look at this mess."

I looked. I wrinkled my nose. Peters was tossing manure and soiled straw into a spreader wagon. "I'm no expert but isn't this the wrong time of year to spread manure?"

"You got me. All I know is, it's got to be cleaned out and this's the wagon you haul it in." He mumbled some rakledly rikkenfratzes and colorful commentary on Snake Bradon's ancestors, then added, "I have enough to do without this. What's up, Garrett? And why don't you grab a fork and help while you're resting?"

I grabbed a fork but I wasn't much help. I was always lucky, even in the Marines, and never had to learn the practical side of keeping horses. "What's up is, I've found the fence who bought the stolen stuff. One of my associates will bring him out this afternoon."

He stopped pitching. He stared long enough to start me wondering if maybe he wasn't less than thrilled. He said, "So you are doing something after all. I was starting to think you were a drone. That the only effort you were putting out was trying to get Jennifer to put out."

"Nope. Not interested. Not my type." I guess there was an edge to my voice. He dropped it.

"You just wanted to give me the news?"

"No. I need your help. My associate is bringing a doctor, too."

"And you want me to distract the old man while this croaker gets a look at him?"

"I want you to go down the road and meet them, explain to the doc so he don't get himself booted before he gets a look. Not that I have any hopes he can tell much without laying hands on."

Peters grunted and started throwing horse hockey. "When are they coming?"

I tried guessing an optimum turnaround time. With Saucerhead there wouldn't be many delays. He'd just grab them by the collar and drag them. "I'd think two more hours. If we can, I'd like to get the fence in without anybody seeing him. So we can spring him on whoever."

He grunted again. "You're slacking." We tossed. He said, "I'll manage. I'll have to see the old man first. Always something around here."

I told him, "I have hopes for this."

"Yeah?"

"Maybe it'll start things unraveling. If it goes right, we could get it tied up by tonight."

"You always were too optimistic."

"You don't think so?"

"I don't. You're not dealing with your average idiots. These guys aren't going to rattle. They aren't going to panic. Watch your back."

"I intend to."

He put his fork down. "You go ahead. I'm going to go clean up."

I watched him walk toward the open doorway, grinned. Those ears stuck out like the handles of jugs.

I tossed about three more forksful and quit. Mama Garrett didn't raise her boy to be a stable hand.

• • •

I'd gone a dozen steps toward the house when I had a thought. I turned back and invited myself into Snake Bradon's den. I fiddled around for five minutes getting a lamp going. Snake wasn't there anymore. I wondered what they'd done with him. Nobody had done any digging in the cemetery.

Damn! I'd meant to ask Peters about Tyler and the draug!

I missed the Dead Man's nagging. I just wasn't alert enough. Getting too turned inward or something. Not paying close enough attention. I didn't do that when I had the Dead Man to tell me what to do. I went down the list, by the numbers.

All right. I would. I'd failed to meet Snake in time. That didn't mean Bradon couldn't still tell me something, as the Dead Man would remind me. They could all tell me things, want to or not, if I concentrated. So let's start here, now, Garrett.

I did the things I'd done when we'd found Snake. I didn't learn anything this time, either. But I did pay attention to the paint-splashed worktable. I hadn't before. I hadn't considered that side of Snake at all.

Cook said he'd had tremendous artistic talent. Someone else said he might have painted the sorceress Invisible Black. Here, there, there'd been remarks to the effect that he remained an active artist. That side of the man didn't fit the rest of the Bradon image, to my mind. Artists sponge off the lords of the Hill. However good they are, they can't make a living doing what they do. I hadn't considered Bradon an artist because he hadn't fallen into the groove.

That table was evidence he'd worked plenty. But where were the results? The table wasn't his product.

I started a thorough search, working outward from the center of Snake Bradon's life. I found nothing interesting in his room except squirreled stuff for making paints. I recalled that he'd been messy when we were checking what had happened to Hawkes. He'd been working on something recently.

There was a fifteen-by-twenty tack room next to Snake's hole. The place had been torn apart.

I just stood there, surprised. Somebody was worried about Snake after he was gone? My, my. And Garrett hadn't been smart enough to get to it first.

If the searcher found something, he did a fine job of getting rid of it. There was nothing there now but a scatter of brushes, some broken underfoot. I wondered if Bradon's hobby had been a secret. One of those kind everybody knows but nobody mentions. Painting pictures wasn't a manly, Marine sort of thing to do. He might not have shared with the others.

I was having a little trouble making sense of these people. Again. Still.

I paused to wonder where I'd have hidden something if I'd been Snake. As the searcher probably had, knowing him better.

Brilliant thinker that I am, I came up with a big nothing.

Nothing for it, then. A general search. Every nook and cranny. Whoever had gone before me wouldn't have had a lot of time. He'd have to be seen places when he was supposed to be. Hell. Maybe he'd done his hunting before Morley and I came along last night. Or maybe while he was supposed to be loading manure?

Whatever, there was a chance he hadn't found anything.

If anything existed.

I did a quick tour of the ground level. Nothing caught my eye. I felt the imminence of the confrontation with the thief and kept getting more hurried, somehow hoping to have an extra dart when the showdown came.

I climbed into the hayloft, perched on a bale, and muttered, "What the hell am I looking for, anyway?" Paintings? He'd painted, obviously. And the product wasn't in evidence. But what could paintings tell me if I found them?

I shrugged, got up, looked around. Snake had gotten a damned good hay supply in, considering. All neatly baled, too. From what I recalled the country boys saying back when, that wasn't common. Ordinary folks filled their lofts with loose hay.

"Ha!" A story recalled. A guy in the outfit, Tulsa something, hell of an archer, did our sniping. Farm kid. Poor background. Died on that island. But he used to laugh about games he'd played with the daughters of the lord of a nearby manor. They'd done it in a secret room they'd built in the hayloft of the lord's main barn.

I raised my lamp high and stared at all that hay, too much for the state of the place. Might that pile be hollow? I muttered, "That has to be it."

I poked around the outside, trying to guess how Bradon would have gotten inside. Elimination left me three good spots to find entrances. I set the lamp on a beam and went to work.

I moved maybe ten bales before I decided I'd tried the wrong place first. I went to the next spot, moved another ten bales and felt foolish. Looked like I'd outfoxed myself again.

My activities drew the attention of the natives. Three ugly cats joined me, including an evil old calico. Me moving the bales got the mice stirring. The cats were snacking. They worked as a team, not something cats usually do, as far as I know. When I'd turn a bale, one would jump into the vacated spot to scare mice toward the others. At one point the calico had one mouse under each forepaw and another in her mouth.

"See?" I told them. "I'm not all bad."

One more try.

Third time was the charm, as they say. I tipped a few bales. Cats flew around. And, behold! A three-foot-high, eighteen-inch-wide hollow, black as a priest's heart, ran back into the pile. I got the lamp. I asked the cats, "One of you want to run in there and let me know what's up? No? I didn't think so."

I got down on hands and knees and crawled.

t smelled in there. Not too bad a smell, but a strong one of moldy hay. It didn't do my cold any good. My nose ran like a fountain.

There was a room inside the hay, larger than I'd expected. Snake had spanned it with planks to support the bales on top. It was maybe six feet wide and ten feet long. His paintings were there, along with other treasures, mostly what we'd consider trivial or trash. Junk from the war, mostly. And medals. Snake had accumulated a potful of medals, proudly displayed on a tattered Karentine banner against the narrow end wall.

I couldn't help feeling for the guy. A hero had come to this. A life for his country, for this.

And our rulers wonder why Glory Mooncalled is a folk hero.

Both side walls were lined with paintings, none of them framed, all just leaning there, stacked three and four deep. They were every bit as good as Cook said they could be. Better, maybe. I'm no expert but they looked like the product of a driven genius.

They weren't cheerful paintings. They were the spawn of darkness, visions of hell. One caught my eye immediately and hit me like a blow in the gut. It was a swamp. Maybe not the swamp that became my home away from home during my stint, but a place just as horrible. And that painting was no simple, brooding landscape faintly touched with the dark side. Swamp things swarmed there the way they seemed after they'd driven you mad for months. Mosquitos the size of hornets, eyes that watched from the dark, stagnant water. Human bones.

In the foreground was a hanged man. The scavengers had been at him. A dark bird perched on his shoulder, pecked his face. Something about the way he hung left you certain he'd hanged himself rather than go on.

A couple of guys in the company *had* killed themselves when they couldn't take it anymore.

Gods. I felt like I could fall into that painting and tumble right back through time.

I turned it around. It got to me that much.

Shaking, I went down the row on that side, then up the other. No other piece had the personal impact that one did but the same genius drove them. They'd have as much power for the right viewer.

"He was crazy," I murmured.

I couldn't hear anything well but it seemed the horses below were restless.

I went around again, checking the paintings behind the ones displayed.

Most seemed less maniacal, more illustrative, yet there was no doubt they portrayed places beheld by the same eye that had interpreted the war in the others. One I recognized as a view of Full Harbor contorted into a hellish dreamscape, more proof that Snake had put his memories or haunts onto his canvases.

Snake hadn't been just a painter of places. The first portrait I encountered was of Jennifer, I'd guess, at the time the General had come home. She was indefinably younger and maybe more beautiful—yet interpreted by mad eyes.

I studied it hard but couldn't figure it out. Yet Snake had done something with Jennifer that gave me the creeps.

There were portraits of the others, too. Kaid looked old and tired and worn out and you got the feeling that death was watching over his shoulder. The General had some of the creepiness that illuminated Jennifer and something of the fox about him. Chain looked plain mean. Wayne looked like a greedy burgher. I got it! Part of it. Part of the interpretation was how Bradon had clothed them. That was the crude statement. But there were the faces, too, painted like the man had been able to read the bones and souls beneath.

There was a later portrait of Jennifer, crueler than the first but with the lady more beautiful. Then a couple of guys I hadn't met, presumably among the missing. Then one of Dellwood that reminded me of a basset hound. I guess Snake saying he was a faithful old dog without a soul or mind of his own. Then one of Peters, either a failure for the artist or observer. I couldn't read anything into it. Then one of Cook that must have been romantic excess because she came off like a saint, like a mother to the world. Then still another of Jennifer, almost repulsive in its portrayal of the dualities, beauty and horror.

Once I got over being startled, I examined it more closely. Part of the effect came at a subconscious level, almost. I don't know how he did it but he'd painted two faces, one over the other, the outer one of blinding beauty and the other the skull face of death. You didn't see that one without staring long and hard.

The horses were excited downstairs. I wondered why but was preoccupied with the magic—yeah, the *sorcery*—of Snake Bradon's artistry.

If it was a sin that Jennifer's beauty should be hidden, it was the crime of the century that Bradon's paintings should go unseen, certain to fall victim to mold and moisture.

Before I left Jennifer, I vowed I'd find some way to bring the paintings out. Snake Bradon wouldn't go unremembered.

Had he been in love with Jennifer? She was the only subject he'd painted more than once, excepting a scene that looked like a before and after of a nonhuman holy place that had had the misfortune to stumble into the middle of a human battle. The later painting reeked of defilement by the corpses and ravens and bones. It felt like a parable of the world.

I blew my nose, hit the mother lode. Before it watered up again, I caught a whiff of a new odor. What? I shrugged and went on.

"Damn! Ah, damn my eyes!" That was no curse, friends. That was a squeal of triumph.

Snake had painted my lady in white. He had caught her as the incarnation of beauty—yet she, too, had some of the creepiness he'd put into his portraits of Jennifer.

She was in a wind, running, frightened. A darkness lay behind her. You knew it was in pursuit, yet you could not define what it was. The harder you looked the harder it was to tell it was there. The woman looked right into your eyes. The artist's eyes. Her right hand was just starting the motion of reaching out for help. Her eyes said she knew the person she was looking at knew what was behind her.

It transfixed me. It had the impact of the swamp painting. And this time I couldn't figure out why, because this one couldn't be explained in terms of my own past.

I blew my nose again. I got another whiff of that odor. This time I recognized it.

Smoke!

The damned stable was on fire! No wonder the horses were excited!

I scrambled out of there, to the edge of the loft.

Flames roared at the end where Peters had been working. The animals had gotten out and run. I heard shouting outside. The heat was savage.

I wasn't trapped—yet. If I moved fast I could get clear.

I knew the mileage Morley would get out of the gesture as I dove into the hole leading to Snake's cache. He'd be on me for a year, risking my life over some daubs on canvas.

I slapped a dozen of those daub-hickeys into a pile as big as I could manage and dragged them out. The fire was spreading fast. Flames were almost to me when I burst out. The heat beat at me. I felt my eyebrows curl, my eyes dry out. I staggered away. The flames came after me.

"Damned fool," I muttered to myself. The heat seared the back of my neck. Now my eyes watered, nearly blinding me. My chances were slim enough without the damned paintings.

I couldn't let them go. They were that important. They were worth risking a life. Part of me already mourned those I'd had to leave behind.

The fire had spread below faster than it had up top. It was ahead of me now, at the end where Snake had lived. I wasn't going to get out that way.

I could see daylight through cracks between the vertical boards that formed the outside wall, rough-cut timber that had shrunk with the years till some of the gaps were half an inch wide. It was like looking through the bars at the gates of hell. From the inside. That close. And so far.

As panic closed in, I threw myself that way.

The stable was old and damned near falling down, and, if it was half as rotten as it looked, I might be able to bust out. I hit the wall with my shoulder, low. Both creaked. Neither broke but I figured the wall had the edge. I got down on my back and shot my feet out. One board gave an inch. That gave me hope and maybe some manic strength. I let fly again. An eight-inch-wide board tilted outward, then fell away under its own weight. Mad as I was, I flipped Bradon's paintings out before trying to make the hole wide enough for me.

The smoke almost overcame me first, but I made it. I jumped.

I lay around panting a while, vaguely aware that I was out there alone, away from the hollering on the other side of the barn. I climbed a fencepost and got myself upright, looked around, counted limbs to make sure I hadn't left any behind. I was still alone. I gathered my priceless salvage.

If there are gods, they agreed with me about those paintings. They hadn't been damaged. I got them together, limped over to the cow barn, hid them in the hayloft. My fuddled sense of humor told me that was appropriate. Then I stumbled back around the far side of the stable.

The whole gang was running around like chickens, doing the hopeless, bringing buckets of water from the wellhouse. Only the General and Peters were absent.

"Garrett!" Jennifer squealed. "What happened?"

I'm such a handsome devil, they just go to pieces when they see me. "I was taking a nap in there," I lied.

She got a little pale.

I gave her my heroic grin. "Not to worry. I just busted through a wall and here I am." A coughing jag hit me. Great timing. Damned smoke. "Can't stop the true of heart."

"You could've been killed."

"I could have. But I wasn't. Too light on my feet."

Kaid said, "Somebody tried to kill you, boy," as he staggered past with a five-gallon bucket.

I looked at the growing inferno. That hadn't occurred to me, though it should have.

No. You don't kill somebody by setting a barn on fire. Too easy for him to get away. Maybe you start a fire to flush him out, but . . . That wouldn't have worked here. Too many witnesses.

Even in my fuzzy state, it was obvious the arsonist had wanted to get rid of the stable and whatever contents he'd been unable to find during a hasty search.

Wonderful. Snake's information had escaped me again.

Even Cook was out lugging water. But no Peters. I worked up a case of the suspicions before I recalled why he wasn't around.

Hell. Saucerhead was overdue. I said, "You guys are wasting your time. Just keep it from jumping to the other buildings."

"What the hell you think we're doing, dipshit?" Chain growled. "If you're not going to help, get the hell out of the way."

Which was just the advice I needed. "I'm going inside to treat these burns." I had a few but didn't know how bad they were. Not too bad, I hoped. I didn't need them distracting me. The cold was bad enough.

I stumbled away. The others didn't pay any attention.

walked straight through to the front of the house, past the dueling champions and all the dead Stantnors. I'd been in that stable longer than I'd thought. Saucerhead was way overdue unless I'd guessed badly about how long it would take to recruit a doctor and jump a couple of fences through hoops.

I stepped out the front door. My burns, not bad, made their presence felt. I hoped that doctor would have something for the sting.

Nothing in sight. "Saucerhead, what's holding you up? How long does it take to twist a guy's arm?"

A few raindrops hit the steps leading to the porch. I glanced at the sky. Old slabs of lead again. I wondered if the Stantnor place ever had any other kind. It was getting to me.

The wind was rising. That wouldn't do the firefighters any good. Maybe their best hope was that the rain wouldn't play around.

It did become a steady fall. Not quite a downpour, but it should help. I guess that took fifteen minutes to develop. The wind started gusting, throwing water onto the porch. I started to retreat. A coach came out of the rain.

That damned Saucerhead. Now it was a hired coach.

It pulled up. People tumbled out. Peters galloped up the steps, followed by a tall, distinguished character whom I presumed to be the doctor. A weaselly little character followed him, then Saucerhead and Morley Dotes. I asked Morley, "Where the hell you been? I been trying to find you all morning."

He gave me a funny look. "Home taking care of business."

Saucerhead interrupted, "Let's do it, Garret. This here is Doc Stones." He indicated the weaselly guy. Which goes to show you what it's worth, judging by appearances. "He'll get an arm and leg off you for this. That's your fence there. We got an agreement. No names."

"Fine with me. As long as he points a finger. Peters. Let's get upstairs."

Peters wore a puzzled look. "What's happening?"

"Somebody tried to burn the stable down. With me inside. Let's go. Doc, you got anything to take the sting out of burns?"

We moved inside as I asked. Saucerhead asked me, "You want to give him the other arm and leg?"

"What took you so damned long, anyway?" Peters led the way, headed for the stairs.

"Morley. He pooted around finding a doc he thought would look like a fence's partner."

That made sense. "Yeah. I guess I can appreciate that. Morley, I thought you were going to prowl around the house, do the stuff I don't have time to do because I've got to be onstage all the time."

He looked at me funny again, like I was maybe talking too much. So did Peters. Dotes said, "I did what I could, Garrett. But I have a business to run and not a whole lot of time to spend working on the cuff."

"But I heard you come in and go out a couple times."

He stopped. "I roamed around an hour after you hit the sack, didn't find squat, decided I better get back and see if Wedge had robbed me while my back was turned. I didn't go back to your room."

I shuddered. The old cold rats pranced up and down my back. "You didn't?"

"No."

"Oh, my. But I'd swear I even saw you once."

"It wasn't me."

I was sure. I'd gotten up to use the chamber pot. I'd even grumbled a hello and gotten something growled in return. I told him that.

"It wasn't me, Garrett. I went home." Dotes said it in a flat, disturbed voice.

"I'll take your word for it." My voice was just as flat. "So who was it?"

"Shape-changer?"

I'd run into one of those before. I didn't want to do that again. "How? Changers have to kill the people they mimic. Then they absorb their souls, or whatever. And even then they can't always fool people who knew them."

"Yes. And this one had me pat?"

"I was pretty damned tired. There was only one lamp burning. And I just walked through, not paying that much attention. But I'd have sworn it was you."

"I don't like this. It makes me nervous, Garrett. Real nervous."

Me too, yeah boy. All we needed was some villain prancing around able to pretend he was somebody else. That would complicate things real good.

Morley was just concerned about Morley Dotes, not everything else. He had troubles enough in life without having somebody else running around doing dirty deeds in his name and face.

I had a broader perspective on it. If somebody here could fake Morley, he could fake me or anybody else, anytime. So none of us could ever be sure who we were dealing with. Which undermined the roots of reality. Some fun coming up.

Morley suggested, "You'd better get out while you still can."

I was tempted. Tempted like I've never been tempted before. But, "I can't. I took the job. If I quit because it's getting tough, it won't be that long before I find some good reason to drop another one. That happens a couple times and I won't get work at all."

He politely refrained from mentioning the fact that I spend most of my energy avoiding work. "Figured you'd say something like that. So. Let's get on with it. I want out of here even if you don't." He started up the final flight of stairs. "You drink much milk, Garrett?"

"No. Beer."

"I sort of figured."

"Why?" The others watched us like we were a road show.

"Not sure what it is about milk. But it's good for the teeth and bones and brain. A man who drinks milk always has a healthy sense of self-preservation. Beer guzzlers get increasingly feeble in that area."

He was dressing up a cautionary message as one of his crackpot dietary theories. That way it was easier to tell me he was afraid I was in way over my head.

Peters said, "I don't know what you're talking about, Garrett. I don't much care. But I do think we ought to get on with it." He stared at the glass at the rear of the house. The glow from the burning stable shone through. He looked like he wanted to rush off and get involved.

"Right. Go get the old man set." I stared at the firelight while the rest moved toward the General's suite.

"Garrett!"

"Coming."

I caught a glimpse of the blonde across the way, behind a pillar. She smiled and looked like she might wave back if I started it.

I growled and headed down the hall.

Her portrait was one I'd saved from the flames. I'd bring it in and ask some questions. And I was, by damn, going to get some answers.

I was getting tired of being nice.

eters moved on into the deeps of the old man's suite. The rest of us waited in the study. I killed time by tossing logs on the fire and exchanging puzzled glances with Morley. Each of us wondered how much the other was pulling his leg.

The General arrived, bundled as though for an expedition to the Arctic. He looked at the fire, at me stirring it around so I could get a few more logs on, beamed approval. "Thank you, Mr. Garrett. Thoughtful of you." He surveyed the crowd. "Who are these people?"

"Mr. Morley Dotes, restaurateur and an associate of mine." Morley gave him a nod.

"Indeed?" The old man seemed startled, like maybe he knew the name. He looked at me hard, reconsidering his estimate of me.

I said, "You've met Mr. Tharpe. The other gentlemen prefer to remain anonymous, but they've agreed to point out your thief."

"Oh." A hollow sound, that. Faced by the imminence, he wasn't that anxious to know. I recalled his instructions: Don't let him evade the truth. He asked, "Where are the others?"

I told Peters to get them. He didn't move till the General agreed. I said, "They're out trying to contain a fire somebody set in the stable."

"A fire? Arson?" He was confused.

The doc and Morley studied him intently.

"Yes sir. Near as I can figure, whoever killed Bradon was afraid something in the stable could connect him with the murder. The place had been searched. Whoever did it probably thought he didn't have time to do it right so he took second best."

"Oh." Again that hollow sound.

I walked over to the door, peeked out. Nothing out there. "Saucerhead, want to warn us when the mob comes?"

He grunted, came over. I whispered, "Did you rehearse those two?"

He grunted again. He didn't have time to explain. I had to trust his judgment. "General, shall I take the position I did last time? Mr. Tharpe and Mr. Dotes can hold the door."

"I suppose. I suppose." As the fire grew and threw more light, I saw that his color was as bad as it had been the other day.

I took my place. A few minutes later Saucerhead announced, "People coming."

"Let them in but don't let them back out."

"Check."

The doctor retreated into a corner. So did the fence. Morley moved to the side of the door opposite Saucerhead.

They came in looking tired and wary and dispirited. They looked at Morley and Saucerhead like they all thought they'd been caught doing something. Even Peters, and he knew what was happening.

The General said, "Mr. Garrett has some news."

Mr. Garrett looked at the fence. So did Mr. Tharpe, glowering like the man wouldn't get out of the house alive if he didn't point a finger.

He didn't have to. The bad boy gave himself away.

I said, "Somebody's been stealing doodads from around here, about twenty thousand marks' worth. The General wanted to know who. Now we know that, Dellwood. I'm curious why."

He took it pretty well. Maybe he'd figured that being found out was inevitable. "To meet household expenses. There was no other way to raise the money."

The General sputtered through a bad case of not wanting to face the truth. He ranted. His people kept blank faces but I got the feeling their sympathies didn't lie with their employer.

For one second I entertained the possibility that they all wanted to do him in.

Dellwood persisted, "The General provides funds suitable for maintaining a household of ten at the time he left for the Cantard. He won't believe that prices have risen since then. Not one copper has gone into my pocket. Not one has been spent needlessly. Our suppliers refused to extend further credit."

Must be hell to be rich and broke.

The General managed, "You might have told me instead of subjecting me to this humiliation."

"I told you repeatedly, sir. For two years I told you. You had your eyes firmly fixed on the past. You refused to believe that times have changed. I had the choice of doing what I did or allowing you to be hounded by creditors. I chose to shield you. I'll collect my things now." He turned to the door.

Saucerhead and Morley blocked his way. I asked, "General?"

The old man didn't say anything.

"For what it's worth, sir, I believe he's telling the truth."

"Are you calling me a miser?"

"I said nothing of the sort. But you do have that reputation." I was piqued. I've never gone out of my way to cuddle up to a client—of the male persuasion, anyway.

He sputtered some more.

Then he had one of his fits.

For a moment I thought it was a ploy. The others did, too. Maybe he'd cried wolf a few times. Everybody just looked till it was over. Then they all moved in, tripping over each other. I gave Saucerhead the signal to turn the fence loose.

Dellwood led the charge. Nobody hung back. Which did not bode well for my hope that breaking one of the cases within the case would start everything unraveling.

"Back off," I told them. "Give him some air." He was past the worst. "Saucerhead, let Dellwood go, too."

Dellwood managed his exit with considerable dignity. I reflected on the fact that my pay, and Saucerhead's, and everyone else's, was likely being financed by his efforts. I glanced at Cook. She'd told me the old man didn't have a pot to pee in. Here he was, living on his principal without even realizing it.

Was some other helpful soul trying to salvage the estate by hurrying an incompetent, tightwad manager to his reward?

The General got himself under control. "I shan't thank you for what you've done, Mr. Garrett, though I asked for it. Dellwood. Where's Dellwood?"

"He's gone, sir."

"Get him back. He can't leave. What'll I do without him?"

"I have no thoughts on the subject, General. I think we've accomplished all we can here."

"Good. Yes. You're right. Leave me. But get Dellwood back here."

"Everybody out. Peters, you'd better stay. Kaid? Morley, Saucerhead, I want to talk to you." I scooted out first.

caught Dellwood in his quarters. He hadn't bothered to close his door. He was stuffing things into bags. "Come to make sure I don't take the family jewels?"

"I came to tell you the old man wants you to stay."

"I've spent most of my life attending his wants. Enough is enough. It'll be a relief being my own man." He lied. "A man's loyalty will only stretch so far."

"You're upset. You did what you had to do and it brought you trouble. Nobody holds it against you. Not even me."

"Bull. He'll hold it against me the rest of his life. That's the kind of man he is. Whatever my reasons, I rubbed his nose in something. He doesn't forgive, no matter who was right."

"But—"

"I know him. Give me credit for that."

I did. "You walk, you lose everything."

"The bequest never meant much to me. I'm not poor, Mr. Garrett. I had few expenses while I was in service. I saved my money and I invested it well. I don't need his bequest to survive."

"Your choice." I didn't move.

He stopped throwing things into bags and looked at me. "What?"

"The General didn't just hire me to find out who was kyping the family trophies. He also wanted me to find out who's trying to kill him."

He sneered. "Kill him? Nobody's trying to kill him. That's just his imagination at work."

"So was theft when I arrived. Except to you. He was right about that and I think he's right about this."

"Bull. Who'd profit?"

"Good question. I don't think the estate has anything to do with it. I can't supply another motive, though. Yet." I looked at him expectantly. He didn't say anything.

"Any friction with anybody? Any time, ever?"

"I can't give you what you want, Mr. Garrett. We've all had our troubles with the General—none of them the kind you kill over. Matters of discipline, that's all."

"None of these people are inclined to hold grudges?"

"Chain. He's a big, stupid farm boy gone to fat at the hips and between the ears. He can hold a grudge forever, but he's never had one against the General. If you'll excuse me, sir?"

"Not yet. You've known this moment was coming since I got here, haven't you?"

"I wasn't surprised you found me out. I *was* startled that you found the man who bought from me. Will that be all?"

"No. Who killed Hawkes and Snake?"

"I wouldn't know. I expect you'll find out. You're a first-class finder-outer."

"It's what I do. You didn't perchance try to discourage me when you decided I could cause you trouble, did you?"

"Sir?"

"There have been three attempts on my life since I arrived. I wondered if you'd thought you could cover your tracks—"

"That's not my way. I made it through a Marine career without killing anyone. I have no intention of starting now. I told you I have nothing to lose here."

Maybe. And maybe he was just a convincing liar.

I shrugged. "For what it's worth, I don't think you did wrong and I don't feel that proud of rooting you out."

"I bear you no ill will. You were only the agency by which the inevitable arrived. But I would like to get on the road before dark."

"You won't reconsider? I don't think the old man will last without you."

"Kaid can handle him. He should've been all along, anyway."

"Do you know who the blond woman is?" He had nothing to lose by telling me now.

"A figment of your imagination, I suspect. There's no blond woman here. No one but you has seen her."

"Bradon did. He painted her portrait."

That stopped him cold. "He did?"

"He did."

He believed me. He didn't get much push behind his "Snake was crazy."

I was pretty sure he knew nothing about any blonde. Which made her that much more interesting an enigma.

I moved out of the doorway, indicating he was free to go. I said, "You can't tell me anything that might keep somebody else from getting killed?"

"No. I'd tell you if I could."

He picked up his bags. I suggested, "Catch a ride with my associates when they go."

He wanted to tell me to go to hell. He didn't. "Thank you." It was raining and those bags were heavy.

I asked, "One more thing. What happened to Tyler and the draug from out front?"

"Ask Peters. I don't know. My duties confined me to the house."

"The draug that tried to get in the back isn't accounted for. It didn't go back to the swamp. Where could it hide out during the day?" Assuming, like story draugs, that it didn't dare hazard daylight.

"In the outbuildings. I really must go, Mr. Garrett."

"All right. Thanks for talking to me."

He headed out, back stick-straight, unapologetic. He'd done what had to be done. He wasn't ashamed. He wasn't going to be talked out of leaving, either.

Another one down, I reflected.

Now there were six heirs. The cut for the minority people was up near a half million apiece.

Morley, Saucerhead, and the doctor awaited me beside the fountain. I didn't approach in any hurry. I was trying to figure out how to launch a draug hunt.

Cook came out as Dellwood headed for the front door. They went into the entry hall arguing. She didn't want him to go, either.

joined Morley and the others. "What's the verdict?"

Morley shrugged. "He didn't shake enough or have trouble enough talking for it to be what I thought. He show any of those symptoms earlier?"

"Some shaking. No real trouble talking. What about the fit?"

"I don't know. Ask the doc."

I did. He said, "I don't quite know. I should've had a closer look and a chance to interview the patient. But from where I stood it looked like you need an exorcist more than a doctor."

"A what?"

Morley was as startled as I was. I'd never seen his eyes bug before. The remark had caught him from the blind side.

"An exorcist. A demonologist. Maybe a necromancer. Possibly all three. Though the first step should be a physical exam to make sure I'm not imagining things."

"Start over. You've got me all turned around."

"Between us, Mr. Dotes and I have a comprehensive knowledge of poisons. We know of none that produce the combination of symptoms the man shows. Not without affecting him more dramatically, physically, leaving him unable to control his speech and extremities—if he stayed alive at all. Disease is more probable than poison. Who knows what he brought home? I spent eight years down there. I saw a lot of strange diseases, though nothing quite like this. Is he taking any medication?"

"Are you kidding? He'd die first." I had a thought. "How about malaria?" I'd been one lucky Marine. I'd never contracted malaria. "Or some kind of yellow fever?"

"I thought of that. A virulent strain of malaria, with massive quinine treatments, might produce most of the symptoms he shows. Tainted medication might account for the rest. But you said he'd die before accepting medication. I really must know his medical history before I hazard a guess."

"Why that business about an exorcist?"

"My chief suspicion lies in the supernatural realm. Several varieties of malign spirit could produce the symptoms we see. My advice would be to examine his past. You might find something there to explain what's happening. You might also look for an origin in unfriendly witchcraft. An enemy may have sent a spirit against him."

Black Pete showed up in time to catch most of the discussion. I asked, "You make anything of that? The General have enemies who'd off him that way?"

He shook his head. "The answer is here, Garrett. I'm sure. He doesn't have enemies who'd want to kill him. The worst ones he does have are the kind who'd send somebody like your friend." He twitched a hand toward Morley.

"There's no sorcerer around here. Unless you count Bradon, who's gone. Doctor, could an amateur necromancer have sicced something on him, say accidentally, that would stick after the spirit-master died?"

"An amateur? I doubt it. Somebody really potent, maybe. If they stuck around themselves, as a ghost. Hatred is the usual force animating spirits that devour a man from within. And I mean hatred strong enough to bend the laws of nature. Hatred that wants its object to suffer for all eternity. But I'm no expert. Which is why I suggested a demonologist, an exorcist, a necromancer. You must discover the nature of the spirit, then banish it. Or raise it up, find out what animates its hatred and appease it."

Peters said, "This is crazy, Garrett. The General *never* made that kind of enemy."

"We're talking possibilities. The doc says the whole thing could be physical. He needs to do a hands-on physical exam. And he needs a detailed medical history. What're the chances?"

He looked at me, at the doctor, glanced at Morley and Saucerhead. "Better than you think." His voice turned hard. "The old bastard can only threaten so much. We don't have to give him a choice. I'll be back in five minutes." He strode toward the kitchen.

Morley settled on the fountain surround, in the shadow of the dragon's wing. "Now what?"

"Let's wait. He'll talk to Cook. If she goes along, you'll get to look at Stantnor." Cook might not be mother to the world but she was queen of the Stantnor household. "Doctor. Can you suggest any experts who might help?"

"Let's see if we get to examine the patient. If I find no physical cause, I'll provide referrals. They won't come cheaply, though."

"Does anybody but me?"

Morley had a big yuk. "This is the man who paid cash for a house with the take from one case."

"And for every one of those, I have fifty where I give Saucerhead half my fee to get them to pay up. You know anything about the art world?"

"That's a change of subject. I know something about everything. I need to. What do you need?"

"Say I discovered an unknown painter genius whose work deserves display. Who would I see to get things moving?"

He shrugged, grinned. "Got me. Now if you had some hot old masters I could help. I know people who know morally flexible collectors. If you have something like you're talking about, you should see your friend with the brewery."

"Weider?"

"He's got fingers in all the cultural pies. Honorary director of this and that. He has the contacts. You *don't* have some old masters, do you?" He glanced around. I'm sure he'd been inventorying potential plunder.

"You won't find anything here but portraits of old guys with whiskers who scowl a lot, all painted by people you never heard of."

"I noticed the welcoming committee. I wondered how long it takes the Stantnors to train their young not to smile."

"Might be hereditary. I've never seen Jennifer do more than fake it."

"Your buddy's coming."

Peters was coming from the kitchen under a full spread of sail. I knew what he'd say before he said it. He said it anyway. "We don't give the old man a vote."

"He'll cut you out of his will."

"Ask me if I give a damn. Let's go." But he hung back, gave me a look that said he wanted a private word. I let the others move upstairs a flight.

"What?"

"That crack about the will. In all the excitement I plain forgot to tell you before. The copy the General burned wasn't the only one. He always made two of every document. Sometimes three."

"Oh?" Interesting. That meant nothing had changed, if the killer knew. "How many are there?"

"One for sure. He gave it to me to give to you. Like you asked. I put it in my quarters, then got distracted till I was talking to Cook and she said the same thing you did, about getting cut out."

"It wasn't that important to you?"

"No. I did you a favor, then forgot to carry through. Till it hit me what that copy could mean."

"It could mean the killer won't back off. If he knows about it. Who knows?"

"Dellwood and Kaid. They were there. And everybody else knows the General made copies of documents."

"Where'd you put it? Give me your key. I'll grab it now. You go ahead and get after the old man."

He gave me a nasty look. I knew what he was thinking. I wanted to toss his quarters. I told him, "I don't think you've got anything to hide."

"You're a bastard, Garrett. Put me in a spot where I'm damned whatever I do."

"You do have something to hide?"

He glared. "No!"

"Then get it yourself. I'll take your word." I recalled the fire, for which he could have been responsible. I hung in there, taking a chance on my guts. "But hurry."

He gave me the key. "In the drawer of my writing table."

Cook came rumbling up, the stair shuddering to her tread. "We going to do this?" she demanded. "Or we going to gossip?"

Smart woman, Cook. The old man couldn't dismiss her. If she went in and sat on him, all he could do was cuss and take it. "Thanks," I told her.

She gave me half a sneer. "What for? He's my baby, ain't he?"

"Yeah." I watched them hurry to overtake the others. The General would be in the worst tactical position of his life. He couldn't do anything to Morley, Saucerhead, the doc, or Cook. And he'd be damned stupid if he did anything about Peters. If he ran Black Pete off, he'd be damned near out of help. He had to think survival in more than personal terms. He had to think about keeping the estate in shape.

I suspected its value was dropping fast.

I fingered Peters's key, glanced around. I had the feeling I was being watched, but I saw nobody. My blonde again, I thought. I wondered where the others were. At work, presumably.

A vampirous spirit, eh? On top of draugs? What a lovely place to live.

31

Something wasn't right. Black Pete's door wasn't locked. He wasn't the sloppy type.

It worked before, so I grabbed a shield and stormed inside. And didn't find anything this time, either.

The damned place was haunted by practical jokers. I tossed the shield against the doorframe, put up my head-knocker, went to the writing table. The room was a mirror image of my sitting room. I sat down at an identical table.

I guess I heard a sole scuff the carpet. I started to turn, to duck. That's all I did, started.

Something hit me like a monument falling. I saw shooting stars. I think I howled. I lurched forward. My face met the tabletop. It wasn't a friendly meeting.

It's pretty hard to knock somebody out. You either don't hit hard enough, in which case your victim gets after you, or you hit him too hard and he croaks. If you have any idea what you're doing, you don't bash him up top the head. Unless you want to smash his skull.

This blow was aimed at my skull. I moved that much. It hit the side of my neck and bounced off my shoulder. It didn't put me out—not more than ninety-nine percent. It paralyzed me. For half a minute I was vaguely aware of a shape in motion. *Then* the lights went out.

Got to stay away from the hard stuff, I thought as I came around. Getting too old for it. The hangover isn't worth it.

I thought I was slumped over my desk at home. The truth dawned as I tried to get up. I saw unfamiliar surroundings. My head spun. I fell, banged my jaw off the edge of the table, curled up on the floor, and dumped Cook's lunch. When I tried to move, the heaves started again.

Sometime during the fun somebody ran past, headed for the door. All I saw was a flash of brown. I didn't much care.

Concussion, I thought. That scared me. I'd seen guys with their brains scrambled after getting hit on the head. I'd seen them paralyzed. I'd seen them go to sleep and never wake up.

Got to stay awake, Garrett. Got to stay awake. That's what the docs say. Get up, Garrett. To hell with the heaves. Take charge, Garrett. Make the flesh obey the will.

Trouble was, there wasn't much will left.

After a while I got my knees under me and crawled to the door. I fell down a few times during the trek. But the exercise did me good. I arrived so chipper, I was afraid I wasn't going to die. I worked up so much ambition that I swung the door open and moved out a yard before I collapsed and passed out again.

Gentle, delicate fingers slid lightly over my face, feeling my features the way a blind woman once did. I'd turned over somehow. I cracked one eyelid a millionth of an inch.

My sweetheart in white had come to succor me. At least she looked concerned. Her lips moved but I didn't hear anything.

Panic. I'd heard of guys who'd lost their hearing, too.

She jumped away. Not that she needed to. I was in no shape to run down a brigand snail. More, Black Pete's door had closed on my legs. I was caught like a mouse. I managed a feeble "Don't go. Please."

The investigative mind was at work. It wanted to know.

She came back. She settled onto her knees, resumed massaging my head. "Are you badly hurt?" Her voice was the ghost of a whisper. She sounded concerned. She looked concerned.

"Only in my heart. You keep running away." We investigator types are tough. We keep our eye on the prime objective. "You're the loveliest woman I've ever seen."

That put a light in her eyes. Strange how women like to be told they're pretty. Strange like a rock falling when you drop it. She even smiled for a hundredth of a second.

"Who are you?" I thought about telling her I loved her, but that seemed premature. I'd give it ten more minutes.

She didn't tell me. She just massaged my forehead and temples and sang something so softly I couldn't make out the words.

Who was I to question the will of the gods? I closed my eyes and let it happen.

The song got a little louder. A lullaby. A hush-my-love kind of thing. Fine by me. The hell with business. This was the life.

Something brushed my lips, light as falling eiderdown, warm. I cracked my eye. She was an inch away, smiling.

Yeah.

Then everything drained out of her face. She jumped up and fled. Bam! Before I overcame inertia and turned my head, she was gone.

Feet pounded up the hallway, businesslike, then hurriedly. "Garrett! What happened?" Peters dropped to his knees. He wasn't nearly as attractive as his predecessor.

I managed to croak, "Somebody in your room. Bopped me on my bean."

He jumped up and shoved inside. I had smarts enough left to drag my legs out before the door closed. That's all I did. Seemed like a good day's work.

Peters bounded out. "They tore the place apart." He had something in his hand. "Here's the will. What else could they have been after?"

"Probably was that."

He scowled at me. "Did you have to puke all over?"

"Yeah. A man's got to do what a man's got to do."

"Why didn't he get it, if that's what he wanted?"

"I fell over the desk. He couldn't get at it without moving me and maybe having me wake up. Lit out when I did start coming to. Who could have heard us talking?"

"Couldn't have been Cook or Kaid. They were upstairs with the old man. Wayne's out burying Snake, Hawkes, and Tyler."

I let him help me into a sitting position. "Where were they?"

"In the wellhouse. It's cooler in there. What difference does that make?"

"That leaves Chain, doesn't it? Or Dellwood, if he doubled back."

"Chain's supposed to be out keeping an eye on what's left of the fire and trying to salvage something from the stable."

"Wasn't any ghost. And it wasn't a draug. Did we find the third draug?"

"Nobody's had time to look."

"He'll find us, then." I lifted a hand. He helped me up. Between him and the wall, they managed to keep me upright. "What was the verdict on the old man?" My head hurt so much, I no longer felt my burns. The old silver lining.

"They were looking for you to tell you."

"You tell me."

"He fired me and Kaid, too. We told him to go to hell, we're not going anywhere."

"I guess you aren't going to tell me."

"I don't want to say it. Not something that's easy to believe."

That told me enough. But I let him help me downstairs, to the fountain, where I perched on the fountain surround and tried to work out which way was up till Morley and the others showed. I said, "I take it that I'm shopping for a demonologist."

"Don't look at me like that," Morley said. "I didn't do it."

"You look spooked."

"Spooks spook me, Garrett. Even a vampire or a werewolf, I can do something about. I can't get ahold of a spook."

"Yeah." He didn't want to believe we had a haunt here. I wasn't quite ready to buy it. It would be easier to swallow without a legacy at stake. It wouldn't be the first fake ghost used to cover a little bloodletting.

It sure wasn't any spook who offed Hawkes and Bradon. No spook tried to trap me, ax me, burn me, knock a hole in my head.

Everybody stood around looking at me like I was in charge. So I said, "My head's killing me." And, "Morley, you want to stay over tonight? Give me a hand?"

"I was afraid you'd ask."

Just his sweet-natured way of saying yes.

"Cash money," I promised.

"How are you going to get cash when that old man doesn't have any?"

I didn't tell him I'd grabbed it off going in, though the expenses had about devoured their allowance. "I'll figure something. How'd he take it?"

"He wasn't pleased. To put it mildly."

I looked at the doctor. "You couldn't find a physical cause?" Oh, please. Please?

The weasel shook his head. "Not saying it isn't something I don't recognize. Or a combination. But bring in a demonologist. Hell, I'll send one. Eliminate the mysterious first. If there's no supernatural cause, send for me. Be an interesting challenge."

Morley grinned slyly. "You two work it right, you could have careers here. Him trying to root out an unknown disease and you trying to find a killer who's smarter than you are."

I grumbled, "My part's easy. I just stay alive till there's only one suspect left." My head was killing me. That didn't do wonders for my temper. "Doc, you got something for a headache?"

"What happened?"

I told him.

He insisted on examining me and offering the usual advice about concussions. Maybe he wasn't a pure thief. I have a low opinion of professionals, notably doctors and lawyers, supported by experience.

He gave me a dose of the old standby, syrup heavily laced with nasty-tasting stuff boiled out of the inner bark of willow branches. With that perking in my stomach I decided to get on with getting on. "Peters, it'll be suppertime soon. These guys might be hungry. Square it with Cook, if they want to eat. I'm going to drop in on the General."

Peters grunted, asked if anybody wanted supper. Saucerhead and the doctor were all for that. And Morley was staying anyway.

As I climbed the stairs, I recalled that I'd told Dellwood he should ride into town in the coach. Was he out there waiting, freezing with the coachman?

It was still raining. I felt for Wayne and Chain, too. Though Chain not so much. I had him. All I needed to do was push him into a box and put a bow on him.

"Throw him out," Stantnor rasped at Kaid, when I invited myself in.

Kaid eyed me. "I don't believe he'll let me, sir." He said it with a straight face. There was a twinkle in his eye. He turned to the fire to hide a smile.

I asked, "Did you hear the diagnosis, General?"

"Mr. Garrett. I didn't employ you to interfere in my life. I employed you to find a thief."

"And a killer. And a would-be killer who wants your scalp. And that implies that part of the job is to keep you alive. And to do that I need to know how they're trying to kill you. The assumption was poison. The assumption was wrong."

He appeared surprised. Maybe they hadn't told him. Maybe he'd become so obnoxious, they'd just walked.

"Mr. Dotes is an expert on poisons. Likewise the doctor, who's also an expert on tropical diseases." Could it hurt to exaggerate? "They say you're not being poisoned, unless it's a poison so exotic they've never heard of it. And you're not suffering from any known disease, though the doctor says you're anemic and jaundiced. Have you had malaria, General?"

I think he was secretly touched that people cared enough to look out for him in spite of himself. "Yes. Hard to avoid it in the islands."

"Bad?"

"No."

"You taking quinine on the sly? The doctor says impure quinine might explain some of your problems."

"No! I won't . . ." He suffered one of his spasms. Was it his heart?

It was a minor one. He'd begun to recover before Kaid reached him. He croaked, "No, Mr. Garrett. No medication. I'd refuse if it was offered."

"I thought so. But I had to make sure before I tell you what they think."

"Which is?" He was coming back fast.

"You're haunted."

"Eh?" That blindsided him. He looked at Kaid. Kaid just looked baffled.

"Your problem is supernatural. Your enemy is a ghost. Or somebody who can send a spirit against you. Peters says you don't have that kind of enemies. The doctor says look at your past for somebody."

I wouldn't have believed it possible, but his color worsened dramatically. He damned near turned gray.

There *was* something. Some dark past moment unknown to anyone else, so dreadful someone might reach out from the grave to restore the balance. Hell, a place like the Stantnor shack wouldn't be complete without a horror in its past, without a curse.

"We'd better talk about it," I said. "We'll have to hire experts." I gave Kaid a meaningful look. The old man wouldn't want to confess ancient evils in front of a crowd. "A demonologist. An exorcist. Possibly a medium or necromancer to communicate with the spirit." Kaid was as thick as a brick. He didn't move.

The General said nothing till he was sure he'd say only what he wanted to be heard. And that was, "Get out, Garrett."

"When you're ready to talk, then."

"Get out. Leave me alone. Hell, get out of my house. Get out of my life . . ."

He had another fit. This was a big one. Kaid yelled, "Get that doctor up here!" His expression lacked any forgiveness for having gotten the old man so excited.

Strange people, every one.

joined Cook in the kitchen. We were alone. "Can you use a hand?"

"Come to try sweet-talking me out of something, eh? I see right through you, boy. You ought to know by now I don't run my mouth. I don't tell nobody nothing that ain't none of their business."

"Of course." I rolled up my sleeves, eyed the heap of dirty stuff distastefully. Not much I hate more than washing dishes. But I stole a pot of hot water off the stove, prepared a sink, put more water on to heat, dug in. Ten minutes of silence passed. I waited till I felt her curiosity becoming palpable.

"You were up there when they looked at the General. What did you think?"

"I think that croaker is as crooked as the General says." She didn't sound convinced. She sounded worried.

"Know what he thinks is wrong?"

"I know what he said. He's crazy if he believes it. Ain't no haunts around here."

"Three draugs."

She grunted. There lay the core of her doubt. If those draugs hadn't come, she wouldn't have given the doctor's idea a glance.

"People keep telling me, the General doesn't have enemies of the killing kind. And there's no incentive here for anyone to hurry him along, despite the size of the estate."

"What'll be left after he lets it wither. I swear, his damnfool sickness has infected the whole place." Her voice was weak. She wasn't the woman she'd been. Things were going on inside her head. She had no attention to spare.

"If nobody from today wants to kill him, to torment him with slow death and the hell between when he passes, who in his past might? My gut feeling is, it goes back to before his move to the Cantard."

She grunted and threw utensils around and didn't say anything.

"What happened? The only trauma I know of is his wife's death. Could that have something to do with it? Her parents . . . Jennifer says she thinks they were a firelord and stormwarden but she doesn't know who. Is this a legacy from them? A delayed curse?"

She still didn't have squat to say.

"Were they involved in the Blue cabal that went after Kenrick III?"

"You put a lot together out of nothing, boy."

"That's what I do. I get paid for it. I think the grandparents *were* involved. I think Jennifer's mother came here partly to hide from reprisals if the plot failed. Lucky her. It did. And Kenrick devoured everyone remotely related to it. I wonder if the doctor who administered an incorrect drug was on the royal payroll. Maybe Jennifer survived only because he couldn't murder a newborn."

"You do put it together."

I kept quiet, hoping she'd fill the vacuum.

I washed, set stuff out to dry. There was enough work for me to make me a new career when I got tired of the old one. I was tempted.

"The missus's mother called herself Charon Light. Her daddy was Nightmare Blue."

"One fun-loving guy." Nightmare Blue had put the Blue plot together. He'd been as mean-spirited and vicious as they came. The story was that only the threatened defection of key conspirators forced him to confine his scheme to the King. He'd wanted to scrub Kenrick's whole house. The bad blood between the men stemmed from a mysterious childhood incident.

Charon Light, supposedly, was as innocent as a wife could be. She'd apparently been ignorant of the plot till the last hours. There was reason to suspect she'd been responsible for its failure, in the penultimate moment warning the King.

We'll never know—unless someone raises the dead to ask. None of those people survived. I doubt anybody would try. Raising a sorcerer is a fool's game—unless you're a more powerful sorcerer.

"Eleanor's mother brought her here to hide her?"

Cook grunted, having second thoughts about talking. She kept her peace for a few minutes. I got more hot water.

"Her mother brought her. In the middle of the night, it was. A devil's own night, thunder and lightning and the wind howling like all the lost souls. She was some distant relative of the Stantnors', was Charon Light. Don't recall her born name. Something Fen. She brought the child in so frightened, she wet herself. As bad as Jennifer, she was—never been out of her own house before. Such a pretty young thing, too."

"Like Jennifer."

"She was more retiring than Jenny. Jenny can work herself up. She's an actress, our Jenny. She puts on a role like a dress, that child. Not young mistress Eleanor. Scared of her own shadow, that one."

I grunted this time.

"The old General and Charon Light, they worked it out right here in this kitchen. I was here, serving tea. They'd marry the child to young Will, in name only, so she'd be safe. This was only a couple days before the storm broke. Kenrick couldn't do nothing to upset the old General. He was the only rock between Karenta and defeat in the Cantard in those days."

"The war hadn't meant much to me back then. My father had been dead for years, killed down there, and I wasn't old enough to worry about going. But I did recall that, at about that time, Karenta's fortunes had been at low ebb and there'd been talk about the elder Stantnor being the only man who could handle the Venageti of the day."

"You want the benefit of my suspicion, I think Charon Light was going to deal. Going to sell the plot for immunity. I don't know if that's how she went. She didn't survive."

I told her, "I'm starting to get confused. I thought Jennifer was born about then. And she had an older brother."

"Half brother. His mother was the General's first wife. Have-to wedding when he was sixteen. Daughter of a serving woman. But you don't need to know that."

"I need to know everything if I'm going to make sense of what's happening. Hidden things kill. What happened to the first wife?"

"They stayed married till the boy was old enough for tutors and nannies. Then he put her aside. The old General sent the family away."

"Hard feelings involved?"

"Plenty. But the old General bought them off. He reminded young Will every day. Especially if he spent a night out wenching. A terror, he was, when he was a lad. Obsessed, you might say." She didn't sound like she'd thought him an amusing rake. He didn't sound like somebody I'd have liked.

For fifteen minutes I tried to get her to tell me more. I got only enough to guess the young Stantnor was a crude ass, a driven philanderer whose life had gained direction and meaning only after his permanent move to the Cantard.

"So he wasn't a nice guy. Who from those days hated him enough to—"

"No." There was no equivocation there. "That's life, Garrett. The hurt don't hang on. Everybody does stupid things when they're young."

Some don't ever stop.

"Everybody grows out of them. You don't laugh at them when you look back, but you don't take a killing grudge to your grave, neither."

I don't know. The Stantnors seemed pretty skewed. If that extended to their circle, someone in contact might hold a grudge over something normal people would call bad luck.

"Then you tell me. Who's haunting him?"

She stopped working, looked at me. She'd remembered something she hadn't thought about in years. For a moment she teetered on the brink of telling me. Then she shook her head. Her face closed down. "No. It wasn't that way."

"What wasn't?"

"Nothing. Some cruel gossip. Nothing to do with us today."

"You'd better tell me. It might have some bearing."

"I don't repeat no lies about no one. Wouldn't have nothing to do with this, nohow."

I got my third pot of hot water. I was tearing them up. I bet she hadn't seen so many clean dishes in years. I'm good for something. Can't keep people from killing each other, but I'm a whiz at washing dishes. Might be time to consider a career change.

After a while, she said, "What goes around comes around. He sure fell for Missus Eleanor. She was his goddess."

We all want what we're not supposed to have. I tried an encouraging grunt. When that didn't get any response I tried a direct question. She said, "I think I done talked too much already. I think I done said things I shouldn't have said to no outsider."

I doubted that. I thought she'd weighed every word and had told me exactly what she wanted me to know. She'd give me another ration when she thought I was ready.

"I hope you know what you're doing. I'd bet there're things in your head that could save lives."

Maybe I pressed a touch too hard there. She didn't have to be told what she already knew. She resented it. She gave me a dirty look and clammed up till dinnertime. Then she only growled and gave orders.

33

After supper, having finally gotten the doctor and Saucerhead off, Morley and I headed for my suite. As we climbed the stairs, I said, "I guess old Dellwood got tired of waiting." He'd abandoned the coach hours earlier, according to the coachman, who wasn't pleased with his own lot. It hadn't occurred to anyone to ask him in out of the cold.

Morley belched. "That woman tried to poison me. That mess wasn't fit to feed a hog."

I chuckled. He'd made only one oblique negative comment and had gotten invited to cook his own meals.

His presence didn't thrill the natives. His charm, stoked to a white heat, had been wasted on Jennifer. His feelings were hurt. He wasn't used to being looked at like something from the underside of a rock.

They didn't know who and what he was, only that he was somebody who had invaded their weird little world. Me, I'm not such a sensitive guy.

"A lovely bunch, Garrett. Truly lovely. The girl should work at an ice-house. Where do you find these people?"

"They find me. People who aren't troubled don't need me."

He grunted. There was a lot of that going around. "I understand that."

I suspect his clients are weirder than mine. But he doesn't have to deal with them on an extended basis.

I checked the telltales at the door. There'd been no sloppy visitors. We stepped inside. I said, "I'm going to take a nap. I had a hard night last night. Don't turn into a spook again."

He gave me a sour grin. "Not this time." He started unwinding a piece of cord he'd scrounged up while I was helping Cook clear supper dishes.

"What's that for?"

"To measure with. You say somebody's getting in and out without using the door, there's got to be a way." He measured off a foot of cord, tied a knot, folded the cord, tied another knot. Not a perfect ruler but it would do.

"I was going to do that myself. When I got time."

"You never get time for detail work, Garrett. You're too busy bulling around, trying to make things happen. What do you expect tonight?"

I'd hinted that we could expect some excitement. "I figure that one draug will come back. What else, who knows? Getting so I think anything can happen here. While you're fiddling around, think of a way to get Chain to give himself away."

"The fat guy with the garbage mouth?"

"That's him."

"He the baddie?"

"He's the only one I can line up who had opportunity with Hawkes and Bradon and the attempts on me."

"Turn you into bait. Catch him in the act."

"Thanks a bunch. He's screwed it up three times already. Maybe four. How many shots should I give him?"

"Take your nap. You're safe. Morley's here."

"That's not the comfort you think it should be." I went into the bedroom, shucked my clothes, and slithered in between the sheets. There was something sinful about being naked in such comfort.

For about thirty seconds I listened to Morley putter, measuring and talking to himself while rain tippy-tapped on the windows. Then the lights went out.

The lights never came on. Not quite.

But there were fires to light the night. Well, there was the threat of fire, anyway.

I woke up no longer alone. My blond friend was back. Checking my head, touching my face, all that. This time she didn't move fast enough. But she was leaning way over, off balance, and I didn't think before I grabbed. I got her wrist and gave her a come-hither tug. She fell on top of me.

It was dark. She'd have been invisible if she'd been a brunette wearing dark clothing. Still, from four inches her face was visible. She wore a sort of

smile, like she wanted to look kittenish and playful. The rest of her couldn't
fake it. She shook like she was terrified.

"Talk to me," I whispered. "Tell me who you are." I put an arm around
her, caressed the back of her neck. Her hair felt fine as spider silk, light as
down. I did it to keep her from getting away, but it took only about four
seconds for me to start having trouble keeping my mind on business.

She kissed me instead of answering me.

Man, oh, man. It had the kick of straight grain alcohol. It got me repeat-
ing mantras just to remember who I was.

Shaking like she was running naked through a hailstorm, she turned up
the heat. She worked her way under the covers. This was what the old man
needed to keep him warm. Boy, could he save on firewood.

Then I lost my mantra and kissed her back. About twenty seconds later
she forgot about shivering.

Morley pounded the door. "Hey! Garrett! You going to nap all night?"

I sat up so sudden I made myself dizzy. I felt around. Just Garrett, all by
his lonesome. What? I've got a vivid imagination and a rich fantasy life,
but . . .

"Bring a light in here."

"What about your booby trap?"

What about it? "It's not set."

Morley found me on the edge of the bed draped in a sheet, looking croggled and feeling four times as croggled as I looked. "What happened?"

"You're not going to believe it."

He didn't. "I never left the other room. Well, only long enough to use the
pot. Nobody could've gotten past. You had a dream."

Maybe. But, damn! "I could use more dreams like that. If it was. I don't
think so. I've never had one like that."

"Man gets on in years, he starts living his adventures in his head." He
grinned a big one full of pointy elf teeth.

"Let's don't start. I'm too flustered to keep up my end. You find anything?
What time is it?"

"Yes. Your cloak closet is two-thirds as big as it should be. It's about
midnight. The witching hour."

"I could probably make it through the night without cracks like that." I
got up, dragged the bedclothes with me.

Morley got a funny look, stepped over, picked something up.

It was the red belt my blonde always wore, even in Snake's painting.

He looked at me. I looked at him. I maybe smiled a little. "Not mine," I told him.

"Maybe we ought to get the hell out of here, Garrett."

I pulled my clothes on. I couldn't think what to say. I agreed, mostly. Finally, I just muttered, "You ever back out on a job once you took it?"

He got him another funny look and said, "Yes. Once."

I couldn't picture that. That wasn't Morley Dotes. He delivered. He wouldn't back down from the kingpin or from a nest of vampires. I'd seen that with my own eyes. "I don't believe it. What were you up against? A herd of thunder-lizards?"

"Not exactly."

He didn't like talking about his work. I dropped it. "Let's look at that closet."

The situation had him more spooked than he let on. He said, "A man hired me without telling me anything about the mark, just where he'd be at a certain time. I had the biggest surprise of my life when I got there."

I opened the closet door. "All right. I'll bite."

"You were the mark."

I turned slowly. For about ten seconds I had no idea where I stood. Had we reached a moment I'd prayed would never come?

"Easy. That was six months ago. Forget it. I wasn't going to mention it."

He wouldn't have unless he'd gotten so rattled most bets were off. I tried to recall what I'd been working on back then. Nothing significant. One missing person thing that had smelled from the start, but that had petered out when I found the missing guy dead.

"I owe you one."

"Forget it. I shouldn't have mentioned it."

"You forget it. Let's see where the missing space went." I thought I got it. That missing person thing had smelled because I'd thought there was more to it than the client would admit. She'd seemed vindictive when nothing in her story indicated a reason. Looking for a man she'd claimed was an associate of her late husband.

Pieces toppled into place belatedly. The guy she was looking for could have been blackmailing her over the husband's demise. She hadn't needed me once she knew the guy was dead.

The guy might have hired Morley if he'd heard I was after him.

Hell with it. Water under the bridge. Nothing to do with what we were into now.

But I owed Morley. That more than balanced the stunt with the coffin full of vampire.

"On this side," Morley said.

It was obvious once you knew it was there. On the right the closet was twenty inches smaller than it should be. "Give me the light."

I examined the wall inside. Nothing out of the way. No door, nothing to release one or open one. "Has to be out there somewhere."

I went out, examined the wall, looked for some hidden device, cunningly disguised, like those I'd seen before. I didn't find any such beast.

"I got it," Morley said.

He tipped a two-foot section of wainscoting outward like a kitchen flour bin. Bam. No sign it was there when it was in place. "Clever," he said. "Every secret gizmo I ever saw leaves marks on the floor or something if it's used much." The section didn't quite drop to the floor. A leather strap kept it from falling all the way.

We eyed each other. I said, "Well?"

He grinned. "We can either stand here and stare at it or we can do something. I vote we do something."

"After you, my man."

"Oh, no. I'm just the hired help. I hand the knight his lance when he's ready to charge the Black Baron. When I'm in a real helpful mood, I polish a few rust spots off his armor. But I don't stomp into traps for him."

"I love you too, boy." He was right. It was my game to play.

Didn't hurt to try, though.

I got another lamp, made sure both were full, started to crawl into the opening. "Stay close."

"Right behind you, boss. All the way."

"Wait." I backed out.

"Now what?"

"Equipment." It seemed like a good time to arm up. Just in case.

Morley watched me ferret stuff out, grinned when he saw the colored bottles. "I wondered if you kept those."

"Smart man never throws anything away. Might come in handy someday." Loaded for thunder-lizard, I returned to the passageway. This time I kept going. Morley had less trouble in there, being a foot shorter and a half ton lighter. I kept banging my head. The passage ran straight ahead fifteen feet. It ran under the counter in the dressing room.

We emerged in a two-foot-wide dead space behind the bedroom and dressing room. It was claustrophobic in there. It was dusty and cobwebby, too, and there was nothing to be seen but studs, lathing, and plaster. The wall at my back was identical. It was the wall of the suite next to mine.

There were peepholes. Of course. A couple for the dressing room and three for the bedroom. The thought that I might have been watched left me real uncomfortable.

Morley said, "Here's how you get out."

At the end of the dead space, against the wall of the hallway, there was a two-by-two hole in the floor. Wooden rungs were nailed to the studs.

I sneezed ferociously. The dust and my cold were ganging up.

My head hurt from being banged. My skin burns gave me no respite. I had no reason to be amused. I chuckled anyway.

"What?"

"No way I'm going to get past you. You have to go first."

"Think so?" He ducked into the passageway from my sitting room. "After you, my man."

"You're so slick, you'll slide out of your casket." I tested the rungs. They were solid.

Ever go down a vertical ladder carrying a live fire? Lucky I'm a paragon of coordination.

The third floor was identical to the fourth except for the cover over the hole opening on the second. "There's a big open storage loft below here," I told Morley. And sneezed so hard, I almost killed my lamp. I listened for movement below. Nothing. I lifted the cover. It swung to the side on hinges.

How would we get down? I'd seen no ladders when I'd explored the storage area.

Crafty builders. Right under the hatch was the end of a rack. The shelf supports made neat rungs.

I dropped to the floor. Knowing what to look for, I spotted trapdoors that would take me to every room in the wing.

"Pretty simple," Morley said. "Think it's set up for spying or for escapes?"

"I think it's probably for whatever's to the advantage of the Stantnors. I wonder how it works in the east wing. That layout is different."

"You've already checked this wing, right?"

"Except for the cellar."

"You didn't find any place your girlfriend could be hiding?"

"No."

"You ask the cook about food shortages?"

"No." I should have. She'd have to eat. I thought of her portrait. I'd better get the paintings into the house tonight.

"Let's do this systematically. The cellar first, then the other wing. Seems probable the passages there start in the cellar."

"Yeah." As I recalled the layout, the walls all sat atop one another from the first floor upward.

We descended to the pantry quietly, listened. Nothing. On to the cellar.

It was your typical earthen-floor cellar, deeper than my own, where I have to stoop, but vasty, dark, and dusty, a wilderness of stone pillars supporting beams that supported joists. At first it seemed mostly empty and dusty and dry—though dry wasn't a surprise. The house sat atop a hill. The builders would have arranged good drainage.

As we moved toward the east end we encountered evidence that an earlier regime had maintained a large wine cellar. Only the racks remained.

"Great place to get rid of bodies," Morley remarked.

"They have their own graveyard for that."

"Somebody sank a couple, three guys in that swamp."

He had a point.

We completed a circuit of the east end finding little but the wine racks, broken furniture, and, near the foot of the steps, sausages and stores hanging so mice couldn't reach them. I sneezed almost continuously.

"That's the easy half," Morley said. We started our circuit of the western end.

That end had less to recommend it or make it interesting, except for the supports and plumbing beneath the fountain. Those would have been of interest mainly to a plumber or engineer. There were no entries to hidden passages.

I said, "We just wasted three quarters of an hour." And sneezed.

"Never a waste when you find something out. Even if it's negative."

"That's my line. You're supposed to grumble about wasted time."

He chuckled. "Must be infecting each other. Let's get out before the spiders gang up."

I grunted, sneezed. Interesting. The cellar was almost vermin-free. Other than spiders there was very little wildlife. I'd have expected a sizable herd of mice.

I recalled the cats. "Can you smell anything? I'm deaf in the nose here."

"What am I supposed to smell?"

"Cat shit."

"What?"

"No mice. If there aren't any, the cats must be on the job. The only cats I've seen are out in the barns. If they're getting in here, there's a way into the basement from the outside."

"Oh." His eyes got a little bigger. He started watching the edges of the light more closely. There was still a draug around somewhere.

He said, "We're not going to find anything here. Let's do the west wing." He was uncomfortable. Usually he's cool as a rock. That creepy house really worked on you.

I was about halfway up to the first floor when I caught the end of a cry. "Oh, damn! What now?"

Don't ever try to run through unfamiliar territory in the dark, even with a lamp. Between us we nearly killed ourselves a half dozen times each before we made it to the great hall.

34

We burst into the light of the hall, where the Stantnors spared no expense on illumination. "What was it?" There was nothing shaking.

"Sounded like it came from here," Morley said. "Looks like we're first to arrive."

"Oh, damn! Not quite. Damn! Damn! Damn!"

Chain had beaten us there. The dragonslayer and his victim had masked him from us at first. He was on the floor, crumpled in a way no man should be. He'd bounced once, some, and had left a big smear. Blood still leaked out of him.

"Looks like he came from the top balcony," Morley said, with an artisan's dispassion. "Tried to land on his feet and didn't quite make it." He glanced up. "He didn't jump. And I'd bet you he didn't trip over the rail. If I was a betting man."

"Wouldn't touch the bet at a thousand to one." The fall wasn't much more than thirty feet. For Chain it must have seemed like a thousand.

Thirty feet is a bad fall, but people have survived it. If they have themselves under control or they're lucky. Chain hadn't been either.

I glimpsed movement on the opposite balcony, whirled. I expected to see my mystery blonde. I saw Jennifer instead, in her nightclothes, at the rail at the end of my hall. She looked down in a sort of daze. She was very pale.

Peters appeared right above us a moment later. "What the hell?" he bellowed, and came bounding downstairs.

"Stay with him," I told Morley. "I'm going up there." I indicated Jennifer.

Black Pete galloped up to Morley as I trotted away, mouthing questions too fast for anybody to shove an answer in sideways.

I was puffing my lungs out when I reached Jennifer, swearing that, when this one was over, I was going to work out every day. Right after I spent a week catching up on my sleep.

She was flushed now, so red she looked like she'd run a mile. She snapped, "Where were you? I've been trying to wake you up for ten minutes."

"Huh?"

She stared at the floor, shivering. "You said . . . I thought you wanted me to . . ."

Hell. I'd forgotten. Damned good thing she hadn't come earlier. Especially damned good thing I hadn't given her a key.

Standing there shy and shamefaced and looking vulnerable, in night-clothes that did little to hide the fact that she was one gorgeous hunk of woman, she made me react after all. I got all set to howl at the moon. Only Peters's chatter downstairs kept my mind on business. Part of my mind on business. A small part of my mind.

"What do you know about this?" I jerked a thumb at Chain.

Her eyes got big. "Nothing."

"Come on. You had to see or hear something."

"All right. Don't bully." She eased a little closer, still shivering. Business, boy, mind on business. "I sneaked out of my room about thirty minutes ago. When I got to the end of my hall, Chain and Peters were down by the fountain. They were just sitting there. Like they were waiting for something to happen. I couldn't get to the stairs without them seeing me. So I waited. The more I waited, the more scared I got. I was ready to chicken out when Peters said something to Chain and started upstairs. Chain turned his back, so I hurried up to the fourth floor, before Peters saw me . . .

"Chain must have seen me when I was sneaking toward the loft stairs. He yelled. I went up and over. When I got to your side he was on the fourth floor, going into the hall to my father's suite. I ran down your hall to your door and tried to get you to answer. You didn't. I kept trying. Then I heard that yell. I didn't know what to do. I was scared. I tried to hide in the shadows at the end of the hall until I heard your voice."

"You didn't see anybody but Peters and Chain?"

"No. I told you."

"Huh." I thought a moment. "You'd better get back to your suite. Before anybody else comes out. Peters's questions will be troublesome enough."

"Oh!"

"Yeah. Let's go." I followed her to the stairs, up to the loft and across. The darkness there didn't bother her a bit. We parted at the head of the stair to the third-floor balcony. I said, "I'll come talk to you as soon as we've settled things down."

"All right." A quavery mouse voice. She was scared as hell. I didn't blame her. I was scared myself.

Chain was dead. Helped along. My favorite suspect. My almost certain killer. Gone. Out of the picture. Meaning I'd wanted to nail the wrong hide to the wall. Unless he'd tried to do unto another and got it done to him in self-defense.

I walked along the balcony to the point where, I guessed, he'd gone over. Morley and Peters were quiet now, watching me.

"He got wool pants on?" I asked.

"Yes," Morley replied.

There were strands of wool on the rail. There were scratches and flecks of skin, too, like he'd tried to grab hold as he'd gone over. Minute scraps of evidence but they made me certain he'd been shoved. I pictured him standing there, looking down, maybe talking to somebody, when he got a sudden boost with barely enough oomph on it. Maybe he'd even needed a little extra help after he'd started going.

Sometimes I suffer too much empathy for men who die untimely deaths. I picture the thing and conjure the feelings they must have felt as the realization hit them. Falling scares the hell out of me. I had more than the usual ration of compassion for Chain.

What would it take, about a second of free fall? All of it intense with fear and wild desperation and vain hope, trying to adjust to take the fall and maybe, just maybe, survive?

I shuddered. This one was going to haunt me.

Trying hard not to think about it, I clumped down to the ground floor. I hurt everywhere. I wasn't in a good mood at all. "What's your story, Sarge?"

He was taken aback by my intensity. But he excused it. "We were waiting for the draug." There was a collection of instruments of mayhem lying in the fountain. I hadn't noticed before. "Kaid and Wayne were going to take the next watch, in about an hour. I had to take a leak. I didn't want to go outside so I headed for my room."

"You took a long time taking a leak."

"Found out I had to do more once I got there. You want to check? It's still warm."

"Take his word for it, Garrett." Morley isn't your dedicated investigator, willing to stir fouled chamber pots in search of damning evidence. I'm not that devoted myself. Anyway, I believed Peters. He'd have come up with an alibi less dumb if he was going to toss somebody off a balcony.

I was about out of suspects.

Which meant I had to open the whole thing up and suspect everybody again. Even the unlikelies.

Shares of the legacy were worth over six hundred thousand now. If the value of the estate wasn't falling faster than the murderer could expand his share.

Peters. Cook. Wayne. Who? For no sound reason I gave Wayne top billing. And Cook was starting to look better, though she had pretty good alibis. But alibis aren't everything.

"I guess the killer knows there's a copy of the will," I told Peters. "That means the General could be in double jeopardy."

"What?"

"After last night the killer has to worry about the other copies going, too. They do, all his risks have gone for nothing. So maybe he'll want the old man to check out before the last copy of the will does. Better find out exactly how many there were and where they're at now." I tapped my shirt to make sure I had my copy.

Not that it was particularly safe with me, considering I was no more immortal than Chain, Hawkes, or Bradon.

Snake popped into mind, and after Snake, his paintings. I had to get those inside.

But it was pouring out. Maybe headed for something worse. There was the occasional flash of lightning. I said, "Getting around to the kind of weather that suits this place. All we need is something howling and ghost lights puttering around outside."

Peters snorted. "You get the next best thing. A frisky draug." He pointed.

There it was, back at the rear again, trying to get in. A lightning flash illuminated it. I got my first good look. It was more decomposed than the others.

Peters selected a few items from the stockpile in the fountain. "Shall we take care of it?"

"That's my old sergeant, Morley. Cool in the face of the enemy."

"Uhm." He went through the arsenal himself. Here was something he could get a hold on.

"All right. I guess we should take care of it. Get it out of the way." I checked their leavings. They'd taken all the best stuff already. "Hell with this." I went and disarmed a retired knight.

I had to be getting close to the end. There weren't many suits of armor left for me to vandalize.

35

Morley sat on the fountain surround hugging cracked ribs. Peters was curled up on the floor in a pool of vomit, clutching his groin. He did his manly best not to whimper. Me, I'd been luckier. All I'd come up with was a shin bruise and a badly stomped foot. Not on the same leg. "Maybe next time I'll save myself some grief and let whoever wants kill me."

Morley gasped, "Why didn't you say the man was a hand-to-hand specialist when he was alive?"

"Don't look at me! I didn't know anything about him. Not even who he was."

Pieces of draug were scattered all over. Some still moved.

"What now?"

"Eh?"

"You burned the other two. Right?"

"One of them, I know."

"Both," Peters groaned. He got onto his knees, his forehead on the floor. His knuckles were bone white. He'd gotten hit bad. "They dumped the other one into the stable fire when they saw there wasn't no stopping it." He didn't say that in one chunk but in little gasps, a word or two at a time. The effort cost him a spate of dry heaves.

I felt for him, though not as much as I would have if I hadn't been hurting myself.

I got up. "Better make sure we got the job done." The thing looked like it was trying to get itself back together. The pieces were trying to get to a central point. I hobbled, pitching random limbs back.

"What the hell's going on down there?"

I looked up. Wayne and Kaid had appeared for their shift, at the third-floor rail. "Come on down. We're in no shape to finish this."

Wayne beat Kaid by a floor. He looked at what was left of Chain, at the pieces of rotted corpse, at Chain again. "Man. Man, oh, man. Man." He didn't say anything else till he asked, "What happened?"

I told him. Kaid arrived in time to get it all.

"Man. Man, oh, man." Wayne was scared. For the first time since I arrived I saw one of those people convinced of his own mortality.

"Hell. You're all a hundred thousand richer now."

"Man. I don't care about that. I don't need it. It ain't worth it. I'm out of here soon as it's light enough that nothing can sneak up on me."

"But . . ."

"Money ain't everything. You can't live it up if you're dead. I'm gone." The man was almost hysterical.

I glanced at Peters. He was preoccupied, though he'd made it to the fountain surround. He hoisted himself up and perched with his misery. He had no attention left for anything else.

Morley was no help. But he couldn't be. He didn't know the people.

I looked at Kaid. He was as pallid as a man could get, as shaken as Wayne, equally eyeball to eyeball with death. It had come home. The field was so narrow, each knew he might be next.

He swallowed about three times, then managed, "The General. Some-body's got to take care of the General."

Wayne snarled, "Let that bastard take care of himself. I'm gone. I ain't dying for his money or for him."

Pain will distract you some, but mine wasn't so all-devouring that I couldn't spend some effort trying to figure out what the hell would happen next. I wondered which of the three was acting and how he'd gotten so good.

I wondered some about Cook, Jennifer, even the old man, and how I could figure one of them for the killer. Or more than one. That was an angle I hadn't given much thought. Maybe there was more than one killer. That would take care of alibis.

And my ivory lover. What of her? The mystery woman suddenly looked like a top bet for the villain.

Who the hell was she?

I plunked myself down on the fountain surround, as nimble as a quadraplegic dwarf. Kaid and Wayne came out of shock enough to start thinking and doing. Kaid went to the kitchen, got some big burlap sacks. He and Wayne stuffed them with pieces of draug and tied them shut. They gagged while they worked. My cold was that much of a blessing. I didn't have to take the smell.

Morley was three feet away. I asked, "How you doing?"

"Be running windsprints in the morning." He grimaced, spat on the floor, winced again as he leaned to look at it.

"What?"

"Wanted to see if I was spitting blood."

"Come on. You rolled with it."

He flashed me a down-under smile. He was putting on a show. He wanted folks to think he was hurt worse than he was. Might be an edge for him later.

I shut my mouth.

Peters managed to say, "What now, Garrett?"

"I don't know."

"How do we stop this before we're all dead?"

"I don't know that, either. Unless we just scatter."

"In which case the killer wins by default. Wayne walks tomorrow, it's the same as if he got killed."

Morley said, "Makes your job easier, Garrett." He did a grimace. He was overacting.

"Eh?" I was at top form.

"Shortens the list by another name."

Black Pete grunted out, "Garrett. How're you going to catch him?"

Him? I wasn't so sure now. If Wayne walked and Peters was clean, the crowd was so small I'd have to lynch Kaid. But I thought Kaid was too old and feeble to have done all the killer had.

"I don't have a clue, Sarge. Don't press me. You people know each other better than I know you. You tell me who it is."

"Shit. It isn't anybody. Logically. One way or another you can discard everybody. Except maybe your phantom blonde, that nobody sees but you."

"I saw her," Morley said. I looked at him, puzzled. Was he lending moral support?

Hadn't he said something about seeing her last night? Or was that the other Morley?

I'd forgotten that. The thing that could be somebody else. Probably the spook that the doctor was sure was here.

It didn't get any easier.

"Your picture," Morley whispered.

I frowned.

"Get it and find out who she is. Besides a hot tumble."

Maybe he was right. Maybe. I wanted to say the hell with it for now. We were out of the woods for a while. That draug had been cared for. The killer wasn't likely to make another move for a while. I hurt everywhere. I just wanted to slither upstairs and finish what I'd started before I'd been interrupted.

But I'd put off seeing Bradon for a few minutes and look what that had cost. Not just Snake but Chain. Not to mention the stable, those paintings, and however many horses had vanished into the sunset because there was no one to round them up.

I got my feet under me. "Peters. Any rain gear handy?"

Morley got up, too. He scrunched over, held his side with his left arm.

"Rain gear? What the hell you need to go outside for?"

"Got to get something while it's still there."

He looked at me like he thought I was crazy. Probably right, I thought. "To your left at the end over there, through that arch. The old guest restrooms." He still wasn't talking in big gobbling chunks.

Morley and I went to the arch, which was barely five feet wide. A crack of a doorway for this place. It opened on an alcove, eight by eight. There was a door in front of me and one to my left. "Check that one," I told Morley, and opened the one in front of me.

Mine was the women's, the only pissoir I'd seen in the house. I hadn't noticed any plumbing downstairs. Maybe it wasn't there anymore. The place was dried up, used only for storage.

There were no raincoats.

I went to check on Morley.

His room was the men's. Surprise, surprise. One wall was all marble that fell to a trough. The flush pipe whence water ran, at eye level, had rusted out. I spied the rain gear but not Morley. "Where are you?"

"Here." His voice came from beyond a copse of brooms and mops and whatnot in the left-hand rear corner. He'd found another movable panel. He was halfway up the narrow stairway behind it.

"We can check it out later." I spied a lantern amongst the junk on the marble four-holer. It smelled like it had been used in the modern era. When Morley came down I was getting it lighted.

Morley said, "If there weren't people hanging around, you'd think the place had been abandoned for twenty years."

"Yeah." I shrugged into an oilcloth coat so big it hung long on me. "Let's get with it." While Morley tried to find something smaller than a circus tent, I snapped up a few extras to wrap Bradon's artwork. We put on hats and dashed out into the storm.

Actually, we stumbled. I wasn't getting any friskier. Neither was Morley. I had to spend most of my energy keeping the lantern from blowing out.

There was a brisk wind blowing, throwing barrels of water around. It came from every direction but up. The thunder banged away. Lightning, over the city, carried on like a battle between hordes of stormwardens. We reached the barn in spite of all.

"Thank heaven we found rain gear," Morley said. "We might have gotten soaked."

Sarky bastard. I was wet to the skin. I rooted through the place where I'd squirreled the paintings. "Damn me! Something's gone right."

"What?"

"They're still here."

"Watch out for a booby trap, then."

I almost took him seriously. That's the way my luck runs.

I shook the water off the extra coats. Morley held the lantern and cursed and dodged bats. "Those coats aren't going to be enough. Let me look around." He scurried off, leaving me halfway convinced I'd never see him again.

He came back with a couple of heavy tarps. We wrapped the paintings in two bundles. We took one apiece and slogged into the storm. I got soaked all over again. I had mud up to my knees when we reached the house, but the paintings arrived dry.

We shed our gear.

"Guess we better take these up to the suite," I told Morley. He was looking at the paintings. "What do you think?"

"The man was disturbed."

"And good, too. That's her."

"I'm in love." He stared at the portrait like he might dive in.

"Let's admire her upstairs."

But we had to pass Kaid, Wayne, and Peters to get to the stairway. Black Pete asked, "What's all that?"

No reason not to tell the truth. "Some of Bradon's paintings. I saved them from the fire."

They wanted to see. They hadn't seen Bradon's work before. The man never had shown it.

"Yech!" Kaid said after a couple of war scenes. "That's sick."

"It's good," Wayne said. "That's how it felt."

"But it doesn't look like—"

"I know. It's how it *felt*."

"Man," Peters said. "He didn't like Jennifer much, did he?"

Somehow I'd managed to save four portraits, the blonde and three Jennifers. Just as well I hadn't salvaged any of these guys. They wouldn't have appreciated them. I'd gotten more than one Jennifer by accident. It had gotten hurried toward the end.

Peters lined the portraits up against the fountain. The third and probably most recent Jennifer stood out from the others. It was the ugliest. Jennifer was radiant yet something horrible about her made you doubt the artist's sanity.

Kaid said, "He was crazier than we thought. Garrett, don't ever let Miss Jennifer see these. That would be too cruel."

"I won't. I took them by accident more than anything. I was just grabbing. But the blonde, now. I took that one on purpose. That's the woman I've been seeing. Who is she?"

They looked at me, at the painting, at me again. Their studied blandness said they were unsure about my sanity. They thought I'd let my imagination attach itself to the first thing handy.

Peters played it straight. "I don't know, Garrett. Never seen her before. You men?"

Wayne and Kaid shook their heads. Wayne said, "There's something familiar about her, though."

That seemed to cue something in Kaid's head. He frowned, moved a step closer. I asked, "You know something, Kaid?"

"No. For a second . . . No. Just my imagination."

I wasn't going to argue with them till I could produce physical evidence. "Let's get these tucked away, Morley."

We started gathering the paintings. Now Peters was frowning at the blonde, something perking in the back of his head. He was a little pale and a whole lot puzzled.

He didn't say anything, though. We collected the paintings and headed for the stairs.

Maybe intuition nudged me. When I reached the fourth floor I went to the rail. Peters and Kaid had their heads together, yakking away. They kept their voices down but were intense.

Morley's ears are better than mine. He told me, "Whatever they're talking about, they're determined to convince each other it's impossible."

"They recognized her?"

"They think she looks like somebody she couldn't be. I think."

I didn't like the sound of that.

36

Morley perched the mystery woman on the mantel in my sitting room, contemplated her intently. I misread his interest. I seldom do that because his interest in the female tribe is definite. "Can't have her, boy. She's taken."

"Be quiet," he told me. "Sit down and look at the painting."

He wouldn't be sharp if it wasn't important. I planted myself. I stared.

I began to feel like I was part of the scene.

Morley got up and snuffed a few lamps, halving the light in the room. Then he threw the curtains open, apparently so we'd get the full benefit of the storm. He settled and resumed staring.

That woman came more and more to life, grabbed more and more of my being. I felt I could take her hand and pull her out, away from the thing that pursued her.

The storm outside intensified what was going on in the painting's background. That damned Snake Bradon was a sorcerer. The painting, once you looked at it awhile, was more potent than the swampscape with hanged man. But this one was more subtle.

I could almost hear her begging for help.

Morley muttered, "Damn her. She's too intense. Got to block her out of there."

"What?"

"There's something else there. But the woman pulls your attention away."

He'd lost me. The rest of the painting was decoration to me. Or arrows pointing out the crucial object.

Morley got paper from my writing table, spent ten minutes using a small knife to trim pieces to cover the blonde. "You damage that thing, I'll carve you up," I told him. I had a notion where it ought to be displayed. There was a big bare spot on the wall of my office at home.

"I'd cut my own throat first, Garrett. The man was crazy but he was a genius."

Curious, Morley calling him crazy without having met him.

Morley killed another lamp. He hung his cutouts over the canvas.

"I'll be damned." The painting was almost as intense without the woman. But now the eye could rove.

Morley grunted. "Let your mind go blank. Just let it sink in."

I tried.

The storm carried on outside. Thunder galloped. Swords of lightning flailed. The flashes played with the flashes in the painting. The shadow seemed to move like a thunderhead boiling. "What?"

It was there for just a second, I couldn't get it back. I tried too hard.

"Did you see the face?" Morley asked. "In the shadow?"

"Yeah. For a second. I can't get it back."

"Neither can I." He removed the cutouts, settled again. "She's running from somebody, not something."

"She's reaching out. You think Bradon has her reaching for somebody particular?"

"Running from somebody to somebody?" he asked.

"Maybe."

"Him?"

"Maybe." I shrugged.

"You? You're the one who—"

"You said you saw her."

"I saw somebody. Just a glimpse. The more I stare at this, the more I think it could have been the other one."

"Jennifer?"

"Yes. They look a lot alike."

I tried to see Jennifer in the blonde. "I don't know. There's a lot of Stantnor in Jennifer but I don't know about this one."

I guess I squeaked. He asked, "What?"

"That face in the background. There was a lot of Stantnor in it."

"Jennifer? Bradon did her bad."

"I don't think so. I got the feeling it was male."

"Around thirty and stark raving mad."

The lightning had fits outside. I shuddered, jumped up, started lighting lamps. I couldn't shake the chill. "I'm spooked," I confessed.

"Yes. The more I look, the creepier it gets."

The chill stayed with me. I wondered if we were being watched. "Think I'll start a fire."

"Whoa! What did you say?"

"I'll start a fire. I'm freezing my—"

"You're a genius, Garrett."

"Nice of you to notice." What did I genius? It went right by me.

"Fire in the stable. You figured right, too. Not for you at all. For something Bradon had hidden. What did you find hidden? The paintings." He gestured at the blonde. "*The* painting."

"I don't know—"

"I do. What were the others? Crazy stuff. But people we've seen and places in the Cantard."

So I looked at the painting again.

Morley said, "There's the key to your killer. That's why Bradon died. There's why the stable burned. That's your killer." He laughed. It was a crazy noise. Hell. Everything was crazy in this place. "And you slept with her." He started to say something else, caught himself, reflected. "Oh, man." He came and put a hand on my shoulder.

He could have slept with a mass murderer and thought nothing of it. Maybe he'd have smiled and cut her throat afterward. A lovable rogue most of the time, but there's a cold subterranean stream inside him.

He knew how it would hit me before it hit. He was there when I started to rattle.

It wasn't as bad as I feared, but the idea did shake me. "I've got to pace."

He let me get up and try to walk it off. That didn't do much good. The whoopee-making noises outside didn't help. The thunder ripped at my nerves like cats howling at midnight.

Then I recalled promising Jennifer I'd see her later. The old mind fixed on that, telling me I could clean out a whole bird's nest with one stone.

"Where you going?" Morley demanded.

"Something to do. Promises to keep. Almost forgot." I got out before he pressed me, sudden as that, not quite sure I was thinking right.

glanced over the rail. Kaid and Wayne were seated on opposite sides of the fountain, not talking. They'd cleaned up Chain. Peters had gone. I wondered why they bothered. Maybe they couldn't sleep. I couldn't see me getting much sleep, despite exhaustion and hurting everywhere.

I made it to the loft, crossed, slipped down to the third floor without attracting attention. It was a great house for sneaking. I tiptoed to Jennifer's door. I tapped. She didn't answer. I shouldn't have expected her to, as long as it had been. I tried the door. Locked.

Only reasonable. Any fool would have taken that precaution. I tapped again and still got no response.

"So much for that idea." I started for home.

And stopped. And without understanding why I turned back and went to work on the lock. I had it undone in moments.

Jennifer didn't like the darkness. Half a dozen lamps burned in a sitting room identical to her father's. Not knowing the layout of these end suites, I decided the best place to find her would be behind the same door the old man used to make his entrances. I locked the hall door and headed that way.

I don't know what you'd call the room beyond. It wasn't a bedroom. It was more a small, informal sitting room with only a few pieces of furniture and one big window facing west. It was gloomy, lighted by a single candle. Jennifer was there, in a chair facing the window. The drapes were open wide. She'd fallen asleep despite the excitement outside. I doubted she'd have heard my knock had she been awake.

Now what, bright boy? Make the wrong move and they'll turn you into a eunuch.

Hell. It'd been tried before. I shook her shoulder. "Jenny. Wake up."

She shrieked and jumped and stumbled away and . . . The gods were kind. One of those barrages of thunder absorbed her cry. She recognized me and got herself under control—more or less.

She held her hands over her heart and panted. "You scared me to death. What're you doing here, Garrett?"

I fibbed a little. "I told you I'd come by. I knocked. You didn't answer. I got worried. I fiddled the lock and came to see if you were all right. You looked so pale I just reached out to shake your shoulder. I didn't mean to scare you."

Did I sound sincere? I poured it on. I do sincere pretty good. Been studying Morley's technique. She relaxed some, moved a little closer.

"Gods. I hope I didn't wake the whole house yelling like that."

I apologized some more. Then it seemed only natural to hug her to comfort her. A minute after that, when she'd stopped shaking so bad, she found a little girl voice and asked, "You're going to ravish me now, aren't you?"

For me it was the perfect thing for her to say at the moment. I busted out laughing. It took the built-up pressure out of me. It took almost too much. I had to fight it to control it.

"What's so damned funny?"

Her feelings were bruised. "No. Jenny. Honey. I'm not laughing at you. I'm laughing at me. Honest. I really am. No. I'm not here to ravish you. The condition I'm in, after today I couldn't ravish a chipmunk. I've been burned, bludgeoned, and kicked half to death. I hurt all over. I'm so tired I could pass out on the spot. And I'm totally upset about Chain. If there's anything I'd want from a woman now, it would be for her to comfort me, not for me to ravish her."

You slick talker. Pay attention. Talk like that, it's eight to five you'll wind up getting comforted by a vestal virgin. Just be harmless, helpless, and in need of mothering, and pour on the sincere.

Well, what with one thing and another, I talked myself right into something without consciously planning it. Fifteen minutes later we were in her bed. Fifteen minutes after that I was trying hard to stay harmless, helpless, and in need of comfort.

There's something reassuring about just lying around holding somebody after you've been bruised and abused and treated like a wolf treats a fox that isn't fast on its feet. But there's also something about being comforted by somebody put together like Jennifer that makes you forget they shoved you through the meat grinder sideways—hide, hooves, and all.

We'd been whispering, mostly just talk, innocent enough but she couldn't lie still. She was relaxed enough now, considering. She moved, seemed startled, asked, "Is that what I think it is?"

Body pressure left no doubt what she meant. "Yeah. Sorry. Can't help it. Maybe I'd better go." I didn't make any move to leave, though. Not me.

"I can't believe it. No. It's impossible."

It wasn't impossible at all.

For a while I forgot the painting, the storm, all my aches and pains. I even got to sleep some. Though that was more like catnaps between tests of the limits of possibility.

I knew I was going to hate myself in the morning.

It was just my body that hated myself in the morning. It felt about a hundred and two years old. My head was fine, not counting my cold. I kissed Jennifer on the forehead, nose, and chin, headed for my own quarters while it was still early enough that I might not be noticed.

Wayne and Kaid were on duty still. Sort of. Kaid was nodding. Wayne was sprawled on the fountain surround, snoring. Cook was in the kitchen cursing. I heard her all the way to the fourth floor. I wondered what was bothering her. I was sure we'd all know before long, what with her closed-mouth, stoic ways.

I went up, through the loft, down. I glanced across as I started into my hallway. The blonde stared at me from the hall to the General's suite. I waved feebly. She didn't respond. "Oh, boy." I headed for my door.

For a second I thought she'd gotten there before me. Then I realized it was the painting. It seemed so creepy, I turned it to face the wall.

"You have a nice time?"

Morley was in a big overstuffed chair. He looked like he'd been asleep. "Ghastly."

"That's what puts that smug look on your face. I'll remember that. Get cleaned up. It's almost time for breakfast."

Him eager for one of Cook's breakfasts? "I'll give it a skip and take a nap instead."

"You're working, Garrett. You don't take time off to nap whenever you feel like it, do you?"

"That's the beauty of being your own boss." He was right. More right than he knew, really. I could go get some sleep, sure. And if somebody got killed while I did, I'd be haunted for years. "Yeah. All right."

Now he looked smug. Bastard. He knew right where to poke me. I went into the dressing room, threw some water on my face, mixed up some lather, hacked and slashed. Morley planted himself in the doorway. He watched the show awhile, then said, "I'd better move on the cook fast. Or you'll have every woman in the place wrapped up."

"You're out of luck. She was my first conquest."

He snorted.

I said, "I had to move fast because I knew you'd head for her like a moth to a candle." I wiped my face. "On the other hand, I won't stand in your way. She's definitely your type. I'll sing at your wedding."

"Don't think you can provoke me into a battle of wits with an unarmed man."

"Huh."

"I know it's your diet talking. Maybe I ought to talk to the cook about that. Dietary improvements could do your General more good than squadrons of doctors and witches."

"Got you on the run already?"

"What?"

"Last recourse, old buddy. You start talking about red meat and celery juice and boiled weeds."

"Boiled weeds? You ever actually *buy* a meal at my place? I mean, pay for it out of your own pocket?"

I was tired enough to forget how well he does sincere. I made the mistake of offering an honest answer. "I don't recall doing that. Every time it's been on the house." And not that bad, but who was going to admit that?

"And you complain about free meals. You know how much it costs to gather those 'weeds'? They're rare. They grow wild. They aren't cultivated commercially." He put on a lot of sincere. I wasn't sure if he was yanking my leg or not. I know it isn't cheap to eat at his place. But I'd always figured that was part of the ambience. Make his customers think they were buying class.

"We're getting too serious," I said, by way of ducking possible issues. "Let's go see how she'll poison us today."

"Not the best choice of words, Garrett, but let's."

38

Sometime back a hundred years ago, Cook whumped up one big breakfast and she'd been rewarming leftovers ever since. The same old greasy
meats and biscuits and gravy and all that, so heavy it would founder a
galleon. Your basic country breakfast. Morley was in pain.

He concentrated on biscuits and muttered, "At least the storm passed."

It was quiet out. The rain had fallen off to a drizzly mist. The wind had
died down. It was getting colder, which I didn't interpret as a positive omen.
I figured it meant the snow would be back.

Jennifer didn't show, which I didn't find mysterious and nobody else
mentioned, so it must not be unusual. But Wayne wasn't around either and
he wasn't the kind who missed his meals. "Where's Wayne?" I asked Peters,
who looked groggy, crabby, and like he still hurt plenty.

He gave me the answer I was afraid I'd hear. "He pulled out. Soon as
there was enough light, just like he said. Kaid said he had his stuff all packed
and at the front door. He was raring to go."

I looked at Kaid. Kaid looked like I felt. He nodded, which seemed to
take all the energy he had. I muttered, "And then there were three."

Peters said, "And I'm having a hard time talking myself into sticking."

Cook rumbled, "What are you boys on about now?" I realized she probably hadn't heard. I told her about Chain. And when I thought about Chain
I wished I hadn't, because Wayne the gravedigger was gone and that meant
either Peters or I or both of us would have to hike over to the graveyard and
wallow in the mud till we got Art Chain planted. I knew Morley wouldn't

do it. He hadn't hired on for that, as he'd remind me with a shit-eating grin while he kibitzed my digging style.

Eight hundred and some thousands apiece now. And all the survivors improbable suspects.

I thought about burning my copy of the will right there. But what good would that do if they didn't know it was the last copy? Then I had a terrible thought. "Was the will registered?" You can do that to keep your heirs from squabbling. It means filing a copy of the document. If Stantnor's was registered, then the villain did not have to worry about my copy or about the General having torched his.

They all looked at each other, shrugged.

We'd have to ask the General.

I started to say I wanted to see him, but a racket out front cut me off. It sounded like a cavalry troop arriving.

"What the hell is that?" Kaid muttered. He shoved himself off his stool, started moving like he was forty years older than his seventy-something. Everybody but Cook toddled along behind. Cook didn't leave her bailiwick for trivia.

We swarmed onto the front porch. "What the hell?" Peters demanded. "Looks like a damned carnival caravan."

It did. And the mob with the garish coach and wagons boasted every breed you could imagine.

None of the vehicles were pulled by horses or oxen or even elephants, which you sometimes see with a carnival. The teams were all grolls—grolls being half giant, half troll, green, and from twelve to eighteen feet tall when they're grown. They're strong enough to tear out trees by their roots—*big* trees.

A pair of those grolls waved and hollered. Took me a moment. "Doris and Marsha," I said. "Haven't seen them for a while."

A skinny little guy bounced up the steps. I hadn't seen him for a lot longer. "Dojango Roze. How the hell are you?"

"A little down on my luck, actually." He grinned. A strange little breed, he claimed he and Doris and Marsha were triplets born of different mothers. I'd given up trying to figure that out.

"What the hell is this, Dojango?" Morley asked. I've never been sure but I think Dojango is some distant relative of his.

"Doctor Doom's medicine show, carnival, and home spirit disposal service, actually. Friend of the Doc said you had a bad spirit needing handling." He grinned from ear to ear. His brothers Doris and Marsha boomed cheerfully, not giving a damn that I didn't understand one word of grollish. They and the other grolls and all the oddities with them got to work setting up camp on the front lawn.

I glanced at Peters and Kaid. They just stared. "Morley?" I raised an eyebrow about a foot high. "Your doctor friend's referral?"

His smile was a little weak around the edges. "Looks like."

"Hey!" Dojango said, sensing my lack of enthusiasm. "Doc Doom is the real thing, actually. Real ghost tamer. Exorcist. Demonologist. Spirit talker. The works. Even does a little necromancy, actually. But there ain't much call for those skills, really. Not when you're not human. How many you humans would think of using a nonhuman to call up your uncle Fred so you can find out where he hid the good silver before he croaked? See? So Doc has to make a mark here and a mark there some other way. Peddles nostrums mostly, actually. Hey. Let me go get him, bring him up, let you judge for yourself." He spun around and headed for the coach, which hadn't disgorged any passengers yet.

He ran halfway down the steps. I muttered, "I don't believe this. The old man would foul his drawers if he saw it."

Morley grunted. His eyes were glazed.

Roze came back. "Oh. Doc Doom is kind of a quirky guy, actually. You got to give him some room and be a little patient. If you know what I mean."

"I don't," I told him. "Better not be too quirky. I've got quirky enough right here and no patience left over for more."

Dojango grinned, managed to leave without using his favorite word again. Actually. He dashed down to that ridiculous coach, which was so brightly painted it would have blinded us on a sunny day. Breeds swarmed around it. A couple got up a giant parasol. Another one brought a set of steps. Somebody else laid out a canvas dingus from those steps to the steps to the house.

Morley and I exchanged glances again.

Dojango opened the coach door and bowed.

Meantime, grolls set up a circus on the lawn.

I asked Morley, "You heard of this guy?"

"Actually, yes." He smiled. "Word is, he's the real thing. Like Dojango says."

"Actually."

Kaid sputtered and went back into the house.

A figure seven feet tall and maybe six hundred pounds wide descended from the coach. What it was wasn't immediately obvious. It was wrapped up in so much black cloth, it looked like a walking tent. The tent was covered with mystical symbols in silver. A huge hand came out and made a benevolent gesture to the troops. One of the taller breeds dragged something out of the coach and planted it atop Doctor Doom's head. It added three feet to his height. Priests should wear something so bizarre and ornate.

He came toward us as though the star of a coronation processional.

"You Doc Doom?" I asked when he arrived. "Give me one good reason why I should take you seriously after that clown show."

Dojango, bouncing around like a puppy, seemed stricken. "Hey. Garrett. You can't talk to Doctor Doom that way, actually."

"I talk to kings and sorcerers that way. Why should I make an exception for a clown? You better pack your tents and get rolling. The nitwit who sent you made a mistake."

Morley said, "Garrett, don't get excited. The man is for real, he's just kind of into drama and maybe has a little bit of a puffed-up notion of his own importance."

"I'll say."

Doom hadn't spoken yet. He didn't now. He gestured. A breed beside him, female, about four feet tall who looked like she had a lot of dwarf and ogre in her—she was *ugly*—said, "The Doctor says he'll excuse your impertinence this once because you were ignorant of who he is. But now you know—"

"Bye." I turned. "Sarge, Morley, we got work to do. Sarge, maybe you better see if you can find a horse. We may have to send for the garrison." There isn't much law anywhere in Karenta, but guys like the General have access to a little. Somebody irritates them, they can always get a hand or two hundred from the army.

Dojango had a fit. He pursued us into the hall, where he lost the thread of his thoughts as he looked around at the paintings and hardware and bellicose scenes in glass. He mumbled something about, "He's desperate for work, actually."

Cook strode onto the scene, as formidable as a war elephant. Now I knew where Kaid had gone. She damned near trampled Roze. I said, "I don't think we'll need the army."

Morley said, "You're being too hard, Garrett. One more time. The man is the real thing."

"Yeah. Right." I went back to the door to watch Cook in action.

The action was over, essentially. She stood in front of the marvelous doctor with hands on ample hips looking like she might breathe fire. He was out of his wonderful hat already and getting rid of the tent.

Like I thought, the guy inside went more stone than I had fingers to count, but I had to revise his tonnage downward. He didn't go more than four-fifty in his work clothes.

He had some troll in him and three or four other bloods; once you saw him without the costume, you figured maybe he was smart to wear it. He made his little mouthpiece look gorgeous.

"Mr. Garrett. I'll dispense with the showmanship. As my good friend Dojango has assured you, I am the genuine article." His voice was down a well's depth below bass. Somewhere along the line somebody had popped him in the Adam's apple. That added a growly, scratchy character to his voice and made him hard to understand. He knew that and spoke slowly. "You have a problem with a malign spirit, I'm told. Unless it's of a class two magnitude or greater, I can deal with it."

"Huh?" I'm not up on the jargon. I try not to hang around with sorcerers. That can be hazardous to your health.

"Will you reconsider and allow me a preliminary examination of the premises?"

Why not? I'm an easygoing guy when people don't shuck me. "As long as you knock the horse apples off your boots and promise not to wet on the carpets."

He was so ugly his expression was hard to read. I don't think he appreciated my humor, though. I asked, "What do you need from us?"

"Nothing. I brought my own equipment. A guide, perhaps, to show me those places where the spirit most commonly manifests."

"It doesn't. Leastwise, not when anyone is looking. The only evidence we have that there is one is the doctor's opinion."

"Curious. A spirit of the sort he suspected ought to manifest frequently. Dojango. My kit."

Morley asked, "Could it appear to be somebody familiar?"

"Explain your question, please."

I told him about having a Morley in my room who wasn't.

"Yes. Exactly. If it wanted, it could cause a great deal of confusion that way. Dojango, what are you waiting for?"

Roze scampered off to the Doctor's coach. Meantime, Doom said, "Perhaps I should apologize for distressing you with my arrival. The sort of people who usually employ me won't believe I'm real unless they get a show."

I understood that. Sometimes I have that problem in my business.

Potential clients look at me and wonder, especially when they catalog the marks on my face. I have to remind them that they should see the other guys.

Dojango staggered up the steps with four big cases. They probably out-weighed him. His face was frozen in a rictus of a grin.

Cook seemed satisfied that everything was under control. She headed into the house. Never said a word to me. My feelings were hurt.

But not much.

Dojango arrived panting like he'd run twenty miles. Doctor Doom said, "Shall we begin?"

39

Once the good doctor stopped clowning, he impressed me as quite professional.

He started at the fountain, about which he made several remarks, suggesting he thought it one of the great sculptures of the modern age. He asked if it might be for sale in the foreseeable future.

Peters and I exchanged glances. Peters was way out at sea, encountering a side of the world about which he'd only heard before. He said, "Unlikely, Doctor. Unlikely."

"A pity. A great pity. I'd love to own it. It would make a wonderful prop." He shuffled through his cases as Dojango popped them open, took out this and that—and nobody else knew what they were. For all I could tell they had no use at all and were just stuff to impress the peasants.

Three minutes later he said, "A great many traumatic events have occurred in this house." He looked at something in his hand, drifted to the spot where Chain had made his exit from this vale of tears. The boys had cleaned up good. I guessed Chain was taking his ease in the wellhouse till planting time.

"A man died here recently. Violently." Doom looked up. "Pushed, I'd guess."

"On the money," I admitted. "Maybe an hour after midnight last night."

He wandered around. "The dead have walked here. Zombies . . . No! Worse. Not under control. Draugs."

I looked at Morley. "I guess he knows his stuff. Unless he's got a friend on the inside."

"You're suspicious of everything."

"Occupational hazard."

The spook hunter spent fifteen minutes just standing by the fountain with his eyes closed, holding some doohickeys to his ears. I'd begun to wonder if we weren't getting shucked after all when he came back from wherever he'd been. "This is a house of blood. The very stones vibrate with memories of great evils done." He shuddered, closed his eyes for another three minutes, then turned to me. "You're the man who needs my help?"

"I'm the guy the General hired to straighten out a mess that only gets more tangled by the minute."

He nodded. "Tell me what you've learned. There have been so many evils done here that it's impossible to separate them."

"That'll take awhile. Why don't we get comfortable?" I led him to one of the rooms on the first floor west where, I presumed, in better times the business of the estate had been managed. We settled. Peters went off to sweet-talk Cook into providing the next best thing to refreshments in a household where alcohol was banned.

"A twisted place indeed," Doom said when he learned that. I decided maybe he wasn't so bad after all.

I told him what I'd learned, which wasn't that much when you came down to it. Mostly a catalog of crimes.

He asked no questions till I finished. "The spirit seems content to victimize your principal? The other deaths are the work of other hands?"

"Hell, I don't know. The longer I'm here, the more confused I get. Every time somebody dies or emigrates, the list of suspects gets more improbable." I explained how I'd had Chain locked in as the villain—till he took his tumble.

He considered. He reflected. He took his time. He was one guy who didn't get in a hurry. He said, "Yours isn't my field of expertise, Mr. Garrett, but I would, as a disinterested layman, suggest that you may be following false trails because you began with faulty assumptions."

"Say what?"

"You think you're after someone who wants a greater share of the estate. Have you considered another motive? The heirs keep demonstrating a lack of interest in the legacy. Perhaps there's another cause for murder entirely."

"Perhaps." I'm not exactly a dummy. I'd considered that. But I couldn't come up with anything to connect these people any other way. Only the legacy offered any normal basis for bloodshed. I told him that. "I'm open to suggestions. I'll tell you I am."

He did some reflecting. "How separate are your separate investigations?"

I explained it the way I saw it. Morley fretted, thinking my perspective too narrow.

"Good heavens!"

"Huh?"

Doom was staring past my shoulder. I had my back to the doorway. I turned.

Jennifer had appeared.

"Good heavens," I said.

She looked like death warmed over.

Doom said, "Come here, child. Instantly."

I got up, put an arm around her waist. She was almost too weak to walk. She hadn't had strength enough to dress herself properly. "Garrett . . ." There were tears in her eyes.

That's all she said. I led her to the seat I'd vacated. The light was better. What it showed me wasn't. She'd taken on the color the old man showed. "It's after her," I croaked. "The spook."

Doom looked at her a long time before he said, "Yes."

Morley looked at her, too. Then he looked at me. "Garrett, let's take a walk. Doc, see what you can do for her. We'll be back."

Numb, I didn't say anything till Morley started leading me upstairs. "What are we doing?"

"That spook's been gnawing on the old man for a year, right? It never bothered anybody else. Right?"

"Yeah." We were headed for my suite.

"Something changed that between last night and this morning."

We reached the fourth floor, me puffing and renewing my vow to get in shape. "I guess. But what?"

He unlocked the door with my key, held it for me. Once we were inside, he took down the portrait of my mystery blonde. "Where'd you spend the night, Garrett?"

I looked at her. I looked at him. I recalled seeing her as I wandered home. I said, "Oh." That's all I had to say. It was a lot to swallow.

Morley went back into the hall, me tagging along. He said, "Time to get an opinion on this from everyone."

"Morley, this isn't possible."

"Maybe not. I hope not." He has no mercy sometimes. His tone was a hot flensing knife.

We returned to the room where Doom and Jennifer were. Doom was disturbed. Jennifer looked a lot better, though. He'd done something for her. She had strength and attention enough now to put herself into better array. Morley placed the portrait on a table nearby, facedown. "Peters. Would you get everyone in here? Garrett has something to show everybody."

Peters had been hovering over Jennifer. He looked at me. I said, "Please?"

"The General, too?"

"We can do without him for the moment."

He was gone longer than I expected. I found out why when he came back. "Cook and Kaid were up feeding the General. Garrett, he's damned near gone. Can't even sit up. Can't talk. It's like he's had a stroke. Or had all but the last ounce of life sucked out."

Doom listened but said nothing.

"How soon will they be here?"

"Soon as they get him cleaned up. He fouled his bed. He's never done that before. He always got hold of Kaid or Dellwood. Most times he had enough strength to make it to his chamber pot."

After that there wasn't much to say. I watched Doom fuss over Jennifer and Jennifer continue to improve. I tried not to dwell on what Morley had said without saying it in so many words.

There are things you just don't want to believe.

Kaid and Cook came in, Cook grumbling steadily about the interruptions in her schedule. Morley said, "Sit down, please. Garrett?"

I knew what I had to do. I didn't want to, for some reason that seemed almost outside me. But Garrett's got willpower. I looked at Jennifer. Too bad Garrett don't have a little more won't power.

"Snake Bradon was a remarkable artist but it seems he never showed his work. Which is a damned sin. He was able to capture the essence of what it felt like in the Cantard. He painted people, too. With a very skewed eye. This is one of his portraits. I managed to save it from the stable fire. It could be the key to everything. I want you all to look at it and tell me about it."

Morley brought a lamp closer so there'd be more light. I lifted the painting.

Damn me if Jennifer didn't let out a squeak and faint. And Cook, who hadn't deigned to seat herself, collapsed a moment later.

"Hell of an impact," I said.

Doc Doom stared at the blonde. He got the look Morley had last night. He shook himself loose, said, "Lay it down again, please." Once I had, he said, "The man who painted that had one eye in another world."

"He's got both of them there now. He was murdered night before last."

He waved that off. It was irrelevant.

Morley asked, "You see what was in the background?"

"Better than anyone with an untrained eye, I suspect. That painting tells a whole story. An ugly story."

"Yeah?" I said. "What is it?"

"Who was the woman?"

"That's what I've been trying to find out since I got here. Nobody but me ever sees her. The rest of these people say she doesn't exist."

"She exists. I'm surprised you're sensitive . . . No. I did say she'd manifest frequently. Sometimes they will attach themselves to a disinterested party, gradually trying to justify themselves before an impartial court."

"Huh?"

Morley said, "I get it. I was wrong, Garrett. She's not the killer. She's your ghost. She didn't need secret passages to get in and out."

"Morley! Morley. You know damned well that's impossible. I told you about . . ." Some sense wormed through my confusion. There was a crowd here. Was I going to be dumb enough to tell them all I'd fooled around with a spook?

Was I dumb enough to believe it myself?

"She's the haunt," Doom agreed. "There's no doubt. That painting explains everything. She was murdered. And it was the culmination of a betrayal so immense, so foul, that she stayed here."

I had it. "Stantnor killed her. His first wife. The one he got rid of. Supposedly he bought her off and sent her away. He murdered her instead. Maybe there is a body in the cellar, Morley."

"No."

"Huh?"

That was Cook, getting up off the floor. "That's Missus Eleanor, Garrett."

"Jennifer's mother?"

"Yes." She moved to the table. She lifted the painting. She stared. I was sure she saw everything Snake Bradon put there, maybe stuff Morley and I missed. "So. He did it hisself. He's lived a lie all these years because he can't give up that alibi. It wasn't no fumble-fingered doctor at all. That lousy bastard."

"Wait a minute. Just wait a damned minute—"

"The story is there, Mr. Garrett," Doom said. "She was tortured and murdered. By an insane man."

"Why?" My voice was in what you'd call the plaintive range. I wasn't calming down any. I couldn't get last night out of my head. That hadn't been any spook . . . Well, if it was, it was the warmest-bodied, friskiest, most solid spook there ever was. "Doc, I need to talk to you in private. It's critical."

We went into the hallway. I told him. He went into one of his reflections. When he came out a week later, he said, "It begins to make sense. And the child? Jennifer? Did you sleep with her, too?"

Well, hell. They say confession is good for the soul. "Yes. But it was kind of her idea. . . ." Stop making excuses, Garrett.

He smiled. It wasn't a salacious grin; it was a eureka kind of grin. "It falls together. The old man, your principal, whose life she's been leeching slowly as she sets his feet upon the path to hell, is drained this morning. She'd have had to do that to assume solid form with you. Then the other—her own daughter?—wounds her by taking you to her bed. You, the focus she's chosen to justify. You've been tainted. That has to be punished." He got reflective again.

"That's crazy."

"We're not dealing with sane people. Living or dead. I thought you understood that."

"Knowing it and *knowing* it are two different things."

"We have to talk to the troll woman. It would be wise to know the circumstances of those days as well as possible before we take steps. This isn't a feeble haunt."

We went back inside. Doom asked Cook, "What reason would General Stantnor have had for doing what he did? From what Mr. Garrett tells me, she was frightened of everything, had almost no will of her own. It would take great evils to animate her to the point where we'd have the situation that exists here now."

"I don't tell no stories—"

"Cook. Can it!" I snapped. "We have the General nailed here. He murdered Eleanor, evidently in extremely traumatic fashion. Now she's getting even. That doesn't bother me too much. I kind of like the idea of retribution. But now she's started on Jennifer. I don't like that. So how about you just puke up some straight answers?"

Cook looked at Jennifer, who hadn't yet recovered.

"I kind of hinted at it but I guess not strong enough. The General . . . Well, he was obsessed with Missus Eleanor. Like I told you. But that never stopped him from rabbiting around hisself, tumbling every wench who'd hold still while he threw her on her back. He wasn't discreet about it, neither. Missus Eleanor, naive as she was, figured it out. I can't tell you what she felt for him. She wasn't never one to talk or show much. But she had to be his wife. She didn't have nowhere to go. Her parents was dead. The king was out to get her.

"She was hurt bad by the way he done. Real bad. Maybe, because she was the way she was, lots more hurt than a deceived wife ought to be. Anyway, she told him if he didn't straighten up, she'd see if what was good for the gander was good for the goose. She wouldn't never have done it. Not in a million years. She didn't have the nerve. But that didn't make him no never mind. He thought everybody worked inside like he did. He beat her half to death. Maybe would've killed her if I hadn't of got between them. Anyway, he just went crazy after that. Poor child. Only time she ever stood up to him. . . ."

I wanted to tell her to make the long story short, but it might not be smart to interrupt while she was puking her guts.

"Well, the poor child was pregnant with Miss Jennifer. She didn't know it yet. Naive child. Once she did figure it out, it was a day too late. I like to pounded his head for him but he wouldn't believe he was its dad. Not till she was gone. Him thinking that poor child was as loose as him! With who? I asked him. Was there anybody around the house? Hell, no. Not but him. And the child never went outdoors. Half the time she didn't even come out of her room. But try to convince a fool with logic.

"He put her through hell. Pure hell. Tormented her. Tortured her, I think. She had bruises all over. Trying to get her to tell him the name. I done what I could. That wasn't never enough. Only made him worse when I wasn't looking. And it got worse when the old General passed." She looked at me. There were tears in her eyes the size of larks' eggs. "I swear, though, I never thought he killed her. I never believed that even when there was some whispers. If I'd of known it then, I'd of plucked off his fingers and toes and arms like plucking feathers off a chicken. How *could* he have killed her?"

"I don't know, Cook. But I'm going to ask." I looked at Doctor Doom.

He asked, "You intend to confront him?"

"Oh, yes. I sure do." I grinned like a werewolf. "He hired me to unravel his troubles no matter how much he didn't like what he learned. I'm going to give him apoplexy."

"Take it easy," Morley said. "Don't get so upset you can't think straight."

Good advice. I've been known to gallop around like a beheaded chicken when I'm excited, doing more damage to myself than to the bad guys. "I've got it under control." I glanced at Jennifer. She'd begun to recover while Cook was talking. She looked a little goofy, still, as she stared at the portrait of her mother. She seemed amazed and puzzled. She mumbled, "That's my mother. That's the woman in the painting in father's bedroom."

I looked at Peters. "Why didn't you tell me that last night?"

"I didn't believe it. I guessed, but this painting doesn't look anything like that one. I thought I had to be wrong. That it was just a coincidence. Snake never saw her, anyway."

Cook said, "That's not true."

"That's right," I said. "He came from the estate, didn't he? I should have thought of that. Did he know her at all?"

Cook shook her head. "He never came in the house even back then. She never went out. But he would have seen her from a distance."

Peters just shook his head. "I didn't believe it."

I recalled him and Kaid arguing after Morley and I left. Now I knew why. They'd been trying to make up their minds. "What do we do about the ghost, Doctor?" At the moment I was on her side, despite what she'd done to Jennifer.

Not hard to understand. Last night she'd added adultery to the punishments visited upon Stantnor, twenty years after he'd convicted her. Then Jennifer and I had . . . But why shouldn't she consider Jennifer my victim, the way she'd been Stantnor's? Was there more to it than I knew? I supposed Doom could explain but I couldn't ask.

I shrugged. Go try to unravel motives and you'll drive yourself crazy. In my line you're better off dealing with results. That's much more straightforward.

Doom said, "She has to be laid to rest. Her staying here and walking the night . . . That's far more cruel. That's more punishment that's undeserved. She needs peace." He paused, apparently expecting comment. When he got none, he added, "It's not my place to be judgmental. I suspect the man who killed her deserves all he's gotten and more. But my own ethics don't let me let the victimization go on."

He was starting to look like a right guy despite his clown show. Most of the time that's the code I follow myself. *Most* of the time. I've been known to get involved and consequently stumble into some homegrown justice sometimes. "I agree. Mostly. What next?"

Doom worked his ugly face into a smile. "I'm going to work a constraint on the shade that will keep it from draining any more substance off the living. The principal will begin to recover immediately. Once he regains some strength—this is just a suggestion—I'd like to call her up to confront him. A direct confrontation will leave her less reluctant to go to her rest, I think. And I have a feeling that an exorcism against a hostile shade would be very difficult here."

"Yeah." I reckoned he knew what he was talking about. And a confrontation sounded good to me.

"You can't do that," Jennifer protested. "That might kill him. He might have a stroke."

Nobody else much cared if he did. At the moment there was very little love for Stantnor around that place. Cook looked like she was considering ways she could help him across to the other shore. She'd raised him like her own but she was less than proud of him.

She said, "I got to get back to work. Lunch is going to be late as it is." She stomped out.

"Keep an eye on her, Sarge," I suggested. "She's pretty upset."

"Right."

40

Doom didn't need help doing his constraint thing. In fact, he wanted to be alone. "There are always risks in these things. I have a tendency to underestimate ghosts. It would be safer for everybody if you stayed away till I finish."

I said, "You heard him."

The party broke up. Nobody said much to anybody else. There was a lot of thinking going on.

Peters went to the kitchen to ride herd on Cook. Kaid went up to take care of the old man, probably with severely mixed feelings. I had them. It was hard to reconcile the General Stantnor of the Cantard War with the vicious monster we'd uncovered here.

Morley went outside to talk about old times with Dojango and his big green brothers. I took Jennifer up to her suite and put her back to bed, alone, to rest. She was badly shaken, seemed to want to curl up and make the world go away.

I didn't blame her. I'd be the same way if I found out my father murdered my mother.

I didn't tell her why she was in such bad shape physically. She had enough troubles. And I still wasn't sure I could accept that myself.

Nothing much to do till Doom was ready to go. I put my coat on and walked out to the Stantnor graveyard. I stared at Eleanor's marker awhile, trying to make peace with myself. It didn't work. I noticed a shovel leaning against the fence. Wayne had left it behind, as though he'd known there would be more graves to dig and why bother lugging tools back and forth? I found a spot and started digging, trying to lose myself preparing Chain's resting place.

That didn't work very well.

It especially didn't work when, after I was about three feet down, I noticed Eleanor by her tombstone, watching me. I stopped, tried to read something from features that were none too clear in daylight.

She'd been pretty substantial last night—because she'd sucked so much life out of Stantnor. Had she taken on substance at other times, to attack him by eliminating his servants? A ghost could make murder out of even apparently accidental deaths, by maddening a bull or maybe causing heart attacks. "I'm sorry, Eleanor. I never meant to hurt you."

She didn't say anything. She never did, except that once, when she found me outside Peters's room.

She seemed to gain substance. What was taking Doom so long? Was she giving him more trouble than he'd expected? I tried to think about that, the grave I was digging, lunch, the killer still to be caught, anything but the sad, futile, brief life this woman had lived.

It didn't work.

I sat on the edge of the grave, in the muck, and cried for her.

Then she was sitting opposite me wearing that look of concern, the same one she'd worn when she'd found me hurt. She didn't have enough substance not to be transparent. I told her, "I wish it could have been different for you. I wish you could've lived in my time. Or I in yours." And I meant it.

She reached out. Her touch was like the impact of falling swansdown. She smiled a weak, sad, forgiving smile. I tried to smile back but I couldn't.

There are evils in this world. It's the nature of things that there are, though it's a struggle accepting that. Because what Eleanor Stantnor had suffered, through no fault of her own, was an evil beyond ordinary evils. It was the kind of evil that goes beyond Man and rests squarely on the shoulders of the gods. It was the kind of evil that had left me an essentially godless man. I can't give allegiance to sky-beasts who'd let things like that happen to the undeserving.

General Stantnor would suffer in turn but the guilt wasn't all his. Nor did it belong to Eleanor's parents. Her mother had tried to protect her. Nor did it belong to the world as a whole. If there are gods at all, *they* deserved equal pain.

I looked up. Doom must have been finishing up, maybe getting an edge because she was distracted by me. She had little substance left. But she smiled as she faded. At me. Maybe the guy who had been best to her, ever. And you can guess how little that made me feel. I said, "Be at peace, Eleanor."

Then she was gone.

I dug some more, in a fury, like I was going to open a gate to hell and shove all the evils of the world down that hole. When I had a grave a foot deeper than necessary I came to my senses, sort of. I hoisted myself out and headed for the house. I had so much mud on me I feared somebody might mistake me for a draug.

stopped and chatted with Dojango and the boys but my heart wasn't in it. I gave up after five minutes and headed for the house. Morley watched me go, worried. About the time I reached the head of the steps he said something to Dojango, trotted after me. Dojango sighed one of those sighs I recalled meant he felt immensely put upon, hitched up his pants, and started running down the drive.

What the hell?

I went inside. As I passed the dead Stantnors I told them what I thought of them and their ways and especially the last of their line. Morley caught up when I was halfway through. "Are you all right, Garrett?"

"No. I'm feeling about as bleak as I can and still be breathing. But I'll be all right. Just frustration over all the mindless wickedness in the world. I'll come back."

"Oh. Pure essence of Garrett. Wishing he was triplets so he could straighten up three times as many messes."

I smiled feebly. "Something like that."

"You can't take it all on your own shoulders."

You can't, no. But it's a hard lesson to learn. And knowing that doesn't keep it from getting to you.

A tremendous metallic crash came from the main hall, punctuated by a high-pitched scream like a rabbit's death cry. We charged through the doorway, bouncing off one another.

Kaid lay six feet from where Chain had died, smashed by a suit of armor.

He wasn't dead. Not yet. He made me think of a smashed bug. His limbs still moved.

They stopped before we got the armor off him. The light went out of his eyes as I knelt beside him.

"And then there was one," Morley whispered.

"And I know which one, now." I hated myself. I should have known sooner. It was there to be had. Doctor Doom had been right. I'd looked at it from the wrong angle all along. But we all miss what we don't want to see. I'd just concentrated way too much on motive, blinded by the one motive I could see. Sometimes the motive doesn't make sense to anybody who isn't crazy.

"Yeah." Morley had it, too. Pretty obvious right now. But he didn't mention it. He said, "Can't do anything for him. Can't do anything about it this minute. You go get yourself cleaned up."

"Where's the point? I've got to dig another grave."

"That can wait. You need to get clean. I'll keep an eye on things."

Maybe he was right. Maybe he knew me too damned well. A bath probably wouldn't help, but it would be symbolic. I went to the kitchen. Cook and Peters had lunch almost ready. They hadn't heard the crash, amazingly. I didn't tell them what had happened. I just swiped all the hot water and headed for my suite. They didn't ask questions. I guess I looked too grim.

I didn't feel any better when I came back down, clean and changed. Some things won't wash off. "Anything?" I asked Morley.

He shook his head. "Except Doom wants to see you."

I went to the room where I'd left the Doctor. He had heard but still was startled when he looked at me. "You look bad."

I told him. He said, "I suspected it. I've done everything I can here, till we bring her up to face her husband."

I told him about my parting with Eleanor. He was a kind soul under that ugly exterior. "I know how you feel. I've been there a few times. Your business, mine, they have their painful sides. You'll get another chance to say good-bye."

"Let's do it."

"Not yet. You're not ready. You need to calm down. Your state is too emotional right now."

I started to argue.

"I don't tell you your business. You don't tell me mine. I'm not thinking about you. We can't operate properly if there's too much extraneous emotion. There'll be plenty involving the key characters."

He was right. I need to learn to separate myself more from my work. "All right. I'll get myself under control."

Morley stuck his head in. "Lunch. You'd better take time to have some, Garrett."

Great. Everybody was looking out for Garrett's mental welfare. I wanted to scream and holler and carry on. I said, "I'll be right there."

I guess I looked a little less ferocious now. Black Pete watched me gobble whatever it was I wasn't seeing or tasting. He asked, "Did something happen?"

"Yeah. Something did. A suit of armor jumped off the fourth floor and squashed Kaid. Dead."

"Huh?" He frowned. He looked at Cook. She looked at him. It took them maybe five seconds each. Then Cook started crying quietly.

I told them, "Soon as we're done here, we're going up to see the old man. We'll wrap it up."

Peters said, "It's almost not worth the trouble anymore. And I'm almost sorry I ever came looking for you."

"I'm sure sorry you did." I finished stuffing my face, never having tasted a bite. Nobody else was in as big a hurry. Morley watched me like he was afraid I was going to blow. I told him, "I've got it under control. Iceberg Garrett. Cucumber Garrett." I'd turned off everything inside. But I didn't look it outside yet. Like the heat going out of a corpse, it would take awhile for the fury and frustration to radiate away.

They ate slower and slower, like kids knowing they were going to get taken to the woodshed after supper. I told Morley, "I'm going up to the room. Be back in a minute." I'd forgotten something, one of Snake's paintings.

When I returned, everybody was done eating. Doctor Doom was there with his tools, Snake's masterpiece under his arm. He was ready to go. He checked everybody over, seemed satisfied with my emotional control. He asked me, "You want to get the girl?"

"Sure. Morley, you carry this."

We trooped across the hall, past Kaid, averting our eyes. We climbed stairs. I broke away at the third floor and went to Jennifer's room. The door was locked but I had my skeleton key this time. I went through the big room into the sitting room where I'd found her during the night. She was there again, in the same chair, facing the same window. She was asleep. Her face was as untroubled as a baby's.

"Wake up, Jennifer." I shook her shoulder. She jumped.

"What?" She calmed down quickly. "What?" again.

"We're going up to see your father. Come on."

"I don't want to go. You're going to . . . It'll kill him. I don't want to be there. I couldn't handle it."

"I think you can. And you have to be there. Things won't work out unless you are." I took hold of her hand, led her. She hung back, making me pull her, but she didn't fight me.

The rest were in Stantnor's sitting room, waiting. As soon as Jennifer and I arrived, Peters pushed on. The next room was a private sitting room like the one in Jennifer's suite. We trudged through into the bedroom.

42

The old man looked like a mummy that hadn't gotten the word and kept on breathing. His eyes were closed and his mouth was open. Some kind of slime bubbled out and dribbled down his cheek. Every third breath sounded like a death rattle.

We got to work. I collected paintings. Morley planted himself beside the door. Peters wakened the General and sat him up. Cook started feeding the fire.

The old man looked like hell but his eyes were bright when they focused. His mind hadn't deserted him. He saw how grim everybody looked, knew I'd come with my final report.

I told him, "No point you wasting strength talking, General. Or arguing. It's final report time. Won't take long but I warn you, it's worse than you dreamed. I won't make recommendations. I'll give it to you and you can do what you want with it."

His eyes sparked angrily.

I said, "The man you don't recognize is Doctor Doom, a specialist in paranormal activities. He's been a big help. You don't see Wayne because he quit. He left this morning. Chain and Kaid aren't here because they were taken suddenly dead. Like Hawkes and Bradon. By the same hand. Doctor."

Doom started doing his part. I gave him a little time to get rolling. Lips tightened into a colorless prune, Stantnor watched. Only his eyes moved. They weren't filled with gratitude when they turned my way. There was something behind the anger in them, too. He was worried.

I told him, "First we'll talk about who's been trying to kill you."

Doom let out a howl. Everybody jumped. A flash filled the room. I'm no pro but that didn't feel right. "You all right?" I asked.

He gasped, "It's fighting me. But I'll get it here. Stay out of my way and don't bother me."

It took him a few minutes more.

Eleanor materialized at the foot of Stantnor's bed. But not as Eleanor. Not right away. First she did a good Snake Bradon, then a less credible Cutter Hawkes before surrendering to Doom's will. I compared her to the portrait they said Stantnor stared at all the time. It didn't look much like her and nothing like the woman in Bradon's painting.

Stantnor's eyes got huge. He sat up straight. "No!" he squeaked. He threw up an arm to shield his eyes. "No! Get her away!" He started whimpering like a whipped child. "Get her out of here!"

"You said my job was to make you face the truth no matter how unpleasant that truth might be, General. One truth I've uncovered is this. I'm going to enjoy making you face it. The woman you tortured and murdered—"

Jennifer burst out, "I still can't believe it! My mother!" She staggered.

"Keep her under control, Morley." Morley left the door, moved to support her. She started blubbering. Words dribbled out but none of them made sense.

Stantnor sputtered like he was going to run a bluff. Spittle ran down his chin. He couldn't talk. He was too rattled. He looked like he might have the stroke Jennifer had predicted.

I faced Eleanor. "Go now. Rest. You've done enough. It doesn't become you. Don't darken your soul any more." Our eyes locked. We stared at one another till the others grew restless. I said, "Please?" And wasn't quite sure what I was pleading for.

"She'll rest easy, Mr. Garrett," Doom said, gently. "That's a promise."

"Turn her loose, then. She doesn't need . . ." I shut my mouth before I said something that might cause me more trouble than I could handle. I closed my eyes, got myself under control. When I opened them Eleanor was little more than a wraith.

She smiled for me. Good-bye.

"Good-bye."

I took another minute before I faced the old man. He was gasping and wheezing but less distressed. "I brought along a little something for you to remember her by, General. You'll love it." I took down the junk portrait of

Eleanor, flipped it away, replaced it with Bradon's masterpiece. "Isn't that better?"

Stantnor stared at it. And the longer he stared the more terrified he became.

He screamed.

I looked at the portrait.

I damned near screamed.

I can't tell you what it was. It hadn't changed in any obvious way but it had changed. It told Eleanor's story. You couldn't look at it and not be crushed by her pain and her fear of the thing that pursued her, that mad shadow that wore the face of a young Stantnor.

I tore my gaze away just before Doom did it for me. He told me, "You still have work to do." His voice was soft and calm. It reached way down inside me, like the Dead Man's can, and gentled that part of me about to stumble over the brink.

"What are you doing?" he asked.

"I want him to know he has to spend the rest of his life looking at that."

"Not now. Let's go on."

"You're right. Of course. Peters, get his attention away from the painting for a minute."

Peters turned the old man's head. I watched madness fade from Stantnor's eyes . . . No, it wasn't madness. Not exactly. He'd just been focused on something far away, that only he could see. On his own vision of hell. He was back now. For a few minutes, at least.

"I have another present for you," I told him. "You'll like this one, too." To make sure he paid attention I turned Eleanor's portrait to the wall. I replaced it with Snake's last portrait of Jennifer. "Your lovely daughter, so like her father."

Jennifer screamed. She threw herself forward. Morley caught her. She didn't notice the pain.

Cook stopped feeding the fire, elbowed Morley aside, took Jennifer into her arms, took the knife away from her, controlled her, held her, wept over her, murmured, "My baby, my baby. My poor sick baby." Nobody else said anything. Everybody knew. Even the General knew.

"There's why your stable burned. That painting. She sat for Bradon several times. But Snake Bradon had an eye that could see the true soul. Which is probably why he retreated from the world. A man with his eye would see a lot of awful truths.

"I look for truth but this time I didn't see it soon enough. Maybe I didn't want to. Like so many of the darkest evils, this one came in a beautiful package. Maybe the painting of Eleanor preoccupied me too much. Maybe I should have studied this one more closely."

Stantnor coughed.

"Eight murders, General. Your baby killed eight mostly good men. Four she lured to the swamp on the Melchior place." Once I'd accepted Jennifer as the villain the pieces had fallen together. "Took a while but I finally figured what they had in common. They were all chasers. She pretended she was catchable. She got them out there and killed them and dropped them in. That got her past the stumbling block I came up against whenever I wondered if she might be the killer. How did she move the bodies? I missed the obvious answer, that she got them to move themselves. The heaviest work she ever did was shove Chain off the fourth-floor balcony and drop a suit of armor on Kaid.

"Maybe I was slow because the murders weren't the kind you associate with women. I just didn't face the fact that in a house full of Marines *everybody* might think like Marines and be straightforward and bloody. Who'd picture a woman being daring enough to take on a trained commando with a Kef sidhe strangler's cord?"

I looked at Jennifer, thought of our stroll to the graveyard. She'd planned to kill me out there, I knew now. I'd offered her an unexpected moment of kindness. That had saved my life and had cost her her chance to get away with everything.

"I know who and how. But I sure as hell don't understand why."

She cracked. She laughed and wept and talked a yard a second and never made a lick of sense. It seemed to have to do with a fear that, if there were any heirs but her and Cook, parts of the estate would get sold off and once it was dismembered she'd be forced to leave for that deadly world she'd visited only once, when she was fourteen.

I was wrong about one thing. She hadn't committed eight murders. She'd committed eleven. She'd done in the three men whose deaths had seemed natural or accidental. She admitted it. She bragged about it. She laughed because she'd made fools of everybody till now.

Stantnor stared at her the whole time, aghast. I knew what he was thinking. What had he done to deserve this?

I started to tell him.

"Garrett!" Morley took hold of my arm.

"What?"

"It's time to go. The job's done."

Doom had gone already, his part complete, Eleanor laid to rest. Cook was trying to comfort and control Jennifer and to work out some separate peace with herself. The girl wasn't the daughter of her flesh, but . . . Stantnor had become fixated on his daughter's portrait, seeing deeper than anyone but Bradon had. Maybe seeing the hand he'd had in creating a monster. I had no pity for him. I did try to find it. It just wasn't there.

Then he had one of his fits.

This one went on and on and on.

"Garrett. It's time to go."

The old man was dying. Rough. Morley didn't want to stay for the show.

Peters just stood there, numb, doing nothing. He didn't know what to do. I did pity him.

I shook off the hold emotion had on me. I told Morley, "Stantnor owes me. I spent my whole fee and then some getting him his answers. It don't look like he'll hang around to be billed."

He looked at me weird. That kind of cold remark wasn't in character. "Don't," he said, though he had no idea what I was going to do. "Let's just go. Forget it. I won't charge you for my time."

"No." I snagged the painting of Eleanor. "My fee. An original Bradon." The General didn't argue. He was busy dying. I looked at Peters. He just shrugged. He didn't care.

Morley snapped, "Garrett!" He was sure I was going to do something I'd regret.

"Wait a damned minute!" I still had a responsibility here. "Cook, what're you going to do?"

She looked at me like I'd asked the dumbest question possible. "What I always done, boy. Look after the place."

"Get hold of me if I can do anything." Then I followed Morley. I didn't think another thought about the old man. If there'd been a doctor outside who could have saved him, I doubt it would have occurred to me to mention his distress.

Peters was at the vestibule door when Morley and I got there, carrying paintings and my stuff. He was staring at the great hall the way I'd stared at Bradon's painting of the swamp and hanged man. He had a shovel in one hand. He had graves to dig. I wondered if anybody would bother giving Stantnor a marker. He said, "I don't think I can say thanks, Garrett. You came when I called, but I don't think I'd have visited you if I'd known—"

"I wouldn't have come if I'd known. We're even. What're you going to do?"

"Bury the dead, then go somewhere. Maybe back into the Corps. They'll need veterans with Mooncalled running amok. And it's all I know, anyway."

"Yeah. Good luck. See you again someday, Sarge."

"Sure." We both knew we'd never see one another again.

A terrible scream came from upstairs. It went on and on till it seemed no human throat could have produced it. We all looked up. Peters said, "I guess he's dead." He said it with a complete lack of passion.

The scream came again. Now it was filled with mad rage. Cook boomed, "Miss Jenny, you come back here!"

The girl had cracked completely. She flew out of the fourth-floor hallway carrying a dagger, screaming. Shocked, I realized she was yelling my name.

"Get moving, Garrett," Morley said. He'd seen berserkers before. Even a ninety-five-pound woman could tear me apart.

She was so far out of her mind, she didn't know where she was. Realization hit her too late. She hit the balcony rail full speed.

The heroic knight caught her in his lap. Broken, she dribbled down off him, wound up at one of the dragon's feet. She looked like the monster's prey. The hero had come to her rescue moments too late.

But this hero had been way too late to save anybody.

I turned and walked. Morley stayed behind me, just in case I did some damnfool thing like try to go back.

Morley and I didn't talk much on the way home. Once I muttered something about finding another line of work, and he just told me not to be a damned fool. I asked if he'd filled his pockets while he was there, or planned to drop back in some midnight. Usually if I ask something like that he just looks at me like he hasn't got the faintest idea what I'm talking about.

"I wouldn't take anything out of that place if you paid me, Garrett. Not if you begged me. There's a darkness in every stone, every thing, in there."

We didn't talk again till we were coming up Macunado Street toward my house. Then he said, "Go in there and get roaring drunk. Falling-down, puking drunk. Get the poison out."

"That's the best idea you've had in years."

43

D ean let me in. He looked older and leaner, though it'd been only a few days. "Mr. Garrett. We were concerned, not hearing from you for so long."

"We?" I grumbled. He was going to fuss over me.

"Him." He jerked his head toward the Dead Man's room. "He's been awake since you left. Expecting you to ask for help."

"I handled this one alone." Boy, did I handle it.

"Oh." He'd gotten the sense of my mood. "Guess I'd better draw one."

"I might drink a whole barrel."

"That bad?"

"Worse. Find me a hammer, too." I eased into my office, checked the spot where I meant to hang Eleanor.

Dean went. He moved with a swiftness I should remember next time he went at his customary snail's pace. He was back with a beer, a hammer, and a cup of nails in less than a minute. I drained the beer mug. "More."

"I'll start a meal, too. You look like you could use one."

Old sneak. Going to get something in my stomach before I started my serious drinking. "I did miss your cooking where I was." I drove a nail into the wall. Dean brought beery reinforcements before I unwrapped Eleanor. This time he brought a pitcher as well as a mug.

I unwrapped the lady and hung her, stepped back.

It wasn't the same picture.

Well, yes, it was. But something had changed. The intensity, the passion, the horror weren't there. But it looked the same. Except Eleanor seemed to be smiling. She seemed to be running *to* something instead of *from* something.

No. It was the same. Nothing had changed but me. I turned my back on it. Snake Bradon hadn't been that great a painter.

I glanced over my shoulder. Eleanor smiled at me.

I downed another mug.

Dean scurried off to get something cooking before I downed enough to pass out.

The Dead Man dragged me into his room almost against my will and dragged the story out of me. He didn't criticize, which was unusual. We didn't get into an argument, despite my best efforts. Instead of climbing all over me for my mistakes, for not having recognized that Jennifer was crazy and a killer earlier than I had, he made thoughtful sounds in my mind. When I finished he meandered off on an extended review of the latest news from the Cantard.

I got interested despite myself.

Glory Mooncalled had attacked Full Harbor. He'd postured and threatened too much. He'd had to prove he wasn't all wind. He'd done his damnedest, launching night attacks from the sea and air, using Cantard creatures. He'd tried to capture the city gates so he could get his ground troops inside. And he'd gotten his ass whipped. Just as I'd predicted.

"There goes the myth of his invincibility," I told the Dead Man.

He responded with a huge mental chuckle. *Not at all. Now they will chase after him, to finish him off. Into his country.*

"Oh."

So. If he whipped them out there, there wouldn't be enough defenders to hold the city next time he attacked. Maybe. And our boys would chase him. In a mob. We don't have enough competent commanders. Our last really capable man retired three years ago.

I am curious, Garrett. Why would the woman hit you in the head in the sergeant's quarters? You had rendered yourself immune by plying her with your adolescent charm. He couldn't resist getting in a small needle here and there.

"I don't think she wanted to kill me. She just wanted to get the copy of the will before I did."

Why?

I had the feeling he'd figured it out and wanted to see if I had. "For exactly the opposite of the reason I assumed at the time. She wanted to destroy it. If she could get rid of the copies, she wouldn't need to kill people. There'd be no evidence there were any other heirs. The law would pass the estate to her. No dismemberment, no need for her to leave."

And how did she know where to find the copy?

"I think she was behind the wall listening when I talked to Peters. I think a lot of the time she was supposed to be in her rooms, she was creeping around in the walls, listening in. Look, I really don't want to talk about it. . . . I have one for you. Why did Eleanor pretend to be Morley? And *how* could she do it so slick that I never suspected a thing?"

She did it because she wanted to know more about you. Your fatal charm again. You had caught her eye. How is quite simple. Especially for one with her antecedents. She simply opened your mind and made herself a mirror. She did not have to know a thing about Mr. Dotes, she just had to make you think she did. You did all the work. Almost like a dream.

There was an implication, remote, that I didn't like. If Eleanor had been inside my head, she knew all about why I was there. She probably could have told me about Jennifer anytime. She could have saved . . . I didn't want to think about it. "That's a little much to swallow."

Watch.

Suddenly that fifth of a ton of dead meat was gone, and in his place was a guy named Denny Tate who was so real, we talked about things the Dead Man couldn't possibly know.

Solid proof. Rock solid. Denny Tate had been dead more than a year. A good choice by the Dead Man. I couldn't call it a trick. He wasn't somebody who could be sneaked in for a little sleight of eye. And Denny was one of the few people important to me who'd died untimely without violence. The silly sack had fallen off a horse and broken his neck. "Enough, Old Bones. I'm a believer."

Denny Tate vanished. What replaced him was ugly as sin but I didn't tell him so. Not today.

My mood hadn't vanished. I almost asked him to conjure Eleanor.

Man, a guy could set up a hell of a racket faking calling up the dearly departed.

Think about something else, the Dead Man suggested.

"I'd love to, Chuckles. But it isn't that easy." Hell. I couldn't do anything right. Not even get drunk. I was barely light-headed.

You need a distraction.

"Right." So conjure me a miracle, Old Bones.

Somebody hammered on the front door.

The Dead Man *is* dead. In the flesh, anyway. But I swear he looked like he was smiling.

Dean hollered, "Can you get that, Mr. Garrett. I'm right in the middle, here. I've got both hands full."

Muttering, I stomped down the hall and flung the door open without bothering to look first. "Maya?"

"Hi, Garrett." Bright, perky, like she'd never been gone, except maybe to step around the corner. She walked in like she belonged. Which she did.

As I started to close the door I caught a glimpse of Morley Dotes holding up a wall down the street, smiling.

That slick bastard. He'd sent Dojango ahead to set this up. I bet he knew where Maya was all along. Maybe they all had.

From the kitchen Dean called, "Welcome back, Miss Maya. Dinner will be ready in a minute." He never looked to see who it was.

Set me up good, they did.

Maya took my hand and led me down the hall. For a second I resented everybody ganging up on me. But I didn't spend a whole lot of time worrying about it. Maya was there.

I was distracted.

•••Dread Brass Shadows

●●●1

hew! The things I get me into!

We had snow hip-deep to a tall mammoth for four weeks, then it turned suddenly hot and the whole mess melted quicker than you could say "cabin fever." So I was out running and banging into people and things and falling on my face because the girls were out stretching their gorgeous gams and I hadn't seen one leg, let alone two, since the snow started falling.

Running? Garrett? Yeah. All six feet two and two hundred pounds, poetry in motion. All right. Maybe it was bad poetry, doggerel, but I was getting the hang of it. In a few weeks I'd be back to the old lean and mean I'd been when I was twenty and a crack Marine. And pigs would be zooming around my ears like falcons.

Thirty isn't old to somebody who's fifty, but when you've spent a few years making a career of being lazy and the belly gets a little less than washboard and the knees start creaking and you start puffing and wheezing halfway up a flight of stairs, you feel like maybe you've skipped the twenty in between, or maybe just started spinning the digits over on the left-hand side. I had a bad case of got-to-do-something-about-this.

So I was out running. And admiring the scenery. And huffing and puffing and wondering if maybe I ought to forget it and sign myself into the Bledsoe cackle factory. It wasn't a lot of fun.

Saucerhead had the right idea. He sat on my front stoop with a pitcher

Dean kept topped. Each time I lumbered past he got his exercise by throwing up fingers showing the number of laps I'd survived without a stroke.

People shoved me and cussed me. Macunado Street was belly button to elbow with dwarves and gnomes, ogres and imps, elves and whatever have you else, not to mention every human in the neighborhood. There wasn't room for pigeons to fly because the pixies and fairies were zipping and swooping overhead. Nobody in TunFaire was staying inside but the Dead Man. And he was awake for the first time in weeks, sharing the euphoria vicariously.

The whole damned city was on a peak high. Everybody was up. Even the ratmen were smiling.

I churned around the corner at Wizard's Reach, knees pumping and elbows flailing, gawking ahead in hopes that Saucerhead would be struck as dumb as he looks and would lose count, maybe a couple of laps in my favor. No such luck. Well, some luck. He showed me nine fingers and I figured he wasn't lying much. Then he waved and pointed. Something he wanted me to see. I cut to the side, apologized to a couple of young lovers who didn't even see me, bounced up the steps with all the spring of a wet sponge. I looked out over the crowd.

"Well."

"Tinnie."

"Yeah." Well, indeed. My gal Tinnie Tate, professional redhead. She was still a block away but she was in her summer taunting gear, and wherever she walked, guys stopped and bounced their chins off their chests. She was hotter than a house afire and ten times as interesting. "There ought to be a law."

"Probably is but who can keep his mind on legalities?"

I gave Saucerhead a raised eyebrow. That wasn't his style.

Tinnie was in her early twenties, a little bit of a thing but with hips that were amply ample and mounted on gimbels. She had breasts that would make a dead bishop jump up and howl at the moon. She had lots of long red hair. The breeze threw it around wilder than I suddenly hoped I might in about five minutes if I could run off Saucerhead and Dean and get the Dead Man to take a nap.

She saw me gaping and panting and threw up a hand hello and every guy in Macunado Street hated me instantly. I sneered at them for their trouble.

"I don't know how you do it, Garrett," Saucerhead said. "Ugly dink like you, manners like a water buffalo. I just don't know." My pal. He got up. Sensitive guy, Saucerhead Tharpe. He could tell right away when a guy wanted to be alone with his girl. Or maybe he was just going to head her off and warn her she was wasting her time on an ugly dink like me.

Ugly? A vile slander. My face has gotten pushed around some over the years, but it has all the right parts in approximately all the right places. I can stand to look at it in a mirror, except maybe on the morning after. It's got character.

As I grabbed my mug and took a long drink, just to replace fluids, a dark-skinned, weaselly little guy with black hair and a pencil-stroke mustache grabbed Tinnie's chin with his left hand. His other hand was behind her, out of sight, but I never doubted what he was doing.

Neither did Saucerhead. He let out a bellow like a wounded bison and flew off the stoop. His boots never touched the steps. I was right behind him yowling like a saber-tooth with his tail on fire, eyes teared up so I couldn't see who I was trampling.

I didn't run into anybody, though. Saucerhead broke trail. Bodies flew out of his way. It didn't matter if they were two feet tall or ten. Nothing stops Saucerhead when he's mad. Stone walls barely slow him down.

Tinnie was down when we got there. People were clearing out. Nobody wanted to be near the girl with the knife in her back, especially not with two madmen roaring around.

Saucerhead never slowed down. I did. I dropped to one knee beside Tinnie. She looked up. She didn't look like she was hurting, just kind of sad. There were tears in her eyes. She reached up with one hand. I didn't say anything. I didn't ask anything. My throat wouldn't let me.

Then Dean was there. I don't know how he knew. Maybe it was our bellowing. He squatted down. "I'll take her inside, Mr. Garrett. Maybe His Nibs can help. You do what you have to do."

I grunted something that was more of a moan than anything, lifted Tinnie into his frail old arms. He was no muscleman, but he managed. I took off after Saucerhead.

Tharpe had a block lead but I gained ground fast. I wasn't thinking. He was. He was pacing himself, matching the assassin's stride, maybe following to see where he led. I didn't care about that. I didn't care about anything. I didn't look around to see what else was happening on the street. I wanted that blademan so bad I could taste blood.

I came churning up beside Saucerhead. He grabbed my shoulder, slowed me down, kept squeezing till the pain took the red out of my eyes. When he had my attention he made a couple of gestures, pointed.

I got it. First time, too. Must be getting smarter as I age.

The skinny guy didn't know his way around. He was just trying to get away. There aren't many straight streets in old TunFaire. They wander like they were laid out by drunken goblins blinded by the sun. This character was sticking to Macunado Street even though we had passed the point where it changes its name to Way of the Harlequin and then again to Dadville Lane after it narrows down.

"I'm gone." I cut out to the right, into an alley, through, darted down a narrow lane, ducked into a breezeway, skipped over some ratmen wasted on weed and a couple of blitzed human winos, then blasted out into Dadville Lane again, where it finishes the big, lazy loop around the Memorial Quarters. I chugged across the street and leaned against a hitching rail, waiting, puffing, and wheezing and grinning because, boy, was I in shape for this.

I was ready to dump my guts.

And here they came. The gink with the mustache was going all out, scared to death, trying so hard he wasn't seeing anything. All he knew was the pounding feet were catching up.

I let him come, stepped out, tripped him. He flew headlong, rolled like he had some tumbling experience, came up going full speed—*wham!* Right into the end of a watering trough. His momentum kept his top half going. He made a fine big splash.

Saucerhead got on one side of the trough. I got on the other. Tharpe slapped my hand away. Probably that was best. I was too upset.

He grabbed that gink by his greasy black hair, pushed him under, pulled him up, said, "Winded as you are, you ain't gonna hold your breath long." He shoved the mustache under again, pulled him up. "That water's going to get cold going down. You're going to feel it going and know there ain't one damned thing you can do to stop it." The big louse was barely puffing. The guy in the trough was wheezing and snorting worse than me.

Saucerhead shoved him under, brought him up a half second before he sucked in a gallon. "So tell us about it, little man. How come you stuck the girl?"

He would have answered if he could. He wanted to answer. But he was too busy trying to breathe. Saucerhead shoved him under again.

He came up, swallowed an acre of air, gasped, "The book!" He gobbled some more air—and that was the last breath he drew.

"What book?" I snapped.

A crossbow bolt hit the guy in the throat. Another thunked into the trough, and a third put a hole through Saucerhead's sleeve. Tharpe came over the trough in one bound and landed smack on top of me. A couple, three more bolts whizzed past.

Tharpe didn't bother making me comfortable. He did stick his head up for a second. "When I roll off, you go for that door." We were about eight feet from the doorway to a tavern. Right then, that looked like a mile. I groaned, the only sound I could make with all that meat on top.

Saucerhead rolled off. I scrambled. I never really got myself upright. I just sort of got my hands and feet under me and made that door in one long dive, dog-paddling. Saucerhead was right behind me. Crossbows twanged. Bolts thunked into the door. "Boy!" I said. "Those guys are in big trouble." Crossbows are illegal inside the city wall.

"What the hell?" I gasped as we shoved the door shut. "What in the hell?" I dived over to a window, peeked through a crack in a shutter still closed against winter.

The street had cleared as though a god had swept a broom along it, excepting a mixed bag of six nasties with crossbows. They spread out, weapons aimed our way. Two came forward.

Saucerhead took a peek. Behind us the barkeep went into a "Here, now! I won't have trouble in my place! You boys clear out!" routine.

Saucerhead said, "Three dwarves, an ogre, a ratman, and a human. Unusual mix."

"Odd, yes." I turned. "You got trouble already, Pop. You want it out of here, lend a hand. What you got under the bar to keep the peace?" I wasn't carrying anything. Who needs an arsenal to lumber around the block? Tharpe didn't carry, usually. He counted on his strength and wit. Which maybe made him an unarmed man twice over.

"You don't get going you're going to find out."

"Trouble's the farthest thing from my mind, Pop. I don't need any. But tell that to those guys outside. They already killed somebody in your watering trough."

I peeked again. The two had pulled the mustache out of the water. They looked him over. They finally figured it out, dropped him, eyeballed the tavern like they were thinking about coming inside.

Saucerhead borrowed a table from a couple of old boys puffing pipes and nursing mugs that would last them till nightfall. He just politely asked them to raise their mugs, picked the table up, and ripped a leg off. He tossed me that, got himself another, turned what was left into a shield. When those two arrived, he bashed the dwarves' heads in, then mashed the ogre against the doorframe with the table while I tickled his noggin with a rim shot.

One of their crossbows didn't get broken. I grabbed it, put the bolt back in, popped out the door, and ripped off a one-handed shot at the nearest target. I missed and pinked a dwarf ninety feet away. He yelped. His pals headed for the high country.

Saucerhead grumbled, "You couldn't hit a bull in the butt with a ten-foot pole if you was inside the barn." While I tried to figure that out, he grabbed the ogre, who was as big as he was, and tried to shake him awake. It didn't work. Not much of a necromancer, my buddy Saucerhead.

He didn't try the dwarf. That guy had gotten pounded down a foot shorter than he started out. So Tharpe just stood there shaking his head and looking baffled. I thought that was such a good idea I did it, too. And all the while, that old bartender was howling about damages while his clientele tried to dig holes in the floor to hide in.

"Now what?" Saucerhead asked.

"I don't know." I peeked outside.

"They gone?"

"Looks like. People are starting to come out." A sure sign the excitement was over. They would come count the bodies and lie to each other about how they saw the whole thing, and by the time any authority arrived—if it ever did—the story's only resemblance to fact would be that somebody got dead.

"Let's go ask Tinnie."

Sounded like a stroke of genius to me.

●●●3

Tinnie Tate wasn't some mousy little homemaker for whom the height of adventure was the day's trip to market. But she wasn't the kind of gal who got messed up with guys who stick knives in people and run in packs shooting crossbow volleys at citizens, either. She lived with her uncle Willard. Willard Tate was a shoemaker. Shoemakers don't make the kinds of enemies who poop people. A shoe doesn't fit, they bitch and moan and ask for their money back, they don't call out the hard boys.

I thought about it as I trotted. It didn't make sense. The Dead Man says when it doesn't make sense, you don't have all the pieces or you're trying to put them together wrong. I kept telling me, Wait till we see what Tinnie has to say. I refused to face the chance that Tinnie might not be able.

We had a curious and rocky relationship, Tinnie and me. Sort of can't live with and can't live without. We fought a lot. Though it hadn't been going anywhere, the relationship was important to me. I guess what kept it going was the making up. It was making up that was two hundred proof and hotter than boiling steel.

Before I got to the house, I knew it wouldn't matter what Tinnie had done, wouldn't matter what she'd been into, whoever hurt her would pay with interest that would make a loan shark blush.

Old Dean had the house forted up. He wouldn't have answered the door if the Dead Man hadn't been awake. He was, for sure. I felt his touch while I was pounding on the door and hollering like a charismatic priest on a holy roll.

Dean opened the door. He looked ten years older and all worn out. I was down the hall pushing into the Dead Man's room before he finished bolting the door behind Saucerhead.

Garrett!

The Dead Man's mind touch was a blow. It was an ice-water shower. It stopped me in my tracks. I wanted to scream. That could only mean . . .

She was there on the floor. I didn't look. I couldn't. I looked at the Dead Man, all four hundred fifty pounds of him, sitting in the chair where he'd been since somebody stuck a knife in him four hundred years ago. Except for a ten-inch elephantlike schnoz he could have passed for the world's fattest human, but he was Loghyr, one of a race so rare nobody has seen a live one in my lifetime. And that's fine by me. The dead, immobile ones are aggravation enough.

See, if you kill a Loghyr, he doesn't just go away. You don't get him out of your hair that easy. He just stops breathing and gives up dancing. His spirit stays at home and gets crankier and crankier. He doesn't decay. At least mine hasn't in the few years I've known him, though he's a little ragged around the edges where the moths and mice and whatnot nibble on him while he naps and there's no one around to shoo them away.

Do not act the fool, Garrett. For once in our acquaintance astound me by pausing to reflect before you leap.

That's the way he is. Usually more so. My tenant and sometime partner, sometime mentor. Despite his control I croaked, "Talk to me, Chuckles. Tell me what it's all about."

Calm yourself. Passion enslaves reason. The wise man . . .

Yeah. He does go on like that, hokey philosopher that he is. Only not in the really grim times . . . I began to suspect something.

Once you get used to a particular Loghyr, you can read more than words when he thinks into your head. He was angry about what had happened but not nearly so outraged and vengeance hungry as he should have been. I began to control myself.

"I did it again, eh?"

You get more exercise jumping to conclusions than you do running.

"She's going to be all right?"

Her chances seem good. She will need the attention of a skilled surgeon, though. I have put her into a deep sleep till such time as one becomes available.

"Thanks. So tell me what you got from her."

She had no idea what it was about. She was involved in nothing. She did not know the man who wielded the knife. He left out his usual stock of sarcastic comments when he added, *She was just coming to see you. She went to sleep completely bewildered.*

He loosened his hold on me, let me settle into the big chair that's there for me when I visit.

Till you lumbered in with your recollections, I assumed it was random violence. Meaning he had sorted through my memories of the chase.

Saucerhead joined us. He leaned on the back of my chair, stared at Tinnie. He jumped to the same conclusion I had. I admired his self-control. He liked Tinnie and had a special place in his heart for guys who wasted women. He'd lost one once, that he'd been hired to protect. No fault of his own. He'd wiped out half a platoon of assassins and had gotten ninety percent killed himself trying to save her. He hadn't been the same since.

I told him, "Smiley over there put her to sleep. She'll be all right, he thinks."

"Sons of bitches must pay anyway," he growled, hanging on to the tough, but he looked relieved all over. I pretended I didn't see his show of "weakness."

The book? the Dead Man asked. *That is all you got before the sniping started?* Like it was my fault. Some sniping was about to get started here. He knew damned well that was all we'd gotten. He'd sifted our minds.

"That's all." Play it straight. That was my new tactic. It drove him crazy when I didn't fight back.

There was nothing in her thoughts about a book.

"Ain't much to go on," Saucerhead said. He had lost his mad urgency. Tinnie was going to be all right. He didn't have to go out and lay waste. Not right away, anyway. He—and I—would keep an eye out for the characters responsible, though.

No. I suggest you both calm yourselves, then recall those blackguards carefully. Any insignificant detail might be consequential. Garrett, if you feel this is of great importance, you might consider collecting the debt that Chodo Contague imagines he owes you.

A reflection of my thoughts, that. "I will if I have to. Too soon to think about that. I need to see Tinnie taken care of and get my mind straightened out before I go off on any crusade." That was a straight line of the sort he scarfs up usually, but this time he let it slide. "Something happens and she goes, I'll ring in Chodo like that. . . ." I snapped my fingers. I'm a fountain of talent.

Chodo Contague, often called the kingpin, is the grand master of organized crime in TunFaire. In some ways he's more powerful than the King. He's no friend. He's damned near the embodiment of everything I hate, the kind of creep I got into my line to pull down. But just by doing my job I've managed to do him some accidental favors. He has an obsessive, if skewed, sense of honor. The slimeball thinks he owes me, and I'll be damned if he won't do almost anything to pay the debt. If I wanted, I could say the word and he'd put two thousand thugs on the street to make us square.

I've avoided collecting because I don't want my name associated with his. Not in any way. Be bad for business if people suspected I was on his pad.

Hell. I haven't really said what I do. I'm what the guys who don't like me call a peeper. An investigator and confidential agent, the way I put it. Pay me—up front—and I'll find out things. More often than not, things you didn't really want to know. I don't dig up much good news. That's the nature of the racket.

On the confidential-agent side I'll do a stand-in, like pay off a kidnapper or blackmailer for you, and make sure there's no last-second comedy. I've worked hard to build a rep as a straight arrow, a guy who plays square, who comes down like the proverbial ton if you mess with my client. Which is why I wouldn't want anybody to think I'd roll over for Chodo.

If Tinnie died, I'd change my rules. For Tinnie it would be dead ahead full speed, and whoever got in my way had best have his gods paid off because I wouldn't slow down till I ate somebody's liver. If Tinnie died.

The Dead Man said she ought to pull through. I hoped he was right. This once. Usually I hope he's wrong because he's damned near infallible and works hard reminding me of that.

Dean came in with a tray, beer, and stronger spirits if we needed them. Saucerhead took a beer. So did I. "That's good. That hits the spot after all that running."

The Dead Man sent, *I suggest you go see her uncle. Inform him what has happened and find out about arrangements. Perhaps he can give you a clue.*

Yeah. He had to bring it up. I'd been wondering about who was going to tell the family. There had to be *somebody* I could stick with that little chore.

The candidates constitute a horde of one, Garrett.

He figured that out all by himself. He is a genius. A certified—and certifiable—genius. Just ask him. He'll tell you about it for hours.

Any other time I would have given him a ration of lip. This time the specter of Willard Tate got in the way. "All right. I'm on my way."

"Me too," Saucerhead said. "There's some things I want to check out."

Excellent. Excellent. Now everything is under control I can catch up on my sleep.

Catch up. Right. In all the years I've known him his waking time hasn't added up to six months.

I let Saucerhead out the front door. Then I headed for the kitchen, got Dean to draw me another of those wonderful beers. "Have to replace everything I sweated out."

He scowled. He has some strong opinions about the way I live. Though he's an employee, I let him speak his mind. We have an understanding. He talks, I don't listen. Keeps us both happy.

I hit the street without much enthusiasm. Old Man Tate and I aren't bosom buddies. I did a job for him once, and for a while afterward he'd thought well of me, but a year of me playing push-me pull-you with Tinnie had somehow soured his outlook.

4

The Tate place will fool you. It's supposed to. From outside it looks like a block of old warehouses nobody bothered to keep up. You can see why from the street out front. First, the Hill. Our overlords are buzzards watching for fortunes to flay through the engines of the law. Second, the slums below. They produce extremely hungry and unpleasant fellows, some of whom will turn you inside out for a copper sceat.

Thus, the Tate place pretending to be poverty's birthplace.

The Tates are shoemakers who turn out army boots and pricey stuff for the ladies of the Hill. They're all masters. They have more wealth than they know what to do with.

I gave their gate a good rattle. A young Tate responded. He was armed. Tinnie was the only Tate I knew who faced the world outside *un*armed. "Garrett. Haven't seen you for a while."

"Tinnie and I were feuding again."

He frowned. "She went out a couple hours ago. I thought she was headed your way."

"She was. I came to see Uncle Willard. It's important."

The kid's eyes got big. Then he grinned. I guess he figured I was going to pop the question. He opened up. "Can't guarantee he'll see you. You know how he is."

"Tell him it can't wait till it's convenient."

He muttered, "Must have been hell being snowed in." He locked the gate. "Rose will be devastated."

"She'll live." Rose was Willard's daughter, his only surviving offspring, hotter than three little bonfires and as twisted as a rope of braided snakes. "She always bounces back."

The kid snickered. None of the Tates had much use for Rose. She was pure trouble. And she never learned.

"I'll tell Uncle you're here."

I went into the central garden to wait. It looked forlorn. Summertimes it's a work of art. The Tates all have apartments in the surrounding buildings. They live there, work there, are born and die there. Some never go outside.

The kid came back looking pained. Willard had scalded his tail for letting me in but apparently hadn't told him to get hurt trying to throw me out.

The thought made me grin. The kid was as big as any Tate gets, about five two. Willard once told me there was elvish blood in the family. It made the girls exotic and gorgeous and the guys handsome but damned near short enough to walk under a horse without banging their heads.

Willard Tate was no bigger than the rest of his clan. A gnome, almost. He was bald on top, had ragged gray hair that hung to his shoulders in back and on the sides. He was bent over his workbench tapping brass nails into the heel of a shoe. He wore a pair of TenHagen cheaters with square lenses. Those don't come cheap.

One feeble lamp battled the dark. Tate worked by touch, really. "You'll ruin your eyes if you don't spring for more light." Tate is one of the wealthiest men in TunFaire and one of the tightest with a sceat.

"You have one minute, Garrett." His lumbago was acting up. Or something. Couldn't be me.

"Straight at it, then. Tinnie's been stabbed."

He looked at me for half the time he'd given me. Then he put his tools aside. "You have your faults, but you wouldn't say that unless you meant it. Tell me."

I told him.

He didn't say anything for a while. He just stared, not at me but at ghosts lurking behind me. His had been a life plagued by loss. His wife, his kids, his brother, all had gone before their time.

He surprised me by not laying it off on me. "You got the man who did it?"

"He's dead." I ran through it again.

"I wish I could have had a piece of him." He rang a bell. One of his nephews responded. Tate told him, "Send for Dr. Meddin. Now. And turn out a half dozen men to walk Mr. Garrett home." Now I had me a "mister."

"Yes sir." The nephew bounced off on a recruiting tour.

"Anything else, Mr. Garrett?"

"You could tell me why anybody would want to kill Tinnie."

"Because she was involved with you. To get at you."

"A lot of people don't like me." Present company included. "But none of them work like that. They wanted to get my goat, they'd burn my house down. With me inside it."

"Then it has to be senseless. Random violence or mistaken identity."

"You sure she wasn't into anything?"

"The only thing Tinnie was involved in was you." He didn't say it but I could hear him thinking, Maybe this will learn her a lesson. "She never left the place except to see you."

I nodded. Undoubtedly he kept track.

I wanted to believe it was random. TunFaire is overcrowded and hagridden by poverty and hardly a day passes when somebody doesn't whittle on somebody with a hatchet or do cosmetic surgery with a hammer. I would have bought it except for those guys who danced the waltzes with me and Saucerhead.

I said, "When we caught him, the guy said 'the book' just before his friends croaked him." *If* those were his friends. "Mean anything to you?"

Tate shook his head. That straggly hair pranced around.

"I didn't figure it would. Damn. You get any ideas, let me know. And I'll keep you posted."

"You do that." My minute had stretched. He wanted to get back to work.

The nephew returned and announced he had a squad assembled. I said, "I'm sorry, sir. I'd rather it had been me."

"So would I." Yes. He agreed a hundred percent. Man. You be nice to some people . . .

plopped into my chair, reported to the Dead Man while the Tate boys collected Tinnie. They had a cart to carry her home. The best medical care would be waiting. It was out of my hands now.

Nothing gained, the Dead Man sent when I finished.

"I think Tate hit it. They got the wrong woman. You've been around awhile." Like half of forever. "You sure 'the book' doesn't ring any bells?"

None. There are books and books, Garrett. Even some men would kill for, considering their rarity or content. I do not hazard uninformed guesses. We cannot, now, be sure that man even meant a book as such. He may have meant a gambling book. He may have meant a personal journal capable of indicating someone. We do not know. Try to relax. Have a meal. Accept the situation, then put it behind you.

"Nobody came around asking about the dead men?" TunFaire's Watch aren't exactly police. Their main mission is to keep an eye out for fires or threats to our overlords. Catching criminals is way down their list, but sometimes they do bumble around and nab a baddie. TunFaire is blessed with some pretty stupid villains.

No one came. Go eat, Garrett. Attend to the needs of the flesh. Allow the spirit to relax and become refreshed. Forget it. All is well that ends well.

Good advice, even coming from him. But he's always so damned reasonable and wise—when he isn't trying to play games with my mind. He got my goat, being cool and sensible. I headed for the kitchen.

Dean was in shock still, distraught because uncaring fate had cast a cold eye so close to home. His mind was a thousand miles away as he stirred some kind of sauce. He didn't look at me as he handed me a plate he'd kept warm. I ate without noticing what, which is a crime itself, considering the class cook Dean is. I was drifting around a few yards away myself. I didn't interrupt the old man's brooding. I was pleased that he cared.

I rose to leave. Dean turned. "People shouldn't ought to do like that, Mr. Garrett."

"You're right. They shouldn't ought. You're a religious sort. Tell the gods thanks for not making it worse than it was."

He nodded. He's a gentle sort generally, a hardworking old fellow trying to support an ungrateful gaggle of eligible but terminally homely nieces who give him more grief than any ten men deserve from their female kin. Generally. Right now he had him a bloodthirst bigger than a vampire who hadn't fed for a year.

I couldn't relax. It was over, but my nerves just wouldn't settle. I prowled up the hall to the front door, peeked outside. Then I checked the small front room to the right like there might be a forgotten blonde cached in there. I was fresh out. I trudged back to the deluxe coffin I call an office, waved at Eleanor on the wall, then crossed the hall to the Dead Man's room. That takes up most of the left side of the house. It contains not only himself but our library and treasury and everything we particularly value. Nothing for me there. I glanced up the stairs without going up, went into the kitchen, and got a mug of apple juice. Then I did the whole route over, taking a little longer at the door to see if my place had become a dwarfish tourist attraction. I didn't see any watchers. Time dragged.

I got on everybody's nerves. That's what I do best, anyway, but now I was fraying my own. Now even I resented my mumbled wisecracks. When Dean growled and tested the heft of his favorite frying pan, I decided to take myself upstairs.

For a while I looked out a window, watching for Saucerhead or somebody in a black hat watching me back. The watched pot didn't boil.

When I got tired of that, I visited the closet where I keep the more lethal tools of my trade. It's a nifty little arsenal, something for every occasion, something to go with every outfit. You never catch me carrying a weapon that clashes.

Everything was in tip-top shape. I couldn't work off any nervous energy sharpening and polishing. I eyeballed the ensemble. Nothing I had was worth much in a scrimmage with crossbowmen.

I did have a few little bottles left over from the time I'd done undercover work for the Grand Inquisitor. I took the case down, looked inside. Three bottles, one emerald, one royal blue, one ruby, each about two ounces. You threw them. Once they broke, the stuff inside took the fight right out of guys. The contents of the red one would melt the flesh off their bones. I was saving that for somebody who really got on my nerves. If I ever used it, I'd have to stand back a ways.

I put the case away, secreted knives all over me, hung the longest tool legal on my belt, then took down my most useful all-round instrument, an oaken head-thumper eighteen inches long. It had a pound of lead inside the business end. It did wonders making me more convincing when I got into an argument.

So what was I going to do now? Go looking for some villains, just on general principles? Sure. Right. The way my luck runs, I'd have a building fall on me before I found any bad boys to astonish and dismay.

I managed to kill time till supper came along. I spent most of it trying to figure out why I was restless and uneasy. Tinnie had been hurt, but she was going to make it. Saucerhead and I had—sort of—dissuaded her attacker from becoming a repeat offender. Everything had turned out all right. Things were going to be fine.

Sure.

6

I didn't get much sleep that night.

It was a time of weirdness for TunFaire, maybe because of the weather. The whole world had turned cockeyed, not just me with my running and my going to bed early so I could get up before anybody sane was oriented vertically. Mammoths had been seen from the city wall. Saber-tooth tigers were at large within a day's travel. There were rumors of werewolves. There were rumors of thunder-lizards being sighted near KirtchHeis, just sixty miles north of TunFaire, two hundred south of their normal range. To our south, centaurs and unicorns, fleeing ferocious fighting in the Cantard, had penetrated Karentine territory. Every night, here in the city, the sky filled with squabbling morCartha, weird creatures who traditionally confined their brawls to rain-forested valleys on the marches of thunder-lizard country.

Where the morCartha disappeared during the day no one knew—nobody gave a big enough care to find out—but all night they zoomed over the rooftops settling old tribal scores or swooped down to mug citizens or to steal anything not nailed down. Most people accepted their presence as proof the thunder-lizards were migrating. In their own country morCartha lived in the treetops and slept during the day. That would make them easy snacks for the taller thunder-lizards. Some of these stand more than thirty feet tall.

Despite the morning's excitement I tried going to bed at what Dean and the Dead Man perversely call a reasonable hour. My theory was that if I rolled out early, my neighbors wouldn't be out to giggle and point at the spectacle of Garrett running laps. But that night the morCartha brought their flying carnival to my neighborhood. It sounded like the aerial battle of the century. Blood and broken bodies and war cries and taunts rained down. Whenever I threatened to drift off, they staged some absurd, cacophonous confrontation right outside my window.

I decided it was time somebody on the Hill suffered a stroke of smarts and enlisted them all as mercenaries and sent them down to the Cantard to look for Glory Mooncalled. Let him lose sleep while they squabbled over his head.

Old Glory probably wasn't getting much sleep, anyway. The Karentine powers that be had thrown everything into the cauldron down there. They were grinding his upstart republic fine, inexorably and inevitably, permitting him no chance to catch his breath and turn his genius toward their despair.

The war between Karenta and Venageta has been going on since my grandfather's time. It's become as much a part of life as the weather. Glory Mooncalled started out a mercenary captain in Venageti service, had a major falling out with the Venageti warlords, and came over to our side swearing mighty oaths of vengeance. Once he had smashed everybody who offended him, he suddenly declared the Cantard—possession of which is what the war is all about—an autonomous republic. All the Cantard's native nonhuman races supported him. So, for the moment, Karenta and Venageta have a common cause, the obliteration of Glory Mooncalled. Once he's gone, it'll be back to war as usual.

All of which is of more interest to the Dead Man than me. I did my five years in the Marines and survived. I don't want to remember. The Dead Man does. Glory Mooncalled is his hobby.

Whatever, I didn't sleep well and I was less cheerful than usual when I got up, which is saying something. On my best mornings I'm human only by charity. Morning is the lousiest time of day. The lower the sun in the east, the lousier that time is.

The racket in the street started about the time I got my feet on the floor.

A woman screamed. She was frightened. Nothing galvanizes me so quickly. I was down at the door with a small arsenal before I started thinking. Somebody was pounding on that door now, yelling my name and begging to be let in. I peeped through the peephole. One ounce of brain was working. I saw a woman's face. Terrified. I fumbled at bolts, yanked the door open.

A naked woman stumbled inside. I gawked for half a minute before my brain started chugging. Then I checked the street. I saw nothing till a thing slightly larger than a spider monkey, built along similar lines but hairless and red, with batlike wings instead of arms and with a spadelike point at the end of its tail, crashed and flopped around, squealing. A city ratman ambled over. The moment it stopped moving, he shoveled it into his wheeled trash bin. The creature's kin didn't protest or claim the body. The morCartha are indifferent to their dead.

So now they were doing it in the daytime, too. If you could call it daytime just because it was light out. Personally, I don't believe daytime really starts till the sun is straight overhead.

I slammed the door, spun around. The woman had collapsed. What I saw in that bad light was enough to make my hair stand up and get split ends.

Not a stitch on her, like I said, but she had the body to wear that kind of outfit. She clutched a raggedly wrapped package in her left hand. I couldn't pry it loose.

The word *flabbergasted* gets bandied about in this age of exaggeration, but you don't often get into a situation where it's appropriate. This was a time when it was appropriate. I didn't know what to do.

Don't get me wrong. I've got nothing against naked women. Especially nothing against naked women when they're beautiful and running around my house. Most especially not when I'm chasing them and they have no intention of getting away. But I'd never had one come to the door all ready to race. I'd never had one drop in and instantly transport herself to dreamland with such diligence that I couldn't wake her again.

I was still trying to figure out what to do when Dean showed up for work.

Dean is my housekeeper and cook, in case you haven't figured that out. He's a sour-faced but sentimental guy about a thousand years old who should have been born a woman because he'd make somebody a great wife. He can cook and keep house and has a tongue to match the nastiest of them. He took one look at the woman. "I just cleaned that carpet, Mr. Garrett. Couldn't you confine your games to the second floor?"

"I just let her in, Dean. She came this way, right off the street. I opened the door, she stumbled in and passed out. Maybe she was hit by the morCartha. She's gone into a fugue. I can't wake her up."

"Must you stare so shamelessly?"

"I don't notice you studying the fly specks on the ceiling." He wasn't *that* old. Nobody ever gets *that* old. And the lady deserved a stare or two. She was the nicest package I'd had stumble in in a long time. "Hell, yes, I must. How often do the gods bother to send us the answer to our prayers?"

He's more alert at that hour than I'll ever be. He honestly believes that getting up before sunrise is a virtue, poor misguided soul. "Attempt at levity noted, Mr. Garrett. Noted and found wanting. I suggest we move her to the daybed and cover her, then get some breakfast into you. You're less at the mercy of adolescent fantasies once you've gotten your blood moving."

"How sharper than a serpent's tooth is the tongue of an ingrate servant."

He knew I couldn't be talking about him. He wasn't a servant. He was an in-house working partner.

He grabbed the woman's ankles. I took the heavy end. Maybe he was put out because the woman had gotten several of his nieces' shares of natural goodies. "Red hair, too," I muttered. "Isn't that nice?" I'm a sucker for redheads. I've been known to favor the occasional blonde, brunette, whatever, too.

Dean would just say I'm a sucker. He might have a point.

We put her on the daybed in the small front room, on the right side of the house. Your left, coming in the front door. She hung on to her package. Once she was set, I moved to the kitchen. Reluctantly. I was thinking maybe I should be there for her when she woke up, just in case she needed to throw herself into somebody's arms and be comforted.

Dean filled me up with breakfast. As I finished up Saucerhead arrived, to supervise me in my pursuit of physical excellence. Or incapacitating cramps, whichever came first. We yakked over tea for a while, me somehow forgetting to mention my nude. Would you tell a pirate where you'd found buried treasure? Then we went outside and got busy with our respective exercise regimens. I wore him down. He ran out of fingers before I ran out of laps.

Puffing and panting and aching, I forgot my mystery guest. Puffing and wheezing is a full-time job.

L ast lap. Beer ahead. Relief only a few yards away. I came off Wizard's Reach full speed, about a walk and a half, snorting like a wounded buffalo, listing from side to side, steering like a ship without a rudder. Only my neighbors watching kept me from getting down and crawling the last hundred feet.

I'd lost count of my laps. Saucerhead had slipped a few extra in on me. I hadn't figured that out till a minute ago. If I lived, I'd get even with him if it was the last thing I did. If that involved running, it *would* be the last thing I did.

I had my chin down. You're not supposed to do that, but I had to keep an eye on my feet. Otherwise they might quit. Meanwhile, I tried to figure how many laps Tharpe had shafted me. I'd lost count because there had been no landmark events to separate one lap from another. There were none to help me come up with an actual number, either. But I knew he'd done it to me.

I reached the foot of the steps honking and snorting, grabbed the handrail, dragged myself up toward the pitcher that would help put the misery behind me.

"This the character I'm looking for?" The voice wasn't familiar.

"That's him." Saucerhead.

"Don't look like much."

"I can't help that. I ain't his mother."

My pal. I got my chin up. Huff. Puff. Saucerhead wasn't alone. Being brilliant, I'd worked that out already. What I hadn't figured out was that he was talking to a woman. Maybe.

At first glance she looked like Tharpe's big sister. Maybe she had a touch of giant in her. She was taller than me by an inch. She had stringy blond hair that would've been nice if she'd washed and combed it. In fact, she had nice stuff in all the right places, only she was so damned big. And so uncaringly kempt. And looked so damned hard.

"The name's Winger, Garrett," she said. "Hunter." Her stance dared me to treat her like a lady. She wasn't dressed like any lady. Lots of worn leather and stuff, that needed cleaning as much as she did. Lots of metal, stuff hanging all over her. She looked like a hunter. She looked like she could whip thunder-lizards with one hand tied behind her. Hell, she could knock them down with her breath.

The name meant nothing to me. She had to be new in town. I would have heard of an amazon like her if she was a regular.

"Yeah, I'm Garrett. So what?" Still gulping air by the bucket, I couldn't get gracious.

"I'm looking for work. New in town."

"No kidding?"

"People I talked to said we might could kind of team up sometimes." She looked at Saucerhead, jerked her head at me. "Kind of puny to have such a big rep."

Tharpe grinned. "Things get exaggerated." He was loving it. The big goof. The way he was grinning I was sure there were wonders yet to come.

"Not much call for hunters in the city," I told her. "We can catch our dinner at the corner butcher."

"Not that kind of hunter, Ace. Manhunter. Bounty hunter." Just in case I'd mistaken her meaning. "Tracker." Her gaze was hard and steady. She worked at being tough. "Trying to make contacts. Trying to get set up. I don't want to have to cross the line to make it."

She had small hands for a woman her size. Her nails were trimmed neatly. But her palms were used to hard work. Looked like she could bust boards with them. Or backs. I wanted to chuckle but decided I might be smart to keep my amusement to myself. Not more than ten thousand people ever said I wasn't smart. "What do you want from me?"

"Whyn't we get in out of the sun, set a spell, down a few brews, let me tell you what I can do?"

Saucerhead was behind her now. Grinning from ear to ear. She must have tried to sell him already. I kept a straight face. "Sure. Why not?" I hammered on the door, glared Tharpe a dagger or three. He thought he'd set me up. I was going to get him for this. Right after I got him for skewing the lap count. Right after I got him for about seven other things on my list.

Dean opened up. He looked at Winger in awe. She snapped, "What you staring at, runt?" Still working hard at that tough.

"Dean, we'll be in the office. Bring us a pitcher. After you lock up." No more free drinks for Tharpe.

I stepped out of Winger's way. "Straight up the hall." I followed her while Dean locked up. She looked around like she was trying to memorize every crack in the walls. I guess Saucerhead was outside har-harring.

"Take that chair," I told Winger, indicating the client's seat. It's wooden, hard as a rock. It's supposed to discourage prolonged visits. They're supposed to sit there only long enough to tell me what they have to, not long enough to bury me in trivia. Theoretically. The real whiners enjoy being miserable.

Winger kept looking around like she was sneaking through enemy territory. I asked, "You looked for anything in particular?"

"You stay alert when you're a woman in a man's racket." Another dose of tough.

"I imagine. What can I do for you, anyway?"

"Like I said, I'm new here. I need to make contacts. You could use an extra hand sometimes, probably. Finding people."

"Maybe." Her alertness had me wound up now. She had something on her mind.

Dean brought the pitcher. I poured. Winger downed a mug, stared at the painting behind me. She shivered. Eleanor can have that effect. The man who painted her was a mad genius. He filled her portrait with indefinable creepiness.

I glanced back. And Winger moved so fast I barely had time to face her again before she had a knife at my throat. A long knife. A knife that looked like a two-handed broadsword right about then. "I'm looking for a book, Garrett. A big one. You wouldn't have it, would you?"

Sure I wouldn't. "I wish I did." But her tone said she wasn't going to believe that. She wasn't going to get confused by facts.

Her knife pricked my throat. Her hand was steady. She was a pro. Not even a little nervous. Me neither. Not much. "I don't have it. How come you think I do?"

She didn't tell me. "I'm going to look. I'm going to take this place apart. You want to stay healthy, stay out of my way. You want your house to stay healthy, give me the book now."

I gave her a look at my fluttering-eyebrow trick. I tossed in a big smile. "Have fun."

She smiled back. "Think you can take me? Don't even think about trying."

"Little old me? Perish the thought. Hey, Chuckles. Time to do your stuff."

Winger glanced around. Her knife hand remained steady. She couldn't figure out who the hell I was talking to. "Who the hell you talking to?"

"My partner."

She opened her mouth. That was as far as she got. The Dead Man turned her into a living statue. In the last instant her expression turned to horror. I edged away from her knife, got out of my chair. "You got nerve," I said. She could hear and understand. "But nerve isn't everything." Nobody who'd studied me would try to take me in my own house. The Dead Man doesn't get out much, but that hasn't kept him from acquiring a reputation.

I patted Winger's considerable shoulder. It was rock hard. "Live and learn, sweetheart." I finished my mug, strolled across the hall. "What's the story, Smiley?"

No story, Garrett. She has told you everything. She is looking for a book. This is her first job in TunFaire. She was hired by a man named Lubbock. He paid her thirty marks to shake you down. He will give her forty more if she finds the book.

"Interesting coincidence. What's she know about that gang yesterday?"

Nothing. Obviously she was selected for that reason. She can tell no one anything because she knows nothing.

"I guess friend Lubbock did *his* research."

Perhaps.

"She has an accent." She was Karentine but from way out there somewhere.

Hender. West Midlands.

"Never heard of it."

Not surprising. Population less than a hundred. A farming village. A suggestion. Assuming your curiosity has been piqued, as mine has, have her watched. Her contacts might prove interesting. It seems likely that Lubbock is not her employer's real name. She believes it to be a pseudonym herself.

Sounded good to me. Something was going on. And I don't like sitting around waiting for things to happen. "Right. Can't use Saucerhead, though. She knows his face. I could dash over to Morley's."

Quickly?

Sarky old clown can put a lot into a single word. He'd recovered from his earlier consideration for my feelings, was back to letting me know what he thought of my ways.

"I'm gone."

I got back faster than either of us expected. I had some luck.

Saucerhead was still loafing on the stoop. He hadn't finished the pitcher Dean had provided for my run. He had company again, a local blackheart called Squirrel. I don't know Squirrel's real name. I never heard him called anything else. He was a skinny little gink with atrocious posture, a pointy face and buckteeth, and huge ears that stuck straight out from the side of his head. He'd have trouble making any headway walking into a light breeze.

They didn't call him Squirrel because of his looks. Somebody left something out when they gave him his brains. He was a first-class goofball.

And a second-class thug.

He worked for Chodo Contague. He was more than a gofer but not one of the heavyweights, like Sadler and Crask. I didn't know Squirrel well but did know he wasn't somebody who was going to elevate the standards of the neighborhood.

I looked at him. He gave me a grin full of teeth. Friendly as hell. That was Squirrel. Always trying to be your pal—till it came time to put a knife in your back. Squirrel desperately wanted to be liked. And wanted to make Chodo's first team even more. "Garrett. The boss heard about your trouble." Chodo hears everything. "Sent me over to help. Said if you need anything, just yell. Said he don't hold with anybody hurting women."

Sure he didn't. Unless they worked for him, showed a wisp of independence. But he probably doesn't consider hookers women.

I didn't want to take anything from Chodo, but, on the other hand, using Squirrel was so damned convenient. So what the hell. "You showed up at the perfect time."

Squirrel grinned. He loved praise. If that was praise. Weird little guy. "How's your woman, Garrett? I should've asked. Chodo wanted to know. Said he'd send somebody to look after her if you want."

"She'll be fine. Her family is taking care of her." They could afford the same quality care Chodo could provide. "If something turns bad, they'll let me know." Willard would do that. He'd expect me to hunt down everybody even remotely responsible if Tinnie died. Then he'd cut out their livers and eat them.

"So I'm right on time. What can I do for you?"

I shivered. Squirrel had a whiny voice to go with an ingratiating manner. Slimy little weasel. But dangerous. Very dangerous.

"There's a woman going to come out of here. Tall blonde amazon type. Follow her. See where she goes. Be careful. She's maybe some bad road." I had no idea how good Squirrel was. His only recommendation was that he had stayed alive so far.

"I can handle it." Like he heard me wondering.

"What's up?" Saucerhead asked.

"She pulled a knife on me. Wanted a book. The Dead Man put her in freeze."

"A book again?"

"Yeah."

"You getting into it even if Tinnie's all right?"

"Say I'm curious." I wasn't getting into anything. I didn't have a client. I don't like work, anyway. I mean, why bother as long as I've got a roof over my head and something to eat?

On the other hand, I might fish a fee out of this somehow. And it does take money to pay Dean and to keep the house from falling down.

"Spread out," I told those two. "Saucerhead, take off. She'd recognize you."

"Sure. You need me, check Morley's place."

I waved them good-bye, slipped inside, stuck my head into the Dead Man's room, whispered, "Turn her loose?" I whispered because I didn't want Winger to hear me.

Yes.

I returned to my office, pried the knife out of Winger's hand, settled myself, started cleaning my nails. The Dead Man turned loose. If somebody could jump out of their skin, Winger would have. "Welcome to the big city, Winger. Something to keep in mind. Everybody has a trick up his sleeve here."

She gobbled air and headed for the hallway. I asked, "You mind telling me where to find Lubbock? Can't say I like people I don't know siccing hired blades on me."

That shook her even more. She hadn't mentioned the name.

I followed her to the door, adding more questions calculated to rattle her so she wouldn't look for Squirrel. She was almost running when she hit the street.

I looked around. I didn't see Squirrel or Saucerhead. I didn't spot anybody interested in my place, either. I went inside to talk to Dean about supper.

••••8

Dean didn't want any suggestions. He never does, but he doesn't mind having me offer. Then he can turn me down.

I settled at the table. Dean asked, "What was that all about?"

"I'm not sure. Somebody called Lubbock sent her to shake me down for a book."

He frowned. He's mastered the art. His face turns into a badland of shadowed canyons. "That fellow who stabbed Miss Tinnie . . ."

"Yeah."

"There's something going on." Another genius. My place is lousy with them.

"Yeah."

"You going to find out what?"

"Maybe." I didn't have much inclination. The world is full of mysteries. Do I have to solve them all? Without even anybody paying me? But I did wonder why Winger had come to me.

Somebody pounded on the front door. I grumbled something about maybe it was time to move. Too many people knew where I lived. Dean said, "That's Mr. Tharpe."

"You can tell from here?"

"I know his knock."

Right. Sure he did. But why argue? Let him have his little fantasies. I headed up the hall. . . . "Whoa!" There was Saucerhead. Inside. "What the hell?"

He looked a little croggled himself. "It just opened up when I knocked." He stared at the door like it would maybe sprout fangs.

Couldn't be. I'd locked it myself. That's a prime rule. There are people on those mean streets dumb enough to drop in. Dumb enough not to worry about the Dead Man. I just sent one packing.

I puzzled it for half a minute before I caught a glimmer of a possibility. "Three geniuses!" Saucerhead scowled, baffled. I popped my head into the small front room.

My guest had vanished. "Dean!" I'd forgotten her in the excitement of my run and those cozy moments with Winger.

"Mr. Garrett?"

"Something's missing." I indicated the small front room. "And Saucerhead found the door open."

Dean looked properly amazed. He went into the room and sniffed around, making sure everything was there. Like it was his own stuff. "The blanket is gone."

She would've taken something. You have to work to attract attention on a TunFaire street, but naked will do it every time.

Saucerhead asked, "What's going on?"

"You know as much as I do. Dean, get Mr. Tharpe a beer. I'm going to talk to the Dead Man."

Dean herded Saucerhead toward the kitchen. I dropped in on my permanent guest, who—I sensed before I said a word—had fallen into a surly mood. His natural state. "What's eating you all of a sudden?"

You failed to mention this visitor who has vanished.

"Why should I?" He knew all the comings and goings.

He was so disturbed he didn't prance around it. *I was unaware of her presence. This is unprecedented. I had not thought it possible.* He went off somewhere inside himself, looking for explanations for the impossible.

He was disturbed? I was beside myself. On both sides. All three of me were one breath short of a panic. Somebody could come and go around here without us having any warning?

"This doesn't sound good, Mr. Garrett," Dean said from behind me.

"Not only a genius but a master of understatement." I considered. "She can't have much of a head start. She'll stand out in the crowd. I better catch her."

"Catch who?" Saucerhead asked. So I explained.

"Naked women just falling through your door." He sneered "How do you do it? That don't never happen to me."

"You don't live right. We don't have time to hang around yakking."

"We? You got a pixie in your pocket?"

"You'd be impressed. That is, if you ever saw her. Imagine Tinnie but with a little more in the lung department."

"I wasn't up to much else anyway. Let's go."

But that little weasel of a god who watches out for Garrett's affairs didn't figure I ought to go chasing redheads. No sense of proportion at all.

Maybe he was just trying to save my legs. He did deliver another one to my door.

Dean was there already. He'd been fixing to let us out when the knock came. Now he was wringing his hands. I asked, "What have we got?"

"Another woman."

I opened up and looked her over. That took a while. You're going to do a job, do it right. There was plenty there to appreciate, though in a small package. I was surprised the whole neighborhood wasn't howling. Hot stuff. All the right goodies packed together in all the best ways. Big green eyes. Big, big green eyes. Lips a dangerous red and puffy, the kind that yell, "Come and get it, I can take it, what are you waiting for?" Breasts like man oh man how did she get that on and how does she keep them in there?

But . . .

She *was* a little thing, maybe five feet two on her tiptoes. And she was another redhead. She had lots of wild red hair the way Tinnie had wild red hair. The way my naked visitor had had wild red hair. In fact, she was a ringer for that gal but definitely not the same woman. I wondered if she was a sister. Or was that little weasel in the sky just poking me in the eye by piling on the redheads?

I didn't say anything. I couldn't. I just led her into that pretentious closet I call an office. Dean brought a pitcher without being asked. He looked numb. The way I was going to be numb if I kept getting pitchers delivered. Another redhead. I hoped some light was going to get shed here. Real soon.

All of a sudden I was convinced that guy with the mustache had thought he was hitting this woman, or the naked one, when he'd stabbed Tinnie. I settled, drank a mug, studied her. She looked back boldly, still without having spoken. She didn't go for come-hither but, damn, it was built in, part of the package. She was the kind of woman who'd sit there and smolder while darning her grandfather's socks. The kind that makes me want to run out back and yell at the sky in sheer joy that I share the same world.

I squeaked, "I'm Garrett. I guess you want to see me." Sometimes I'm so cool I amaze even me.

"Yes."

Yes what? I took a drink so I wouldn't pant all over her. I believe in long courtships. Fifteen minutes at least. I swallowed and croaked, "So?"

"I need someone to help me. Someone like you."

I grinned from ear to ear. Could I help her? You betcha . . . I'd give it my best shot. . . .Hey! Garrett! Let's calm down a little. Let's get the chemistry under control. Anyway, I'd already begun to suspect that this wasn't a match made in heaven. She was smoldering, but that wasn't my fault. That was just her being her. Whoever she was. "Well?"

"I need someone to find something for me."

"That's what I do. Find things. But sometimes people are sorry when I do."

She just sat there heating the place up while I started to sweat. I turned sideways and studied Eleanor out of the corner of my eye. A tall, cool, slim, ethereal blonde, Eleanor has what it takes to bring me back to earth. I talk to Eleanor when no one else will listen. She's my rock in turbulent seas. I wondered what the real Eleanor would think if she knew how I used her portrait. I didn't think she'd mind.

The redhead asked, "Is that someone special?"

"Yes. Her name was Eleanor Stantnor. She was the wife of a client. I never really met her. He murdered her twenty years before he hired me. All he got for his trouble was found out for his old crime. I took the painting for my fee. Yeah. She's special. And if she was around, she'd be as old as my mother. But I'd probably fall in love with her anyway." I faced the redhead. "Let's get down to it."

"Have I come at a bad time?"

"You've come at the perfect time. You're almost a ringer for a friend of mine somebody tried to kill out front yesterday. I have a feeling you could maybe shed some light on why."

She started to say something. What I'd said sank in. Her mouth made an *O*. Her eyes got even bigger. She started to get up, sank back, shook fetchingly.

"My friend's name is Tinnie Tate. She never hurt anybody. She's got hair like yours and she's about your height. A little less rounded, here and there, near as I can tell from here, but not enough so anyone could make a case of it. She was coming to see me when some scumbag stuck a knife in her. For no damned reason I could figure till I got a look at you."

"Oh, my," she breathed. "I've got to get out of here. He knows. I've got to go."

"You aren't going anywhere, sweetheart. Not till I know what the hell is going on."

She just sat there oh-mying and heating up the room. I thought about having Dean throw cold water on her, but that would just steam the place up and cause the wallpaper to peel. I said, "Tinnie getting hurt makes me mad. Some other guys, too. Some bad people. Rich people. Her people. They want blood. You look like a gal who knows how to take care of herself. Maybe you wouldn't want to get caught in the middle of all those angry people."

Her pretty little face turned puzzled.

Was I trying to scare her? You bet I was.

She just said, "Oh," like it wasn't very important.

"I figure the guy who stuck Tinnie thought he was getting you." Sure, I was fishing. You don't throw out a hook, you never get a nibble. "That's the only way it makes any sense. He mistook her for somebody else. So let's you and me get to the point." I got up and walked around the desk.

"I made a mistake coming here." She started to get up.

I sat her down. "You made your mistake when you told somebody somewhere that you were thinking about coming here. That worried somebody. He tried to off my lady. Spill. I'm not in a good mood anymore."

Actually, I was being gentle. I had the Dead Man across the hall. All I needed to do was keep her mind frothing so he could get at anything interesting in there.

She tried to get up again. I sat her down with more force. She looked more irritated than scared. That didn't fit.

"The story, lady. Maybe starting with your name."

She looked down at her hands. Man, those were fine hands.

"My name is Carla Lindo Ramada. I'm a chambermaid in the home hold of Lord Baron Cleon Stonecipher."

"Never heard of him." But if all his help looked like this, I'd consider relocating. "Out of town, I take it. What about this baron?"

"He's kind of at the edge of the story. He's about two hundred years old and just lies in bed waiting to die. Only he has a curse on him. He can't. He just keeps getting older. But that's not important. The witch is. The one that put the curse on him. They call her the Serpent. She lives in the castle, too, only nobody ever sees her. Nobody knows what she looks like except her own men. All anybody really knows is she won't take the curse off the baron until he makes her his heir."

"Huh?"

"She wants the castle. It sits way up in the Hamadan Mountains, near the border between Karenta and Therpra. Both kingdoms claim it, but neither has any real control. The Serpent wants the castle because it's invulnerable."

I wondered if Miss Ramada could be half as slow as she sounded. I glanced at Eleanor. She didn't give me a clue. Hell. If she wasn't a genius, so what? She'd never had to use her head. In this world women who look like that never have to work for anything. The only lesson they need to learn is how to pick the times to wag their tails.

"To the point. What're you doing here? I want to know why Tinnie got stabbed. We'll get into background if it seems important."

She showed that flicker of irritation again. "The Serpent was making a book. They called it a book of dreams or a book of shadows. The Baron thought she was putting most of her powers into it. He thought if he could grab it, he would run her out of the castle. He told his men to steal it. They waited till her guard was down. They grabbed the book. There was a fight. Most of the Baron's men were killed. So were a lot of the Serpent's guards. A man named Holme Blaine escaped with the book, but he didn't take it to the Baron. He brought it to TunFaire. The Baron sent me to get it back because I was the only one he trusted. When I asked around for someone who might help me your name kept coming up. I decided to see you. Here I am. But I think I made a mistake."

I had a strong feeling she wasn't telling me the truth, the whole truth, and nothing but the truth. But the Dead Man could straighten out the little details. "See me why?"

"I want you to find the book of dreams."

Sure. I looked at Eleanor. She gave me a blank stare in return. Not much help there, honey. I checked the redhead again. Damn, she was a sizzler. "So who tried to kill my friend? And why?"

"The Serpent's men, probably. I know they're here. I've seen them. Did you see them?"

I described them carefully.

"The man with the mustache sounds like Elmore Flounce. Even his friends won't mourn him. The ratman might be Keem Lost Knife. Nastier than Flounce. The ogre could be Zacher Hoe, a hunter and tracker. But the Serpent has other ogres. The dwarves . . . I don't know. She had dozens around."

"Hunh. Somewhere to start." I hoped the Dead Man was taking her apart inside.

The redhead started wringing her hands. That isn't something you see much, especially in younger people. The only wringer I know is Dean. It seemed studied. "Will you help me find Holme Blaine, Mr. Garrett? Will you help me recover the book of dreams? I'm desperate."

All alone and desperate, battered by powerful forces. A sure way to sew Garrett up. Only I didn't *feel* her desperation. I was becoming disenchanted so fast I almost had to work to pant. String her along, Garrett. What's to lose? "I have problems of my own. But if I come across your book, I'll snap it up."

She gave me a look that melted my spine despite my restored cynicism. It made me want to grab up Dean and the Dead Man and toss them into the street. She took out a doeskin sack, removed five silver coins. "I have to keep a little to live on while you find the book. I'm sorry I can't give you more. It's all we could scrape together. The Serpent grabs all the silver she can find."

Silver had gotten scarce since Glory Mooncalled took over the mines in the Cantard. I opened my mouth to tell her she didn't need to beggar herself. The sucker side of me was wide-awake.

Take it.

The Dead Man seldom sends a thought beyond the confines of his own quarters. If he does, I don't argue. His reasons generally stand up. But having him jump in ruined my concentration. There were a hundred questions I should have asked the woman, but instead I said, "I'll have a friend of mine see you safely to wherever you're staying." Saucerhead was hanging around somewhere.

She stood. "That's not necessary."

"I think it is. There's been a knife used once already. Probably meant for you. By now I expect the people who did it know they missed. Understand?"

"I suppose." That irritation again. "Thank you. I'm new at this. I don't expect people to be that way."

Really?

She was good. Give her that. She really was good. I called out, "Dean, tell Mr. Tharpe to see the lady safely tucked away home. Ask him to scout the area, see if she's being watched."

Dean stepped into the doorway, nodding. As I'd suspected, he'd been out there eavesdropping. "Miss? If you will?" He could turn on the charm for a guest, that old boy.

I didn't think about the questions I should've asked till after I heard the door close. But what the hell? I could get the answers from the Dead Man.

ean came back from the front door as I headed across the hall. "She was lying, Mr. Garrett."

"She wasn't telling the whole truth, that's for sure."

"Not telling a word of it if you ask me."

"It shouldn't matter. Let's find out what old Smiley plucked out of the air between her ears."

Dean shivered. I can't figure it. After all this time he ought to be used to the Dead Man.

I added the Ramada woman's money to the pile under the Dead Man's chair. I settled into my own, glanced around. Dean had been slacking again. He gets the creeps in there, so he lets cleanup slide till I jump on him or do it myself. The bugs were ready to take over. "What did you think of my visitor?"

Will you never outgrow that adolescent sense of humor?

Crumbs. Now he was getting on me for what I was thinking. "I hope not, Chuckles." There. Damned for it, I might as well say it. "Grown-ups are so stodgy."

As Dean observed, she was lying.

"So what's her real story?"

I dare not hazard a guess.

Oh-oh. This didn't sound good.

I was unable to capture any but the most fleeting surface thoughts.

Oh, my. What the hell? "I thought you could read anybody." This was getting to be a bad habit. Was he getting near the end, slipping over the edge?

Only simple minds.

Ouch! "And you complain about my sense of humor? What's it mean?"

That she is no chambermaid. She bears close observation—not that way—though we have no real business mixing in here. I got the distinct impression he wanted to mix.

Not in the manner you have in mind.

"What's wrong with mixing business with pleasure? She was. . . ."

Yes. She was. And what else?

"Hey! She's a client now. A paying client."

And it is quite obvious why. Amaze me sometime, Garrett. Think with your brain instead of your glands. Just once. Astonish your friends and confound your enemies.

I considered sulking. I considered mentioning the fact that I hadn't broken a sweat over Winger—though even that wouldn't have been a definitive truth. Winger's only distracting feature was her size. "Hell. You're just being sour grapes because you can't anymore."

Which was near enough the truth that he changed the subject. *How do you propose finding the book she wants? With no more information than you cozened out of her? You are such a clever interrogator.*

"How was I to know you'd gone feeble?"

You have to learn to carry yourself, Garrett. I cannot do it all for you. Rather than start a quarrel, I suggest you try to overtake Mr. Tharpe and engage him to watch the woman.

"How about the book she wants? It has to be the book we heard about before. What about it?"

Nothing about it. A book of shadows, a book of dreams, you tell me. Something mystical, presumably. But the concept is unfamiliar. Knowing what that book is might well illuminate everything else. She suggested a great many dwarves were associated with the woman she called the Serpent. That is unusual. Even unlikely, I would suspect. Perhaps you should visit the local enclave and see if anyone can elucidate. I believe the dwarf Gnorst, the son of Gnorst of Gnorst, is still canton praetor. Yes. By all means. Go see him. Invoke my name. He owes me a favor.

The old bag of bones was getting going. He was more interested than I was. But he's a sucker for a puzzle.

"Come on, Old Bones. Not even a dwarf gets stuck with a name like a hay-fever attack. Does he? And how can he owe you one? I've never seen any dwarves around here."

They are long-lived, Garrett. They have excellent memories and a delicate sense for the proprieties of balance.

That was supposed to put me in my place. Water off a duck, man. Us short-lifers don't have time to worry about gaffes.

Once you visit the dwarves, you might enlist Mr. Dotes. If Mr. Tharpe learns nothing useful, and the Squirrel person likewise, you might begin researching the woman's story, detail by detail. Heraldry and peerage experts should know this baron and his stronghold. Traders and travelers who visit the region might cast light on events there.

"Go teach Grandma to suck eggs. You're on my turf now."

I am? I am talking legwork here, Garrett. Remember that facet of this business to which you are allergic?

A base canard. The sour grapes of a guy who hasn't gotten out of his chair for four hundred years. Though it *is* easier just to stir the pot and see what floats to the top. "Guess I'll see if Dean will hang around. If he'll stay late, I'll head for Dwarf Fort."

I went to the kitchen, hoisted me a brew. Of course Dean would stay over. Now that things were happening I couldn't run him off. Tinnie was one of his favorite people. He wanted to see somebody get hurt for hurting her. "So hold the fort," I told him. "His Nibs has me off to the realm of the short and surly."

"Don't be out too late. I'm making deep-dish apple cobbler. Better when it isn't reheated."

Surprise, surprise. That old boy knows how to take my mind off my troubles. One more talent and I'd marry him.

I trotted up to my special closet and dressed myself for the street, then headed out. Not for the first time I didn't have the foggiest notion what the hell I was doing. Or maybe it was the first time and it just hadn't ever stopped.

11

The Dead Man had suggested a stop, coming back, at the Joy House, owned and operated by one Morley Dotes, friend of mine, professional vegetarian, assassin, and elf-human breed. I gave it a think and decided to skip it. Morley is handy when the going gets rough, but he has his liabilities. Most of them are female. No sense bringing him in where he'd face so much temptation. Besides, not having him in meant the odds were better for me.

The Joy House. Some dumb name for a restaurant with a menu fit only for livestock. How about the Manger, Morley? How about the Barn? Or the Stable? Though that kind of smacked of upscale chic.

What people call Dwarf Fort or Dwarf House sits on four square blocks behind the levee in Child's Landing. The Landing abuts the river north of the Bight, where the big water swings sharply southwest and the wharves and docks start and go on for miles, all the way to the wall. Legend says the Landing was settled when humans first came into the region. First there was a fort, then a village that grew because it lay near the confluence of three major rivers. Then there were more fortifications and a growth of industry during the Face Wars, when human insecurities compelled our ancestors to prove they could kick ass on the older races.

The Face Wars were a long time ago. Things have come full circle. Now the Landing is occupied by nonhumans come to grab at the wealth floating around because of Karenta's endless war with Venageta.

I can always work up a case of indignation about the war and its spin-offs. One is, the nonhumans are picking our pockets. Our overlords are cheering them on. Someday they'll be picking our bones.

That's not racist, either. I get along with everybody but ratmen. Our rulers, in their wisdom, in their infallible opportunism, made treaties with these other races that shield them from military service even if they've lived as Karentines for ten generations. They gobble the privileges and don't pay the price. They're getting fat making the weapons carried by youths who couldn't be conscripted if the nonhumans weren't there to replace them in the economy.

If you're human and male, you'll do five years in service. Nowadays, with the Cantard in the hands of Glory Mooncalled and his mercenaries and native allies, they're talking about making that six years. Meaning even fewer survivors coming home.

I'm bitter. I admit it. I survived my five and made it home, but I was the first of my family to do so. And nobody thanked me for my trouble when I got back.

Hell with it.

Dwarf House covers four blocks. A north-south street cuts through the middle. A canal spur runs through east to west. Rumor says the blocks are connected by tunnels. Maybe. They're connected by bridges four stories up. Make that four human stories. Dwarves are dwarves. There would be more floors.

The buildings have no outside windows and few doors. Humans seldom get inside. I had no idea what to expect. All I knew was if they let me in and didn't want me out, I was sunk. Not even my pal the King would come rescue me. Dwarf House enjoys virtual extraterritoriality.

I looked the place over before I knocked. I didn't like what I saw. I knocked anyway. Somebody has to do these things. Generally somebody too dim not to back off.

I knocked again after a reasonable wait. They weren't in any hurry in there.

I knocked a third time.

The door swung inward. "All right! All right! You don't have to break it down. I heard you the first time." The hairy runt in red and green was probably six hundred years old and had been assigned to the door because of his winning personality.

"My name is Garrett. The Dead Man sent me to talk to Gnorst Gnorst."

"Impossible. Gnorst is a busy dwarf. He doesn't have time to entertain every Tall One who wanders past. Go away."

I didn't move except to insert a foot into the doorway.

The dwarf scowled. I guess. He wasn't much more than eyes inside a beard big enough to hide storks' nests. "What do you want?"

"Gnorst. He owes the Dead Man."

The dwarf sighed. What might have been a conciliatory smile stirred the brush on his face. He grunted and made noises that would be considered rude at the dinner table. "I'll inform the Gnorst." *Bam!* He slammed the door. I barely saved my foot. Then I snickered. These characters had to get a little more imaginative. I mean, Gnorst Gnorst, son of Gnorst, the Gnorst of Gnorst? Hell. I guess they don't have much trouble remembering who's related to who. If Gnorst lost his voice, he could answer most personal questions by blowing his nose.

I bet it makes perfect sense to dwarves.

The hair ball was back in five minutes. Probably record time for him. "Come in. Come in." Either the Dead Man's name was magic or they were short on chow for their pet rats. I hoped the character with the imaginative name was impressed with my credential. "Follow me, sir. Follow me. Mind your head, sir. There'll be low ceilings."

The door dwarf did me the added courtesy of lighting a torch off a lamp that yielded a light so feeble it would have done me no good at all. He gave me a look that said this was first-class treatment, properly reserved for visiting royalty.

Dwarf House inside was all gloom and smell, like tenements where families crowd in four to the flat. Only more so. Ventilation was nonexistent.

We trudged up stairs. We went down stairs. I stooped a lot as we marched through workshops where dwarves by the platoon worked on as many projects as there were dwarves working. The lighting was uniformly abysmal, but my guide's torch added enough to reveal that these were all proud craftsmen. Each dwarf's product was the best he could fashion. Which would make that item the best of its kind. Dagger, shield, plate armor, clock, or clockwork toy, each was a work of art. Each was unique. Each artisan was a master.

My lower back was gnawing at me before we were halfway where we were going. I breathed through my mouth because of the smell. I hoped nobody took offense. The racket was incredible. Those dwarves banged and clanged and scraped and squeaked like crazy, all for the sake of maintaining an image as industrious little buggers. I bet they started loafing the second I was out of sight.

12

The dwarf with the silly name didn't look silly. Mostly he looked hairy. I assumed a beard was an emblem of status. He was two beady black eyes peeking out of gray brush. I couldn't tell what he was wearing behind all the foliage. He did have a standard-issue sort of dwarf's hat perched on top, complete with pheasant tail feather.

Gnorst of the many Gnorsts met me in a shaded garden on top of one of the buildings. Very stylized and arty, that garden, with white marble gravel paths, teensy trees, little wooden bridges over fish ponds. The works, all in a style usually associated with high elves.

I rubbed the small of my back and gawked. Gnorst said, "An affectation of mine, Mr. Garrett. My tastes are very undwarfish. My worldly successes allow me to indulge my peculiarities." This before the introductions and amenities.

"It's restful," I said. "I'm surprised to see it atop a building."

My guide faded away. Another hair ball brought refreshments. The goodies included beer. Maybe they'd heard of me. I took a long drink. "You all make beer like you do everything else."

It wasn't that good but I had to be diplomatic. Gnorst was pleased. Maybe he'd had some hand in its brewing.

Dwarves shun alcohol and drugs, so wouldn't have any real standard by which to judge the product.

"I wish I had time for a relaxed chat, Mr. Garrett. I'd love to catch up on the adventures of my old friend, your partner."

"My partner?" Maybe he is but I don't go around admitting it in public. I laughed. "I'll forget you said that. I don't want to give him ideas."

"To be sure. He's stubborn at times. I'll drop in someday. It's been too long. Meanwhile, indulge my impatience. I'm pressed."

"Sure. I'm in a hurry myself."

"What brought you, then?"

"The Dead Man's idea. A friend of mine was knifed yesterday. The gang that did it were mostly dwarves."

Gnorst popped up. "Dwarves! Involved in a killing?"

"Attempted killing. So far," I explained.

"Strange. Very strange." But he relaxed visibly, like maybe he'd concluded his own bunch couldn't be responsible. "I don't see how I can help you."

"The Dead Man hoped you could give me a line on those guys. The dwarf community is pretty tight."

"This one is. But there are dwarves who aren't part of this enterprise. Still . . . The behavior isn't to be countenanced. It aggravates prejudice. That's bad for business. I'll quiz my people. Someone may know those dwarves—though I hope not. A dwarf gone bad is a bad dwarf indeed."

That sounded like a proverb. I told him, "Thanks for your time. I didn't think it would help. One more thing. You ever heard of something called a book of shadows? Or a book of dreams?"

He jumped like somebody goosed him with a hot poker. He stared at me a whole minute. I exaggerate not. Then he squeaked, "A book of dreams?"

"A woman came to the house before I came over here. She looked a lot like my friend who got stabbed. I think she was the intended victim. She wanted to hire me. Gave me a long story about a witch called the Serpent and a book of dreams that got stolen from her and is supposed to be in TunFaire now."

"Excuse me, Mr. Garrett." Gnorst scuttled off, mumbled at the guy who'd brought the beer. He stomped back over. "I just canceled some appointments. You have more time."

"Did I ring a bell or something?"

"A gong. A carillon. I guess you're unfamiliar with early dwarf history."

"Everybody else's, too. What's up?"

"You've recalled an ancient terror."

"Maybe you'd better explain." Before I got dizzy.

"The Book of Dreams, more often called the Book of Shadows, is infamous in dwarfish legend. It must be unimaginably ancient to you. It dates from before men walked the earth."

Yesterday's breakfast is unimaginably ancient to me most of the time, but I didn't say so. I didn't want to seem shallower than I am. Wipe off that sneer.

"In those days dwarfish sorcerers were quite powerful, Mr. Garrett. And some were quite dark. The most powerful and darkest was Nooney Krombach, who created the Book of Shadows."

Praise me, I kept a straight face. Nooney Krombach. I reminded myself that they probably find our names just as quaint. "Nooney Krombach?"

"Yes. Quite possibly fanciful, of course. Like so many saints in human mythologies. But he doesn't have to have existed to have influenced his future."

"I understand." I did, because just a few months ago I'd survived a case involving several of TunFaire's religions. This city is cursed with a thousand cults.

"Krombach's legend has led thousands of would-be masters of the world to attempt to create their own Book of Shadows."

That was fine by me but didn't make anything clearer. "What was it?"

"A book of magic. One hundred sheets of brass hammered paper thin, bound in tooled mammoth leather, every page bearing a spell of immense potency. And every spell created and set down with our dwarfish passion for perfection."

I began to see why people were after this book. But not why they were after me. I didn't have any grimoires lying around the house. Gnorst mistook my frown for puzzlement.

"These spells are very specialized, Mr. Garrett. Each enchantment, one to the page, properly employed, will allow the book's user to assume a different form and character. In other words, the book's user is able to assume any of a hundred guises by turning to the proper page and reading aloud. He is able to become any of a hundred people—or whatever creature might be inscribed."

"Huh?" I wasn't being dumb. But that was a big load. My imagination grabbed the idea and darted around. I gulped. "You saying this Serpent had the Book of Dreams and somebody stole it?"

"*The* Book of Shadows was destroyed, at great cost to the ancients. The characters it contained were all wicked. If your visitor told the truth, the witch she mentioned was trying to create her own book of shadows. What could she have possibly offered them?"

"Who?" I was having trouble keeping up.

"Those dwarves. The ones you encountered. It isn't possible to create a book of shadows without dwarfish craftsmen. But no sane dwarf would lend himself to an evil of that magnitude. . . . But you don't care about that."

I did and I didn't. I was way out at sea, without a rudder, taking waves and wind on the beam.

Troubled, Gnorst started pacing. He looked like a hairy egg on stubby legs, wobbling. "This is bad, Mr. Garrett. This is very bad." He repeated himself several times. I didn't say anything back because I figured I'd said everything I had to say. "This is awful. This is grotesque. This is *terrible*." I'd started to get the idea he thought this wasn't good. He spun on me. "She said the book is here, this woman? Here in TunFaire?"

"She said she thought it was."

"We have to find it and destroy it before it can be put to use. Did she say it was complete?"

"She said it was taken. Stolen by a character named Holme Blaine. That's all. She didn't go into details. She just wanted to hire me to find it."

"Don't. Don't go near the thing. An evil that great . . . Let us handle it. No human is pure enough of heart to resist." He wasn't talking to me anymore. He went on not talking to me. "This will ruin me. My production schedule will go to hell. But I have no choice." He remembered me, whirled. "You're a cruel man, Mr. Garrett."

"Say what?"

"You've made it impossible for us to get any work done while this monstrosity is loose. Our entire industry may collapse."

Right after the moon fell into the sea. He was overreacting. "I don't get it."

"Imagine yourself to be deeply evil. Then imagine yourself with the power to become any of a hundred other people, each designed to your specification. One might be a superassassin. Another might be a master thief. One might be . . . anything. A werewolf. You see what I mean?"

"Oh. Yeah." I'd begun to catch on but not clearly enough. The possibilities I'd imagined originally had been much too picayune.

"Armed with a completed book, that witch would be almost invincible. And as long as she lived in the Book of Shadows, she'd be immortal. If you killed the persona she was wearing, she'd still have ninety-nine lives. If she prepared properly. Plus her own. And she'd only be vulnerable in her natural form. Which she would avoid assuming because she *would be* vulnerable."

I got it. Sort of. It didn't make a lot of sense the way he said it, but nothing much about sorcery does, to me. "We've got big trouble, eh?"

"The biggest if the book is complete. I doubt that it can be, though. But even incomplete, it's a powerful tool. And almost anyone who knew what it was could use it—if she was foolish enough to write it in a language someone else could read. You wouldn't have to be a sorcerer. You'd just look up the page for *sorcerer* if that's what you wanted to be."

I thought about it. Hard. The more I thought, the more possibilities I saw and the less I liked this book. It sounded like a triple shot of Black Plague. "You think there's a chance it really exists? That it isn't just somebody's fancy?"

"*Something* exists that people are willing to kill for. But it just can't be complete." He sounded like he was whistling in the dark. "Else the thief wouldn't have gotten to it. But it would be dangerous in any state. It has to be destroyed, Mr. Garrett. Please go straight to the Dead Man. Urge him to exercise his entire intellect. My people will do everything within their power."

Tinnie's place in the mess was fading fast. The stakes seemed huge. I should've known it couldn't stay simple. My life never does. "Let me know if you come up with anything."

Gnorst nodded. He had given me more time and information than either of us had planned. Now he seemed anxious to see me go. I said, "We ought to excuse ourselves and attack our respective tasks."

"Indeed. My life has been complicated no end." He signaled. The old boy from the front door popped out of nowhere. He took me back the way we had come. Somebody scampered ahead to warn all the dwarves. They were all hard at work when I passed by.

Nobody is that industrious all the time.

••• **13**

slipped out into the afternoon, leaned against the wall a dozen feet from Dwarf House's door, pondered my place in this exploding puzzle. The Book of Shadows. A real nasty. Did I have a moral obligation here? Gnorst and his gang knew how to handle it.

I understood the danger better by the minute. I was tempted by the book and didn't yet know how it could be useful to me. Pretty easy to see why Gnorst was scared of it.

If I stayed involved, I was going to have to cover my behind. There were some rough players out there. I didn't know them, but they knew me. Maybe it *was* time to drop by the Joy House, see if Morley had anything cooking.

I started toward his place, not hurrying, still trying to figure angles.

I didn't get there.

There was a whole gang of them but they were dwarves, so I had the reach. And for once in my young life I'd had the sense to go out dressed. I dented three heads and chucked one dwarf through a window. The owner came out and cussed and howled and threatened and kicked a dwarf I knocked down. Nobody paid him any attention. The rest of us were having too good a time.

I started out not really trying to hurt anybody. I just wanted to fend them off and get away. But they were playing for keeps. I decided I'd better argue more convincingly. My stick wasn't getting the message across.

Somebody whapped me up side the head with a house. It had to be a house. Nobody dwarf size could hit that hard. The lights went out.

• • •

Usually I come around slowly after I've been sapped. Not that I have a lot of experience with that. This time I wasn't slow, maybe because I was so excited about finding myself still alive, if a little run-down.

I was bouncing along facedown. Cobblestones slid past inches from my nose. The hairy runts were taking me somewhere rolled into a wet blanket. They were skulking along through an alley. Maybe they wanted us to party some before they let me swim the river with rocks tied to my ankles.

I didn't like the situation. Naturally. Would you? But there wasn't a whole lot I could do about it. I couldn't even yell. My throat felt like I'd tried to swallow cactus.

However . . .

The dwarves stopped. They chattered gutturally. I strained, lifted my head, looked around. My temples throbbed. I saw red. When my eyes cleared, I saw a man blocking the alleyway ahead. He was alone and there were eight dwarves around me, but the numbers didn't bother him.

His name was Sadler. He was one of Chodo Contague's top boys, pure death on the hoof. The dwarves chattered some more. Someone was behind us, too. I couldn't twist around enough to see him, but I could guess. Where Sadler went Crask was sure to follow. And vice versa.

Those two are hard to describe. They're big men, have no consciences, will cut a throat with no more thought than stomping a bug. Maybe less. And you can read that in their eyes. They're scary. They probably eat lye for breakfast.

Sadler said, "Put him down." His voice was cold and creepy.

Crask said, "And get out of here." His voice was so much like Sadler's, people had trouble telling them apart.

The dwarves put me down, all right, but they didn't get out of there. Which made it sure they were from out of town. They might be thugs, but any thugs native to TunFaire wouldn't have argued for an instant. Nobody in his right mind bucks Chodo without having an army behind him.

Sadler and Crask were efficient and ruthless and not even a little sporting. They didn't argue, they didn't negotiate, they didn't talk. They killed dwarves till the survivors decided to get the hell out of there. The two didn't chase anybody. They had what they had come for, which was one broken-down confidential agent named Garrett.

Crask grabbed the edge of the blanket and gave me a spin. Sadler said, "You're keeping weird company, Garrett."

"Wasn't my idea. Good thing you guys happened along." Which I said knowing they hadn't happened along at all. They probably wouldn't have lifted a finger if they hadn't been sent.

"Maybe you won't think so." That was Crask. "Chodo wants we should ask you a question."

"How'd you find me?"

"Your man told us you went to Dwarf House." Dean would. Even with the Dead Man watching over him. He isn't that brave. "We saw you get knocked down. You got to learn to control that tongue, Garrett." I didn't remember saying anything but I probably did. Probably asked for it. "We don't want to lose you." That was Sadler talking. And what he was really saying was that he didn't want me to get myself smoked before the day came when Chodo decided the world would be better for my absence. Sadler looks forward to that day like it might be for the heavyweight championship of Karenta.

"Thanks anyway. Even if you didn't mean it." Crask helped me to my feet. My head whirled. And ached. It was going to ache for a long time. "Maybe we're even now."

Sadler shrugged. Damn, he's a big one. Two inches taller than me, fifty pounds heavier, and not an ounce wasted on flab. He was losing a little hair. I'd guess him at about forty. A real ape. A doubly scary ape because he had a brain.

Crask is the other half of a set of bookends, almost like he stepped out of some mirror where Sadler was checking his chin for zits.

Sadler shrugged because he wasn't going to put words into the kingpin's mouth. Chodo has the idea he owes me because a couple of my old cases helped him out in a big way. In fact, I saved his life once. I'd rather not have. The world would be a better place without Chodo Contague. But the alternative had been worse.

"Let's us guys walk," Crask said. He got on my left and supported me by the elbow. Sadler got on my right. They were going to ask some questions and I'd better give some answers. Or I'd be very unhappy.

There's my life in a nutshell. Cheerfully skipping from frying pans to fires.

I couldn't for the life of me think why they were interested in me now, though. "What's up?"

"It ain't what's up, Garrett, it's who's down. Chodo got kind of crabby when Squirrel turned up dead."

I stopped. "Squirrel? When did that happen?" I nearly fell on my face because they kept on going.

"You tell us, Garrett. That's why we're here. Chodo sent him down to help you. A favor, because he owes you. Next thing we know a city ratman finds him in an alley with his guts hanging out. He wasn't much, but Chodo considered him family."

Catch that? Always Chodo, never Mr. Contague? I've never figured it out. But I didn't have time to wonder or ask. It was time to talk. "A woman came to the house. Called herself Winger. Not a local. She pulled a knife on me in the office. The Dead Man froze her." I awarded myself a smirk when Crask and Sadler jumped. The only thing in the world that bothers them is the Dead Man. He's a force they can't cope with because they can't kill him. "I was going to go get Morley Dotes to tag her after I pushed her out, but Squirrel turned up right then and volunteered. I told him to find out where she went and who she saw. The Dead Man said somebody named Lubbock sent her."

"You know anybody named Lubbock?"

"No. I never saw the woman before, either. She was real country."

They spread out a little. They were going to indulge me, give me the benefit of a shadow of a doubt. Maybe. Sadler asked, "This tie in with the hit on your woman?"

"Maybe. This Winger was looking for a missing book of some kind. I don't know why she thought I had it. She didn't say and the Dead Man couldn't get it out of her. Later, though, another woman showed up. Wanted to hire me to find a guy called Holme Blaine who stole a book from her boss, who wanted the book back bad. She was a redhead Tinnie's size and age and build. Maybe somebody mistook Tinnie for her."

They thought. Crask said, "It don't add, Garrett." Accusing me of holding out.

"Damned straight it don't. It might start to if I can find this Holme Blaine."

They grunted. They've spent too much time around each other. They're like those married couples that get more and more alike as time goes by. Crask asked, "Why visit the dwarves?"

"There're dwarves in the thing."

"No shit. Your pals back there. You smartmouth somebody in Dwarf Fort?"

"Different gang. From out of town."

"Figured that." They're that confident of their reputation.

Sadler asked, "How do you get into these weird things, Garrett?"

"If I knew, I wouldn't get into them anymore. It just sneaks up on me. You going to show me where Squirrel bought it?"

"Yeah."

I was doing something right. We were on the street now. In view of witnesses. I was a little less nervous. Not that those two would scruple against icing me in front of the whole world at high noon if they thought the time was right. Half the unresolved killings in TunFaire can be pinned on the kingpin's boys. I don't see anybody rounding them up for it.

Chodo's secret of success is he doesn't muscle in on our overlords' rackets. He works his own end of the social scale. He's much more at peril from his own than from the vagaries of law or state.

Equal justice for all. As long as you make it yourself.

They had me glad I'd done some running by the time we got to Squirrel. It was a hike and a half, all the way to the skirts of the Hill, where our masters have raised their fastnesses upon the heights. I knew our trek was at an end when we reached a block where a few hardcases loafed around, holding up walls, and the street was otherwise empty.

Squirrel had gone to his reward in an alley that ran downhill steeply. We entered from the high end. Sadler told me, "He got it here," about fifteen feet into the shadows. It would have been light there only briefly, around noon. "You can't tell 'cause of the light, but there's blood all over. He ended up down there about fifty feet. Probably tried to run after it was too late. Come on."

The body lay ten feet from the bottom end of the alley. Somebody with a sharp blade and strong, probably using a downward stroke, had sliced him from his right ear down the side of his throat and chest all the way to his belly button. Bone deep. "Last time I saw a wound like that was when I was in the Corps."

"Yeah," Crask said. "Two-handed dueling saber?"

Sadler demurred. "Couldn't get away with lugging one around. I say just sharpness and strength."

Crask squatted. "Could be. But how do you get that close to hit that hard with a legal knife?"

They meandered off into a technical discussion. Craftsmen of murder talking shop. I squatted to give Squirrel a closer look.

Some of us never get used to violent death. I saw plenty in the Marines and didn't get numb. I've seen more than enough since. I still don't have calluses where Crask and Sadler have them. Maybe it's hereditary. Squirrel probably earned what he'd gotten, but I mourned him all the same. I noted, "He wasn't robbed or anything."

"He was plain hit," Crask said. "Somebody wanted rid of him."

"And him such a sweetheart. It's a sacrilege."

If those guys have a weakness, it's lacking a sense of humor. Their idea of a joke is promising a guy to turn him loose if he can walk on water wearing lead boots. My crack didn't go over.

Sadler said, "Chodo doesn't like it, Squirrel getting offed. He wasn't much good but he was family. Chodo wants to know who and why."

"You guys using carrier pigeons now?" Chodo lives way the hell and gone out in the sticks, north of town. There shouldn't have been time for all the back and forth implied here.

They ignored me. They get that way about trade secrets—or anything they don't think I need to know. Crask said, "You get anything here we don't?"

I shook my head. All I could tell was that Squirrel wouldn't be doing much dancing anymore.

Sadler said, "Bet the iceman used both hands. You'd get more on it that way."

Crask told me, "We're going to keep an eye on you, Garrett. Something don't add up here. Maybe you didn't tell us everything."

Hell, no, I hadn't. Some things Chodo doesn't need to know. I shrugged. "I find out who did it, you'll be the first to know."

"Take it to heart, Garrett. Take it to bed with you. Get up with it in the morning. Chodo is pissed. Somebody is going to pay." He turned to Sadler and started in on whether the killer had cut upward or downward. Ignoring me. I'd been dismissed. Warned and dismissed. Chodo owed me, but not the life of one of his men. Maybe I was nearer even with him than I'd thought.

I checked Squirrel again, but he still wasn't sharing any secrets. So I got out of there.

Heading home, I saw something I'd never seen in TunFaire before, a centaur family trotting down the street. The fighting in the Cantard must have gone berserk if the natives were fleeing it, too. I'd never heard of centaurs ranging this far north.

Things must be going real bad for Glory Mooncalled and his hatchling Cantard republic. He'd be gone soon and the world could get back to normal, with Karentine killing Venageti in the never-ending contest for control of the mines.

I'd have to mention the centaurs to the Dead Man. Glory Mooncalled is his hobby. The mercenary turned self-crowned prince has lasted longer than even my career houseguest expected.

hile walking home, I noticed that, though it was still too early for morCartha high jinks, there were plenty of fliers aloft. Like every fairy and pixie in the known universe, with a random sample of other breeds. I nearly trampled a band of gnomes while gawking at the aerobatics. The gnomes yowled and cursed and threatened mayhem upon my shinbones. The tallest didn't reach my kneecap. They were feisty little buggers.

I stood and gawked while they stomped off, cocky because they'd intimidated one of the big people. I didn't get around to cussing back because I was numb. You don't often see gnomes. Not in town. They look kind of like miniature dwarves who sometimes find time to shave. "What next?" I muttered, and "Never mind! I don't want to find out." Just in case my guardian angel was going to grant my every wish.

I reported to the Dead Man. He seemed more interested in the gnomes and centaurs than in what had happened to me. I held my tongue while he mulled what I'd gotten from his pal Gnorst, then digested the news about Squirrel. Then he queried, *Why do you not want the killer to have been the woman Winger?*

"I liked her. In an off-the-wall sort of way. She had balls that drag the ground."

You get your priorities scrambled. You mentioned her name to Mr. Crask and Mr. Sadler.

"I did indeed. I wasn't thinking clearly at the time. A mistake, but with some justification." They would find her and ask her some hard questions. Unless she did the unlikely and headed for her home village fast. Like about the day before yesterday.

You did not mention the book.

"I was playing with pain. I managed to think a little. I thought I should keep something to myself."

Wise decision. If for the wrong reason. Consider the power of the book, then consider that in the hands of Chodo Contague.

I did. And maybe had before, unconsciously. "Not a good plan."

Not for anyone but Chodo Contague. A fancy keeps floating through your mind. It may not be as difficult as you think.

"What?" He'd blindsided me again.

To find an eyewitness to the Squirrel person's demise.

"You're kidding. Chodo's in it. People are going to sew their lips together."

He does not intimidate everyone.

"You weren't there, O Fearless One. Everybody that he doesn't intimidate is buried. Or soon will be."

You noted considerable aerial activity out there. How often do fairies and pixies catch your attention? More often than children and pets? Generally such remain part of the background unless they force themselves upon you. And in that you are not unique. The Squirrel person's killer probably was careful about witnesses, but did not think to check the air above.

"It's an idea. One of your more outrageous ones, but an idea. How am I supposed to con some witness into talking?"

Pass word to the fairy and pixie communities saying you will pay for information about what happened in that alley. Those people are not afraid of Chodo Contague. In fact, they hate him. They would not help him. If he has a similar notion, they will thumb their noses at his men. They can fly faster than his thugs can run.

Legwork again. He was coming up with these things just to get more hoofing around town.

Still, it might be worth a shot. If I could get the message across. It's hard to communicate with those people. They speak Karentine but somehow it isn't always the same language I speak. You have to be careful what you say and precise in how you say it. No ambiguities. No words or phrases that can be understood in more than one way. You do and ninety-nine times in a hundred they'll take you the wrong way. I think they do it on purpose to give us a hard time.

I'd never thought much about it, but there are people with little to fear from Chodo. It might behoove me to find friends among them. Sure as the sun will rise in the east, there'll come a day when Chodo and I go head-to-head; I don't want that day to come and I expect he doesn't, either, but we both know our natures make it inevitable.

I said, "Crask and Sadler got me spooked."

They did more good than harm.

"I heard that. Those dwarves weren't taking me to a party."

Time to consider taking on backup.

"Yeah." He was being awful practical. "I wanted to keep the little leaf-eater out of it but I'm really not at my best when the odds are eight to one."

I sensed faint amusement over there. *There are other possibilities. The groll brothers, Doris and Marsha, make effective bodyguards.*

"They also tend to stick out in a crowd." Grolls being part giant, part troll, and the brothers in question being twenty feet tall and green. And they don't speak Karentine. The only man I know who speaks grollish is Morley Dotes. I'd have to enlist him anyway. "Why don't I sleep on it?"

Because if you sleep now, you may waste the chance to enjoy sleeping a few thousand times more. It is not legwork that is going to kill you, Garrett. It is lack of legwork.

"Who walked twenty miles today? And who stayed home contemplating his own genius?"

I pondered the mystery of Glory Mooncalled.

"That'll help us out." How old Chuckles preens and crows when he guesses right what the mercenary will do next. And how he cringes and whines when that sumbitch surprises him.

I hate to admit it, but I kind of long for the old days last year when Mooncalled was on our side and just gave the Venageti fits and made our generals look like simpletons.

Maybe I should worry more. Mooncalled may be the most important man alive today. The fate of his republic will shape that of Karenta and Venageta. If the two kingdoms can't squash him and regain access to the silver mines that are the object of the ancient war, sorcerers on both sides will soon be out of business. Silver is the fuel that makes their magic go.

Mooncalled's strategy is to hang on till the wizards fade. He doesn't fear our mundane generals. Most of them can't find their butts with a seeing-eye dog. They get their jobs through brilliant selection of parents, not competence. Mooncalled may not be a genius, but he can find his butt with either hand, in the dark, which is plenty good enough when dealing with Karentine generals or Venageti warlords.

I said, "I take it you think something is about to happen down there."

Perhaps. And the news may be less than favorable to those who find hope in Mooncalled's mutiny. Both Karenta and Venageta have kept the pressure on but have not run blind into his traps. His native support appears to be dwindling. You mentioned spotting a centaur family today. A few months ago centaurs were Mooncalled's most devoted allies, vowing to fight till they were extinct if that was the price of ending foreign domination of the Cantard.

I hadn't thought about the political implications of a centaur presence here. Did it mean negotiations for a sellout? Usually I turn a deaf ear to such speculation. I have the romantic, silly idea that if I ignore politics steadfastly, maybe politicians will ignore me. You'd think I'd have learned after having spent five years helping kill people on behalf of politicians.

Don't tell anybody on the Hill, but I—like almost everybody who doesn't live up there—have rooted for Glory Mooncalled in my secret heart. If he actually manages the impossible and hangs on, he'll break the backs of the ruling classes of both of the world's greatest kingdoms. In Karenta's case that could mean the collapse of the state and either the return of the imperials from exile or evolution into something entirely new and unique, built upon a mixture of races.

Enough. Whatever happens on the Hill, or in the Cantard, it won't change my life. There'll always be bad guys for me to chase.

You had better get on your horse.

"Yuk! Don't even mention those monsters." I hate horses. They hate me. I think there's a good chance they'll get me before the kingpin does. "I'm on my way."

orley Dotes's Joy House is only a short way from my place, but by the time you get there you wonder if you haven't fallen through a hole into another world. In my neighborhood—though it's not the best—the nonhumans and baddies are mostly passing through. In Morley's, the Safety Zone, they're there all the time.

TunFaire is a human city, but just about every other species has an area of its own staked out. Some are a quarter unto themselves, like Ogre Town or Ratman Creek. Some occupy only one tenement. Even though individuals may live anywhere in town, somewhere there's a home turf that's fiercely defended. There's a lot of prejudice and a lot of friction and some races have a talent for that which makes our human bent toward prejudice look wimpy. Thus the Safety Zone evolved, of its own accord, as an area where the races can mix in relative peace, because business has to get done.

Morley's place is right in the heart of the zone, which seems to have gelled around it. It was always a favorite hangout for baddies who mix, before the zone became an accepted idea. Morley is becoming a minor power. I've heard he's turned into a sort of judge who arbitrates interracial disputes.

Useful, but he'd better not get too ambitious. Chodo might feel threatened.

Chodo only tolerates Morley now because he owes him. Morley spiffed his predecessor and created a job opening at the top. But Chodo remains wary, maybe even nervous. What Morley did once he might do again, and there's no more sure an assassin than Morley Dotes.

Killing people is Morley's real line. The Joy House started out as cover. He never expected the place to become a success and probably didn't want it to.

Thus do the fates conspire to shape our lives.

It was getting on dusky, with the first morCartha out reconnoitering, as I approached Morley's place. "Well," I muttered unhappily as I turned into the street that runs past the Joy House. And "Yeah, hello," as a couple of overdeveloped bruisers fell into step beside me. "How's the world treating you guys?"

Both frowned as though trying to work through a problem too difficult for either. Then Sadler materialized out of shadow and relieved them of the frightful and unaccustomed task of thinking. Sadler said, "Good timing, Garrett. Chodo wants to see you."

They must have seen me coming. "Yeah. I suspected." A big black coach stood in front of Morley's. I knew it better than I liked. I'd ridden in it. It belonged to that well-known philanthropist, Chodo Contague. "He's here? Chodo?" He never leaves his mansion.

Crask appeared, completed the set. I had me bookends who would strangle their own mothers not only without a qualm but who wouldn't recall it a day later with any more remorse than recalling stomping a roach. Bad, bad people, Crask and Sadler. I wish I didn't, but whenever I run into them I waste half my little brain worrying about how bad they are.

I'm glad they don't make a lot like them.

Crask said, "Chodo wants to talk, Garrett."

"I got that impression." I kept my tongue in check. No need to mention that Sadler had told me already.

"He's in the coach."

They couldn't have been sitting there waiting for me. That wasn't their style. They must have had business with Morley and I was just a target of opportunity.

I walked to the coach, opened its door, hauled my carcass inside, settled facing the kingpin.

You take your first look at Chodo, you wonder why all the fuss. Everybody's scared of this old geek? Why, he's in such lousy shape he spends his whole life in a wheelchair. He can barely hold his head up, and that not for long unless he's mad. Sometimes he can't speak clearly enough to make himself understood. His skin has no color and it seems you can see right through it. He looks like he's been dead five years already.

Then he works up the strength to meet your eye and you see the beast looking out at you. I've been there several times and still that first instant of eye contact is a shocker. The guy inside that ruined meat makes Crask and Sadler look like street-corner do-gooders.

You get in Chodo's way, you get hurt. He don't need to be a ballerina. He has Crask and Sadler. Those two are more loyal to him than ever any son was to a father. That kind of loyalty is remarkable in the underworld. I wonder what hold he has on them.

He has them and a platoon of lieutenants and those have their soldiers on the street. Those have their allies and informants and tenants. Chodo flinches or frowns, somebody can die a gruesome death real sudden.

"Mr. Garrett." He had the strength to incline his head. He was having a good day. Wiry wisps of white hair floated around.

"Mr. Contague." *I* call him Mr. Contague. "I was considering coming to see you." But not very seriously. His place is too far out. It's a disgustingly tasteless mausoleum (sour grapes, Garrett?) that dwarfs the homes of most of our overlords. Crime pays. And for Chodo it pays very well indeed.

"I thought you might when I heard from Dotes."

Thanks a bunch, Morley. There you go thinking for me again.

"I know how a man feels in such a situation, Mr. Garrett. I once lost a woman to a rival. A man grows impatient to restore the balance. I thought I would save time if I came to the city."

Huh? Didn't he know Tinnie was going to be all right? Or did he know something I didn't? That was likely, since almost everybody knows something I don't—but not about Tinnie, he shouldn't. "I appreciate it more than you know." He had a girl once. Funny. I'd never thought of him having been anything but what he is right now.

"You're surprised. It's a pity you're so determined to maintain your independence." That's a problem between us. I want the world to know I'm my own man. He'd like to get a hold on me. He said, "I admire you, Mr. Garrett. It would be interesting to sit and talk sometime about have-beens and might-have-beens. Yes. Even I was young once. Even I have been in love. I once considered getting out of this life because a woman caused me such despair. But she died. Much as yours did. I recall the pain vividly. For a time it left my soul as crippled as my flesh is now. If I can help, I will."

For the first time I began to suspect there was something going on between me and Chodo that was on a level having nothing to do with antipathies and favors accidentally or knowingly done. Maybe he'd glommed me as some kind of tenuous lifeline from his shadow world to one where "higher" standards reigned. And maybe his continued attempts to seduce or coerce me into his camp had something to do with tempering that life-line.

Whoa! Hip boots time, Garrett. "Sure. Thanks. Only, Tinnie didn't die, see? She was hurt, but they say she should get better. Squirrel was supposed to tell you, only . . ."

His face darkened. "Yes. Squirrel. Mr. Crask and Mr. Sadler told me what you said. I failed to make sense of it."

"I can't, either. But the whole world is going crazy. We got morCartha fighting all night, mammoths and saber-tooth tigers roaming around, thunder-lizards maybe migrating south. Today I saw centaurs on the street and almost tromped a gang of gnomes. Nothing makes sense anymore."

He made a feeble gesture with one hand, a sure sign his blood was up. He seldom spends the strength. "Tell me."

"You have a professional interest?"

"Tell me about it."

My mama didn't raise many kids dumb enough to argue with Chodo Contague while hip-deep in Chodo's headbreakers. I gave him most of the bag. Exactly what I'd given Crask and Sadler. I didn't contradict myself. The Dead Man taught me well when it comes to retaining detail. I added some speculation just to give the impression that I was making a special effort for him.

He listened, relaxed, chin against chest, gathering his strength. What went on inside that strange brain? The man was a genius. Evil, but a genius. He said, "It makes no sense in terms of the information at my disposal."

"Not to me, either." I arrowed to the key point. "But there're dwarves under arms roaming the streets."

"Yes. Most unusual."

"Is there a dwarfish underworld?"

"Yes. Every race has its hidden side, Mr. Garrett. I've had contact with it. It's trivial by human standards. Dwarves don't gamble. They are inca-pable of making that mental plunge into self-delusion whereby others be-come convinced that they can beat the odds. They don't drink because they make fools of themselves when they're drunk and there is nothing a dwarf fears more than looking foolish. They shun weed and drugs for the same reason. There are individual exceptions, of course, but they're rare. As a breed, they have few of the usual vices. I've never known one to become excitable enough to employ lifetakers."

"Pretty dull bunch."

"By your standards or mine. All work, all business, very little play. But there is one game they do enjoy. One weakness. Exotic females. Any species will do, though they gravitate toward big-busted human women."

So do I. I made an unnecessary crack about, well, if you've taken a look at your average dwarf woman . . . He shut me up with a scowl.

"They can't resist, Mr. Garrett—if you give them half a chance to convince themselves that they won't get found out. They can be as vulnerable as priests that way. In the area around Dwarf Fort there are half a dozen very discreet and exclusive hook shops catering to dwarves. They are quite successful enterprises."

Which meant they were pouring gold into Chodo's pockets. I wondered if he was trying to tell me something. Probably not. He isn't one to talk around the edges of something—unless he's handing you a gentle admonition concerning a possible catastrophic decline in the state of your health. "You make anything of the book angle?"

"They would get excited if someone got hold of one of their books of secrets. But that can't be done."

Such a flat statement. He'd tried. I flashed on what the Dead Man had said. Damn! I shouldn't have gotten him thinking about books.

He said, "There's no way to get enough leverage on a dwarf to make him turn over any secret. Those people are perfectly content to die first."

"How about a thief?" Maybe I could nudge this into safer channels.

"Their books are too well guarded to be reached." Again that flatness. He knew whereof he spoke. "That enclave is a puzzle box, a series of fortresses going inward. You need a guide to get through it. The army, backed by every wizard off the Hill, couldn't take the place fast enough to keep them from destroying whatever they don't want to get out."

"It was a notion. I thought it might explain what's been happening."

"What's going on is something else entirely. You tell me your young lady is alive and mending. Does that mean you're out of it?"

I answered honestly. "I don't know where I stand. Every time I decide I don't have any stake, something happens. Those dwarves Sadler and Crask ran off . . . They were out to get rid of me. It can't be sound business practice to let people get away with something like that."

He looked at me in a way that told me he knew I was holding out, but he said only, "That's true, Mr. Garrett. A first principle. Don't let anyone get away with muscling you. For the moment, let me counsel patience. Let me put my eyes out. These people have dragged me into their affairs. Someone beholden to me will know something about them. It's impossible for those people to exist in the cracks without being noticed. My people will catch some of them and ask questions. If I learn anything of interest to you, I'll inform you immediately."

"Thank you." I couldn't tell him to get out of my face, go home, I didn't need him stomping around in my life. Even if I'd wanted to.

"I'm going to have Mr. Sadler set up headquarters here so my people have a central reporting site." He meant the Joy House. That would thrill Morley all to hell. It would shoot the guts out of his business.

Chodo read that thought in my face. He's good at reading people. "Mr. Dotes won't lose because of it."

"I don't know how to thank you, Mr. Contague." I managed to keep sarcasm from creeping in. Dean and the Dead Man would have been amazed. They don't think I can do that.

"Don't thank me. You've done me numerous good turns. This may be my chance to pay some back. Maybe to lay a little good karma on my soul."

Another surprise. That old boy is full of them. I thanked him again, climbed out of the coach. It rolled away immediately. Most of Chodo's bodyguards went with it.

orley's place was deserted. I stepped into half the usual light and none of the usual uproar. I looked across the desert at Puddle, behind the serving counter, polishing glassware. "What the hell?"

"Not open tonight, buddy. Come back some other time."

"Hey! It's me. Garrett."

He squinted. Maybe his eyes weren't so good anymore. He was going to flab fast, but that didn't keep him from being a bad man. "Oh. Yeah. Maybe I ought to say we're double not open for you, pal. But it's too late. You done got Morley dragged in."

"Where is everybody?"

"Morley shut the place down. You think anybody's going to come in here with that circus parked out front?"

"He here?"

"Nope." He didn't volunteer any information. Most of Morley's people think I take advantage of his good nature. They're wrong. He doesn't have a good nature. And he owes me for a couple stunts he pulled on me back when he was hooked on gambling and he had to cut things fine to keep from taking that long swim in the river. "What you want him for?"

"Just talk."

"Right." His tone said I was full of it.

"He leave any word for me?"

"Yeah. Have a beer. Hang in there till he gets back."

"Beer?" Morley never has anything drinkable around except a little brandy upstairs for special guests of the female persuasion. The kind that always scurry for cover when I show up, afraid I work for their husbands.

Puddle swung a pony keg onto the bar, grabbed the biggest mug he had, drew me one. I arrived as he topped it off. I noted that the keg had been tapped already. I noted that Puddle had brew breath. I grinned. Another of Morley's bunch who didn't share his boss's religion. Puddle pretended he didn't know why I was showing my teeth.

"Seen Saucerhead?"

"Nope."

"Morley supposed to be back soon?"

"I don't know."

"Know where he went?"

He shook his head. Probably afraid he was going to get a sore throat with all this yammer. A real heavyweight conversationalist, Puddle. Always ready with a lightning riposte. Rather than subject myself to any more abuse, I went to work on my beer.

It went down smooth. Almost too smooth. I let him draw me another and finished half before I thought about all I'd put away already today. Where was the point of the running if I was going to fix myself up to look like Puddle anyway?

"You got anything back there ready to eat?"

A big, wicked grin grew on Puddle's homely face. Before he turned toward the kitchen, I was sorry I'd asked. He was about to make me pay for my sins.

He came back with something cold smeared on a bed of soggy noodles. "Chef's surprise." It looked like death and didn't taste much better.

"Now I know why all those breeds are so damned mean. Can't help it, eating like this."

Puddle chuckled, pleased with himself.

I ate. To get through a mess like that, all I have to do is recall what I'd had to eat as a Marine. I could dig in and feel pampered.

Saucerhead ambled in. "Where you been, Garrett?"

I filled him in.

"I heard about Squirrel. Can't figure it."

"What about the redhead?"

He frowned. "She went home meek. And disappeared." He shook his head. "Went in the place where she stayed. Wanted to ask her a question. I looked all over. She wasn't in there no more. And I know she never come out. Only two people ever did and she wasn't one of them. And she never came back." He shrugged and forgot it. Not his problem anymore. "They tried to ice you, eh?"

"Yeah."

He sighed. "Hey. Puddle. Whup me up a double load of whatever this glop is Garrett's got." He asked me, "Where's Morley?"

"I don't know. Puddle ain't saying."

"Hmm. Chodo's in it now. Account of Squirrel. What you going to do?"

"I don't know. I have a couple grudges. And like Chodo told me, letting them slide isn't good for business."

"You think that Winger smoked Squirrel?"

"Maybe. I think Chodo's going to find out."

"Pretty pissed, eh?"

"Yeah. Probably hasn't had a good excuse to off somebody for days."

Saucerhead drank about a quart of beer, inhaled the food Puddle brought him, shoved back, said, "Well, it's been an interesting day. I got to get on home. Got a little gal waiting." Off he went.

I sat quietly for a while. It got dark outside. I waited some more. I asked Puddle, "You sure Morley didn't say when he'd be back?"

"Nope."

Puddle seemed to be the only body in the place. Where were all the help? Where was Sadler, who was supposed to set up his headquarters? Where the hell was Morley Dotes?

I waited some more. Then I waited some. And when I didn't have anything else to do, I waited. Then I got up and said, "I'm going home."

"See ya." Puddle grinned me out the door. He locked it behind me in case I had a change of heart.

The morCartha were zooming around, trying to undress the night. I recalled Dean saying we were going to have cobbler for dessert. I cussed. I'd eaten that sludge at Morley's place and now I wouldn't have room for decent cooking.

Story of my life.

almost made it home without getting distracted.

I'd just crossed Wizard's Reach. I was beginning to feel optimistic. I'd decided I was going to wrap myself around another gallon of beer, then throw myself in bed and sleep till noon. The hell with running and everything else. I justified future loafing the old-fashioned way. I told me I'd earned it.

Somebody hissed at me from the shadows beside a neighbor's stoop.

I took a deep breath, sighed, looked for signs of trouble, looked at that shadow, didn't go any closer. I couldn't make out whoever was there. Mama Garrett didn't raise many fools who lived to be thirty. I didn't go over there. "Come out, come out, whoever you are. Allee allee in free."

"I can't. They might be watching."

"Too bad." Very too bad.

My mood had plunged. I didn't bother asking *who* might be watching.

The voice sounded a tad familiar. I couldn't place it, though.

I laid a hand on my belt. No head-knocker. Still down somewhere near Dwarf Fort. I resumed walking, wondering if I'd see that billy again. I wasn't ready to go looking. Too many dwarves down there and I can't tell one from another. I don't think they'd accept a kill-them-all-and-let-the-gods-sort-them-out approach.

My egg might be scrambled some but it does me just fine, thank you.

The dark behind me moaned. Feet pitty-patted toward me. I eyed the house, wondered if I'd have time to get Dean's attention before somebody did something unpleasant and maybe left the old boy a mess to clean up.

That's the power of positive thinking there. After having had my head redesigned—it was throbbing and pounding—I saw no dawn on any horizon. Funny how one little thing can cause your mood to change so fast.

I sidestepped, dropped into a crouch, and came around with a fist meant to drive right through somebody's ribs and let me get hold of his backbone from the front. Then, if I was feeling mean, I'd shake him till his ears fell off.

I tried pulling it. I fell on my face, rearranged my nose into an even less appealing mess, and still folded the little darling up around my fist.

I got myself up, wobbled around a little, wiped the fuzz out of my eyes. The girl stayed down, holding herself and making strangling noises. Hoo, boy. What a lady-killer, Garrett. It wasn't my week for women. If it kept up, it wasn't going to be my year.

I felt my nose to see if anything was left. Hard to tell from here, but there seemed to be a nub under the ick. It hurt enough to be my nose. I shook some more cobwebs and knelt. "You shouldn't ought to run up on a guy like that."

She made noises like she was trying to heave up her stockings. I scooped her up and headed for home, caveman Garrett bringing home the goodies.

She felt like a real treat, curled in my arms. It was hard to tell by eyeball in the available light. Curious morCartha cruised around as I climbed the steps, kicked the door, and hollered. They didn't bother me. I felt the Dead Man touch me, just to make sure it wasn't somebody trying to get past Dean disguised as a freshly slaughtered side of beef.

Dean opened the door after peeking through the spyhole. He looked at the girl. "Got lucky again, eh?" He stepped aside.

I took her into the small front room, put her down on the daybed. "See what you can do while I clean up." I sketched what had happened. He gave me one of his better looks of exasperation.

"You missed supper."

"I ate out. At Morley's. Get a light in here so we can see. I'll be back in a minute." I left him and dashed upstairs faster than a wounded snail. After I washed my face and rechecked it for missing parts, I put on clean clothes and scooted downstairs and stuck my head into the Dead Man's room. "Company, Smiley."

I am aware of that, Garrett. Try to restrain your animal urges. She may be of some help, though I cannot get anything yet. She is too frightened and confused.

"Restrain myself? I'm a paragon of restraint. I'm the guy they invented the word for. I've never burned the house down around you."

It was one of those rare times when he didn't try to get in the last word. Chalk one up in the history books. Might not happen again in my lifetime. *She knows something, Garrett.*

Hell. Score one for him. That was worse than one of his standard digs. It was tone rather than words. He was accusing me of goofing off.

I stomped into the small front room.

Dean was bent over the woman, blocking her from view, talking softly. I paused, looked at him with an affection I'd never show to his face. He had been the luckiest find of my life. He did everything around the house that I hated, cooked like an angel, put in absurd hours, and more often than not was as emotionally involved in my cases as I was. I couldn't ask for much more but maybe a little less lip and a little more enthusiasm about keeping the Dead Man clean.

If he has a failing, it's his disapproval of my work habits. Dean believes in work for its own sake, as a tonic for the soul.

I coughed gently to let him know I was there. He didn't hear. Was he going deaf? Maybe. He had to be pushing seventy, though he wouldn't admit it.

"How is she, Dean? Settled down any?"

He tossed a glower over his shoulder. "Some. No thanks to you."

"I should let somebody run up on me and maybe change the shape of my head?" I was getting irritable. Can't understand why. My face hurt? My head ached? My shoulder throbbed? My legs were cramping from all the walking and running? That's no excuse. I was headed for despair mode, where you keep on fighting the fight but you've decided it isn't worth it. You just can't stop.

Facts don't bother Dean much. He's still fifteen years old inside. He never stopped believing in the kind of magic kids carry around inside them before reality beats them down. He gave me another look at his glower. He was on a roll. He said, "Give me a couple more minutes."

"I'll go report, then." I went and told the Dead Man about my excursion into that world where Dean's brand of magic has died.

He had no direct comment. *Go meet the girl.* Chuckle. *You will be surprised.*

• • •

The Dead Man scores his points. I was surprised.

She was gorgeous. Luscious. I'd had my suspicions, of course. I'd carried her in and there's nothing wrong with my sense of touch. But there hadn't been light enough to reveal all that red hair.

Yeah. She was a ringer for the gal who'd told the Baron Stonecipher story, who was a ringer for the naked gal. This one with a difference. This one had an air of innocence. "It's raining redheads, Dean."

He grunted. Like he didn't care.

She was sitting up now, no longer green around the gills. She looked at me. Green eyes. Again. Gorgeous big naive green eyes. Lips like I only dream about. Freckles.

Down, boy.

I gaped. Dean gave me the evil eye. I said, "We need a name for this case. Maybe call it Too Many Redheads."

"Mr. Garrett?" Whoo! That voice! Like the last redhead's voice, but with added bells and promises . . . whatever.

"That's me. Garrett. Ferocious dragon fighter and unwitting stomper of damsels in distress. And that's on my good days."

She looked puzzled.

"Sorry. It's been a rough day. I'm on edge. Let's start over. I promise not to sock you if you promise not to run up behind me in the dark." In the street, anyway. We could put the Dead Man to sleep and run Dean off and she could chase me all over the house if she wanted. I wouldn't try too hard to get away. In the interest of science, of course. To see how closely she compared with my nudist visitor, say.

She smiled. The freckles on her cheeks danced. That almost made my day worthwhile.

Almost.

"Dean explained," she said. Funny how he gets on a first-name basis so fast. "I should apologize. That wasn't smart. I'm not used to the city." She stood. My eyes bugged. Her movements were unpretentious and unaffected, and I had to grind my teeth to keep from howling and whistling. She was a natural heart-stopper. Wherever she came from, she'd been wasted on them there. They'd been dumb enough to let her get away. Send more of her kind to TunFaire. Take our minds off poverty and war and despair. Talk about your bread and circuses. This gal was a three-ringer all by herself.

She stuck out a hand. It wasn't half as big as mine. I took it. It was a chock full of warmth and life—which reminded me that Tinnie almost wasn't.

That brought me back to earth. She said, "I'm Carla Lindo Ramada, Mr. Garrett. I came here from—"

Oh boy. "Hold it. Let me guess. The castle of Baron Stonecipher in the Hamadan Mountains. Where you're a chambermaid. The baron sent you after a guy named Holme Blaine who kyped a book from a witch called the Serpent."

Her jaw dropped.

Outside, overhead, the morCartha started up. The racket was so close and so loud it sounded like they were using my roof for landings and take-offs. I told Dean, "They're going to make themselves unpopular if they keep that up."

The redhead realized her pretty little mouth was open, so she closed it, but it sagged open again. She stood there like a goldfish gulping air.

I asked, "Was I close?"

"How did you . . . ?"

I wanted to brag about what a great investigator I was. No point exaggerating, though. "Take it easy. I'm not a psychic." *He* was in the other room. "You're at least the second gorgeous redhead named Carla Ramada who turned up today. You want me to find the book, right?"

"Carla *Lindo* Ramada," she said. Apparently that was important. "But . . . How . . . ?"

"I don't know." There wasn't any doubt in my mind that this wasn't the woman who had been here earlier. I was pretty sure she wasn't the naked woman, either. I couldn't tell you what it was. A subtle clue of some kind. I had only minimal reservations about her being the real Carla Lindo Ramada. She wore the name more comfortably.

Her face went through the changes, all of them fetching. I was thinking the thing to do was get her out of town before she started riots because there was only two or three of her to go around—then I finally started wondering how come there were two or three. Or were there four or five? Was there a whole legion of her out there? Did redheads grow on trees in the Hamadan? Gods, get me into the forestry racket.

Her features settled into solid fear. "It must have been *her*! She must have a page in the book that's me."

"What?" It sank in. "The villain of the piece came here masquerading as you?" Well. Well again. And she was my client. More or less. "But how? If she doesn't have the book anymore?"

She didn't ask how I knew what the book did. She thought about my question. "First draft? Maybe she brought draft pages with her. You couldn't *really* mistake her for me, could you?"

She wasn't that naive after all.

No. I couldn't mistake her, having seen her. I thought back to that earlier visit. It wouldn't come clear. That was odd. The Dead Man has taught me to pick up details and retain them. But I found only mists where I should have had clear, crisp recollections.

"Dean, make us a pot of tea. I have a feeling it's going to be a long night." And who could get any rest with all that racket going on outside? I was beginning to hope they'd wipe each other out. "We might as well relax before we start."

He gave me the hardeye like he wondered if something so sweet would be safe if he visited the kitchen, decided maybe I could restrain myself that long, stalked out. Carla Lindo Ramada told me, "Dean is a sweet man."

"Yeah. Sometimes we have trouble keeping the bees off him. We use him to bait our flytraps. And he's a sucker for a girl in trouble." But not me. Oh, no, not Garrett. Garrett is hard as nails. "How come you were hiding out there?"

"When I arrived in TunFaire, I stayed with people the Baron knows. On the Hill. I asked everybody I saw who might be able to help me. Everybody recommended you."

Gahk! I hadn't thought my name was common coin on the Hill. That could be bad news.

"They say you're honest but you do things your own way and you have a reputation as a chaser." Her eyes sparkled. She definitely wasn't as naive as she looked.

"Me? They must've been thinking about somebody else. I'm pure of heart and soul. Pure as the driven slush."

"But maybe a little lax in mind and body?" More eye twinkle. She was coming back from her fright. Fast. I bet she kept that mountain castle simmering.

She smiled. Her freckles danced. And I knew why she stood out from the other redheads. They didn't have freckles. Even Tinnie doesn't have them. Many. Where they show.

We could've gone on like that all night, but there was a job to do. And Dean would be back any second, pushing his scowl before him. "Guilty more often than not. Let me tell you about the Carla Lindo Ramada who was here before. You tell me when her story doesn't match up with yours."

She listened attentively. Her eyes never stopped sparkling and her freckles never stopped dancing, even when Dean brought our tea. He looked at her looking at me and sighed. He never does quite abandon hope that he can stick me with one of his nieces.

Carla Lindo sipped her tea, seemed startled. Dean had broken out one of his reserve blends. She took another sip, told me, "That's exactly the way it happened, Mr. Garrett. I think."

"You think?"

"I wasn't there. He sent me away so I'd be safe."

"He did? He wanted you safe from the rowdiness at home, but he packed you off to the wicked city alone?" That didn't seem consistent.

"He didn't want to send me. Probably she got here before I did because he spent so much time making up his mind. But he didn't have any choice. I was the only one left that he could trust."

"Why?"

"The Serpent tried to enlist everybody else. Some of them had to be with her. The trustworthy ones all got killed trying to get the book. She never tried to get to me because she knew I'd never do anything against him."

"Why not? We all can be tempted."

"Because he's my father, Mr. Garrett. My mother was a chambermaid, too, so there was no way he could legitimize me, but their relationship wasn't any secret. He never denied me, even to his wife. She hates me and my mother. But she hasn't dared do anything." She shivered, suddenly frightened. There was a big *yet* unspoken there. If Dean had been anywhere else, I would've bounced over to comfort her.

This was getting more complicated by the minute, at the far end, where the story started, but I wasn't a step nearer getting things unraveled here. "Wait up. I'm getting confused. We have a wife and a witch and a mistress and a daughter, all for a guy who's supposed to be two hundred years old, bedridden, and under a curse that won't let him die?"

She looked at me funny. I ran past her what the other Carla Lindo told me. Maybe she hadn't been listening the first time.

"Oh. That's not quite true. Father is old and bedridden, but he wasn't always. And he's not two hundred; she just says that. He's sixty-eight. She put the curse on him when I was four, when he stopped even pretending about my mother and sent her to live in the other tower."

"Huh?"

Dean got it first. "His wife would be the Serpent, Mr. Garrett. He exiled her to a separate part of the castle." So much for my steel-trap mind. Maybe if I was a little less pained and tired . . .

The girl nodded.

"Oh. Right. I got it now. Should have said so." I wondered if that changed anything. I wondered why I cared. The carryings-on of the denizens of a faraway castle were no business of mine. Unless those people wouldn't leave me alone. I thought out loud, "It seems we know who and why, Dean. You think?"

"That Serpent person. Wanting to keep Miss Carla from reaching you and getting your help."

"That's one. What about Squirrel? Her doing?"

He shrugged. "That blond woman?"

"Maybe. Now we know this, what should we do?"

Carla Lindo didn't correct *Dean's* lapse. So she was the kind who would let *him* get away with stuff.

She interrupted my thoughts. "Will you help me, Mr. Garrett?"

I wanted to tell her I wouldn't let her out of my sight. That that would be too painful, like taking away my vision. My eyes couldn't stand the darkness when she was gone. But I kept it businesslike. Barely. "Yes. I think our interests run parallel." Wouldn't be the first time I'd turned on a client who turned out to be shady.

My comments puzzled Carla Lindo. I glanced at Dean. He shrugged. He hadn't told her about Tinnie or that the imposter Carla Lindo had hired me.

"Miss Ramada . . . I became involved in this on a personal level yesterday. A good friend was coming to visit. She's about your height and has red hair. A man tried to kill her out front. One of the Serpent's men, evidently. Mistaking her for you, I suspect. So I have a score to settle, I suppose."

The Dead Man touched me, a summons. He had something he wanted to stick in, in private. "Excuse me. I have to step out for a minute. Finish explaining, Dean."

The old man nodded. He was looking hurt all over again. Like Tinnie had just gotten hit. He'd probably tell it better than I could. He didn't pretend to be tough.

I sure didn't *feel* tough and invulnerable.

slid into the Dead Man's room, starting to feel sorry for myself. I hadn't had me a good dose of that yet. I suppose it was due. Part of being human.

"What's up? This one a ringer, too?"

This one is genuine. She is an open book, easily read—though the truth be told, there is not much written there. Her light does not shine brightly. Be kind to her, Garrett.

"Aw, hell. That ain't playing fair."

He filled my head with a chuckle. *There is kindness and kindness, Garrett. I would not ask you to cease being human.*

"Big of you." Not much, he wouldn't. "What's up?" Looking at all of him here and thinking of all of Carla Lindo over there, I was headed into withdrawal.

One significant factor has escaped you. No. You need not feel slow. Indulgent of him. *It escaped me until you told Miss Ramada about Miss Tate's narrow escape.*

That's the way he is. Nothing straight out. Try to make me figure it out for myself. "Well?"

He didn't play with me long. *You related the same account to the pretender earlier. That woman, if she is indeed the Serpent—and I now believe she is—then knows that Miss Ramada had not been harmed and was in fact ignorant of that threat, so was in no danger of being scared away. Presumably she had something to do with your adventure near Dwarf House. So. Assum-*

ing the house was not watched while you were away, because you were not expected to return . . .

"I've got it. Do you think she figured out that you were here?"

That is of no consequence. It is no secret that you share the home of a Loghyr. She will know once she starts to ask questions.

I skipped his invitation to feud over whose house it was. I considered what we knew about the Serpent. Damned little, but if she was heavyweight enough to create the kind of book that was the root of the excitement, she could be heavyweight enough to cause us trouble. The Dead Man can do incredible things, but strength isn't everything. Sometimes you have to bob and weave and he just isn't light on his feet. There are disadvantages to being dead that even he can't get around.

"Let's back off and look at this. Why is she here? To get her book back. That's the big thing. Keeping me out of her way ought to be secondary. When she was here, she got everything I knew. She gave me stuff back, but only because then she figured me to do her legwork." But if she wanted me to do legwork, why try to hit me? "Maybe she changed her mind when she got wind I was seeing your pal Sneezy."

Sneezy?

"Gnorst Gnorst Gnorst, and so forth. Maybe she started feeling the heat, realized how much she'd stirred up. She's got me and Saucerhead and you and the Tates after her on account of Tinnie, as soon as we figure out she isn't Carla Lindo. She's got the kingpin after her because he wants whoever cut Squirrel. I visit the head dwarf, he squawks like a stuck turkey when I mention the Book of Shadows, goes into a panic, says he's going to put his whole mob on the warpath. They're after her, too. She's got to make some moves. Maybe she figures if she gets rid of me, everybody will sit back for a while because I was the common denominator tying her enemies together."

I'd gone from explaining to thinking out loud. "She's going to push hard, going after that book. She might take another whack at me when she finds out I got away from her boys. Now I can raise the heat even more."

Yes.

"Can there really be a book where you just read a page and turn into whoever's written there?"

She believes it. Gnorst believes it. The girl and those who sent her believe it. The man who stole the book believed it. Miss Tate was wounded because people believe it. What I believe does not matter. This has become a race, Garrett. You have to find that woman before she finds the book.

"How about I just find the book and wait for her to come to me?"

An admirable strategy, simple and direct. I should have seen it myself. How do you propose to execute it?

Sly, sarcastic old devil. Of course it would be easier to find the witch than the book. She was running with a strange pack. Even in TunFaire, it would stand out like pants on a mare.

"I shouldn't be here. I should be at Morley's, in case Sadler gets an interesting report."

Mr Dotes's establishment would be convenient. I can get a message to you there. Though perhaps a modicum of rest would better serve you at the moment.

"Right." He was. "I'm on my way."

Dean looked expectant when I returned to the small front room. "He wanted to remind me that we told the other woman about Tinnie. Which means she knows Carla Lindo is still kicking."

The redhead's eyes got huge. Damned if that didn't make me want to charge over there and set her in my lap and tell her everything was going to be all right. Even if I didn't know everything was going to be all right. Because things would be plenty all right with me as long as she remained perched there.

I said, "We figure there's no reason for you to worry. The cat's out of the bag. Killing you won't chase it back in. She'll concentrate on finding the book."

"You can't let her find it!"

"Take it easy. She'll need some fantastic luck to find it before she gets found herself. In about a minute I'm going to take a walk and tell a man about her, and before you can wink there'll be about three thousand bad people looking for her." I had a thought, which sometimes happens. Sometimes even before it's too late. "What's she look like when she's not being you?"

Carla Lindo just looked at me.

"Well?"

"I'm trying to think. I don't know. I don't think I ever saw her. At least not and know it was her."

"Say what?" The Dead Man had warned me. "You lived in the same place and you never saw her? She had to see you if she put a page in her book that was you." Had to see her pretty damned close. About all she'd left out was the freckles.

"She stayed locked up in her tower. Nobody went in there but people she wanted in there. All those dwarves and ogres and creepy ratmen. If I ever saw her, I didn't know it was her. I'm sure I never saw her."

The Baron's castle had to be some weird place. Not one where I'd like to spend a lot of time. Unless Carla Lindo had her four or five sisters. Maybe I ought to find out if there were any more at home like her.

I must've been showing my thoughts. She gave me a look like she was reading my mind. I stammered some, then managed to say, "You can't give me anything to go on?"

"No. Yes. I never saw it, but they say she wears a ring. Middle finger of her right hand. She never takes it off. It's a snake that wraps around her finger three times. It has a cobra head. They say there's venom in the ring that can kill you instantly."

"That's handy to know." I reflected. "The woman who was here wasn't wearing a ring. I don't think." That was still foggy. "Did you see one, Dean?"

"No." Good man. He refrained from mentioning the extra redhead.

"Then she will take it off in some circumstances. Is there anything else?"

Carla Lindo reddened, which was surprisingly fetching considering her coloring. But I couldn't imagine her doing anything that wasn't fetching. She only had to breathe.

She said, "She has a tattoo. They say. It's how she got her name. The Serpent."

"Huh?" Vagrant memory, of a guy in my company when I was in the Marines. He'd been stuck with the name Donkey Dick till one night he'd gotten all drunked up and had a tattoo artist go to work. After that we called him Snakeman. If he's still alive, I'll bet he regrets it. Unless he's turned it into a carnival act.

The girl stood up. "The whole front of her is supposed to be a snake's face." She gestured. "Her breasts are supposed to be the snake's eyes."

Boy. There was a thought. Imagine waking up and looking over at that next to you. That would dampen your ardor. No wonder old Stonecipher took up with a chambermaid. "That's a vivid image. Anything else?" I could just see me going around ripping open the blouses of suspects.

She shook her head. All that copper hair flying around left me with another vivid image. But this one faded to red hair against cobblestones.

I wondered if Tinnie was going to haunt me. Maybe I'd better go see how she was doing. Tomorrow.

"I have to go out, Dean. Over to Morley's."

His face pruned up with concern. "Is that wise?"

"It's necessary. Put Miss Ramada in the front guest room. She'll be safe enough there."

His look said she'd be safe only as long as I was out of the house. I didn't argue. I seldom do. There's no way to change Dean's mind. Maybe he should've gone ahead and become a priest. You sure can't rattle him with facts.

He'd make a great little old lady, too.

Probably comes of having to live with all those nieces. I hate to wish them on anybody, but I do wish they'd find husbands and get out of his hair.

Dean nodded. I stepped out of the room, deaf to the girl's appeals. I went upstairs and rearmed, then came down and stopped by the office to say good-bye to Eleanor. "Wish me luck, lady. Wish me better luck." I hadn't saved a soul in the case that had involved her. Unless, maybe, in a way, I'd saved me. After the hurting went, I'd found a renewed resolve to do my bit to make the world a better place.

19

Y ou get wary when people have been pounding on you. Even when you're so tired even snazzy redheads have begun to lose their appeal. Before I'd gone a block I sensed I was being watched. I'm not sure what it was. Certainly nothing I could spot. The watcher was that good. Maybe it's a sense you develop in order to survive in this business, in this city.

I decided I'd stay out of places so tight I'd have nowhere to run, which was just common night sense anyway.

I was halfway to Morley's place, dodging low-flying morCartha, when suddenly I was no longer alone. "Shee-it! You guys got to stop doing that. My heart can't handle it." Despite my wariness, Crask and Sadler had surprised me, appearing out of nowhere. An object lesson, most likely. In case I ever became inclined to line up against them. They like to play those games.

I supposed it was their people who had tracked me from my place and sent them word I was coming.

Sadler smiled. At least I think that was supposed to be a smile. Hard to tell in the dark. "Really thought you'd appreciate some good news, Garrett. But if you ain't happy to see us . . ."

"I'm overjoyed. I'm thrilled right down the quicks of my toenails." Thrilled like they were double pneumonia with a raging dysentery tossed in. "Why can't you guys just walk up to me like normal people? You always got to be jumping out of alleys and stuff."

Crask said, "I like to see the look on your face." He wasn't smiling. He wasn't kidding.

Sadler said, "My, my. We're crabby tonight. Did we have a bad day?"

"You got your kicks. So tell me what's the good news?"

"We found your man Blaine."

"Huh?"

Sadler said, "Come on. You ask, we deliver."

Deliver, sure, but without any guarantees about condition.

It's hard to read those two, but I did get a feeling all was not well during our stroll to see Blaine. So I wasn't surprised when, after we'd passed a platoon of henchmen and climbed to a third-floor one-roomer, he turned out to be in a poor state of health.

Some unaccountably thoughtful soul had covered the body with a blanket.

I glanced around. The room's door had been busted off its hinges. And I don't mean just kicked in but torn up like it had gotten in the way of a troll in a hurry who didn't want to be bothered with latches. The room itself was ripped all to hell, like a squad of werewolves had gone berserk there. But there wasn't any blood. "You guys get a little overwrought?"

Sadler shook his head. "Somebody else. We come here when he heard about the racket."

"Who did it?"

He shook his head again. "Everybody cleared out before we got here. You know how it goes. See no evil, hear no evil, you don't got to worry about comebacks. We only caught one old guy who was too slow. He didn't know nothing but the dead guy's name. Dipshit was so thick he used his own name."

"Bright." But what did that mean? None of us knew Holme Blaine. The dead guy could be anybody and we wouldn't know the difference.

I glanced around again. Looking more closely, I could see the damage wasn't just insane destruction after all. "Somebody wanted it to look like crazies did it."

Crask smiled at me like I was a dull pupil who had seen the light at last. "Somebody was looking for something. Maybe some of them looking while some of them were asking. Then we come along unexpected, they do a quick cleanup and fade."

Ha! "So where are they?"

"Gone. Saw us coming."

Huh. I wondered why anyone would bother hiding the fact that they'd searched Blaine's place and fixed him so he couldn't talk about it. Did we have somebody looking for the book who didn't want somebody else looking for it to know they were looking, too?

That came to me off the wall but felt so right I went into a trance trying to figure out why.

Sadler said, "You want something to exercise your mind, check this out." He yanked the blanket off Blaine.

I gaped. I managed a one-syllable expletive after about fifteen seconds, and a quarter of a minute later said, "That's impossible."

"Yeah. Prime example of a mass hallucination."

Damn. Everybody was getting sarky.

Blaine was half-man, half-woman. Actually, more woman than man. Running from three inches above the waist on the right diagonally to his left shoulder, he was a he. Down below he was a she. Very much a she. In fact, a familiar one. I'd seen that end before.

"What do you think of that?" Crask asked.

I chewed some air. I made my eyes bug. "Looks like he had trouble making up his mind." I made funny noises. "Bet he had trouble on dates." They must've thought the circus was in town and I was practicing for my audition.

"First time I ever seen him without some wiseass remark," Crask said. I bet he'd waited a year to pick a time to drop that one.

Sadler asked, "What you know about this, Garrett?"

"I know it's weird. I never saw anything like it." Well, like part of it. That bottom had been in my small front room for a while. "It's like something out of a freak show."

"Not what I meant."

I knew that. "Zip."

"You sure? You wanted this guy."

"Because he was supposed to have the answers."

Sadler gave me the fish eye. "Don't look like anybody's going to get to empty him out, now."

"No. I guess that's the point." I leaned against a wall, where nobody could get behind me, and gave the room another look. But there wasn't anything there to see. Except that body. Whoever did the job, they left nothing of their own. And they didn't find what they were looking for, else they wouldn't have been there still when Crask and Sadler showed. "Nobody saw nothing, eh?"

"This's TunFaire. What do you think?"

I thought they were lucky to have caught the old man they'd caught. I told him so. He grunted.

"You sure you ain't got nothing to tell us, Garrett?"

"Actually, I do. But let it ride a minute. I want you to understand something. I don't have a client. There's no percentage in me holding out." What's a little white fib amongst friends?

Crask said, "Would you look at this?" He'd gotten distracted in a big way.

"What?" Sadler.

Crask pointed at the body. We looked. I didn't get it till Sadler said, "It's changing." A little more of it was male than had been before.

Crask knelt, touched it. "And it's dead enough it's cooling out. This is weird."

"This is sorcery," Sadler said. "I don't like this. Garrett?"

"Don't look at me. I can't change water into ice."

They both scowled, sure I was holding out. Sure. Blame it on Garrett when weird things start to happen.

Crask said, "I don't like it. We ought to get out of here."

I said, "That sounds like a good plan." I headed for the door. "You guys rounded up any other news? You get a line on those dwarves yet?"

They both got a funny look. Sadler said, "Not yet. And that's weird, too."

Crask said, "Yeah. They *got* to leave a trail. They *got* to be staying somewhere."

True. Curious. It bore some thought. Where could they stay and not catch the eyes of the kinds of people who work for Chodo, or who work for the people who work for Chodo? Couldn't be many places like that around.

I paused in the doorway. "Somebody really blew in here."

"Yeah," Crask said. "Hope I never have to arm-wrestle him."

I went over the fragments, looking for maybe a thread from a knit sweater that came only from one small island off the coast of Gretch, or something. You go through the motions even when you think they're pointless. A matter of discipline. They pay off sometimes, so you do them all the time. When I found a big lot of nothing, I wasn't disappointed. I'd fulfilled my expectations. If I'd found something, I'd have been overjoyed, having struck it rich beyond my wildest fancy.

Sadler said, "Let's not slide out so fast, Garrett. You had something to tell us."

"Yeah." I'd been vacillating. Information given up is advantage surrendered.

"Well?"

"Found out about another character who's got something to do with whatever's going on. Called the Serpent. She's the one this guy is supposed to have stolen a book from." Blaine was changing faster, maybe because he was getting cold.

"Well?"

Sadler ought to get together with Puddle for a gabfest. Sparkling. "The Serpent is a witch. She hangs out with dwarves." I took it from the top. They had some of it already but I didn't know how much. I gave them everything I thought they needed to know. I was real ignorant about why the book was a big deal.

"Witch, eh?" Crask eyed Blaine. That was the salient point for him.

"Tattoo?" Sadler asked. He lifted an eyebrow. "That would be a sight to see."

It would, but I was surprised he thought so. He never showed much interest along those lines. He asked, "You figure she cut Squirrel?"

"If she didn't, she knows who did."

"We'll find her. We'll ask."

"Be careful."

He gave me a look. Mostly it wondered about my smarts. He'd be careful. He'd survived his five in the Cantard. He'd survived in his line of work long enough to get to the top. Careful was his middle name right between bad and deadly.

I took a final look at Holme Blaine, who hadn't been careful enough. He still didn't have anything to tell me. I didn't have anything to say to him either.

I'd done my duty. It was time to get my bones moving toward a bed. If the morCartha took pity maybe I could get some sleep.

20

Morley's place wasn't far out of the way. I ignored my weariness and the racket overhead and the doings of a night proceeding in the streets and headed for the Joy House.

Ratmen were out doing what they do, picking up after everyone if they worked for the city, stealing anything loose if they were self-employed. There were more goblins and kobolds and whatnot out than I was used to seeing. I guess the weather had turned for the night people, too.

I still had that feeling I was being watched. And I still couldn't spot a watcher. But I didn't try hard.

Morley's place was a tomb. Nobody there but a couple of the kingpin's men. Even Puddle was gone, home or wherever. That gave me pause to reflect. I don't often think of guys like Puddle, or Crask and Sadler, in human terms. Home. Hell. The guy might have a family, kids, who knew what all. I'd never considered it. He'd always been just another bonebreaker.

Not that I wanted him to ask me over for dinner, to meet the missus and little bonebreakers coming up. I was just in one of those moods where I start wondering about people. Where they came from, what they did when I wasn't looking, like that. Probably got started when Chodo told me about his girlfriend.

It isn't a mood I enjoy. It gets me thinking about myself, my own lack of place and depth in the scheme. No family. Hardly any friends, and them I don't know that well. What I don't know about Morley or Saucerhead could fill books, probably. They don't know me any better, either. Part of being a rough, tough, he-man type, I suppose. Onstage all the time, hiding carefully.

I have plenty of acquaintances. Hundreds. We're all tied together in a net of favors done and owed, all of us keeping tabs on the balance, sometimes thinking it friendship when it isn't anything but a shadow of the obsession that drives Chodo Contague.

Comes out of the war. There isn't a human male in this city who didn't do time in hell. I even have that in common with the nabobs of the Hill. Whatever privileges they claim or steal, exemptions aren't among them.

Down in the Cantard witch's cauldron, you keep track of all the little stuff and strive to keep a balance because you don't want anybody checking out owing you. And, even though you share a tent, cooking utensils, campfires, clothes, even girls, you never get too close to anybody because a lot of anybodies are going to die before it's over. You keep your distance and it don't hurt so much.

You dehumanize the enemy entirely and your comrades enough so—though you'll charge into hell behind them or storm heaven to rescue them—you never open your heart and never let them open theirs.

It makes sense when you're down there in the shitstorm. And once you've survived the storm and they send you home, you're saddled with that baggage forever. Some come home like Crask and Sadler, purged of everything human.

That got me wondering what those two had done during their duty. I'd never heard. They'd never said. A lot of guys don't. They put it all behind them.

Then I started wondering why, though the night people were busier than usual, it was so quiet out. Night isn't just the time of those races who have to shun the sunshine, it's the time of the bad boys, the time when the predators come out. I wasn't seeing anybody dangerous or suspicious.

I guess Chodo had the baddies beholden to him busy, and the freelancers, not clued in, were lying low so they wouldn't catch his attention. Or maybe it was just the morCartha being so obnoxious nobody came out who didn't have to.

The morCartha weren't that much trouble if you hugged the edge of the street and kept an eye out. They seldom risked crashing into a building just to swoop down and steal a hat.

Speaking of whom . . .

The tenor of their aerial pandemonium changed suddenly, radically. A violent outcry spread. It sounded like terror. Hasty wings beat the air frothy. The sky cleared. An almost total silence fell. It was so remarkable I paused to look at the sky.

A broken fragment of moon lay somewhere low in the east, out of sight, casting barely enough light to limn the peaks and spires of the skyline. But there was light enough to show a shape circling high up.

Its wings sprawled out a good thirty feet. It wasn't doing anything but making a wide, gliding turn over the city before heading back north.

A flying thunder-lizard. I hadn't known they were night hunters. I'd never seen one before. What I saw of this one made it look a lot like a prototype for all those dragons guys in tin suits are killing in old paintings. I hear they are. The dragons of story are mythical. Which makes them about the only imaginary creatures in this crazy world. Hell, I've even run into a god who thought he was real.

"Garrett."

I turned, less surprised than I expected. There must have been subconscious clues. "Winger. Kinda hoped I'd run into you again. Wanted to warn you. You got some bad people looking for you. Not in too good a mood, either."

That surprised her. "You can tell me about it on the way. Let's go."

I didn't think to ask where or why because her attitude tapped my anger. "I have a previous engagement. With my bed. You want to talk to me about something, come around in the morning. And try to ask nice."

"Garrett, you seem like a pretty good guy, considering. So let's don't butt heads. Let's don't do it the hard way. Just come on."

She had a problem. A serious problem. Now I wouldn't have gone anywhere with her even if I'd planned to before. "Winger, I kind of like you. You got balls and style. But you got an attitude problem that's going to get you hurt. You want to make it in the big city, you got to learn some street manners. You're also going to have to know who you're messing with before you mess. You cut somebody who has friends like Chodo Contague, your chances of staying healthy just aren't good."

She looked baffled. "What the hell you talking about?"

"That guy you cut in the alley off Pearl Lane. A couple thousand of his friends are looking for you. They don't plan to slap you on the back and tell you you did a great job."

"Huh? I never cut nobody."

"I hope not. But he was following you when it happened. Who else could've done it?"

She thought about it for half a minute. Then her frown cleared as she decided not to worry about it. "Come on."

"Not smart, Winger. You're pressing where you don't know what you're doing."

She was one stubborn woman. And just a whole lot too confident. Maybe where she came from men wouldn't defend themselves against a woman. Maybe she was used to them hesitating.

Hell, I might have myself. But she'd let me talk and that had given me time to get my mind right.

She got out a nightstick not unlike my head-thumper. So I got out mine, a replacement for the one I'd left down by Dwarf Fort. She came in figuring to feint a few times and tap me upside the head. I didn't cooperate. My head had taken enough dents already.

I just slipped her guard, rapped her knuckles, then her elbow when the pain froze her for an instant, then jabbed her in the breadbasket as her stick tumbled toward the street. "That's how you use one of these things." She wasn't very good. All bull offense.

She didn't seem upset because she'd been disarmed so easily, just surprised. "How'd you get so damned fast?"

"There's two kinds of Marines, Winger. Fast ones and dead ones. Better get something through your head right now, before you run into somebody who won't cut you some slack. There isn't a man in this town, over twenty-three, who wasn't tough enough and fast enough to survive five years in the Cantard. A lot of them, you make a move on them, they'll leave you for the ratmen and not look back. Especially the bunch that are looking for you. They *like* to hurt people."

"I said I didn't cut nobody. Not yet."

"Then you'd better be able to tell them who did. Fast."

She raised both eyebrows. A strange woman. She wasn't afraid. You have to worry about the sanity of somebody who doesn't have sense enough to be afraid of Chodo Contague.

"You be careful," I told her. "Come by in the morning if you still want to talk." I turned to head for home.

Damned if she didn't try again. Barehanded.

The reflexes still worked. I heard her move, pranced aside, stuck out a leg and tripped her, grabbed her by the hair on the fly. "That's twice, Winger. Even nice guys run out of patience. So knock it off." I turned loose, started walking.

This time she listened to the message.

21

Dean almost got his marching orders when he went to get me up for my morning run. He's worse than a mom about not buying excuses. "You started it, you stick with it," he told me. "You're going to run, you're going to run every day."

Grumble grumble grikkle snackfrortz. Go take a flugling fleegle at a frying forsk. I said something like that. I fought the good fight till he went for the ice water. Then my yellow stripe came out. He'd do it, the driggin droogle. I didn't want to stay in bed that bad.

Carla Lindo was heating up the kitchen when I stumbled in. I grumbled a greeting.

"He always such a ball of sunshine in the morning?"

Dean told her, "This is one of his better mornings." Thanks, old-timer. He plunked honeyed tea down at my place at the table. He had bacon frying, biscuits baking. The smell of the biscuits was heavenly. I gathered he hadn't bothered to go home. Not much point. Wouldn't have been much time to sleep.

His nieces were used to it. They'd know I was into something. Now, if they'd just forget to use him not coming home as an excuse to come hang around, cooking and baking and batting their eyes and uglying up the place . . .

I sipped tea and stared into a fog, nothing much else happening inside my head. Carla Lindo stared at me but didn't say anything. She wore a teensy frown. Maybe her confidence was rattled.

You may suspect that morning isn't my best time. You may be right. I'm waiting for some genius to figure out a way to do without it. The sad truth is, too often it sets the tone for the rest of the day.

"How do you feel this morning?" Carla Lindo finally asked.

"Black and blue. My bruises got bruises." I hadn't been a lovely sight when I got dressed. I'd seen corpses in better condition.

Dean took the biscuits out, set the baking sheet directly on a trivet on the table. "You ought to figure a way to trade with His Nibs. He could get out and run while you loafed all you want."

He takes advantage of me mornings. Snipes away, knowing my brain isn't working. The best I can do is threaten to send him job hunting. A hollow threat if ever there was one. Crafty old dink don't play fair. He made himself indispensable.

He asked, "Did you learn anything last night?" as he brought the bacon.

"Yeah. That Winger character's only got one oar in the water." I told him about it.

He grinned. "I didn't think she killed that man."

"World's best judge of character," I told Carla Lindo. "Somebody sent Squirrel to the promised land, Dean. That character Blaine, too."

That got Carla Lindo. "What?" She looked stricken.

"Somebody did him. Busted his door down, tore his place up, left him dead."

"The book!"

"I guess."

"Damn it! Now *she* has it again." She jumped up, started pacing. I wasn't so far gone in the morning blahs that I wasn't distracted. "What will I do? Father was counting on me."

"Take it easy, love." My, wasn't she a sight when she was excited, bouncing and jiggling and . . . "Whoever did it didn't find the book. If that was what they were after. They were still trying when they were interrupted."

"Then . . ."

"It wasn't there to be found. Carla Lindo, my sweet, sit down. You're doing things to my concentration. That's better. You sure there isn't something you haven't told me? You been holding back something that would make sense of what's been happening?"

Big-eyed, looking shocked and hurt, she shook her head. I doubted she was telling the truth. Well, maybe, by her own lights, she was telling her own version. But it sure felt like there ought to be something more.

Breakfast usually brightens my outlook. I had been known, recently, to go into my morning runs with a smile on my puss. This morning was going to be an exception. This morning my mood just got blacker. I didn't finish eating.

I pushed back from the table. Carla Lindo was still shoveling it in. Where do those little ones put it? "I'm going to see Himself." I walked out. Dean looked hurt, like I'd made some nasty remark about his cooking.

I was no bundle of sunshine falling on the Dead Man, either. I stepped into his room, grumped, "You awake?"

I am now, O Shield Against Darkness.

"Huh?"

An attempt, however futile, to cajole you away from your gloom. I abandon it forthwith. There is no hope. Review events of last night.

I reviewed events of last night. I spared no detail. I finished, said, "I'm open to suggestions." My own best notion was to lock the front door and not answer it till the world straightened itself out.

Hardly practical, Garrett. Blaine's death is a setback, yes. But, I agree, it seems unlikely his murderers obtained the Book of Dreams. Unless Mr. Crask and Mr. Sadler were not telling the whole truth.

"Huh?" I was ready to get in there and mix it up with Puddle.

I suspect that Chodo Contague would be very interested in the Book of Dreams if he became cognizant of its capacity and function. Very interested, indeed, considering his personal circumstances.

"Huh?" Again. I was on a roll.

Think! A flash of impatience. *We have discussed this already!*

Yell, hell. Yeah. Shoot, fire. If Chodo knew what the Book of Shadows could do, he'd be after it like an addict ratman after weed. I'd bet there wasn't a page in the whole one hundred that was a crippled old dink in a wheelchair. He could be young again. He could dance at weddings and funerals. Mainly funerals. He could chase girls and be able to do something when he caught them. Not to mention all the wonderful ways he could use it in his business.

Yeah. Chodo and the book were not meant for each other. "I got it, Smiley. I'm slow but I get there."

Excellent. So. What you really came for was to get me to tell you what to do. To avoid the unwonted labor of deciding for yourself. Very well. First, avoid contact with Mr. Chodo's people as much as possible. Try to create the appearance of disinterest in pursuing the matter further. By way of establishing a foundation for that pretense, I suggest you visit Miss Tate. Assuming, as is probable, you find her mending quickly, you have your basis for proclaiming no further interest. See to that immediately after your morning run.

"What morning run?" I had me a bad feeling here.

Off we went into a grand fuss about me maintaining my training regimen. He got in the last word. He usually does. He's more stubborn, but that's only because he has more time. He can argue for the rest of my life if he wants.

You must also reconnect with the woman Winger. An encounter with her principal could be most instructive.

"Fatal, too, maybe."

We have no idea who he is or where he fits. His very existence lends credence to your ill-formed suspicion that there are more than two parties to the search for the Book of Dreams.

I can't keep anything from him. Not in the long run. Hell. I'd thought I was covering that idea pretty cleverly.

I felt his gloating as he continued, *There are two additional areas deserving pursuit. As time permits. The movements and contacts of the Blaine person before his encounter with misfortune. And the whereabouts of our friend Mr. Dotes.*

I sensed a touch of concern for Morley. I was a touch concerned myself. Nobody had seen him for a while. He wouldn't disappear. . . .Unless he'd gone under to do a job or was sincerely concerned about his health. If his health wasn't gone already.

Seemed a little premature to start worrying, though. He hadn't been gone that long. "He probably isn't anywhere. He just hasn't been at his place when I have. No law says he's got to hang around waiting for me to drop in."

Perhaps. Even so . . .

"I'll check him out." It looked like another full day. I looked forward to it with the same enthusiasm I look forward to arthritis.

Go. Do your running. Visit Miss Tate. Visit Mr. Dotes's establishment. Be back in time for lunch. I will interview Miss Ramada in the interim and prepare additional suggestions.

He would, too. Probably suggestions involving trotting down to the Cantard and back.

Ah. Indeed. Thank you for reminding me. Do keep an ear open for news of Glory Mooncalled. I anticipate word of major events soon.

What? Had he figured some angle nobody else saw? Maybe. He'd anticipated Mooncalled's mutiny, more or less.

Him and his damned hobby. Why couldn't he collect coins or used nails or something?

Hell, I'd have to do the legwork there, too.

I went back to the kitchen for another cup of tea. Breakfast had started working inside me. I could appreciate Carla Lindo a little more. I indulged myself till Dean started grumbling about me being in the way. Never said a word about Carla Lindo, did he? Even though he hates having anybody help him because it disturbs his rhythm and routine.

"Well, I'm off on my campaign of self-torture."

Nobody seemed very excited.

Once on the stoop, I paused to suck in a couple of lungfuls of TunFaire's chunk-style air. Because of the warm spell, it was thinner than usual, what with nobody needing to heat their homes. Didn't have much spice at all, actually. I didn't miss it. I looked around.

Dang me. The sun wasn't even up yet, hardly, and already I knew this wasn't going to be one of my better days.

Winger was hanging out down the way, not hiding at all, just about ten yards beyond the Dead Man's usual effective range. She must've gotten around to doing some homework.

She didn't bother me nearly as much as did several other studious types hanging out trying to be invisible. There wasn't a dwarf among them. They were all human, by courtesy. Not the type you want your daughter to bring home. Bent-nose boys, collective intelligence level about that of a slow possum. There were four of them. With Winger? I couldn't tell. She didn't seem to notice them. Nor they her. Chodo's boys? They didn't have that feel. Took me a moment to figure why.

They weren't neat. In fact, they were pretty scraggly. Chodo's troops have to meet a certain minimal level of personal hygiene, dress, and grooming. These guys never heard of those words. Anyway, Chodo has more respect for me. He'd send Crask and Sadler.

Who, then? The Serpent? But she seemed to prefer dwarves and ogres and whatnot.

All that passed through my head in a couple seconds. I considered going inside and locking up and saying the hell with it all. Then I got mad.

All this time I was stretching and yawning and carrying on like I didn't see a thing. I skipped down the steps and turned right, away from Winger, skipped around a little warming up, then took off running.

Fast. It caught them off balance. The two in the direction I was headed pushed off walls, then exchanged "what now?" looks. I was past the first before anybody made a decision.

Then I started flying.

Somebody else got into the game.

Three quarrels zipped past me, plunging bolts loosed from a rooftop across the street. I don't know why they waited till I was moving to start sniping—though I wasn't all that long getting started and maybe they had to wake up first. The best-sped quarrel passed a few inches ahead, high. I tossed a glance back, saw a little ball of hair duck out of sight atop the only flat roof on that side of the street.

I sailed past the second thug, heeling and toeing and whooping for all I was worth. People scattered like startled chickens. I bounded over piles of horse apples deposited since the ratmen passed through. The last watcher came pounding after me but it was obvious he lived a dissolute life. He couldn't keep up for a block.

I zigged into a breezeway, zagged through an alley, leaped and dodged assorted snoring drunks and weed-puffing ratmen, scavenging dogs and hunting cats and even one crippled morCartha, zoomed into always busy Wodapt Street, and faded into the crowd.

Easy as that. No problem now till I decided to go home.

Well, it did take a minute or two to really blend in. For a while I was whoofing and puffing so bad everybody backed away.

I got mad all over again. What was this crap, dwarves trying to snuff me all the time? What did I ever do to them? I don't have to put up with that. And Winger . . . I had a mind to turn her over my knee. Only she was as big as me and that might take more turning than I could manage. But I'd had about enough. I was ready to start pushing back.

I ambled up to the Tate compound and spent an hour at Tinnie's bedside. She was mending fine. Full of fire and vinegar. We had us a good little spat, and because she wasn't in any shape for making up, I went away grouchier than ever.

Barely past breakfast time and already it was a memorably lousy day.

One of the innumerable nephews caught me before I made good my escape. "Uncle Willard wants to see you, Mr. Garrett."

"Right." Just what I needed. A fuss with the head Tate. No matter how rotten I felt, I couldn't get my heart into an argument with him. He'd suffered so much sorrow in the time I'd known him, unearned, that it just didn't seem right to give him any grief.

I went peaceably, ready to absorb whatever aggravation he wanted to give me.

He was at his workbench. Where else? He'd told me once that the family had a touch of elvish blood. I wondered if he hadn't fudged a little and it was really dwarfish. He was addicted to work.

He gave me the fish eye, face unreadable. "Sit if you like, Mr. Garrett." Maybe I wasn't high up his list after all.

"Something on your mind?" I sat.

"I understand you're looking for the people responsible for what happened to Tinnie."

"Sort of."

"What does that mean? Sort of."

I explained. I wondered how many times I would have to tell the story, in how many versions, before the dust settled.

Tate listened closely. I know he picked out those points where I slipped past something I wanted to keep to myself. He said, "I see." He reflected for half a minute. "I'd like to meet the person who sent that man to kill Tinnie, Mr. Garrett."

"It was mistaken identity. Had to be."

"I realize that, Mr. Garrett. Even so, Tinnie was hurt. Badly. She would have been killed had not you and your friend been nearby. Had you not intervened. I've given this considerable thought. I want to meet the person responsible. I'll pay well for the opportunity."

He'd have to get in line, but why not? "I'll find her. Or him."

"Him? I was under the impression you believed this witch . . ."

"The Serpent? Seems likely. But, like I said, as time goes by I become more convinced there's another party involved. Somebody working against the Serpent. And anybody else who gets in the way."

"The blond woman." He nodded. "You might question her."

"Yeah." Like she was going to let me. "Speaking of her, she says her principal's name in Lubbock. Mean anything? Ever heard the name?"

He didn't hesitate. "Lubbock Crister, tanner. Lubbock Tool, drayage. Frith Lubbock. Wholesale greengrocer. Yon Lubbock Damascen, shipping agent. All men I've done business with, one time or another. Surely there are others. Historically, you have Marshall Lubbock, the imperial general. You have Lubbock Candide, the sorcerer, and his daughter Arachne, who were so black-hearted and vicious mothers still use their names to frighten children."

"All right. All right." I'd never heard of any of them but the last two, but he had a point. "There're plenty of Lubbocks out there. And this Lubbock probably isn't named Lubbock at all. Could even be the Serpent under an assumed name."

The little old guy nodded again, his hair floating around his head. He picked up his TenHagens, perched them on his nose. The interview was over. He was going back to work. "Thank you, Mr. Garrett. Please do keep me posted, when you have the odd moment. And do make time to visit Tinnie. She hasn't many friends."

"I will."

"Leo!" He called for one of the nephew horde. "See Mr. Garrett to the gate." Just to make sure I didn't get lost somewhere along the way.

I hit the street feeling oddly relieved, like I'd taken care of an unhappy duty, comparable to a visit to an unpleasant maiden aunt, and now I could get on with work that mattered. I didn't much like me when I recognized the feeling. Tinnie was no old lady turned to vinegar in her solitude. I would have to examine my feelings toward her more closely.

I stopped walking, leaned against a wall, started the process of self-examination while considering my next move.

don't figure I set a record for the standing high jump but I did go up like I had wings.

"Garrett!"

I came down facing Winger, knowing I'd have been dead if she'd wanted me that way.

This was a free one. The gods wouldn't hand me another chance to get away with napping on the street. "Hey, Winger." I hoped my voice didn't quaver too bad.

How had she found me so fast?

Homework. I'll bet she took my advice and did her homework. There was hope for her.

I looked around. I didn't see the guys who'd chased me. "Where are your brunos?"

"Huh?"

I'd forgotten she was from out of town. She wouldn't know the argot. Brunos are low-grade hired thugs. "The hard boys who were with you outside my place."

"They weren't with me. I didn't know they were there till you took off and they went after you."

"Oh?" The gods shield fools, all right. "Maybe you better think about getting into another line of work. You aren't going to stay alive long in this one."

She shrugged. "Maybe not. But if I go, I'll check out doing what I want to do, not worn out from pulling a plow and making babies."

She had a point. One of the reasons I do what I do is because I get to be my own boss, not a creature caught in a web of commitments and responsibilities. "I got you."

"It's tomorrow, Garrett. And Lubbock is getting impatient."

Tough, I thought. I said, "All right. Lead on."

She headed toward the Hill. I let her lead and set the pace, kept my mouth shut. She walked like she was still behind a plow. Kind of a waste. If you took time to look her over, you saw she wasn't a bad-looking woman at all, just put together on a large scale. Way too big for my taste. I figured she would clean up pretty nice. If she wanted.

I asked, "You happen to get a look at those clowns who were sniping at me off that roof?"

She grinned. "I did better than that, Garrett. I ambushed them when they came down. Kicked their butts and broke their toys."

"All of them?"

"There was only four of them. Little hairy fellas. Stubborn. Trick with them is, stay in too close for them to use them crossbows but don't get so close they can reach you. Work on them with your feet." She skipped, kicked a foot high. I hadn't seen boots like those since I got out of the Marines. Those would do a job on somebody. If you had the strength to lift them.

"How come you did that?"

"They was horning in on my game. You ain't no good to me full of them little arrows."

"I wouldn't be much good to me, either. Wish I knew where they came from."

"Them fuzzballs?"

"The very ones, Winger. That makes three times they've come after me." Recalling that I started watching my surroundings with more enthusiasm.

We *were* headed toward the Hill. Her principal had to be a stormwarden or firelord or . . . I tried to recall which of our sorcerer elite might be in town. I couldn't think of one. Everybody who was anybody and old enough was down in the Cantard helping hunt Glory Mooncalled.

If I was the political type, I'd figure this was a great time for an uprising. Our masters hadn't left anyone to keep us in line. But I'm not a political type. And neither is anyone else. So we'll just keep going on going on the way we've always gone on—unless Mooncalled pulls off his greatest coup yet and arranges it so none of them come home.

After deliberating, Winger told me, "I don't know where they come from, Garrett. But I got a good idea where they went."

"Ah?" Turn up the charm and cunning, Garrett. Shuck and jive this rube right out of her socks.

"Twenty marks. Silver. After you see Lubbock."

I'm nothing if not adaptable. "I'll give you three." I wasn't carrying much more than that.

"It's your ass. You don't figure it's worth twenty marks, I'm not going to argue with you."

Some of these rubes have a certain low cunning and a nose for sniffing profit out of disaster. "Make it five, then."

She didn't say anything, just led me on toward the Hill. All right. She'd come around. Five marks was a lot of money to a country girl.

A couple of dwarves ambled across an intersection ahead. I blurted, "Ten." And they hadn't even looked our way. Hell, they never did. They were just a couple of short businessmen.

Winger ignored me.

All right. I know. I gave myself away there. But I was nervous. You'd be nervous if you had dwarves trying to poop you every time you stuck your head out of the house.

Dean doesn't let me do the marketing, either.

I didn't let up on keeping a lookout. Not for a second. I didn't see anything disturbing, either, except once I caught a glimpse of a guy who could have been Crask, but he was a block away and I couldn't be sure. I did grin, though. That might be something to bargain with.

stopped, studied our destination.

"Come on, Garrett. Quit farting around."

"I want to look it over first." The place looked like some nut's idea of a haunted castle, in miniature, a hangout for runt werewolves and vampires too limp of wrist to fly. It was a castle, all right, but no bigger than the surrounding mansions. About quarter scale. All black stone and dirty. "Cheerful little bungalow. This where Lubbock lives?" I'd seen the place before but hadn't paid attention. Just another hangout for some nut on the Hill. I knew nothing about it.

"Yeah. He owns it. Only, tell you the truth, I don't think his name is really Lubbock."

"No! Really?"

She gave me a double dirty look.

"What do you know about him?"

"He's in metals smelting. That's his business, I mean. Royal contracts. Very rich. I picked that up keeping my ears open. He's a little peculiar."

"I'll say."

"Try to keep a straight face."

I started moving again. Slowly.

I expected zombie guards at the gate. Maybe gnome zombies, since the place was so shrunk down.

Black steel bars covered its few windows. A toy drawbridge spanned a toy moat five feet wide. Nonhuman, fangy skulls hung over the gate. Smoke dribbled out of their nose holes. Oily torches burned in broad daylight. Somewhere a group of musicians played spooky music. A dozen morCartha perched on the battlements, living gargoyles. I'll say somebody was peculiar.

A guy who goes to live on the Hill usually buys or builds his dream house there.

I stopped, considered the morCartha. They seemed lethargic beyond what was to be explained by the fact that it was daytime. Winger said, "Let's don't stand around in the street." She crossed the drawbridge without a qualm. "You coming?"

"Yeah. But I'm beginning to wonder if this is such a bright idea."

She laughed. "Stop worrying. It's all for show. He's a crackpot. He likes to dress up and play sorcerer but the only magic he can do is make food disappear."

Probably so. If he had any real talent, he'd be in the Cantard trying to outwaltz Glory Mooncalled.

A cadaverous old guy met us. Without a word he led us to a small, spooky receiving room. The walls were decorated with whips and chains and antique instruments whose function I didn't even want to guess. By way of art there was a rogues' gallery of demonic portraiture. Also a couple of real people I probably should have known, did I pay much attention to history. They looked like they'd shaped our past.

Lubbock joined us.

He made the Dead Man look slim and trim. He had to go six hundred pounds if he went a stone. He wore a silly black wizard's outfit that looked like he'd made it himself. It had enough material in it to provide tents for a battalion. The powers that be got wind of it, they'd have him up on charges of hoarding.

Lubbock smiled a smile that got lost in the ruddy landscape of his face. It made me think of the wax dripping down around the top of a candle. "Ah, Winger. You've managed to get the man here at last. Pay her, Pestilence." A woman who looked like she might be the old guide's grandmother brought Winger a small leather bag. Winger made it disappear fast.

"Mr. Garrett." Lubbock tried to bow. I tried to keep a straight face. Neither of us was completely successful, though I managed well enough.

That old boy had one spooky voice. It sent chills scampering around my back. I bet he spent hours practicing to get that effect. "I had begun to wonder if I hadn't made a mistake employing you."

I thought she'd made the mistake, taking him on as an employer. But sometimes you have to do what you have to do to keep body and soul together. I asked, "How you doing, Lubbock?"

He threw up his hands and crossed his wrists in front of his heart, palms toward me. He made fists but left his little fingers standing. He waggled his pinkies furiously. He had nails almost two inches long. I guessed that was some kind of sorcerer's move. I think I was supposed to be impressed.

And some people I know say *I* belong in the Bledsoe cackle factory because I don't have a firm grasp on reality.

Winger whispered, "At least pretend to be courteous, Garrett."

"I asked him how he was when I don't care, didn't I? What more do you want?" Blame it on nerves. When people give me the creeps, I get flip. "Get him talking." I wanted answers from Lubbock but had the heebie-jeebies bad enough to think of walking.

He got himself started. "Mr. Garrett," again. "Good day. I have awaited our meeting anxiously."

"Pleased to meet you. Whoever you are." See? Courteous. I could have said *whatever* you are.

Another smile tried to break through and died young, smothered by fat. "Yes. As you surmise, my name is not Lubbock. No sir. That is merely wishful thinking, the heartfelt desire to walk the same path as the great Lubbocks of centuries past."

He rolled his fists over heel to heel with their backs toward me, looked at me between raised forefingers that, more or less, made the ancient sign against the evil eye. "Unfortunately, my dream is denied me by harsh reality."

I recalled Willard Tate mentioning a couple of dead double nasties named Lubbock. Sorcerer types. This guy obviously had less talent than I do. His harsh reality. So he was playing some wacky game.

If you're rich enough, you're allowed.

"As you surmise, sir," he repeated, "my name is not Lubbock. Hiding the truth from a man of your profession would be foolish. You need but poll the neighbors to learn that madman Fido Easterman lives here."

"Fido?" People don't even name their dogs Fido anymore.

"It means 'faithful,' Mr. Garrett. Yes sir. Faithful. My father, rest his soul, was an aficionado of imperial history. Fido was an imperial honorarium. Rather like a knighthood today. Though it could be bestowed upon anyone, not just those nobly born. Yes sir. The man whose name I took in vein, like a momentary domino, my kinsman Lubbock Candide, attained that very distinction. He was an ancestor of mine, you know. The glittering star atop my family tree. Yes sir. But the power in the blood failed after his daughter, Arachne. How I abuse the gods for that jest."

Man. This clown was a one-man gale. "What's that got to do with me?" Trying to get to the point. "Why am I here?" I tried to figure the color of his eyes. I couldn't make them out behind all that fat.

"Patience, my boy. Patience. One never hurries the headsman." He chuckled wickedly. "Just my little joke, sir. Just my little joke. You are in no danger here."

Like hell. Wouldn't take too much of this to get me foaming at the mouth and talking to little men who weren't there.

I kept an eye on the staff. They came and went in the background, eager to see their boss in action. He was a real three-ringer. They all wore costumes and spooky makeup. Easterman could afford to pay people to pretend that he was bad.

Hell, maybe he was. In a more mundane way. Amongst the remote voyeurs I spotted one of the men who had chased me away from my place.

Don't call him crazy, though. The Eastermans of the world are never crazy. When you have money, you're eccentric.

"Fido Easterman, yes sir." He put all his fingers together and made a spider doing push-ups on a mirror. Then he pulled his hands apart slowly, as though he was pulling against tremendous forces. His fingers shook like he was coming down with a disease.

"I've been hearing rumors about a marvelous book, Mr. Garrett. Yes sir, a masterpiece. I wish to obtain that book, sir. I will pay very well indeed to obtain it. Winger has been doing my legwork for me, searching. As you can see, I am not cut out for strenuous effort, however much I might wish it to be otherwise. She has been hunting diligently, of course hoping to separate me from a substantial portion of my wealth. But fortune has not been kind to her. Her only success has been to discover that you may have some knowledge of the book's whereabouts." He beamed at me. Before I could get a word in, he continued, "Well, then, sir, from what I have learned of your situation, it's likely you could use a substantial sum. Paid in the metal of your choice."

"I sure could. I wish I had something to sell. I don't know where she got the idea I know anything about any book."

"Come, sir. Come. Let us not play games with one another. Let us not bandy words. I have said that I will pay well to obtain that book, and I will. My word is good, as any fool can discover by posing a few questions in the ores and metals community. But if you do go asking about me there, you will also discover that I have a reputation for getting what I want."

I didn't doubt it a bit. "All I can tell you about the book is that it exists, maybe, supposedly incomplete. But I don't have the faintest idea where."

"Come, sir. Surely you don't expect me to . . ."

"I don't expect you to do anything but stay out of my hair."

"Sir . . ."

"I told you I don't know where it is. You did some checking on me, eh? I tell the truth? The truth is, I was looking for it myself. For a client. I succeeded only in finding the man who stole it."

"Ah, sir. Now we're getting somewhere."

"We're getting nowhere. The guy was dead."

He chuckled. "Unfortunate. Most unfortunate." I got the feeling this wasn't news.

I spotted another of those guys who had chased me. It finally sank in. Here was my third force. This nut and his brunos. Those guys probably sent Blaine to the promised land. Maybe they'd done the same with Squirrel. I said, "I don't want anything more to do with this book. It's gotten a bunch of people killed already. It's got the Dwarf Fort dwarves on the warpath. It's got Chodo Contague out for blood because one of his men got cut." That got a small reaction. "It's got a witch called the Serpent and a bunch of renegade dwarves running around the city sniping with crossbows. I don't need to get in the middle of any of that."

Easterman closed his eyes and started talking. Actually, he made some kind of speech, but it wasn't in Karentine. I'd guess Old Forens, which is still around as a liturgical language amongst some of the more staid of Tun-Faire's thousand cults. I don't know ten words of Old Forens but I've heard it used and this had that cadence.

Good old Fido was a linguist like he was a sorcerer. But what he lacked in talent he made up in enthusiasm. He howled and foamed at the mouth.

I'd come with Winger hoping to ask some questions. Now I didn't care. All I wanted was out. Things were sane outside. There were thunder-lizards in the air for the first time since TunFaire's founding. There were thunder-lizards at the gates. There were centaurs in the streets. There were saber-tooth tigers and mammoths and morCartha and gnomes. My friends had disappeared. Crask and Sadler were acting spookier than ever. But it was sane out there. I could survive in that world out there. I told Winger, "I'm thinking about becoming a bricklayer. Bricklayers don't have these problems."

She shrugged, kept staring at Easterman like he was a genius revealing the secrets of the universe. Maybe she understood him. She was a little bit twitchy herself.

I gave up and more or less went to sleep on my feet, paying just enough attention so nobody walked up and bopped me with a battle-ax without me noticing. I stayed only because Winger wasn't ready to leave. I couldn't leave her with this spook. He might hold a virgin sacrifice, figuring, hell, she used to be and maybe that was close enough. Also, she knew something I wanted to know.

Easterman finished having his fit. "Well, sir. Well," he said, not the least embarrassed. "Do we have an understanding, then?"

"No."

His people did manage to be embarrassed. But they covered it and didn't walk out. I suppose he paid very well indeed. He'd have to.

He looked puzzled. As much as he could with all that fat to mask expression. "I thought I made myself crystal clear, sir."

"If you made a lick of sense somewhere, I missed it in the smoke."

"Garrett!" Winger cried.

Easterman smiled again. I think that was a smile back in there. "Very well, sir. In words even you will understand, then. I want that book. I mean to have that book. I get what I want. Those who help me to obtain it will be well rewarded. Those who attempt to thwart me will not be so fortunate. Is that clear enough?"

"I got it." I returned his smile. "I'll pass the word to Chodo Contague and the Serpent if I run into them. I'm I sure it'll set them to shaking in their boots so bad they'll scurry out of the way so you'll have an open field." Threat and counter. All very friendly, with knives held behind our backs.

Winger started apologizing for my barbarism. The more I saw of her, the more I couldn't figure her out.

"No matter, child. No matter. The man has an image to maintain. As we all do, of course. As we all do. Very well, sir. I think our business is quite concluded. We understand one another. I was about to dine. Will you join me? I do set a fine table."

I pleaded press of business. I didn't want to see what kind of table this creep set. Could be hazardous. Wasn't lunchtime, anyway.

"Very well, sir. As you will. I hope to be seeing you again soon, in circumstances profitable to us all. Plague." He gestured at the cadaverous old man. "Escort our guests, if you will."

The old man bowed, then led me and Winger to the castle gate. I kept a sharp eye on the old boy. I didn't need to get pushed through any secret doors. I tried making conversation about his boss. He wasn't having any. Maybe that wasn't smart for a guy in his position.

Winger took up the slack. "I'm disappointed in you."

"I'm disappointed in me a lot, too. What did I do to break your heart?"

"That guy is a ripe fruit."

"A whole orchard."

"Worked right . . ."

"I couldn't take the clown. He could probably tell me something I need to know, but . . . I'd like to hold his toes in a fire for a while."

"Garrett!"

"You got yourself tied in with a loony, Winger. He'll get you killed. I'll take your word you weren't working with those guys who chased me a while back. But I noticed some of them were there, hanging around in the background. You better keep your eyes open." I had a feeling they'd been dogging her since Easterman hired her. A character like him would use a tactic like that.

I had no sympathy for Fido. I didn't owe him squat. And now I had an idea who'd done Squirrel. I'd pass it on next time I saw Crask or Sadler.

We got out of that bughouse. I didn't look back. "Winger, you know anything about the book?"

"Only that it's supposed to be about so by so and weigh fifteen to twenty pounds. The pages are brass."

"Brass. Brass shadows. It's what the dwarves call a book of shadows. Each page has a character described on it. Whoever reads the page can become the character written there."

"Say what?"

We were safely away, without any tail I could spot. I led her to the steps of a public building. They still consider public buildings public here. For now. Subjects gather on the steps. Sometimes they live there in good weather. We could plant ourselves and talk without getting bashed over the head and told to move along by the hired thugs who police the Hill's streets. "Think about it, sweetheart."

"About what? How?"

"Say a guy has a dream. No matter how crazy the guy or how insane the dream. Eh? Then all of a sudden he gets a real chance to grab it. Eh?"

"You lost me, Garrett."

I didn't think she was that slow. I played it out, explained a little more about what the book was supposed to be. "That creep Fido wants to be a wicked wizard more than anything in the world. But he doesn't have the talent it takes to trip over his own feet. He's so bad at what he wants it's almost easy to feel sorry for him. Almost. But I can't when it comes to the Book of Shadows. A nut like him gets it . . ."

Her eyes widened. "Oh."

"Oh. Yeah. You got it. But he doesn't have the book. Yet. We know that for sure because he's so crazy he'd be taking his wicked-wizard act all over town if he did."

"Let me think about this, Garrett."

"You know him better than I do."

"I said let me think." Her face furrowed up exactly the way Saucerhead's does when he concentrates. I had a feeling she was like Tharpe in ways other than size. She'd be one of those who think slow but steady, sometimes getting there more surely than those of us who are quicker of wit.

After a while I said, "He must have been in touch with Blaine sometime. Else how would he know about the book?"

"Yeah. Blaine did offer to sell it to him, I think. But something happened. He backed off."

"And got killed for his trouble."

"My fault, probably. I found Blaine for Lubbock."

"Huh?"

"I told you, I'm a manhunter. He wanted Blaine found, I found Blaine."

I glimmed Easterman's hangout. It wasn't far away. Not far enough. Somebody was up top trying to lure a flying thunder-lizard down. I guess Fido wanted to catch him his very own dragon.

"But he didn't get the book."

"I guess not. I don't know why. Unless Blaine spotted me and guessed who I was."

Curious. Blaine hadn't had the book when they'd killed him, logically. But he'd had it earlier, and had tried to use it, because he'd been Carla Lindo when he'd stumbled into my house. The Serpent couldn't have it any more than Fido did, else she wouldn't be trying to kill me. She'd be headed out of town.

Gnorst? I'd seen no evidence he was even looking. I'd guess he didn't have it, either.

So where the hell did it go?

Why should I care? Tinnie was going to be all right.

I asked, "You think anybody ought to have that kind of power?"

"Me, I could handle it. But I don't know nobody else I'd trust."

"And I don't know about you."

"How much you pay me not to find it?"

"What?"

"I come to the city for the money, Garrett. Not to save the world."

"I like a straightforward thinker. I like a girl who has her priorities straight and knows what she wants. I'll give you a straight answer. Not a copper. You don't have a glimmer where it is."

"But I will. I find things real good. Tell you what. When I find it, I'll give you a chance to outbid Lubbock."

"And the Serpent? You maybe ought to think about that some. While you're at it, think about what happened to Blaine."

"That's no problem."

"Look, Winger, it's stupid not to be scared. There's some bad people in this town. And you got some of the baddest looking for you. On account of Squirrel. If they catch up with you, you can kiss your tail good-bye." I mentioned it because once again I'd glimpsed somebody who looked like Crask.

"I can take care of myself."

"I saw when you tried to jump me."

"Damn it, Garrett, I'm not your responsibility. Back off."

Something about the way she flared there, and her choice of words, made me wonder if the Winger I was seeing was the real Winger. "All right. All right. Tell me where those dwarves went."

"Twenty marks."

"Mercenary bitch. You'd sell your own mother."

"If the price was right. Two marks. To cover expenses. Won't do you much good. She's dead."

"I'm sorry."

"Oh, she's still breathing. She's just been dead from the chin up for the last thirty years. All she knows how to do is whine and bitch and make babies. Sixteen, last time I counted. Probably a couple more by now. Her almost bleeding to death having the fourteenth, then keeping on pumping them out, was what made up my mind I didn't want to be like her."

"Twenty marks." I didn't blame her. Peasants live short and ugly lives, uglier for the women. Maybe she didn't have anything to lose, considering. "But I don't have it on me right now."

"I'll trust you. They say your word is good. Just don't get yourself croaked before I can collect."

"So talk to me. Where are they?"

"You going there right now?"

"Yeah. If you tell me."

"Mind if I just show you? Might find me something interesting, too."

We'd hardly begun walking. Suddenly people started running around cackling at each other like the world's biggest chicken herd. They didn't act scared, they just wanted to know what was happening. Me too, you bet. I got no sense from the confusion till everybody stopped, faced the same way, and pointed.

The shadows came first, rippling over us. Then came the monsters, out of the morning sun, a good dozen of them. Instead of drifting way up high, they were down at rooftop level, wing tip to wing tip, necks snaky and heads darting around. They screeched as they went over. MorCartha appeared from nowhere, diving for safety below.

Nobody panicked. There was no cause. Those things were big but not massive. They couldn't carry anyone off. Maybe a cat or small dog. They didn't have the wing power to go flapping away with anything heavier.

Somebody nearby observed, "They're cleaning out the pigeons." Which was why their heads were darting around. "One comes along ahead of the others and flushes those feathered rats, then the rest get them on the fly."

Somebody else said, "I hear they's a bunch of the big meat-eaters in the hills up north."

Grimmer news, that. Some of those critters stand thirty feet tall, weigh a dozen tons, and snack on mammoths. The farmers would be in for some excitement. I told Winger, "There you go, you want to make money. I know a guy pays prime rates for thunder-lizard hides." Willard Tate used thunder-lizard leather for the soles of army boots.

Winger spat. "Easier money here." Like I'd made a serious suggestion. Not subtle, friend Winger.

We started moving again. When we hit a quiet stretch, she said, "I didn't know you had those things around here."

"We don't. Usually. Something must be pushing them south. They don't like it down here. Too cold and unfriendly."

Which sparked a thought. If there *were* big carnivores rampaging through the hills, they wouldn't last. One chilly night and that would be that. The farmers would sneak around and feed them a few hundred pounds of poisoned steel while they were too sluggish to protect themselves. Then Old Man Tate would find himself with more hides than he could handle.

One reason thunder-lizards stay away from the sapient races is they always get the dirty end. They're pretty dim, but they've learned that. Teeth and claws and mass are only so much use against brains and sorcery and sharp, poisoned steel.

Which is another reason we didn't see much fear. Not to mention the fact that TunFaire is surrounded by a wall no thunder-lizard could climb.

The excitement made it difficult to tell if we were being tailed by Fido's boys or Chodo's. I took it for granted we had company. I worried more about Easterman's clowns than Chodo's troops. The latter would be pros. They'd be predictable. All I knew about the brunos was that they could be deadly.

As we walked I hammered away at Winger, trying to get through. She couldn't believe things were as black as I claimed. She didn't understand how potent the Book of Dreams could be. Or she didn't want to.

We'd just passed Lettie Faren's cathouse, which clings to the skirts of the Hill like a malignant parasite, and I'd started telling Winger a story about something that had happened there. I was worried about the woman. She didn't get the chuckle she should have. . . . Sadler stepped out of an alley. Just for a second. Nothing special to someone who didn't know him. But I knew him. I glanced back. I doubted any tail would have spotted him.

He wanted to talk to me. Did I want to talk to him? Particularly, did I want to walk down a dark alley with him?

Well, maybe I could get him off my tail. "Winger, I got to see a man about a dog. Hang on a minute." I headed toward that alley hitching my pants. Watchers would buy it if I didn't take all day.

I was at a disadvantage stepping out of the brightness into shadow. If Sadler wanted me, he had me. I said, "Make it fast."

"Right. Heard you had a close scrape."

"Yeah. Dwarves. Again."

"I heard. That the woman we been looking for?"

"The very one. Only she didn't cut Squirrel. I think I know who did. Brunos who work for a guy called Fido Easterman."

He snickered. "Fido?"

"It's an imperial title. Don't make mock. Yeah. He's crazy as a platoon of loons. Real candidate for the ha-ha house. Got a place up the Hill looks like a haunted castle. Wants to be an evil sorcerer."

"He isn't?"

"Like a stone isn't. He's just crazy. Maybe it's his business. Metal smelting. Maybe he's breathed too many fumes off the crucibles. He's got four brunos that I spotted. Not first water. I think he went for cheap over competent."

Sadler clicked his tongue, looked thoughtful. He seemed distracted. Odd. He'd wanted to talk to me, not the other way around.

I said, "There's a good chance they offed Blaine, too."

Sadler clicked again, looked even more thoughtful. Maybe he was turning into a philosophical cricket. It could happen. Stranger things have.

"What?" I asked. Impatient me. Just because a whiz don't take twenty minutes.

"These guys are second rate, eh?"

"Looked it to me." Was he paying attention?

"What about that door? Who cut Squirrel so deep? Somebody with a little strength, eh?"

I hadn't thought of that. "Yeah. I guess."

"You guess. That's you, Garrett. Guessing and stumbling around in the dark till you fall over something. Reason I wanted to talk to you, we got a line on some dwarves. Probably won't do you no good. They was in a big dustup down on the Landing. Dwarfish gang fight. One bunch jumped another bunch. After, some headed for Dwarf Fort, some headed toward the Bledsoe. I'd call it a draw, far as how it turned out. I got some guys trying to track the ones went toward the hospital. Thought you'd want to know."

"Yeah. Thanks." I forgot to mention Winger and I were on a trail. Better to have the hard boys headed somewhere else. "This is turning into the longest leak in history. Anybody was watching me they'd be getting suspicious."

"You worry too much. Crask can handle them. But go on. Catch you later." He drifted into shadow, taking his aura of menace with him.

"Yeah. Later." I stomped out of there hitching my pants and shaking my head.

Winger said, "You must have a five-gallon bladder, Garrett." She was breathing heavy.

"Yeah. Something happen?"

She gave me a mocking smile. "Nothing I couldn't handle. Some guy tried to pick me up. I discouraged him."

"Oh. Let's move." I wanted to see what I could see before Chodo's boys stumbled into my way. Always seemed to be people turning up dead when they did.

Winger seemed disappointed that I didn't have any banter or follow-up questions about her encounter. I shrugged it off.

It was hard to make any speed. The streets had filled with people gawking at the pigeon exterminators. One glided over, pathfinding. I said, "I hear those things only go thirty, forty pounds." This one went right over the Tate compound, which wasn't far away. I wondered if Tinnie was watching, too. For no reason I could finger I was feeling blue.

"Cheer up, Garrett. We'll find that book and get rich."

Or dead. Lots more likely dead.

26

T he longer we walked the more certain I became that I'd have to rene-
    gotiate with Winger. I glanced at her, big as me, strutting along like she
    dared the world to take its best shot. Something about her unjustified
cockiness appealed to me. Give her a dose of sense, she might be all right.

"Hey, Winger. That twenty isn't an open offer. I won't buy a pig in a poke.
You got to deliver dwarves."

"No cat in this bag, Garrett. You'll get dwarves."

Cat and pig, both expressions come from an old country con. Once upon
a time peasants took piglets to market in a "poke." Some grifter got the idea
of stuffing the bag with a cat and selling it to somebody gullible enough not
to look inside before he handed over his money. So. Pig in a poke, cat out of
the bag.

I wanted dwarves. I got them. But not exactly in mint condition.

"What's going on?" Winger muttered. People were milling around a tenement that had seen its best days a hundred years before I was born. People
who weren't interested in the ongoing air show.

"Trouble," I told her. "Past tense. Else we'd have a desert here."

"Ghouls?"

"You could say that."

She pushed through the crowd, not caring who she shoved or elbowed.
She was mad, perfectly willing to get in a fight. I wondered if I ought to be
around somebody who had herself a war on with the whole world.

The first dead dwarf lay sprawled in the tenement entrance, hacked and stabbed and twisted up into an unnatural position. He clutched the hilt of a broken knife. "Got swamped in a rush, looks like," I said. "Anybody see it happen?" I'm a dreamer.

The nearest vultures looked at me like I was crazy. I shrugged, pushed inside. No crowd in there, which suggested the folks outside expected city busybodies any minute. People not worried about the Watch would have been inside collecting anything the dead couldn't use anymore.

The Watch seldom bothers doing much policing or chasing, but they do grab folks found on the scene, then make life miserable for them. I told Winger, "We'd better do this quick."

"Do what?" She sounded depressed. I supposed she was thinking about all the things she couldn't buy with the money I wasn't going to pay her.

"Look the place over. See what's to be seen."

"Why? All you're going to see is more dead guys."

She had a point. There was another on the first-floor landing and three in the hallway on the second. Two of those may have been attackers. They were better kempt, better clad. Gnorst's bunch.

The fight had proceeded along the hallway, scourged a half dozen sleeping rooms, and tumbled down a cramped rear stairwell. None of the rooms had doors. Most had been torn apart by somebody in a hurry looking for something. We found a ratman and a dwarf, both critically wounded and a lot of nothing else. I asked, "Was this the place you wanted to sell me?"

"Sure was." Still depressed.

"You tried."

"That don't put money in my pocket. What's that racket?" She meant the yelling out front.

"Watch must be coming. People telling each other to make themselves invisible. Which isn't such a bad idea." I stomped down the back stairway. Behind me, Winger muttered about her luck couldn't turn worse if she prayed. Her vocabulary wasn't unique or imaginative, but it was colorful.

The back way out featured a broken door. I squeezed through. The mess beyond suggested somebody tried to hold Gnorst's dwarves there while the renegades made their getaway. One of Gnorst's dwarves lay partially buried in litter, alive enough to groan. I tried asking him questions. If he spoke any Karentine, he was too involved in his own misery to respond. He did manage one dwarfish outburst filled with fireworks, the only word of which I caught was "ogre." I told Winger, "This one will be all right. If the Watch don't lynch him just to make believe they're doing something useful."

"I think they're in the building." There was a racket inside.

"Time to go. Watch your step." TunFaire's alleys serve many unplanned uses, especially those of trash dump and public relief facility. The quality of cleanup attention they get from the city ratmen declines as one moves farther from the Hill. What the lords don't see don't exist. We were far from the hub of the wheel here, in a stretch so foul it boasted no homeless tenants.

A Watchman stepped into our path as we approached the street. Being a naturally courteous kind of guy, I'd let Winger go first. The Watchman was about five six and tricked out in those gaudy blues and reds, a pretty little devil who got him a nasty grin when he saw he had somebody boxed. He started to say something.

What did he want to say? Who the hell knows? Winger grabbed him by the throat, planted one on his nose, hoisted him up, and flipped him into the mess behind us. Like he weighed about six pounds. I wanted to gawk but knew it wouldn't work. He had friends. "Bright move, Winger. Real bright." I hoped he hadn't seen me well enough to know me if we met again.

I put the old heels and toes to work doing what the gods intended and didn't slow down till I was ten blocks away. Huffing, puffing, snorting like a bilious dragon, I looked for Winger. Not a sign of her. She'd gone her own way. Which was maybe an excellent idea and one I ought to hope she'd pursue indefinitely. A guy could get hurt hanging around with people like her.

27

I trust the light was feeble there, the Dead Man sent. Winger's behavior amused him. *Is there any likelihood the Watchman recognized you?*

"Why should he?"

You are a known character.

That sack of petrified lard was worried about losing his free ride!

He wouldn't have admitted it if I'd set a fire under him but the truth smoldered through. If he lost me, he might actually have to work to keep a roof over his head. There's nothing in this world he loathes more than work.

The fact that he was worried worried me. It was out of character. I take my life in my hands every time I go sniffing around after the bad boys. That never bothered him before. It got me thinking and that's always dangerous. Wondering if he hadn't had some premonition. Wouldn't surprise me to find he could peek into the future. Especially after the way he'd been guessing what Glory Mooncalled would do.

"What's happened?" I thought it a perfectly reasonable query. He ignored it. "Be that way, then." I took my question to Dean.

"Nothing," Dean told me. "Except that he did hint that he was getting something like a black vibration out of the Cantard. I think he meant he felt something happening down there."

"Oh, my. It'd have to be big." Oh, my, oh, my.

I couldn't believe it was anything but imagination. Dead men got nothing to do but fantasize. But . . . If something that big was happening, it *had* to involve Glory Mooncalled.

• • •

When the going gets tough, the tough get going. When the going gets tough, Garrett puts his feet up and has a beer. I took a pitcher into the office and snuggled up with Eleanor. We had us a chat about whether or not I had any obligation, anywhere, now I could be sure Tinnie was going to be all right. Eleanor didn't have much to say, but somewhere along the way, after things got a little dizzy, I recalled that I'd taken on a client, a wee lovely who thought me finding an improbable book could save her father's bacon.

I didn't want to believe in the thing, but people and dwarves were dropping like flies. We were playing morCartha down here on the ground, I was caught in it, like it or not. Somebody wanted me to join the flies.

Dean brought beer and a stern look. I asked, "Where's Carla Lindo?"

"Guest room. Worrying." He assumed his human roadblock stance. "She doesn't need comforting. She needs help."

"Yeah. Sure. So do I. You don't see me getting any. Hell. I'm done waiting for it to come to me. I'll go round it up." I drained another mug of courage, checked my portable arsenal, headed for the door. Dean trotted along behind grinning like an old death's-head.

His romantic notions would be the death of me yet.

I'm immune to romantic notions, of course. I'm a block of heavy metal unshakably planted at the center of a plain of common sense, illuminated by the sun of reason.

Right. Look up. See the swarms of pigs flying south for the winter?

I hadn't been inside, isolated from the city ambience, for long, but something had changed. Some new level of tension had been reached. There were fewer people out. Those who were seemed nervous. I could see no real reason.

I visited Morley's place but found no Morley. I went away puzzled, headed for Saucerhead's shabby den.

Tharpe was out, too. Not one of his mouse-size lady friends was there to clue me where he'd gone, either. 'Twas a puzzlement.

I went away frowning. Something had to be going on. Especially with Morley. He faded from sight sometimes, but I'd never known him to take his whole crew with him. There'd always been some way to get in touch.

I headed for home.

I got the news from a neighbor moments before I reached the house.

• • •

"Big roughhouse in the Cantard, Old Bones," I told the Dead Man. "Word's just in. All mixed up. Sounds like our troops and the Venageti caught up with Mooncalled at the same time, some place called Broken Back Canyon. No word how it came out yet, though." All the neighbor knew was that the battle had been all-time big. I assumed the northbound dispatches had been sent immediately on contact. The mere catching of Mooncalled was news of major importance.

I suspected as much. To yield vibrational energies I can detect here . . . It must be the battle of battles and still going on. I would not have expected Mooncalled to be capable of so violent a defense.

"Cornered rats." But Mooncalled always did the unexpected.

Perhaps. Let us not concern ourselves overmuch before more coherent information arrives. I sense that you are troubled.

"What a genius. Amazing how you figure things out." I told him about my day, such as it was so far.

Go eat. Let me think.

I did that, without a squabble. I was that down, feeling that inadequate.

"He's had an hour," I told Dean, who was thoroughly sick of me hanging around the kitchen. "That ought to be long enough for even a genius." Stomach full, now optimistic enough to have put aside thoughts of suicide, I hit the hallway.

Carla Lindo stepped out of the Dead Man's room. She carried a broom and dustpan. I stopped to gape. Behind me, Dean started apologizing. "She wanted to do something, Mr. Garrett. And he doesn't bother her."

"Fine." No broom ever took my breath away. No. She'd just turned my spine to jelly with a look that should have gotten the fire bells sounding all over town.

I grabbed myself by the collar and dragged me into the Dead Man's room before I soaked the carpet with drool.

She is attractive, is she not?

"Huh? You too?" We lived in an age of wonders indeed. The millennium was at hand. He never said anything nice about persons of the opposite sex. But maybe Carla Lindo was opposite enough to touch even the dead.

You have something to report?

"Huh?"

Report. It may help you avoid hyperventilation.

"I already told you everything."

Oh. So you did.

Somebody started pounding on the front door. The Dead Man didn't appear interested. I ignored it. Whoever might go away. It was time to uncomplicate my life.

I have been thinking, Garrett.

"Hey, that's great! I'm glad to hear it. Especially since that's what you get paid for."

Garrett! Time is of the essence.

"So quit wasting it. I've only got maybe thirty years left."

I have been mulling this Book of Dreams. It occurs to me that Chodo Contague must soon, if he has not already, discover the nature of the root of all this excitement. It occurs to me that, then, his interest will intensify, passing beyond professional revenge.

"Huh?" He does go on like that. "You lost me." Not really, but he does like to feel smarter than the rest of us and the best way to keep him moving is to appeal to his ego.

The more I consider this Book of Shadows, the more sinister and seductive it seems.

I made appropriate noises indicating awed curiosity.

We all play roles all the time, Garrett. We all develop multiple faces we don according to the situation and companion of the moment and, perhaps, according to the advantage we hope to acquire. How terribly convenient it would be to have the ability to become whatever we wanted, filling the role to perfection, whenever that suited our whim. He sounded wistful. Having a Carla Lindo around can do that to anybody. *How very convenient if we happen to be afflicted with terrible handicaps.*

Like being dead, maybe? "I get you. But my inclination is just to squat here till we see how the wind's blowing."

Unacceptable. There is a balance that must be rectified. Not to mention the fact that we have undertaken to aid Miss Ramada. I must do some additional thinking on how best to proceed. While I do so, I suggest you cross the hall. Dean has installed Mr. Tate in your office. He appears to need reassurances.

"*Willard* Tate? Here?"

The same.

"The old boy never leaves his compound. What the hell is he doing here?"

You might ask.

Nothing like a subtle hint. "Yeah. Right." I headed for the office.

Tate had taken the guest chair. He didn't fit. Too small. Like a wispy, gray old gnome. Dean had settled him with a pitcher. He was working on that and flirting with Eleanor. I said, "Three minutes more and you wouldn't have caught me home." Just to suggest that I was a busy man.

He glowered. "Tinnie's taken a bad turn, Garrett." He gestured reassuringly, though. "Won't kill her, they tell me. But it's enough to leave me an emotional wreck. I came here to find out if you've learned anything new."

"Not a lot." I told him about my day.

He shook his head slowly, angrily, looked at Eleanor as though he was talking to her. "I'm wasting my time and yours. I know that. But I couldn't work. Couldn't sit still." As he spoke he changed, gaining an edge of steel. "I want to meet this woman who calls herself the Serpent. I want to tell her a thing or two."

"She's a witch, Mr. Tate. And not any tea-leaf reader, either. Not easy to reach and big trouble if you do. Moreover, my partner has cautioned me that Chodo Contague should be developing a more than passing interest in her." I explained why.

Tate rose. He would have paced had there been room. "I don't like seeing Tinnie hurt, Garrett. Nor any Tate. Especially not for no reason. I won't endure it. Chodo isn't a problem. I have money. I have proven connections. I can buy myself a stormwarden if I care to."

"Sounds like the frying pan to the fire to me. Suppose you do buy you one. What happens when he figures out what the book is?"

"I don't much care."

"You ought to. I do. We have obligations that transcend—"

"Crap."

"It's not quite law of the jungle and survival of the fittest out there, Mr. Tate. Not yet. And that's mainly because some of us do what's right. Listen to me. That book is evil incarnate. Even if every character recorded in it is as sweet and naive as Tinnie, the book is an instrument of darkness. Its only use can be to do evil."

Was this me speechifying? My oh my.

I'd started thinking about how I could use the book myself. I suspected anybody who heard about it would do the same. Human nature. How could anyone who possessed it resist abusing the power it would confer?

"Think about this. If the Book of Shadows didn't exist, would Tinnie be a step from death's door? How about all the people who've already died because of it? It's pure evil because it brings out the worst in everybody."

In his best moments Tate looks like he's noshing lemons. This wasn't one of his best times. "I think you're splitting hairs, Garrett. That book didn't kill anybody. People made decisions and acted on them. Only then did people die."

"Those decisions were warped by knowledge of the existence of the book."

"You're quibbling. We're quibbling. Why? Are you trying to get money out of me? Why on earth are you sitting there talking to me at all?"

Best question he'd asked so far. "Courtesy, Mr. Tate. Courtesy."

"Why don't you toss me out? I'm just an old pain in the ass who's keeping you from doing something useful."

He was in a mood, he was. "You have a suggestion what? Maybe I should rent a horse and go galloping around yelling 'Come out, come out, wherever you are.'"

His control had grown ragged, but he actually gave my question consideration.

"I'd like to do something, Mr. Tate. I want to do something. My style is to grab loose ends and keep picking till things unravel. But I'm having trouble finding any loose threads. All I can do is keep getting in the way and hope that leads somewhere. Meantime, I keep tripping over all these other people who're looking themselves."

Willard Tate wasn't a wealthy man because he let his emotions rule him. He clamped down. He thought. He told me, "You have resources. The girl. The dwarf chieftain. Those men who work for Contague. Find those two. Keep an eye on them. Let them do your hunting "

He was a storehouse of ideas, all right. Crazy ideas. Follow Crask and Sadler around? Why not just tie boulders to my toes and go for a swim? Save us all time and trouble.

"They're only men, Garrett. Chodo's just a man. You've faced down stormwardens. You've invaded a vampire nest. Did those things use up all your courage and leave you a crippled old man, too?"

He was a manipulator, that guy. "No." What did he want, really? I hadn't yet gotten a real grip on the fact that he was here. Had he slipped his moorings?

"Money and contacts, Garrett. I've got them. Chodo Contague doesn't intimidate me. I want this Serpent creature. Get her for me. Destroy her book if you want. It means nothing to me. Just get me her. My mind is set. I'll pay whatever it costs. If you have to work through Chodo Contague, do it. Tell me what you need and I'll provide the tools. But don't sit there cringing."

I wasn't cringing, but wasn't going to argue. He'd started sounding like a candidate for the cackle academy. Having him behind me was all right but preferably far behind and not on any crusade.

How do I get into these messes? I glanced at Eleanor. "Why me?"

Hell. I should get out of this racket. Weider still wants me at the brewery. I could handle security there, work regular hours, and never worry about getting caught up in any wackiness.

A book of shadows that lets somebody change characters like I change socks. Come on. I don't need it.

Tate and I looked at each other for a while. We drank some beer. He had his anger worked out now and seemed abashed. I'd never seen him that way, but in this world anything can happen.

The pitcher went dry. I called Dean. Carla Lindo came. Tate squeaked. The resemblance to Tinnie was strong in the weak light. I said, "This is Carla Lindo Ramada, Mr. Tate. The lady the assassins were after."

He stared. "I understand their mistake. Speaking of which, I made a big one coming here. Made a real fool of myself, eh? Let me get out of your way, Mr. Garrett." He rose, still staring. Carla Lindo was embarrassed.

His sudden change of attitude left me twitchy. I didn't believe it but didn't know him well enough to guess what he was thinking.

But I had the Dead Man to explain it to me. I said, "I'll see you to the door."

Tate was still looking at Carla Lindo when I closed the front door. A platoon of his relatives awaited him out there. Tinnie was the only Tate who went around alone. I wished that just the once, she'd clung to family custom. I'd just as soon I'd never heard of the Book of Dreams.

joined my permanent houseguest. "What was that all about?"

He wished to discover if you had learned anything new. He is considering taking matters into his own hands. Miss Tate's relapse appears to have unhinged him.

"You ask me, his hinges never were on tight. Damn. He's one stubborn runt. He could cause a lot of grief."

That appears to be his intent.

"You get anything useful out of that thick head?"

The best time to purchase leather futures. Should you care to get into the shoe and boot trade.

"You're a scream, Old Bones. Har-har."

Gnorst has been in the thick of it lately. Go see if he will tell you anything.

"Right." It was getting dark out. I really wanted to take a stroll amongst the screeching morCartha and lurking dwarves. "Hell, why not? I still got places that don't have bumps and bruises. Maybe if I get out there fast enough, I can even get myself killed."

He knew no mercy. *Do not forget to inquire after the latest from the Cantard.*

Probably had a bet on with himself. Loghyr can do stuff like that if they're inclined. They have multiple brains and sometimes multiple personalities.

I huffed out of there and told Dean I was going for a walk. Carla Lindo was there with him. I salivated all over the place. She smiled and posed. Saucy. That was a good word for her. Along with about twenty others.

Dean hammered me with dirty looks. That old boy knows me too damned well. I ought to fire him and get somebody less opinionated. But where could I luck onto somebody who'd do half the job he does?

I checked the street good before I stepped outside. I checked again after I stepped out. I saw nothing obvious but stayed ready to duck. No bolts came whispering death. The only noise was that of the aerial circus. The morCartha had taken their show to the riverfront tonight.

I headed for the Safety Zone. It wasn't out of my way.

Morley's place was closed up and dark. I went around back. Nothing. Amazing. Even when the front door is closed, there's always somebody in the kitchen.

I was getting worried.

I tried Saucerhead's place next. This time I got an answer but not from Tharpe. A little blonde about big enough to sit on his palm told me she hadn't seen him all day. She got worried because it was me looking for him. She thought he was with me. I told her to relax, we'd just missed each other. She didn't relax.

I didn't either. There was something going on. And I was zooming around in the middle of it like a blind moth amongst a thousand candles.

A sane moth would have landed and saved his wings.

Speaking of flames. I'd accumulated a tail again. I sensed it as I moved away from Saucerhead's place. I didn't run any games on him. Let him think I didn't know. Let him relax. I'd move fast when I wanted to shake him.

I did change my mind about where I'd go next. I'd been thinking of making the rounds of every shady character I knew willing to sell somebody for a copper. None of those people were friends, but they did trust me not to bring down any heat. I'd lose a lot of sources if I went around fingering them even by accident.

So I headed for Dwarf Fort. Gnorst's crowd could take care of themselves.

I went to the same door. The same old boy—or his evil twin—answered my knock. "I'm Garrett," I reminded him, in case his memory was feeble or a different dwarf had taken up residence behind all the facial brush. "I need to see the Gnorst again." I figured if this wasn't the same dwarf, he'd at least have heard of my previous visit.

Same dwarf or not, he had the same talent for public relations. "You Tall Ones are all alike. Think nobody's got nothing better to do than hop when you say frog, even in the middle of the night. All right. All right. If you must. If you insist. Himself, the very Gnorst, said bring you if you turn up again." His manner suggested he thought his boss was a damned fool.

I stepped inside. "Whoa. Let me close that." I pushed the door shut, to a crack, peeked outside.

Whoever was out there didn't show himself. This was starting to spook me. I'd known only one man that good. He'd died. And there wasn't any doubt he was still dead.

Gnorst met me in the same garden. Maybe that was the only place outsiders were entertained. "How can I help you tonight, Mr. Garrett?"

"Just checking in. I wondered if you'd learned anything since we talked."

He shook his head. "Not one damned thing." Man. He lied with such style I wanted to believe him anyway. You got to admire a character who can jerk you around and make you like it. Only I didn't like it. He almost snarled as he said, "I would have sent a message if I had. I thought I told you I would."

Oh really? When? "None of your people knew anything?"

"No."

"That's curious."

"How so?"

"There've been fights amongst dwarves all day. We've had dead dwarves turning up everywhere. I'd have sworn some were yours."

"You're a victim of your prejudices and preconceptions, Mr. Garrett. Gods bring on the hour when you stop thinking we all look alike."

I could plead guilty except the little clown was trying to divert attention. He was lying. I knew he was lying. He knew I knew he was lying. He knew I knew he knew, and so forth. But this was his house and no place to challenge him.

I said, "When I came here before, I didn't know anything about any Book of Shadows or what dwarves might have to do with making one. Right?"

Gnorst nodded. "Agreed. So?"

"You think finding out would make me more dangerous to somebody?"

"Possibly. Not many nondwarves know the story. Even among us it's mostly forgotten. It has been said by the wise, knowledge is dangerous."

"That's what I thought."

"Sneaking up on something, Mr. Garrett?"

I thought some before I explained. I wanted it to stay airborne when I shoved it out of the nest, though it would never soar. "The bad boys paid me no attention before I came down here. They've been trying to kill me ever since I walked back out. Makes a guy wonder. How was I different? How did they know? Not to mention how come is it that all these skirmishes between dwarf gangs keep turning out inconclusive?"

Gnorst darkened behind his face fur. He started pacing. "I did hear about you being attacked up the street. I didn't put it together before. Yes. I see your point. One of your points. They weren't keeping an eye on you, but all of a sudden, they knew you'd seen me and had become a danger. Though it leaves me embarrassed and ashamed, Mr. Garrett, I must admit that it looks like one of my people is an informer."

Putting it mildly. "That's my guess."

"Out of curiosity, Mr. Garrett, how is it that you're alive to visit me again? I would think that dwarfish efficiency would extend to setting an ambush."

"I got lucky. Chodo Contague's men turned up the first time. Second time I started running before they started sniping. I hope there won't be a next time. I hope they're on the run from whoever has been hitting their hideouts."

He chuckled. It wasn't a nice sound. It was a noise something like the *glug-glug* of water coming from a ten-gallon bottle crossed with fingernails scraping a slate board.

"I don't find any of this amusing."

"I'm sure you don't, Mr. Garrett. What are you doing?"

I was sneaking toward the edge of the roof. "Somebody's been following me. I thought I might get a look at him from here."

I didn't, though. It was so damned dark down there he could have danced in the street without me getting a look. I lied, "So that's mainly the reason I came by. To let you know I think you've got a spy on board."

Gnorst grunted irritably. My experience is, his kind are naturally crabby. Gnorst was a paragon of manners and patience. Maybe that was why he was the local boss dwarf. He told me, "You didn't bring me any news I wanted to hear. Now I have to deal with it."

It's hard to read a being who grew up in an alien culture yet looks human enough to make you jump to conclusions. But I had a strong suspicion Gnorst was a lot less unhappy than he wanted me to believe. Maybe he thought having a renegade handy was an asset. I could think of ways that would be true.

"I know what you mean. I've been a regular fountain of bad news all day. Everywhere I go I'm telling somebody something they don't want to hear."

We fenced awhile with words. He wouldn't give up a thing I could use. I surrendered to the inevitable, told him I was going to go dump it all on the Dead Man. He let me go without another word. He wasn't as gracious as he'd been. That questionable attitude infected my guide. The dwarf took no pains to make my passage through the place a comfort.

I froze the moment I hit the street, looked around carefully. Garrett don't get bitten by the same snake twice. I saw nothing. Even so, I moved away ready for anything.

Nothing ever happens when you're ready.

The silence overhead seemed almost ominous. The morCartha had retired, for whatever reason. I almost missed them. They had become part of city life.

had the night to myself. Unless you count sharing with a tail. It wasn't a happy feeling. Empty streets always mean trouble to me.

Whoever was after me was spooky. I only ever knew one guy that good, Pokey Pigotta. Maybe this was Pokey's ghost.

I'd outthought Pokey once when he'd been on me. Maybe I could use the trick again. It was hard to beat for a guy working alone. I looked for a busy tavern I knew would have a back door.

Not my day. It didn't work. I didn't catch anybody sliding in the front door by sprinting around from the back. It was like the guy was psychic. All I accomplished was to let whoever know I knew he was there. Go match wits with a rock, Garrett. Chances are the rock will come out ahead.

Having somebody dog you works on your head. You start out wondering who and why. Pretty soon you're into what if and then imagination flares and you've got a vampire or werewolf or ghoul pack just waiting for you to walk down a dark alley with your eyes closed. . . . There ain't no comforting thoughts, come a dark night.

Hell with the clown. Let him walk his behind off. He didn't seem interested in messing with me, just in seeing what I got me up to. If I kept moving, he'd have no time to report to whoever sicced him on me.

I was tired and depressed and short on zest for life. Maybe even a little cranky. I get that way when things keep on not going my way. Call me spoiled.

I was near the Bledsoe Infirmary, a charity hospital supported by surviving descendants of the old imperial family, when I sensed a change in the night. It wasn't obvious, just a difference. Nothing I could pin down. My shadow was there still. The morCartha weren't making much racket. Random flying thunder-lizards still ghosted overhead, chasing bats. The streets remained underpopulated. I wondered if it might not be some holiday among the night people.

I paused to consider the Bledsoe, a monument to good intentions having become a symbol of despair. A place of fear, where the poor went to die and the mad screamed out their souls in overcrowded, locked wards. The imperial family did all they could, but their best wasn't enough. Their money and donations of labor barely kept it from falling down. It was huge, gray, ugly, and may have been imposing in its prime, a couple of hundred years ago. Now it was just another shabby old building, bigger than but no better than ten thousand others in TunFaire.

I shook my head, startled by an original thought. I couldn't recall ever having seen new construction anywhere in the city. Was the war that big a drain on resources?

The war is the most important thing in all our lives, whether or not we're directly involved. It shapes our selves and surroundings and forges our futures as every minute passes.

Whatever was happening in the Cantard, so heroic the Dead Man could sense it from here, would have a crashing impact on all our lives.

That scared me. I'm not fond of things the way they are, but the only changes I can see will be for the worse. The bigger the change, the more for the worse.

Some tiny sound reached me, some ghostly flicker of motion teased the corner of my vision. I'd been a step too far away from here and now realized it, and my reaction was maybe more vigorous than it should have been. I did me a wild roundhouse kick toward the movement, brought my foot down, ducked and pivoted and lashed the air with a knife.

Crask was saved by the fact that my tippytoe brushed his chin lightly, pushing him back. He'd thrown himself away at the same time. Now he sat on his duff looking up at me with a goofy expression.

"Say . . ." he said. "Say, what's wrong with you?"

I had so much juice in me so sudden I started shaking. I'd blown it, really. I took some deep breaths to calm me down, put the knife away, extended a hand. "Sorry. You startled me bad."

"Yeah? Well, you got no call . . ." I shut up as he reached with his left hand. I didn't like the look in his eye. I pulled my hand back before he grabbed it and went to chewing on it.

He got up slowly, using only his left hand. I noticed he had his right arm strapped to his stomach. "What happened to you?" Hard to tell in that light but his face looked a little worse for wear, too. He looked less intimidating than usual.

He got up slowly, rubbed his behind. Damn, he looked embarrassed! Maybe it was the light leaking from the Bledsoe. . . . He didn't have an answer.

I leaped to a conclusion. He'd been the guy Winger had discouraged when Sadler had me in that alley. No proof, and he'd never tell, but by damn I'd put money on it. A copper or two, anyway. I grinned. "You shouldn't ought to sneak up that way."

"I didn't sneak. I walked right into you, Garrett."

I didn't argue. You don't with a Crask or a Sadler. "What you doing here?"

"Looking for you. Your man said you were headed for Dwarf Fort. I come down this way figuring you'd be headed back by now."

I was going to have to have a talk with Dean. Though it was understandable he'd answer Crask's questions if Crask put on his nasty face. "What's up?"

"Couple things. You seen Sadler?"

"Not since . . . Not for a long time. Why?"

"Disappeared." Crask didn't waste many words. "Come to see Chodo right after . . ." He wasn't going to talk about the incident. "Talked some, then went away. Nobody seen him go. Wasn't told he was supposed to. Nobody's seen him since. Chodo's concerned."

Chodo was concerned. That would be an understatement, as were most statements about the kingpin. In language the rest of us would use, it meant Chodo was mightily pissed.

I don't usually volunteer information, especially to the kingspin's people, but I made an exception. "Guys have been disappearing all over. I can't find a trace of Morley Dotes. Likewise Saucerhead Tharpe. You might say I'm concerned, too. I don't hear anything on the street. You?"

He shook his head first, some top skin flashing in the hospital light. "I thought Dotes was sulking on account of we used his place."

"I thought so, too. At first. Only that wouldn't be his style, would it?"

"Nah. Feisty as he is, he'd have busted our heads and kicked our asses out of there if he was really pissed."

"He'd have tried, anyway."

Crask smiled. He did that so seldom it was startling. "Yeah. Tried. I got some business I got to get on with, Garrett. I'm late, I been chasing all over after you to find out about Sadler. I want you should walk along, talk to me. Maybe we can brainstorm out where people are disappearing."

I didn't feel like it but didn't argue. It wasn't that I was afraid of offending him. I thought I might learn something. Call it intuition.

The first thing I learned was that Crask wasn't, for the moment at least, the man I knew and loathed. He was so busy working on something inside him that some of his barriers against the world leaked. He seemed almost human at moments—though not so much I'd want my sister to marry him, if I had a sister. I don't and I'm glad. My friends are hostages enough for fortune.

30

For some hours I'd entertained the notion that Chodo had eliminated Morley and Saucerhead in order to deprive me of resources should I discover he'd become interested in the Book of Dreams. Sometimes you get that way, thinking you're the center of the universe. But once I ran into Crask, the speculation collapsed under the weight of reason.

You grab straws when nothing makes sense.

Morley had dropped out before Chodo could have discovered the book's nature. Even now I had no real reason to suspect he knew about the book. Him looking for a missing Sadler only made everything murkier.

Who might be making people disappear? The Serpent shouldn't be interested in those guys. She was after the Book of Dreams. Headhunting wouldn't help. The same reasoning applied to happy old Fido Easterman.

So who had reason to eliminate my acquaintances?

Plenty of people, if you took them individually. But nobody was the only answer when you considered them as a group. They didn't share many enemies.

Crask agreed.

We trudged along, me leaning into the bitter wind and grumbling about not having a clue. Then about having so many clues I didn't know which had to do with what.

"Where we headed?" I asked. This wasn't helping me any yet. I glanced back. I still felt the presence of that shadow that had been with me off and on. I didn't see anything. Like I'd maybe expected I would?

"Tenderloin," Crask mumbled. The wind was getting to him, too. He was trying to shelter his injured arm. "Got an appointment with some dwarves."

Ah. So. "Why didn't I think of that?"

The Tenderloin is sin's homeland in TunFaire. Anything goes, nobody asks questions, nobody interferes with anybody else. Missionaries not welcome. Reformers enter at your own risk. Likewise everybody else. The Serpent's whole gang could hide there in plain sight easy, despite everyone and everything being owned by Chodo. They'd just need to remember not to run in a pack.

I really *should* have thought of it. The Tenderloin isn't far from Dwarf Fort. It's just a few blocks past the Bledsoe and I'd been told the renegade dwarves had fled that way after one of their skirmishes with Gnorst's bunch. Had I been from out of town and needed to hide, that's where I'd have gone to ground.

So why hadn't I thought to come poke around? I must be getting senile.

The Tenderloin never sleeps, it just slows down late. When we arrived, lamplighters were out snuffing lights, conserving oil. During peak hours the area is awash with light, a carnival, but the management doesn't waste a copper that won't return ten. This was the hour of the diehard, when light and darkness were irrelevant.

The Tenderloin is like the whores who are its chief commodity, all paint and makeup on the outside. Behind the flash lies rot and stink and human despair. Even where they could, they don't put makeup on that. By the time you look it in the eye, they've already gotten your money and are interested only in processing you through as fast as can be managed.

The wind grew more bitter by the minute. Maybe that was why the morCartha had taken the night off. Their native valleys are much warmer. The lamplighters hunched inside their ragged coats and cursed into their beards. The barkers for various establishments watched the street through doors cracked scant inches, waited till we drew abreast to jump out and wax rhapsodic about wonders unimaginable available within. They retreated when we signaled lack of interest. Nobody pressed. They all recognized Crask.

I let him show the way, wandered off inside me in search of one good reason why I kept charging around looking for the Book of Dreams. I'd begun to distrust me. I feared there was a part of me that wanted it the way the Serpent and Easterman wanted it. The way maybe even the local prince of dwarves wanted it.

There was a new idea. It deserved a look. It might explain why Gnorst was uncommunicative. He might be thinking of trying on Nooney Krombach's shoes.

"Uh-oh." While I was scouting the badlands within, the outer landscape had changed. The streets had emptied. Crask had stopped hurrying. Now he tread softly, clung to shadows.

Something was about to go down.

Crask had a few steps on me. I zagged to the side, up stairs that climbed the face of an old tenement. He didn't notice. His attention was focused ahead. I flattened out on the landing in front of a second-story doorway.

I trust my hunches, usually. I'd had a sudden, strong one that this was no time for Garrett to be out in the open and a worse one to dive into shadowed alleys. I thought shadow and tried to become one with the chilly darkness, nothing but watching eyes.

My hunch was good. I'd barely flattened myself out when every alley in sight barfed hard boys. Crask made hand signals. They all headed for the place that was the target of Crask's good hand.

About then he noticed I wasn't with him anymore. He looked around, startled, spat, cursed, and I knew I'd come one step short of stepping into a big pile of it, maybe.

Had he been leading me to the slaughter?

Joining his party sure didn't look like a brilliant move. I stayed where I was and froze my tail and wondered.

What was wrong with the Serpent? I'd been told and told that somebody who could make a book of shadows was a real heavyweight in the sorcery game. But she didn't act like a heavyweight. Her sort, when they have any weight at all, aren't bashful about throwing it around. But she did her pushing and shoving with second-string hired hands. It was confusing.

The state TunFaire was in, with all our witches and wizards and whatnot off to chase Glory Mooncalled, somebody like the Serpent ought to be able to do whatever she damned well pleased. But she was going about her search like she had no more power than crazy Fido.

Had she put it all into her book, then let that get away?

Sounded good. Sounded like she would be one desperate witch, cranky as a dragon with bad teeth.

Chodo's hordes swept silently toward a tenement. The silence didn't last. A big uproar broke out as soon as a couple got inside. There were enough illegal weapons in evidence to arm a company. The uproar inside reached battle pitch. People were getting hurt in there. . . .

It didn't last. The kingpin's men started dragging captives outside, began forcing them to undress.

Uh-oh. The Dead Man's prophecy had come true.

I couldn't hear the orders and threats Crask issued but didn't need to. He had to be looking for tattoos.

I didn't see the Serpent among the prisoners. Neither did Crask. He stomped around and cussed theatrically. I rested my chin on my forearms, shivered, and wondered how he'd known about the tattoos. Had I mentioned them? I couldn't recall. I guess I must have when I was trying to direct Chodo's attention toward the Serpent.

Crask didn't accept defeat. He had his troops drag out the dead and wounded, lined everybody up, started his inspection all over again. The prisoners shivered and whimpered. The wind was merciless.

He found her. She'd assumed the form of a ratman. Short fur hid her tattoo. The second he made her he popped her upside the head, got a gag stuffed in her mouth and about forty-three miles of rope wrapped around her. She looked like a mummy. He wasn't going to take no chances with a witch.

He barked orders. The wind stole them away. I didn't need to hear them. The hard boys started marching prisoners toward the river. I had a suspicion their life expectancies weren't those of immortals.

Chodo isn't a forgiving sort. These people had stomped on his toes, sort of. . . . He has no trouble conjuring justifications.

A half dozen thugs shuffled off with the Serpent. Crask and a few buddies hung around.

Well, I thought to me, I thought, I guess this means Chodo wants him a little light reading, just to pass those chilly winter nights. A little something to peruse beside the fire.

He wouldn't get the book from the Serpent. She didn't have the foggiest where it was. But he'd get something. He always did. And she had managed to become a credible ratman. . . . Ah. There Crask went, back into that tenement, shoulders set like he meant to find something.

That would have been a good time to stroll on out of there—if about four of Crask's buddies hadn't been hanging out, keeping a wary eye.

I got me comfortable in a good position for shivering and thought about Holme Blaine. Why had he come to me as Carla Lindo? Why had he come at all? How had he known to come to me? Through contact with Easterman? I could pursue that. Come morning. After a good sleep. If I thawed out enough. Sure be nice to head for bed. Why wouldn't Crask's clowns clear the street?

They didn't do me any favors. In fact, I was getting suspicious that they had something on their pea brains besides the Serpent and her improbable book. They spread out, started poking into shadows and alleys. So.

Crask passed below me, massaging his arm. He muttered something about the cold and "I don't get it. One second he's right there beside me, the next he's gone. He ain't no spook. How'd he disappear?"

Who? Bet you guessed as fast as I did.

What a bunch of guys.

I'd suspected it for a while. The kingpin's boys don't generally do you many favors. I'd tried setting it aside because I didn't want it to be true. But there it was. Chodo had something special in mind for a guy named Garrett. Maybe just a fancy dinner, a dip in the inside pool he's got out to his place, with the hot and cold running blondes. Maybe. Maybe just a friendly chat, old times, like he'd mentioned in the coach. I didn't want to find out. The streets aren't filled with guys who have had chats with Chodo.

One of Crask's boys came over and mumbled something I couldn't catch. Crask cussed and growled. "Keep looking!" Then he did an odd thing, for him. He went and perched on the steps of the raided tenement, rubbed his arm for a minute, rested his chin on his good fist, went away somewhere inside. If he hadn't been Crask of the Crask and Sadler torture show, I'd have pegged him for a man wrestling with his conscience.

He stuck with it till all his boys had given up and gone away. Naturally, I stayed put. Me and my frozen fanny. Ever have yours up in the air with a winter breeze tickling it? I wasn't in any shape to outrun or outfight Crask, or even somebody's granny, had no interest in trying and even less interest in visiting Chodo or maybe checking out the attractions on the bottom of the river. Frostbite can have its attractions.

Garrett is tough and patient. I outstubborned Crask. He finally had enough and went away. I pried my stiff bones loose from that porch and did the same. In another direction.

Boy, was I glad people never think to look up.

swung through the Safety Zone, found exactly what I expected to find. A big nothing. Morley's place was dead and dark. I was beginning to wonder if it wasn't time to start thinking about a wake.

I approached my place carefully. Crask might have it staked out.

Here was a problem that deserved some thought. I was too dependent on my home. If the bad boys wanted to hand me real trouble sometime, they'd just have to cut me off from my base.

Didn't seem to be anybody around. Even that off-and-on presence behind me was absent. Nice that whoever that was occasionally slipped up or needed rest.

I hustled to the door and banged away. Dean opened up. I crabbed, "What took so long?" He answered me with one of his better glowers. He hadn't taken long at all. The house was quiet. "Carla gone to bed?"

"Yes, I shall do so myself, now."

"Where? Across her door?"

"The daybed."

He didn't give me what I deserved for my crack. Oh, well. "Sleep well." I clumped into the Dead Man's room. "Awake there, Old Bones?" It would be like him to take a two-week nap in the middle of things.

Yes. I gather you were frustrated again.

"It just gets worse," I told him. "Any suggestions?"

Get some sleep. While the implications are disturbing, the information is tenuous. I will have to do considerable thinking.

"Get some sleep? That's the best idea you've had in years."

Do not allow frustration to embitter you, Garrett. We all suffer our unproductive days.

Easy for him to say. He had unproductive centuries. "Your talent for noting the obvious remains unblunted."

Indeed. But we cannot indefinitely continue to be in the wrong place or to arrive too late.

"We can't? Want to bet?"

Despair does not become you, Garrett. Dawn follows the darkest hour as surely as the rains fall to earth. Put Chodo Contague out of mind. Rest. That is the most useful thing you can do at this point. Relax. And rejoice. He does not have the book itself.

He was right. The dead fat genius usually is. Sometimes he can't be wrong if he wants. But: "No. He's just got somebody who knows how to make a book. That son of a bitch would write his own." I was in one of those moods where you're contrary for contrariness's sake. But maybe I've grown up some. I didn't overindulge. "While you're pondering, conjure me up a theory that explains the disappearances of Morley Dotes, Saucerhead Tharpe, and Sadler. And figure out who's following me like a ghost, so good I've never caught a glimpse."

As to those disappearances, I do have a hypothesis. Two, in fact. But they must be tested. And I refuse to discuss them till you have slept.

I knew better but wasted time trying to pry something out of him. He wouldn't budge. Does anybody ever budge? I don't think they can. They only don't or won't. It's always negative. How come?

See what kind of mind is out there leading the war on evil? Tsk-tsk.

He wouldn't budge. And even a boulder anchored to bedrock is less stubborn than a dead Loghyr.

I gave up, shambled toward the doorway.

What news from the Cantard, Garrett? As though he hadn't read my mind and found that I hadn't bothered asking around. Just a little nudge, there—nudge, unfortunately, being one of those words that doesn't come standardly negative. Old Bones nudges me a lot. Hinting that maybe if I cooperated more with him, he'd help me more. Right. Laziness is his reason for hanging around. He's too damned lazy to finish dying.

I didn't answer him. I tramped upstairs and threw myself into bed still clad, lay there searching my soul, tossing and turning, for at least seventeen seconds.

32

Dean wouldn't let me sleep in. I got four hours of the kind of sleep that fires and earthquakes can't interrupt, then he arrived. The ultimate disaster.

I cracked one eye a hundredth of an inch, heaved one leg over the side of the bed. That seemed good enough for a day's work, but that old man wasn't satisfied. He went for a bucket of water he had cooling out back. He found me sitting up when he got back. I grumped, "How come you couldn't send Carla?"

"Because you wouldn't get up. The sausages would burn, the biscuits would blacken, the kettle would boil dry while you tried to lead her astray."

"You're one suspicious and negative old goat." I made an epic attempt to stand up. It didn't work.

Dean chuckled. "I know you. If I don't stay between you and Miss Carla, nothing will get done around here for the next two weeks."

"I'm hurt. I'm in pain. Why don't you just bring breakfast up here?"

He hefted the bucket of ice water.

"Whoa!" I blinked several times, taking my morning exercise. Dean eased over to a better spot, started to wind up. The man doesn't know the meaning of mercy.

He sneered. "Maybe that's not such a bad idea."

"Huh?"

"My niece Ruth brought me fresh clothing. She's downstairs. She'd love to serve you breakfast in bed."

I groaned. The man won't play fair. Talk about your double-whammy threat. Ruth is a nice kid. Lots of personality. You know how that translates. Dogs don't howl when she goes by, they whimper and slink, hoping she won't notice them. "I'm out of my class now."

He chuckled again. Evil old man.

Then I didn't think well of myself for a minute. Ruth *was* nice. She couldn't help her looks.

I got completely vertical and wobbled toward the hall. I made it downstairs without killing myself. I even pasted on a wan smile for the ladies in the kitchen. Carla and Ruth had a contest to see who could beam back the brightest. It was like staring into the rising sun. I dropped into a chair and shielded my eyes.

Dean was a prophet. Breakfast was sausages and biscuits, with hot tea. My condition improved radically, though I never achieved sparkle. I staggered up and made the long march to the Dead Man's room. "I'm here, Chuckles." Plop into the chair.

Barely.

"Huh?" I had to figure it out. I'm not at my best in the morning. You may have noticed.

We have only one real option left. We have to be the first to find the book. I consider that imperative now. If we fail, it could mean disaster for TunFaire.

"Eh?" It *was* too early. I'd left my brain upstairs snoozing.

After sustained reflection I have come to distrust the motives of my friend the Gnorst. The cues are small but there. He has succumbed to temptation.

"I thought so."

We can, for the moment, ignore the Serpent. She has been neutralized. Easterman is of little account.

"You think? He's got Winger playing for him."

She is lucky to stay alive. Her luck will not last. No, Chodo Contague is the hunter who concerns me. The focus has shifted to his forces and those of the Gnorst. Both parties are far more formidable than the originals commanded by the witch and the madman. We now have the potential for a substantial conflict, perhaps fired by some personal animus, considering hints you picked up during your interview with the kingpin.

I had to slap me upside the head to get the clockwork ticking well enough to understand what he was saying. Yeah. Chodo had sounded bitter about dwarves and Dwarf Fort. He hadn't been able to corrupt the place. Knowing him, he'd like to get in there and kick some ass. He doesn't like it when folks aren't afraid.

"We're off to a scintillating start today, aren't we? With your brains and my brawn I just know we'll wrap it all up before lunch."

You appear to be coming to life.

"Easy for you to say. All I got to do is breathe."

We do have a lead, Garrett. An oblique angle that should not be difficult to pursue.

"Could have fooled me."

Assume our unclad guest was Holme Blaine.

"We know that for a fact."

Not exactly, though it is highly probable. Now. Listen. You have spent considerable energy trying to guess why he came here but none on why he chose us in particular.

I was coming around. I could see both fragments of the hair he was split-ting. "I thought about that." But not very much.

You thought of the lead, too. The possibility that he came because he knew Miss Ramada was going to come.

"So you think I should see the people she talked to, find out if he talked to them, too, see if he left something with somebody."

Exactly.

"Guess I might as well ask her, then get cleaned up and changed and climb on my horse. The house being watched?"

Not obviously.

"You got any idea who's been following me?"

No.

"Great. Well, what's become of everybody who's disappeared?"

You have not yet reasoned that out?

"No. I have not yet reasoned that out. Would I ask if I had?"

You remain as lazy as ever.

"Damned straight. I got you to figure for me. So give me the benefit of your wisdom. Without the standard shilly-shally."

Dotes and Tharpe have gone underground because they expect you to bestride your white horse and charge Chodo Contague. I suspect. They read the signs early and moved quickly, seizing the head start.

"Wonderful friends I have."

I have doubts myself. But I am not as mobile as they. My options are re-duced. I am at your mercy. I have to stand and fight.

I grumped.

That is but a hypothesis, Garrett. Though a good one, I think. They know you. You are wont to fly in the face of good sense. Do you truly believe that it is your duty to rescue the world from Chodo Contague?

I grumped some more. How come everybody assumes whenever some baddy poots I'll grab me my rusty sword? Hell. Considering how Crask wanted to round me up last night, even Chodo thinks that way. Hell again. I don't want to think I'm predictable any more than the next guy does.

"What about Sadler?"

More difficult, as I have not had as many exposures to Mr. Sadler's thought processes. My best guess is that he saw the implications of Mr. Contague obtaining the book and exhausted his patience.

"Say what?"

Have you never wondered about his unswerving loyalty?

"Only about a million times. Along with anybody else who ever had anything to do with the underworld."

Reflect on that patient loyalty in light of what you suspect Mr. Contague might do with the Book of Dreams.

It took me a minute. Hell, it was still early in the morning, remember? I had an excuse. "Say what?" Tell me black is white. Tell me princes of the church are saints, our overlords are philanthropists, lawyers have consciences. I might believe you. I might give individuals the benefit of a doubt. But don't try to sell me the notion that Sadler would turn on Chodo. "I don't believe it."

Have I not yet convinced you that what you believe is of no consequence? It is obvious, based on his questions, that Mr. Crask suspects a defection. If he acts upon that, the truth and your belief will not matter. My own inclination is to believe he would be correct in his assumption, considering hints underlying your last discussion with Mr. Sadler.

It's a fact, perceptions have more impact than absolute truths. We humans belong to a tribe steadfast in its refusal to be confused by the facts. Still . . . "Yeah, but Sadler just wouldn't." Would he? Even if the cripple he expected to replace any day came up with a way not only to evade death but to get healthy in the bargain?

Ah. You begin to use your head for something besides a device which keeps your hair from getting in the way when you eat. Excellent.

"Even I have a thought sometimes." Not much of a comeback. Hell. It was *still* morning.

There is some excitement outside. Perhaps news from the Cantard, long overdue. You might investigate.

Him and his hobby. "Sure. Why not? I'll have plenty of time. Hell, I'll borrow Dean's broom and help the ratmen clean streets in my spare time."

Mental sneer. Sometimes he has a higher estimate of my abilities than I do.

I was losing the war there. Just too damned early. I retreated to the kitchen. "Carla Lindo, my lovely, I need your help. The Dead Man says Holme Blaine must have been in touch with some of the people you were in touch with when you were looking for somebody to help you. I need to talk to them. Soon as you tell me who they were."

She eyed me about ten seconds, smoldering and crackling. The homely Miss Ruth lost her smile. I didn't blame her. It plain wasn't fair that the gods would give one woman so much advantage over another.

They ought to make them all gorgeous. Right?

"Actually, I only asked at the place where I was staying, with friends of my father. Everyone there who could think of anyone mentioned you."

Oh, wonderful. Now I'm a household name. "So where do I go? Who do I see?" I'll get the Dead Man one of these days. He knew already.

"I'd better go with you. They're a little odd there."

"Wouldn't be safe."

"Why not? Your friend Chodo Contague captured the Serpent, didn't he?"

Oh, boy. There just aren't any secrets around my house.

I tried arguing. Carla Lindo turned deaf as a post. She wasn't telling me nothing. It was show me or nothing. "I'll be ready in a minute, Garrett." She breezed out, leaving some sort of vacuum there in the kitchen. Dean grinned at me. He enjoys seeing me nonplussed. Actually more than nonplussed. Very minused. Even Ruth got a kick out of it, though I could see she envied Carla her power.

I never had a chance once Carla Lindo went to work on me. Someday, in about a thousand years, I'm going to develop an immunity to female charm. I don't know if I look forward to that or not.

I made a tactical error. I was the one who took a while getting cleaned up and changed. They never let you forget.

Sometimes I have to wonder if I'm as smart as I think. I mean, Carla gave me some pretty good hints, but I didn't tumble to the facts till we'd damned near walked through old Fido's front door.

stopped dead, stared at that bughouse, and thought I wasn't going in there never again.

"Garrett? What's the matter?" Carla Lindo was a couple steps ahead now, looking back, smoldering. How the hell did she do that? I stared at her some, too. I got a little less reluctant to head that way.

There wasn't much traffic, but what there was seemed determined to run over any guys who stood around with their mouths hanging open, staring at pretty women.

I gobbled, "I've had it, babe. All I can take of this mess. I'm up to here with running around like a short-necked chicken, not knowing what the hell is going on, who's going to do what to who, or why, always being a step too late." I couldn't tell her I was afraid to go back in there with that lunatic Easterman. Hell, I wasn't going to admit that part to me. I just told me the same stuff I told her and added that I don't much like hanging out with guys whose brains are off in fairyland.

Without a word she turned up the heat, piled on the come-hither, stacked up the promises. I kept the drool off my chin, but she did get me shivering. "You sure you're no witch yourself?" She couldn't be that old and crafty. She couldn't have discovered my weakness that quick.

She just smiled and tossed another sack of coal on the fire.

I muttered, "You're going to carrot me right into somebody's whipping stick, woman."

"What?"

"Yo! Garrett! Just the clown I want to see."

Oh, hell. Winger. Coming on like a galleon under full sail. Right behind her was the cadaverous old butler guy with the absurd name. I wondered if they were running a race. The old guy had stamina.

Carla Lindo gave Winger a look all trimmed up with daggers but lost it in about a second. Then she just gaped and tried to keep a straight face.

"Picked you up some new duds, eh, Winger?"

Winger stopped to do a pirouette. The old guy gained on her. "What do you think?"

"Colorful." Old Mom Garrett's favorite boy is shooting for another forty years. He tries to stay neutral when somebody as mean as that dressed like that asks a question like that.

"Knew you'd like it." Her eyes narrowed suspiciously.

Colorful was understating the truth.

Nobody has lousier taste and a worse idea how to dress than an ogre. This outfit would have stunned a nearsighted ogre. Splashes and panels of howling purples and screaming oranges and a limish green so virulent it fried your eyes. Some other colors in there that swirled venomously when she so much as breathed. Which meant what you saw was changing all the time. The total picture was so awesomely ugly it was almost hypnotic.

"Bet you're surprised to see me in a dress."

"Yeah." Kind of a half-breed croak and squeak. I was in pain. I didn't dare beg for mercy. That outfit should have been illegal. It was a deadly weapon.

"A dress? Is that what that is?" Carla Lindo asked.

Winger's grin vanished. I got between the women fast. "Peace. Child's new in town."

"Who is that dung beetle, Garrett? Just so I can apologize polite like after I squish her into frog food."

"Easy. She's a friend of your boss."

"He ain't got no friends. That old spook—"

The old man caught up with her. He grabbed onto her arm and hung there puffing like he'd sprinted six miles. However dire his message, he couldn't squeeze it out. In fact, he lost his grip and started to go down on his beak. Winger caught him by the scruff and hoisted him up. "Watch out you don't kill yourself, Pop."

Carla Lindo stared at the old man. She wanted to say something, too, but couldn't.

"You come to see the boss, Garrett?"

"Yes."

"Right. Then what I got can wait a couple. Maybe when we don't got so many mouse ears around." She turned the old man around and headed for home, holding him up with one hand. He kept trying to say something but couldn't get it out. His collar was choking him.

"What was *that*?" Carla Lindo finally managed.

"That was Winger. Try not to aggravate her. She's kind of like an earthquake. Not a whole lot of self-restraint."

"I believe it," in a tone of total disbelief. Then, "Look at that!" as excited as a little kid. Her attention span wasn't much longer than Winger's.

I looked.

Easterman had him a dragon.

A flying thunder-lizard was tethered atop the battlements of the runt black castle. It was being tended by a whole gang of morCartha doing their best to look like little devils. Easterman had them outfitted in some kind of suits but I couldn't make out details. When they realized we were watching, they started howling and carrying on. The thunder-lizard started screeching. It seemed more bewildered than put out.

Carla asked, "Isn't that neat?"

I was beginning to wonder about that girl. "The loonies have taken over. Maybe I ought to start cutting out paper dolls and practicing talking backward."

Carla Lindo didn't get it.

Winger dropped the old man inside the entrance. He had caught his breath and, despite all, had lost none of his dignity. "If you will follow me, sir? And madame." Some kind of look passed between him and Carla Lindo.

What now?

He led us to the room where I'd met Easterman before. The place had changed. A wall or two had been knocked out to make it bigger and it had been redecorated in black and red. They'd brought in a big ugly black throne carved all over with the ugly sisters of those gals you wake up with the morning after a night when you drank one gallon of popskull too many. There was a lot of indirect, shifting red light that was supposed to make you think it had been piped in from Hell itself. And the resident mental basket case had added some new employees to the payroll. They included six of the biggest, ugliest, fangiest ogres I've ever seen. Tittering morCartha in formal evening wear were all over the place.

Easterman's regulars, the old thugs with seniority, seemed embarrassed by the company they were keeping. One actually whispered, "He pays *real* good."

"God, I hope so." I began to wonder if Fido hadn't picked out Winger's wardrobe.

Easterman waited till he could make an entrance.

The fat man had him a new outfit, too. He'd chosen a few square miles of red accented with acres of black. I realized the black consisted entirely of little eyes. . . . Oh, my. Every eye was alive and looking around, blinking, or maybe winking over some private joke.

Easterman struggled up the steps of his throne, finally fell into its seat. There's why I'm running, I told myself. So I don't get like that . . . Oh, my, all over again. When his well-larded behind hit the seat, all those uglies carved on the throne got excited and started whispering to each other.

I gaped and gawked and wondered how he had come up with all this when he couldn't enchant a rock into falling down. Then I got worried. Had he won the race? Had he grabbed the Book of Dreams?

I'd almost rather Chodo laid hands on it first. Chodo was predictable.

Fido got himself settled. He beamed down benevolently. More or less. "Mr. Garrett. I'm so happy you came calling, sir. What do you think, sir?" He gestured. "Is this not an impressive setting?"

"Yeah. It's that." It was. "But I'm kind of partial to the old setup. Know what I mean?" It was only ninety-percent whacko before.

"We must change with the times, sir. We must change with the times. These present changing times are intriguing, are they not, sir? Here you are, an appellant, when but a short time ago you turned your back on me, a strutting cock. Yes sir, changing times."

Carla Lindo gave me a puzzled look. I guess she didn't know about my earlier chat with Fido. I asked, "Where did you get the idea I came here to beg for something?" That fat clown had my nerves frayed already. I should have been amused, should have had trouble keeping a straight face, but something kept making me want to hop up there and plant a boot in his face.

Not a smart move with all those ogres there to save his jowls.

"Plague!"

The old man did the hopping.

Easterman and the old guy traded melodramatic whispers while taking turns staring at me. Fido's gaze flicked to Carla Lindo. He started looking puzzled. I had the impression he'd expected me to drop on my knees and crawl. I wasn't and didn't look like I would and maybe had no idea why I was supposed to.

Puzzled turned to troubled. Easterman stared at me, eyes narrowed more than seemed possible. "Are you making mock, sir?"

"I'm not doing anything but standing here. I don't know what your problem is, Fido. Sorry I'm not doing what you expect. I just dropped by with my friend Carla Lindo to ask who all you told about her business here in town."

"What?"

"Miss Ramada stayed here when she first came to TunFaire, right? She asked who could help her find a little bauble somebody swiped from her dad. . . ."

"I've never seen this woman before, sir."

"People told her to come to me. Right? So . . ." I stopped chattering.

Fido popped up and glared around. He eyeballed Carla Lindo. He sputtered. Spit flew. For a second I thought he was going to have a seizure.

I didn't really get it till Carla Lindo unfroze and started tugging on my arm and shaking her head. Long after the whole herd of cats had flown out of the bag. She maybe stayed here, but old Fido hadn't been in on it.

Easterman started roaring endearing sobriquets like Famine, War, and Pestilence. He took a moment out to tell his ogres, "Get that man out of here! I don't want to look at his ugly face another second." Then he went to foaming at the mouth.

Well. I never. Ugly? Maybe a little battered around the edges, but the dogs don't howl. . . . I didn't wait for the ogres. I latched onto Carla Lindo and headed for the exit. No sense dancing with those boys. The mood I was in, suddenly I'd have tried to break a head or three. I wouldn't have been able to do the job justice before the sky collapsed on me.

"That was real bright, Garrett," Carla Lindo said as soon as we hit the street. "You have a real golden tongue."

"You could have told me something up front. You could have given me one teensy hint. The Dead Man is the mind reader, not me." I spun around and dared an ogre to bring it out into the street. He looked over his shoulder to see how much help he'd get. He had no cavalry on the way. He just waved bye-bye. An ogre with sense. The times they are a-changing.

I faced Carla Lindo. "So what else haven't you told me, sweetheart? You want me to help, you got to give me the tools. What the hell was that all about in there, anyway?"

She shrugged, stared at the pavement. "I didn't know. . . . I never saw any of that before. I stayed with my uncle. My mother's brother. One of the servants. When they took us to that room . . . I only ever saw that man from a distance before. My uncle just said he was a little potty."

"A little, yeah. Here you had me thinking you had an in with some Hill bigwigs." I added another score to the list needing settling with the Dead Man. He could have warned me. His idea of a joke, probably, letting me find out the hard way.

"I sort of wanted you to think . . ."

"I figured that out."

A shadow fell on the conversation, which was about to sneak on toward making up. Making up is always full of promise when a guy and a gal are doing it.

"Yo, Garrett! That was some brilliant show you put on in there. You foxed the old boy right out of his garters."

"Don't you start on me, Winger. You want something, spit it out. If you don't, you better scoot back in there and make sure old Fido don't choke on his rug. You might miss a payday."

"Hey. Here I come trying to be friendly, trying to build some bridges, and all you want is to start a fight."

"Want to build a bridge?" I grumbled. "Tell me what's with the new look in there. What's with the zoo on the roof?"

"Old goof is getting set for the new era. Getting his props together so he'll have the right look once he gets hold of the Book of Dreams."

"Huh?" That's Garrett. Swift on the uptake.

"Claims he knows where it is."

"Where?"

"He didn't tell me. He don't trust me."

Couldn't say I blamed him for that. Winger would sell him out to the highest bidder if she got the chance. "Any hints?"

She shook her head. "Just said it's there for the taking soon as he figures how to get past one big obstacle."

Probably like not knowing where it was. "The Serpent? Chodo Contague grabbed her last night." Finding some guile at last, I figured maybe I could keep an eye on Fido, grab the book from him after he grabbed it, before he could start using it.

"We heard. Who cares? He isn't interested in her, except to stay out of her way and grab the book before she does."

All hell broke loose overhead. Daytime or not, the morCartha from

Fido's roof went on the warpath. Easterman's human servants yelled at them to come back or get fired. I asked, "What the hell?"

Winger said, "They do that. Probably spotted a critter from another tribe."

"I should've stayed in bed." This was all Dean's fault.

"*You* know where the book is, Garrett?"

"If I did, I wouldn't be here, would I? I'd be waving bye-bye to my friend at the west gate." I gave Carla Lindo a one-armed hug. I'd at least be trying to collect a suitable reward.

Winger ignored Carla Lindo. "We got to have a sit-down, see what we can come up with if we put our heads together."

"Right."

She didn't catch my sarcasm. I think she was immune to it, or at least deaf. Besides being color-blind. She said, "That thing's still worth a fortune, Garrett. Word is, there's a dwarf willing to put up *big* money for it. More than Easterman would."

"You going to turn on him?"

"If there's money in it." Like maybe I had that kind of cash. Sure. In my sock. She said, "He never did nothing to make me want to stay loyal. He treats them damned ogres better than me and they don't have my seniority."

I chuckled. "You're one in a million, Winger."

"I know. But don't let it get to you. I ain't ready to settle down. But you'll be first on my list when I am."

I don't often get caught without something to say. I did that time. I just stood there with my mouth open wondering if maybe she wasn't a whole lot sharper than I thought.

She said, "You get a line on that book and you need some help, get in touch. I'll go in for a split." She marched back toward Easterman's hovel.

Carla Lindo snickered. "You've made a conquest."

I bellowed. She took off, giggling. I took off after her. People stared. She didn't run too fast. I didn't either. The view was much too entertaining from second place.

This was more like life ought to be.

I caught her. She leaned against me, panting, making it plain she was willing to be caught. Hell. There we were in the middle of a street with no-where to go.

That's the story of my life. Whenever I do win the prize, I can't collect. "Let's go home and try to figure out where the hell Easterman thinks that book is." I had a feeling he *was* sure he knew where it was. Thinking that gave me an idea. "Any chance this uncle of yours would know what his boss is thinking?"

"No." She looked sad. "And if he did he wouldn't tell. He's really afraid he'd never get another job if Easterman throws him out. He's too old."

"Wonderful." We walked a ways, snuggling. I felt just a touch guilty doing that only a couple of blocks from Tinnie. Must be getting old. "You really still need the book? Chodo's got the Serpent. I'd say it's a safe bet she won't be back to haunt your dad."

She had to think about that awhile. Most of the way home, in fact. Then she said, "I could go home without it, I guess. But only if I was sure it'd been destroyed. My father would never forgive me if I didn't."

Well, hell.

was still explaining to the Dead Man and getting hell for not having snatched Fido by the short hairs and twisted till he sang when Dean stuck his head in the room. "There's a gentleman to see you, Mr. Garrett."

I'd heard the knock. I'd hoped it was for me. The Dead Man was way up on his high horse, really smoking. I couldn't get a word in to suggest he consider the facts of the situation. I guess I was supposed to have taken care of Fido's troops with my free hand while I was twisting and yanking and humming along.

The gentleman at the door wasn't. That was Dean's way of making a snide social observation. The guy was a mixed-breed kid of obscure antecedents sneaking up on adolescence. His outstanding feature was the most awful set of teeth I've ever seen. He could pass as an ugly ogre or uglier human if you needed a stand-in for one of those. He said, sneering, "You Garrett?" Like he'd heard of me and wasn't impressed.

"Last time I checked."

"Got a paper for you." He shoved something at me and lit out before he saw if I had a grip on it. I didn't. It fell onto the stoop, started tumbling on the breeze. I dashed out and hunted it down. Naturally, the door swung shut behind me. The latch fell and caught. I cussed it and kicked and pounded till Dean let me in. He didn't say anything, just smirked. "Go scrub a pot or something," I grumbled.

I took myself to my office, planted me in my chair. I asked Eleanor, "Why the hell don't I take that job at the brewery? There something wrong with me? I enjoy abuse? I could get me a room right there in the plant. You and me. I could go tap a vat whenever the mood hit me. I could spend the rest of my life holed up there."

Eleanor didn't have any answers. She just gave me her enigmatic look. Nobody was on my side anymore. I uncrumpled the wad of paper.

It was a note, but it took me a while to decipher the primitive printing. Before it became a vehicle for deathless prose, it had been used to wrap fried fish or something.

We got to talk. Sinkler. Statue. Soon. Sadler.

Interesting. I hadn't thought he could read or write. He wasn't a threat to anybody doing illuminated manuscripts but he was a match for any educated seven-year-old. And he had all the words spelled right. Amazing.

Sadler. One of my many missing men. I couldn't turn him down.

But when to meet? He didn't state a time.

I didn't jump up and run over, though. Despite my interest. That sort of thing isn't done if you care to survive in this line. There are proprieties one observes when dealing with mysterious messages. Like sending some sucker . . . er, friend . . . to scout the terrain. "Hey, Dean." I didn't have anybody else left.

"I have dishes and laundry to do, Mr. Garrett. One extra body seems to triple the workload around here." This from the kitchen, shouted.

"Wait a minute. . . ."

"I don't have time to run any errands."

Who the hell is the mind reader around here? "How did you know . . . ?"

"That's your favor-asking voice. Perhaps you could send Miss Ramada."

He sucked me in there. I wouldn't send Carla Lindo. And because I wouldn't, he'd know I hadn't been about to send him after rutabagas so we could have rutabaga pie tonight. In the following silence I could almost hear his brain creaking and squeaking as he mulled over how to get even for me even considering getting him involved in something chancy.

I caught the edge of a mental chuckle from across the hall. I was everybody's entertainment. I got up and plodded into the kitchen, drew me a beer. "You're going to stay on after I get married, aren't you? We're going to need all the help we can get."

Dean's face brightened. He forgot all about me thinking of sending him out where the bad winds blow. He knew he wasn't going to get rid of one of his nieces but having me shackled to any woman was the next best thing. He was a born-again advocate of marriage, though he'd managed to evade martyrdom himself. "It would be an honor to serve Miss Tinnie, Mr. Garrett."

I felt almost bad, digging at him like that. Almost. "Not who I've got in mind."

"Miss Maya certainly is devoted to you, but don't you think she's a bit young for a man of your years?"

My years? He'd get no mercy now. "Not Maya. I'm thinking about asking Winger. You got to admit, she's more my type. We'd make a hell of a team out on those mean streets."

He looked scandalized, horrified, proceeded rapidly toward apoplectic. His face got red. He gulped for air. I poured it on. "I'm not really cut out for these sleek little beauties, Dean. I need somebody who can be a real partner. A pal. A real man's man everywhere but in the dark. I think Winger is the gal I've been waiting for. She's a take-charge type. She'd get things straightened out around here."

Garrett!

I must have overdone it. That squeak of horror came from up front.

I'm used to Dean taking everything too serious, to him taking forever to figure out he's being ribbed. But not the Dead Man. I finished up, "Don't you think?"

Dean just stood there with a pan dangling from one hand, his mouth open and his eyes crossed. He looked so forlorn I almost let up. If Carla Lindo hadn't been upstairs, I would have. Instead, I headed for the front door. "I'd better take care of it right away."

oes anybody know who this guy Sinkler was? Does anybody care? Somebody put up a statue, didn't they?

Hell, maybe that ugly hunk of rock was there when they built the city. It looks worn out enough. If anybody does know, they haven't been talking. Whatever Sinkler did, it's a secret from me. Only the pigeons have much use for him. They perch on his upraised arms and tricorner hat and wait for primo targets to come by. Once upon a time he was covered with copper. Thieves took care of that ages before I was hatched.

Sinkler stands in the center of a small square where five streets butt heads, maybe half a mile northwest of my place. His main significance to me is he marks the frontier between your ordinarily dreadful city and the Bustee, which makes any part of town you care to name look like a suburb of heaven. The Bustee is where the *real* poor folks live. The Bustee is a quarter Chodo Contague wouldn't enter without an army, let alone wimps like the Watch. Hell, it's gotten so bad lately some of the landlords have gotten chicken to collect their rents.

Of course, a Chodo wouldn't bother going into the Bustee. People there are so poor they can't afford names. They survive by looking poorer than their neighbors.

Hell on earth. In the Marines I met guys out of there. They thought the Corps was great, despite the war. They got food to eat, clothes to wear, shoes on their feet, their life expectancies were better in the Cantard than at home, and they even got paid. So how come you rich boys are all pissing and moaning?

My folks never had a pot to pee in, but I'd grown up rich compared to those guys.

You'd think those people would bust out and go berserk. They never have. Like nobody is taking advantage of the fact that all the lords of the Hill are off to catch Glory Mooncalled. People have a sense of order and place and caste. Most figure if they're poor and dying of starvation, the gods want it that way. Probably they earned it in a former life.

It's a strange world. Its people are stranger.

What am I on about? What's this got to do with Sadler or the Book of Dreams? Not a damned thing. Just indulging the social observer within.

Speaking of Glory Mooncalled, there was a lot of talk. News had come north. People were telling perfect strangers. They'd grab you by the shirt to get you to hold still long enough so they could get the thrill of being first to tell you.

Mooncalled had engineered some apocalyptic collision between the massed Karentine and Venageti armies but lost most of his own making it happen. He was on the run. Or maybe not, depending on your informant. I hung out with Sinkler and absorbed stories. I'd hand them all to the Dead Man when opportunity arose. If ever it did.

I'd spent an hour perched on the pedestal where Sinkler stood, spreading his benevolence. I was beginning to suspect I'd been tricked. At best Sadler wasn't making it easy. Whatever he had in mind. If it was Sadler who sent that message.

It was. He showed eventually. He came creeping out looking around like he was into the loan sharks for half a million and hadn't made his vigorish in a year. I didn't recognize him till he was almost in my lap. He looked like a bum. He wasn't the lethal character I knew and loathed.

He settled beside me, all scrunched up so his size wouldn't give him away. He started throwing crumbs to the pigeons. Nobody would recognize him doing that.

"Where you been?"

"Underground. Had to do some thinking. Couldn't just keep on after I knew why Chodo wanted that book."

"Um?"

"Think what he could do with it."

"I have been. One reason I'm not fond of the idea of him glomming on to it."

"Me neither. Crask too."

"Crask?"

"Took him a little longer but he figured it out. He got a message to me. We met up and talked. We decided we got to do something. We want to bring you in."

His crumbs had brought in pigeons from miles around. They'd been climbing over each other. Now they exploded off the pavement. I glanced up, figuring a flight of thunder-lizards was coming in. But the birds had panicked because of one lone morCartha who appeared to be drunk. Sadler expressed my sentiments for me. "Out in the daytime now, too. Somebody ought to do something. Put a bounty on them, maybe. Give the kids something to do besides cut purses and roll drunks."

Yeah. Things just aren't the way they were in the old days. We had us some respect when we were kids. And so forth. I knew that routine by heart. "How come you're coming to me?"

"You just said you don't want Chodo getting that book."

"I don't want anybody to get it. Not him, not you, not Crask, not the Serpent, not Gnorst Gnorst or Fido Easterman. Hell, I wouldn't trust the old guy who keeps house for me with it. There isn't anybody alive who could resist the temptation."

He thought a minute. "Maybe. I can figure all I could do with it if I could read for shit."

"You can't?"

"My name. A few signs and things I seen all my life. I never got a chance to learn. In the army they didn't teach guys like they did you Marines."

"That was luck." That was something I'd brought away with me. I suspect, though, that I'd been more motivated than Sadler had. "But you sent a note."

"Crask wrote it. He picked up a little here and there. I been thinking we could get us a tutor after Chodo croaks and we take over. Only now it don't look like he plans on checking out, ever."

"So you're figuring on helping him along."

"Something like that."

"I don't do assassinations."

"You was in on the old kingpin biting the big one."

"He didn't bite it, it bit him. And you know how it went down. Morley Dotes set me up. If Saucerhead or I had known what was happening, we'd have been on the other side of town instead of helping Dotes lug his vampire."

"You help us, Garrett, you'd have friends could help you back."

"How? Chodo embarrasses me now, carrying on like I was his favorite kid."

Sadler was startled. Why? He grinned but didn't say. He had lousy teeth. "Maybe so. But he sure as hell ain't never going to give you that book."

"Would you?"

"I can't read and Crask ain't much better. You figure we could hire somebody to read it for us? You figure we could have that thing and hang on long enough to learn how to read? Without everybody in the world coming after us?"

"You have a point. But I have a problem." I don't do assassinations. I didn't have much use for Chodo but didn't want in on sending him to the big rackets in the sky. He hadn't earned it from me.

I didn't not want in badly enough to tell Sadler no, though. He might decide I had to be put to sleep so I wouldn't tell anybody his plan. "It doesn't look like I have too many options. How you going to do it?" It's called temporizing.

"Old Chodo, he's going to be partying tonight. Going to be distracted. His daughter is in town for the wingding he throws her every year. . . ."

"His what?"

"His daughter." Sadler laughed. "Not a lot of people know about her. You'd like her. She's a looker. Must take after her old lady. I never saw the broad. Before my time, Chodo put her away himself 'cause he caught her screwing the guy who was the boss back then. So what? History is history. Important thing is, he's throwing a birthday party tonight. Goes on like they have before, everybody will drink themselves blind and pass out. Me and Crask figure if we hit about three in the morning, it'll be a walk."

"Why do you need me, then?"

He grinned again. He was doing more of that than in all the time I'd known him. "Garrett, you do that innocent so damned good. Man, I wish I could do that."

"Glad you get a kick out of it. Because I really don't know what the hell you're yapping about."

"Sour today. Little chickie tell you no? Okay. You remember a while back we all had us a problem with that thing that thought it was a dead god? Wanted to bring itself back to life?"

That wasn't all that long ago. I didn't want to remember. That had been a hairy one. There'd been some sick people involved. Only good that came out of it was Maya. "I remember."

"No wisecrack? You must be getting old. So. One day you come out to the house. Dotes was with you. We gived you a little stone. An amulet, like. Eh? Maybe you thought we forgot to take it back."

I'd been hoping. That stone was hidden in the Dead Man's room with our most precious possessions. I'd expected to have to use it someday.

It was a magical gizmo that kept the thunder-lizards away. Chodo isn't fond of unannounced visitors. To discourage them, he has his grounds walled. Behind the walls he keeps whole herds of small, carnivorous thunder-lizards. They're more efficient than dogs, though he has packs of those, too. Thunder-lizards don't leave much evidence lying around. No telling how many valiant adventurers have scaled Chodo's wall only to become monster munchies.

"You set me up."

"We thought it might be handy someday, having one on the outside."

"You guys are too damned smart for me."

"That's a fact."

I doubted it, but he and Crask *were* a lot smarter than they let on. "So you need the stone to get through to the house, where everybody's going to be polluted. Then what?"

"Then Chodo expires in his sleep. Maybe because they're all drunk and not watching what they're doing, a couple thunder-lizards get inside and gobble up a few guys who been trying to take over me and Crask's spots."

"You think you can run the outfit?"

"Between us we can. It don't take a lot of running. We got the machine all oiled up. We go break somebody's head once a month or so, it keeps running smooth. We can handle that."

No doubt. "And I get the book, eh?"

"Soon as we find out where it is. That's a promise. And we'll find it. You know that."

They would if they wanted. But would they really deliver? That is, would they bother collecting it if it turned out to be in the clutches of a Fido Easterman or would they just point me in the right direction? "Three in the morning, eh?"

"I know you been keeping regular hours. But that's the way it is."

Another night without much sleep. And no nap between now and then because I'd be trying to think of a way to slide out of being part of a gangland killing.

Morley would say this was an opportunity to show I wasn't under Chodo's thumb, forgetting it would give Crask and Sadler a rather ferocious hold on me. Speaking of Morley Dotes, where *was* he? Now I needed a helpful hand. Not to mention Saucerhead. "Hey, you got any idea what's become of Dotes and Tharpe?"

"Nope. Still sulking?"

"Looks like." Something about his answer told me he really didn't know. Probably it was the fact that his tone said he didn't care.

He asked, "You aren't thinking about bringing them guys with you?"

I caught the edge of something there. "No." This deserved some thought. "Just haven't seen them since this mess started. I'm concerned."

"Um. I been sitting still too long. Got to keep moving. Don't want to let anything catch up. We'll meet you at the milestone on the hill down the road from Chodo's place. Two o'clock. Bring that amulet stone."

"Sure."

Sadler went away, stooped like he was a hundred and ten. He did it pretty good. I wouldn't have recognized him from a distance.

I wondered what they would do if I didn't show.

He'd left his packet of crumbs. I fed the pigeons while I mused, till some jerk came up and pounced, wanting to tell me all the latest from the Cantard.

hadn't gone a block when Winger fell into step beside me "Must be my lucky day."

She asked, "What was that about?" No sensitivity, Winger. I wondered if she could be insulted.

"What's what about?"

"Your little cheek-to-cheek with Chodo's boy Sadler."

So she had an eye. His disguise hadn't fooled her. "You're too nosy, along with all your other charms."

"That's what they tell me." She gave me a big grin, followed with a comradely punch to the shoulder. Would I ever get used to her? Tell the truth, I hoped I didn't have to. There were moments when I wished the odds would hustle up and overtake her. "Bet I can figure it."

"Go right ahead." I did my surly best to lengthen my stride till she couldn't keep up. Lot of good it did me. She cruised along, had me huffing and puffing before I was halfway home. Big old country girl.

"How's this, Garrett? Sadler and his boyfriend figure out their hopes for moving up ain't worth squat if their boss grabs that book. Eh?" Big chuckle, up from the gut, like a Saucerhead Tharpe chuckle. "They put in their time, played it straight, figure they deserve better. Eh?"

"That you been following me all over?" I hadn't sensed her presence at all. Nor that other presence, if that hadn't been her. Scary, her that close and me not feeling a thing. And her in that outfit.

"Only since you left Easterman's hangout. Them guys want you to help them promote themselves, don't they?"

Was I giving myself away? Usually I do good hiding my thoughts. She laughed. "Yeah. I thought so. When they going to do it?"

"What're you babbling about? You been smoking weed?"

"Sure. My imagination's gone berserk. You ever seen that place that Chodo lives?"

"I've been there."

"Bet whoever cleans that out would be set for life."

"Be a short life if somebody tried."

"Them thunder-lizards? No problem. Your pals got some way to get past them. I ride in on their coattails, stay low while they're doing the dirty deed, grab a sackful of the best loot, hightail out in the confusion afterward. No big deal."

Incurable optimism. "When did you get out to look at the place?"

"I get around. You made a big deal about the guy being bad, I figured I had to check him out."

"You ever sleep?"

"I got a lot of energy. You do when you got ambition. You, you're an old box turtle. Never move unless you're starving and then only far enough to get yourself fed. You're never going to amount to anything, Garrett."

Was she taking lessons from Dean? "I manage. I have my own house. Not many can say that."

"I heard about how you made the money, too. People kept sticking pins in your ass till you did something. Then you fell in the shit and came up with a sack of gold."

It really was something like that. But I do think I gave value for money. I stomped up the steps to my front door. Winger invited herself along. I thought about tossing her back when I recalled my little joke on Dean. What the hell? It would do his old heart good to get to pounding. I knocked.

Dean opened up. He took a look at Winger. His face scrunched up but he didn't say anything. Winger said, "How you doing, Pops? You got any more of that good beer? I'm dry as a mummy." She gave him a friendly thump on the chest. He almost went down. He regained his balance, took off down the hall shaking his head.

Only after I shut the door behind her did I recall how things had gone last time Winger visited. I had to see the Dead Man and couldn't let her run amuck while I did. No telling what would leap into her pockets. "Come on.

It's time you met my partner." I shouldn't use that word so close to him. He'd make a point of bringing it up.

My partner was as thrilled to meet her as he'd be to be the star at a witch burning. Carla Lindo could charm him some, but even she was a woman, and I'd not be forgiven for having her around so long. Winger was something else. Say she lacked Carla Lindo's grace.

"What the hell is that thing?"

"The Dead Man. My sidekick. Not as frisky as some, but he does his part. If you light a fire under him."

"That ain't no man, Garrett. That's some kind of *thing*. Gots it a snoot like a mammoth. Gods, it's ugly. Kind of ripe, too." Like I said, a real charmer. All the sensitivity of a dire wolf.

Garrett!

We must have caught him dozing. I expected him to get peckish sooner. "News from the Cantard, Old Bones. Your boy maybe weaseled out one more time. Got the big boys butting heads . . ." He wasn't going to buy.

This time you have gone too far! Why have you brought that creature into my home?

Oh-oh. He was piqued. He's very precise in his word choices. If he had used *my house*, he'd just have wanted to squabble to kill time. *My home . . .* Well, he was not pleased. He felt violated.

"So I can keep an eye on her. Wouldn't want some unscrupulous rake making a move on her before—"

Stuff that nonsense. Play that game with Dean if you like, but I know you better.

"Had you going there, didn't I?"

Do what needs doing, then get her out.

Hey! He was willing to work to get shut of her. All right. I'd finally found a way to twist his arm.

Garrett!

"Right."

Winger looked at me like I was foaming at the mouth. The Dead Man wasn't giving her his half of the conversation. She asked, "You talking to that thing?"

"Sure. He's just dead, he isn't gone."

Report, Garrett! Get on with it.

I did. Every little detail.

I suggest you play along for the time being. He let Winger catch that. She jumped about a foot, grabbed the sides of her head. Her eyes got big as she wondered if he could look inside there as easily as he put thoughts in. I think she would've attacked him if she hadn't been so shocked.

"Play along. Right. My sharpest skill. And when the crunch comes, how do I get out of committing murder? Or at least becoming a heavyweight accessory to same?"

The Dead Man sent the mental equivalent of a shrug. *You will manage. You always do. Tell me more about what has happened in the Cantard.*

Back to normal. He had his bluff in again. He thought. "How about you suggest a way I can keep them from killing me once I've helped with the dirty work."

Really, Garrett. Your stubborn refusal to think for yourself is becoming a burden. He paused. *Since you have developed a fondness for this Winger person, and she has the intent anyway, why not take her along? She has shown herself capable of handling one of them already. I foresee an unbeatable team here.*

Did I walk into that one? I sprinted. And did all the setup work, too. I couldn't raise a fuss without Winger maybe getting upset and busting me upside the head.

A hint of mental snicker, private, for me alone. The devil.

It wasn't my day. It wasn't my week. If I went along to help ice Chodo, it might not be my lifetime.

"Sounds good to me," Winger said. It would. She'd already invited herself along once. Now she had the Dead Man's blessing.

I noted that she had caught her balance fast. The Dead Man had become old news. She watched me expectantly, like she wondered how much originality I'd show trying to weasel out.

"I should've been a clown," I grumbled. "I'm everybody's entertainment anyhow."

The Dead Man's laughter was silent but evil.

Winger's wasn't silent.

I heard a sound, glanced back. Dean was in the doorway. Grinning.

My get-even list was getting too long to keep in my head. I was going to have to get me a diary to keep track.

don't know why I left the house after I got rid of Winger. I guess because the Dead Man was riding me with spurs on, digging them in deep. My joke about Winger had turned on me. I didn't dare go to the kitchen without Dean ragging me, too.

Out seemed like a good idea at the time. Especially when the Dead Man said he'd like to know what Gnorst was up to now. I grabbed the out.

So I went to see the sneeze man. Actually, I just left a message at the door. Gnorst wasn't receiving. I suspect he especially wasn't receiving people with connections to old pals.

I headed for home. I got the notion I could root Carla Lindo out of her room and weep on her shoulder. She hadn't ridden me. She'd been especially understanding, in fact. The more I thought about it, the more I was sure we were going to become great friends real soon now. I started getting high on anticipation.

You may have noticed that things have a way of catching up with me whenever I feel too positive. The god who hands out the towels in the heavenly loo has a sideline. Messing with Garrett. He's such a puny, useless god they couldn't find anything better for him to do. But he's really good at messing with me. He works at it so hard I think he's bucking for a promotion.

I was a block from my place, trotting toward Macunado on Wizard's Reach. I stopped suddenly.

They came out of nowhere. They closed in carefully. There were six of them. I didn't know them but they had to be Chodo's boys.

The street cleared magically. I struck some martial-arts poses, made me some nifty yells. That just kept them from getting overconfident.

They were good. They would be, of course. Otherwise they wouldn't be on the first team. And they'd been briefed on what to expect, which was to expect the unexpected. I've been known to yank tricks out of my sleeves.

Today I was fresh out, not counting the old-fashioned lie. I got one guy to turn his head by yelling, "Hey! Morley! Just in time for the party."

That was the only good Morley did me all week, and he wasn't even there. I laid that guy out with a flying kick and just kept going for about six feet. Then I was out of running room. A building jumped in my way.

They closed in. I hauled out my stick. We mixed it up. I dinged two pretty good. I wasn't worrying about how bad I hurt them. They apparently wanted me alive. At least a little. Nobody bothered explaining anything to anyone.

The scuffle lasted longer than they planned. Our dancing and prancing brought some of the bolder neighbors back outside, especially the kids. Some were kids I knew. Did they lend a hand? Did they run to the house to tell somebody I was in trouble? They did not.

These are the little people, the ones I thought needed a champion when I outfitted myself with creaky idealistic armor. Sometimes people make it damned hard to care about people. Sometimes they do their damnedest to make it seem they deserve whatever they get.

Oh, well. I made a showing till somebody got my stick away from me and tried it out on my skull.

A black pool opened at my feet. . . .

I didn't dive in. I sort of belly-flopped and floated there with my nose above the surface. I vaguely recall sagging between two thugs while a third summoned a waiting coach. The coach came. My buddies helped me dive inside. Somebody did a drumroll on my noggin, then they dumped their injured in on top of me.

My head stuck out of the pile. The guy with my stick tapped it every little bit, like he was trying out different patterns of lumps. I would fix him with some patterns of his own if I got the chance.

Even my skull has limits. I went off to dreamland.

The sandman isn't all bad. Before we left the city, before I wakened with an all-time headache, he got rid of the three guys piled on top of me. Hell. I had it whipped. I outnumbered them now.

The headache was a memorable effort. At least I remembered it better than any I had before. I'd been thumped hard enough to generate a small concussion. I'd puked all over the coach floor. Recently, too. The guy with the stick was still cussing me. His partner, riding with his back to the horses, observed, "You bopped him too many times. What you expect?"

"Hell, we'll probably just end up croaking him. Why'd he got to go make a mess?"

"Inconsiderate of him."

"Sure as hell was. I'm gonna gotta clean it up. I always get stuck with the shit jobs."

A philosopher and a complainer. The philosopher said, "You don't plan to go messy when your turn comes? You just going to take the hit and fold politely?"

"I ain't going." Sullenly.

The philosopher chuckled. How could a guy with his realist's outlook stay in the niche he'd chosen? He said, "Least we know he ain't dead yet. I never saw a stiff puke. I was worried. Chodo'd have a litter if we delivered a deader."

"Why? He's gonna be dead anyway."

"We don't know that. He didn't *say* that."

"Shit."

"All right. There ain't much doubt. But Chodo wants to talk to him first. To apologize, maybe. They used to be buddies or something."

Or something. I'd never counted on Chodo's gratitude being bottomless. I wondered if there was a connection between this and my chat with Sadler.

"Shit. He's crazy," the complainer said.

"Sure. And he's the kingpin, too."

Grumble grumble. Lots of use of that favorite four-letter word. I wondered if they knew I was awake. I wondered if I was being snookered.

The philosopher began rhapsodizing on the passing scenery. A nature lover. Some city boys get that way in the country. A plain old willow is a cause for wonder. His observations suggested we were on the road to Chodo's place already. We were in some wooded hills. That meant we weren't more than a mile or two from the place I was supposed to meet Crask and Sadler later. The woods would give way to vineyards on the north slopes, though there would still be patches of trees alongside the road. If I wanted to stay healthy, I ought to do something before we reached the vineyards. There wasn't cover enough to make an escape over there.

Only my body didn't feel like doing anything. Maybe next week. Maybe after the swelling went down.

It's real hard to find much ambition after you've had your noggin used for a drum.

The way the horses were straining I guessed we were climbing Hornet Nest Hill, a long steep climb. Near the top the road makes a backward S-curve, climbing what amounts to a bluff, before it leaps the ridge and heads for the end of the woods. Perfect. I could dive out the door and over the side, roll down the hill, and disappear before these thugs could get their mouths closed. I told my body to get ready.

My body said go to hell. It wasn't moving. Moving hurt.

The carriage stopped.

The complainer opened a door, asked, "What's up?"

"I don't know," the driver told him. "The horses don't want to go any farther."

Say what? Me and horses don't get along. If there's any way for them to mess me around, they will. I couldn't picture them not galloping all the way to carry me to my execution. Unless they wanted to mess with me some themselves before letting Chodo have me. . . . Hell. I couldn't keep that game going. I felt too lousy.

The philosopher edged the complainer out of the doorway. "Hang on, Mace. Don't push them. Maybe they know something." He got out of the coach. His buddy followed him. "Could be that shoemaker's bunch. Was I to set an ambush, I'd put it right up there, just before the top. Where the cut is, with the drop on the right. Leaves you nowhere to duck."

They debated. The sullen one tossed in two sceats' worth of let's get rolling, there ain't no damned ambush. The philosopher suggested, "Why don't you go up and look?"

They argued. The complainer sneered. "Candyass! I'll show you." I heard his feet crunch the road surface. He sent opinions back meant to keep the curl in the philosopher's hair.

Come on, Garrett! This is it. They've handed it to you. All you have to do is fall through a door and roll down a hill. Or the other way around. You have the necessary skills.

My body told me, all right, I'll let you open one eye.

I did. I couldn't see squat because I wasn't facing the door.

The driver observed, "Something's up. He's slowing down." Like maybe the philosopher had bad eyes.

The philosopher called, "What is it, Winsome?"

I wished I had the energy to laugh. Winsome? Was that a nickname? Did I have a death wish? The philosopher was talking from near the head of the team. They were handing me it on a platter and all I could do was turn my head enough to look outside and see that we were exactly where I'd guessed.

Come *on,* Garrett!

I reached back for the old reserves and found I had enough to lever myself up enough to see that they hadn't dressed me up in ropes or shackles. I could leap up and dash away after leaving my dreaded mark slashed into the property of the evildoers.

Winsome yelled something about a bad smell.

I heard a footstep. Cunning me, I lay down where I'd been and made like a guy who was going to snore for another week. The philosopher must not have watched many guys come back from a thumping. He bought it. He pulled an illegal sword from beneath his seat, told the driver, "Don't move," and went stomping up the road.

The driver cussed the horses. The animals were getting restless.

My body began to yield to my will. I got onto my knees slowly so as not to rock the coach and alert the driver. I looked out the open door at the woods. I don't usually have much use for the country, but from where I knelt at that moment ticks and chiggers and poison ivy didn't sound bad at all. I eased forward, poked my head out far enough to look uphill.

One guy was almost to the top. He seemed uncomfortable. Only his brags were keeping him up there. The other was striding toward him, sword in hand.

One quick dive over the edge, Garrett. Your best chance.

Ha! said my body. No you don't.

I was recovering. And they were giving me time I could use to recover some more, talking up there. I wondered what was going on. I wondered even more about that reference to a shoemaker.

Maybe if I lived, I'd figure it out.

●●●**38**

If I didn't get off my ass soon, I was going to lose a lot of respect for me. Not to mention aforesaid ass. I'd regret it the rest of my life. So I did something, on the old Corps theory that doing anything is better than doing nothing at all.

I swung my feet over the side and settled them on the road. That took most of my energy. Unfortunately, it also wakened the driver. I'd hoped to have another minute before I went down the hill. But the guy up top yelled.

Winsome spotted me. He roared. The philosopher yelled. You'd have thought we'd won the war. They started running downhill.

The driver hollered again, but he wasn't worried about me now.

I heaved myself upright and tottered forward. I didn't look where I was going. I was too busy gawking at the scaly green barrel of a head, sleepy-eyed, that had risen above the ridge line. The monster made a puzzled whuffing noise, then grinned a grin filled with about ten thousand gigantic teeth, got up from where it had been napping. And got up and got up and got up.

The bottom went out from under me as the horses began a brief debate about the quickest way to get the hell out of there.

The slope was steeper than I'd remembered it. I couldn't control my descent. I went down ass over appetite, sliding, rolling, ricocheting off trees, bouncing through underbrush. Every stick and stone autographed my body. I ended up spread-eagle in a patch of last year's thistles. I wondered if it was worth it.

Up top, the horses had found a way to turn around and were headed south. The driver cracked his whip like maybe they needed encouragement. The philosopher and Winsome were fifty feet behind hollering for the driver to wait up. Big Ugly had gotten all of himself upright and over the ridge and was fixing to put on a burst of speed.

The whole thing would have been amusing had I not been part of it, down there in the ravine trying to blend into the landscape so I wouldn't look killable or edible either one.

No team and no men are going to outrun a critter that makes its living chasing things and has legs fifteen feet long. On the other hand, no critter thirty feet tall will have a lot of luck sprinting down a twisty road less than eight feet wide in the turns. The thunder-lizard overhauled Winsome as the man headed into a sharp turn with a cut on one side and a forty-foot drop on the other. The critter smacked into the hillside, rebounded, and off the road he went. He cussed in thunder-lizard all the way to the bottom.

The big greenie had stick-to-it-ivity, I'll give him that. He got up, shook himself off, tore up some timber just to express himself, then got rolling again. He wanted to catch *something* for all his trouble. He limped a little. Maybe he'd twisted an ankle, or whatever thunder-lizards have.

I barely breathed till the excitement took itself out of hearing. Then I moved carefully. I've heard that those things sometimes run in packs. And maybe he'd spotted me going over the side. Maybe he was waiting for a Garrett snack to come to him. Probably what he was doing up there on the ridge—just letting breakfast, lunch, and dinner come trotting up from town.

I glanced up the slope I'd descended. "I got to find another line of work." I started limping. "People don't want to be saved anyway." Weider's standing offer at the brewery looked better all the time. Nobody to beat on me, no hills to fall down, nobody wanting to take me for a ride, all the beer I could drink. Just lean back and pour it down until I was as fat as the Dead Man. What a life.

The job would look good till the hurting stopped.

My myriad aches and bruises wakened the anger that had grown feeble since I'd learned that Tinnie was going to make it. I remembered her lying in the street with a knife sticking out of her, and that reminded me that complain as I might, I did have an interest in all this confusion and insanity. A very personal interest.

There will be Serpents with us always. With the best will it can muster, the race wouldn't be able to exterminate them all. And the race, of course, has no universal will to see them become extinct. We all have a bit of the Serpent in us, just waiting for the right moment to bloom.

Witness all these characters who wanted the Book of Dreams. Not all of them had been bad to begin.

I'd even begun to doubt Carla Lindo's honorable intentions.

We can't get shut of the Serpents but we can sure as hell lower the price in pain by snipping one off the social bush now and then. My attitude underwent adjustment as I limped along. My get-even list rearranged itself. Sometime during my trek homeward, my resistance toward participating in Crask and Sadler's adventure evaporated. I donned my pain like a badge, let it flow through me, refused to be daunted by anything.

It's only six miles from Hornet Nest Hill to my place. A couple hours, loafing along. I didn't loaf but I didn't make that good a time. Too many injuries slowing me down.

I never saw the nest for which the hill is named, I never saw a hornet. I didn't see friend Winsome or the philosopher again, either. I did, at a distance, spy some busted black wood that might have been fancy coachwork. I didn't go look for survivors.

By the time I got home I was mad at myself for letting the Dead Man get my goat and run me out to see the head dwarf. I'd known it was a pointless exercise when I left.

Dean let me in. He saw I was in no mood or shape for any discussion. He did a fade. I went into my office, shut the door, wouldn't even let Dean bring my beer. I communed with Eleanor. We made a pact. Despite the pain and discouragement, I'd keep plugging. I'd get that book, one way or another. I'd thin the ranks of the villains. Eleanor gave me one of her rare smiles.

"Hell, honey, I guess I can't help being Garrett, anyway." I headed upstairs, paused halfway to tell Dean to bring the pitcher and our first-aid stuff to my room.

39

It had been a full day and it wasn't yet suppertime. I decided to eat light then lie down. Maybe my subconscious would produce a miracle while I napped and I'd end up turning the adventure against Chodo into a coup for the good guys. Assuming I didn't get so stiff and swollen I couldn't move at all.

That's how I figured. The rest of the world didn't share my vision.

Dean wakened me before I was completely asleep. "His Nibs wants you. He accused you of neglect."

So I hadn't taken time to report. He feels no pain. He doesn't get physically tired. He forgets that the rest of us do. Poor spirits and defeatism he understands better. His existence is entirely cerebral.

I went down to report.

Carla Lindo was just slipping out. She gave me a smile that set my backbone vibrating despite my state. Old Bones was chuckling to himself. She had his ego puffed up enough to swamp small cities. I wondered if she'd goaded him into disturbing me. She did seem to be getting impatient.

He took a quick riffle through my mind, saved me the trouble of talking. *Any doubt that those were Chodo Contague's men?*

I couldn't give the answer he wanted to hear. "None."

I hoped it would never come to this.

"You and me both. I was lucky. I got a pass. The bastard was sentimental enough to want to explain why he had to send me off. I won't get that option again." As soon as Chodo was sure things had soured he'd put the word out. Maybe even an open contract.

It is premature for that. First he will have to learn that you were not de-voured with the others. Then, considering the highly public nature of his past favor, he will want to avoid public reversal because he cannot yet answer questions sure to arise and threaten his credibility. He is proud and vain and his power in great part rests upon a widespread belief that he is an honorable man within criminal lights. To tell the world he wants you dead would compel him to provide reasons. He cannot tell the truth. It would bury him.

"That wouldn't keep the hard boys from carving me up for the bounty."

No, he admitted.

"So? Suggestions?"

Survival now heads our priorities. Finding the Book of Dreams has be-come secondary.

And people wonder why he's considered a genius. Would I have thought of that myself? "Only way out is to take out Chodo first."

Indeed.

"I've never deliberately set out to kill somebody."

I know. He wasn't taking it lightly.

"Is being able to live my life the way I want worth another man's life?" I could get out of town. Permanently. Because if I went, there'd be no one else to slow Chodo down—unless Crask and Sadler got lucky without me.

That is a decision you must make.

"You and Dean have a say."

I survived for centuries before we met. Whatever you decide, I will get by.

No doubt. "You really know how to pump a guy up." But his welfare was only one consideration. My ego was going to take a whipping whatever I did. Run and I'd spend the rest of my life questioning my courage. Kill Chodo and I'd have to endure big dents in my self-image. "I can't win."

There is no question of winning or losing. Nor one of right or wrong. If you have one fatal weakness, it is your thinking too much. Your insistence upon viewing any choice as a moral decision. It is not immoral to fight for your life. Stop posing. Cease overcomplicating. Decide if you would prefer to spend your remaining days in TunFaire or elsewhere, then act to support your preference.

He can strip a thing to its bones when he wants. And he's damned good at twisting something till it looks like something else.

Dean stuck his head into the room. "There's a person to see you, Mr. Garrett."

"Who?"

Hint of a smile. "A most unusual person."

I looked at the Dead Man. He didn't give me a clue. I went into the hall. "At the door?"

"I couldn't make up my mind whether or not to let her in. Personally, I don't feel she's your type."

"Huh?" My type is female, in the three primary colors, blonde, brunette, and redhead.

"Ordinarily you do tend toward a certain physical type, Mr. Garrett. Mr. Dotes once observed that they could all wear the same underwear."

"Oh?" I thought of myself as an eclectic. I opened the door.

"About damned time," Winger said.

I gaped. Dean laughed. I'd forgotten events earlier.

Winger said, "I got to thinking. We ought to get an early start. We let them bozos Crask and Sadler call all the shots, then we only got ourselves to blame if we get hit by a stray bolt."

She had a point, but I didn't feel like conceding it.

"You going to leave me out in the weather or you going to invite me in for a brew?"

40

Joking aside, Dean was right. Winger wasn't my type. She wasn't any-body's type. I led her to my office, suggested Dean bring beer. I planted myself. Winger took the other chair, looked at Eleanor like she could read the truths of the painting. Maybe she could.

"One slick character painted that, Garrett."

"An unsung genius named Snake Bradon. A total lunatic. How come you're early?" I'd set a time figuring I could slide out earlier. She probably figured that's what I'd try. The woman wasn't stupid.

"Nice place you got."

"A couple of big cases broke right. You sneaking around before you get to something?"

"Broke right? Word on you is you're lucky. But it's dangerous to be your friend."

"Huh?"

"You got a sharp line of patter, don't you? Word's going around that somebody wants to take you down. Word is, stay away. It might rub off."

So, maybe just to keep myself awake, I told her about my adventures since we'd parted.

Carla Lindo brought the beer for Dean. That woman was turning into a spook, around sometimes, but more invisible than not. She looked at Winger like she'd stumbled into the men's loo. Winger looked back at Carla Lindo like she was trying to figure out what she was. Carla Lindo lost the staring match. She deposited the supplies and deserted. "You got something going there?" Winger asked.

"Just a client."

"Not much to her."

Debatable. Highly debatable, from where I sat. But I didn't feel like debating. I felt like finding out what Winger was up to. Even more, I felt like taking a nap. The beer didn't help.

Winger said, "Interesting Chodo should take a poke at you right after you talked to his renegade. Think he'll be looking for company tonight?"

I shrugged. "He's no fool."

"Um. I got to thinking about them pets of his. Went out looking for some thunder-lizard hunters, figured on buying them a few drinks, pumping them for tricks of the trade. Know what? Ain't a whole lot of them around. Somebody's been hiring them up. Some shoemaker."

Shoemaker, eh? I could guess which one. That damned fool. "Shoemakers use a lot of thunder-lizard hides making army boots."

She said, "You know you got somebody watching you?"

"I've had that feeling for several days. I thought it might be you."

"Not me. Dwarves. Every time I come around here, there's dwarves. And morCartha. Somebody's hired one of the morCartha tribes to keep track of you. I couldn't find out who."

"MorCartha?" Things fell into place. No wonder I'd never been able to spot anyone following me. I hadn't looked up any more than anyone else does. If I had, I'd've accepted the morCartha the way I accept pigeons. One of the inevitable nuisances that are part of life.

MorCartha tails would explain the erratic nature of my intuitions about being watched, too. MorCartha are neither organized nor responsible. The watching would go on only when somebody actually felt like watching.

"Want me to take them off you? Ten marks, I'll do a job that'll have them staying ten miles from you."

"Not before I find out who wants me watched." I had ideas. Gnorst Gnorst seemed a likely candidate. Backup for his ground-bound dwarves. The kind of thing a dwarf would do. Cover every angle possible. I figured Chodo a likely candidate, too. He was cunning enough to see that morCartha would go unsuspected.

There had been morCartha aloft when I'd met with Sadler. Maybe Chodo ought to be number one on my list. "Thanks for the tip."

"One on me. For letting me come along tonight."

I hadn't planned it to go that way, but now I knew that I had to take a legitimate shot at Chodo I didn't mind as much. Any friend is better than no friend.

Again I wondered where the hell Morley and Saucerhead were. That was becoming a big worry, but events kept pushing it farther and farther down my list.

Winger considered Eleanor again. "You had something going with her, didn't you?"

How to answer that one? If I said yes, there might be more questions and I might end up mentioning that she'd been dead twenty years before I'd met her—and not like the Dead Man is dead. How to explain an affair of the heart with the ghost of someone who died when you were a child? "Something. I don't know what you'd call it and I sure can't explain it."

"That picture explains it good enough."

She *was* seeing everything that madman Bradon put into it. Would she ever stop surprising me?

"I can understand you not wanting to talk about it. So. What say we get going? I got some things lined up, give us an edge. You got to have an edge. You in any shape for this?"

She was nervous. She was getting close to chattering, which was how it showed. "Hell, no, I'm not. But I have to take my shot. If people haven't lied to me too much, tonight's the only night I'll ever have half a chance of doing what I've got to do." I told her about the supposed party.

"There's our edge right there. Even if the guy knows we're coming, he's giving up some advantage if he doesn't cancel his party."

Chodo wouldn't. He was a character who wouldn't let the gods themselves nudge him into changing his plans. "Guess we take what we can get." I was getting more down by the minute.

"Won't get nothing done sitting here."

"Sure. Back in a jiffy." I went across and got the amulet stone from the Dead Man's room, wondering what the hell a jiffy was. He didn't have anything to say. I rolled upstairs and outfitted myself as well as I could from my depleted arsenal. I included the little padded case with the bottles. This was no time to wimp out. I'd do what I had to.

Winger awaited me in the office doorway, eyes sort of glazed. I frowned. She'd had another run-in with the Dead Man. What now? I didn't ask.

Being a born gentleman, I opened and held the front door for her. Even if she was a Saucerhead type in physical drag. She stepped outside. "You hang on here."

"What?"

She eyed the street. "Wait here." She took off down the steps and up the street. Fast. She ran without throwing her arms and legs all over, the way so many women do.

I closed the door and leaned against the wall, trying to stay awake, trying to avoid thinking about my aches and pains.

A knock. I peeked. Winger's eye stared back at me. She backed off only far enough for me to see her grin. I opened up.

She had a dwarf slung over her shoulder, out cold. "He was a feisty little bugger."

"Huh?"

"He was watching your place. Thought you might want to talk to him before we shove off."

"Bring him back here." I led the way to the Dead Man's room. "Hey, Chuckles. You want to take a look at this and tell me what we've got?"

A dwarf.

"What an eye. Could you maybe give me a little something more?"

He has been watching the house for about three hours. My old friend Gnorst sent him. I will send him back bearing a strong protest.

"Wonderful. You do that. Why was he on us?"

In case you locate the Book of Dreams, I presume.

"Anything else useful?"

He was selected for his lack of direct knowledge.

Naturally, Gnorst knew the Dead Man. Wasn't much point putting the little hair ball through the wringer. "See you later, then."

Have you come to an accommodation with your conscience?

"A man's got to do what a man's got to do."

He got a chuckle out of that. *Right.* My moral discomfitures always amuse him. He'd have no trouble slicing Chodo into cold cuts.

"I can do it. The alternative is unacceptable."

A sneer radiated from that pile of lifeless lard.

"He's the one made it him or me."

You need not justify. The day has been inevitable for some time. He and I knew. Mr. Dotes and Mr. Tharpe knew. Mr. Crask and Mr. Sadler knew. Only you insisted on pretending otherwise.

Hell, I'd known it, too. I'd hoped it would come to a more clear-cut case of good guy against bad guy, though.

Take care, Garrett.

"I plan to."

followed Winger once we hit the street, lost in my own thoughts. After a few blocks, she asked, "You scared?"

"Yes." I was. Nothing to be ashamed of. A body who wasn't afraid of a Chodo Contague was a damned fool. Or worse.

"Thought you were a heavyweight tough guy."

"I eat nails with acid on them for breakfast. Then I kick thunder-lizards around for my morning workout. Hell, I'm so tough I don't change my socks but once a month. But tough don't help when the kingpin is after you and your only pal can't get out of his chair to help."

She was amused.

I asked, "You sure you know who Chodo is?"

"Sure. Bad mojo." She laughed. "Doing him will be good for my reputation."

"His reputation doesn't bother you?"

"Who needs to live forever?"

I slipped the little padded case out of my pocket. I eyed those little bottles. The red one, the deadliest, seemed to sparkle all by itself.

"What's that?"

"Something left over from another job. Might come in handy."

"So don't tell me."

"I won't. Knowing you, you might knock me over the head and grab them. This way I can feel confident that if you pull something, you'll kill yourself messing with them."

"You're a suspicious wart."

"Helped me reach the ripe old age of thirty. Where the hell are we going?" She was headed south instead of north.

"I told you, I made arrangements. Figured we'd come in from a direction nobody'll expect."

"Like what?"

"I got us a boat. Well go up the river to the Portage. From there it's four miles over a range of hills, mostly through vineyards, to Chodo's place."

I groaned. I was dragging already. Every ache and pain was still with me. I'd taken a powder for those and the headache, but relief was marginal.

"I take it you ain't overwhelmed by my brilliance."

"Ha. That's the trouble with being a boss, Winger. Whatever you do, you're always in the wrong. Whatever you do is dumb and could be done better, faster, cheaper, by your minions."

She got a laugh out of that. "I noticed that when I went to work for Easterman. My smarts level went way up."

"Probably because you knew he had to be dumb to hire you."

"You got such a line of sweet talk."

The boat was one of those usually devoted to ferrying people to the east bank, to the side sometimes called Nether TunFaire. Winger had chosen one run by a breed family with no prejudice against rowing upriver if we paid in advance. I paid up and snuggled down amongst cargo and sails and closed my eyes. I might still get my nap.

Winger seemed content to do the same.

The chief ferryman stirred me with his toe. His name was Skid. He was about a hundred years old but spry. The river life was healthy. I snorted and gurgled and otherwise made it seem my intelligence approximated that of a turtle, cracked an eye, and asked, "We there already?"

"Nope. Got a boat following us. Shouldn't be." Maybe Skid was still alive because he hadn't used up his ration of words.

Winger was one of those freaks of nature who just open their eyes and are wide-awake. She was upright, looking aft, before I managed to sit up.

"Where?" I could see lights back there, sure. On about two hundred boats, most of them just like our own, what landlubbers politely call bumboats, home and business for the families operating them.

Skid got down so I could sight along his arm. "Skylar Zed's tub. Works the east-west, same as us. Don't come north."

"Oh." I couldn't see the boat he wanted me to see, let alone tell who owned it. I faked it. I told Winger, "This is getting irritating."

She grunted. She'd sprawled out again, completely without self-consciousness. She reminded me of Saucerhead more and more. Yet she was different. Less intense, more relaxed. Tharpe does worry about what people might think. Winger plain didn't care—or faked that so well it made no difference. I guess when you're as oversize as she is, you make adjustments.

I looked some more. At least in the light of the running lamps there was nothing wrong with the way she looked. She was just big. "Hey. Tell me about Winger." I wasn't sleepy anymore.

"What's to tell? I was born and I'm still around. What you see is what you get."

"The usual stuff. Where are you from? Who were your people? How come you're out here with me instead of holed up somewhere with a house full of little Wingers?"

"Where'd you come from, Garrett? Who're your people? How come you're here instead of back to your place with a pack of little Garretts?"

"I see. Only I don't mind telling." I told her about my family, none of whom are alive. I told her about my years in the Fleet Marines. I tried but couldn't really explain what I was doing on the boat. Not in terms she understood. "As for kids, I like them fine but I think I'd make a lousy father. I still have some growing up to do myself, at least by the accepted standards."

"That ain't fair, Garrett."

"Hey, I was just passing the time. You don't have to tell me anything."

"We going to be friends, Garrett?"

"I don't know. Could be. Hasn't a lot gotten in the way so far."

She chewed that some, leaned back, spat over the side, turned to check our tail, lay down again. "How old you figure me for?"

"My age. A little younger, maybe. Twenty-eight?"

"You're more generous than most. I'm twenty-six. I do have a kid. Be almost twelve now. I couldn't handle that life. I walked. It's usually the man leaves the woman with the brats."

I didn't say anything. Not much you can say when somebody tells you something like that. Nothing that doesn't sound judgmental or insincere.

"I lug around a lot of guilt. But no regrets. Funny, huh?"

"Things turn out that way sometimes. I've been through some of that."

"Like this little jaunt?"

"Huh?"

"You don't hide so well behind the smart mouth and weary attitude, Garrett. We ice this Chodo, you're going to take on a shitload of guilt."

"But no regrets."

"Yeah. And you know something? That's why I wanted in. The money and the rep I can use, but it wasn't just for that. It's 'cause I figure you for one of the good guys."

"I try." Probably too hard. "But when you get down to it, there isn't much difference between the good guys and the bad guys." I used some of my cases to illustrate.

She told me how she'd become a bounty hunter. Mostly by accident. Right after she'd left her family she'd killed a much-wanted thug who'd tried to rape her. She traded the remains for a reward and had found herself with a reputation for having more guts than sense and a big chip on her shoulder.

"The rep's the thing, Garrett. You build it right, you nurture it, you save a lot of trouble. You take this Chodo. Nobody bucks him because of his reputation."

"He backs it up."

"You got to do that. Ruthlessness is the key. You, now, your rep is wishy-washy except for keeping your word and not letting people mess your clients around. You might he tough, but you ain't hard. You get what I'm saying? Somebody hires you to get him out from under blackmail, you don't just go cut some bastard's throat and have done with it. You try to finagle it so nobody gets hurt. Lot of people figure you for soft in the center, you go that way. Figure they've got an edge."

"Yeah." I understood. But I didn't make any sudden New Year's resolutions.

"I figure you'll waste this chance. You off Chodo, you'll never let anybody know."

"You're beginning to depress me."

She laughed. "You heard the one about the nuns, the bear, and the missing honey?" She told the story. It was about what I expected. She followed it with another. She kept telling them. She knew every bad, off-color joke ever invented—and this world, with all its tribes, offers plenty of absurd possibilities.

"I surrender," I said. "I won't be depressed if you won't tell any more stories."

"Great. So now let's figure out what we're going to do about that other boat."

I glanced downriver. I still couldn't tell anything. "Skid. Can you run inshore and let us off without them back there knowing?"

He reflected. "Around Miller Point, up ahead. Be out of their sight maybe twenty minutes. But I thought you wanted to go to the Portage."

"You go ahead upriver after we get off. Lead that boat along with you."

"You're paying the freight. You heard the man, ladies. Cut it close going around the point. Lucky for you," he said to me. "Channel's close in there."

When the time came, we did it fast. It worked. Skid headed upriver. Winger and I heard the second boat creak past as we worked our way through the dense growth beside the river. She punched my arm, grinned.

We started our hike cross-country. My body kept threatening to put a curse on me for mistreating it so.

guessed it was just past midnight. We were a mile from Chodo's place, which was easy to see. "Party must be roaring," I observed. "Either that or there's a forest fire over there."

"We're coming in from the north, we better head over there, move in closer later."

"Yeah. Better stay behind this ridge, too. Never know who might spot us if we don't." We were in a vineyard. There were grapegrowers' houses nearby.

"You said that already."

"You said that about heading north three times, too."

"You nervous, Garrett?"

"Yeah. You?"

She seemed cool. "Scared shitless."

"It doesn't show."

"You learn."

The sky went berserk toward Chodo's place. I said, "Sounds like the mor-Cartha brought their show to the country." We couldn't see them, light or no, with the ridge in the way. We decided not to go over and look. Everybody at the kingpin's place would be out gawking.

We found us a comfortable jump-off place fifty yards north of Chodo's property line. The morCartha were still at it, off and on. "Those flying rats could wake the dead," I grumbled.

"We got time to kill. We're ahead of schedule." The plan was to wait for

Crask and Sadler to draw the thunder-lizards around front once they gave up on me and decided to take their best shot. Then we'd move, hoping my amulet still worked.

"Yeah." I tried making sense of the racket. "I don't like that." I stood up. Standing, I could see the occasional dot swoop through the light over the kingpin's house. A deadly battle over there, near as I could tell. "Why did they bring it out here?"

"Oh, sit down and sweat blood like I am."

If there was no attack by Crask and Sadler, or none we could detect, we would move about three o'clock, the coolest hour of the night, when the thunder-lizards would be sluggish. With them slow and maybe ignoring us on account of my amulet, we'd only need to worry about dogs, armed guards, booby traps, and whatever I didn't know about.

Winger lay back and stared at the stars. "Be enough light, anyway. I can handle the dogs. Better hope those morCartha clear off, though."

I grunted. Dogs make me nervous. Not afraid, just nervous.

"You got a special woman, Garrett? That little Sparky, hanging around your place?"

"Sparky?"

"The carrot top. I put the name Sparky on her in my own head."

"Oh. Yeah. I have one or two."

"One or two?"

"Tinnie Tate. The one who got stabbed. And one named Maya I kind of like. I haven't seen her lately."

"I heard some about her. People talk. Besides them two. Anything going? You got kind of a rep that way, you know."

"Highly exaggerated, I'm sure. Those things have a way of getting blown out of proportion. Nah. Nobody else special. Except maybe Eleanor."

"That Sparky?"

"No. The blonde on my office wall. She's a good listener."

"Nothing going with Sparky, eh?"

"Just wishful thinking. Why?"

"No reason. Just wondering. We got time to kill."

What? "Oh." Sometimes I'm real slow. I started fumbling for excuses that wouldn't leave any hurt feelings. "I don't know. Condition I'm in . . ."

Boy, howdy! Who'd a thunk it . . . ?

Winger started grabbing stuff. "Somebody coming. And we're running late."

No lie. Me, the mission-oriented old Marine, forgot why I was out in the middle of a grape orchard freezing my aching body in the wee hours. You betcha. My weakness again. When that Winger decided to be a woman, she popped and sizzled. Sparky . . . Carla Lindo had nothing on her then.

Amazing. Utterly amazing.

"Easy, Garrett." Dark shapes drifted closer. "Crask and Sadler."

Winger and I finished our scrambling around. Those two settled on the hillside. Crask said, "Sneaky, sneaky Garrett. You was supposed to meet us around front. We'd've never found you, wasn't for all the puffing and snorting."

"Easy, lady," Sadler said. "Easy. Ain't gonna be no trouble. I don't blame you for not showing, Garrett. Not after this afternoon."

"You heard, eh?"

"Yeah. Some. We was too late to save your ass. We did try. We figured you was gone and counted you out when we heard about the coach and the thunder-lizard."

Crask said, "Bunch of farmers took it down right after sundown, you care about that. They was still skinning it when we come out."

Sadler continued, "Along about sundown we heard from a friend what seen you talking to the sheela here. We counted you out anyhow."

Crask said, "You got to be the luckiest bastard that ever lived. We changed the whole plan when we heard about the coach. Then we changed it again when we heard you was alive."

Sadler said, "We figured we wouldn't show where you was supposed to meet us, just in case you did. But we'd watch, and then we'd follow you in when you went."

"Follow me? What made you think I'd do it on my own?"

"You got to. Chodo's after your ass. You got to get his first or kiss yours good-bye. You're mush on the inside, but you ain't stupid. You do what you got to."

Crask chuckled. What a pair of bastards. And not the least bit ashamed of themselves. Crask said, "We changed the plan again. Now we figure we ought to hit in a bunch. Something weird's going on over there."

Sadler asked, "You guys got any idea what the hell all that racket's about?"

"MorCartha wars."

"At Chodo's place?"

I shrugged. "They hold them wherever they can get enough of them together."

"Sounded like more than that to me. You miss it?" He kept a straight face. Crask did, too. Those guys were inhuman.

Winger said, "Ready when you are, Garrett."

No kidding. I dreaded having the Dead Man find out about tonight. I'd never hear the end. Probably deserved it, too. "You guys want to rest up first?" I wasn't going to tell them they couldn't horn in. Not here. Not now.

"We're ready," Sadler replied. "You bring the stone?"

"I'm slow but I'm not stupid. Winger says she can handle the dogs."

"They shouldn't be no problem. We came prepared." I could see him well enough to tell he thought I hadn't. He and Crask carried military spears and Venageti two-handed sabers. They were loaded down with enough other hardware to start their own war. "Whenever you want," he added.

"Let's do it, Winger." We started walking.

hodo's north wall wasn't much. Was that intentional?

"Yeah," Crask told me. "Farther to the house here. Most of them that try come this way. Sets them up so the dogs and lizards got more time to work."

Wonderful. Being a genius, I'd selected exactly the course Chodo wanted me to choose.

Sadler said, "It's sure turned quiet." He was right. The morCartha had moved on.

"Gone dark, too," Crask said.

It took me a moment to understand. The lights round the house had been extinguished. "What about armed patrols?" We'd have trouble spotting them in the dark.

"Maybe." That was Sadler. "But they'll stay near the house. The lizards get unpredictable when they're excited."

"Glad you warned me." Like I'd really counted on the amulet stone to turn the beasts blind.

We moved ahead a quarter mile, those two leading. They knew their way. Then Crask stopped. Sadler stopped. Crask said, "Something's up. We should've run into a dog or lizard by now."

I told him, "I'm not going to complain."

"Watch out."

We moved again. Seconds later I tripped, fell on my face. Just what I needed. Bruises on my bruises. I did manage to go down without hollering. "Hey!" I hissed. "Check this."

This was a dead thunder-lizard. Healthy, it would have been my size. Cause of its poor health seemed to be a bunch of crossbow bolts. Hard to tell how long it had been unhealthy because those things are cold to begin with.

Crask and Sadler were not pleased. Sadler speculated, "Somebody got here before us."

Crask muttered, "That explains the quiet."

I asked, "You think somebody did our job for us?"

"Maybe. Maybe not. One lizard is down. That ain't the whole pack. Maybe the rest are curled up with full bellies."

Real helpful, those guys.

We found two more thunder-lizards turned into pincushions. Then a dead dog. "Something strange here," I said. "I was a scout in the Marines. One guy couldn't do this. It would take a gang. But they didn't leave any sign. The only grass down was put that way by the animals."

Crask and Sadler grunted. Winger observed, "The arrows are all in the back."

They were. "So?"

She jerked a thumb skyward. The morCartha?

We were halfway to the house. Despite the absence of light, I could sense a hulking darkness where it stood.

The silence ended. So did the darkness.

An uproar broke out around the house, suddenly. Heavy fighting. The light developed more slowly. Sadler suggested, "Let's don't get in a hurry just yet, Garrett."

I'd started moving. He was right. No sense galloping into something. We advanced slowly. The crash and clang declined.

The animals came out of nowhere. Crask and Sadler each skewered a thunder-lizard. Winger moved like a bullfighter, slashed a dog's throat on the fly. Blood flew everywhere. It was over before I could decide who to help. I gurgled, "Don't look like the stone is much good."

Sadler snapped, "They didn't come after you."

Crask muttered, "Now we know they ain't all dead." We reached a barn. Crask said, "Let's scope it out from the loft."

We did, but that didn't help much. Most of the light had faded. We saw two armed men directly opposite us, beside the house. Six more were doing something along the side of the house, toward its front. Winger said, "I see bodies."

There were a lot of them. The men toward the front were moving some inside. Chodo must have brought a small army in for the festivities. Not mentioning the men down, there were thunder-lizards and dogs and mor-Cartha all over the place. It had been ferocious out.

"Whatever happened, it's over now," I said.

So naturally the gods had to make me out a liar before I even finished talking. One of Chodo's men took an arrow in the chest. The rest charged the darkness. After some noise and screaming most of them came back. Apparently they decided not to do any more picking up.

"Dwarves," Sadler decided.

"Huh?" My repartee was up to standard.

"Dwarves attacked the place. Some of those stiffs are dwarves."

What the hell was going on?

Either the Serpent's buddies had tried to rescue her or Gnorst had taken a shot at getting her away from the kingpin. I put my money on Gnorst. But that didn't explain the morCartha. I didn't think.

I said, "I hope Chodo is as confused as I am. And drunk, too."

Sadler said, "They ought to all be sobered up by now."

"Don't count on it. You remember how ripped they got last year."

"I don't see any more animals," Winger said.

"No patrols, either," Crask observed. "That'd mean he's used up all the men he can afford. He's keeping the rest in close."

I said, "He'll have the entrances covered. How do we get inside?"

"From up top. We climb the stonework on the northwest corner, swing out onto those beams, get onto the roof. We move across there, drop onto that balcony in the middle. See it? It shouldn't be covered if he's short on bodies and is thinking dwarves. Dwarves couldn't get up there."

"One of my favorite hobbies, climbing unfamiliar buildings in the dark."

Sadler told me, "You done it before. I was there. I brought a rope. I'll go first." He sounded like he had serious reservations about me.

Hell, I had serious reservations about me. I didn't think I could get to the roof up a ladder, all the pains I had. I thought about calling everything off. Didn't seem too bright, charging in when we didn't know what the hell was going on.

We moved across to the house unchallenged. Sadler monkeyed up the northwest corner, dropped the rope. Winger went up like climbing was her calling. Crask told me, "After you, sir. Age before beauty."

"Right. I'll just tie it around my neck and let them hoist me up." I grabbed the rope and went at it. I got to the top somehow, though I had my eyes closed half the time. Crask arrived right behind me.

Sadler told him, "I'm starting to get a good feeling about this, Bob."

Crask had a first name? Amazing. I figured even his mommy called him Crask.

"Yeah, looking good. Let's slide on over there."

We were getting set to drop to the balcony when the morCartha returned. One, singular. It whispered down out of the night, zipped past, nearly panicked us all. We figured it was a scout and a herd would be right behind it. But nothing happened.

We were trying to get inside when the excitement brewed up again around front. We paused, listened. Winger said, "That's weird."

"What?" I think I squeaked.

"Chodo's guys are all inside. So who's fighting who?"

I didn't know and at the moment I didn't care. "Let them have fun. Let's get on with it."

To my complete astonishment we broke in without any trouble at all.

44

We were on the highest of three floors. Crask and Sadler insisted on checking every room there before we started down. They didn't want to leave anybody behind us. Winger and I took one end of a long hall, those two the other half. We met again at the head of a stair in the center.

"Find anybody?" Sadler asked.

I told the truth. "A few drunks so far out of it they're barely alive." I'd recognized some and had been surprised by a couple supposedly honest men, big in business or society. Chodo's reach seemed infinite.

"Same over there. Nobody who has the balls to do anything but squeal, anyway. Party must really have roared before the shit came down."

"Head downstairs now?"

He nodded. "Stay low. Part of the stair can be seen from the ballroom."

I'd never visited this wing before. I'd never been off the ground floor, up front, except to visit a guy locked up in what passed for Chodo's dungeon.

We listened before we moved. There was a racket toward the front of the house. Men cursed down below, angry and scared. It had nothing to do with us.

Crask led off, still encumbered with his arsenal. It seemed impossible that he should move silently carrying all that clutter, but he managed. As did Sadler and even Winger. Me, carrying next to nothing and a trained Marine sneak, I felt like I was banging a drum.

We found no one on the second floor, just plenty of small sleeping rooms with no one home. "Bodyguards and staff," Sadler explained. "They'll be sober and near Chodo—if they're still alive."

"Where'll he be?"

"In his office."

Meant nothing to me. I'd never visited his office.

Crask dropped. I did, too, pushed my nose against the banister. A half dozen colorful, shaggy dwarves light-footed past below, headed toward the front of the house. An uproar broke out as soon as they disappeared. Crask chuckled, "Ambushed them little shits."

One dwarf hustled back bent over, holding his guts in. A limping man overtook him, cut him apart with a heavy naval sword. I asked, "Can we get around that ambush?"

"Nope."

"You're a Marine," Sadler said. "Hey diddle diddle, straight up the middle."

That didn't sound any more appetizing now than it had back then.

Crask said, "The runts used it up. Or there'd have been more guys after the dwarf."

We moved down to the ground floor, passed the dwarf, headed toward the ballroom and possible ambush. To our right were kitchens and laundries and whatnot. To our left, too, I assumed. I'd heard, during one of my visits, that such took up most of the ground floor, except the showy stuff up front and the ballroom and pool area.

The ambush was pretty basic. Crask and Sadler sprang it entering the ballroom. The guy who'd slaughtered the dwarf was the healthier of the two trying to hold the fort. Crask bopped his head with the haft of his spear.

Winger whistled. "Some party room. Some party, too."

The ballroom was a cozy eighty-by-one-hundred feet and three stories high. Party detritus lay everywhere. Looked like the celebration had run its course before the bloodletting started.

Crask and Sadler tied the victims. They were going to need soldiers when they took over. Sadler said, "Straight to the pool."

"I'll take rear guard," Winger said. When I glanced back, she was slipping something inside her shirt.

The pool room dwarfed the ballroom. The pool itself was that big. There was nobody there. Except Chodo's dead. Had to be thirty of those laid out amidst the party debris. We skirted the flotsam-covered pool and headed for the reception hall.

That hall runs to the front door through the front wing of the house, though wing isn't the right word. The house is a huge box with the center, inner court roofed to form the ballroom and pool areas. We took turns peeking into the hall. Several men were guarding the front door. They were all scared and they were all injured.

"Not many left," Sadler observed.

I grumbled, "Maybe we've just jumped into a trap with the kingpin."

"Maybe. Let's check his office." He trotted to a closed door that would let us into the east wing, leaned against it, listened. "Not that way. Mob in there." He headed for the rear of the house. Back the way we had come.

I looked at Winger, shrugged, followed. But I was considering fading away. Things had gotten too deadly and mysterious.

We entered the east wing by means of second-floor halls built for the cleaning staff. Sadler led us into a residential suite. "Chodo's kid uses this when she's in town."

"Nobody's home now." I wondered if most of the house was a mystery to Chodo. He wouldn't get to see the upper floors unless his men carried him.

"Don't look like."

Crask and Sadler started poking around in closets and tapping walls. They found what they were hunting before I became mystified enough to ask. A panel opened beside a fireplace. Of course. Chodo would have his hidden passages and whatnot. Sadler said, "We're going down to a room hidden off Chodo's office. Be real quiet." Like we needed warning.

Our destination was big for a secret room, a good eight by twelve. Winger's eyes bulged when she saw it. Stacks of moneybags lay against one wall. She gulped air and chewed it. Impressive pile, I thought, but only Chodo's day-to-day working capital. His petty cash.

A racket developed while we were crawling through the walls, the mob from outside attacking again.

Crask and Sadler moved directly to a wall, opened peepholes. Crask indicated one I could use. I'd always suspected that the kingpin employed hidden watchers during his meetings. I pulled a cork out of a hole, peeked into a room about twenty-five by forty. There were only two men in the room, Chodo and a character who provided the power to move the kingpin's chair. Chodo sat in the middle of the room, facing an open door. He looked content, not afraid. Behind him, piled furniture barricaded two outside windows.

I pictured Chodo as a big trapdoor spider calmly awaiting a victim.

Sounds of fighting came from elsewhere in the house. Chodo's pusher tensed up. Then he relaxed as two men entered the room. They supported a naked, bound woman between them.

"Ha!" I muttered. "That's her."

"Who?" Winger asked.

"The Serpent. Check out that tattoo." It was uglier than I'd imagined. The witch herself was not a disaster, but she'd begun to show the ravages of time. More evident were the ravages of stubbornness. It looked like Chodo had asked a few polite questions, and when it had come time to answer, she'd demurred.

She was lucky he'd had a birthday party to preoccupy him. He might have gotten serious otherwise.

Chodo examined her critically from a few feet away. "Five pages? These are all?" He strained to lift several sheets of brass out of his lap. He seemed unaware that his place was being invaded.

"That's it, old man." The Serpent wasn't bothered by her situation, either. It seemed.

"They're damaged. Useless."

"Of course."

"Where is the book?"

A huge thug leaned in the door. "They're in the house." My heart jumped. But he didn't mean us. "Too many of them. Can't hold them off."

"Hold them in the hall out there, then. You ought to be able to handle a few dwarves. Don't kill Gnorst. I need him alive."

"Yes sir." Like if Chodo said do it, it could be done.

I watched the witch. Damned if she wasn't happy about the way things were going.

So was Chodo.

Interesting.

The kingpin eyed the witch again. "Where is the book? I won't ask again."

"Fine. Then I won't have to listen to you anymore."

Chodo didn't get mad. He smiled, said, "Take her into that corner there." He murmured something to the man behind his chair, who moved him over behind a big barricade of a desk to my left. I couldn't see him anymore.

Crask gave Sadler a thumbs-up.

The uproar from the rest of the house had been moving closer. Now the huge thug stumbled into Chodo's office. "I'm sorry, sir." He collapsed. Chodo still didn't get upset.

A bunch of dwarves galloped in, Gnorst in their midst. He took in the setup, barked orders in dwarfish. For a moment there were a good thirty of them in there. Then some started drifting out. Most didn't want to go and a few flat refused. Gnorst smoldered. I guessed he didn't want anyone figuring out that he had visions of becoming the new Nooney Krombach.

There were a dozen left when the flow stopped. Gnorst strutted over to the kingpin. His beard waggled like he was fixing to say something.

Chodo trampled his line. Amazing. Put a little pressure on that old boy and he found all kinds of energy reserves. "Looks like six of one and half a dozen of the other, eh, Chet?"

Chet was one of the guys holding the Serpent. "Maybe seven to five."

The dwarves were baffled. Chodo was supposed to be dribbling in fear.

"I've waited a long time, Gnorst," Chodo said. "But patience pays. Today I get to see you die."

Dwarves peered around nervously. Gnorst's wicked little eyes went squinty. He wondered if he'd walked into a trap.

Chodo managed a little chuckle. "You're going to do it to yourselves. Because half of you are her creatures and half are Gnorst's." He continued, stirring them up. The old boy had balls that dragged the ground. And he was telling the truth. That was obvious. You could tell as soon as the short folks started eyeballing each other.

The witch yelled, "Don't!"

Chodo laughed.

The fur started flying.

How'd he set them off so easy? One second they were calculating their chances, the next flying around hooting and hollering and stabbing.

The men holding the witch eased along the outside wall, toward Chodo. She didn't look so chipper now. Chet paused once to stick a shiv into some short guy who thought he'd be a hero and rescue the maiden not so fair.

It wasn't all dwarf hacking dwarf into chop meat, though. Chet got his before he could get behind the desk with Chodo and his coolie.

Crask made another thumbs-up sign. He and Sadler moved over some, got set.

Gnorst's loyalists were getting the best of the witch's boys. The last two broke for the doorway. The rest whooped in pursuit. I heard Chodo laugh again, softly, now through a gap opening in the wall of the secret room.

Gnorst caught on a step too late. Chodo made good his escape. . . . Only it wasn't so good, was it?

Crask and Sadler bopped the two guys with Chodo, cracked the witch a good one, made sure the wall was solidly in place. Gnorst had him a fit on the other side.

Crask said, "Hi, Boss."

Chodo was fresh out of good humor. He sighed. "You place your bets and take your chances, don't you, Mr. Garrett? But you can't beat the house forever. The wheel is fixed."

"You ought to know."

"I've rigged it often enough. I knew I should have tried harder to find that missing stone."

I tossed it into his lap. "I didn't need it. They killed all your pets." I nodded toward the wall. The dwarves out there had gotten awful quiet. I went to peek.

They were quiet, but there were a good forty of them out there now. Most just stood there staring at Gnorst. Gnorst didn't look a whole lot like Gnorst anymore. He was scared shitless.

His buddies had caught onto him. He'd been using them so he could grab the Book of Shadows and turn himself into another Nooney Krombach. And he'd given himself away here. His pals had fallen into what you might call an unforgiving mood.

He'd told me what dwarves thought about Nooney and his book.

He started trying to yak his way out, but there was no hope in his voice and nobody was listening. Short folks started edging toward him, growling. I put the plug back in the wall.

"Well?" Chodo said, like he was in a hurry to get it over. Like he wanted to see if I had what it would take.

The witch wobbled to her feet. "Let's get a leash on her," I suggested. "Chodo asked a question I never heard answered. I'd like to know myself."

Chodo smiled feebly. "I knew you had a price, Mr. Garrett. It's a high one, admittedly, but it turns out you're human."

"I want to destroy it. If I have to lug it up to thunder-lizard country and dump it into a volcano."

He eyed me while Crask and Sadler rummaged for a choker for the Serpent. His smile faded, then returned. "You really would." He shook his head. "You understand about this afternoon?"

"Not really."

"I believe you. My error. I appear to have been misinformed and thereby have moved to a false conclusion. But more than one source suggested you knew the whereabouts of the book. I wanted to ask about that. All I accomplished was to activate your enmity. Well. You can't beat the house."

"Why the hell would anybody think I'd know where the damned book is? I've been running myself crazy trying to get a lead on it."

Winger muttered, "We going to stand around jawing all night? We're going to have those runts out there after us real soon now. Let's do what we got to do and get."

"I think they're done. I don't think they'll be any more trouble."

She went to check through the peephole.

I looked at Chodo.

I couldn't do it. And he knew I couldn't. He smiled. And not like he'd won some victory but like I'd won one and he was pleased. He smiled even knowing he wasn't going to get out of anything. Crask and Sadler didn't have my sensibilities. They wouldn't forgive and forget.

Bigger smile on a devil's ugly face. "Look out for my baby, Mr. Garrett." I nodded.

"She'll be fine," Crask said. And she would. That's the way those people worked. They counted women and children out, untouchable.

"Gods," Winger said from the peephole. She turned away pale, shocked. I decided I didn't want to see anything that would shock Winger.

Crask and Sadler eyed her, responding to the grim awe edging her voice. . . .

The Serpent let Crask have it in the crotch. He folded up. She leaped at Chodo. . . .

like to make out that I'm fast on my mental feet, but usually I'm no quicker than anybody else. When a woman is involved, I can be frightfully slow. But I do have a knack for seeing right and doing right when my tail is on the line.

Everything seemed to slow down as the Serpent lunged toward the kingpin. I noted that she was not totally naked. She wore a ring. A big ugly snake thing probably still on her because they hadn't wanted to chop her finger off till after she died. I started to yell but it was too late.

She hit Chodo while Crask was still folding and Sadler was turning to see. She didn't know where she was going but knew she couldn't stay. Anywhere would be safer than here.

I yelled, "Winger! Come on! Let's get her!"

She responded without thinking. Good for her.

It had occurred to me that this was the ideal moment to separate ourselves from Crask and Sadler. Before they started considering who ought to follow the kingpin down that dark road.

The witch had a good sense of where to run. We couldn't corner her. She found her way out of the hidden passages. She fled the house from the rear. And gained on us while doing it.

I pounded around the side of the house just as she reached the front and almost landed in the middle of the departing dwarves. She whirled and headed east, toward the false dawn just beginning to define the vineyard hills.

Now Winger and I gained ground. We had longer legs and no need to worry about scratches from weeds and brush.

A winged shape dropped out of nowhere, brushed the Serpent's right shoulder, staggered her. Another followed it, then another, forcing her to change course.

Winger grabbed my arm. "Slow down. We might not ought to catch up."

"Huh?" I'd stopped thinking much.

"They're steering her."

They were indeed. I slowed to a trot and tried getting my brain to perking again. But I'd used my daily ration of smarts in Chodo's secret room.

The Serpent scrambled over the estate wall, raced for the cover of a woodlot following a small creek. MorCartha swarmed around her as Winger and I cleared the wall. They ignored us completely. The witch stopped just short of the trees, looked around wildly. MorCartha were there to cut off any attempt at retreat.

Men came out of the woods. Little guys, all of them, but men, not elves or dwarves or whatever. They surrounded the Serpent. A little old guy with glasses hobbled after them.

Willard Tate.

"Whoa," I said. "Stop right there, Winger. Good. Now, real careful, let's stroll toward the road." In half a second I'd overcome an impulse to go down and talk some sense into the Tates. That might not be any healthier than going back to hang around with Crask and Sadler. Willard Tate appeared demonic in the feeble light. He was set to get even with the world.

"What's happening?" Winger asked.

"You don't really want to know." Old Man Tate had his tools with him. I kept easing toward the road, hoping I wouldn't catch anyone's eye. "That old man there. His niece was the one the Serpent's thugs hit by mistake." I wondered how much he'd spent to arrange this encounter. I wondered how much had been engineered and how much was pure luck. I didn't have any urge to go ask. Uncle Willard might decide it was a fine time to uncomplicate Tinnie's life by removing her favorite ex-Marine.

The Serpent screamed.

"You going to do something?"

"Yeah. Get my dearly beloved ass out of here. Too many people with their blood up in this neighborhood. I'm going to go home and lock myself in for a month, then I'll start trying to figure out what the hell became of that damned Book of Shadows."

I had an idea. It weighed five hundred pounds and was mad as a hatter.

Process of elimination. Everybody else who had the slightest interest *didn't* have the book. Therefore, Easterman did or knew where it was. Maybe he wanted the excitement to settle down some before he started playing Fido the Terrible.

The Serpent had one hell of a set of lungs. She howled steadily. I didn't look back.

I'd make my peace with me about that later. After I got used to the idea of still being healthy.

46

Six hundred yards southwest of Chodo's gate the road to TunFaire crosses a small stone bridge over the creek that supports the woodlot where the Tates had waited in ambush. A pair of unsavory sorts were perched on the sides of that bridge. Seedy morCartha inhabited the trees overhead, for once uncontentious. Presumably they belonged to the same tribe, perhaps the same family.

The shorter character stood, dusted his seat, gave me a big smile filled with pointy dark-elf teeth. "Everything come out, Garrett?" He was a handsome devil.

I kept cool. Cucumber Garrett, they call me. Icicles for bones. "You see before you the infamous Morley Dotes," I told Winger. Obviously, he wanted me to ply him with questions. I didn't. I'd show him. I'd spoil his whole day.

"He sure don't look like much."

"That's what the girls all say."

Saucerhead, still seated, grinned, spat into the creek. He glanced upstream. "Some excitement, huh?"

"Routine. They never had a chance once I got rolling. I'd love to hang around and swap lies, but I haven't had my breakfast."

Saucerhead got up. He and Morley tagged along after us. Dotes sounded wounded when he said, "Routine? Your tail was an inch short of going down for the last time all the way. If I hadn't had you covered every step . . ."

Saucerhead told me, "We hired these morCartha to watch and report so we could jump in if you got in too deep."

"Oh. It was you guys that got me away from Chodo's kidnappers and that thunder-lizard?"

Morley hemmed and hawed. "You know the morCartha. Short attention spans. They kind of lost you that time. But your luck held. We were on you the rest of the time."

"Maybe half the time," Saucerhead admitted. "Well, maybe a quarter of the time. People got to sleep some."

"My pals," I told Winger. "They look out for me."

"Hey," Morley protested. "Don't be that way. I set it up so it came out in the end, didn't I?"

"I don't know. Did you?"

Morley isn't one to blow his own horn, not any louder than the trumps of doom, anyway, so he let Saucerhead explain. Seems Morley smelled something in the wind early, something that would get me and Chodo butting heads. He'd stopped hiding and sulking over Chodo's having commandeered his place, had made arrangements. He'd gotten in touch with most everyone looking for the book and offered to become their warlord. Gnorst's bunch had no practical experience hunting and fighting. Likewise the Tates. And his reputation was dark enough to endear him to the witch's gang. Naturally, he'd gotten all parties to pay him in advance. Then he'd nudged everybody together for the final free-for-all.

"*I* thought it was pretty slick," Morley grumbled.

"Yeah," Saucerhead said. "Way it came out, it even halfway solved the morCartha problem." He looked around to see if any hired hands were following. They'd lost interest. He was relieved.

Morley chuckled. "Don't worry about them. They're back there cleaning out Chodo's place."

I didn't have much to say. Let Morley think he'd covered me. He was a friend, sort of, and he'd tried. I guess it was his morCartha I'd sensed when I'd had that feeling of being watched. It had been him and Tharpe and the Tates in the boat that had followed me and Winger up the river. Let him think what he wanted. *I* was sure his contribution didn't mean much. Things couldn't have turned out much different, the nature of the greedy beast being what it is.

As we entered the city I asked Winger, "You still on Fido's payroll? I still have to go after that book."

"I don't think so." She was puffing.

I chuckled. "Want we should stop somewhere, get you a mule?"

"For what?" She did a good puzzled look.

"So you don't collapse. You must be lugging a hundred pounds of loot. I was amazed you kept up when we were chasing the Serpent."

She got huffy but denied nothing.

Hell, she clanked when she moved.

Morley was thoughtful. He observed, "We may be in for interesting times, what with the kingpin's spot up for grabs."

"Crask and Sadler are smarter than they act. Who could challenge them?"

"Each other."

Winger eyed him hard. "Is he that naive, Garrett?"

I skipped answering because I'd figured those two out only recently myself. "Power changes people. Some get greedy."

"They're going to worry about the world, not each other."

"Whatever," Morley said. And: "All's well that ends well." We were in the Safety Zone then. "I've got to go see if I have a place left."

"Yeah," Saucerhead said. "I better check in with Molly. She might be a little worried. I never let her know what was up."

As he headed for his place a flight of thunder-lizards swept over. Only the pigeons got excited. Folk in the street scarcely noticed. That was Tun-Faire. Anything can happen so everyone gets used to everything quickly.

Winger clanked a little closer. She looked as bad as I felt. "Your friend was right. All's well that ends well."

"But this isn't over. I haven't taken care of that damned Book of Shadows."

"Let's get some shut-eye first, though. Eh?"

"I could handle a few weeks of that." I didn't have much energy left but there were loose ends. Tinnie. Carla Lindo. The book. Maybe Fido Easterman. Not to mention Crask and Sadler. But I couldn't concentrate on them. With home and bed so near, I was fading fast.

So. Trudge trudge, drag drag, off Wizard's Reach into Macunado Street . . . "Oh, hell! Now what?" I drifted over and parked the back of my lap on a neighbor's steps.

There was a crowd in front of my place, oohing and ahing. But the attraction wasn't anything as commonplace as flying thunder-lizards.

A huge character in star-spangled black floated twenty feet above the street, twisting and spinning and making motions like he was trying to swim. He didn't get anywhere. Fido Easterman.

He spotted Winger, started bellowing like a potato auctioneer.

I dragged myself to my feet, ambled closer. I noted that Fido's whole gang was with him, though no one else was airborne. The rest were in the street, stiff as hardened leather. Some, caught in midstride, had toppled.

"What the hell?" Winger said. "What the hell?"

"He pissed the Dead Man off somehow."

There were ogres on my stoop, also rigid. My door was open. Busted open. No wonder Old Bones was peckish.

I didn't hurt myself getting in a hurry. The Dead Man had it under control. I slithered through the crowd stopped to eyeball Easterman.

"Get me down!"

"Why? You want more trouble than you've got?"

Easterman flailed at the air, snarled something about somebody was getting away, then started laying on the threats.

He popped up fifteen feet, then fell, howling. People scattered. He started darting around like a feeding bat. People clapped and cheered and yelled suggestions about what he should try next. He really had the Dead Man's goat.

I shouted, "What did you do? Try to break in? Why do a dumb thing like that?"

Fido glowered as he whizzed by.

The Dead Man tossed him high and let him fall till his nose was four inches from the pavement, then flipped him up again. How long had this been going on? The Dead Man's powers are amazing, but there are limits to his endurance.

"The book!" Easterman wailed. "I meant to snatch the book."

"I can understand that. I'd like to snatch it myself. But why bust up my place?"

He didn't have anything more to say. Not yet. The Dead Man set him spinning. He got busy dumping his last six meals. People scattered again, grumbling. This part of the show wasn't so attractive.

Winger told me, "He's always been convinced that you have the book hidden at home. That's why he sent me in the first place. To root around."

"Huh? Then he's even crazier than I thought. Don't go away, Fido." I headed for the house. Mounting the steps, I removed the big green litter there, tossing it into the gutter where it belonged.

They'd chopped my door all to hell. Dean could use it for kindling. I wasn't pleased.

The door to the small front room stood ajar. Had the Dead Man let them get that far before he reacted? No. Dean was in there. "Dean? What's the matter?" He was seated on the daybed, sniffling, fiddling with gray burlap he had wrapped around one hand.

He needed time to respond. "Oh! Mr. Garrett!" It was shock. "I tried to stop her. I couldn't."

Winger had invited herself aboard. She said, "He's been cut, Garrett." Yes. The floor between his feet was bloody.

I moved then, thinking he was badly hurt. But he wasn't. His left hand had been laid open to the bone, though, like he'd grabbed a blade. "What happened?"

"She took the book, Mr. Garrett. Right after those creatures tried to break in. I caught her unwrapping it. I tried to take it away."

What was he babbling about? "What are you babbling about?" Then I spotted a torn brass page under his foot. The page that had cut his hand.

"That Book of Shadows. It was here all the time. Under the daybed. And she knew it."

She knew it? How did she know it? How come he hadn't found it while he was cleaning? We were maybe going to have to have a talk about his housekeeping. Under the daybed? How the hell did it get under there?

"Oh, my." I recalled a certain naked vision of a morning past. She'd carried a bundle wrapped in cloth like that wrapped around Dean's hand. I'd paid no attention because there'd been distractions. If I'd thought of that package at all, I'd assumed she'd taken it with her when she'd done her fade. "Carla Lindo grabbed it? She knew where it was and took off with it?"

Dean nodded.

I catch on real quick. "Winger, see what you can do about that hand. I need to go yell at my partner."

You had best not, the Dead Man sent as I charged into his den. *I was as surprised as Dean.*

"You couldn't be. You know the inside of everybody's head. You playing some kind of game?"

I was ignorant of what was happening at deeper levels of her mind, though now it is obvious that her principal motive for staying here was to locate and remain near the Book of Shadows. Note that I was unable to read the mind of the Serpent and unaware of the presence of the other while they were here in the guise of Carla Lindo Ramada. This suggests that there is something quite unusual about that young woman.

"Really?" I was angry. Needless to say. One half-wit thought after the naked woman's departure and I could have saved us all a peck of trouble. I could have poked around, found the book, and destroyed it publicly. End of excitement. But no! I had to let myself get distracted by acres and acres of redheads.

I am doing my part here, Garrett. But I have no legs.

"Say what?"

It has not been twenty minutes since the little devil fled. You know where she is going.

I thought I knew where I was going. Upstairs. To bed. "More power to her."

Garrett! It has been demonstrated to my satisfaction that that woman is not one of the good people either. I suggest you consider what use she or her father might have for the Book of Shadows. Take into consideration their supposed base of operations, an unassailable fortress.

His feelings were hurt because he'd been taken in. He wanted blood. "All right. All right." I needed this like I needed another vacation at the kingpin's place. What I did need was rest, about thirty quarts of cold beer, a ten-pound steak, rare and smothered in mushrooms. A long soak in a tub wouldn't hurt, either. "I'm on my way." Why do I do these things to me?

On my way where? There was a whole world out there.

She has to head west, Garrett.

That narrowed it down. There's only one way out of the city if you're headed west.

47

Winger invited herself along. I didn't argue. She could stick pins in me, keep me awake.

We set our watch against the wall, outside the west gate, among the most optimistic beggars in the world. I mean, half the people inbound are destitute peasants looking for the streets of gold.

"Think we got here in time, Garrett?"

I'd taken our lives in my hands and cut through the Bustee, following the most direct route. "She doesn't know the city. Even if she hired a coach, she couldn't have gotten here first." True, logically, but I was whistling in the dark. After recent events, logic didn't seem very trustworthy.

I mean, the Dead Man getting swindled not once but three times? That was damned hard to swallow, though for the sake of peace in the house I'd take his word.

I suspected wishful thinking had helped Carla Lindo sucker him. He'd been exposed long enough to have smelted something. He'd overlooked it because she'd charmed him. . . . Hell. I should talk?

"She have any money?" Winger asked.

"I don't think so. Why?"

"I wondered if she could hire a coach or buy a horse."

"She gave us everything she had to hire us."

"She'll be walking, then. Can she read?"

"Why?"

"If I was her and I could read, I'd open that book and turn me into somebody else in case somebody came after me."

I hadn't thought of that. I couldn't recall if she could read or not. My memory plays tricks when I'm tired. "Assume the worst. Watch for anybody with something that might be the book."

"How big?"

I made gestures, as best I could recall what I'd seen in the naked woman's arms.

Winger scrunched down in the shade of the wall, ignoring the glower of the beggar next to her. She closed one eye like she was going halfway to sleep. "Think there'll be trouble because of what your sidekick did to Easterman?"

"Nah. Shit happens. Pretty often around our place. The neighbors will be happy it was just entertaining this time. One time half the houses got busted up. That's why all the new brickwork and stuff. People that don't like excitement moved out. Nobody else gives a damn. They don't own, they rent."

"I noticed that about TunFaire. Nobody gives a damn about anything but themselves."

Not entirely true, but close.

Nothing happened for a while. I got into a discussion with a bum who was a fellow ex-Marine, mostly about Glory Mooncalled's exploits in the Cantard. During the night, while I was preoccupied, word had come that Mooncalled's magnificent maneuver down there hadn't panned pure gold. Our fearless leaders had, in fact, anticipated it. They'd gone ahead and jumped into a brawl with the Venageti but had held back powerful reserves. Those had continued the pursuit of Mooncalled and had carved him up pretty good.

From the sound of it, once the dust settled there would be no predominant force in the Cantard. We'd be back to the old endless terror, only now with the balance teetering three ways instead of two. That should make the situation there crazier than ever.

I was glad I was past all that.

Winger nudged me.

One gorgeous redhead had come hiking out the gate. She was dressed for rough travel and carried a big pack. She was in a hurry. Literate or not, she hadn't changed her appearance.

She was in too much of a hurry. Thus, she didn't notice us or know that she'd acquired other admirers, city thugs who thought they had them an easy mark. They cruised along behind, knowing the road ahead would provide ample opportunity. Three miles past west gate you're into wild country already. The hills out there are better suited to raising sheep than to grape growing.

Winger rose with me. She understood the situation without my pointing it out. "I got a suggestion you ain't going to like."

"Which is?"

"Let those three clowns have first crack, then take the book from them."

"You're right. I don't like it."

"Think about it. No telling what's up her sleeve. Right? So why not let somebody else take the lumps?" She did have her own style of thinking. She had a point, too.

I was in a foul enough temper to accept it. "You come to TunFaire this way?"

"Yeah. So?"

"There's a big curve in the road a couple miles ahead. Runs around the end of that ridge yonder, to a town called Switchback."

"I remember."

"If somebody was to go over the ridge, they could save a mile and a half, get ahead, and come back this way. We could come at them from two directions. My guess is they'll jump her at the knee of the ridge, Maiden Angel Shrine, or the spring just past there."

"Does somebody mean me?"

"There's a thought."

"Here's another one. She going to be watching behind her or ahead? She running to or from? Who's she going to recognize?"

Damn her black heart. She was right. Carla Lindo would recognize me in a second. I bellyached a lot, but when the time came I headed uphill, cussing all the way.

It wasn't so bad going down the far side. I tripped and rolled part of the way. No work at all, that. But I didn't make the time I should have. I was late getting to the Shrine of the Maiden Angel.

The bad boys had had time to catch Carla Lindo and Winger had had time to catch them in an indelicately exposed posture. When I came puffing along, one was dead and another working on it while the third was unconscious. Winger had just finished tying a half-naked Carla Lindo to a sapling. "You stop for a couple of beers, Garrett?"

"My pins aren't short enough for running down hills." A westbound peasant family studiously ignored us. They would report us at Hellwalker

Station, the cavalry barracks two miles beyond Switchback. Riders would come to investigate. Highwaymen aren't tolerated the way criminals are in the city.

Carla Lindo had gotten batted around some. It took her a while to recognize me and turn on the heat. I gaped. Winger spat, shook her head, grabbed Carla Lindo's pack in one hand and my arm in the other. "You going to stand there drooling or are you going to haul ass?"

I shuddered and shivered and broke the spell. "Haul ass. One minute." I squatted, told Carla Lindo, "The cavalry will be here soon, sweetheart. They'll turn you loose. If you don't want to spend the rest of your life explaining to every firelord and stormwarden there is, tell the soldiers that these guys jumped you, then some travelers came along and broke it up. But they took off before anybody thought of cutting you loose."

"Garrett! Please." Could she ever turn on the heat. She wasn't human. I turned to hot wax. "I have to have the book. I can't go home without it."

I repeated my shudder-and-shiver routine. I can withstand them when I have to. "No way, darling. It's too wicked. It's killed too many people already. It's got to be destroyed. And I don't trust anybody to do that. Maybe not even me." I wasn't tempted anymore, though. I'd suffered too much. I just wanted to put an end to the damned thing.

I touched Carla Lindo's cheek. "I'm sorry, sweetheart. It could have been something."

"Garrett, you can't do this to me. You loved me. Didn't you?"

"Maybe I did, some. That don't mean I'll let you use me. That don't mean I'm going to go to hell for you. I wouldn't do that for anybody." Except maybe Tinnie. I'd skipped through a suburb of hell for her trying to get this straightened out. I had to go see her again. . . .

Carla Lindo changed. She stopped being that delicious little morsel, turned into a wildcat with a mouth like a dock walloper, speaking the true shadows in her heart. She became the real Carla Lindo Ramada, no better than the other two who'd worn her face.

Winger grumbled, "You ready now? Or you want to hang around and put yourself through some more punishment?"

Right. I put a cap on my hurt, turned my back on Carla Lindo Ramada, walked toward TunFaire. Winger and I didn't talk much. Wasn't much to say. I told myself it could have been worse. I could have gotten involved with Carla Lindo. That wouldn't have been hard. But events had conspired to keep me distanced. Lucky me, I'd ended up just getting another lesson revealing the basic blackness lying below the human heart. Once again I'd seen that, given incentive and opportunity, most anybody will jump at the chance to turn wicked. And the wicked will turn wickeder still.

Priests of a thousand cults proclaim the essential goodliness of Man. They must be fools. All I see is people flinging themselves at the chance to do evil.

I said a lot of that out loud. Winger told me, "You're depressing."

"So they tell me. If they run into me at a time like this. Afterwards. Hang around me much longer, you'll see me really black."

I wondered how black it would get. She had Carla Lindo's pack. She might get a notion to cash in off Easterman.

I'm not sure where the idea came from. Maybe it was spur-of-the-moment. Maybe it was in there all along because the route I picked through the west end was not the fastest. Whatever, suddenly we were at the corner of Blaize and Eldoro. Across the way, alone, hunched, as though shunned by its neighbors, aware of that, cringing, stood a building of ocher brick. Most TunFaire brick is red. Smoke wisped from a stack. The idea hit me. "Come on over here."

I pushed through the front door of that place. A cowbell arrangement announced me. A wizened kobold appeared. A squirrel on two feet. His hands permanently washed one another over his heart. "How may I help you, sir and madam?" His smirk told us he knew. All his kind have a fawning companionship with death.

"I saw smoke from your chimney. You all fired up?"

Puzzled, he replied, "No sir. We keep the fire burning so we don't have to spend time preheating the kiln.

"Let me have the pack," I told Winger. She gave it up reluctantly. She was puzzled, too. She came from an area where they had few nonhumans. If she'd known what was up, she might have resisted. I told the kobold, I want to run this through." I let him look at the pack.

"Sir?"

"I'll pay the usual fee."

"Very well, sir." Even kobolds don't usually argue with money, whether or not they understand. He reached for the pack.

"I'd rather send it off myself. So I'm absolutely sure. You know?"

"As you wish." He didn't move. Time to show him the color of my money. I did. He smiled, put it into a cash box that appeared magically, and disappeared even more quickly. He washed his hands some more, suggested, "If you'll follow me, then?"

"What the hell we doing, Garrett? What is this place? It has a weird smell."

"You'll see."

We went down a hall that passed between several small rooms. In one a kobold family kept vigil over an old, still form on a stone table. Winger got it then.

Many of the races, and even some humans, prefer not to bury their dead. The reasons vary. For kobolds and some others burial supposedly leaves the dead the option of getting up and walking again. Or so they fear. For us humans expense is usually the major consideration. TunFaire is short on cemeteries. Burial ground is expensive.

The kobold took us to the kiln room. He shouted in his own language. More kobolds, likely family, popped up, threw coal into the kiln's firebox, pumped bellows furiously. In seconds waves of heat beat at us.

"You're going to burn it?" Winger asked.

"Going to chuck it in there and cremate it. Won't be anything left but slag." It gets *hot* in those kilns. Has to, to reduce bone.

The little folk shoveled coal and pumped. The whole place got toasty warm. Winger argued with herself. She wasn't much at hiding her thoughts. "Garrett . . . I got to go outside. I can't handle the smell." It was a bit thick in there but she just needed an excuse to remove herself from temptation. If she could stand herself, she could stand a crematorium.

Soon enough the old kobold told me the kiln was ready. I wrestled with myself a little, finally managed to pin the dark side of me long enough. I tossed the bundle in onto the rack where they usually parked the bodies. I leaned my nose against a mica porthole and watched.

Carla Lindo's pack burned quickly, exposing the book. First time I'd seen it. It was pretty much as described, big, thick, bound in leather that went fast. Its brass pages started to curl.

I'm sure it was imagination. I don't know what else it might have been. But as those pages yielded to the fire I thought I heard tiny, distant screams. I thought I saw frantic shadows scurrying over the glowing coals.

48

I stepped out of the crematorium. "Well, that's the end of that. . . ." A young couple passing spared a wide-eyed look for a goof who carried on conversations with thin air. I clammed. Winger wasn't there. I hung around half a minute, probably looking as silly as I felt. Then I shrugged. What the hell? She had work to do, Chodo's plunder to pawn while the pawning was good.

Now what?

I figured my best bet was to go home and catch up on my sleep. So naturally I decided to punish myself a little by delaying gratification. I headed for the Tate compound.

It would be just a quick stop, just a minute to see how Tinnie was doing. If I could weasel my way around the Tate at the gate. After last night they'd be less friendly than ever.

But they did let me inside. I did see Tinnie. She was all better, full of vinegar. The old redhead again. She put on a big, wicked grin and threatened to try visiting again, as soon as I did a little recovering myself. "You might even try getting near some warm water, fella. I think your fleas have all died and started to ripen."

I gave her a little peck on the lips, about ten minutes' worth, on account, and a grin for interest, and said, "I'll run all the way. Don't let me get too old before you. . . ."

"You're already too old but I like you anyway. I'll probably give in to my baser nature. . . .You'd better scoot before Uncle Willard finds out you're here."

I scooted. I didn't exactly run home, but I didn't waste much time. People tell me I was humming. I went straight to bed.

Which is probably where I ought to stay, and say good-bye to running and redheads and whatever else. If I had the sense to stay in bed and keep my head under the covers, I wouldn't get into these crazy things.

•••Red Iron Nights

When I shoved through the doorway of Morley's Joy House you'd have thought I was the old dude in black who lugs the sickle. The place went dead quiet. I stopped moving. I couldn't push uphill against the weight of all those stares. "Somebody sneak lemons into your salads?"

Quick check of the talent. It looked like somebody with an ugly stick had gone berserk. That or those guys spent a lot of time diving into walls and shaving themselves with hatchets. I saw enough scars and bent noses to open me a sideshow.

The Joy House boasts that kind of clientele.

"Aw, damn! It's Garrett." That was my pal Puddle, safe behind the bar. "Here we go again, troops." Puddle goes two-eighty, maybe more. His skin is the hue of somebody who's been dead awhile. You ask me, rigor mortis set in above the neck twenty years back.

Several dwarves, an ogre, miscellaneous elves, and a couple of guys of indeterminate ancestry chugged their sauerkraut cocktails and headed for the door. Guys I didn't even know. Guys who knew me did their damnedest to pretend they didn't. A murmur spread as the ones who didn't know me got clued in.

What a charge for the ego. Call me Typhoid Garrett.

"Hi, everybody," I chirped, going for cheerful. "Ain't it a grand night out?" It wasn't. It was raining cats and dogs and the critters were quarreling all the way to the ground. I had dents in my head from random volleys of hailstones, not being bright enough to wear a hat. On the plus side, flash floods might clear the garbage festering in the streets. Some of that was ready to get up and walk.

The city ratmen get lazier every day.

"Hey, Garrett! Come on over."

Well. A friendly face. "Saucerhead, old buddy, old pal." I steered for the shadowy corner table Tharpe shared with another guy. I hadn't spotted him because of the gloom back there. Even close up I couldn't make much of Tharpe's companion. The guy wore heavy black robes, like some species of priest, complete with cowl. He exuded gloom like a miasma. He wasn't the kind you'd have over to liven up a party.

"Drag up a chair," Tharpe said. I don't know why he's called Saucerhead. He don't like it much but ranks it higher than "Waldo," which a parent or two hung on him.

I planted my behind. Tharpe's companion observed, "Seems you're less than welcome here. Are you diseased?" He wasn't just gloomy, he was forthright, a social handicap worse than bad breath.

"Ha!" Saucerhead snorted. "Ha-ha-ha. That's good, Licks. Hell. This's Garrett. I told you about him."

"The mist begins to clear." But not around him, it didn't.

"I'm starting to feel a little hurt here," I said. "You're wrong." Louder, "You're all of you wrong. I'm not working. I'm not into anything. I just thought I'd drop in and catch up on my friends."

They didn't believe me.

At least nobody cracked wise about me not having any friends.

Saucerhead said, "If you'd come around and socialize sometimes, instead of just when you're up to your crack in crocodiles, maybe folks would smile when they saw you."

Grumble grumble. Hard to argue with that.

"You're looking good, Garrett. Lean and mean. Still working out?"

"Yeah." More grumbles. I don't much like work. Especially not workout-type work. I figure in any rational world a man will get all the exercise he needs catching his share of blondes, brunettes, and redheads.

Got it so far? I'm Garrett, investigator and confidential agent, not animated by any overwhelming ambition, with a penchant for figures of a certain kind and a knack for stumbling into things friends and acquaintances don't find enthralling. I'm a young thirty, six-feet-two, ginger-haired and blue-eyed, and the dogs don't howl when I go by, though the hazards of my profession have left traces which give my face character. I say I'm charming.

My friends disagree, say I just won't take life serious. Well, you do too much of that and you end up as dark as this friend of Saucerhead's.

Puddle arrived with a huge tankard of my favorite food, that divine elixir that makes it necessary for me to work out. He'd drawn it from his private keg, hidden behind the bar. The Joy House doesn't serve anything but rabbit food and the squeezings thereof. Morley Dotes is a rabid vegetarian.

I took a long drink of bitter beer. "You're a prince, Puddle." I fished out a silver mark.

"Yeah. I'm in line for the throne." He didn't pretend to make change. A prince indeed. You could buy a pony keg wholesale for that, the price of silver being what it is. "How come you're in here instead of gamboling through acres of redheads?" My last big case involved whole squads of that delightful subspecies. Unfortunately, only one of the bunch turned out palatable. Redheads are that way. They're either devils or angels—and the angels are no angels. I think it's because they try living up to an image from an early age.

"Gamboling, Puddle?" Where did Puddle pick up a word like "gamboling"? The man had trouble with his own name on account of it had more than one syllable. "You been going to school or something?"

Puddle just grinned.

I asked, "What is this, teak on Tommy Tucker night? With easygoing old Garrett playing Tommy?"

Puddle's grin widened into an unappealing smear of rotten and missing teeth. He was one guy who should convert and become one of Morley's born-again vegetarians.

Saucerhead said, "You make yourself a fat target."

"I must. For everybody. You hear what Dean did?" Dean is the old boy who keeps house for me and my partner and cooks for me. He's about seventy. He'd make somebody a fine wife.

While we jawed, Tharpe's tablemate filled and tamped, filled and tamped the biggest damn pipe I ever saw. It had a bowl like a bucket. Puddle snagged a brass coal bucket off the bar. Licks used copper tongs to transfer one small coal to his pipe. He puffed clouds of weed smoke potent enough to sky us all.

"Musicians," Saucerhead muttered, as though that explained the ills of the world. "I didn't hear, Garrett. What's he done now? Found you another cat?" Dean was going through a stray-collecting spell. I'd had to get firm to keep from ending up up to my belt buckle in cat hair.

"Worse. He says he's moving in. Like I don't get a vote. And he goes on about it like he's making some kind of supreme sacrifice."

Saucerhead chuckled. "There goes your extra room. No place left to stash you a spare honey. Poor baby. Gots to make do with one at a time."

Grumble grumble. "Ain't like I'm overstocked. I been doing with none at a time since Tinnie and Winger ran into each other on my front steps."

Puddle laughed. Heathen.

Tharpe asked, "What about Maya?"

"I haven't seen her in six months. I think she left town. It's me and Eleanor now." Eleanor is a painting on my office wall. I love the gal but she has her limitations.

Everybody thought my situation was hilarious—except Tharpe's friend. He wasn't hearing anybody but himself anymore. He started humming. I decided he couldn't be much of a musician. He couldn't carry a tune in a handcart.

Puddle stopped snickering long enough to say, "I knew you was up to something. Not your usual, but you still looking to get bailed out."

"Damn it, I just wanted out of the house. Dean is driving me buggo and the Dead Man won't take a nap on account of he's expecting Glory Mooncalled to do something and he don't want to miss the news. I defy anybody to put up with those two for half as long as I have."

"Yeah, you do got a hard life." Saucerhead sneered. "My heart goes out. Tell you what. I'll trade you. I take your place, you take mine. I'll throw in Billie." Billie being his current flame, a little bit of a blonde with temper enough for a platoon of redheads.

"Do I detect a note of disenchantment?"

"No. You detect the whole damned opera."

"Thanks anyway. Maybe next time." Saucerhead's place was a one-room walk-up without furniture enough for company. I lived in places like that before I scored big enough to buy the house I share with the Dead Man.

Saucerhead tucked his thumbs into his belt, leaned back, smirked and nodded, nodded and smirked. A smirk on his ugly face is a wonder to behold. He ever holds one too long the Crown might declare it a national park. He claims he's all human, but from his size and looks you've got to suspect he has a little troll or giant in him. "You ain't ready to deal, Garrett, I can't say I got a lot of sympathy for you."

"I could've gone to some second-rate swillhouse and drowned my sorrows in ardent spirits, pouring my woes into the ears of sympathetic strangers, but no, I had to come down here. . . ."

"That works for me," Puddle kicked in when I hit the part about ardent spirits. "Don't let us hold you up."

I never did count him as a friend. He just came with my friend Morley— though Morley's friendship can be suspect enough. "You take the joy out of the Joy House, Puddle."

"Hey, Garrett. The place was rocking till you walked in."

Saucerhead's pal Licks wasn't even gurgling now, but he kept puffing like a volcano and grinning. I was getting the smoke secondhand but was ready to start humming myself. I lost track of what I was saying, started wondering why the place was called the Joy House, which made it sound a lot more exotic than the vegetarian hangout it is.

Licks suddenly shot up like he'd been goosed. He headed for the door, sort of floating, as though his toes barely reached the floor. I'd never seen anyone do weed so heavy. I asked Tharpe, "Where'd you find him?"

"Licks? He found me. Him and some other guys want to organize the musicians."

"Say no more." I could imagine their interest in Saucerhead. Tharpe makes his living convincing people. His technique involves bending limbs in unnatural directions.

Two or three Morleys descended the stair from the second floor, staring toward Licks as the musician hit the exit. Morley had heard about me. Puddle had warned him through the speaking tube to his office upstairs. Hard to tell through the smoke, but Dotes looked irked.

Morley is a breed, part dark-elf, part human. The elf side dominates. He's short, trim, so handsome it's a sin. And sin he does, as often as he can with anybody's wife who'll hold still. He'd grown a little pencil-stroke mustache. He had his black hair slicked back. He was dressed to kill—though his type looks good in anything. He drifted our way, showing a lot of pointy teeth.

"What's that thing living under your nose?"

Saucerhead offered a crude suggestion. Morley ignored him. "You quit working, Garrett? You haven't been around."

"Why work if I don't have to?" I tried looking smug—though my finances weren't comfortable. It costs to keep house.

"You have something going?" He occupied the chair vacated by Licks, waved at persistent weed smoke.

"Not hardly." I gave him my sad tale of woe. He laughed too.

"Imaginative, Garrett. I almost believe you. I have to admit, when you make them up they sound like things that *could* happen. So what is it? Something hush-hush? I haven't heard about anything shaking. This town's getting dull."

He talked that long only because I was stammering. "Damn! Not you too!"

"You never come around except when you need muscle to hoist you out of a hole you've dug yourself."

Not fair. Not true. I've even gone so far as to eat some of the cow chow his joint serves. Once I even paid for it. "You don't believe me? Then tell me this. Where's the woman?"

"What woman?" Dotes and Saucerhead and Puddle all grinned like shit-eating possums. Thought they had me on the run.

"You claim I'm working. Where's the woman? I get into one of my weird cases, there's always a lovely around. Right? So you see a honey on my arm? Hell, my luck's so bad I'd almost go to work just to . . . Huh?"

They weren't paying attention. They were staring at something behind me.

2

She liked black. She wore a black raincloak over a black dress. She wore high-top black boots. Raindrops shimmered like diamonds in her raven hair. She wore black leather gloves. I imagined she'd lost a black hat and veil somewhere. Everything about her was black except her face. That was as pale as bone. She was about five-six. She was young. She was beautiful. She was frightened.

I said, "I'm in love."

Morley's sense of humor deserted him. He told me, "You don't want anything to do with her, Garrett. She'll get you dead."

The woman's gaze, arrogant from amazing black eyes, passed over us as though we didn't exist. She chose to perch at a table isolated from those that were occupied. Some of Morley's patrons shivered as she passed, pretended they didn't see her.

Interesting.

I looked some more. She was about twenty. She wore lip paint so red it looked like fresh blood. That and her pallor gave me a chill. But no. No vampire would dare TunFaire's inhospitable streets.

I was intrigued. Why was she afraid? Why did she scare those thugs? "Know her, Morley?"

"No. I don't. But I know who she is."

"So?"

"She's the kingpin's kid. I saw her out there last month."

"Chodo's daughter?" I was stunned. Also a lot less romantically inclined.

Chodo Contague is TunFaire's emperor of crime. If it's on society's underbelly and there's a profit in it, Chodo has a piece of it.

"Yes."

"You went out there? You saw him?"

"Yes." He sounded a little vague, there.

"He's really alive, then." I'd heard but I'd had trouble believing it.

See, my last case, the one with all the redheads, ended up with me and my friend Winger and Chodo's two top lifetakers going after the bastard. Winger and I took a powder before the dirty deed, figuring we'd be next if we hung around. When we left, Crask and Sadler had the old boy ready to go on the meathook. But it hadn't taken. Chodo was still boss wazoo. Crask and Sadler were still his top headcrushers, like they'd never had a thought of putting him to sleep.

That worried me. Chodo had seen me plain enough. He wasn't the forgiving sort.

"Chodo's daughter! What's she doing in a dump like this?"

"What do you mean, a dump like this?" You can't even hint that the Joy House might be less than top of the mark without Morley gets his back up.

"I mean, obviously she thinks she's a class act. Whatever you or I think, she's got to figure this's a dive. This isn't the Hill, Morley. It's the Safety Zone."

That's Morley's neighborhood. The Safety Zone. It's an area where folks of disparate species get together for business reasons with a lessened risk of getting murdered. It's not your upper-crust part of town.

All the time we're rattling our mouths, whispering, I'm trying to think of some good excuse for going over there and telling the girl she's made me her love slave. And all the time I'm doing that, my little voice is telling me: Don't make a damned fool of yourself—any kid of Chodo's is going to be murder on the hoof.

I must have twitched. Morley grabbed my arm. "You're getting desperate, hit the Tenderloin."

Common sense. Don't stick your hand in a fire. I hung on to my ration of sense. I settled back. I had it under control. But I couldn't help staring.

The front door exploded inward. Two very large brunos brought half the storm in with them. They held the door open for a third man, who came in slow, like he was onstage. He was shorter by a couple of inches but no less muscular. Somebody had used his face to draw a map with a knife. One eye was half-shut permanently. His upper lip was drawn into a perpetual sneer. He radiated nasty.

"Oh, boy," Morley said.

"Know them?"

"I know the type."

Saucerhead said it for me. "Don't we all."

The scar-faced guy looked around. He spotted the girl. He started moving. Somebody yelled, "Shut the goddamned door!" The two heavies there took their first good look around and got a read on what kind of people hang out in a place like the Joy House.

They shut the door.

I didn't blame them. Some very bad people hang out at Morley's place.

Scarface didn't care. He approached the girl. She refused to see him. He bent, whispered something. She started, then looked him in the eye. She spat.

Chodo's kid for sure.

Scarface smiled. He was pleased. He had him an excuse.

There wasn't a sound in the place when he yanked her out of the seat. She betrayed pain by expression but didn't make a sound.

Morley said, "That's it." His voice was soft. Dangerous. You don't mess with his customers. Scarface must not have known where he was. He ignored Morley. Most times that's a fatal error.

He was lucky, maybe.

Morley moved. The thugs from the doorway got in his way.

Dotes kicked one in the temple. The guy was twice his size but went down like he'd been whacked with a sledge. The other one made the mistake of grabbing Morley.

Saucerhead and I started moving a second after Dotes did. We circled the action, chasing the scar-faced character. Morley didn't need help. And if he did, Puddle was behind the bar acquiring some engine of destruction.

Rain hit me in the face, like to drove me back inside. It was worse than it had been when I'd arrived.

"There," Saucerhead said, pointing. I spied the loom of a dark coach, figures struggling as Scarface tried to force the girl inside.

We pranced over, me unlimbering my favorite oak head-knocker as we went. I never leave home without it. Eighteen inches long, it has a pound of lead in its business end. Very effective, and it don't usually leave bodies littering the street.

Saucerhead beat me there. He grabbed the scar-faced guy from behind, twirled him around, and threw him against the nearest building with a force that drowned the rattle of distant thunder. I slithered into the vacated space, grabbed the girl.

Somebody was trying to drag her into the coach. I slipped my left arm around her waist, pulled, pushed my head-knocker past her, figuring I'd pop a bad boy between the eyes.

I saw eyes, all right. Eyes like out of some spook story, full of green fire, three times too big for the wizened little character who wore them. He had to be a hundred and ninety. But he was strong. He hung on to the girl's arm with hands like bird claws, pulled her in despite her and me both.

I swished my billy around, trying to avoid seeing those eyes because they were poisonous. They scared hell out of me. Made me feel cold all the way down to my tailbone. And I don't scare easy.

I got him a good one upside the head. His grip weakened. That gave me a chance to line up another shot. I let him have it.

His mouth opened wide, but instead of a scream, butterflies poured out. I mean like about a million and two butterflies, so many the coach was filled. They were all over me. I stumbled back, flailed around. I'd never been bitten by a butterfly, but who knew about the kind that come flapping out of some old geek's mouth?

Saucerhead pulled the girl away from me, tossed me back like a rag doll, dived in there, and pulled that old guy out. You don't want to get in Saucerhead's way when he's riled. He breaks things.

The old man's eyes had lost their fire. Saucerhead lifted him with one hand, said, "What the hell you think you're pulling, Gramps?" and tossed him over to ricochet off the same wall that had been Scarface's undoing. Then Tharpe went over and started kicking, one for this guy, one for that, no finesse. I heard ribs crack. I figured I ought to calm him down before he killed somebody, only I couldn't think how. I didn't want to get in his way when he was in that mood. And I still had a flock of soggy butterflies after me.

Tharpe calmed himself down. He grabbed the old man by the scruff of the neck and pitched him into the coach. The old boy made a sound like a whipped puppy. Tharpe tossed Scarface in on top of him, then looked up. There wasn't anybody on the driver's seat, so he just whacked the nearest horse on the rump and yelled.

The team took off.

Hunching down against the rain, Tharpe turned to me. "Takes care of those clowns. Hey! What happened to the girl?"

She was gone.

"Damned ingrate. There's a broad for you. Hell." He looked up, let the rain fall into his face a moment, then said, "I'm going to get my stuff. Then what say you and me go get drunk and get in a fight?"

"I thought we just had a fight."

"Bah. Bunch of candyasses. Wimps. Come on."

I had no intention of going trouble-hunting. But it did seem like a good idea to get in out of the rain, away from the butterflies. I told you I hadn't used up my ration of sense.

One of the two thugs was blocking the water flow in the gutter in front of Morley's door. The second came flying out as we started in. "Hey!" Tharpe yelled. "Watch where you're throwing your trash."

I looked around inside. The girl hadn't gone back in there. Morley and Puddle and I settled down to wonder what it was all about. Saucerhead went off looking for a real challenge.

did my best to get my money's worth out of Puddle's keg while Morley and I dissected cabbages and kings and butterflies and the old days that never were that good—though I'd had me a moment now and then. We solved the ills of the world but decided there was nobody in authority with sense enough to implement our program. We were disinclined to take on the job ourselves.

Women proved a topic of brief duration. Morley's recent luck undershone my own. It was too much to take, seeing that great blob Puddle tipped back in his chair, thumbs hooked in his belt, grinning smugly in regard to his own endeavors.

The rain continued relentless. At last I had to face facts. I was going to get wet again. I was going to get a lot wet if Dean failed to respond to my pounding and whooping at the door. With set jaw and scant optimism I took my leave of Morley and his establishment. Dotes looked as smug as his man. He was home already.

I hunched my chin down against my chest and wished I'd had the sense to wear a hat. I wear one so seldom it doesn't occur to me to top myself off when that would be wise. Right away rain started sneaking down the back of my neck.

I paused where we'd rescued Chodo's mysterious daughter from her more mysterious assailants. There wasn't much light. The rain had swept away most of the evidence. I poked around and was on the verge of deciding half had been my imagination before I found one big bedraggled butterfly. I salvaged the cadaver and carried it as carefully as I could, cradled in my left palm.

My place is an old red brick house in a once-prosperous stretch of Macunado Street, near Wizard's Reach. The middle-class types have all abandoned ship. Most of the neighboring places have been subdivided and rented to families with herds of kids. Usually when I approach my house I pause to inspect it and reflect on the good fortune that let me survive the case that paid me enough to buy it. But cold rain down the back of the neck has a way of sapping nostalgia.

I scampered up the steps and gave the secret knock, *bam-bam-bam*, as hard as I could while bellowing, "Open up, Dean! I'm going to drown out here." A big flash of lightning. Thunder rattled my teeth in their sockets. The sky lords hadn't been feuding before, just tuning up for another Great Flood. Thunder and lightning suggested they were about to get serious. I pounded and yelled some more. The stoop isn't protected from the weather.

Maybe my ears were still ringing. I thought I heard something like a kitten crying inside. I knew it couldn't be a cat. I'd given Dean the word about his strays. He wouldn't lapse.

I heard shuffling and whispering inside. I did some more yelling. "Open this damned door, Dean. It's cold out here." I didn't threaten. Mom Garrett didn't raise no kids dumb enough to lay threats on somebody who could just go back to bed and leave me singing in the rain.

The door creaked open after a symphony of curses and clanking bolts and rattling chains. Old Dean stood there eyeing me from beneath drooping lids. He looked about two hundred right then. He is around seventy. And real spry for a guy his age.

If he wasn't going to get out of the way I was going to walk over him. I started moving. He slid aside. I told him, "The cat goes as soon as the rain stops." I tried to sound like it was him or the kitten.

He started rattling bolts and chains. I stopped. All that hadn't been there before. "What's all the hardware?"

"I don't feel comfortable living somewhere where all there is is one or two latches to keep the thieves out."

We needed to have us a talk about assuming and presuming. I knew damned well he didn't buy that hardware out of his own pocket. But now wasn't the time. I wasn't at my best.

"What's that you've got?"

I'd forgotten the butterfly. "Drowned butterfly." I took it into my office, a shoe box of a room behind the last door to your left heading back to the kitchen. Dean hobbled after me, bringing a candle. He has decrepitude down to an art. It's amazing how incapacitated he gets when he has a scam running.

I used his candle to light a lamp. "Go back to bed."

He glanced at the closed door of the small front room, a door we shut only when there's somebody or something in there we don't want seen. Something was scratching its other side. Dean said, "I'm wide-awake now. I might as well get some work done." He didn't look wide-awake. "You plan to be up long?"

"No. I'm just going to study this bug, then kiss Eleanor good night." Eleanor was a beautiful, sad woman who lived once upon a time. Her portrait hangs behind my desk. I go on like we're into a relationship. That drives Dean buggy.

I have to balance the scale somehow.

I settled into my worn leather chair. Like everything else around my place, including the house, it was secondhand. It was just getting adjusted to a new butt. Just getting comfortable. I pushed my accounts aside, spread the butterfly on my desk.

Dean waited in the doorway till he saw I wouldn't react to the accounts being out. Then he huffed off to the kitchen.

I popped a quick peek at the last entry, made a face. That didn't look good. But go to work? Gah! Sufficient unto the day the evil thereof.

Meantime, there was this raggedy old green butterfly. It could've been a beauty before, but now its wings were cracked and chipped and split, bent and washed out. A disaster. I suffered a moment of *déjà vu*.

I'd seen its cousins in the islands while I was doing my five years in the Royal Marines. There're a lot in the swamps down there. There's every kind of bug the gods ever imagined, except maybe arctic roaches. Maybe creation was handled by a heavenly committee. In areas where departmental turfs overlapped, the divine functionaries went to competing. And they all for sure dumped their bug-production overruns in those tropical swamps.

But the heck with the bad old days. I'm all growed-up now. What I had to ask was, what was I doing with the flutterbug in the first place?

I was definitely, for sure, guaranteed, not even a little bit interested in anything involving dried-up old geezers with stomachs so sour they belched up butterflies. I'd done my good deed for the decade. I'd rescued the maiden fair. It was time to get on with things dearer my heart, like hustling Dean's latest fuzzball charity out my back door.

I swept the bug cadaver into the trash bucket, leaned back, started thinking how nice it would be to put myself away in my nice soft bed.

Garrett!

"Hell!" Every time I forget my so-called partner . . .

4

The Dead Man hangs out in the larger front room that takes up the whole front side of the house opposite my office, an area as big as my office and the small front room together. A lot of space for a guy who hasn't moved since before TunFaire was called TunFaire. I'm thinking about putting him in the basement with the other junk that was here when I moved in.

I went into his room. A lamp was burning there. That was a surprise. Dean doesn't like going in there. I glanced around suspiciously.

The room contains only two chairs and two small tables, though the walls are hidden by shelves of books and maps and memorabilia. One chair is mine. The other has a permanent resident.

If you walk in not knowing what to expect, the Dead Man can be a shock. First, there's just a whole hell of a lot of him. Four hundred and fifty pounds' worth. Second, he's not human, he's Loghyr. Since he's the only one of that tribe I've ever seen, I don't know if he'd set the Loghyr girls swooning, but by my standards he's one homely sucker. Like he was the practice dummy when the guy with the ugly stick was doing his apprenticeship.

After fat you notice he's got a snoot like an elephant, fourteen inches long. Then you notice that the moths and mice have nibbled him over the years.

The reason he's called the Dead Man is that he's dead. Somebody stuck a knife in him about four hundred years ago. But Loghyr just don't get in a hurry. His soul, or whatever, is still hanging around in his body.

I gather you have had an adventure.

Since he's dead, he can't talk, but he doesn't let that slow him down. He just thinks right into my head. He can also go rummaging around in there, amongst the clutter and spiders, if he wants. Mostly he's courteous enough to keep out unless he's invited.

I took another look around. The place was too clean. Dean had even dusted the Dead Man.

Something was up. Those two had gotten their heads together. That was a first. That was scary.

I'm nothing if not cool. I covered my suspicion perfectly. Knowing it was going to be something I wouldn't like, I decided to get even first.

The Dead Man made a big mistake when he taught me to remember every little detail of everything when I was working. I started talking about my evening.

The theoretical basis of our association is I do the legwork and suffer the slings and arrows and thumps on the head and he takes whatever I learn and runs it through his self-proclaimed genius brains and tells me whodunit or where the body is buried or whatever it is I'm trying to find out. That's the theoretical basis. In practice, he's lazier than I am. I have to threaten to burn the house down just to wake him up.

I was dwelling in lingering detail upon the charms of the strange Miss Contague when suspicion bit him. *Garrett!*

He knows me too well. "Yes?" Sweetly.

What are you doing?

"Filling you in on some odd occurrences."

Occurrences, incidentally, of but passing interest. Unless your passions have overcome your brain yet again. You could not possibly be considering involving yourself with those people, could you?

I thought about lying just to rattle his chain. We do a lot of that, back and forth. It passes the time. But I said, "There *are* limits to how much I'll let a skirt override my good sense."

Indeed? I am amazed and surprised. I had concluded that you have no sense at all, good or bad.

We do get going. Usually it's play, wit and half-wit. It's up to you to guess who's who.

"One point for you, Old Bones. I'm going to go put myself on the shelf for the night. If Dean explodes in another mad burst of energy and decides to dust you again, tell him he can wake me at noon." I have this thing about mornings. No sane man gets up then. They come too damned early in the day.

Think about it. All those early birds out there, what do they get? Ulcers.

Heart trouble. Caught by homeless cats. But not me. Not old Garrett. I'm going to lean back and relax and loaf my way to immortality.

I wish you could sleep in. After your valiant rescue job and your heroic attempt to turn a profit off that Puddle creature, you deserve a reward.

"Why do I get the feeling you're about to stick it to me? Why shouldn't I sleep in? I don't have anything else to do."

You have to be at the gate of the Al-Khar at eight o'clock.

"Say what?" The Al-Khar is the city prison. TunFaire is notoriously short on law enforcement and justice, but once in a while some clown is so clumsy he stumbles into the arms of the Watch. Once in a while some brain-damage case actually gets himself some time. "What the hell for? There's people up there don't like me."

If you were to avoid every place where someone does not like you, you would have to leave town in order to find room to breathe. You will be there because you have to tail a man who is to be released at eight.

I had it scoped out. Him and Dean had found me work on account of they were worried about our dwindling funds. The brass-bottomed nerve! They were both getting big-headed. But sometimes it helps to play dumb. I'm a past master at playing dumb. I'm so good I fool myself sometimes. "What would I want to do that for?"

Three marks a day and expenses. It should take only a modicum of creativity to shift our household budget into the latter category.

I got down and peered under his chair. There were still a couple little sacks down there. "We aren't broke yet." That's where we keep our cash. There's no place safer. Any thief who gets past the Dead Man is somebody so bad I don't want to mess with him anyway. "If I kick Dean and his cat out and cook for myself, that'd be beer money for months."

Garrett.

"Yeah. Yeah." It really was getting time to hustle up some money. Only I didn't like the idea of jobs being handed to me. I'm the senior partner in this chicken outfit. The boss. Har. "Tell me about it. And while you're doing that, put one of your spare brains to work thinking about who keeps a roof over whose ungrateful head."

Phsaw! Do not be petty. This is the ideal job. A simple tail. The client simply wishes to trace the movements of the convict.

"Right! So this clown makes me, leads me into an alley, practices the latest dance steps on my face . . ."

This man is not violent. Nor should he expect to be followed. It is easy money, Garrett. Take it.

"If it's that easy, why me? Why not Saucerhead? He always needs work." I sent a lot his way.

We need the money. Get some rest. You will be rising early.

"Maybe." How come it's me that has to get out and do the hustling? "But first, how about you drop me one or two more hints here? Like maybe a description. Just in case more than one guy graduates from college tomorrow. Like maybe the initials of the guy who's hiring me. So I can practice my deducing and figure out who I'm supposed to report to."

The client is one Bishoff Hullar. . . .

"Oh, great. You got me working for a sleazy taxi-dance operator from the Tenderloin. Bring me down in the world, why don't you? I used to play with real villains, like Chodo and his boys. Who do I follow? Somebody who stiffed one of his girls? And why?"

The target is one Barking Dog Amato. A colorful name. . . .

"Gods! Barking Dog? You got to be kidding."

You know him?

"Not personally. I know who he is. I thought everybody over ten knew Barking Dog Amato."

I do not get out much anymore.

I resisted temptation. He'd want me to be his wheels. "Barking Dog Amato. AKA Crackpot Amato. Given name, Kropotkin F. Amato. I don't know what the F stands for. Probably Fruitcake. The man's a total loony. Spends all his time hanging around the Chancery steps with a brass megaphone, yelling about how the powers that be swindled his ancestors. He's got a whole road show he hauls around, signs and banners and displays. He hands out broadsides to anybody who gets close enough to let him shove one at him. He's got conspiracy theories that boggle master conspiracy theorists. He can connect anything up with anything and produce a diabolical plot to rule the world or fleece Kropotkin Amato of his birthright. He's big on the Emperor being behind everything."

The empire that preceded the Karentine state fell ages ago, but there's still an imperial family hanging around awaiting the call. Its only influence on today's world is it provides some small funding for the Bledsoe charity hospital. Nobody but Barking Dog could imagine them being secret masters of anything.

Interesting.

"Entertaining. In small doses. But if you get too close you'll get grabbed and told the whole story of how his noble family got defrauded of its title and estates. Hell. His father was a butcher down on Winterslight. His mother was some kind of breed out of the Bustee. The only conspiracy that victimized him was the one that got us all. Conscription and the war. He started his barking after they mustered him out."

Then the man is harmless, a deluded fool?

"That'd cover it. As harmless, deluded, and foolish as they come. One of our more entertaining street characters. Which is why they let him hang out with his megaphone."

How did this harmless fool get himself thrown into jail? Why would anyone want him shadowed? Can he be more than he seems?

I was working on that already.

It had been a while since I'd seen the Barking Dog in action. But then, I hadn't been onto his turf.

I hadn't missed him. He wasn't the sort anyone would miss if he disappeared. Maybe once in a while somebody would ask: Whatever happened to that cacklehead who used to howl on the Chancery steps? He'd get a shrug and forget it. Nobody would get excited and go looking.

I was sure Barking Dog would have inventive things to say about his prison time. Maybe devils from another world were after him now. He'd never rattled anybody from this world enough to get himself locked up. Maybe it was Venageti secret agents. Or the little people. Or the gods themselves. The god gang don't need excuses to turn malicious.

"I'm going to bed, Chuckles." I got out before he could change my mind, muttering, "Three marks a day to tail Barking Dog Amato. It can't be true."

The foot of the stairs is just a couple steps from the kitchen door. I leaned in to wish Dean a good night. "After you get rid of that cat, start thinking about the floor in the Dead Man's room, since you two are such good buddies now. It could use sanding and refinishing."

He looked at me like he was seeing spooks.

I chuckled, headed for bed. He pulled any more stunts, I'd have him in there for three months, sanding and polishing and painting and generally getting himself a good dose of employer vengeance.

I hit my room, shucked my clothes, brooded about having to go to work for about as long as it took me to plop my head into my pillow. Insomnia isn't one of my shortcomings.

5

There are those, old Dean among them, whose major personality flaw is a compulsion to spring up with the first bird chirp. That's a dandy habit—if you've *got* to get to the worms first. Me, I swore off exotic chow when I parted ways with the Corps. I won't get into that situation again.

Dean suffers from the delusion that sleeping till noon is a sin. I've tried and tried to show him the light, but his brain hardened along with his arteries. He flat won't admit the truth of my theories. No fool like an old fool.

I made the error of observing that aloud.

Hell, it was barely sunup. You expect me to *think* at that time of night?

I got me a drizzle of ice water down my spine.

I screamed. I cussed. I said stuff to set dear old mom spinning in her grave.

I got up, to no avail. The old boy had him a head start.

I sat on the edge of my bed, put my elbows on my knees and my forehead in my hands. I asked the gods, which I believe in once a week, what I'd done to deserve Dean. Hadn't I always been one of the good guys? Come on, fellows. Let's all play a prank on the universe and let true justice reign for a day. Get that old sucker.

I blinked. Between the heels of my hands I glimpsed Dean peeking around the doorframe. "Time to get up, Mr. Garrett. You have to be outside the Al-Khar in two hours. I've started breakfast."

My suggestion about breakfast reversed the traditional alimentary process. He wasn't impressed.

He clumped downstairs. I groaned vigorously and stumbled to a window. There was barely enough light to see. The city ratmen were banging and clanging their trash carts while they pretended to do something useful. A herd of dwarves hustled past, carrying bundles bigger than they were. They were a sullen, surly, silent gang. See what getting up early does?

Except for dwarves and street sweepers, the thoroughfare was barren. Sane folk were still in bed.

Only impending poverty kept me from easing back into mine.

What the hell? I could turn old Barking Dog into a career. Anybody dumb enough to have him tailed deserved to have his purse looted. Sure be safer than most jobs that come my way.

I prettied myself up and moseyed downstairs. I paused outside the kitchen to put on a heavyweight scowl—though at that time of night, if my rest is disturbed, scowling comes naturally.

Which did me no good. I stepped into the smells of spicy sausages, stewed apples, fresh hot tea, biscuits just out of the oven. I didn't have a chance.

He won't cook like that when I'm not working. I'm just hanging around, it's maybe a bowl of cold porridge developing a crust. If I want fresh tea, I've got to put the pot on myself.

What do you do with these work-ethic fanatics? I mean, I don't mind if he busts his butt working for me—which I've never noticed him doing. My problem is, he's one of those characters who wants to redesign the rest of us. His ambition is to see me collapse from overwork, rich, before my thirty-first birthday. I'm going to fool him. That won't ever come. I'm going to stay thirty forever.

I ate. Too much. Dean hummed as he cleaned his pots. He was happy. I was employed. I felt abused, trivialized. Such a vast array of talents and skills wasted trailing a nut case. It was like using a rosewood four-by-four to swat flies.

Dean was of such good cheer about my employment that he forgot to kvetch till I was halfway through my second helping of apples. "You go past the Tate compound to get to the Al-Khar don't you, Mr. Garrett?"

Oh-oh. When he Misters me he knows I won't like what he's got to say. This time he was pretty transparent. "Not today." He was going to nudge me to make up with Tinnie. Which I wasn't going to do on account of I'd decided I was done apologizing to women for things I didn't do. "Tinnie wants to make up, she knows where to find me."

"But . . ."

I got up. "Something you need to think about, Dean. Maybe while you're finding a home for that cat. And that's what you'll do if I suddenly find me a wife to manage the house." That would hold him.

I headed for the front door. I didn't get there. The Dead Man's voice rang in my head. *You are leaving without taking adequate precautions, Garrett.*

He meant I was leaving the house unarmed. I said, "I'm just going to follow a crazy man. I won't get into trouble." Without bothering to go into his room. He doesn't hear physically.

You never plan to get into trouble. Yet each time you assume that attitude and go out unprepared, you end up wishing you had had the foresight to carry something. Is that not so?

That was uncomfortably close to the truth. I wished it wasn't. I wished we lived in a more civilized age. But wishing never makes anything so.

I went upstairs, to my closet of unpleasantries, where I keep the tools I use when the tools I prefer, my wits, fail me. I grumbled all the while. And wondered why I resisted good advice. I guess I resented the fact that I hadn't thought of it myself.

Lessons you don't want to learn come hard.

TunFaire is not a nice city.

I hit the street in a black humor. I wasn't going to make the city any nicer.

6

L ike most public buildings in this town, the Al-Khar is generations over-due for renovation. It looks like the prisoners could walk through the walls if they wanted.

The Al-Khar was a bad idea from the beginning, a pork-barrel project making somebody rich through cost overruns and corner cutting. The builder used a pale yellow-green stone that absorbed grunge from the air, reacted with it, streaked, turned uglier by the hour, and did not stand up, being too soft. It chipped and flaked, dropping talus all around the prison, leaving the walls with a poxy appearance. In places there'd been mortar decay enough that stones were loose. Since the city hardly ever jailed anybody, there seemed to be no financial provision for prison maintenance.

It was raining still, though now the fall was just a drizzle. Just enough to be a misery. I posted myself under a forlorn lime tree as down-and-out as any alley-dwelling ratman. It didn't know the season. But its sad branches offered the only shelter around. I recalled my Marine Corps training and faded into my surroundings. Garrett the chameleon. Right.

I was early, not something that happens often. But since I started my exercises I move a little faster, with more energy. Maybe I should go for a mental workout too. Develop some energy and enthusiasm in that direction.

The trouble with me is my work. Investigating exposes you to the slimy underbelly of the world. Being a weak character, I try to make things better, to strike the occasional spark in the darkness. I have a notion my reluctance to work springs from the knowledge that if I do I'll see more of the world's dark side, that I'll butt heads with the Truth, which is that people are cruel and selfish and thoughtless and even the best will sell their mothers at the right time.

The big difference between good guys and bad is the good guys haven't yet had a fat chance for profiting from going bad.

A bleak world view, unfortunately reinforced by events almost daily.

A bleak view that's scary because it keeps on telling me my turn is coming.

A bleak street, that dirty cobbled lane past the Al-Khar. Very little traffic. That was true even in good weather. I've felt less lonely, less touched by despair, alone in the woods.

The street was a problem professionally as well as emotionally. I didn't blend in. People would start wondering and maybe remembering—though they wouldn't come outside. People in this town avoid trouble.

Barking Dog came stomping out of prison, thumbs tucked into his belt. He paused, surveyed the world with a prisoner's eye.

He was about five-feet-six, sixtyish, chunky, balding, had a brushy graying mustache and ferocious huge eyebrows. His skin was tanned from decades in the elements denouncing conspiracies. Prison hadn't faded him. His clothes were old and tattered and filthy, the same he'd worn when he'd gone inside. The Al-Khar doesn't offer uniforms. Barking Dog, so far as I knew, had no relatives to bring him anything.

His gaze swept me. He didn't react. He raised his face, enjoyed the drizzle, then started moving. I gave him half a block before I followed.

He had a unique way of walking. He was bowlegged. He had arthritis or something. He sort of rolled along, lifting one whole side of his body, swinging it forward, following with the other. I wondered if he hurt much. Prison wouldn't do wonders for arthritis.

Barking Dog wasn't in a hurry. He ambled, savoring his freedom. I'd hang out in the rain myself, enjoying it, if I'd been locked up. But I wasn't terribly empathetic at the moment. I muttered and sputtered and grumbled. Such thoughtlessness! Keeping a crack investigator out in the rain.

Wasn't his fault, though, was it? I started plotting vengeance on the Dead Man.

Always an interesting mental exercise, that. What sanctions can you exercise against somebody who's been murdered? Aren't many options left.

Even us masters of the game get sloppy. It's easy when you don't feel threatened. I didn't feel threatened. Barking Dog wasn't the kind of street bruno I run into ordinarily, somebody big as a house and half as smart and just as easy to shove around. Barking Dog was damned near a little old man. Little old men don't get violent. Or, if they do, they pay some big, stupid bruno to do it for them.

I strutted around a corner and—oooph! Right in the breadbasket. Lucky for me, Barking Dog was damned near a little old man and little old men don't get violent.

I folded up, tried to prance away from his follow-up. Wonder of wonders, I made it. He was, after all, damned near a little old man. I gagged and hacked and got my breath back. Meantime, Barking Dog added things up and decided he hadn't gotten enough oomph on his punch and his best move now was to apply heels and toes vigorously to the cobblestones.

Not unwise tactics, considering the mood I was in all of a sudden.

I got me trundling after him. Lucky me, I'd been working out so I was in good enough shape to come back quickly. Before long I was keeping up, then I started gaining ground. Barking Dog looked back only once. He saved his energy for streaking away.

Me, I started taking corners more carefully.

It didn't take me long to catch up, grab him by the shoulder, block his futile blows, and force him to sit on somebody's steps. "What the hell was that for?" I demanded.

He looked at me like I was a fool. Maybe he was right. I hadn't exercised a lot of wisdom so far. He didn't answer me.

It didn't look like he was planning to make a break, so I sat me down beside him, far enough off so he couldn't cream me with a backhand. "That hurt, guy. How come?"

That look again. "What you take me for, bruno?"

Oh. That hurt more than the whack in the gut. I'm an experienced investigator, not a street thug. "A crazy old man, ain't got sense enough to get in out of the rain."

"I'm one with nature. You going to get to it?"

"To what?"

"The threats. The arm-twisting."

Ha! My turn to do the looking.

"You don't fool me with that dumb look. Somebody sent you to keep me from telling the truth."

Craftily I asked, "What truth would that be?"

Craftier, he told me, "If they didn't tell you, they don't want you to know. Wouldn't want to get you in as deep as I am."

Crazy. And I was sitting there talking to him. In the rain. Downwind. They hadn't given him a scrubbing before they turned him loose. "No threats. I don't care what you do."

He didn't understand. "Hows come you're dogging me?"

"To see where you go." Get him with a new technique. Tell the truth. Confuse him all to hell.

It worked. He was puzzled. "Why?"

"Damned if I know. Guy paid my partner, who took the job without consulting me. Naturally, he's housebound. So I'm the one out here drowning."

He believed me, probably because I wasn't twisting limbs. "Who'd want to know that?" He seemed lost. "Nobody takes me serious. Hardly nobody, anyway."

I checked to see if we were drawing a crowd. Barking Dog had one voice level, loud. Like he'd been yelling so long, that was all he could do. Too, I wondered what they'd fed him in jail. He had breath like a buzzard. Not to mention he wasn't appetizing visually, what with his wild eyebrows, mustache, bulbous nose, and buggy eyes. At least he didn't try to handbill me or want me to sign a petition.

Might as well push my experiment to the limit. "Guy called Bishoff Hullar."

"Who? I don't know no Bishoff Hullar."

"Runs a taxi-dance scam in the Tenderloin."

He looked at me queer, sure I was lying or crazy. Then he frowned. "A nominee! Of course."

"Say what?"

"A nominee. A stand-in who hired you for somebody else." He began nodding, grinning. Somebody was out to get him. He liked that idea. After all these years, somebody was out to get him! Somebody was taking him seriously! He was about to be persecuted!

"Probably so." I'd never spent much time wondering about Barking Dog. Occasionally I'd given thought to whether or not he believed what he said. It was common knowledge his claims about his family were exaggerated. None of his conspiracy claims had borne fruit, and that in a town where everybody who was somebody wanted scandal ammunition to use against other somebodies. Nobody tried to shut him up.

"What did they nick you for?" What the hell. I wasn't going to get much wetter. And the damp was toning down the miasma around Amato.

"Sixty days."

A comedian. "What was the charge? It's a matter of record. Wouldn't take me an hour to get the story."

He mumbled something.

"What?"

"Public nuisance." He didn't boom this time either.

"They don't give you two months—"

"Third complaint." His excitement over being persecuted had faded. Now he was embarrassed. He was a convicted public nuisance.

"Even so, more than a few days seems excessive."

"I kind of got carried away at my hearing. Fifty-five days were for contempt."

Heavy time, even so. The magistrates I knew were pretty contemptible. They ran their courts like feeding time at the zoo. It would take some barking to aggravate any of them.

I recalled outrageous claims I'd heard Amato make. Yep. He had run into somebody with no sense of humor, somebody who didn't know Barking Dog was a genuine loony, harmless in the extreme. Nobody else could get away with the stuff he said. "Maybe you were lucky," I told him. "You get somebody really pissed, they could toss you into the Bledsoe." Part of the charity hospital is a madhouse. You get stuffed in there, you won't get out unless somebody outside springs you. There are plenty of stories about people who have gone in and been forgotten for decades.

Barking Dog went pale under his tan. *That* scared him. He started to leave.

"Hang on, old-timer."

He settled, resigned. He thought the threat had come. The Bledsoe. Just sitting there beside him, talking to him, I'd begun to feel like a candidate for the cackle factory. "You won't talk, eh?"

"No."

I shook my head. Water from my hair dribbled into my eyes. "I'm getting paid, which maybe ought to be enough, but I'd sure like a hint why I'm spending time with you."

I suspected that, on reflection, he'd decided that *he* didn't know. A cold drizzle can be a great cure for a case of the fantasies.

My thoughts flitted like drunken butterflies, trying to make sense of what was happening. The only answers I found were that this was a practical joke, or a mistake, or a sinister plot, or something. It couldn't be the job advertised.

I heard the Dead Man: "Three marks a day and expenses." I hadn't thought to ask if we'd taken a retainer.

"What're your plans?" I asked. "Right now."

"You're going to get wet, son. First I'm going to go see if I still got me a place to live. If I do, then I'm going to go buy me a bottle and get drunk. You want to hang around, wait for me to sneak off and make contact with your boss's secret enemies, you just go ahead." He spoke with conviction when he mentioned getting drunk. That wouldn't be the first thing I'd go for after leaving jail, but he was maybe a little past catching honeys. As a second choice it didn't sound bad. "How about tomorrow?"

"Tomorrow it's back to the old grind. Unless it's raining. Then I'll stay in and make the acquaintance of another bottle."

I got up. "Let's walk over where you live, then. Get you tucked in. Then I'll see this Hullar clown, find out what's shaking." Nobody likes being made a fool—and I was developing the sneaking suspicion I'd done it to myself. I should've asked more questions when I was talking to the Dead Man.

I decided to start with him, work my way back to Bishoff Hullar.

ean let me in. "What in the world are you doing home?" He hoisted his nose at the dripping I did.

"Need to consult the genius." I pushed past but hung a surprise left into the small front room. Huh. No cat. No sign of a cat. But I smelled it.

Dean shuffled from foot to foot. I gave him my most evil look, pretended to twist a neck to the accompaniment of dramatic noises. I headed for the Dead Man's room.

He was pretending to sleep.

I knew he wasn't. He wouldn't nod off before he heard the latest from the Cantard. He was obsessed with Glory Mooncalled and expected news of the republican general's adventures momentarily.

I went inside anyway. Dean hustled in with a raggedy blanket he tossed over my chair so it wouldn't get wet. I settled, stared at the Dead Man, said, "That's a pity, him drifting off just when we finally hear something from the war zone. Make me a quick cup of tea before I hit the street again."

What news from the Cantard? . . . You are a treacherous beast, Garrett.

"The treacherousest. As bad as the kind of guy who'd send you out to follow a nut case as a joke."

Joke?

"You can come clean. I won't hold a grudge. I'll even admit it was a good one. You had me out there for hours before I figured it out."

I hate to disappoint you, Garrett, but the fact is we have *been hired to report the movements of Barking Dog Amato. The client paid a fifty-mark retainer.*

"Come on. I admitted it was a good one. Let up."

It is true, Garrett. Though now, seeing the thoughts and reservations and questions rambling across the surface of your mind, I grow curious myself. I wonder if I, too, have not been the victim of an elaborate hoax.

"Somebody *really* paid fifty marks to have Amato watched?"

There would be nothing under my chair otherwise.

I was sure he wouldn't take a joke that far. "You didn't ask questions?"

No. Not the questions you wish I had. Had I known what a Barking Dog Amato was, I would have asked them.

Somebody had begun pounding on the front door. Dean, apparently, was too busy to be bothered. "Wait a minute."

I looked through the peephole first. I'd learned the hard way. I saw two women. One was hugging herself, shivering. Neither seemed to enjoy the weather.

I opened up. "Can I help you ladies?"

I used "ladies" poetically. The younger had twenty years on me. Both were squeaky clean and wore their finest, but their finest was threadbare and years out of style. They were gaunt and threadbare themselves. One had a trace of nonhuman blood.

Both put on nervous smiles, as though I'd startled them by being something they didn't expect. The younger screwed up her courage. "Are you saved, brother?"

"Huh?"

"Have you been born again? Have you accepted Mississa as your personal savior?"

"Huh?" I didn't have the foggiest what the hell was going on. I didn't even realize they were talking religion. That doesn't play much part in my life. I ignore all the thousand gods whose cults plague TunFaire. So far I've seldom been disappointed in my hope that the gods will ignore me.

Apparently my not slamming the door was great encouragement. Both women started chattering. Being a naturally polite sort of guy, I halfway listened till I got the drift. Then I grinned, inspired. "Come in! Come in!" I introduced myself. I shook their hands. I turned on the old Garrett charm. They became uneasy almost to the point of suspicion. I probed only deeply enough to make sure their brand of salvation wasn't limited to humans. Most of the cults are racist. Most of the nonhuman races hold to no gods at all.

I confessed, "I'm not free to entertain a new system of beliefs myself, but I do know someone who should see you. My partner is the most ungodly sort you can imagine. He needs . . . Let me caution you. He's stubborn in his wickedness. I've tried and tried . . . You'll see. Please come with me. Would you like tea? My housekeeper just put the kettle on." They chattered steadily themselves. What I had to say mostly got shoved in in snatches.

They followed me. I had a hell of a time keeping a straight face. I sicced them on the Dead Man. I didn't stay around to watch the fur fly.

As I hit the rain I wondered if he'd ever speak to me again. But who needed spiritual guidance more? He was dead already, already headed down the path to heaven or hell.

But the grin on my clock wasn't any smug celebration of my ingenuity. I'd had me another attack of inspiration. I knew how to turn the Barking Dog business into a scam that would make us both happy.

The man could read and write. He did his own signs and broadsides. And he was harmless. And he needed money. I'd seen that where he lived. So why not have him keep track of himself? I could hand his journal over to my client, split my fee with Barking Dog, save myself hunking around in the weather.

The more I thought about that, the more I liked it. And who'd know the difference?

So the heck with Bishoff Hullar. I wouldn't press my luck there. I'd stay away except to collect. I chose a new destination.

I went off to sell Barking Dog. I didn't anticipate any trouble. I would appeal to his sense of conspiracy.

Some white knight, eh? Our hero, third-string con artist.

I didn't suffer much guilt. The Bishoff Hullars of the world deserve what they get. Hell, before I got to Barking Dog's place I was chuckling.

8

Some of us take a notion we're what the world perceives us to be, so we create images the world feeds back. You see it especially with kids. You get some pathetic louse of a parent, always sniping at his kid, telling him he's no good and dumb, pretty soon he's got a dumb, no-good kid. That's your one-way version. I'm talking about creating yourself.

I worked at it, not always consciously, when I wanted the world to think I was bad. I didn't make my bed. I changed my socks only once a week. I cleaned house once a year whether the place needed it or not. When I wanted to look real mean, I stopped brushing my teeth.

Barking Dog must have lived in those same two rooms for about eleven thousand years without cleaning once. The place could become a museum where mothers showed their kids why they ought to pick up after themselves.

The smell suggested it was the one place in TunFaire not infested by vermin. The smell was the smell of Barking Dog Amato, confined and reinforced by time and made heavier by oppressive humidity. Barking Dog had no handle on the principles of hygiene.

Thank whatever gods he'd been out of there awhile.

I'd never seen that much paper anywhere, not even in the offices of royal functionaries. Once Barking Dog muffed both sides of a handbill sheet, he flipped the cull over his shoulder. When he brought in food, its wrappings, paper or cornhusk, joined the rejected handbills. The broken cadavers of earthenware wine bottles lay everywhere. Unscathed survivors apparently returned for the deposits.

The entire history of Barking Dog Amato lay there, in sedimentary layers, ready to be excavated by a historical adventurer unencumbered by a sense of smell.

I took that in at a glance after Amato invited me in. I wasted a second glance on his furniture. That amounted to an artist's easel where he painted posters and placards and a rickety table where he calligraphed handbills. A semiclear corner boasted a ragged blanket.

Two steps inside, I saw that I'd leapt to an erroneous conclusion. Barking Dog did indeed clean house. There was a second room, with no door in its doorway, where he moved his trash whenever his primary got too deep.

He didn't apologize. He seemed unaware that his housekeeping varied from the norm. He just asked, "What did you find out from that Hullar?"

"I didn't go see him. What happened was, I had an idea."

"You didn't strain nothing doing that?"

It must be on my forehead in glowing letters that don't show up in a mirror. "You'll like it. Be good for both of us. Here's the plan." I told him how we could make a few marks. His eye developed a malicious twinkle.

"Son, I'm maybe gonna like you after all. You ain't as dumb as you look."

"It's my disguise," I grumped. "Want to do it?"

"Why not? I can always use an extra mark. But don't you figure we ought to go fifty-fifty? When I got to take time out of my busy schedule to do all the work?"

"I figure the split's fine at two for me and one for you. I have the contract. I'll have to rewrite whatever you give me. And I'll have to hike over to the Tenderloin to deliver it."

Barking Dog shrugged. He didn't argue. "Found money," he muttered.

"Speaking of money. How do you live? Not to mention pay for all that paper?" Even junk paper isn't cheap. Papermaking is a labor-intensive industry.

"Maybe there's some with enough sense to see the truth and want to spread it." He glowered. He wasn't going to tell me squat.

Could be a helpful believer. TunFaire boasts a fine crop of lunatics, with more ripening daily. Or maybe he was stealing paper. Or maybe he had a fortune stashed with the gnomish bankers. You never know. In this town, almost nobody is what he seems.

I answered surliness with a shrug. "I'll catch you every couple days."

"Yeah. Hey! Maybe you could give me a hand."

Only at long range. His breath had taken on new freight, a heavy wine odor that combined with its previous fetor in a lethal gas. Maybe we could bottle it and send it to the Cantard. It could discourage entire Venageti brigades.

"How?"

"Some religious nut grabbed my spot while I was away."

"Set up next to him, stick close, outlast him." The man's faith wouldn't outlast Barking Dog's aroma. "That don't work, then ask me."

"All right." He was doubtful. He couldn't smell himself. His nostrils were corroded to the bone.

"See you." I had to get out. My eyes were watering. My nose was running. My head was spinning.

I didn't hurry home. I let the rain rinse the smell off me. I wondered if it would ever stop raining. Should I invest in a boat?

The weather had a bright side. Flying thunder-lizards hadn't pestered TunFaire since the rains started.

Everyone cheered when those monsters first appeared. They gobbled rats and cats and squirrels and, most especially, pigeons. Pigeons don't have many fans. But the thunder-lizards shared some of the pigeons' worst habits. The missiles they launched were both larger and more precisely targeted.

There was talk of bounties. The monsters tended to be attracted by the Hill, where the rich and powerful live. They favor high places. The upper classes and thunder-lizards both. If the latter had had the sense to stick to the slums, there would have been no dangerous talk.

9

The only warning was Dean's smirk, filled with so much childish malice I knew something was going on.

Garrett!

Oh-oh. I'd forgotten I'd left him with those evangelists.

I considered taking a powder. But, hell, it was my house. A man is king in his own castle. I stepped into the Dead Man's room. "Yeah?"

Sit down.

I sat, warily. He was too calm.

Have you contemplated the state of your immortal soul?

I believe I screeched. Next thing I knew, I was headed down the hall, staring back at his closed door with bugged eyes. Somewhere a cat meowed. This couldn't be happening to me. It wasn't real. I was going crazy. If this kept up, I'd be out there howling at the sky alongside Barking Dog.

It got worse. I ducked into the kitchen for a beer, found Dean at the table having tea with the religion women. One had a kitten in her lap. Dean seemed spellbound by the ropes of sand the other was spinning. The cat woman said, "Won't you join us, Mr. Garrett? We were just sharing the wonderful news with Dean. Won't you share the joy with us too?"

Joy? She was as joyous as the piles. She didn't know the meaning of the word. The fraud. She was smiling, but that was a domino. Everything behind it was holier-than-thou sour. She would remain constipated as long as she suffered the suspicion that somebody, somewhere, was having a good time. "Sorry. Some other time. I'm just going to grab a biscuit and run." I knew her kind. A Barking Dog with a bath, only her fantasy contained a harsh, metallic flavor of violence. Barking Dog was determined to expose imaginary devils. She wanted to scourge them with fire and sword. Yet she was painfully formal and polite. If I stopped moving for a second, she would pin me and soon drive me over the edge. She wouldn't let go till I'd gotten so damned rude I'd be embarrassed for a month.

I grabbed my biscuit and fled to my office. I asked Eleanor, "You haven't gone gaga on me too, have you?"

She gave me her best enigmatic look.

I settled behind my desk. Things were falling apart around me. I had to take charge before chaos conquered all. I had to get this storm-tossed ship back on a steady keel.

It was my own damn fault, trying to pull a fast one on the Dead Man.

I groaned. I'd just gotten comfortable, and now somebody was pounding on the front door. Nobody ever comes around except to see me. Nobody ever wants to see me unless they want me to work. Nobody ever wants me to work except when I've just gotten comfortable. Then my attitude improved. Maybe it was more evangelists. I could turn the new bunch loose on the pack already infesting the place. They could go to the theological mattresses right here. I could have a ringside seat while they fought it out, toe to illogical toe.

See. I'm an optimist. Whoever said I always look on the dark side? I did? Right. Well, when you do that, your life fills with pleasant surprises, and seldom are you disappointed.

Answering the door provided one of the disappointments.

did peep through the peephole first. I did know I wouldn't be happy once I opened up. But I didn't have much choice.

His name was Westman Block. He was the law. Such as the law is in TunFaire. He was a captain of that same Watch that couldn't catch anyone more dangerous than Barking Dog Amato. I knew him slightly, which was too well. He knew me. We didn't like each other. But I respected him more than I did most Watchmen. When he took a bribe, he stayed bought. He wasn't *too* greedy.

I opened up. "Captain. I nearly didn't recognize you out of uniform." Polite. I can manage it sometimes. I glanced around. He was alone. Amazing. His bunch run in crowds. That's one of their survival skills.

"Can we talk?" He was a small, thin character with short brown hair graying around the edges. There was nothing remarkable about him except that he seemed worried. And he was almost polite. He'd never been polite to me before. I was suspicious immediately.

A healthy dose of paranoia never hurts when you deal with the Westman Blocks.

"I have company, Captain."

"Let's walk, then. And don't call me Captain, please. I don't want anyone guessing who I am." Damn, he was working hard. Usually he talked like a longshoreman.

"It's raining out there."

"Can't put anything past you, can they? No wonder you have that reputation."

See? Just not my day. I pulled the door shut without bothering to holler to Dean. What did I have to worry about? I had a heavenly host on guard. "Why don't we scare up a beer, then? I feel the need." For about a keg, taken in one big gulp.

"Be quicker if we just walk." His little blue eyes were chips of ice. He didn't like me but he was working hard not to offend me. He wanted something bad. I noted that he'd acquired a little mustache like Morley's. Must be something going around.

"All right. I'm a civic-minded kind of guy. But maybe you could drop me one little hint?"

"You figured it already, Garrett, I know you. I need a favor I hate to ask for. A big favor. I got a problem. Whether I like it or not, you're probably the only guy I know of can solve it."

I think that was a compliment. "Really?" I swelled with newfound power. It almost matched the growth of my paranoia. I'm the kind of guy gets really nervous when my enemies start making nice on me.

"Yeah." He grumbled something that must have been in a foreign language, because no gentleman would use words like the words I thought I heard. Watch officers are all gentlemen. Just ask them. They'll clue you in good while they pick your pocket.

"What?"

"I'd better just show you. It isn't far."

I touched myself here and there, making sure I was still carrying.

After a block, during which he muttered to himself, Block said, "We got a power struggle shaping up up top, Garrett."

"What else is new?" We haven't had a big shake-up or a king bite the dust for a couple years but, overall, we change rulers more often than Barking Dog changes clothes.

"There's a reform faction forming."

"I see." Bad news for his bunch. "Grim."

"You see what I mean?"

"Yeah." I'd heard grumblings myself. But those were there all the time. Down here in the real world we don't take them seriously. All part of politics. Nobody *really* wants change. Too many people have too much to lose.

"Glad you do. Because we got something come up that gots to be tooken care of. Fast. We got the word. Else it's going to be our balls in a vise." See? He even talked like a gentleman.

"Where do I come in?"

"I hate to admit it, but there ain't none of us knows what to do." Damn!

He *was* in trouble. He *was* scared. They must have showed him a vise heated red hot, with ground glass in its jaws. "I put in some time thinking. You was the only answer. You know what to do and you're straight enough to do it. If I can get you to."

I didn't say anything. I knew I wasn't going to like what I was about to hear. Keeping my mouth shut kept my options open. Marvelous, the restraint I showed in my old age.

"You help us out with this, Garrett, you won't be sorry. We'll see you're taken care of fee-wise. And you'll be covered with the Watch from here on in."

Well, now. That would be useful. I've had my troubles with the Watch. One time they laid siege to my house. It took some doing to work that one out.

"Right. So what is it?" I had a creepy feeling.

Didn't take a genius to figure it would be something big and nasty.

"I better just show you," he insisted.

Despite his fine-sounding offer I was liking this less and less.

11

We walked only a mile but that mile took us over the edge of the world into another reality, into the antechamber of hell, the Bustee. Now I understood why he was out of uniform.

TunFaire boasts peoples of almost every intelligent race. Mostly they clump like with like in closed neighborhoods. Likewise with humans not of the ethnic majority. Breeds fall into the cracks, live in between, catch as catch can, often welcome nowhere. Two-thirds of the city is ghetto slum. Poverty is the norm.

But the Bustee is to those slums as the slums are to the Hill. People there live in tents made of rags or in shanties put together from sticks and mud and trash scavenged before the ratmen could collect it. Or they cram in a hundred to the building meant for five or ten two hundred years ago, when the structure had windows and doors and flooring that hadn't yet been torn up to burn for heat during the winter. They lived in doorways and on the street, some so poor they didn't have a grass mat for a mattress. They lived amidst unimaginable filth. The ratmen wouldn't go in there without protection. The soldiers wouldn't go in less than company-strong—if at all. Too many soldiers had come out of there and wouldn't go back even to visit.

The Bustee is the bottom. You can't roll downhill any farther. You roll that far, chances are you'll never climb back. Not till the dead wagons come.

Only the deathmen are safe in the Bustee. Each day they come with their wagons, wearing their long gray robes with the veils that conceal their faces, to collect the dead from the streets and alleys. They chant, "Bring out your dead! Bring out your dead!" as they work. They won't leave the streets to collect. They load their wagons and make their deliveries to the city crematoriums. They work from dawn to dusk, but every day they get a little further behind.

Death in the Bustee is as ugly as life.

In the Bustee there is no commodity cheaper than life.

In the Bustee there is only one commodity of any value at all. Young men. Hard young men who have survived the streets. These fellows are the only real beneficiaries of the Cantard war. They enlist as soon as they're able and use their bonuses to get whoever they can out of hell. Then, despite their hard and undisciplined youths, they work hard at being good soldiers. If they're good soldiers they can make enough to keep their families out. They go down to the Cantard and die like flies to keep their families out.

That such love should flourish, let alone survive, in the Bustee is ever an amazement to me. Frankly, I don't understand how it does. In the more affluent slums, youth seems to victimize those closest to it first.

Another world, the Bustee. They do things differently there.

Block stopped walking. I halted. He seemed to be having trouble getting his bearings. I looked around nervously. We looked too prosperous. But the streets were deserted.

Maybe it was the rain. But I doubted that. There was something in the air.

"This way," Block said. I followed, ever more alert. We saw no one till I spotted a pair of obvious Watchmen, though out of uniform, peeking from a narrow passageway between two buildings that might have been important back at the dawn of time. They were as big as they get in the Bustee. The men faded back into the passageway.

My nerves worsened. I was supposed to go back in there with a guy loved me the way Block did? But he didn't dislike me that much. Not enough to bring me down here for that kind of fun.

I stepped into the passage—and almost tripped over an old man. He couldn't have weighed more than seventy pounds. He was a skeleton with skin on it. He had just enough strength to shake. The deathmen would collect him before long.

"All the way back," Block said.

I didn't want to go. But I went. And wished I hadn't.

I like to think I developed a solid set of emotional calluses in the Marines, but that's only because my imagination can't encompass horrors worse than those I saw and survived in the war. I keep thinking there's no devil's work that can surprise me anymore.

I keep on being wrong.

There was a little open area where porters had made deliveries in a by-gone age. Several Watchmen were there. They had torches to break the gloom. They looked like they hoped the rain would drown the torches.

I didn't blame them.

The girl had been about twenty. She was naked. She was dead. None of that was remarkable. It happens.

But not the way this had happened.

Somebody had tied her hand and foot, then hung her from a beam, head down. Then they had cut her throat and bled her and gutted her like a game animal. There was no blood around, though the human body is filled with an amazing amount. I muttered, "They caught the blood and took it away." My meals for the month wanted to desert me.

Block nodded. He was having his troubles too. So were his boys. And they were angry besides. Hell, I was angry, but my anger hadn't had time to ripen.

No telling why she'd been gutted. Maybe for some of her organs. Her insides had been dumped on the ground but were gone now, carried off by dogs. They had been at the body too, some, but hadn't done much damage. Their squabbling had brought about the discovery of the corpse.

Block told me, "This is the fifth one, Garrett. All of them like this."

"All in the Bustee?"

"This's the first one down here. That we know of."

Yeah. This could happen here every day. . . . I looked at her again. No. Even in the Bustee there are limits to the sickness they'll tolerate. They don't kill for sport or ritual, they kill for passion or because killing will, directly or indirectly, put food in their mouths. This girl had been killed by some-body insane.

I said, "She came from outside." She was too healthy, too pretty.

"None have been Bustee women, Garrett. They've turned up all over town."

"I haven't heard about anything like this." I hadn't been out listening, though.

"We been trying to keep it quiet, but word's starting to get around. Which is why we're about to go in the vise. The powers that be want this lunatic and they want him sudden."

On reflection, I said, "Captain Block, sir, I don't believe you're being entirely forthright. Maybe if there'd been fifteen or twenty of them and people were getting panicky, they'd bestir themselves up there. But you're not going to convince me they give one rat's ass what happens to four or five street girls."

"They don't care, Garrett. But these ain't street girls. They was all from top families. All of them gave some perfectly good, even trivial reason for going out the days they were killed. Extended errands. Visits to friends. Everything perfectly safe."

"Yeah? There's no such thing as perfectly safe in TunFaire. And that kind of woman doesn't go anywhere without armed guards. It's a status thing. So what about their guards?"

"Most of them don't got no idea what happened. They delivered their charges to friends' houses, went on about their rat-killing. There's something going on, but the guards aren't it. Though maybe their memories would improve some on the rack. Only we ain't been authorized to go that far. Yet."

"Any leads at all?"

"Diddly. Nobody's seen or heard nothing."

That's the standard state of affairs throughout TunFaire. Nobody sees anything.

I made a sick grunting noise and forced myself to look at the victim yet again. She'd been a beauty, slim, with long black hair. Unpleasant as the truth may be, you feel it more when they waste the pretty ones. Block looked at me like he expected some blast of wisdom. "So what do you want from me?" As if I didn't know.

"Find out who did this. Give us a name. We'll take it from there."

I didn't have to ask what was in it for me. He'd told me. His word was good. Like I said, he stayed bought. "What else do you know?"

"That's it. That's all we have."

"Bullshit. Come on, Block."

"What?"

"That right there tells you a bunch just by being what it is. Especially if the others were like it."

"They were."

"All right. They gutted them. They took their blood. That stinks of dark religion or black sorcery. But if it's a cult, it can't have a base, else the bodies would have been disposed of there."

"Unless they wanted them found."

"There's the weakness in my thinking. Maybe we're supposed to think it's ritual when it's just crazy. Or maybe crazy when it's ritual. Though it's crazy for sure. Nobody sane would do that."

"You keep saying 'they.' You figure on more than one?"

I thought about it. It'd been a gut reaction. "Yeah. Somebody had to get her away from her bodyguards. Somebody had to bring her here. Somebody had to strip her and tie her and string her up and do that. I don't think a solo crazy could manage."

I flashed on a kidnapping I'd helped break up one rainy evening, went stiff and cold. Any connection seemed unlikely, but . . . "These girls got anything in common besides being high-class? They know each other? They all the same physical type?" This one couldn't have been confused with Chodo's brat, but she did have a similar build, black hair, and dark eyes.

"Age range is seventeen to twenty-two. All with dark hair and eyes except for one blonde. All between five-four and five-eight. Built pretty much alike, near as I could tell, seeing them this way."

"Five of them."

"That we know about."

There was that. In TunFaire there might be that many more not yet found or reported. "You have yourself a blue-assed bitch of a problem, Captain. These things are hard to untangle because there's nothing to grab hold of that makes any sense to anybody who isn't crazy. If you get many more, the thing will turn into a circus."

"I know that, Garrett. God damn it, that's why I came to you. Look, you want me to beg, I'll beg. Only—"

"No, Block. I don't want you to beg." That had its appeal, but I couldn't stomach it. "I want you to calm down. I want you to come walk with me in the rain and tell me everything you know. And I mean everything. Whatever little thing you hold back, to keep from embarrassing somebody important, might be the key."

I hadn't decided to get involved. Not yet. I wanted to distract him long enough to walk him over to my place so he could have a sit-down with the Dead Man. The Dead Man could sort everything stashed in his feeble mind and, probably, hand him what he needed to solve his case. Thus would I satisfy my civic obligation. I could feel smug without having to stick my neck out.

Only thing was, going back out that narrow passage, Block's boys went with us, carrying their torches. Those spat and sputtered in the drizzle and gave me more light than I'd had coming in. Which meant there was enough light for me to spot the butterflies.

There were three of them. They weren't anything special. Just little green butterflies. But how come there were butterflies dead in an alley in the Bustee?

I stopped when we reached the narrow street. "Take that old man somewhere and feed him. Get a doctor to look after him. Do whatever you have to do to get him well enough to tell us what he saw. If he saw anything."

Block told his men, "Do it."

I headed for home, Block hustling along beside me, telling me anything he thought might help. I didn't listen as closely as I could have. Besides being horrified, I was bemused by the fact that I might hold the fate of the Watch in my hands. I could destroy the useless bastards. Or maybe even force them to become some small percentage of what they were supposed to be. Hell, people will do anything to keep their jobs. Sometimes even *do* their jobs.

I wasn't used to that kind of power. Maybe I'd have to have Dean follow me around whispering in my ear to remind me I was mortal.

Dean had noticed that the door was unlocked. He'd locked it. I whooped and pounded till he tore himself away from his evangelists. When he opened up, he had a gleam in his eye that had nothing to do with salvation.

"You rogue, you." He pretended he didn't understand what I meant. Hell, a fling would be good for him and them both. If it didn't kill him.

I'd never let Westman Block enter my house before. He did so warily, like a soldier visiting an enemy stronghold.

The Dead Man is no secret. Anyone interested in such things would know he lives with me. But hardly anyone has seen him. They go into his room with all sorts of wild prejudices, then find out the real thing is worse than anything they imagined.

I told Block, "You take the chair. I need to pace."

He couldn't stop staring. "What're we doing here?"

"Old Bones there is a genius. You don't believe me, ask him. I thought we'd lay it out for him. He'll find connections, tell you where to start looking." Old Bones wasn't talking. I couldn't tell if that was a good sign or bad. I did know that if he cooperated he would bring more than genius to bear here. He'd been around a long time. Something from yesteryear might be the key to today's horror. It had happened before.

There are horrors that recur in long cycles, like locust plagues, but separated by generations. If these murders were cultist, they might fit one of those cycles.

The Dead Man wasn't talking but he was listening. He was poking around. He's damned subtle, but when he starts prying, I can tell. If I'm paying close enough attention.

Garrett. Shall we set all sham aside? Shall we abandon all childish efforts to abrade one another's nerves? I will not yet admit that we must pursue this monster, but I will stipulate that we owe the situation a close look.

"You grow up, I'll grow up."

Block gave me a strange look. He hadn't heard the Dead Man's end. The Dead Man can do that if he wants. It makes some of our conversations spooky.

Excellent. I will set my concern for your soul in abeyance for the moment.

Oh, boy. He wasn't going to let me off. Those women had offended his sense of rationality. He hates people who won't examine beliefs critically. Most of the time he hides it when he deals with me, but he holds the majority of humankind in contempt. Of the gods-know-how-many sentient species in the world, we humans are the only ones who insist on fervent belief in things logic and our senses demonstrate to be implausible. Amongst other races those who stumble into never-never-lands of wishful thinking are considered insane and are dealt with about the way we deal with Barking Dog. Or more harshly. Other races don't make priests out of their nuts, then give them money and follow them wherever they lead.

"I take it you're going to handle this, Garrett," Block said. He was nervous as hell. Most people are around the Dead Man. He has a considerable reputation, all of it deserved. He's done some amazing things since I've known him.

"We're considering it." I was fighting myself. Laziness and the desire not to get involved in another bizarre case warred with outrage. Outrage was ahead by a nose. The white knight had been on the shelf too long, his only chance to strut his stuff his rescue of Chodo's spooky daughter. But the white knight has his weaknesses. While he doesn't mind charging full tilt against a visible villain, rusty sword flailing, he hates having to hunt the villain down. Legwork buries his resolve faster than anything the hard boys can do by way of threat or violence. And this thing would be solved by legwork.

Relax, Garrett. It should not be so bad as you anticipate. I saw Block jump, so knew the Dead Man had included him in this time. *Captain Block. I sense that you have a great deal hanging upon the outcome of the investigation you propose.*

Block turned pale, took on kind of a green tinge around the edges. Having somebody talk right into your head is not a reassuring experience. Not

the first time. And especially so when you're a guy who has a whole ency-
clopedia of corruption stashed and doesn't want it out where the world can
see. I guess you'd say it was a measure of his distress and determination that
he coped so well. He bounced back quickly. "Yes. There's a lot of heat from
the top of the Hill. It'll get hotter every time some dizzy bitch gets herself
offed."

You are certain there will be more?

"Damn straight. What do you think?"

I think you are correct. The Dead Man was all business now. *The killings
will continue and will come more and more rapidly until the people responsible are destroyed. I think we are up against something like nothing any of us
has seen before. The evidence I glean from your minds tells me this is the work
of a compulsive killer who cannot help doing what he is doing and who will
have to do it again, ever more often, to appease the devil that drives him. But
it also tells me he is not doing this without help.*

I asked, "You figure there's a connection with—?" With what had happened at Morley's place. Only he cut me short.

Yes. We had something he didn't want handed to Block. *Garrett, I see
you shrinking from the legwork this will entail. You are correct in your estimate. This will require talking extensively with everyone even remotely involved. The families of the dead women. Their guards. The people who found
them, and the Watchmen who followed up. People in the neighborhoods
where the bodies were found.*

He knows how to beat a guy down. I shrank with every word. I was the
size of a mouse. I looked for a hole in the baseboard so I could scoot off and
hide. He was talking about the rest of my life.

I do legwork because it's what I do; talk to people and talk to people and
poke and prod until things start to happen. But I don't like it, partly because
I'm lazy, but mostly because of the people. I never cease to be amazed and
appalled by the sheer scope of human wickedness.

You are not considering our resources, Garrett.

Right. I was busy feeling sorry for myself.

*We have the Watch. A thousand men for legwork. Is that not so, Captain?
Will not every man of the Watch throw himself into this with the greatest
vigor?*

"It's our asses if we don't. They're already hinting. We have another five
murders, I figure the Watch is out of business."

Break my heart.

I saw what the Dead Man meant. I'd been too involved in myself. The

Watchmen would do anything to cover their asses. Maybe even their jobs. We just had to grab them by their instinct for self-preservation.

Then do as I tell you. I want to interview the bodyguards and the parents myself. Also those who found the corpses. Your men will canvass the neighborhoods where the women were found. Also the areas where they were seized. I doubt you will gain much cooperation, but cooperation is unnecessary. Even you Watchmen will have developed a rudimentary sense for when someone is not being forthcoming. Bring any such persons to me. I will open them up.

I marveled. The Dead Man makes me look hyper. Usually I have to threaten mayhem just to get his attention when there's work to do. He was jumping into this one headlong. I hadn't agreed to do anything yet. His enthusiasm suggested a secret agenda. Or he knew something he wasn't sharing. I eyed him narrowly as he continued with Block, telling him what times he wanted whom to come be interviewed.

Suspicion and paranoia become habits in this business. You take fits where you don't even trust yourself.

When the Dead Man takes a notion to snooze, he can hang in there for months. And when he's awake, he can go around the clock for days. He had that in mind. Poor old Dean was going to die answering the door.

Block had to borrow pen and paper to remember all his instructions. It took him half an hour to write them down. I paced and worried and wondered. Then the Dead Man dismissed the Watchman. I walked him to the front door.

"You'll never regret this, Garrett. I guarantee. We clean this up, you got a free pass for life."

"Sure." I know how long gratitude lasts. About as long as it takes for the bill to come due. Especially in TunFaire. The only guy I know who sticks to that kind of promise is Chodo Contague. He used to drive me crazy repaying imaginary debts.

That gave me a shiver. Old Chodo always paid his debts. And he owed me a big one.

I closed the door behind Block, put Chodo out of mind, went charging back to find out what the hell old Chuckles thought he was doing.

N *ot yet, Garrett. Dean!* The Dead Man did not often extend his mind touch beyond his room. That was a courtesy he extended us. *Get rid of those harridans. Commend them to your nieces. We have a commission.*

"His nieces?" I hurried into his room. "You want to create monsters?" Dean had a platoon of spinster nieces, all front-runners for Miss Homely TunFaire. They drove him to despair. Which was why he had conscripted himself as a full-time member of my household. He couldn't take it anymore. "Can you imagine that pack in pursuit of a mission from God?"

Dean has sense enough to avoid that eventuality. While we await him, I will tell you what to do. Backtrack from events at Mr. Dotes's place. But first bring Mr. Dotes and Mr. Tharpe to see me. We will want their help.

" 'We' might want it, but how are 'we' going to afford it? My share of what I'm getting to watch Barking Dog won't—"

Captain Block will assume expenses. You should pay closer attention. I quoted an exorbitant fee. He was desperate enough not to quibble.

"If they're as scared as he puts on, they could put up enough from bribe money to pay anything."

Exactly. We have been handed an unprecedented opportunity. Where he's concerned, money has no provenance. It's never dirty, only the people who handle it are. *I intend to pursue it with vigor.*

With my vigor, he meant. "That's the reason you're jumping on this?" I didn't believe it.

*Let us say that I find my mind growing as flabby and slothful as you al-
lowed your body to become. I must get into shape before it is too late. I am not
yet prepared to slide into oblivion.*

Oblivion. I put that away where I could find it next time he started in on
the condition of my immortal soul.

What he said sounded good. I didn't believe it. And he knew that. But
he didn't let me press. *There is no time to waste. Get Mr. Tharpe and Mr.
Dotes.*

Mr. Tharpe didn't want to get got. He'd gotten rid of Billie and had replaced
her with a little blonde who could have been her sister. The new hadn't worn
off enough for him to see that. He wanted to stay home and play.

"Anyway, it ain't even dark out yet, Garrett."

"You only work at night now?"

"Getting in the habit, doing these odd jobs for Licks."

"So sunlight for me. Talk to the Dead Man. You don't want the work, no
harm done. I'll get somebody else. Won't be as good, but I'll make do."
Never hurts to butter him up.

"What's shaking?"

"A serial killer. A real psycho. His Nibs can fill you in. I don't know why
he wants you. He just started spouting orders like a fountain."

"Okay. I'll talk to him." He looked at his friend. She scorched me with a
lethal stare.

I said, "I got to see Morley," and got out of there before the woman
carved their initials in my trunk.

Morley's place was sparsely populated. It had just opened. His customers
are like the stars, seldom seen before dark. Those in there then were early
bats trying to get a jump on their competition.

Nobody got excited when I walked in. Nobody knew me. The guy behind
the counter was new. He was a skinny little half-elf like Morley, handsome
as hell but barely old enough to think about taking advantage of that. He
was trying to grow a mustache.

It was catching. "I need to see Morley," I told him. "Name's Garrett. Tell
him it *is* business and there's a shitpot in it."

The kid looked me straight in the eye. "Morley? Who the hell is Morley?
I don't know any Morley."

One of those. "Kid, I'll take into account the fact that you're new. I'll take
into account the fact that you're young and dumb, and figure you got to be
a wiseass. When I'm done accounting, I just might pull you over the bar and

pound away till Morley comes down to see about all the screaming. Get on the tube."

The audience wasn't much, but it did exist. The kid thought he had to show me. Quick as an eyeblink he showed me a razor. Elves have a love affair with sharp steel, especially the young ones. He was so predictable I was there with my head-knocker as fast as he was with the blade. I popped his knuckles. He yowled like a stomped cat. The razor flew down the counter. The audience gave us a hand. And a mountain of a man lumbered out of the kitchen.

"Garrett. What you doing?" This was Sarge, another of Morley's old hands. He came out of the same production batch as Puddle.

"I asked to see Morley. Kid pulled a razor."

Sarge shook his head sadly. "What you want to go do that for, Spud? Man wants to see Morley, give Morley a howl. Morley wants to have him friends like this, that's his lookout."

"Spud?" I asked. What kind of name was Spud? Not even a dwarf would tag his kid Spud.

"What we call him, Garrett. Name's really Narcisio. Morley's nephew. His sister's kid. Got to be more than she could handle. Morley brought him down here so he could straighten him out."

Meantime, the kid talked to the voice tube that connected to Morley's office.

I shook my head. Morley Dotes going to set somebody's feet on the straight and narrow? Morley, whose real career is cutting throats and breaking bones and running an occasional con or even a straight rip-off if the stakes are big enough? My pal Morley?

Sarge put on a big grin. "I know what you're thinking. But you know Morley."

I knew Morley. He could believe mutually contradictory things at the same time, with religious fervor. His whole life was a tangle of contradictions. He lived them all with passion. He could sell you anything because he believed every word he said when he said it. That was why he did well with the ladies. And no matter that he might take up a completely new passion five minutes hence. He was completely committed now.

Morley had done some good where Spud was concerned. The kid wasn't happy about being shown up, but he put it away from him. He told me, "Morley will be down in a few minutes. You want something while you're waiting?"

"Puddle still got his keg back there? Tap me one off it. He owes me a couple gallons."

Sarge chuckled. "Whyn't you finish the whole thing? I love to watch him puff up like a big old toady frog when he comes in and finds out somebody's been at his keg."

"I'll do my best. Company?" I jerked a thumb skyward.

"Yeah. His luck's coming back."

"Glad somebody's is."

Sarge chuckled again. "You shoulda married that Maya when she asked. She was all right." He patted Spud's shoulder, said, "You done all right. Just don't be so fast with that razor. Next guy might not be nice like Garrett." He headed for the kitchen. I wondered what he was doing back there. I wouldn't trust him anywhere near food in preparation. Not even the horse fodder they serve at Morley's place.

I figured the kid's ego needed a boost so I sort of sideways apologized for being so hardass. The audience had lost interest, so he could halfway apologize too. "I only been here a couple days, Mr. Garrett." He recognized the name now. "Always somebody coming in here to pester my uncle. You looked like an unhappy husband."

I laughed. "Not a husband, just unhappy." Morley isn't satisfied unless he's taking needless risks. Like refusing to fool around with a woman if she isn't married. He used to have a bad gambling problem too, but he got over that.

Morley came downstairs looking smug. Without saying so, he wanted me to know his life was going great. Way better than mine. I couldn't argue. Lots of people's lives were going better than mine.

"What's going on, Garrett?"

"Need some privacy to talk."

"You on a job?"

"This time. Dead Man says we might need to subcontract. Also, he wants to pick your brain."

"Take the table in the corner."

I picked up the beer Spud had drawn off Puddle's keg. "You have so many of them up there you can't hide them all?" Usually we went to his office to discuss business.

"No. Place is just a mess. Got a little carried away."

That one he didn't make me believe. Maybe it wasn't a woman. Maybe they wanted me to think it was a woman because it had to do with his real business.

I didn't ask. I just went to the table and sat, then told him what there was to tell. He listened well. He can do that when he wants.

"You think there's a connection with what happened the other night?"

"I don't know. The Dead Man thinks so. And he knows how to handi-cap."

"Interesting."

"You'd say something else if you'd seen that girl."

"I expect so. I don't approve of killing people who don't ask for it. I mean, I find interesting the idea of taking money from the Watch for once, instead of seeing it go their way."

I raised an eyebrow. It's one of my finest skills.

He said, "That's the way it works, Garrett. I'm not under Chodo's protec-tion. I don't want to be part of the outfit. There's always a price for indepen-dence."

Made sense when I considered it. There were a thousand Watchmen and only a handful of guys in his bunch. As long as the Watch didn't get greedy, it would be easier for him to pay than fight. Not that he would like it. But he was very much the pragmatist.

The Watch wouldn't bother Chodo, of course. A *lot* of people are be-holden to him. And he wouldn't take kindly to any attempt to muscle his operations.

Morley thought about what I'd told him. "Let me finish up upstairs. I'll walk over to your place with you."

I watched him climb the stairs. What did he have going? He'd set it up so he'd be sure he was with me when I left. So I wouldn't hang around out-side to see who left after he did? That didn't make sense. If I wanted to know, I could ask the Dead Man after Morley talked to him. If I let the Dead Man know I wanted him to peek.

Ah, paranoia.

aucerhead opened the door. "A butler," Morley cracked. "You're coming up in the world, Garrett."

Saucerhead didn't crack a frown. "Who shall I say is calling, sir?" He filled the doorway. A charging bull couldn't have moved him. Morley didn't when he started inside.

"Hey! What gives? Check it out, big guy. It's raining out here."

I said, "I'm thinking about getting into the boat business. Might be the coming thing."

Saucerhead cocked his big ugly phiz like he was listening. He was waiting for the Dead Man's go-ahead. Even on us. Which meant Old Bones had convinced him anything could happen. Saucerhead was the type to make damn sure it didn't while he was on the job.

The Dead Man had him not trusting his own eyes? What was this? What did he suspect?

Saucerhead finally grunted, stepped aside. Like he didn't think it was such a hot idea. Morley shot me a puzzled look, headed down the hall. He ducked into the Dead Man's room. "Garrett says there's something sinister about what happened at my place last night."

For twenty minutes I felt like an orphan. "Five of them?" Morley said. "They're keeping a good wrap on it, then. I only heard about one, last month, down at the Landing."

I jumped in. "That was the one before the one before the one they found this morning. This nut is on a shrinking time cycle. After the first one he waited six weeks. Then four weeks for the one in the Landing. Then three weeks, then a couple days over two weeks to get this last one."

"Unless there's some in there we don't know about."

"They'd be hard to miss, all of them strung up with their throats cut and the guts gone. And the Watch hasn't had any reports of daughters missing from the Hill."

"The guy doing this has got to be doing some homework up front. He's not just hanging out on the corner waiting for the right rich girl. He's picking his targets and he's working several at the same time."

"What makes you think that?"

"He blew the snatch on Chodo's kid but grabbed another woman in time to have her hung up this morning."

Crazy don't mean stupid, my old mom used to say. I've seen that proved often enough. The man doing this *was* doing a lot of planning. He'd be aware that his fun would cause a stir. He'd be real careful.

"Morley, the guy made a real dumb move last night. Maybe double dumb. He did it in front of witnesses. And he went for Chodo's kid. He'd get less heat going after the King's sister."

"You remember she was scared when she came in. I have a notion the snatch was blown once already and somebody was desperate to cover his tracks. Far as going after Chodo's kid . . . What you have to do with this character—and I can't myself—is put yourself inside his head. Try to think like he does. He's a genius and knows it. He's been messed up and playing out psychotic dramas since he was a kid and he keeps getting away with it. Maybe he doesn't quite see the rest of us as real anymore. Maybe we're just things, like the bugs and rats he started out on. Maybe he thinks there can't be any kickbacks as long as he's careful. In his mind Chodo might not be a worry any bigger than Dean is."

I understood but wasn't sure Morley's ideas held any water. I didn't know what to think. TunFaire has killers by the battalion, but none like this. Muckers and cold-blooded pros were the multiple murderers I knew. This monster was a hybrid, a mutant.

"Last night is the only starting place we have," Morley said. "We have to talk to the girl."

I made an ugly noise.

"I know. Means the outfit gets in on the hunt."

I was surprised they weren't already. I said so.

Morley observed, "Means she didn't mention it when she got home.

Maybe she was doing something her father wouldn't approve." He wore a frown, though, like he thought that couldn't be quite right.

"Boyfriend?"

"She's human."

I backed off inside and considered, bitten by sudden suspicion. She'd run into Morley's place when she was in trouble. She'd shown no sign of knowing him, but . . . No. He wouldn't. His need to take risks wouldn't push him that far. Would it?

The Dead Man intervened. *Gentlemen, I sense the approach of persons I must interview. I will be at that all night. Garrett. I suggest you rest till morning. I may have suggestions for you then.* Apparently he'd shuffled through Morley's head and had gotten what he wanted. If there'd been anything there.

Sometimes that was arguable.

I was wound up more than I realized. "I could start—" Like I was eager to get to work.

If I calculate accurately, we have eleven or twelve days before the killer acts again. That should be ample time. The wheels of the law and Mr. Contague's organization will grind every clue fine by then. There is no need to rush and risk doing ourselves harm.

What? He was going to stamp his approval on my loafing? I'm no fool. I hustled Morley out the front door, brought in the couple I ran into there, introduced them to the Dead Man as the parents of the first victim, then headed upstairs.

s soon as I was flat on my back I thought of fifty things I should have discussed with Morley. Like did he have any idea who those brunos were who stormed into his place after Chodo's brat? He would have tried to find out. I knew him. After he'd brooded awhile he'd have decided that booting them around and chucking them out in the rain wasn't good enough. He'd want a whack at the guy who'd sent them.

He might be miles ahead of me.

I let my thoughts drift back to what had happened, went over it, seeking a clue.

Nothing that special about the three men. If you had the money, you could recruit a thousand like them. Only thing remarkable was that they'd dared invade a place owned by Morley Dotes. Local professionals knew better. Those three hadn't had out-of-town accents. Therefore, they weren't professionals. Not streetside, anyhow. I didn't doubt they were professional thugs.

Which led me off blue-skying. Who had thugs on staff who wouldn't get into the streets much? Only priests and people on the Hill. The priest angle was so juicy I set it aside to look at the other first.

Off the Hill? A lunatic up there would be in a fine position to observe the movements of prospective victims. I tried to recall the appearance of the old geek with butterfly indigestion. That didn't match any Hill people I knew.

What about the coach? I recalled it, though details were getting vague.

Big, black, and fancy. A custom four-horse job. Silver brightwork. The killer had money.

Couldn't be many coaches like it.

I fought it for fifteen minutes but it was a struggle foredoomed. Eventually I swung my legs off the bed, got up, and hunked downstairs. So much for good intentions. I donned a cloak and, marvel of marvels, a hat. The hat was Dean's. I didn't think he'd miss it.

Saucerhead came to see what I was up to. "I'm going out for a while. Shouldn't be long." I scowled at the closed door to the small front room. "Tell Dean that if that cat's still here when I get back, they both go out in the rain."

I went to see a friend. His name was Playmate. He was nine feet tall and black as coal, big enough to make Saucerhead nervous. But he was as gentle as a lamb and religious to boot. He was in the stable business. He owed me. Early in both our careers I'd saved him from human sharks.

He never ceased to amaze me. No matter what time I showed, no matter how inconvenient my appearance, he was always glad to see me. This time was no exception. "Garrett!" he boomed when I strolled into his stable. He dropped a curry comb and bounded toward me, swept me up in a ferocious hug. He turned me loose only after I started squawking like a bagpipe.

"Damn, Playmate, sometimes I wish you was a woman. Nobody else is excited to see me."

"Your own fault. Come around more often. Maybe you wear out your welcome."

"Yeah. It's been a rough year. I've been neglecting my friends."

"'Specially that little bit, Maya."

I forgot my mission momentarily. "You've seen Maya? I thought she left town."

"Been a while, come to think. She used to come around, help out some, just 'cause she liked the horses."

"I knew there had to be *something* wrong with her."

The look he gave me told me more than he could have said in words. Maya had cried on his shoulder. I couldn't really look him in the eye. He said, "You've been having troubles all the way around, I hear. Miss Tinnie. Somebody named Winger."

He was implying it, so I said it. "Yeah. I have a way with the girls. The wrong way."

"Come over here and sit. I have a pony keg I've been nursing. Should be a sip or two left."

Which was all right by me, except it would be warm brew. Playmate liked his beer warm. I prefer mine just about ready to turn to chunks. But he was offering beer. Right then I had an inclination to surround several gallons. I settled on an old saddle, accepted a big pewter mug. Playmate plopped his behind on a sawhorse.

"Trouble is," he told me, "those gals all been growing up, getting interested in something besides fun."

"I know." It's hell, getting older.

"Don't mind me. It's the preacher getting out."

I knew that too. Back when I saved his bacon, he'd been thinking of getting into the religion racket on his own. He'd have done good but wouldn't have gotten very big. TunFaire has a thousand cults. Always there are plenty of disenchanted would-be believers eager to sign on with the thousand-and-oneth. Playmate had taken a look around, decided that he was insufficiently cynical and dishonest to make a real go of it. He may be religious personally, but he's practical.

"The preacher is right, Playmate. And it's maybe him I need to talk to."

"Problem?"

"Yeah."

"Thought so, soon as I saw you."

What a genius. With Playmate I commit the same sin as with Morley. I don't go around unless I need help.

I resolved to do better in the future.

Right, Garrett. Duck! Here comes a low-flying pig.

I laid it out for Playmate. I didn't hold back. My story upset him so badly I was sorry I hadn't softened it some. "Who'd want to go and do something like that, Garrett? Killing little girls."

They hadn't been little, but that was beside the point. "I don't know. I mean to find out. That's where I thought you might help. That coach outside Morley's wasn't any junker or rental. I don't think there's another like it. Nearest I've ever seen is Chodo Contague's coach. And it didn't have the gaudy silver brightwork."

Playmate frowned at every mention of Morley Dotes. He didn't approve of Morley. He frowned again when I mentioned Chodo. If Playmate was the kind to keep a little list, the first name on his would be Chodo Contague. He sees Chodo as a cause of social ills rather than as an effect.

"Custom coach?"

"I'd guess so."

"And similar to Chodo Contague's."

"A little bigger and even fancier. Silver trim and a lot of carving. Tell you anything? Know whose it is?"

"Don't know that, but I can make a good guess who built it. If it was built in TunFaire."

Bingo! I almost let out a whoop. Maybe I did let out a whoop. Playmate looked at me oddly for a moment, then grinned shyly. "Helped some?"

"As soon as you tell me that coachmaker's name."

"Atwood. Linden Atwood."

That name meant nothing to me. At my income level I don't buy many custom-built coaches. I don't hang out with those who do. "Where would I find Mr. Linden Atwood, coachmaker?"

"Tinkery Row."

Excellent. That narrowed it right down to a whole neighborhood where potters potted, tinkers tinked, and at least one wainwright wrighted wains. The neighborhood lies south of the Tenderloin and north of the brewery district, stretching east to west beginning a few blocks in from the river, and parallels a street called Tinker's Lane. That is one of the oldest parts of town. Some artisan families have been established there for centuries.

Playmate glanced toward the stable door. "Going to be getting dark soon. You figure on going down there right away?"

"Yes."

"That's not a nighttime neighborhood. Pretty soon they'll all close up, have supper, then the menfolk will head for the corner tavern."

"So it's late. It's already too late for five women. The Dead Man thinks this guy won't kill again for another eleven or twelve days, but I don't count on it."

Playmate nodded, conceding the point. "I'll walk with you."

"You don't need to do that. Just tell me where—"

"Trouble follows you. I better go with you. Takes a certain touch to deal with Atwood, anyway."

"You've done enough." I didn't want to put Playmate at risk. He didn't deserve it. "My job is dealing with people."

"Your style is maybe a touch too direct and forceful for Atwood. I'll walk you down."

Arguing with Playmate is like arguing with a horse. Don't get you anywhere and just irritates the horse.

Maybe if he would get into another line I'd visit more often. Any line where there weren't so many horses around. I don't get along with those monsters. Their whole tribe is out to get me.

"I'll get my hat and cloak," he said, knowing he'd won before I conceded. I looked around, wondering where he'd hidden the circus tent he'd wear. I spied a horse eyeballing me. It looked like it was thinking about kicking its stall down so it could trot over and dance a flamenco on my tired bones.

"Don't waste time. The devils have spotted me. They're cooking something up."

Playmate chuckled. He has one big blind spot. He thinks my problem with horses is a joke. Boy, do they have him fooled.

We stopped to have supper, my treat. Which strained my budget severely. Playmate ate like a horse, but not cheap hay. "You're on expenses, Garrett."

"I was just figuring on cleaning the Watch out of pocket change, not driving them into bankruptcy."

He got a good laugh out of that one. Simple pleasures for simple minds.

Tinkery Row is all light industry, single-family operations that produce goods without producing much smoke. The nastier stuff is down south, the nastiest across the river. The air gets chunky and takes on flavor when the wind is from the east, past the smelters and mills. Their stench can make you long for the heavy wood and coal smoke of winter or the rotten garbage of summer.

Tinkery Row is four blocks wide and eight blocks long, approximately, measuring by normal city blocks. There aren't many of those in TunFaire. There never has been any planning applied to the city's growth. Maybe we need a good fire to burn it all down so we can start over and do it right.

Playmate insisted on sticking with me. He said he knew the neighborhood and knew Linden Atwood. I gave up. I needed to spend some time with somebody who wasn't going to give me a lot of hassle.

I let him lead but insisted on setting the pace myself. My legs weren't long enough to match his prodigious stride. He strolled. I scampered. Once we got into Tinkery Row he chatted up people who still had their doors open hoping for a late sale. I huffed and puffed. Tinkery Row is a safe neighborhood. The villains stay away because the natives have this habit of ganging up. Justice is quick and informal and applied with considerable enthusiasm.

Everyone seemed to know Playmate. Nobody knew me, but my feelings weren't hurt. That's a plus in my line. I puffed out, "You spend a lot of time down here?"

"Grew up here. One street over. Pop made tack." Which explained the interest in horses, maybe. "But I changed in the war. Came back too nervous, just couldn't fit in. Kind of slow and timeless around here. People don't change. Get fixed in their ways. I could probably tell you who is where doing what right now, though I haven't been around for months. Right now Linden Atwood is having supper with his missus at home. His sons are having supper with their families, and his apprentices are eating bread and cheese while they clean the shop. About a half hour from now they'll start drifting into the Bicks and Kittle. Each one will buy a pint of dark. They'll all go into a corner and nurse their pints for an hour, then somebody will say he'd better get on home and get to bed 'cause he has to make an early start in the morning. Old Linden will tell him to stay, have another on him, and he'll buy the round. They'll all sit another hour, find the bottoms of their mugs at the same time, then they'll get up and go home."

A thrill a minute, life in Tinkery Row.

It was the longest speech I'd ever heard from Playmate. While he made it he led me to and into the corner tavern with the name I found unfathomable. Most taverns do have odd names, like Rose and Dolphin, but that's because most people can't read. A sign with a couple of symbols will hang over the door, serving as both name and address. Bicks and Kittle didn't have a sign, and when I finally asked Playmate about the name, he told me those were the families who ran the place.

Some mysteries just aren't worth unraveling.

Playmate studied the layout. The place wasn't crowded. He held me back while he chose a table. "We don't want to trespass on the regulars." Apparently they became disturbed when casual trade usurped their traditional tables. Playmate chose a small one in the middle of the small room. It appeared less shopworn than most.

Playmate ordered but I paid. He asked for the dark beer. "You can get any beer you want as long as you're willing to go down the street for your pale or lager."

"Real set in their ways." I do like the occasional dark beer, though. And this proved to be a fine brew with a strong malt flavor. I like to taste the malt more than the hops.

"Hardheaded. Atwood comes in, let me pick the time and do the talking."

I nodded. Made sense.

The place began filling. Young and old, they were all cut from one bolt. I wondered if there would be a problem, what with Playmate's being the only dark face in the place. Nope. Soon guys started dropping by to exchange a few words of greeting while eyeing me sidelong, curiously, but with manners too steady to express that curiosity aloud.

Playmate identified the apprentice coachmakers when they arrived. "Atwood never took apprentices till a few years ago. The war's fault. He lost a couple sons, then none of his grandsons made it back. Has three still doing their five years, though. Maybe they'll get lucky."

The apprentices were old for that. Middle twenties. "In Atwood's place I'd take kids, educate them so they could avoid the line units. Supply outfits always need wainwrights."

Playmate looked at me like I'd missed the point of everything he'd said tonight. "Where would he find kids? Any Tinkery family with kids would bring them up in the family trade."

All right. I did miss that, sort of.

The surviving sons appeared, then Linden Atwood himself. Linden Atwood was that rare creature, a man who fitted his name and looked like a coachmaker. In my preconceptions. He was a skinny little dink, old, with leathery skin, all his own hair, intelligent eyes, and plenty of bounce. His hands were hands that still did their share of work. He stood like he had a board nailed to his back, seemed confident of his place in the world. He and his crew were one big happy family. He was no aloof patriarch. He, his three sons, and four apprentices got into a spirited argument about whether or not the King's Rules were turning TunFaire's football players into gangs of whining candyassed wimps.

Now there was something worth arguing about. King's Rules went into effect before I was born.

Karentine football, or rugger, is so rough now I wouldn't want my enemies playing. In Old Style football I think the only rule was: no edged weapons.

"I take it football is popular down here."

"Serious business. Best players come out of Tinkery. Every block has a team. Kids start out as soon as they can walk."

Not only hardheaded but not very bright. But I kept that thought to myself. "Not very tolerant" goes along with the other two, most places.

"Played some myself when I was younger," Playmate told me.

"Why am I not surprised?" He'd have made a team all by himself.

Playmate was slick. He managed to insinuate an opinion into an argument so old it was obvious ritual, elicited a response because, apparently, in his olden days he'd been a star. Before I understood what was happening, he and I were part of Atwood's crowd. I pursued Playmate's advice diligently. The Dead Man would have been impressed by how long I kept my mouth shut.

In time the Atwoods veered from the tried and true long enough to betray polite curiosity concerning Playmate's presence. Playmate gave them a big grin, like he was mocking himself for taking anything seriously. "My pal Garrett and me, we're on sort of a crusade."

Those guys understood a crusade. They were religious. Real salt of the earth and backbone of the nation. Hadn't had an original thought in generations.

Pardon. I do get overly critical at times.

Curiosity levels rose. Playmate played with them a minute, then said, "I better let Garrett tell it. He's the one been closest to it. I'm just trying to lend a hand."

I pictured Block exploding if he heard I was hanging out his dirty laundry all over town, grinned, told the story of the dead girls. The Atwoods were properly horrified. I played to that, noted the old man paying closer attention than the others, who just wanted to be entertained.

I said, "So right now it looks like the only way to trace this monster is through his coach."

Everybody got it then. The whole gang got quiet and grim. All eyes turned to the old man. He considered me neutrally. "You suspect that coach came from my shop, Mr. Garrett?"

"I have no idea, Mr. Atwood. Playmate says you're the premier coachmaker in TunFaire. If it was built here, according to him, you're the only man with the talent to have built it."

"I expect so. Describe it again."

I did, recalling every possible detail.

The sons were less skilled than he at concealing their thoughts. I knew that coach had been built by Linden Atwood. The question was, would the man expose his buyer?

He would. "We delivered that coach, built to strict and exacting specifications, about three years back, Mr. Garrett. I do not believe in false humility. It was the finest coach ever built in TunFaire. I will accept responsibility for that, but I refuse any blame."

"Excuse me?"

One son muttered, "Damn thing's jinxed."

The old man glared. "Madame Tallia Lethe, wife and mother of the Icemasters Direfear, commissioned it. Three months after she took delivery, there was an accident. She fell. A wheel rolled over her head."

Oh, boy. "I knew we could get some big-time sorcerers into this." Karentine wizards mainly belong to the Elemental Schools: Earth, Air, Fire, and Water. The Windmasters and Storm Wardens of the Air school are common, Firelords more so. There may be Earth schoolers elsewhere in Karenta, but none in TunFaire. Water-school types are almost as rare. "I didn't know we had any Icemasters here."

"We don't," the old man said. "The woman lived here. The Icemasters are dead, anyway. Crossbones Bight."

Ah. *The* big naval battle of the War. We got our Karentine asses kicked. Unfortunately for the Venageti, a naval triumph hadn't meant much strategically. "I see," I said, not seeing at all.

"Madame had no heirs. The estate passed to the Crown. The Crown agents auctioned everything. Lord Hellsbreath bought the coach."

There was a name to conjure nightmares.

The only Hellsbreath I recalled was no healthier than Madame Lethe. "He had some bad luck himself, right?"

"He was murdered. The assassin got away."

"He was in the coach when it happened," a son volunteered.

"Crossbow bolt right in the eye," another said. He demonstrated with enthusiastic gestures and sound effects.

"Then who got the coach?"

"Duchess of Suhnerkhan. Lady Hamilton."

I knew that one. "Does seem like it was unlucky." The King's great-aunt, Lady Hamilton, had decided to visit the family estate at Okcok. She hadn't bothered with an escort, though there'd been a full moon out. Werewolves had given her a fatal set of hickeys.

Linden Atwood grunted but conceded nothing.

"That was a year and a half ago. I guess it's changed hands a few more times?"

"No. Crown Prince Rupert brought it back to town and stored it in the coachhouse behind Lady Hamilton's town house. Far as I know, it hasn't been out since." The old man produced a pipe and pipeweed. He filled up, lit up, leaned back, closed his eyes, puffed, and thought. The clan waited quietly. I followed their lead. Playmate signaled for another round of the dark. On me, naturally.

The beer's arrival wakened Atwood. He tilted forward, drained half his mug, wiped foam with the back of a hand, belched, said, "I don't put no stock in this jinx stuff, Garrett." We were pals now. I'd bought him a beer. "But was I you, I'd be careful. Seems like everybody that gets near that coach gets dead." He frowned. He didn't like that at all. What if word got out? What if people started thinking it was the coachmaker's fault?

"I'm not much on haunts and jinxes," I told him. "But if that coach *is* jinxed, you got any notion how come?"

"Beats the shit out of me." He guzzled the other half of his beer. "Shit happens. Sometimes it don't make no sense."

Playmate horned in. "Thanks, Mr. Atwood. Sure was good of you to talk to us." He nudged me with a knee, got up. I wondered why he was in a hurry, but I'd promised to follow his lead. I piled on my share of thanks and excused myself, followed Playmate into the rain.

"What was that? How come the run-out?"

"Atwood was getting glassy-eyed. In about a minute he was going to start in on his boys that didn't make it home from the Cantard. I thought you might want to get some sleep tonight."

"Oh."

"Yeah. You got to feel sorry for the guy. But that don't mean you got to go live in his hell with him. He's got to lay his own ghosts himself."

True. But I was surprised that Playmate thought so. I pulled my cloak tighter. There was enough wind to make the night cold.

"Past my bedtime, Garrett. Hope all that helped."

"You hope? Hell, it cracked the thing. All I need now is to find out who's been using that coach." And how hard could that be? I mean, the Crown Prince's duties included running Karentine internal security. The TunFaire Watch were one obscure arm of the many he oversaw. And if what Block said was true, the heat on the Watch had good old Rupert behind it.

"Come around more often, Garrett," Playmate said. "At least soon enough to let me know how this comes out." He strode off like he was late for a date with one of his mares. I stood absorbing some rain for a moment, startled, then shrugged. Playmate did these things. He didn't know he was being rude and unsociable.

What now?

16

Morley's place, that's what now.

It wasn't that far out of my way. I dropped by. My reception was no more charming than before. Maybe not as good. More people departed. The others seemed edgy, except for Saucerhead's pal Licks, who was at the same shadowed corner table stoned out of this world.

Puddle gave me a huge scowl, glanced down at his keg. I told him, "That rat Sarge said he was going to blame it on me. Morley here?"

Puddle already had a finger pointed skyward and an eyebrow up. I nodded to make sure he understood that I wanted to see Morley as well as to know if he was home. With Puddle you have to take it by the numbers. He don't fill in the gaps so good.

He was the kind of guy who thought if you couldn't solve a problem with a right cross or a club, then it wasn't a problem in the first place and therefore didn't need solving. Ignore it and it would go away.

Puddle grunted, growled at the speaking tube, fluttered a hand to indicate that I should go on up. Apparently Morley didn't have company.

I climbed the stairs, tiptoed to Morley's door, listened before I knocked. I didn't hear anything. Usually there was scurrying as somebody's wife headed for cover. All I heard was Morley telling me to come in.

I opened the door. Something zipped past the end of my nose. Morley was behind his desk, his feet up, leaning back, tossing darts. I didn't recognize the painted face serving as his target. "You doing the hoodoo voodoo on somebody?"

"Not really. Found all that in a junk shop. Velvet painting of a guy who looks like my sister's husband." Zip. Wham. Another eye put out. "What's up?"

"No company tonight?"

"Too wet out there these days. Nobody's going to be seeing much company as long as this weather keeps up." Zip. Wham. Right in the end of the nose. "Want to get those darts for me?"

"You're a bundle of ambition tonight."

"Yeah. Long as you're doing my legwork, you see that creep Licks downstairs? So I don't have to go look for myself?"

"He's there. Unconscious, I think. The smoke was pretty thick."

He snagged his speaking tube. "Puddle. Toss that creep Licks out now. Don't leave him where he'll get run over." Morley put the tube down, looked at me. "I hope he gets pneumonia."

"You have a problem with the man?"

"Yes. I don't like him."

"So bar him."

"His money's as good as yours. Maybe better. He spends it here." That didn't get a rise, so he asked, "What's up? You look like you can't wait to get something off your chest."

"I got a line on the coach."

"Coach? What coach."

"The one out front that they tried to drag Chodo's kid into. I found the man who built it. He told me where I can find it," I explained.

Morley sighed, took his feet down. "Isn't that just like you? Here I am, having the time of my life, and you have to walk in and mess it up." He got up, opened a closet, dug out a raincloak and fancy hat that must have set him back a dozen broken bones.

"What you doing?"

"Let's go check it out."

"Huh?"

"Way I see it, that beats hell out of trying to get to see Chodo. You carrying?"

"Here and there."

"Finally started to learn, eh?"

"I guess. What's the problem with Chodo? I thought you were tight. It's me that's on his list."

"I don't know. I sent word I needed to talk. That it was important. I never got an answer. That's never happened before. Then comes a roundabout kind of hint that nobody out there wants to hear from me and if I'm smart I won't bother them ever again."

"Odd." I couldn't figure that. Morley was an important independent contractor. Chodo owed him a listen.

"Been odd ever since you and Winger went out there. And getting odder every day." We were headed downstairs now.

I asked, "What's with the mustaches? That the coming thing?"

"Huh?"

"I'm seeing them all over. On you it don't look bad. On Spud it would look good if he could grow one. But on Puddle it looks like some damn buzzard built its nest on his lip."

"He doesn't take care of it." Morley darted to the counter, spoke to Puddle briefly. I noted Licks's absence and Puddle's wet shoulders. Licks remained with us in spirit. The smoke was thick enough to slice.

17

When it rains and the wind blows, it gets real dark in TunFaire. Streetlamps won't stay lighted, though those lamps exist only in neighborhoods like the Hill and the Tenderloin, where the wraths of our lords temporal and lords criminal encourage thieves and vandals to practice their crafts elsewhere. Tonight the Hill was darker than a priest's secret heart. I didn't like it. Given my choice, I want to see trouble coming.

Morley was as excited as a kid planning to tumble an outhouse. I asked, "What's your thinking on this?" I looked around nervously. We'd approached Lady Hamilton's place unchallenged, which made me just that much more anxious.

I don't believe in good luck. I do believe in cumulative misfortune, in bad luck just lying back piling up interest till it dumps on you in one big load.

"We climb over the wall, see if the coach is there."

"You could give Glory Mooncalled lessons in innovative tactics." I didn't like his idea. We could get ourselves arrested. We could get ourselves hurt. We could get ourselves fatally unhealthy. The private guards on the Hill are a lot less inhibited than their public-payroll counterparts.

"Don't get all worked up, Garrett. Won't be anything to it."

"That's what you said the time you conned me into helping deliver that vampire to the old kingpin."

"That time you didn't know what you were doing."

True. But where would he get the idea I knew what I was doing now? "You're too optimistic to live."

"Comes of living right."

"Comes of eating horse fodder till you have the sense of a mule."

"You could do with more horse fodder yourself, Garrett. Meat is filled with the juices of things that died terrified. They make you timid yourself."

"I have to admit I never heard anybody call a cabbage a coward."

"There they go. All clear."

There who go? Were we hanging around soaking because he'd seen someone? Why didn't he tell me these things?

He did have better night vision. One of the advantages of his elvish blood. The disadvantages, of course, started with a conviction of personal immortality. It isn't true, what you hear about elves being immortal. They just think they are. Only an arrow through the heart will talk them out of the idea.

Morley took off toward the Hamilton place. I followed, watching everywhere but where I was going. I heard a sound, looked for its source as I jumped ten feet high, walked right into the Hamilton wall.

"You must have been some Marine," Morley grumbled, and continued muttering about no wonder Karenta couldn't win in the Cantard if I represented the kingdom's best and brightest.

"Probably a hundred thousand guys down there would be happy to let you show them how to do it." Morley wasn't a veteran. Breeds don't have to go. The nonhuman peoples all have treaties exempting people up to one-eighth blood. The nonhumans you see in the Cantard are natives or mercenaries, and usually both. And agents of Glory Mooncalled besides. Except for the vampires and werewolves and unicorn packs, who are out to get everybody.

The Cantard is a lot of fun.

Morley squatted, cupped his hands. "I'll give you a boost." The wall was nine feet high.

"You're lighter." I could toss him right over.

"That's why you go first. I can climb up there without help."

A point. Not one that fired me up to go first, but a point. This business was more in his line than mine. He wouldn't buy my plan which was to go pound on the front gate and ask to see the deadly coach. That was too prosaic for his sense of adventure.

I shrugged, stepped into his cupped hands, heaved my reluctant bones upward, grabbed the top of the wall in expectation of getting my fingers ripped to hamburger by broken glass. Broken glass is an old trick for discouraging uninvited company.

Oh, my. Now I was really disheartened. There was no broken glass. I pulled my chin up level with the top, peeked. Where was the trap? They had to have something really special planned if they didn't use broken glass.

Morley whacked me on the sole. "Better move your ass, Garrett. They're coming back."

I didn't know who "they" were but I heard their footsteps. I took a poll. Opinion was unanimous. I didn't want to find out who they were. Up and over I went. I landed in a small garden, gently, failing even to turn an ankle. Morley landed beside me. I said, "This's too easy."

"Come on, Garrett. What do you want? You have a closed house here. Who's going to guard that?"

"Exactly what I want to know."

"You ever begin to sound optimistic, I'm going to flee the country. Come on. Sooner we do it, the sooner you're out of here."

I grunted agreement. "Looks like the coach house there." I don't like sneaking, much. I still thought we should have tried the front way.

Morley scooted to a door in the side of the coach house. I let him lead. I noted how carefully he moved, for all he did so quickly. Whatever he said, he wasn't taking chances.

In his line you didn't get old taking anything for granted. My line either, for that matter.

Neither of us had brought a lantern. You do dumb things when you rush. Still, there was light enough leaking from nearby homes to let Morley see a little. He told me, "Somebody was here before us. They jimmied the lock." He tried the door. It opened.

I looked over his shoulder. It was blacker than the inside of a buzzard's belly in there, and about as inviting. Something made noises and shuffled around. Something breathed. Something a lot bigger than me. Always a courteous kind of guy, I offered, "After you, sir."

Morley wasn't that sure he was immortal. "We need a light."

"Now he notices. This the kind of planning you're going to do when you take over in the Cantard?"

"I'll be back in five minutes." He vanished before I could argue.

18

Five minutes? It was more like twenty. The longest twenty I ever lived, excepting maybe a few dozen times in the islands when I was in the Corps, dancing the death dance with Venageti soldiers.

He wasn't gone ten of those five minutes when, from my lurking place under a crippled lime tree—where I was trying to drown less speedily—I noted a light moving past a downstairs window inside the Hamilton house. Probably a candle. It had a ghostly effect, casting a huge, only vaguely humanoid shadow on a drawn shade.

I gulped air.

Damn me if my luck didn't hold. Somebody came outside and headed straight for the coach house. I heard muttering, then realized that there were two of them. The guy with the candle was leading.

Closer. It was my old buddy with the bad stomach. He didn't look like much now, a sawed-off runt in clothes that had been out of style since my dad was a pup. He wore the kind of hat they call a deerstalker. I'd never seen one outside a painting before. He was bent and slow and shaky and a damned near perfect match for my notion of what a pederast ought to look like.

Hunking along behind, having trouble navigating, was Scarface, the guy Saucerhead had bounced around so thoroughly. He moved slower than the old guy, like he'd aged a hundred years overnight. Saucerhead hadn't broken much but he'd left both of them with plenty of pain.

Now what? Jump in and make a citizen's arrest? Accuse somebody of something and maybe get my own bones rearranged? Maybe cause the geezer another attack of dyspepsia and have him belch carnivorous butterflies all over me? Maybe just end up in court for assault? My mind wanders at such times, examining the dark side. I wish I had Saucerhead's capacity for lack of doubt.

There *are* advantages to being simple.

While I tried to decide and wondered where the hell Morley was with the light, those two dragged their bruise collections inside the coach house. Light flowed through cracks as they lit lamps or lanterns. Talk continued, but I could distinguish no words.

I crept to the doorway, still could make out nothing. I heard a horse snort, jumped. Boy, was I glad I hadn't gone in there before. They would've ambushed me for sure.

It sounded like they were fixing to harness a team. The cussing level suggested that was difficult when you were all bruised up. Sounded like some impressive descriptive work being done in there. I wanted to hear more. I need to expand my vocabulary.

I slipped my fingers into the gap between the door and its frame, pulled outward slowly till I had a crack through which to peek. So I could spy on a whole lot of horse stalls and tack racks doing a whole lot of nothing. Pretty dull stuff. I had the wrong angle.

Someone had the right angle to see the door move inward. I heard one voice say something soft but startled. Heavy footsteps lumbered my way, like a stomping troll wearing stone boots. I thought about doing a fast fade but thought too long. I barely had time to duck aside before the door flew open.

I couldn't run, so I did the next best thing. I bopped Scarface over the head with my listen stick. His conk *thunk*ed like a thumped watermelon. He sagged, looked at me like I wasn't playing fair. Well, why should I? That's dumb with his kind. I'd get hurt if I tried. I thumped him again to make my point.

I bounced over Scarface, popped inside, charged the little character with the sour stomach and antique clothes. Don't ask me why. Seems plenty dumb in retrospect. Just say it seemed like a good idea at the time.

He was trying to get the street doors open. I can't imagine why. His team were still in their stalls. He wasn't going to drive away. And he wasn't going to outrun anybody on foot either. But there he went, heaving away and spitting green moths.

He heard me coming and spun around. For him a spin was a slow turn. His one hand dropped to a kind of frayed rope that served him as a belt, hitched his pants. His eyes started glowing green. I got there with my stick.

One of his moths bit me. Stung like hell. And distracted me so the old boy could slide aside enough for me to whap his shoulder instead of the top of his gourd. He howled. I bellowed and flailed at bugs. His eyes flared and his mouth opened wide. I avoided his gaze and the one big green butterfly that flew from his maw. I flailed crosswise, catching him alongside the jaw.

I put too much on it. Bone cracked. He folded like a dropped suit of clothes.

My juices were flowing. I bounced around looking for more trouble, so cranked the horses just backed up in their stalls and waited for me to go away. I checked Scarface. He was snoring, getting soggier by the second. I darted back to the old man . . .

Who wasn't snoring. He was making funny noises that said he wouldn't be breathing at all pretty soon. I'd broken more than his jaw.

A green giant butterfly crept halfway out from between his lips, got stuck. He held on to his crude rope belt with both hands, like he didn't want to lose his pants, and started shaking.

I'm not in the habit of croaking people. I've done it, sure, but never really by choice and never because I wanted to.

Now I *was* wound up. This was the Hill. Up here the guardians of the peace were no half-blind, unambitious Watchmen interested only in collecting their pay. If I was caught anywhere near a dead man . . .

"What the hell is this?"

I didn't quite leap into the hayloft. Just maybe ten feet. Not even a record for the standing broad jump. But I was out the door the old man had wanted to use, thirty feet into the wet, before I recognized Morley's voice.

Still shaking, I went back and told him what had happened. The presence of a dying man didn't rattle him at all. He observed, "You're learning."

"Huh?"

"Case solved and wrapped in a day. You dig up your buddy Block, tell him where to find his villain, end up with your pockets stuffed with gold. You still have the luck."

"Yeah." But I didn't feel lucky. I didn't *know* that that little old man had gotten his thrills carving on pretty girls.

Morley closed the yard door, eased toward the street door. I said, "Hold it. I have to take a look around in the house."

"Why?" He said that sharply, like he didn't want me going that way.

"In case there's any evidence. I need to know."

He gave me the fish eye, shook his head, shrugged. The notion of a conscience was alien to him. "If you have to, you have to."

"I have to."

tripped over the old man's sidekick as I stepped into the garden. Well! Another mystery. Some wicked soul had come along and stabbed him in his sleep.

I scowled at Morley. Morley wasn't abashed. "Didn't need him, Garrett. And now you won't need to keep looking back." Just because the guy had caused a scene at the Joy House.

I didn't argue. We'd had the argument more times than I liked to recall. Morley knew neither pity nor remorse, only practicality. Which, he had a habit of reminding me, was why I turned to him so often.

Maybe. But I think I go to him because I trust him to cover my back.

I'd grabbed the old man's lantern. It was out now, after my spill. I pushed it aside, dragged the body into the coach house, closed the door, and headed for the big house by the light of the lantern Morley carried. I snagged the extinguished lantern as I went.

The house wasn't locked. It took us only moments to get inside and find something.

We entered through a dusty kitchen. We needed go on no farther. Seconds after we entered, Morley said, "Check this, Garrett."

"This" was a three-gallon wooden bucket. A tribe of flies had made it a place of worship. Their startled buzz and the smell told me that it was no water pail. Rusty cakes of dried blood adorned it.

"They had to use something to carry the blood away." I shone my light around, spotted a set of knives on a drainboard. They were not ordinary kitchen knives. They were decorated with fancy symbols. They were decorated with dried blood too.

Morley observed, "They didn't take good care of their tools."

"You didn't see the way they moved. After they'd danced with Saucerhead they probably didn't feel much like doing housework."

"You satisfied now?"

I had to be. "Yeah." No point lollygagging around, maybe getting ourselves hanged with all that evidence.

Morley grinned. "You really are learning, Garrett. I figure maybe another hundred years and you can get by without a babysitter."

I wondered if maybe he wasn't a little too optimistic.

Being no fool, Morley went his own way. I found Captain Block the last place I expected, at the bachelor officers' quarters at the barracks the Watch shares with the local army garrison. Those troops are less use than the Watch, coming out for nothing but ceremonies and to stand guard at various royal edifices.

I got the usual runaround trying to reach Block, but it had no heart in it. Maybe he'd left word a certain battered old Marine might want to get hold of him sometime.

He was dressing when I walked in and started dripping on his carpet. "I take it you've got something, Garrett." For the life of me I couldn't figure why he wasn't thrilled to see me, just because it was after midnight.

"I found your man."

"Huh?" Dumbstruck is really amazing on a naturally dumbfounded face.

"That villain you wanted found? The fellow who entertained himself by whittling on pretty girls? If you want him, I've got him."

"Uh . . . yeah?" He didn't believe me yet.

"Put your slicker on, Cap. I've had me a long, hard day and I want to get on home."

"You found him?"

Ta-da! First thing you knew, he'd figure it out. "Yep. But you'd better get rolling if you want to cash in."

"Yeah. Sure." He was in a daze. He couldn't believe this. For a moment I entertained suspicions. They didn't get too rowdy. "But how? I had a thousand men looking. They never caught a whiff."

"Didn't know where to sniff. You get the nose when you have to make your living at it."

"Sounds like you plain got lucky."

"Luck helps."

"Should I bring some men?"

"You won't need them. They won't give you any trouble."

Must have been an edge to my voice. He looked at me askance but was too shocked still to pursue it. He shrugged into an army overcloak, jammed a waterproof hat onto his head. "You don't know how much we appreciate this, Garrett."

"I have my suspicions. Just show me by making sure you don't forget to drop my fee off at my place."

"What?" He managed to look affronted. Somebody had the audacity to question the integrity of the Watch? "You think we'd screw you?"

"The gods forfend. Me? Think a thing like that about our brave Watchmen? Surely you jest, Captain."

He heard the sarcasm and didn't like it, but had become too excited to take offense. Hell, he took off like the proverbial bat, dashing boldly into the night and rain—till he realized he didn't know where the hell he was headed.

"I'm moving as fast as I can, Captain," I told him. And I was. I did want to get home. I had big ambitions in the night lumber trade. "I put in about two thousand miles of legwork today, tracking these monsters down."

"Monsters? There's more than one?"

The man didn't listen. I shook my head. He fell into step beside me, as bouncy as a five-year-old.

"One more than one, Captain. The big villain was a guy about a thousand years old who was some kind of wizard. The other was your basic street bruno, middle thirties."

"Was?" Now he sounded nervous, even wary. "You keep saying 'was.'"

"You'll see."

e saw. He was less than thrilled. "Did you have to kill them?" He stared at the old man like he hoped the crazy bastard would rise from the dead.

"No. I could've let them kill me. But then you'd still be looking, wouldn't you?" I stared at the old man, rattled. Block didn't notice.

First, the old boy had crawled to the garden door before he'd checked out. Then he'd gotten naked. What there was of him was so dried up it looked like something had sucked out everything inside his skin. That skin was dead white. I wondered if maybe he wouldn't rise from the dead. If he hadn't already, a time or two. Then I shook off the fit of superstition and concentrated on a problem that was real and immediate.

Someone had been into the coach house in my absence. Somebody who had stripped the dead man and had ripped off a crazy miscellany from the tack and tool racks. That smelled of a crime of opportunity committed by some down-and-out amateur. By someone who had seen a door open, had darted in for a nervous peek, had taken what he could use, and had grabbed everything else he could carry that looked like it might sell for enough to make a down payment on a bottle of cheap red wine. Was I to go a-hunting this thief, I'd keep an eye peeled for a short, skinny wino all cocked up in a new suit of old clothes, complete with one of those absurd deerstalker hats.

Block complained, "Would've had a lot more impact if I'd been able to bring them to trial."

"I don't doubt it a bit. It would've been a circus. The show of the year. I would've loved to have seen it. But he was belching butterflies and staring green fire and getting ready to lay some serious sorcery on me. I couldn't talk him out of it. Come on. Let me show you some evidence."

I led him to the kitchen, showed him the bucket. I wanted to show him the knives but they weren't where I'd seen them last. That damned Morley, collecting souvenirs. I felt more comfortable in the house now that I had an officer of the law along to explain to the local custodians. I took time to look around more carefully. I didn't see anything new. "You satisfied?"

"I expect." He held up a big glass jar Morley and I had overlooked. It contained a human heart in a clear fluid. "I'll have my people come take the place apart."

"You know who owns it?"

"I know. Ironic coincidence. There won't be any problems, though. The Prince is determined. He'll just be doubly pissed because somebody dared. He'll breathe fire."

I chuckled. "You're welcome to collect the kudos, Captain. I don't want his kind noticing me. Just see that I get paid. Then you're happy, I'm happy, and TunFaire is happy soon as word gets out. Now, unless you insist on my help, I'm dragging my weary ass home and putting it to bed."

"Go ahead," he said distractedly. "And, Garrett?"

"Yeah?"

"Thanks. You'll get your money. And I'll still owe you for this miracle."

"There you go." I got me out of there while the getting was good.

The Dead Man was still doing interviews when I got home. There were people in with him and people waiting in the small front room. Dean was doing a shift on the door. I gave him my most malicious smile and sneered. "Now you know what it feels like to be up at an absurd hour." I made a quick sally into the small front room in search of feline game but did not find my prey. Dean eyed me nervously and kept his mouth shut.

Excellent, I thought as I trudged upstairs. First thing in the morning we'd have a talk about that cat.

••• **21**

First thing in the morning, I didn't talk to Dean at all. About cats, anyway. He rolled me out at some absurd hour before noon, told me, "His
Nibs wants you in his room. I'll bring your breakfast there."

I groaned and rolled over.

Dean didn't bother with the usual roust. That should have warned me. But
it was morning. Who thinks in the morning? I just grumped some ill-placed
gratitude in the general direction of heaven and burrowed into my pillow.

Bugs started chewing on me.

Felt like bugs biting, anyway. When I started flopping and swatting and
cussing and digging around, I couldn't find a thing. But the nibbling kept
on keeping on.

It was morning. It took me a while to figure it. Old Dean hadn't salted
my bed with insects. The Dead Man was prodding me.

Still cussing and dancing and swatting, I pried myself out of bed. That
part of my mind that was working duly noted the discovery of a hitherto
unsuspected aspect of my partner. He would persecute his allies as readily
as his enemies.

Though my eyes only pretended to be open and my legs rebelled at every
step, I made it downstairs without suffering any disaster. I stumbled into
the Dead Man's room and dropped into my chair, weakly looking around
for something I could use to start a fire as soon as I got the ambition.

Good morning, Garrett. You wouldn't think you'd get much expression
out of his style of communication, but he sure managed to sound as happy

as a clam that didn't know it was being fattened up for a chowder. *I am so pleased you could join me.*

The sentiments I expressed were less sociable. "What the hell you bubbling about? What the hell did you drag me down here for? The sun ain't even up yet." Which wasn't strictly true. Somewhere out there, above the rain clouds, there was a sun that had been up for hours. It just hadn't been up for enough hours.

I could contain my curiosity no longer. The gentlemen of the City Watch came round to pay their respects and debts this morning. They were generous beyond belief.

"Don't mean much. Them showing up with one sceat makes them generous beyond belief. How much?"

The full one thousand marks. Moreover—

"Only a thousand?" I grumped. Naturally, I grumped. A thousand was a major score, but I'd have grumped if they'd brought money around by the wagonload. "You could've waited till a decent hour."

Moreover, he continued, ignoring me completely, *they brought the latest news from the Cantard. My theories have been vindicated at last. The expected collapse of Glory Mooncalled's revolution, indicated by all those defections and desertions, has proved chimerical. He was just biding his time against the ripe moment.*

"Aw, hell." Now I understood why he'd dragged me out. Didn't have a thing to do with money. He'd gotten his big chance to crow—with me in no condition to fight back.

I'd figured Mooncalled was on his last legs. The evidence was there. Defections and desertions had been strong indicators that the rebellion was about to fold. Hell, there were refugees from the Cantard scattered all over Karenta now. I'd seen plenty right here in TunFaire.

I didn't bother asking how Mooncalled had conjured another miracle. The man did these things. I went to work on the breakfast Dean brought and waited on the Dead Man. He would want to rub it in. He loves it when I lose an argument completely.

He let me have it blow by blow, the uneconomical way. The way I do him when I want to yank his beard.

He claimed most of the defections and desertions hadn't been genuine. Furthermore, Mooncalled had just been lying low, staying ahead of the various armies, occasionally encouraging the Venageti forces or Karentine to come to blows while he awaited one of those rare but exceedingly violent storms that sweep into the Cantard from the gulf. I saw a few of those while

I was down there. All you can do is take cover and hope the cover stands up to the wind and rain.

While his enemies were paralyzed, Mooncalled had struck. In both directions. One force attacked Full Harbor, Karenta's biggest bridgehead in the Cantard. He'd tried before and had failed. This time he'd succeeded, taking Full Harbor with all its supplies and munitions.

Another force attacked Quarache, Venageta's logistical bastion in the southern Cantard. Quarache is bigger and far more important than Full Harbor. It surrounds the only big, reliable oasis in that part of the desert. The Venageti war effort hinges on continued control of Quarache. Without it they wouldn't be able to project their power far enough to threaten the silver mines.

Losing Full Harbor would hurt the Karentine effort but not cripple it. Karenta has other bases along the coast. Venageta doesn't.

I tried a weak sally. "Your boy is in deep shit now, Chuckles. They'll send the Marines to take the Harbor back. He's never gone up against Marines."

Except for a sly touch of amusement he ignored me. He continued his story.

Quarache didn't go the way of Full Harbor. Mooncalled hadn't had the strength to carry it completely. Fighting continued as the Venageti rushed reinforcements in from everywhere, were reclaiming Quarache in prolonged, desperate, expensive house-to-house combat.

Like most ordinary Karentines, I've developed an affection for Glory Mooncalled. Not that I want my kingdom to lose a war. But when you spend your whole life a witness to the corruption, incompetence, and greed shown by our overlords, you can't help but admire a guy who makes rude noises in their faces and brassily dares them to do their worst—then dances around mocking them while they stumble over their own feet. Too, I think a lot of us nurture the secret hope that Mooncalled's antics will compel an end to the endless war.

"This is really why you dragged me out of bed?"

This and the fact that I wish to hear details of what happened last night. And he did seem intensely interested. I recalled that he had been from the beginning, like he'd suspected something he didn't want to share. *How was it that you managed to conclude the thing so quickly?*

"Ah? I think I detect a hint of jealousy. A note of disbelief."

The law of averages suggests you should be capable of stumbling through unaided occasionally. It is true that I remain amazed at your ability to flout that law so frequently.

Yes. He was piqued. He'd put all that time into all those interviews, which we hadn't yet discussed, expecting to dazzle one and all with a startling indictment. Then I'd had to go spoil his game by tracking down that jinxed coach. Garrett the Killjoy, that's me. "You want to tell me what you thought was going on when Block first told us about the women?"

Somebody pounded on the door, timing it as though the Dead Man had had him waiting in the wings.

That will be Mr. Tharpe. I allowed him to return home last evening. He had personal matters to settle. Stay seated. Dean will handle the door.

I yelled, "Dean, throw that cat out when you let Saucerhead in." I waited till Tharpe came in before I started my story.

"You got lucky," Saucerhead said when I finished.

"Lucky, hell. That was a prime piece of deducting and detecting."

Tharpe grunted, unconvinced.

"I didn't see anybody else thinking about attacking it by looking for the coach."

"I still say you lucked out, Garrett. How about if the old geezer used some regular coach? How about if he walked?"

"But he didn't. And that's the point. And that's what cost him. He decided to break in on a closed house and use it for his base, and found him a spiffy, neato coach there and just couldn't resist going in style. And it cost him." For a second I wondered if the jinx had gotten old butterfly-breath. But I didn't care. I wasn't much bothered by having croaked him, now. I hadn't run into many people who'd needed killing more. I couldn't feel bad about doing the world a favor.

"You lucked out," Saucerhead insisted. And wouldn't be swayed. Neither would the Dead Man.

Mr. Tharpe, I have an errand for you, should you care to extend your employment.

"You pay, I play." Saucerhead liked the Dead Man for some reason.

This building has become suspiciously free of vermin. That was because I'd burned a dozen sulfur candles one day while he was taking one of his six-week naps. I thought I'd do him a favor. Bugs like to snack on him. *I am accustomed to employing large numbers of insects when I examine the various permutations of action available to the forces operating in the Cantard. I cannot indulge my curiosity without them.*

"You already heard what Glory Mooncalled done, then?"

Yes. I am excited. I need a few thousand insects with which to evolve through the options available to the surviving combatants.

He had a habit of lining bugs up on the wall, like soldiers, and running them through maneuvers. A disgusting vice.

"Now, wait a minute," I protested. "I just got this place deinfested." Bugs and mice are the Dead Man's worst enemies. Left unchecked, they would devour him in no time.

So. You are the villain responsible.

He knew darned well I was, he just hadn't brought it up before.

"I am he," said I. "I'm also the guy what owns this dump. I'm also the guy what's feeling damned put upon on account of I've got a housekeeper who's moved in uninvited and figures it's his duty to drag in every stray cat he can find. I'm also the guy what don't like the floor crunching under his tootsies whenever he starts looking for the chamber pot in the dark. Never mind about the bugs, Saucerhead. Let him use his imagination."

The Dead Man sent me an exaggerated mental sigh. *So be it. I fear, then, Mr. Tharpe, that we have no further need for your services.*

I gave the Dead Man a narrow-eyed look. He'd given up too easily. "He's right. What do we owe you?"

"Not enough so I don't got to go back to raising knots on heads for that creep Licks."

A sad story. Nobody liked Licks. Including me, and I didn't know him. "Guy has to make a living, I guess." I counted out a few coins, not much. Tharpe seemed satisfied. He hadn't done anything but answer the door.

"You might maybe add a little tip on account of personal hardship, Garrett."

"Personal hardship?"

"I had to be here instead of home. Though maybe from what I hear, you done forgot about women."

"Not quite. Not yet. But it's fading fast."

"So be cynical and self-serving. Go apologize to Tinnie." He liked Tinnie. Hell, I liked her. I just couldn't get along with her redheaded temper. For now. The songs you sing do change. Abstinence does make the heart grow fonder.

Saucerhead seemed in no hurry to leave. He and the Dead Man were wondering what might have snapped inside the butterfly man's head and left him wanting to carve up women. I figured this was my chance. I gathered my breakfast leavings, took them to the kitchen. Once I disposed of the evidence, I'd slide upstairs and catch me forty winks.

Somebody banged on the door.

hat was this? I'd worked so hard to discourage customers that I didn't get this many visitors in a week anymore. Dean made like he was too snowed in cleaning up, so I took care of it myself.

Hoping for some randy sex goddess, I got Barking Dog Amato. I'd forgotten him completely.

"You forgot all about me, Garrett," he accused, pushing inside, forcing me back with his personal chemistry.

"No," I lied. "I figured you hadn't had time to get anything ready yet."

"Been raining. Not much else to do. Making signs and handbills gets old."

You'd think a drenching would wash the grunge away. Not so. Water just brought it to life. I considered propping the door open, maybe opening a few windows so the wind could blow through. If I'd lived on the Hill, I might have tried it. In my neighborhood you wouldn't dare. Even during a typhoon there would be some opportunist ready to accept the challenge. Besides, I only had one downstairs window.

Once past me, Amato halted, dripped, reeked, looked around. "You got that thing, that whatsit they call the Dead Man. I'd sure like to take a gander at that, you know what I mean?"

I tried shallow breaths. I don't know why we bother. It never helps. "Why not? You're a man he ought to meet." I wished Old Bones had him a working sniffer. I'd lock them in together till Amato sold him his whole zany conspiracy collection.

I opened the Dead Man's door, held it for Amato. Saucerhead, in my chair, half turned, saw Barking Dog. His face scrunched up into a world-class frown. He didn't ask, though.

He got a whiff, that's why. He gasped, "I see you got a client I'd better go good-bye," all in one long exhalation. He slid out the door almost before I got through. He tossed me a look that told me he wanted to hear all about it. Later. A lot later, after the miasma cleared.

I winked. "Make sure the front door is closed."

Barking Dog said, "My God, it's an ugly sucker. Got a hooter like a mammoth, don't it?"

Another missionary, Garrett?

"This is Kropotkin Amato. You recall the arrangement we made."

You know what I mean. You still intend to harass me? You will recall that your previous effort met with a singular lack of success.

"Me? No. . . ."

Nor did you bother mentioning any arrangement, though I discern the details in your mind. We did not contract to have the man watch himself.

"*We* didn't contract anything, Smiley."

Barking Dog looked baffled. I would have too, hearing only half the conversation. I changed subjects. "You can understand why I did it." I didn't want to bruise Amato's feelings. The Dead Man could peek inside his head, see why we didn't have to mount a major campaign.

You are correct, Garrett. This time. However unlikely, he believes his theories. Which, you will understand, make them the reality in which he lives. I suggest you do meet our principal, try to ascertain why he deems it worthwhile to keep tabs on Mr. Amato.

Good morning, Mr. Amato. I have been anxious to make your acquaintance since Mr. Garrett first undertook to trace your movements.

The rat was going to lay it off on me.

"Uh . . . hi." Barking Dog was at a loss for words. Maybe I ought to check to see if this was really him.

One breath and I knew I didn't have to check. "Look here, Chuckles, don't you go—"

Mr. Amato and I have a great deal to discuss, Garrett. I suggest you visit Mr. Hullar and see if you cannot unearth a reason for his interest.

"Yeah, Garrett. What you been doing, anyhow? You was supposed to . . ."

I fled, defeated. Would Barking Dog care that I'd neglected him only to save TunFaire from a vicious serial killer? He would be sure *they* had bought

me off. Even though he was the subject I was supposed to investigate for
them.

I gave the stairway one longing look, then got into my rain gear. I
checked my pockets to see how much cash I had. Maybe I could rent me a
room and catch a few winks.

I made a sudden sally into the small front room before I left, thinking
I'd snatch Dean's cat and drag it along. But the cat wasn't in evidence, only
the scratches it had left on my furniture.

Then I realized that I had nothing to report to Hullar. I trudged back
and pried Barking Dog's report away from him. He and the Dead Man were
weaving drunken spiderwebs of conspiracy theory already.

23

The Tenderloin is that part of town which caters to the side of people they keep hidden. Any vice can be found there, any sin committed, almost any need fulfilled. The hookers and the drug dens and gambling pits are just the surface, the glamour. At least, those aspects of those things that can be glamorous when seen from the street.

It's a glitzy street. Or streets, really. The area is bigger than Tinkery Row. And more successful. Nothing sells like sin. After the Hill it's the most prosperous, cleanest, safest, and most orderly part of the city. Some very unpleasant people make sure it stays that way.

It all belongs, directly or indirectly, to Chodo Contague's empire.

Bishoff Hullar's taxi-dance place is as tame a dive as you can find there. That's all the girls do, dance and talk to lonely fellows and try to get them to buy drinks. Maybe a few make personal arrangements, but there are no facilities on the premises. The place is as shabby as they're allowed to get down there. Frankly, I don't see how Hullar stays in business, competing with neighbors who offer so much more.

The place wasn't jumping when I arrived, but it was just after noon then. A couple of sad-looking sailors sat at a table talking to a sad-looking girl who sipped colored water and didn't pretend very hard that she gave a damn about what the sailors were saying. A doddering ratman mopped around the other tables. All those had chairs piled atop them. There was nobody on the dance floor, though a couple more girls were loafing by the bandstand, where three worn-out old musicians weren't trying very hard to stay awake.

Both girls glanced at me, wondering if I was worth the effort of making so long a trek. One, who looked like she might break out in a case of puberty any day, lazily packed a pipe with weed.

The guy behind the bar had to be the world's oldest dwarf. He wore the full costume, complete with a pheasant's feather in a peaked little cap. He had a beard that should have kept the floor swept of debris. "What's it going to be, Ace?" He wiped the bar in front of me with the same rag he'd been using to polish mugs.

"Beer."

"Pint?"

"Yeah."

"Light? Dark?"

"Light."

"Lager? Pilsner? . . ."

"Just draw one. Surprise me. Weider's, if you got it." I figured I owed Old Man Weider a little commercial loyalty, what with him having had me on retainer so long.

"Hasty. Always hasty." He drew me a pint. "Wet enough for you out there?"

Oh, my. A talkative bartender. "Wet enough. Hullar around?"

"Who wants to know?" Suddenly he was completely alert.

"Name's Garrett. I'm supposed to be doing something for him."

"Yeah?" He wiped the bar next to me while he thought about that. After a moment he said, "I'll check." Off he trundled. I rose onto my toes, watched, wondering if he'd stumble over his beard.

"Hi. I'm Brenda." The pipe smoker had puffed up enough ambition to hike all the way over. I glanced at her, resumed studying the wasteland behind the bar. The woman was less interesting.

Up close it was obvious she wasn't a child, that that was just her hook. The gamine had gone a long time ago, probably before she was old enough to become a gamine. I said, "I'm just here to see Hullar. Business."

"Oh." Her voice had had little life before. Now it was dead.

I glanced at the musicians. "I could part with a few coppers, though, if you could explain why those band guys are here at this time of day." I didn't know Hullar's place well, but didn't think there was any music during the day.

"Somebody kicked the shit out of them last night after work. They're waiting to talk to some guy about it."

Licks? Coming in to put the arm on them?

"You're in, Ace. The man says come on back."

I dropped a half dozen coppers into the woman's hand. She made an effort to find a smile but had trouble remembering where she'd left it. I wanted to say something to waken her spirit but couldn't think of a thing. So I just said, "Thanks," and hurried after the dwarf. If I let him get too big a head start I'd miss out when he tripped over his beard.

Bishoff Hullar was five feet tall, three feet wide, bald as an egg, in his sixties, ugly as sin itself. The width wasn't fat. I'd heard he was a strongman in his younger days and that he kept up in case there was a call for his talents. "Sit, Garrett." He indicated a rickety antediluvian chair. He had a voice like rocks tumbling around inside an iron drum. Somebody had done the lead-pipe thing on his throat in his once-upon-a-time. "You got anything for me?"

I gave him Barking Dog's report. He took it, started reading. I said, "I have some questions." I glanced around his workplace. You couldn't call it an office. He sat behind a table with some writing tools on it, but also makeup pots, which suggested the girls used the place for a dressing room. Overall, it was as tacky as the rest of the place.

"Huh?" He looked up, piggy little gray eyes narrowed.

"Basic stuff my partner never got around to asking because he thought this job would be a good joke on me."

Hullar's eyes got narrower. "Joke?"

"Barking Dog Amato. Nobody in the world is going to pay somebody to spy on a lunatic. Least of all a guy who runs a place like this down here. I can't see you even knowing Barking Dog."

"I don't. Wouldn't know him if he walked in and sank his fangs in me. What's it to you? You're getting paid."

"I'm the guy what takes his butt onto the street amongst the slings and arrows, Hullar. I kind of like to know why I'm doing that, and who for. That way I have a notion what direction to expect trouble from when it comes."

"You're not going to see no trouble."

"They all tell me that. If there wasn't trouble, though, they wouldn't come to me in the first place. I don't play blindfolded, Hullar."

He put the report down, looked at me like he was making up his mind whether to kick my butt or not. Not won the toss.

"You got a good rep, Garrett. Why I picked you. I'll take a chance."

I waited. He brooded. The dwarf bartender waited at the door, maybe to see if the boss would need help. There wasn't much tension, though. I didn't feel threatened.

"I ain't got much here, Garrett. *We* ain't got much. But we're like family. We take care of each other on account of we're all we've got. This here is like the last ledge before the fall into the pit."

I couldn't argue that. I kept my opinion to myself. My old mom used to suggest strongly that I just might learn something if I could manage to keep my mouth shut long enough to listen. Mom was right, but I didn't get the message for years—and I still forget it far too often.

"Somebody works for me comes to me with their trouble, usually I try to lend a hand. If I can. I do that, maybe they give me a little help when I need it. Right?"

"Makes sense." Only in the real world it doesn't work that way very often. "One of your people wants Barking Dog watched?"

He eyed me, still taking my measure. "You're a cynic. You don't believe in much. Especially not people. Maybe that's a good thing in your line, kind of folks you probably have to deal with."

"Yeah." I was proud of me. I kept a straight face.

He glanced at the dwarf, got a response I didn't catch. "All right. Here's the way it is, Garrett. Amato's kid works for me. When he got himself tossed in the Al-Khar, she—"

"He's got a daughter?" You've heard that one about knocking a guy over with a feather? That feather would have smashed me like a bug.

"Yeah. This Amato, he's a loony. But harmless. You know that. I know that. Only he's got a habit of naming names. She's scared maybe he named the wrong one, some Hill-type asshole what don't got a sense of humor. Maybe the old man is about to get his ass in deep shit. Girl's a little light-headed herself, if you get my drift. But she's family here, and when my people worry, I try to fix it so they don't. So what I want from you is you should keep an eye on the old nut, let me know if he's about to step in it so I can yank him out of the way before he gets run over. Understand?"

Yes. And no. Barking Dog with a daughter? How did he ever manage that? "A bit hard to buy."

"Yeah? Something about it you don't like? You just say you're out. I'll get somebody else. I picked you on account of they say you're almost honest. But I can live without you."

"It's just a big chunk to swallow. You don't know Barking Dog. You did, you'd know why. I can't figure him for having a kid."

"Crunch. Tell Sas to bring us a couple of beers."

The dwarf left. We didn't talk. After a while a woman came with two beers, light for me and dark for Hullar. I'd seen her with the gamine, muttering with the musicians. I hadn't noticed then, but up close the resemblance to Amato was there. She even had those spooky eyes that looked like they were seeing things hidden from the rest of us. She pretended not to study me while I pretended not to study her.

"Thanks, Sas."

"Sure, Bish." She left.

"Sure looks like him," I admitted.

"There you go. Any problems now?"

"Not really." I wondered if she'd studied me because the dwarf had told her who I was. Probably. Maybe he'd sent her back more to give her a look than to give me one. "This supposed to be a secret?"

"Secret?"

"I'll tell my partner, of course. He won't kick it around. But is it supposed to be a secret from the rest of the world?"

"Probably wouldn't hurt. The guy maybe does have an enemy or three."

"Suppose he catches on that I'm watching? Am I allowed to tell him why?"

"I don't figure that would do Sas no good. Look, I know this ain't in your usual line. Pretty tame, you being used to mixing it up with sorcerers and gangsters and Hill folk, but it means something to us. You don't got to make a career out of it. I ain't paying that much. But we'd all appreciate it if you'd let us in on it should he get his ass into something he can't handle. Right?"

I rose. "Good enough." I believed him because I wanted to believe him. You don't much see people do nice things for people. "One of your girls said your musicians are having problems."

"You don't need to worry about that. Tooken care of." For a moment he looked like the evil thing I'd pictured him to be. "Or will be, real soon. How about you take my mug back out to Crunch?"

I took both mugs.

24

The dwarf grunted when I made my delivery. For an old guy—especially for an old dwarf—Crunch was astonishingly polite.

As I headed for the street, I glanced at the bandbox. And almost tripped over my feet.

A man had joined the musicians. He was one guy I'd hoped I wouldn't ever see again. He stared at me. I stared back.

He had nothing on me in height and only a little in weight, but size didn't make this man. He reeked menace the way Barking Dog Amato reeked uninspired personal hygiene. He scared you just by being around, even when he smiled. His name was Crask. He was one of Chodo Contague's top cats. He hurt people for a living. He enjoyed his work.

I realized I'd stopped to stare. He kept staring too. Each of us was wondering what the hell the other was doing there. When my brain unfroze again I had no trouble figuring him. He was there because of the battered musicians.

Old Licks didn't have a license from the outfit. Him and his buddies would be in deep shit if Crask caught up. Especially deep for picking on musicians in the Tenderloin. The Tenderloin was Chodo's. Even the King doesn't mess around down there.

I almost made it to the door before I got stunned again.

The girl blew in as I reached for the latch. I dodged, gaped. For all she reacted, I was a ghost.

She was the one those villains had dragged out of Morley's place. The one Morley claimed was the kingpin's daughter. I turned, stared, maybe panted some, as she strode toward Crunch.

Crask's face went as cold as death. My heart jumped. But it wasn't me he was watching.

The girl glanced his way, stopped, made a little sound of surprise, whirled, and sprinted for the street. She ricocheted off me as she went. I purred. Whip me, beat me . . .

Crask came pounding up behind me as I stepped into the rain to watch her fly away. He halted beside me. "What the hell was that?" I asked.

"What you doing here, Garrett?" He sounded suspicious. Nasty suspicious. Like getting-ready-to-break-arms-and-legs suspicious.

"What are *you* doing here? I thought you were too big-time for legwork."

"She come here to meet you?"

"Huh?" That was a surprise notion. "Uh-uh. No touch. I'll break things." Crask was scary, but I wasn't afraid of him in any head-butting contest. I figured our chances were equal if we got to prancing around pounding on each other. He was scary because he was a killer and a smart one. If he decided to send you over, you might as well start counting your beads.

"You stay away, Garrett. Or they'll find parts of you all over town."

"I didn't know you had a woman. Who is she?" Fact was, I thought he and his sidekick Sadler had a thing.

"Huh?"

"I'm going to tell you this once, Crask. I don't know the girl. I have seen her before. Once. She walked into Morley Dotes's place night before last. Two minutes later a bunch of guys roared in and tried to kidnap her. Me and Morley and Saucerhead showed them what we think of guys who pick up their girls the rough way. She disappeared before we finished. Beginning and end of story. Now it's your go. Who is she? How come you got your balls in an uproar?"

"You don't need to know." The girl was out of sight now. Crask frowned after her, as much puzzled as angry. He'd bought my story, probably because I'd not lied to him much in the past. "What was she doing at Dotes's place?"

"You got me. Never said a word. Just came in looking scared, sat by herself, then three guys blew in and dragged her out."

He grunted. "I didn't know about that. Thanks, Garrett. I'll give you one back. Tell Tharpe it ain't going to be healthy hanging around with those guys trying to mess with the musicians."

"I was going to suggest that anyway after I saw you in there." I started moving, planning to put some distance between us before it occurred to him to bring up old business.

"Garrett."

Damn. "What?"

"You see the girl around again, pass the word. We'd like to know."

"Sure. But why? Who is she?"

"Just do it." He went inside without turning his back.

I hustled away, breathing hard. It had been an encounter I'd dreaded more than necessary. Maybe. Maybe the street in front of Hullar's place didn't strike him as the best stage for my demise.

25

Peace and harmony broke out all over. I had nothing to do but loaf, deliver the occasional report to Hullar, and keep an eye on Dean's crowd whenever he had them over for one of his rehab parties. You wouldn't believe how rowdy old men can get.

There weren't any cats around, and except for his barbs about me not working, Dean wasn't a nuisance. The Dead Man went to sleep, visions of Glory Mooncalled dancing in his head. Saucerhead resigned from the musician-organizing racket just before Morley reported that he was no longer obliged to endure the custom of that human smudgepot Licks. I got out and visited, bought a few rounds for friends, reforged contacts, even dropped by the brewery and spent a few days checking employee theft for Weider. As always, he wanted me to take the job full-time. As always, I couldn't overcome my horror of holding down a real job.

Nobody's life stays on that high and relaxed a level. Especially not mine. The gods have a special Garrett harassment squad dedicated solely to my persecution.

So I should have known the good times were over the morning I went out to run and found that the rains had returned.

I was in my office busting my skull trying to fake up numbers that would impress the tax thugs with the depths of my destitution. Somebody hammered on the door. I groaned. It was nearly suppertime and Dean was fixing a standing rib roast that would be bloody rare and would melt in my mouth, with all the extras. Smelling the odors from the kitchen had me drooling already.

Dean asked, "Shall I ignore it?"

"No. It's probably Saucerhead." Tharpe had been around a lot lately. His flame had walked. His luck hadn't been good since. "There enough to feed him too?"

"Barely." Saucerhead does put it away. "There won't be anything left over."

I shrugged. "I'll get even with him someday."

"You just want to get away from what you're doing." He tottered down the hall to the accompaniment of renewed pounding. Somebody was awfully anxious.

Dean was right. I did want to get away. I hate the whole idea of taxes. What have I ever gotten from the Crown? A pack and a collection of weapons and a five-year adventure in the war zone. I had to give back the pack and weapons. They just wanted to rip me off so they could give some other kid a chance to see the acne on the ass of the world.

I got out of having to be creative, but, all things considered, I'd rather I'd stayed with the taxes.

It wasn't Saucerhead. It was a guy I'd hoped never to see again, Captain Block. Dean showed Block into my office. Block looked frazzled.

I couldn't help myself. "Now what?"

Block planted his behind, settled his elbows on his knees, buried his face in his hands. "Same as before. You'll have to see it."

"Look, I bailed you out once. Isn't that enough? Dean's cooking supper. It'll be ready in half an hour."

"So he told me. Also told me you were busy doing taxes."

"Yeah."

"You wouldn't be the kind of guy who'd forget to report a fat cash payment from the Watch, would you?"

Damned right I would be. "Why?"

"One mission of the Watch is to investigate alleged tax fraud. We don't *do* much of that, but when there's a report, we have to act to cover our butts."

"I'll find my hat. How far do we have to go?"

"Not far." He smiled weakly. "I knew I could count on you. And I'm sure your purse won't get hurt this time, either."

No happiness came through his smile. He looked more stressed than last time. What had him by the short hairs now?

Something that would be politically painful, surely. By getting out, tapping the wind of rumor whispering through the streets, I knew Block had turned catching old bug-breath into a big score. Suddenly there was a lot of stuff going on in the shadows. Prince Rupert was getting behind Westman Block. Block had hidden irons in the fire. It all had the knights of the street feeling nervous.

I made sure I was equipped for trouble, just because of the company I'd be keeping. Trouble followed Block.

We talked about the Cantard as we walked. Glory Mooncalled had abandoned his effort to capture Quarache but had hamstrung the Venageti ability to project their power far into the desert. I'd also been on the mark about the Marines getting the job of retaking Full Harbor. That operation had begun. I had mixed feelings. They brag that when they turn you into a Marine they make you a Marine forever.

The more we talked, the more I realized that Block was thoroughly spooked. Whatever his problem, it was going to be something I wouldn't like.

Now *I* was spooked.

"Identical," I said, staring at the gutted, naked girl. She hung in an alleyway behind abandoned tenements on the near south side. Those tenements had been occupied by ratmen squatters until a few hours ago. They were long gone now.

In the rain and poor light the dead girl was a ringer for the one Block had shown me in the Bustee. "This can't be, Block. I got them." I had to believe I'd gotten them. I'm not made to shake off killing the wrong villains.

Block wasn't so scared for his behind that he couldn't see what was bothering me. "You got the right guy, Garrett. Don't doubt that for a minute. After we got the Prince's go-ahead, we took that place apart. You wouldn't believe what we found. They'd been in there a long time. They kept pieces of all their victims. There were bodies in the cellar, girls, but not the type. My guess is they used them for practice before they went after the real thing."

I stared at the new corpse, listened to the flies sing. "There was one thing . . ." I told him about that missing clothing and knives. I'd discovered that Morley hadn't taken away any souvenirs. I didn't mention Morley's name. It wouldn't appeal to Block.

"You didn't mention any of this before."

"I thought everything was wrapped up before. But—"

"Yeah. But. Elvis!"

A nondescript Watchman hurried over. "Captain?"

"Show Mr. Garrett what you found."

Elvis had a folded scrap of paper tucked into a pocket inside his rain cape. Inside it were three green butterflies. I shivered as though the rain had turned to sleet. "How long since the last murder?"

"Twelve days. This one was right on schedule."

"I was afraid you'd say that." I'd been confident he would. I don't know why I asked. Maybe I hoped he'd show me I was wrong.

"The killer is dead but the killing goes on. How can that be, Garrett?"

Now I understood why Block was so rattled. This wasn't just a matter of his career being in jeopardy.

"I don't know. What happened to the old man's body?"

"It was cremated. I saw them both go into the ovens."

"What did you do with the old man from the Bustee? Did you get anything out of him?"

Block looked embarrassed. "He died."

"Huh?"

"We tried too hard. Gave him too much of everything. He overdid himself to death."

I just shook my head. It could only happen around me. "You recheck the Hamilton place since you found this?"

"Got the report before I came after you. Nothing there. No connection."

"What about the coach?"

"Hasn't moved. The wheels are chained so it can't be. And the horses were sold. They didn't belong there. They were squatters too."

"Know who this girl is yet?"

"No. But it won't be long before we do. She'll be somebody."

He meant she'd be related to somebody. None of the dead girls had been important in their own right yet, but they'd all come off the Hill. "If the pattern holds." I was scared and confused. I told Block I was scared and confused and didn't know what to do now, except, "We'd better talk it over with the Dead Man before we do anything. He did interview all those people."

Block brightened. "Yeah. If there's anything to start on, he ought to have it."

I recalled my roast. That wonderful, expensive roast that had had me drooling for hours.

I wasn't hungry anymore.

"It probably don't mean a thing now," I said, "but did you ever find out who we caught?"

"The old guy?"

No, dipshit. The lead horse in the team in . . . "Yes."

Block glanced around, then whispered, "Idraca Matiston."

"Whoa! Scares me. Who the hell is . . . *was* . . . Idraca Matiston."

"Keep it down, will you?"

"Somebody, I take it, that was enough of a somebody that you don't want word getting around."

Whisper. "Idraca Matiston, Viscount Nettles. Lady Hamilton's lover. Had a bit of a bizarre reputation to begin, which is why we wrapped it fast and quiet and other quarters let it out he'd passed on from complications. He was in and out of the Hamilton house all the time and nobody thought anything of it because he'd always been. Now I know what I know, I'd go back and take a closer look at Lady Hamilton's mishap if the Prince would let me."

"I still don't know who you're talking about. I don't keep up with the ruling class's scandals. Guess it doesn't matter now, anyway."

"No, it doesn't. We're under orders to forget that episode."

I was willing to forget everything except when I looked at the young woman without her entrails. I shut up, did not press Block, but I did wonder about a woman who would take an antique like old butterfly-breath for her lover.

"Your dream came true," I told Dean when he let us in. "I'm employed. You'd better be more careful what you wish for."

"Is it that bad?"

"Worse. Go wake up the Dead Man."

"What about supper? Everything is overdone now." He almost whined. He's proud of his cooking.

"If you'd seen what I did, you wouldn't want to eat either."

"Oh. Then I'll have to get everything off the stove and put away right away." Thus he evaded having to deal with the Dead Man. He has a real talent for getting out of things by having something else to do that has to get done first.

I told Block, "We may have to light a fire under him. I think he's only been asleep about a week. Sometimes these spells last for months. Dean. Since you don't want to handle His Nibs, you get to go get Morley." That would fix him. He was less comfortable at Morley's place than in the Dead Man's room.

The brave Captain Block endured our juvenile maneuvers without comment. Maybe there was a human being in there. Maybe I could grow to like the guy, incompetence and all.

I led the way, storming the ramparts. Or whatever.

I hadn't been into the Dead Man's room since well before his nap began. Things had changed.

"Gods!" Block swore.

I made an inarticulate sound something like a squeal.

The place was full of bugs. Big bugs, little bugs, enough bugs to carry the Dead Man away if they got into teamwork. And I knew who was to blame.

The fat stiff had worked a deal with Saucerhead behind my back. The real question was, how had he worked it so the creepy-crawlies hadn't gotten into the rest of the house to give his scheme away? I muttered, "I hope you're enjoying your dreams about the Cantard." Despite my efforts, chitin crunched underfoot.

"What is this?" Block asked.

"He collects bugs. Believe it or not. And doesn't bother to get rid of them when he's done playing with them. Now I'll have to use sulfur candles again. I hate it when I have to do that." I wondered if Dean had been in on the deal. Probably. That would explain the absence of the cat. He'd know I'd start exterminating as soon as I found out. No cat would survive a thorough sulfur-candle job.

I started considering doing a sulfur-candle job on myself. It had been half an hour.

"He dead?" Block asked. "Like for good?" His Nibs hadn't twitched a mental muscle.

"No. Just napping. Really. He picks his times for when it's most inopportune."

"How come?"

I shrugged. "These things happen to me."

"What do you do?"

"Fuss and fume and threaten to light a fire under him. Scream and yell and run in circles."

"What if that don't work?"

"Then I muddle through on my own." I started loosening up to do my screaming and circling. I'd exhausted fuss and fume and threaten.

Block started wadding scrap paper from a trash box nobody had emptied in an epoch. He tossed the wads under the Dead Man's chair. I got attentive. "What're you doing?" My money was under there. I hoped he hadn't noticed.

"Going to start that fire you mentioned."

"Hell, you got balls after all." I talked about it but never seriously considered doing it. I leaned against the doorframe, watched. This could get interesting.

The bugs started getting excited—more excited than they usually do when someone is stomping around. I began to suspect that my partner wasn't as far away as he'd like me to think.

Block grabbed a lamp.

Damn. He was going to go for it. All the way. I wouldn't interfere in it for anything. Grinning, I observed, "I figure the fire will get his attention before it's big enough to be a threat to the house. After four hundred years he's pretty dried out. Ever hear about how when the Dewife invaded Polkta they couldn't find enough wood to heat their stills—no trees in Polkta—so they dragged old mummies out of the ancient Polktan tombs and burned them instead?"

Block paused. "Really?" He had a big dopey frown on.

"Really. A body dries out for a few hundred years, it'll burn. Not great, but good enough so you don't have to do without your liquor."

"Oh." Block didn't care about curiosa. In fact, he was baffled. What did this have to do with a bunch of drunken barbarian tomb robbers in a far-away land a hundred years ago?

I had to wonder about the man. And my cherished notions about the Watch. Maybe I was wrong. Maybe they weren't all bone-lazy and graft-bitten. Maybe some were well-meaning—like Block most of the time—but were too stupid to handle their jobs.

Block squatted to shove the lamp under the Dead Man's chair.

Call him off, Garrett.

"It lives! Hang in there, Captain. I'm starting to get something."

Garrett!

"Take a peek inside a head or two, Old Bones. We've got a problem."

Block froze, flame a foot from the wastepaper, eyes a hair too high to spot my stash.

I have called you a curse upon my waning years, Garrett. I have been too kind. Many a time have I been tempted to terminate our association. I should have yielded. You are rude, pushy, thoughtless, uncouth. Only a certain crude charm shields you.

"My mother loved me. But what did she know, eh?"

I could spend hours cataloging your shortcomings. But this is not the time.

"You've done it often enough that I know them by heart anyway."

Excellent. You do have your redeeming virtues.

First time I'd heard that from him. Tinnie and Maya and one or twelve other ladies had mentioned an occasional virtue and a more-than-occasional failing, but—

Including an all-consuming laziness. However, this once, you were correct to disturb me.

"Gods, you can carry me away. I've seen it all now."

Your manners are deplorable. You might have found a more civil means of obtaining my attention. But your assessment is correct. You cannot handle this without my assistance.

Smug character, eh? I signaled Block to back off. "He's awake." I breathed easier with the Watchman away from the household fortune.

I feared it would come to this. The hints were there. But I allowed your success on the Hill, come so swift and with such apparent finality, to deceive me. Because I wanted it to be true. Yes. Even master realists such as myself may, in a lifetime, succumb occasionally to wishful thinking. The mind and the heart naturally eschew horror.

Brag about your failures loudly, longly, humbly, and you can make a virtue of them. Make it look like you're a regular guy. I asked, "How come I get the feeling you weren't asleep at all, you were just rehearsing? Cut the aw-shucks comedy, Chuckles. Girls are dying right on schedule. They shouldn't be. You talked to everybody who had anything to do with the others. Did you get anything? Give us an angle. Tell us how to stop this thing for good."

That may not be possible. Not in the sense you mean. If it is what I feared at first glimpse. Captain Block, I need to know about that man you took from the Bustee. Garrett, I want to know about those ritual knives.

I felt him digging into my mind, deeper than usual. Presumably he was doing the same to Block at the same time. Block's eyes got huge. In my case I felt him digging after things I hadn't noticed noticing at the site of the most recent murder.

It's neither fun nor comfortable having somebody prowl through your head. I hate it. You'd hate it too. There are things in there that nobody ought to know. But I didn't shut him out.

I can do that—if I work at it hard enough.

He surprised me. *Butterflies?*

"Yes. So?"

Three times now, butterflies. This is a new twist. Though no one has mentioned butterflies in connection with any of the victims you did not see yourself, I feel that we are dealing with a single killer.

"No shit?" I couldn't see there being a bunch of guys all getting the same idea: Hey, wouldn't it be neat if I found me a pretty young brunette and strung her up and bled her and cut her guts out?

Indeed, Garrett. Absolutely. One particularly interesting fact that emerged from my interview series was that the blond young lady, Tania Fahkien, was not a natural blonde. In fact, the state of blondness had befallen her only hours before her demise.

"Are any of them natural blondes? Not many, in my experience."

Just so. The point is, the coloring of the victims is worth pursuit.

Even Block had gotten that far. I said so.

Of course. But we forgot that in our excitement over having brought the killer to ruin. Correct?

"The details do seem inconsequential when you've got your bad guy nailed down and everything wrapped. You said you feared this. Did you have some idea what was going on before I spoiled everything by getting lucky but not as lucky as I thought?"

Yes. As you suspect, these sorts of murders have come around before. I know of three previous series, though without any direct knowledge of the first two outbreaks. Those occurred while I was still among the ambulatory, surrounded by a people whose foibles and tribulations were, at best, of marginal and academic interest. The victim types and killing methods were similar, but insofar as I recall, there were no butterflies.

"So maybe nobody noticed. You don't see what you're not looking for." But Block's one man had.

Perhaps. There was no reason to look for butterflies. Though, as I noted, I was not that interested in those outbreaks—other than as behavioral curiosities amongst the unwashed and ignorant latecoming barbarian, a creature capable of firing his distilleries with the remains of his dead.

He does like to get his needles in. "All right. You know something. You said you feared this. How about you get to the point before all the brunettes in town are lost to us? I confess to a personal penchant for redheads, but brunettes are a valuable resource in their own right."

Horrors out of olden times, Garrett.

"It's happened before. Right? Surprise me a surprise. Fact me a fact."

I was never involved with those prior cycles. Yet they were dramatic enough to stick in mind, though with few useful details.

"I can see that." I was getting exasperated. And he was enjoying that. "How about remembering what you can remember?"

He sighed mentally but forged boldly into new territory by ignoring my impatience. *Then, as now, the victims fell into a narrow range of physical characteristics. They were female, young, brunette, attractive by human standards, with very similar features. In fact, facial similarities seemed more important than height or weight.*

The faces of many women flickered through my mind, as he had reconstructed them from his interviews and ancient recollections. None were related, but all could have passed as sisters. All had faces much like that of Chodo's daughter—if not as pale—and wore their hair as she had when I'd run into her at Hullar's. . . .

Hey. For the first time I realized that she'd worn her hair differently there. That she'd had a full head of hair, hanging long, not the helmet I'd seen at Morley's place.

Hairstyle could be a key. The Dead Man produced several notions of styles from olden times. The faces and figures remained vague, but the hairstyles were identical with that worn by Chodo's daughter at Hullar's. All the recently departed had had bushels of hair.

"So maybe we got us an unhappy hairdresser," Block said. "Stalking down the corridors of history, eliminating the gauche and passé." The man had a sense of humor after all. Weird, but he had one.

I said, "This mess is getting kind of spooky, Smiley." And I wasn't alone in thinking so. Despite his flirtation with levity, Block was green around the gills.

There is sorcery in it, Garrett. Grim, gruesome, ancient, and evil sorcery. Necromancy of the darkest form. Dead men who have gone to the crematorium do not rise up and resume their atrocities.

"Really?" What genius. "Hell, I figured that out." I'm not a detective for nothing. Deductive reasoning. Or was it inductive? I can never keep those two straight.

There is a curse at work. If this outbreak is indeed connected with those that went before, it is a very potent curse. In those cases, when the guilty parties were apprehended and executed, the killings stopped.

"But did start up again later."

Eventually. Apparently. After generations.

"They started up again right away this time," Block said.

This was the first time the guilty party was caught quickly. This was the first time without a trial and execution. This was the first time the guilty party was cremated.

"What's that got to do with anything?" Block demanded. He was into the thing now. In fact, he was back over by that lamp looking like he was thinking about starting a fire just to make the Dead Man get on with it.

He wasn't as dumb as he pretended.

As I recollect, the earlier killers were caught, tried, convicted, and hanged. Two were hanged. I believe the first was beheaded. Beheading was the punishment in fashion then. In each case the remains went into unmarked graves.

Executed criminals still go into unmarked graves. That's part of the punishment. "And?" I asked.

"So?" from Block.

Garrett, Garrett, must you be so determinedly thick of wit? I have given you everything you need. Use your brain for something more than landfill that keeps your ears from clacking together.

The same old challenge. Use my gods-given mind and talents to figure it out for myself. He's no fun at all. But he thinks he's bringing me up right.

Block grabbed the lamp and headed for the Dead Man's chair.

I waved him off. "He's right. Sort of. He's given us what we need. Anyway, if you bully him, he gets stubborn. It's a pride thing. He'll let you burn him and the house both before he'll give you a straighter answer."

Block eyeballed me a moment before he decided I was telling it straight. "A god damned oracle, eh?" He put the lamp back where it belonged. "So what's he talking about? Where's our point of attack?"

I didn't have the foggiest. All I knew was that the Dead Man had seen some fog, and if he had, then it was right there in front of my face.

Of course, you not being in the middle of it, stressed out and confused and still smelling the stink of a girl who died in terror, you have it all scoped out and you're telling yourself that Garrett, he's too dumb to be believed.

•••28

nearly had it. I started to get a eureka grin. My unconscious was hinting that it might pay off if I was a good boy. But then somebody went to hammering on the door. The front door is the curse of my life. Could I brick it up? Slide in and out the back way? If some pest found himself facing nothing but rough brick, would he persist in trying to inflict himself on me?

I lost whatever was about to surface. I glanced at Block. He looked like he was having trouble figuring out how to spell his own name. No help there. I trudged to the door, glanced through the peephole. I saw Morley and Dean staring back. I was tempted to leave them there. But Morley was the kind of guy who would chew his way through a door if he thought you were letting him cool his heels. Anyway, he didn't deserve to be left out in the rain. And I didn't see how I could let him in without admitting Dean too, so I opened up and let the whole crowd stamp in with their ingrate comments about how long it ought to take to unlock a door.

It occurred to me, not for the first time, that I could sell my place for a lot more than I paid for the wreck it was when I bought it. I could move on somewhere where no one knew me. I could get me a real job, put in my ten or twelve hours a day, and suffer no hassles the rest of the time. Whoever bought my place could enjoy what I left behind. I could make the sale more attractive by offering the house's contents at no extra cost. *Caveat emptor.* So long, Dean. Good-bye, Dead Man.

"You got me over here, you'd better catch my attention fast," Morley told me. Not even a query about my health. But what are friends for, if not to make us feel little and unloved? "I've got a date—"

"Indeed." I tried my Dead Man impression. "You will recall a certain corpse in a certain coach house on a certain Hill, not so long ago? Relating to a certain series of distinctly unpleasant murders?"

"As in the waste of high-grade dalliance talent?"

"Probably for someone far less deserving than you or I, but yes. The one we came across during our evening constitutional one night." Why were we doing this? I'd started it and I didn't know—except that Dean was there to witness whatever we said. But why should I care what Dean thought? The guy liked cats. There's something fundamentally wrong with a guy who likes cats. Why should his opinion concern me?

"What about it?"

"This about it. The gentleman who got his deserts that night, despite having found his way into a city crematorium, hasn't given up his hobby."

"Say what?" Morley couldn't stay with the game.

"There's been another murder. Just like the others. Right on schedule. We don't know who she was yet, but we will soon." I gave a jerk of the head toward the Dead Man's room. "Official company. The Dead Man tells us there's a curse involved. Sorcery."

"No! Really?"

"You don't have to take that tone. Dean! You have work to do. You want to hang out here twenty-six hours a day, you damned well better . . ."

He might be in his seventies, but he didn't let the years slow him a bit. He stuck his tongue out like he was six. Then he headed for the kitchen fast as a glacier, smoke boiling around his heels. As he fled I told Morley about my plan to sell the place, as is, to anybody who had a few marks to invest. He didn't jump at the opportunity. Dean wasn't impressed with the threat. I had to spend more time on the streets, had to learn how to be nasty again.

Dean beat the seven-year locusts to the kitchen. I celebrated the new age by nudging Morley into my office, explaining the situation here. Being Morley, part elf and familiar with things sorcerous and eldritch, he cut straight to the heart of it, immediately finding the thing that had been nagging me since the Dead Man had told me he'd given me enough to go on.

"The man you skragged was naked when you brought the Watch captain. The men buried in the old days would have gone into the ground wearing whatever they had on when they were executed. Which would have been what they were wearing when they were caught. The clothes must be the key.

Or something the old boy had on him. An amulet. Jewelry. Something that whoever got into the coach house took when he stripped the corpse."

"Cut it." By that point I'd gotten the point, if you follow me. It wasn't the man that was cursed, it was something that went with the man. Like maybe some knives.

I shuddered. I shivered. I went cold all over. This was grim.

I would have to do some legwork. One hell of a lot of legwork. I would have to dig out records that went back to imperial times to see what the villains had in common. What piece of apparel, decoration, or whatnot that might carry a curse compelling a man to waste ladies who ought to be conserved for fates sometimes known as worse than death.

Is it really worse, girls?

The case had developed a certain rhythm. I should have expected what happened next, as I was about to rejoin Block and the Dead Man. It was guaranteed.

Somebody pounded on the door. "Three guys with knives," I muttered as I headed that way, Dean having proclaimed himself incapacitated before the pounding stopped.

I peeped through the peephole. "I wish it was three guys with knives." I considered pretending nobody was home. But Barking Dog knew better. He had come around often enough to know our dark secret. Somebody was always home.

I opened up. "Uhm?"

"Been more than a week, Garrett. You ain't been over to get my papers." He bulled in behind the usual aromatic advance guard, dripping. He produced his latest report.

"You writing the history of the world?"

"What else I got to do? It don't stop raining. I don't like getting wet."

"I noticed."

"Huh?"

"Nothing. Nothing. Cabin fever's making me cranky. Maybe you ought to polish your speeches. It can't rain forever."

"No. Only all day every day. You noticed that? It's mostly just raining during the daytime? How did the weather get so screwed up, Garrett?"

I thought about tossing him something flip about the Cantard and stormwardens but feared he'd go off the deep end with some wild new theory.

"You'd think the gods themselves don't want me spreading the truth."

"Them probably more than most mortals." I left it at that, mostly because I didn't get a chance to say anything more.

Barking Dog froze. His eyes got huge, his breathing ragged. He threw one hand up, fingers twisting into the sign against the evil eye. He said, "Gah! Gah! Gah!" in a high squeak, retreated toward the door. "It's him!" he croaked. "Garrett! It's him!"

Him was Captain Block, who stood in the doorway to the Dead Man's room, gaping. When I turned back to Amato, I saw nothing but the door closing behind him.

"Gah! Gah!" I said, making the horns. "What was that?"

Block asked, "What was Amato doing here?"

"Him and the Dead Man are buddies. They get together to make up stories about the secret masters. It's amazing how they get along. What's your story? How do you know Barking Dog?"

Block's cheek twitched. He looked like he wasn't sure where he stood. "In the course of my labors as a minion of the hidden manipulators, the puppet masters who pull the strings on marionette judges and functionaries, I was forced to circumscribe Mr. Amato's freedom."

I laughed. "You arrested him?"

"I didn't arrest him, Garrett. Whatever he claims. I just asked him to come talk to a man who was put out about something he said. He'd have been fine if he could've kept his mouth shut for five minutes. But he just couldn't resist tearing into the best audience he ever had. One thing led to another. I had to take him in front of a magistrate for a formal warning about libel. He couldn't stop running his mouth. Donner doesn't have a sense of humor. He doesn't find Barking Dog an amusing street character. The more he bore down, the more Amato jacked his jaw. So he got pissed, gave Amato fifty-five days for contempt. And all of that is *this* running dog's fault. You never heard such carrying on as when we were walking him over to the Al-Khar. Hell, if he could've kept his mouth shut then, I'd probably have screwed up and let him get away. But he pissed *me* off."

"A different view of events," I said. "Though his version isn't much different. He said it was his own fault."

Block chuckled, but grimly. "I wish all our rebels were as harmless."

"Huh?"

"One of the reasons the Prince wants to get serious is, he thinks we're on the brink of chaos. The way he puts it, if the Crown can't demonstrate its willingness to fulfill its social contract with the Karentine people, in an obvious and popular fashion, we'll head into a period of increasing instability. The first sign will be the appearance of neighborhood vigilante groups."

"We already have those, some places."

"I know. He thinks they'll get stronger and become politicized. Fast, if Glory Mooncalled stays lucky. Each time he makes fools of us, more movers and shakers head down there to help tame him. The more that go, the fewer there are to keep the peace here.

"He thinks the vigilantes may connect up, form private militias. Then different groups that don't agree politically will go to knocking each other's heads."

"Got it. Some might even take a notion to get rid of the folks running things now."

"The Crown could end up as one more gang on the streets."

Good boy me, I didn't say a word about that.

Overall, we Karentine rabble are unpolitical. All we want is to be left alone. We avoid what taxes we can, but do pay some as protection money. You pay a little here and there, the tax goons don't grab everything. Near as I can tell, that's the common man's traditional relationship with the state—unless he's a state thug himself.

I said, "I might have to take a closer look at this prince—if he really thinks the Crown is something besides a mechanism for squeezing out cash to benefit the privileged classes." I buttered too much sneer onto my remarks. Block didn't understand that I was being cynical and sarcastic instead of seditious. He gave me a thoroughly dirty look.

I said, "Maybe I should pay more attention to the fable about Barking Dog's running mouth."

"Maybe, Garrett."

"What did you do down there?"

That's a question every veteran understands. And every human male adult in TunFaire who can stand on his hind legs, and plenty who can't anymore, are veterans. The one thing the Crown does very well indeed is find every man eligible for conscription.

"Army. Combat infantry to begin, then long-range recon. After I was wounded they moved me into military police. I saved a baronet's ass once, which is how I came to get this job."

A hero. But that didn't mean squat. Most everyone who lives long enough to get out does something heroic sometimes. Even some downright nasty scum, like Crask, have medals they trot out. It's a different world in the Cantard. It's a different reality. Regardless of where they stand, heroes or villains, the men with the medals show them off with pride.

Contradictions. Being human is contradictory. I've known killers who were artists, and artists who were killers. The man who painted Eleanor was a genius in both fields. Both natures had tortured him. His torment ended only when he crossed paths with someone even crazier.

I said, "We're wandering far afield. Let's scope out what to do about this killer."

"You buy that about it coming back from the dead?"

"You mean like there's been outbreaks before?"

Block nodded.

"From him, yeah. I buy it. We'd better dig into the old records. You have the manpower and access for that, and the clout to get around functionaries."

"What do I look for?"

"I don't know. A common thread. Anything. If the same spirit is coming back again and again, then it's been caught and stopped before. We see what they did back then, we can do it now. And maybe figure out how they screwed up so the cure didn't take."

"If your buddy don't have something he caught from Barking Dog."

"Yeah. If."

"What're you going to do?"

"I saw the first guy alive and dressed. I'll work the clothes and hope I get lucky again."

He eyed me narrowly. He thought I knew something. I did, but what good would it do to tell him there was a survivor of a murder attempt—and she was Chodo Contague's kid? He'd get himself a case of heart troubles complicated by hemorrhoids.

"Right. So tell me one thing, Garrett. What the hell is Morley Dotes doing here?"

He wasn't dumb enough not to know that Morley and I went way back. "I know what he is, Block. And I know what he isn't." But how to explain that this professional killer never offed anybody who hadn't asked for it? How explain that Morley had standards less flexible than most people on the right side of the law? "He's my window onto the other side of TunFaire. There's anything to find out there, he'll find it." I hoped.

I wasn't sure why I'd sent Dean for Morley, now, though it had seemed the thing to do at the time. Maybe he could conjure me a connection with

Chodo's kid. She had to know something. Her pretty head might hold the one fact we needed to nail this butterfly freak.

Right. She was the type who saw nothing but herself. She'd probably forgotten butterfly granddad as soon as the fear went away.

Block scowled, not liking Morley being involved. Gods spare me the born-again—even when they're born-again only so they can cover their asses. "Don't go righteous on me," I said. "It won't help." How did he know, anyway? Morley was keeping his head down.

Block's scowl deepened. "I'll go get my men started. I'll let you know what they find."

Sure he would. After he milked every ounce of advantage. My opinion of him had improved, but not so much I didn't think he was a born functionary. Him using me was still a desperation measure.

"Do." I saw him into the drizzle, then went to find out what the Dead Man thought.

30

"Another thousand marks if I wrap it permanently?"

So the man promised. He delivered before. The Dead Man was pleased with himself for having wangled another cash commitment from Block.

"Occasionally I've complained about the way you—"

Occasionally? Would you not prefer 'frequently'? Or 'consistently'? Possibly even 'persistently' or 'continuously'?

"Once in a while. Whenever the seven-year locusts sing. But I did want to make the opposite point. That was a coup, getting him to pay again."

He is desperate.

"And desperate times are the best times for those who are alert to opportunity. I understand. What do you think about interviewing Chodo's daughter?"

Morley had invited himself out of my office into the Dead Man's room. Now he invited himself to comment. "This came up before. My overtures were *not* greeted with cries of joy."

"Leave it to me. I got style. Get word to Crask that I want to talk about the girl. Don't say what girl. He don't know I know who she is."

"I don't get it. How can he not know? . . ."

"You don't have to get it. Just tell him I want to talk to him about a girl. You don't say which one, he'll know what I mean. Him and me can take it from there."

"You're working an angle, Garrett. You ought to know better. You always get yourself into deep shit. What is it? Don't try anything with the kingpin's kid. You get a notion like that, slash your wrists and save the rest of us some grief."

"What do you think?" I asked the Dead Man.

An interview with the girl may prove unproductive, but an interview is necessary to demonstrate that. If possible, arrange to see her here.

"The very core of my master plan."

You lie. But I do trust your sense of self-preservation will deflect your inclinations.

"I am a mature human being, sir. I do not look upon all members of the opposite sex as objects of desire."

Morley sneered. "Only those over eight and under eighty."

"You're not helping. Sure, I don't plan to be in bed alone when I go. But I don't plan to go for a couple centuries, either."

Ha. I convinced me. All but one tiny part that wondered what I'd do if Chodo's daughter suffered some miraculous remission and not only became able to see me but decided to whisper sweet nothings. . . . Sometimes even the stoutest-hearted of us white knights find the dictates of reason, conscience, and survival overruled by parts not amenable to the dictates of the mind. There's a sociopath in each of us just waiting to miss the connection between an act and its consequences.

"Right." Morley didn't believe me.

I got the impression the Dead Man didn't either.

My own doubts were less apocalyptic. I'd seen enough of the woman to have become deafened to the sirens of that fantasy. I might snort and stamp, but I wouldn't lose control. She wasn't my type.

We talked about this and that till Morley decided he'd heard enough bad news. He said, "If I'm away too long, Puddle and Sarge and the kid will have me set for the poorhouse."

"Sure. Let's go watch them race the flying pigs." I saw Morley out, rejoined the Dead Man.

What now, Garrett?

"I'm thinking real hard about taking a nap."

Indeed? And what was that Mr. Amato brought? I trust that you do recall that we have another iron in the fire?

"Come on. You want me to drag that mess down to Hullar?"

It occurred to me that doing so might be useful in more than the obvious way. When you deliver the report, invest a few minutes in trying to learn if anyone knows why the Contague woman turned up there.

"I did wonder about that."

But you were not ambitious enough to pursue it. You really must make TNT your motto, Garrett.

"TNT?"

Today, Not Tomorrow. Take it from an expert. The only thing one should defer is one's final appointment with Death.

Hang around with the Dead Man long enough and you can read him well enough to get messages that aren't in his words. What he hadn't said but meant was that if I didn't go make myself a nuisance at Hullar's place, I wouldn't get any peace at home.

You compromise. That's life. Every day you make deals that buy you peace—or an opportunity for a good night's sleep.

I decided the path of least resistance lay through Bishoff Hullar's taxi-dance place.

31

Crunch and I were getting to be buddies. After only five minutes of squinting and thinking he remembered that I preferred beer. That saved him one question in his routine. I saved him the others by asking for a pint of Weider's pale lager, then told him, "Tell Hullar Garrett's here."

"Garrett. Right." He tiptoed away. I waited for his feet and beard to disagree. No such luck. That dwarf defied the laws of nature.

He took a while. I sipped beer and surveyed the place. I'd never seen it so busy. It was jumping. Three couples were dancing while the band snored through something I might have recognized had it been played by real musicians. Three tables boasted customers. There wasn't a girl left over to hustle me—though by now they had me pegged for a waste. They remembered better than Crunch did.

One of the girls caught my eye. She was new. She had some life left. And she was a great actress—unless she really was having a good time. She was younger than the rest, an attractive brunette who looked enough like the brunette I'd seen earlier to cool my fantasies.

"Be out in a minute," Crunch said behind me. I'd turned to lean against the bar while I studied the local wildlife. I glanced over my shoulder. Crunch looked back, puzzled. He didn't understand what was going on. He had an idea I was a bagman for the outfit, only I made deliveries instead of collections.

I'd caught him on a real good day first time around. Most of the time he was like this. Puzzled. By everything.

"Who's the brunette there, Crunch?"

He squinted, had trouble making her out. He fumbled out a pair of cheaters, perched them on his nose, pushed them back with a finger like a dried-out potato. I was surprised. Glasses are expensive. "That there's the new girl, mister."

Right. "Come with a name?" Her or me?

He puzzled it but didn't come up with anything before Hullar descended on the stool beside me, his back to the bar too. He accepted a mug from Crunch. "It don't get no better than this, Garrett."

I glanced his way. I read no more from his expression than from his tone. Was he saying this was heaven on earth? Was he stating a fact about business? Was he being sarcastic? Maybe he didn't know himself.

I handed him Barking Dog's latest.

"Shit. Don't you got nothing else to do? All I want to know is, is the crazy bastard getting his tit in a wringer? I don't need to know every time he picks his nose."

A point I kept trying to get across to Barking Dog. I said, "First time I dropped in here, Crask was here."

"Crask?" Wary, suddenly.

"Crask. Like from the outfit. He was talking to the musicians."

"If you say so. I don't remember."

He remembered fine. Else he wouldn't have so much trouble with his memory. "A girl walked in just as I was going to leave. She headed for Crunch like she had something on her mind, only she spotted Crask and suddenly hightailed it."

"If you say so. I don't remember none of that."

"What can you tell me about her?"

"Nothing." He was real definite about that. So definite it was a cinch I'd be beating my head against a wall if I kept after him. I've used my noggin to dent a few walls in my time. All that banging has taught me how to tell when it's going to be the head and not the wall that gets broken.

I dropped it. "Who's the new girl?"

He shrugged. "They come and go. They don't stick for a while, you never find out. Calls herself Candy. That's not the truth. Why?"

My turn to shrug. "I don't know. Something different about her. She's having fun."

"Get those sometimes. Do it for the kick. Takes all kinds to make a horse race, Garrett." He tapped Barking Dog's report. "What's this shit say? He alive?"

"Same old Barking Dog, only going bonkers because the rain won't let up long enough for him to preach."

"Good. Next time, just tell me that. Never mind you bury me with five hundred pages of every time he picked a zit. I maybe agreed on expenses, but not on that much paper."

I didn't look at Hullar. He wasn't in one of his better moods, but neither did he want to be left alone. Tenderloin people are that way. They want to spend time with somebody from outside who isn't a customer or somebody with a moral ax to grind. They just want to feel like real people sometimes.

They *are* real people. Maybe realer than most. They're more in contact with reality than are those who buy their time or those who condemn them. Their real sin is that they've shed their illusions.

Hullar missed his illusions. He wanted to be distracted from those nights when this was as good as it got. "Up for a story?" I asked.

"What kind?"

"Good guys and bad guys and lots of pretty girls. What I'm doing besides peeping Barking Dog."

"Shoot. But don't look for me to give you no help."

"Gods forfend. It's just an interesting mess." I gave him most of it, edited where appropriate.

"That's sick, Garrett. Real sick. I thought I heard of every freak there was, but this's a new one. Them poor girls. And butterflies?"

"Butterflies. I don't know if they've got anything to do with it."

"Weird. You got a curse at work. Or something. Maybe you ought to find you a necromancer. Hey! I know. I know a guy, weird but real good, goes by Dr. Doom—"

"We've met. I don't think he'd be much help." Weird for sure, Doom was more fraud than expert. I think. He did have a knack for laying ghosts. I'd bring him in if that was what it took.

Hullar shrugged. "You know your situation."

"Yeah. Desperate." I eyed the happy brunette. "In more ways than one." I wondered if there might not be something to the idea of apologizing to Tinnie. Fate wasn't throwing anything else my way.

Hullar saw me looking. He snickered. "Go ahead, Garrett. Give it your best shot. But I'll tell you this. Candy's all talk and no play. She's the kind that, far as she's concerned, it's good enough to know she could've got you if she wanted. She gets you there, she starts looking for the next one."

"Story of my life." I levered myself off my stool. "Catch you later. Got an appointment with an overcooked roast."

••• **32**

Dean does miracles when he wants. The roast wasn't a disaster, considering. The go-alongs were excellent. I ate till I was ready to pop. Then, though it was early, I rambled into the hall and stared upstairs, awaiting a flood of ambition. It was a long climb to a cold, lonely bed.

This is where the sad strings are due—only with my luck, the orchestra would whip into an overture.

Right. It wasn't mood music I got, it was: *Garrett! Come report.* Not quite an overture. But close enough.

No point arguing. The sooner done, the sooner to sleep.

What sleep? When I finished telling about my visit to Hullar I got: *I want you to go back there. Work the Tenderloin for the next nine evenings. Spend time with that Candy.*

"Huh?"

A notion has been brooding in the back of my rear brain. Your assessment of Candy as out-of-place hatched it.

"Huh?" What repartee. "What about all the legwork? The research on olden villains?"

Take care of that days. Work the Tenderloin nights, watching for young ladies off the Hill amusing themselves by playing lower-class roles.

It clicked. Candy. Chodo's kid. High-class girls hanging out in low-class dives. For the kicks? Not unlikely. "If that's some fad—"

I will ask Captain Block to revisit the families of the dead girls. I may have interviewed the wrong people. Sisters and girlfriends might have been wiser. Parents are the last to know what their youngsters are doing.

"You may be onto something." Only a few victims had known one another, and that only casually. But if you put sisters and girlfriends and a fad for slumming into the gaps, you might find a pattern.

We might indeed.

"What do I look for?"

Girls who fit the killer's particulars. Maybe we can identify the next victim before she is taken. We have nine days before the killer must slake his need. If the pattern proves out, if the girls were playing games, we will know how and where the killer selects his victims. With Captain Block's help we can watch all potential victims and grab our man when he strikes.

"I'm way ahead of you now. Only, do we have to start tonight?"

TNT, Garrett. You have not been shortchanged on sleep recently.

True. And I was too fired up to sleep now anyway. Might as well go drink beer and ogle girls in the line of duty.

Hell. All of a sudden this mess had begun to look a little interesting.

TunFaire by night becomes a different city. Especially when there's no rain. It had stopped raining. For the moment. I carried my raincloak over one arm and strolled, checking out the nightside.

The ratman hordes were about their legitimate tasks of cleaning and illegitimate tasks of removing everything not nailed down. Kobolds and gnomes and numerous varieties of little people dashed here and there on business. Sometimes I wonder how so many peoples can live side by side with so little contact. Sometimes I think TunFaire is a whole series of cities that just happen to occupy the same geographical position.

I saw a troll family, obvious bumpkins, gaping at the sights. I got propositioned by a giantess of ill repute who was, evidently, suffering a business slump. I ran into a band of goblins riding red-eyed hounds that looked more wolfish than domesticated. I'd never seen goblins before. I walked with them a ways, swapped stories.

They were bounty hunters. They specialized in tracing runaway wives. They were a ferocious, unpleasant bunch clinging grimly to an old trail. The goblin woman they were after was, evidently, smarter than the bunch of them put together.

They had plans for when they caught up. They never doubted they could outlast a mere woman.

It would seem wives are a premium commodity amongst goblins, where five or six males are born for every female. Goblins don't go in for polyandry or equal rights or homosexuality or any of that wimp stuff. Real macho men, male goblins. One-third will die in fights over females before age twenty-three.

I watched the hunters ride off and didn't blame goblin wives for cutting out first chance they got.

I encountered several families of centaurs, refugees from the Cantard, working together, doing bearer-type jobs. What a concept. Jackasses with the brains and hands to load and unload themselves.

I have almost as little love for centaurs as I do for ratmen. The only centaur I ever knew well was a thorough villain.

There were dwarves everywhere. Day and night, TunFaire teams with dwarves. They're industrious little buggers. All they do is work. If they could figure out how, they'd do without sleep.

What you don't see much of at night, outside certain areas, is human people. You do see a human, be careful. Chances are his intentions aren't honest or honorable.

That, in fact, can usually be counted on to get you by—if you're young and strong and don't look an easy mark. Most people will stay away. Only the nastiest, craziest bad boys prey on other bad boys.

Hell. There I go giving the wrong impression. What I'm talking about is late nights, after the entertainment hours. Much later than it was then. People were out. I wasn't seeing them because I wasn't following the streets they usually chose for safety.

Sometimes I tempt fate.

At one point I joined several ratmen in a fast fade into an alley. We watched a gang of ogres tramp past, grumbling and cussing. They were headed for the north gate, on their way to hunt thunder-lizards. Night is the best time to hunt them. The beasts are sluggish then. There's good money in thunder-lizard hides. They make the toughest leather.

I don't like ogres much either, but wished this bunch luck. The southward migration of the thunder-lizards has been rough on the farmers, who have been losing both fields and livestock. More, it's always nice to see an ogre doing something honest. You don't very often.

runch recognized me right away. He plopped a pint onto the bar. "You back?"

"No. It's my evil twin."

He thought about that, couldn't make sense of it, asked, "Need to see Hullar?"

"Wouldn't hurt. If he's not busy."

"Hullar's never busy. Got nothing to do." Off he went. He didn't step on his beard this time either. He was a magician.

I scanned the place. Business had dropped off, but the girls were still occupied. There were two I hadn't seen before. Two daytime girls were gone. The new girls were a blonde and a brunette not of the sort at risk. Both seemed out of place.

Maybe the Dead Man was right. Maybe the girls were slumming.

The streets are no place to play if you don't know them. You'll make more than your share of lethal mistakes if you come down off the Hill wearing your arrogances and assumptions. The natives won't be impressed.

Of course, if it's a game, maybe you'll forget your superiorities while you're playing. Until you get into a tight place.

Hullar waddled out, dragged himself up onto a stool, sucked up a beer Crunch had waiting, scanned the action, shrugged. You couldn't disappoint Bishoff Hullar. A man after my own heart, he expected the worst. "Slumming, Garrett?"

"Not exactly."

"I can't believe you've taken a shine to the place. A man with your rep."

"No. This has to do with that other thing I'm working."

"The murders. You didn't tell me there was another one last night."

Word was getting around. "I got to thinking over supper. About Candy and the girl who wasn't in here the other day, that you and Crunch never saw and don't know. Occurred to me the rich girls might be playing bad girls, just for fun. Like the blonde and brunette there. Don't look like the sort I'd expect in here."

"Uhm?"

"You know the Tenderloin, Hullar. You know what's going down. There a fad among the rich girls, bored because the guys are off to war?"

"How come you want to know?"

"Maybe my girl-killer spots his victims down here. Maybe I can spot him looking for his next target."

"You in the guardian-angel racket?"

I grunted.

"You been out of touch, Garrett. Yeah. The rich broads been coming down. Not just the kids, neither. Them that only want into it at the edge work places like mine. The wild ones, mostly older ones, end up peddling their asses at the Passionate Witch or Black Thunder or someplace. The outfit goes easy on them. They're good for business. You got a skillion low-lifes would love to throw the pork to some high-tone lady."

"I understand the psychology."

"Don't we all. Don't we all. And that's what'll cause the trouble."

"Hmm?"

"Good for business, having all this fine young stuff down here. Gotten a lot of cash moving despite the weather. But how long before their fathers and husbands catch on? Then what do we got? Eh?"

"Good point." The parents wouldn't be pleased. And, human nature being what it is, the girls wouldn't get the blame. The richer people are, the less they seem able to hold their kids responsible for their actions. "How many of them you figure there are?" Couldn't be a lot or there would've been a lot of excitement already.

"I don't get around much, Garrett. I ain't out there counting heads and figuring who's working the Tenderloin why. You know what I mean?"

"I know."

"But they do stand out. People talk. You ask me, tops, there's maybe been a hundred. Biggest part is over now. Just a few come-latelies and them that gets a special jolt from going bad. You got maybe thirty these days, mostly hard-core. Ones like my Candy are the exception now. Whole thing'll be dead in two months."

"They'll find some other game."

Hullar shrugged. "Could be. I don't worry about rich kids."

"Makes you even. They don't worry about you." I eyed Candy. Didn't look like I'd get a chance to talk to her. She had a couple of sailors on the string. Hullar or Crunch would have to do some bouncing if she led them on too far.

"Going somewhere?" Eagle-eye Hullar had noticed me getting up.

"Thinking about eyeballing any other girls I can find. Any suggestions where to look?"

"You want just brunettes? Candy's type?"

"Basically."

He got thoughtful. He wasn't concentrating on my problem, though. He had one eye on Candy's sailors. He was getting steamed. "Crystal Chandelier. The Masked Man. The Passionate Witch. Mama Sam's Place. I seen your type all them places, one time or another. Not saying they's any there now. These gals, they come and go. Don't do regular hours, neither."

"Thanks, Hullar. You're a prince."

"Eh? What's that?" Crunch snarled suddenly. He came up from behind the bar with a nasty club. "You want to watch your mouth, boy."

Hullar shook his head. "Prince!" he yelled in Crunch's ear. "He called me a prince. Got to pardon him, Garrett. He lip-reads. Sometimes he don't do so good."

Crunch put his stick away but didn't stop scowling. He wasn't sure he ought to trust his boss over his imagination.

Everywhere I go, I get involved with screwballs.

•••34

The Crystal Chandelier, as the name implied, pretended to have class. Hill girls would be just what the management ordered. I headed there first. I was in and out in the time it took to slurp a beer. I didn't learn anything except that somebody there knew my face and didn't like what I did for a living.

I did better at the Masked Man. I knew somebody there.

The name of the place was appropriate again. People donned masks before they showed themselves inside. Likewise, those who worked the place. The Masked Man catered to a select clientele.

The guy I knew was a bouncer, a breed nine feet tall with muscles on his muscles and more between his ears than anywhere else. I downed three beers before he understood what I wanted to know. Even then he wouldn't have talked if he hadn't owed me. And what he had to say wasn't worth hearing. Only one Hill-type gal worked the Masked Man these days, a blonde so screwed up she scared the owners. He hadn't seen a brunette in weeks. The last had quit her second night. But he did remember her name, Dixie.

"Dixie. Right. That's useful. Thanks, Bugs. Here. Have a beer on me."

"Hey, thanks, Garrett. You're all right." Bugs is one of those guys who are always amazed when you do something nice, no matter how trivial. You'd think after a while the whole world would be nice just to watch him be amazed.

I drifted over to the Passionate Witch. The Witch was strange, even for the Tenderloin. I never quite understood the place. A lot of girls worked there, mostly dancing, mostly without wearing much. They were very friendly. They'd crawl all over you if they thought you might stuff a mark into their pants. They were available, but not to everyone. There was a kind of bid board. The girls worked the crowd, getting guys drunker and randier and driving the bidding up till closing. A crafty girl could pull more with one trick there than some who worked all night the traditional way.

Whatever will separate a mark and his money. It's there in the Tenderloin.

"Ever see so many bare boobs in one place, Garrett?"

I jumped. You don't expect your friends in those places.

I hadn't found one. "Downtown. Been a while. Nope. Never. And I shouldn't be seeing some of these here now."

Downtown Billy Byrd was the guy they'd had in mind when they'd decided somebody looked like a ferret. He was a walking stereotype. He looked slimy-sneaky and was. He spied on people, sold information to anyone who'd pay. I'd used him myself, which is how he knew me.

Downtown wore a lot of junk jewelry and flashy clothing. He carried a long-stemmed ivory pipe. He tapped its mouthpiece against his teeth, pointed it at a woman. "Case in point?"

"Right. Bigger don't always mean better."

"She was something before gravity set in." Downtown Billy Byrd was the kind who'd think gravity sets in. "You working, Garrett?"

I didn't have much use for Downtown's type but I stayed polite. I wasn't spending much. It'd help if I stuck with somebody whose cheapness was accepted. Else I might get asked to take my questions to the street.

"Would I be here if I wasn't?"

"Half the guys here would say that if I asked."

I understood, then, what Downtown was doing in the Passionate Witch. He was working. Looking for faces he might sell later. I told him, "I'm working."

"Something maybe I can help with?"

"Maybe. I'm looking for a girl. A special kind. Brunette, seventeen to twenty-two, five-feet-two to five-ten, long hair, reasonably attractive, high-class."

"You don't want much, do you? She got a name?"

"No. It's a type. I'm interested in any woman like that working the Tenderloin."

"Yeah? How come?"

"Because some creep is snatching them and cutting their guts out. I want to find him so I can explain why we don't consider that behavior socially acceptable."

Downtown eyed me a moment, weasel mouth open. "Come on over here, Garrett. I got a table with some pals."

I followed but feared it was a mistake. Byrd ran his mouth steadily. How long before word spread? I wouldn't catch anybody if the girls hid out and the bad guys lay low.

Downtown led me to the worst table in the dive. You had to send carrier pigeons to the bar. Waiters got lost trying to get back there.

Downtown's two pals looked sleazier than he did. Cheap flash must have been in, along with mustaches.

They had bought their night's supplies before lighting.

"Sit, Garrett." There was a spare chair. "Shaker, give the man a beer."

"Screw you, Byrdo." Shaker had a palsy. He had a face like a rat's. It was loathing at first sight. "What you giving away our beer?"

"Don't be a butthead, Shaker. Business. The man might maybe be in the mood to buy. We got something he might want."

Shaker and Downtown glared at one another while the third man contemplated the secrets inside a beer bottle. Then Shaker pushed a bottle my way. It was the old-fashioned stone kind, not used by commercial breweries anymore. Which meant the beer inside was cheap stuff from a one-man cellar operation, fit only for the poorest of the poor. My stomach started whimpering before the first blast headed south.

I couldn't be intimidated. We investigators fear no beer. Besides, I'd swilled so much already that it had become hard to care what went down next.

Downtown didn't introduce anybody. Common practice on the street. Nobody wanted anybody to know them. But Downtown didn't bother not dropping names, either. "Garrett's looking for a guy that snatches girls." He looked at me. "Cuts them open, right? The one doing the jobs we been hearing about?"

I nodded, sipped from my bottle, was pleasantly startled. That was damned good for cellar beer. I found the trademark. It didn't match that on the other bottles, so the brewer was putting his product up in whatever came his way. Too bad. I said, "Way I figure it, he grabs rich girls working the quarter for kicks. I expect he scouts them before he grabs them. I want to spot him doing it before he snatches the next one."

Downtown eyed Shaker. "What do you say now, butthead?"

I asked, "There something that I'm not getting, Downtown?"

"One minute, Garrett." He kept looking at Shaker.

"Well?" His minute had flown.

"I figure you got somebody big behind you, Garrett. Some girl's father. Maybe a bunch of them. Somebody what's got more money than sense and is out to buy revenge. Right?"

"Something like that." Downtown's bunch would melt like salted slugs if I told them who was paying.

"Somebody that might pay damned good if somebody handed them the whole thing on a platter?"

"I don't think you can, Downtown. You're shucking me. Running a game. You heard I was asking around. You decided to see if you couldn't rip me off."

Wound a man to the heart. Downtown Billy was in pain. "Garrett! My man! This is me! Your old buddy, Downtown Billy Byrd. I never done you wrong."

"Never was anything in it for you."

"You just being nasty. You know that ain't my style."

He'd never gotten caught. Everything was his style if he thought he could get away with it. "So I'll give you the benefit of the doubt. What've you got?"

"I tell you, then I don't got nothing to sell."

"I'm not buying a pig in a poke, Downtown. I've got enough cats already."

His face screwed up into a frown that had to hurt. He didn't understand. In the old days, less-than-scrupulous peasants sold gullible city folks baby pigs in tied sacks. Only when the sacks were opened, out jumped some very unhappy cats.

"All right, Garrett. I got your point. Here's the way it is. Gal like the one you're looking for, name of Barbie, worked here up to last night. Ain't in tonight, you'll notice."

"So?"

"So the bidding went outrageous. Way high. And when it come time for her to deliver her half, two guys come in to pick her up and take her somewhere, not upstairs."

It might be a lead. But I was less than excited. I'd dealt with Downtown before. He'd try to make a mountain out of some molehill and sell it for a fortune.

"You aren't impressing me yet. It isn't unusual for the high bidder to take his prize home. Not even unusual for him not to show his face."

"He showed his face when he was bidding. Scruffy little dink. Like a bum somebody cleaned up, but not much. Definitely not no high roller."

"Was a bum." That was the third man.

Downtown grinned. "Dickiebird says he seen the guy before, on the down-and-out. Anyway, it all looked funny. We decided to scout it out. You never know what might be handy to know. Like, here you are already, wanting to know what we saw."

"Maybe I do. What did you see?"

"You want it all for free, don't you? No way, Garrett. We got to live too. You ain't heard enough to know if you want more, then you're gonna have to do without."

I pretended to study it. Then I dug out a few small coins. "I'm interested. But you'll have to talk a lot more than you've done."

Downtown traded looks with his pals. They had to trust his judgment. That put them in a spot I hoped I'd never occupy. I've never understood how Downtown survived his five in the Cantard.

"Going to take a chance, Garrett. Going to tell you more than I would anybody else, but only on account of I know you. On account of I trust your rep for playing square."

"My hair's getting gray."

"Looks to me like it's falling out. Whoa! Touchy!"

"Talk, Downtown."

"Right. Always in a hurry. Here it is. The two guys that come in for Barbie put her into a coach with the dink that did the bidding. Only he'd changed somehow. Gotten spooky. She didn't want to go, but he grabbed her. I thought maybe I'd give her a hand, only the guy's eyes got weird."

"Green?"

"Yeah. Like green fire."

"You're holding my interest, Downtown. But if that's all you've got . . ."

"Shaker knew one of the guys helped push her into the coach."

"Ah!"

"I don't *know* him, see," Shaker said. "It's like I seen him around. He's not somebody I pal with, like Downtown. Just a guy I seen around."

"Here's the one that makes or breaks you, guys. You know where to find him?"

Shaker said, "I know where he cribs."

I dropped coins on the table. "I'll be back in a while. I'm going to bring a guy to talk to you. If you put us together with this guy you know, he'll fill your pockets." I was out of there before any of them could respond.

Morley had company. I had to wait. Then wait. Then wait some more. While I waited, Saucerhead came in. I waved. He joined me, glumly. "Cheer up. I need some muscle," I told him.

"Like now?"

"Right away. Unless your investments—"

"Can't wait?"

"Would I be . . . ? What's the matter?"

"Just don't feel like it, Garrett. Not in the mood."

"Since when do you have to be in the mood to make yourself a mark?"

"Hey, busting heads ain't all the fun it looks like, Garrett."

"I know. I know."

"How would you? You don't whale on nobody unless—"

"You feel good enough to pick up a few coppers running a message?"

"I guess. Yeah. I could handle that."

I sent him to fetch Captain Block. If I had to wait around forever for Morley to finish playing, I might as well pull in the money man while I did.

I did wait. And I waited. And then I waited. I waited so long I got sober. No Morley. Block and Tharpe showed up, dripping. It was raining again. I thought some more about getting into the boat business. When Morley still showed no sign of growing bored with his guest, I said, "The hell with him. We can handle it without him. Let's go."

Block was relieved. He didn't think it would be politic for him to associate with a professional killer.

Saucerhead said, "I'll tag along."

"Thought you weren't in the mood."

"Maybe I'll change moods."

"It's raining out there."

"It's always raining. Let's go."

Block said very little till we enjoyed the privacy of the street. "I hope this is something good, Garrett. I need it."

"Yeah?"

"Pressure again. You don't feel it down here. The Hill is in a panic. Some people up there are carrying on like the Venageti were at the gates. I need something fast. Anything."

"Tell you what. This doesn't pan out, you pass the word for them to keep their daughters out of the Tenderloin."

"Give me a break, Garrett."

"I mean it. There's a fad amongst the deb set. Go down and play sleaze-girl. That won't make their fathers happy, but it's a fact. It looks like our killer picks his victims from rich girls working the quarter."

"That won't make anyone happy."

"Not when it gets out. You recall, none of the stories we got about the victims ever mentioned anything like that. I think we talked to the wrong people. People who didn't know and didn't guess because the bodies weren't found near the quarter."

"Maybe some suspected. I can think of several stories that sounded like somebody trying to make somebody look good." Block sniffed, grunted, hawked. He was working on a cold. "We get lucky, maybe we won't have to deal with any of that."

"We don't get lucky, maybe we can let the word get around without it looking like it's your fault. It will come out if this goes on much longer."

Block grunted again.

I glanced over my shoulder. My instincts were right. We were being fol-lowed. "Did you maybe bring a few helpers?"

Block glanced back. "Yeah. They're mine. Clumsy, aren't they?"

"They don't get much practice."

"Thought it might be handy having a few guardian angels hovering."

"Aw. You don't feel comfortable in the Tenderloin?"

"Make fun while you can, Garrett. Things are gonna change."

Nice talk, but I wouldn't put one copper on it. Good intentions can't overcome the inertia of decades.

• • •

We reached the Passionate Witch. I checked my companions before I went inside. Tharpe was fine. And Block didn't look like the law. "We're going to be talking to some real lowlifes. Let me do all the jawing. No matter what. Understand?"

Saucerhead said, "Means you, Captain. You want to lose these guys fast, let them get a notion what you are." I gave Tharpe the fish eye. He said, "I know Downtown Billy Byrd, Garrett. Bottom of the barrel."

I said, "I'm going to try to bring them out here. You bring money?" I asked Block.

"Some. I won't let them rob me."

"They don't have imaginations that big. What they'd call robbery you'd call a tip." I shoved into the Passionate Witch.

The evening was fading but Downtown and his pals were hanging on, nursing their stone beer bottles, waiting for opportunity to knock. I knocked. Downtown grumbled, "I thought you forgot us."

"Had trouble finding my man."

"Huh?"

"Guy I work for. One who wants to know what you know. He's outside. Wants to listen. He brought money. You ready to deal?"

"Now?"

"You want to wait for the King's birthday? He don't have time to waste."

"Why don't he come in? It's wet out there."

"He don't want to show his face. You have to get wet anyway. You got to show us the way, right?"

"I guess. Shaker. Take care of the bottles." To recover their deposits, of course. "Dickiebird. C'mon."

I led the way. Downtown and Dickiebird followed like they counted on trouble. Each kept a hand inside his shirt. Knives. Shaker wasn't near the bar, getting deposit refunds. He'd vanished. "Awful nervous, aren't you, Downtown?"

"Think about it, Garrett. We got a bunch of murders, Hill gals what probably got daddies that eat no-counters like you and me for snacks. Could get hairy."

"Sure could." I didn't like being included in his no-count family. I'm at least a one-counter. "But it hasn't yet. We're counting on what you tell us fixing it so it never does."

"Yeah?" He was starting to think about holding me up.

Block stepped out of the shadows. "These the men?" Saucerhead wasn't to be seen. Somebody had to watch for Shaker. Block looked damned evil in a bad light. He might do.

"Yes. They say they think they saw the last victim, who called herself Barbie, get snatched. They think they knew one of the snatchers."

Block eyed Downtown and Dickiebird. "What's the deal?"

"Huh?"

I asked, "You have a plan, Downtown? You got a price? Talk to us."

"Uh. Oh." Downtown looked around for eavesdroppers, or maybe to see if Shaker had him covered. "Yeah. Like this. You pay half now. We show you where to find your guy. He'll be home, I guarantee." Like he'd maybe checked while I was collecting Block. "He don't go out. You pay us off. We split. You forget you ever saw us."

"Not bad," I said. "Only let's make it you get the other half after we grab the guy and make sure he's the one you saw."

"Garrett! Take it easy, man. He'll know who fingered him."

"If he's the real thing, you won't have to worry about what he knows," Block said. "How much?"

Downtown tried to get a better look at Block. "This don't sound like nobody off the Hill, Garrett."

"Don't worry about where he comes from. Worry about earning his money."

"Yeah. Right. We figured about thirty marks would be fair. Ten apiece."

Small men have small ambitions. Block had trouble keeping a straight puss. He jingled coins, handed me three gold five-mark pieces. I passed them to Downtown, who stared at them in the light leaking from the Passionate Witch. "Damn." He was stunned by the certainty that he'd just blown a rare opportunity.

"Too late, son," I told him when he started to say something. "You set the price. Time to deliver."

"Uh. Yeah." He led off.

36

We walked maybe a mile, into an area of dense tenements occupied mostly by newcomers to TunFaire. Reasonable enough. The man we wanted couldn't have been in town long. Only the ignorant would've gotten into what he had.

Downtown and Dickiebird led us to a four-story row place in the middle of a long block. Pure people storage, though more upscale than most. Depressing.

The clouds parted, let a moonbeam sneak through. It was the only light, but I didn't complain. It was nice to have the drizzle stop, even for a little while. Downtown said, "Top floor, rear door. Hired a sleeping room all to hisself."

"You did a lot of research, Downtown."

His weasel face stretched in a nasty smile. "I *knew* somebody was going to want the goods on this one."

Block growled but stifled his opinion. Even starry-eyed idealists knew you couldn't sell TunFaire's people the idea of civic responsibility. Not after they'd watched their betters do nothing but look out for themselves for centuries.

"Top-floor rear," I grumbled, thinking of the climb. "Inconsiderate bastard."

"Right. You get him out, we'll finger him, we'll all go home. Right?"

"Right. Saucerhead?"

Tharpe materialized. He lugged a limp Shaker over one shoulder. "Yeah?"

"Just making sure you were there." Why had he bopped Shaker? Maybe just for the hell of it.

Block said, "Ripley, scout the place out."

Shadows detached from shadows. Downtown gawked as two men entered the row building. He knelt beside Shaker, muttered about maltreatment and distrust. I asked, "If you was us, would you trust you?"

He didn't have an answer for that.

Block's man returned, puffing. "Somebody's in there, all right. He's snoring. There's only one door. Ain't no other way out. Unless there's a window."

Downtown volunteered, "There is. If he's got real spring in his legs, he could maybe jump across to the roof behind this place."

I said, "If he's asleep, he shouldn't have time to get up, open a window, make a jump."

"Better let me make sure," Saucerhead suggested, gently pointing out that he was the specialist.

"All right."

Saucerhead and Block and I went upstairs while Ripley went around back, just in case. We tried to be quiet, but there's something about your step when you're headed for trouble. I sensed sudden fear and alertness behind those doors where people were awake.

Block's other man waited upstairs. Block whispered, "Still snoring?"

He had to ask? Hell, yes, he was still snoring. I never heard anything like it. That ripping and roaring had to be one of the wonders of the world. "Careful," I told Saucerhead. He nodded.

Everybody got out of Tharpe's way. He seemed to swell up, then charged. The door exploded. Though I was right behind Saucerhead, it was over before I could contribute anything. Meat hit meat, snores turned to baffled groans, Saucerhead said, "Got him under control."

I said, "Take him downstairs."

Tharpe grunted. Block slid around, opened the window. "Got him, Ripley. Get around front."

We clumped downstairs. I smelled the fear from behind those doors we hadn't destroyed. The more I thought how this was for those people, the less I liked what I was doing.

Our prisoner was groggy when we hit the street. Block demanded, "Is this the man?"

Downtown and Dickiebird stayed out of the moonlight while edging closer. "Yeah," Dickiebird said. "That's him."

I asked, "You saw this man help put the girl into the coach?" I was playing a role now and Saucerhead was good enough to catch my cues. I believed Dickiebird. The prisoner was one of the men who'd tried to kidnap Chodo's daughter. We had a different killer but the same assistants, apparently.

"That's the guy, Garrett," Downtown insisted. "What do you want? Come on. Pay up."

Block had his helpers take the prisoner while he paid up. "You know these three men, Garrett? In case this is a con and I want to find them?"

"I know them." I was still reserving the incident at Morley's place, couldn't explain my confidence in them.

"Hey, Garrett! I ever do a number on you?"

"Not yet, Downtown. Go on. Enjoy yourselves." A man could make ten marks go a long way in this part of town.

Downtown and his buddies flew off like the breeze. With money in hand, they would be hard to find. For a while.

"You want to help with the questioning?" Block asked.

"Not particularly. Only if you insist. What I want is to go to bed. I've been knocking myself out finding this lead. I do want to hear what you find out from him."

"Sure." He shook my hand. "Thanks again, Garrett. Winchell. Get him moving."

I didn't say, "Anytime, Captain," because he was the kind who would take me up on it.

37

The Dead Man wasn't impressed. He refuses to be impressed by anything but himself. He's afraid I'll get a big head.

He did relent, though, when I returned from watching Block and his troops, with great fanfare, before numerous official witnesses, raid an abandoned brewhouse and nab a creepy old man who was, beyond doubt, the perpetrator of the most recent murder. Clothing and body parts were recovered. These monsters liked their souvenirs. Not to mention that the old boy spat a ton of butterflies, some poisonous, before they subdued him.

Subdued meant dead. Again. I didn't see that part, but the dozen Watchmen they carried off on stretchers implied that Block was right when he insisted there had been no choice.

The Dead Man remarked, *I do hope Captain Block exercises appropriate precautions.*

"I think he will."

Excellent. So it would appear that the matter is closed.

"Except for collecting from Block."

Indeed. Take the rest of the evening off. Sleep in tomorrow.

"We're sure generous with time that isn't our own, aren't we?"

Tomorrow you must resume the investigation as though nothing has been accomplished. Continue seeking Miss Contague. Try to identify potential victims. And take a closer look at this fellow you rooted out tonight. He may have had more than one associate.

"He did. But the other guy headed out of town before we finished arresting the first one. He lived in the same dump. So what the hell? You finally gone gaga? You think we got the wrong killer?"

I am confident your famous luck held and you swept up the very villain. But you got the right man before and Death did not miss a stroke.

"You don't think it'll take?"

I have strong hopes. But I think a wise man would prepare beforehand against the wiles of evil and the ineptitude of the Watch. It would be most excellent if everything worked out. But should it not, no time will have been wasted. Not so?

"All a matter of viewpoint. I'm not the guy who gets to sit here day-dreaming. I'm the one who runs back and forth till his legs get worn down to the knees. I'm going to bed. Wake me up when the war's over."

Should the worst occur, you will regret having failed to take minimal precautions.

Sure. All right. So maybe I'd play with it some more. Just in case. What could it hurt? Did I have anything else going? Anyway, there were some pretty pretties around the edges of the thing. I might luck onto one who was sane and sociable.

Staying in just meant doing time with Dean's cronies, anyway. The amount of beer those old boys were putting away while they were supposedly rehabbing upstairs, it would've been cheaper to hire professional help.

t was like nothing in my experience. I couldn't fathom it. The Dead Man was frothing with ambition. He had hold of the case like a starving dog held a bone. He wouldn't let go.

It was easier to get out of the house, into the drizzle, and do legwork than it was to stay in and argue. Especially with Dean taking the Dead Man's side.

It might be time to think about an apartment.

The Dead Man still had Block digging through the records too. Block was our best buddy now. We'd turned him into the Prince's fair-haired boy. He was the hero of the Hill. His name was at the top of the short list to head the new, improved, serious, and hopefully useful Watch. What we hadn't been able to get him to do was pay his bill. He meant to stiff us.

He said he'd pay up just as soon as he was sure we'd given him the permanent solution he'd wanted to buy. Right. He meant to stiff us.

I didn't care if he was the Dead Man's buddy. I didn't care if he was tight with Prince Rupert. I had him on my list to turn over to the Saucerhead Tharpe collection agency.

Meantime, amidst all else, I maintained my thrilling surveillance of that ferocious threat to the peace, Barking Dog Amato, mainly by collecting his reports, skimming them, then passing a few appropriate comments to Hullar so he could give something to the daughter. Barking Dog's autobiographical ambitions dwindled as he foresaw the advent of better weather. I was grateful, especially after he went into rehearsals for his new, more forceful act, designed with the help of the Dead Man.

Days hurried past. I lumbered around town trying to get some line on the old-time killings. I got nowhere. If there was any glory to be had, Block wanted his boys to get it. I wasn't allowed access to any public records.

Evenings fled too. I made and lost friends in the Tenderloin. People down there were appalled by what had been done to those girls—but they were more appalled by what making potential future targets safe might do to business.

The consensus was you got the guy. Don't bother us.

The Dead Man fell back on an ancient and adolescent device for getting some of the women out of the Tenderloin. He sent anonymous notes to their families.

Six days after my amazing coup involving Downtown Billy Byrd, I told the Dead Man, "I've found the girl. In fact, I've found two of them. One of them would have to be it."

Candy, at Hullar's place, of course. And the other?

"Dixie Starr. She works Mama Sam's Casino."

Dixie Starr?

"Really. Call it her business name. Barbie was the only victim who came close to using her real name." The most recent victim had been one Barbra Tennys, daughter of a viscount with obscure connections to the royal family, said family including Prince Rupert. Barbra's mother was a stormwarden on duty in the Cantard. No proofs would convince her father that his daughter had been selling her favors at auction, for kicks, before reality slithered dread tentacles into the fantasy. "Dixie's name came up before, at the Masked Man. This is a girl with problems. Candy, on the other hand, is a real innocent on the street. I don't think it'll be hard to find out who she is. I doubt she'd notice if I just followed her home."

And the identity of the Dixie woman?

"I have it already. She's Emma Setlow. Her father and grandfather are meat packers who found a better way to preserve sausages. They made their mint off army contracts."

And you have gotten nothing useful from your search for information from the past?

"Block's made sure I can't get near any official records. From what I can see, though, he's not doing much looking himself. Whatever he says. He's too busy making political hay and spreading his influence throughout the entire Watch."

I suspect he will change his attitude.

Damn if I didn't think he knew something he wouldn't share.

• • •

There came a dawn when there was an actual break in the rains. Dean became so excited that it was still dawn when he wakened me. I cussed and threatened, but he won out. He got me interested. What did daylight look like without rain? My body whined and dragged, but I hauled out and headed for breakfast.

Dean had the kitchen curtains back and the window open. "Place needs airing out."

Probably. I shrugged, sipped tea. "Streets are going to be crazy."

Dean nodded. "I need to do some shopping."

I nodded back. "Barking Dog will launch his new show, the rain doesn't start up. I can't miss that."

Everyone in town would find some excuse to get out, even knowing everyone else would be in the streets.

"At least the city will be clean," Dean observed.

"It will. The rains lasted long enough for that."

"Now, if people would just keep it that way." He delivered a plate of biscuits, steaming, straight from the oven. Drooling, I left him to do the talking.

I didn't hear it, which meant I'd grown distracted. That had been happening more and more as more and more the women of my heart became the women of my imagination. Anyway, I looked up and found the old boy absent. Puzzled, I started to get up. Then I heard him coming down the hall, talking. He'd answered the door. He'd let someone inside.

Going to have to have a talk with him.

"Someone" just had to be Captain Block.

"Not again," I muttered loudly enough to be heard.

Dean set another place, poured tea. Block settled, went to work daubing a biscuit with honey. I ignored his existence.

"Not sure yet, Garrett," Block said around a mouthful of biscuit. "May be trouble again."

"Ain't my problem. Ain't going to be my problem. Only problem in my life is deadbeats."

Block got hot, sudden and major. He thought we were trying to exploit his misfortune. He was right. But he'd set the terms. And I figured he was getting off cheap, considering the alternative.

Block cooled down before he risked speaking. "Garrett, do you recall the knives from the Hamilton place?"

"The ritual tools? What about them?"

"They've disappeared. We got them back when we went after Spender." Spender having been the accursed bum in the abandoned brewery.

"Huh?"

"They was locked up in the barracks armory. I got space there for keeping evidence. I saw them there day before yesterday. Last night they was gone."

"So?"

"Tomorrow night is the next time the killer would strike."

"Wow. That's right." I laid on my most sarcastic tone, like I was amazed a Watchman could work that out.

"A Corporal Elvis Winchell, who was part of the raid force the other night, disappeared yesterday sometime. He had access to the armory. Apparently he and a Private Price Ripley were isolated with the killer's corpse for about seven minutes during its trip to the oven."

"And you're afraid Winchell will—"

"Yes. I need your help again, Garrett."

"It's wonderful to be appreciated. It really is. But you're talking to the wrong guy. You need to see my accountant."

"Huh?"

I'd lost him. "The Dead Man. But he's put out with you too. With me, it's money, with him, it's information."

"Oh. Back to that."

"Back to that. It's the bottom line. I have a feeling that if you talk him into anything, he'll insist on payment up front."

Block didn't argue. He didn't dare. We were about to discover how desperate he really was. I passed him on to the Dead Man.

slipped out while their backs were turned. It was going to be a long, dull argument. Block hadn't yet panicked.

Negotiations are fun for the Dead Man. My tastes are more earthy, more basic. Maybe not as simple as a hotfoot, but not cerebral. It always helps if there's a lady along. Especially if she's no lady.

Barking Dog got the better of his crackpot religious squatter by showing up earliest. The nut was there when I arrived. He was sullen. He growled a lot. Amato tended his placards and ignored him. Barking Dog looked confident. He was ready.

His return had been noted. His normal audience consisted of functionaries who worked in the area. They kept an eye on him, wondering when he'd start raving. Speculation was rife. His absence had left him looking primed with fresh madness. His reappearance was a happening resented by a single soul.

The holy crackpot finally left in a huff.

Barking Dog's venue is the Chancery steps. Seems appropriate, in a sense. In the old days the Chancery was a court of equity, but time changes everything. Today it's mostly a place to store official records, civil type, for the duchy, plus some royal records. Half the main floor has been occupied by the functionaries who manage military conscription in this end of Karenta. They migrated from the military Chancery years ago, after having been crowded out by procurement offices that grow faster and faster as the war winds down.

The Chancery structure is a relic of the empire, built late, evidently with an eye to impress. To reach the huge brass doors of the main entrance, you have to climb eighty dark granite steps that span the entire front of the building. Each twenty steps there is a level stretch ten feet wide. Vendors and people like Barking Dog take advantage of those. If it can be sold from a tray hung from the neck, you'll find it for sale outside the Chancery.

Amato's spot was at the left end of the first landing. Most of the traffic in and out of the building naturally passed that way, plus Barking Dog was just high enough to be seen and heard easily from the street.

I planted myself on the stone rail alongside the next landing up, nodded to Barking Dog. He acknowledged my presence with a smile. He adjusted his placards. He had four, all on sticks with bases meant to hold them upright.

Whether entering the Chancery or just passing in the street, people slowed, paused, hoping the merriment would break out soon. Several clerk types accumulated, looking uncomfortable. Their superiors had sent them to keep track and to call when the nonsense began.

Barking Dog was as crazy as a herd of drunk possums, but he had his fans.

Judging from his placards, his text for the day would be a traditional crowd pleaser, the international conspiracy which denied Barking Dog Amato his rights and properties.

He let word spread before he spoke. He waited past the commencement of the business day. Then he started, soft and slow, without the brass megaphone, while word spread that he was starting.

I noticed something that had escaped me during more casual viewings. Barking Dog had him a kettle out, marked to encourage donations. Passersby surprised me with their generosity.

Maybe Amato was less the fool than I thought. Maybe this was how he paid for supplies. Maybe this was the whole point. . . . No. That couldn't be true. He'd live better than he did.

He started gentle and slow and sane, almost conversationally. His chats with the Dead Man had paid dividends. His soft voice arrested passersby, made them strain to hear. I couldn't hear from behind him.

"Signs and portents," he said when he did raise his voice slightly. "Yea! Signs and portents! The hour is coming! It is at hand! The wicked shall be revealed in all their ugliness. They shall be found out and rooted out, and we who have endured, who have borne their weight upon our shoulders till we have become hunchbacks, we shall see our agony repaid."

I glanced around. Was there anybody here who might know me? That sounded suspiciously like he was going to take a plunge into sedition. That seemed an unwise career move to me. Sedition was the sort of talk that could get you thrown into a real prison—if you were dumb enough to talk it on the Chancery steps instead of at the bar in your neighborhood tavern. Outside, in broad daylight, it might sound serious instead of just bitching.

Ha! Fooled you, Garrett!

Everyone listening heard hunchbacks and jumped to the same conclusion. The crowd grew quieter, waited for Barking Dog to step into it up to his knees, then shove his foot in his mouth.

How come people get such a kick out of watching a disaster in progress?

Barking Dog veered off ninety degrees. "They have stolen my houses. They have stolen my lands. They have stolen my family titles. Now they strive to steal my good name so they can silence me when I denounce their wickedness. They had me incarcerated in the Al-Khar in their efforts to stifle me. They have tried to silence me through fear. But by stealing everything from me they have left me entirely without fear. They have left me nothing to lose. By stealing everything they have also taken those signs which remind them of who I am. They forget whom they consigned to vile durance.

"Kropotkin F. Amato will not yield. Kropotkin F. Amato will fight on so long as a single breath remains in his abused flesh."

That was all old stuff, excepting the prison references. He began to lose his audience. But then he did something he'd not done before. He named names. And he started moving, stalking back and forth, flinging his hands around, shrieking in rage. Again I thought he was digging himself a grave, but then realized he'd named only names on the public record. And he hadn't said anything objectionable about them, he'd just surrounded their names with racket that might nail them through guilt by association.

The man was damned clever.

40

"**T**he man's damned clever."

I bounced high enough to bruise my skull on low-flying clouds.

"I mean, using the truth to tell lies that way." Crask had appeared out of nowhere, behind me.

I barked, "Why the hell you got to do that?"

He grinned. "Because it's fun watching you jump." He meant it. He would keep trying to make me jump till the day he really did greet me with a knife.

"What do you want?" My mood wasn't what it had been.

"It's not what I want, Garrett. It's never that. It's what Chodo wants. You know that. I'm just an errand boy."

Right. And a saber-toothed tiger is just a pussycat. "I'll play. What does the kingpin want?" I tried to keep one eye on Barking Dog. Amato was into a foaming-mouth frenzy now, excoriating and denouncing everyone and everything and drawing one of the best crowds of his career. But I couldn't keep my mind on him with Crask so near.

Crask said, "Chodo wants to talk about the girl."

"The girl?"

"Don't get cute. She's his kid. It ain't right she's down to the Tenderloin, whatever she's doing there. That don't look good. That can't get out."

"You don't like it, tell her to knock it off."

"There you go again. Cute. You know it ain't that simple, Garrett."

"Sure. It isn't like she was some kid off the street, just slap her around, maybe kick in a few ribs when she don't do right."

"You got a problem with your mouth, Garrett. I been telling Chodo for a long time you got a problem with your mouth. For a while there he couldn't see that. But he's maybe seeing things clearer these days. You'll maybe want to keep a lid on the wise-guy stuff when you see him."

I always had . . . See him? I hadn't planned to see that old coot ever again. I told Crask that.

"We're all entitled to our opinions, and maybe even our little dreams, I reckon. But sometimes they got to change, Garrett."

I glanced around. Crask wasn't alone. Naturally. He'd brought enough help to carry off three or four uncooperative characters my size. "I suppose you have a point." I stood, indicated he should lead the way.

I considered taking a powder. Barking Dog's crowd might have made escape possible. But I had a feeling I wasn't in danger. Yet. Had I reached the head of the kingpin's list, they'd have just hit me. Killing was a businesslike business with Chodo and his main men. They didn't waste time tormenting their victims—unless there was a big public-relations dividend to be gained from killing somebody an inch at a time.

"Pity to miss the rest of this." I nodded at Barking Dog.

"Yeah. Old goof's on a roll. But business is business. Let's go."

Our immediate destination stood at the curb on the far side of the Chancery. It was a big black coach similar to the one the old butterfly man had ridden. Chodo Contague's personal coach.

"How many of these does he have?" It hadn't been that long since I'd fallen out of a similar one scant seconds before it became a lunch bucket for a thunder-lizard taller than most three-story houses.

"This is a new one."

"I figured." Since it looked and smelled new. You can't fool us trained investigators.

That other, earlier ride had sprung from a misunderstanding that had irked me at the time. So much so that I'd decided to whack Chodo before he came after me again. I'd joined forces with this very Crask to see the job done.

But Chodo was still alive, still in charge.

I couldn't figure it.

Crask is smart but he isn't much of a talker. It's a long haul from the skirts of the Hill out to Chodo's estate. You have plenty of time to consider the meaning of life. If you're traveling with a Crask and a couple other stiffs who lack even the redeeming value of having brains, you tend to drift away into philosophy. There's only so much amusement to be had from farting contests and exchanges of grotesque misinformation about female anatomy.

Try as I might, I couldn't get anything better going. All I got out of Crask was an indefinite impression that there was more going on than he cared to tell me.

Which made perfect sense if he planned to break my neck. You don't tell the pig ahead of time that it's come the day for making bacon. All I had going was the dubious comfort I could take from knowing that Crask had no cause to go to all this trouble just to ice me.

I hadn't seen Chodo's place since the night Winger and I broke in planning to hasten Chodo's journey to the promised land. Nothing appeared changed except that the damage had been repaired and a fresh herd of small thunder-lizards had been brought in to patrol the grounds and graze on intruders. "Just like old times," I muttered.

"We've added a twist or two," Crask informed me, grinning evilly, like he hoped I'd think he was bluffing and would have a go at sneaking in. That would appeal to his selective sense of humor.

41

L ike old times. Chodo greeted his company in the pool room.
It was called that because there was a huge indoor bath in there. I've seen smaller oceans. The bath was heated. Usually—though this time was an exception—the poolside was decorated by a small herd of unclothed beauties, there just to lend that final touch of decadence.

While we waited, I asked, "Where are the honeys? I miss them."

"You would. Chodo didn't want them around while his daughter was staying here. He never got around to bringing them back."

What did that mean? That the daughter wasn't staying here anymore?

Patience, Garrett. All will come clear.

The man himself arrived, looking little changed. He was in his wheel-chair with a heavy blanket wrapped around his lap and covering his legs. Hands like tallow claws lay folded upon his lap. I couldn't see his face. His head had fallen forward. It swayed back and forth.

Sadler stopped him at the far end of the pool, fiddled with his chair, tilted him back so his head stayed level. I'd never seen Chodo in anything approaching good health, but now he seemed way worse than ever before. He looked like somebody had poisoned him with arsenic, then he'd suffered severe anemia till the vampires got him. His skin was almost translucent.

He was dressed and groomed as though for dinner with the King—and that only made the sight of him more horrible.

I started forward. Crask caught my arm. "From here, Garrett."

Sadler bent to Chodo's right ear. "Mr. Garrett is here, sir." He spoke softly. I barely heard him.

Nothing shifted in Chodo's eyes. I saw no light of recognition. I saw no evidence that he could see at all. His eyes didn't move and didn't focus.

Sadler leaned forward as though to let Chodo speak into his ear. He listened, then straightened. "He wants to know about his daughter." No pretense about her now. "Whatever you know. All your speculations."

"I already told you—"

"*He* wants to hear it. With everything you left out."

Bullpucky. Maybe I wasn't supposed to notice. Maybe they didn't care if I did. Chodo's lips hadn't moved. He hadn't done anything but drool.

I flashed back to the night we tried to scribble the end of his story. We—Crask, Sadler, Winger, and I—had had him cornered, along with a witch he'd been chasing. The witch did get herself elevated to a higher plane before Winger and I cut out, but she'd made a final gesture before checkout. She'd given Chodo a fist in the face. She'd been wearing a poison ring filled with snake venom.

So. Rather than killing Chodo, the venom had induced a stroke.

How nice for Crask and Sadler. They must have thought themselves beloved of the gods when that happened. Their original plan had been to do Chodo and grab control of the outfit before anyone realized what was happening. That was the historically preferred solution to the problem of the transition of power in the underworld. But it meant a long shake-out period while potential challengers were eliminated.

This way there was no problem with the succession. Chodo was alive. They could pretend he was still in charge while they gathered the reins slowly.

It was grotesque.

I played along.

Not playing along would be a capital crime, I suspected.

Much of the time I function well in tight situations. I didn't betray my thoughts. I pursued a conversation with Chodo, through Sadler, as though I sensed nothing unusual.

I gave them a thorough briefing on the serial killer and young women frequenting the Tenderloin. Sometimes it's best you don't shield people from the truth.

"Seen her lately?" Sadler asked.

"Not since that day at Hullar's."

"You didn't try to trace her?"

"Why? No. I lost interest once I knew who she was."

"You're not as dumb as you look," Crask observed.

"Like you. Protective coloration."

Sadler gave me the fish eye. "You would've known who she was after seeing her at Dotes's place."

"Speaking of Morley, the reason I asked him to contact you is the girl might know something that would help stop this killer. And I didn't figure hunting her up personally would—"

Sadler cut in, "You said the killer was dead." He was determined to trip me up.

"Maybe. We hope. But he's been dead before. The killings didn't stop."

"You don't think they're going to?"

"The ritual knives disappeared. A Watchman who was around the corpse and who had access to the knives has disappeared. That may not mean anything, but why take chances? I've identified two women who fit the victim profile. I'll see them covered like a blanket." Did I sound like I was making sense?

Sadler bent, stayed bent a long time, though Chodo's lips never moved. "Yes sir. I'll tell him that, sir." He straightened. "Chodo says he has a job for you, Garrett. He wants you to find his daughter. He wants you to bring her home."

"The resources he has, he can't find her?"

"Not without everybody knowing he's looking."

Crask said, "He can't go looking himself, Garrett. That would be like admitting he can't control his own family."

Yeah. And folks might even wonder why she'd run away. "I see." I turned away, pretended to pace, finally stopped. "I can handle it. But I could use a little something to get started with. I mean, I don't even know her name, let alone anything about her."

"Belinda," Crask said, "She won't be using it."

Teach your mama to suck eggs, boy. "Belinda? You're kidding. Nobody's named Belinda anymore."

"After Chodo's old granny." The man didn't crack a smile. "She raised him up until he was old enough to run the streets."

Crask had a faraway look. I hoped he didn't wax nostalgic about the old days. Chodo had a decade on him, so they couldn't have run the bricks at the same time, but Crask and Sadler, like most of Chodo's inside boys, had come into the business from the streets, with time out for special education at Crown expense, in the University of the Cantard.

"I can handle it," I said again. I seldom demur when dealing with the kingpin face-to-face. A weakness of mine, being fond of breathing.

Sadler leaned down as though startled, listened. "Yes sir. I'll see to it, sir." He straightened. "I've been instructed to advance you a hundred marks against your fees and expenses."

Maybe it was the season, all these people throwing money my way. "I'm on the job," I said. "Only I hope I don't have to walk ten miles home." Hint, hint. But I wouldn't press the issue. I wanted out of there bad. Soon. Before there was anything more.

··· **42**

I thought a lot during the ride home, concluded that finding beautiful Miss Belinda Contague might not be healthy.

Crask and Sadler might consider me disposable once they had her in hand, under control.

My disposability probably had plenty to do with why they had chosen this particular investigator to investigate. There was one fine chance they figured I knew too much already. In fact, just to be optimistic, I was going to count on that.

So the one thing I had going for me was the fact that I hadn't found the girl yet. As long as she stayed unfound, things would stay just dandy for me.

The more I thought, the more I was convinced I had to simplify my life. I didn't have enough eyes to watch all the directions I needed to watch.

Night fell before I got home. With the darkness came rain, surprising me I don't know why. Wasn't like it was something new.

I headed up the front steps wondering how I could find Belinda Contague without seeming to find her, before I weaseled out of my troubles with Crask and Sadler.

"Where have you been?" Dean demanded before the door opened wide enough to admit me.

"What are you, my mother? You think it's any of your business, you drop in while I'm explaining to His Nibs." I could maybe drop a few housekeeping hints while I was at that. Anything to get a little cleaning done in there without having to do it myself.

Dean read me like a book. He was old and slow but far from senile. He harrumphed, headed for the kitchen, but halted as he came abreast of my office doorway. "I nearly forgot. You have a guest. In the small front room."

"Oh?" A new cat, big enough to rip my leg off? Or Barking Dog on a midnight mission? . . . No. Amato would be across the way swapping insanities with the Dead Man. Evangelists?

Only one way to find out.

I opened the door.

Time passed. I finally came around when the woman cracked, "You like what you see? Or are you just a mouth breather?"

"Sorry. You weren't what I was expecting."

"Then put your eyes back in their sockets, Jocko. Why surprised?"

"Your father just drafted me to find you, Belinda. In his usual smooth-talking way, he offered me the job without giving me any chance to turn him down."

That shut her up. She stared.

"His driver just now dropped me off." I stared back. I liked what I saw. She didn't hurt the eyes at all. She still preferred black. She still looked good in black. "You look marvelous in black. Not many women wear it so well." She would look good in—or out of—anything. She had what it took, though I got the impression she was used to hiding it.

For the moment the cat had her tongue.

I wondered where Dean had the beast hidden.

Belinda didn't match the victim profile tonight. Her hair was short, black as a raven's wing, made more remarkable by the pallor of her skin and the brightness of her lip rouge. I wondered if the pale skin was a family look, if she would resemble her father in a few years. She looked pretty much the way she had at Morley's place and not much the way she had at Hullar's. At Hullar's, probably wearing a wig, she'd fit the profile perfectly.

They're a protean breed, women.

Oh, I love them, I do, I do, however they disguise themselves.

Belinda rose like she meant to make a run for it. "My father? My father is—"

"Your father is in less than total control of his faculties. His lieutenants—who hijacked me and dragged me out to the estate—made a big show of it being his idea. Oh. Excuse me. I'm Garrett. Dean said you wanted to see me. I'm glad, too. I've wanted to meet you since that night at the Joy House."

She looked puzzled. "The Joy House?" She edged sideways. She'd changed her mind about wanting to see me.

"Weeks back. In the Safety Zone? You ran in and stole my heart. Then some brunos tried to steal you. Remember? Big black coach. Old boy with green eyes and butterflies on his breath? Your basic every-night weird kidnapping upset when the gallant knight of the streets rescued the distressed damsel?"

"You've been dieting. You were four inches taller and sixty pounds heavier then."

"Ha. Ha. That was Saucerhead. He used to be my buddy. He helped me a little. My heart was broken when you didn't stick around long enough to say thanks."

"Thanks, Garrett. You're blocking the doorway."

"No shit? You're quick. I told Saucerhead you'd be quick. I told everyone you'd be sharp. Is that a problem? Me not moving? I thought you wanted to see me."

"That was before you told me you work for the ugly twins."

"Did I say that? I didn't say that. I couldn't have said that. I have a long-standing reputation for refusing to work for them or your father—though I might let one or the other labor under the misapprehension." I tried my famous boyish grin, guaranteed to set any girl's little heart going pitty-pat.

"Stow the bullshit, Garrett. Let me out of here."

"I don't think so."

"You're not dragging me off to the uglies."

"No way. Why would I do that? My life wouldn't be worth two coppers if I did."

"Mine either. Mine especially. I don't really know about yours. Let me out of here."

"Not till I hear why you came."

"Doesn't matter now. You aren't the guy I need."

"Because I know Crask and Sadler?" I shrugged as though trying to shake off a broken heart. "Can't win them all. But you *are* the girl I need. I've been looking for you for weeks."

"Why?"

"It's about the people that tried to snatch you. You're their only target that got away."

She got real pale. That wasn't the reaction I'd expected. She asked, "What do you mean?"

"You've heard rumors about the killer who strings girls up and guts them?"

"I've heard talk. I didn't pay much attention."

"That's funny. I would've paid a lot of attention after somebody almost dragged me off."

"Was that them?" She was grim, suddenly. Hard, like her father.

"Yes."

"Oh." In a small voice. An *I feel foolish* voice.

"You and me, we're the only ones who ever saw him face-to-face and lived." She didn't really need to remember Saucerhead, did she? "And I only saw him for a second. You must've had more to do with him and his boys. You were running from them when you showed up at Morley's."

"I was working part-time at Bishoff Hullar's Dance Parlor. I don't know why. For the hell of it. I didn't do anything but dance. Some girls I knew used the place to make dates."

"I know the scam."

"One night—that night—two men tried to pick me up. Their boss had seen me, they said. He wanted to meet me. I'd be well paid for my time. I said no. They persisted. I told them to eat shit and die. They wouldn't take no for an answer. Hullar had to run them out. But they didn't go away. They tried to grab me when I left work."

Plausible. Some guys think that when a woman says no she's only being coy, possibly because so many women have only been being coy when they've said no. From what I saw at Morley's that night, those guys hadn't been long on social skills. "Why the Joy House? Funny place to run."

"Morley Dotes. I hoped his reputation would scare them off long enough to give me time to think. Then, when they came in, I hoped Dotes would get upset about them getting physical inside his place."

"He did."

"I couldn't run to my father's people. I would've had to explain why I was in the Tenderloin in the first place."

"What about the guy who wanted to meet you so bad?"

"I guess that was him in that coach. That was the only time I ever saw him."

Well, hell. Wonderful. She'd be no help unless the Dead Man found something she didn't know she knew. "Great. Back to where I started. So. Even though you've changed your mind, how come you're here? What's up?"

She studied me. "I think he's after me again. Anyway, it's somebody with that same smooth style, sending guys to talk for him. I got scared. I heard you were straight. I thought you could get him off my back."

The butterfly man had good taste if not good intentions. Belinda wasn't dressed for it, but she couldn't hide the fact that she was a looker. Her mother must have been something. She hadn't gotten those looks from her father.

"I could discourage him. Why'd you change your mind? Because I mentioned your father?"

"Because of Crask and Sadler. I'm not going to let them profit from what happened to my father. And they know it."

Should I reveal my past role? Tell her Crask and Sadler had done nothing but exploit a situation that had fallen into their laps? Didn't seem the best strategy. "There's never been any love lost between me and the uglies. When they were your dad's top boys they strained at their leashes, wanting their chance at me. Now they can pick their time. I wish I had time to worry about that. But I have to concentrate on this killer. He's about due to strike."

She was distressed again. "Then he wasn't taken by the Watch? A Captain Somebody was doing a lot of crowing a while back."

"Captain Block. His optimism was premature." I told about the two killers so far and asked her to fill me in on the dandies whose sweet talk had so impressed her that she'd come running to me.

I learned a lesson. Belinda Contague didn't listen any closer than her father ever had. "I don't get it. How come the murders keep happening?"

I shrugged. "Crazy stuff happens."

"Inside somebody's head. You didn't get the right man."

Odd. Mostly, Belinda was a girl of the street, what you'd expect of a thug's daughter. But something kept sneaking through, something suspiciously redolent of refinement. She'd been away from home most of her life, a secret because Chodo hadn't wanted her to become a hostage to fortune. I had a feeling she'd learned to be a lady while she was away.

"We got it right, Belinda. Both times. Without a doubt. The killers liked to keep souvenirs, and the men we caught had them. This time we have an idea who may have caught the curse—if it moved on—but we can't find him. We can guess when his compulsion will make him kill. We've identified his three most likely victims. You're one. And somebody's been bothering you."

"Actually, I thought . . ." Small, sour smile.

"You thought they were Crask and Sadler's beagles and you could leave me in the middle while you did a fast fade on everybody."

She nodded. "You're not as put out as I'd expect."

"That's what I do. Get in the middle. It's easier when a pretty woman wants me there."

"Save that stuff, Garrett. I'm immune. I've heard all about you."

Checking up? I put on my best hurt look. "What? Me? The white knight?"

"The rooming house where I stay—under a name I'll keep to myself, thank you—caters to single women."

Sounded like the antechamber to heaven. I maintained a neutral expression. "And?"

"So I've heard about you. You recall a Rosie Tate?"

I gasped, choked. Should I be outraged or should I laugh? "Good old Rose. Sure, I know Rose. I did her out of a fortune by making sure the lady her brother named in his will got what she had coming. I didn't let her get her way by wagging her tail at me. Yes, I know Rose. She's got a real boner for me. I didn't know they let her out on her own." Rose Tate running loose could be a disaster worse than a platoon of serial killers. The woman was nasty. As gorgeous as they come, but nasty.

"You think she's a joke?"

"Not hardly. Not Rose. Rose is a joke like a starving saber-tooth is a joke. Make that a starving saber-tooth with a toothache." I faked a laugh. "So she still holds a grudge."

"That woman wants your head. She didn't say anything about any money."

"Rose was never one to let little things like truth and accuracy get in the way when she was creating a mood in her audience."

"Tell me about it. Didn't take two weeks before every girl in the place was ready to strangle her."

"Way it goes. It's hard to be a crowd pleaser in my racket. So what about Crask and Sadler?"

"Garrett, I don't really know. I can remember when either one of them would have died to protect me or the family name. They would have done anything to shield me from a breath of scandal. That's the way those people do things. They have this elaborate code of honor."

"I know. And part of it is that women and children are exempt. But. The last thing your father ever said to me was, look out for his baby." I don't know why I told her. It wasn't a smart move. She didn't need to know. I didn't need to hoist up a sign saying here's a way to manipulate me. "I said I would. I didn't think I'd need to. Crask and Sadler said you'd be taken care of. Maybe they had their fingers crossed."

"That sounds like them. Him and them too. My father had a thing about you, Garrett. He used to go on about honorable men. About how there were none left, except for you, and you were going to get yourself killed for your trouble."

"He didn't know me the way he thought. I have my bad moments like anybody else."

"He was funny some ways, Garrett. Besides having crotchets about you, he was always honest with his daughter."

"Meaning?"

"Meaning I was never in doubt what he did. Unlike most females near his kind. As far back as I can remember, he told me all the hows and whys and wheres and dirt that makes the business go. I never thought anything was strange till he sent me off to school. Then I got embarrassed. I lay awake nights. I prayed my little heart out. Then I found out all the other girls were embarrassed by their fathers too, and half of them made up the most outrageous stories to explain why. . . . I realized that no matter what my father did, he did love me. And that was more than most of my classmates could say."

Cue the violins, Bunky. The kingpin was a loving dad. When they were totting up the score at the gates to hell, he could tell them, "I done it all for my little girl."

Chodo was the next thing to dead, and still he kept surprising me. "Belinda, I have to admit I admired your father—even when I hated what he was and what he did to people. But all that's something we can go into later. Right now every minute brings me nearer to the time the girl killer will have to do what he's got to do to stay happy."

"What?"

"Bottom line. Some people need rougher stimulation than others. That's what the Tenderloin is all about. Providing junk for the weird-stuff junkies."

My sweet Belinda surprised me by responding in an accent neither of the street nor of the Hill. "My daddy woulda been proud a you, Garrett. Some people . . . Some people is just sick and cain't get it off."

"That's the heart of it, isn't it? Where's the line between what's unusual and what's unacceptable? When does weird become dangerously perverted?"

She looked me straight in the eye. "I'll let you know."

"Hey . . ."

Garrett.

Of course the Dead Man would yank my chain right then.

43

"He wants to see you."

Belinda looked puzzled. "Who does?"

"My sidekick. Watch him. He's not fast on his feet, but he's sly."

"The Dead Man?"

"You've heard of him. That'll puff his ego."

Garrett, do get on with it.

"I thought I was getting on with it as good as I could, under the circumstances."

Belinda gave me a strange look. The Dead Man sent, *Your love life was not my concern. Get her in here.*

"We're a little hasty today, are we?"

"What the hell are you doing, Garrett? Talking to the walls?"

I wish to speak with you, Miss Contague.

"What the hell is this, Garrett? Get the hell out of my head!"

"It ain't me, babe. I thought you knew about the Dead Man." She wasn't heading for the door, she was pressing closer to me, a development I didn't discourage. I eased her across the hall. "I know. I know. You didn't think you'd have to deal with him. You thought the stories were exaggerated. They are, mostly. Except about how ugly he is."

Garrett!

"And testy. He's real testy. Like a badger with bad teeth."

"My God! Look at that nose!" She clutched my arm. I melted. I tried to slide the arm around her, to comfort her, but she wouldn't let go. I'd have bruises in the morning.

Garrett, take your gloating, less-than-winning personality into the kitchen. Indulge your true nature guzzling beer while the lady and I exchange reminiscences.

"Hey! Let's not get personal."

I went to the kitchen and sulked, indulged in my favorite food, Weider's pale lager.

Garrett!

Hell. Here I was barely through my fourth pint and he was rattling my chain. What did a guy have to do to relax? I stamped in there, past Belinda. She asked brightly, "Where can I find Dean?"

"Kitchen. What do you want, Chuckles?"

The girl is exactly what she appears to be. He was astonished, obviously. *I am amazed that she is so honest and forthright.*

"So it isn't hereditary?"

That is not what I meant.

"What you really mean is, she didn't know a damned thing we could use. And you're thrilled about it."

After a fashion. I convinced her that it would be in her best interest to remain here, out of sight, in our guest room, till we do something about the killer.

"Say what?" He doesn't like women, of any species. He doesn't want them in the house to visit, let alone to hide out indefinitely. "You going through some change? Actually recommending that a female stay here?" He sure wasn't trying to do me any favors.

It would not be the first time.

"That depends on how you add things up."

I would love to match wits with you, but that game has lost its savor. I want you to go see if you cannot charm either the Candy woman or the Dixie woman into spending the night here.

"Why?" He had more faith in me than I did.

I despair of teaching you to employ your reason. Because once you lure the potential victim close enough, I can make sure she is not out there when the killer goes hunting tomorrow night. Because then I would have two of the three most likely targets under my protection, freeing you and Captain Block to concentrate on the remaining woman.

"Right. I've watched those two women in action, Smiley. Candy don't play and Dixie is out of my price range. Snowball-in-hell time."

I have faith. You will find a way.

"Right."

This defeatism amazes me in a man who so regularly disturbs my naps with the gales of whooping and snorting emanating from his room.

"Regularly? I can just about count on the fingers of one finger the number of times—"

Garrett, I am dead, not stupid.

"Yeah. Well. So maybe I underexaggerated. But I do wish I was doing half as good as you think."

I wish you were too. You are more easily endured when—

"Stow that. How're we going to move a bunch of women in here? We don't have—"

Dean can see to their wants. I will see to their safety. You go to the Tenderloin, bring us back one.

"If they're even working. You have to remember, they don't do this stuff for a living. It's part-time, for kicks. Anyway, why should we bother? Did Block catch up on his payments?"

We came to an agreement. There are no financial obstacles.

"Really? Nice of you to keep me posted. I hope you took him so bad he won't come around here ever again."

I suggest you adjourn to the Tenderloin and lay groundwork.

Is that what you call it? "But I have to—"

Let everything else ride. Mr. Hullar will not expire if he misses his regular report on the adventures of Barking Dog Amato. I want to be right on top of this killer if he has survived. I insist.

I was willing to arrange that, only I didn't know how to get him out there—unless maybe I hired a wagon and a dozen sturdy moving men. I could just see him dashing gallantly about town, bringing his special style of derring-do, to the dismay of the wicked and cheer of the downtrodden.

Your brain has become a snake pit.

"But I have only one snake pit." I withdrew, danced lightly upstairs to see how my unexpected guest was settling in. Mostly I got to watch Dean help her settle. He interposed himself like he was her maiden aunt.

Dean had been having his rehab parties for weeks. My bedroom, which lies across the front of the house, and the guest bedroom have been done for a while, but till Dean and his pals went to work, the other two rooms had remained untouched, repositories for junk that should have gone to the basement or street long ago. The parties had gotten the room across the back set for Dean, partly. It wasn't finished. But he no longer had to sleep on the daybed downstairs when we had company. Still, his room needed plenty of work to become really habitable. The more he got between me and Belinda, the more I considered leaving the gaps in the outside walls there for him to handle himself come winter.

"Look, what I really need to know is whatever you know about the girl called Candy. At Hullar's. I have to come up with a way to make her stay away tomorrow night."

"I didn't work with her. I barely knew her to say hi."

"Damn. Somehow I had the idea all you girls should know each other. I'm getting really tired of this whole thing. You can't give me anything?"

Dean scowled, though even he realized I'd intended no double meaning. Belinda caught his scowl, raised an eyebrow—I fell in love all over again, because that's one of my own great talents—then winked when Dean wouldn't see her. "No."

I went away wondering.

44

"Look," I snapped when the Dead Man started in on me during my report, "I did my best. I let Barking Dog drive me crazy telling me about his day so I'd have something to tell Hullar. Then I spent two hours trying to get somewhere with a dame so dizzy she thought me trying to save her life was a new pickup routine. She finally told me to screw off and die. Not exactly a boost for the ego. But I did find out that she won't be working tomorrow night. She has family obligations."

Excellent. If we fail tomorrow, we will have her as bait next time.

"How come you're so sure we'll have more trouble with this killer?"

I am not sure. I am taking a page from your philosophy, looking on the dark side, expecting the worst. If nothing happens, I will have had a wonderfully pleasant surprise.

"Yeah? I hope you get your wonderfully pleasant surprise. I'm going to bed. It was a bitch of a day."

All that beer, in the line of duty.

"There *are* limits. Stand watch. If that woman finds she can't control her urges—"

Ha. She is sound asleep, without a thought of anyone named Garrett anywhere in her mind.

"What is she, then? A nun? Never mind. I don't want to know. I want to sleep. Good night. Tight. Bedbugs. Bite. All that stuff."

I made it upstairs before the summons came. *Garrett! Come down here.*

Rather than prolong the pain by fighting, I went. "What?" This would have to be good.

You did not tell me about the other woman. Dixie. At Mama Sam's. Remember?

"I remember. She didn't show up for work. She was expected in but she didn't make it. Nobody was surprised. That was the way she was. All right? She was time wasted. But she's supposed to be there tomorrow for sure. She'll be our bait. Good night."

Whatever questions he had, he took answers directly, without forcing me to spend more time on one of our famous exchanges. I climbed the stairs again. This time I made it all the way to my room before he prodded me. *Garrett! There is someone at the door.*

Hell with them. Let them come back at a civilized hour. I settled onto the edge of my bed, leaned forward to untie my shoes.

Garrett, Captain Block is at the door. I believe he has brought bad news but he is too excited to read reliably.

Great. For Block I'd make special arrangements. He could come back next week.

Nevertheless, I pried my carcass off my bed and trudged down the hall, downstairs, up the ground-floor hall to the door, peeped through the peephole. The Dead Man was right. That was Captain Block out there. I held another brief debate about whether or not to admit him. I finally gave in and unlocked the door.

I was a tad more frank than usual. "You look like death on a stick."

"I'm considering suicide."

"And you came here for help? That's not one of our services."

"Ha. Ha. He grabbed a march on us, Garrett."

Bring him in here, Garrett.

"Say what? You can't go talking around things tonight. I'm so tired I'm wasted."

"Winchell. He snatched the Candy woman. Tonight. Because he knew we'd be set for him tomorrow night. Ripley was with him."

"How do you know?"

"I saw them. I was down there scouting out how I wanted to do cover tomorrow night. I saw them snatch her when she left work. I chased them till I collapsed. They saw me too. They laughed at me."

"You lost them?"

"I lost them. I'm going to kill myself."

I told the Dead Man, "You want to let him do that now so I can get some sleep? I'll get rid of the body tomorrow."

Nonsense. Captain Block, you must return to your barracks and turn out every man who knew Corporal Winchell or Private Ripley. Determine if any knows where either man might hide. Send squads to check those. Worry more about saving the girl than capturing the villains. A success there will endear you to the public and your superiors alike. I suggest you begin moving now. If, in fact, you do manage to overhaul the villains, do capture rather than kill them. The curse will be easier to control with its carrier still alive.

"I tried that last time. The clown made us kill him."

I suspect that, too, is part of the curse. Whoever cast it originally, for whatever reason—you seem to be taking an inordinately long time examining the official records—was a genius. He did not just toss off a spell that compelled someone to go forth and slaughter a certain sort of woman. He created a curse that interacts with its environment, that learns when it fails, that goes on and gets harder to overcome with time.

Block had grown pale. "There's no way to beat it? If I do stop it today, it gets harder to stop tomorrow?"

I can think of several ways to stop it. None are especially appealing. You can make certain the current curse-bearer dies in the presence of someone so handicapped that he cannot manage a killing. Or with a prisoner who will never be released. I am now convinced that the accursed must be kept alive while the appropriate experts study him and determine how to deactivate the curse, cantrip by cantrip.

Alternatively, inasmuch as each transfer has been from a dead man to a living one through direct association, we might experiment with a live burial. Even better might be a live burial at sea. Perhaps entombment if we could be certain the tomb would remain unopened forever.

"You saying the curse itself can't be stopped, only the guy wearing it?" I asked.

That has been the situation to date. In reality, burial has just been a means of passing the problem to a subsequent generation.

"I smell legwork."

Indeed. Much of it legwork that should have been done already. I suspect actual dismemberment of the curse will require identification of the sorcerer who cast it and a clear picture of circumstances surrounding the casting. Motive may be as important as means. Knowing why the curse was created could provide a clue as to how to get at it, where to start unraveling it.

I told Block, "I'll bet he's been thinking this way since the first time you came around. And you've been sloughing off the research on account of it seemed like too much trouble."

He didn't argue and neither did the Dead Man.

I said, "Whatever's happening now, I'm not involved. I've got sleep to catch up on."

Block opened his mouth.

"Don't start on me, Captain. How many times do I have to drag your ass out of the fire before you're satisfied? You have the same equipment I have. Old Bones here told you what to do. Go do it. Save a life. Get famous. Where's Dean? Can't he let Block out? Gone to bed? Come on." I grabbed Block by the elbow. "Do what he says. Get that research when you can. Good night." Out the door he went, sputtering.

got me a few hours of horizontal, but not hardly enough. A big racket awakened me. I smelled food cooking, so it must've been around the solar dawn, though still a long way from any time when a rational being would be awake.

For whatever irrational reason, I pulled on my pants and stumbled downstairs. I rambled into the kitchen, dropped into my customary chair. "I thought those little shit morCartha were all taken by the army for aerial scouts in the Cantard." MorCartha are a flying race, knee- to hip-high, resembling old-fashioned red devils with bat-style wings, only they're more brown than red. They're a contentious, loud, and obnoxious species possessed of no consideration whatsoever. They came from the north, fleeing thunder-lizards. TunFaire had been plagued by them till somebody suffered a seizure of smarts and hired them as auxiliaries. If they did what they were paid for, they could have a dramatic impact.

"These come from a new wave of immigrants, Mr. Garrett." Dean handed me a cup of tea. "Or so they say. I suspect the hired tribes are returning, hoping they can get paid to leave again."

"Likely. Why couldn't we have lived in imperial times? It's one damned thing after another. Look at all this shit. MorCartha on the rooftops. Thunder-lizards everywhere. One of those five-horned things swam the river and went crazy on the Landing last month."

"I felt sorry for him."

"Huh?" I cracked an eyelid, looked to my left, discovered that I was sharing the table with my houseguest. And me in nothing but my pants.

"I felt sorry for the big stupid thing. It didn't know what was happening. It was terrified, all those little creatures screaming and throwing pointy things at it."

"You hear that, Dean? Ain't that a woman for you? Here's a monster going berserk, stomping people to death, ripping up property, and she feels sorry for it."

"Actually, I rather felt that way myself."

Yeah. And so had I. And probably everyone else who hadn't suffered directly from the poor beast's fear and confusion. When you went and looked at the thing, now caught in a big pen on a vacant lot, it just seemed a big lovable puppy that looked like it had moss and lichen growing on it. I don't see how you can call something that weighs in at fifteen tons cute, but it was cute.

"I guess it was good practice in case one of the big carnivores tries the same trick."

"He always have to play hardass, Dean?"

Come on. On a first-name basis already? The old boy drives me crazy doing that.

"Always, Miss Belinda. Pay him no mind. He means well."

"Dean, you checked how you feel lately?"

"Sir?"

"You said something nice about me."

"This is a nice young lady, Mr. Garrett. I approve thoroughly. I'd like you two to get to know one another."

Holy shit.

"Ah. Yes sir. I know who her father is. We cannot be held accountable for our choice of ancestors. I know who your father was." That was news to me, if he meant that he'd known the old man personally, back in those olden days before Pop went to the Cantard to get himself killed. "As I understand the situation, this isn't a problem. Mr. Contague, begging your pardon, Miss Belinda, is as good as dead, and the real say lies with Mr. Crask and Mr. Sadler."

"Two fun-loving boys who haven't stopped being dangerous because they've started running things by forging Chodo's signature. What're you trying to do, Dean?"

"I'm doing what I always do, Mr. Garrett. I'm matchmaking."

His easy admission struck me dumb. Belinda found nothing to say either. We exchanged helpless looks. I added an apologetic shrug.

Dean said, "I've spoken with Miss Belinda extensively and find her quite your type behind her antagonistic public face."

Belinda snarled, "Is this some kind of teamwork seduction effort, Garrett?"

I protested, "You have to excuse him. He's got this thing about getting me involved."

Dean didn't listen. He hummed and did kitchen work while we traded excuses and accusations, then declared, "The Dead Man is napping. Why don't you two go upstairs, make love two or three times, then finish arguing over lunch?"

I couldn't believe Dean would say something like that. This just wasn't the Dean I knew.

Not that I found the idea repulsive. Something about Belinda got to me.

Belinda just sat there staring while Dean smiled, then winked. I suffered the faintly hopeful suspicion that she didn't find Dean's suggestion entirely repulsive either.

However, this had become one of those situations where you couldn't carry forward if both of you were randier than a cat in heat.

I said, "You're pushing your luck, Dean. I'm going back to bed. I'm sorry, Miss Contague. Please don't think ill of me because of Dean's presumptions."

I thought Dean was going to break out laughing. Was this some scheme to sabotage all hanky before it turned into panky?

Belinda didn't say anything. As I fled, I thought I detected the faintest look of disappointment.

You know how it goes. As soon as I was alone and the risk of her reaction was no longer part of the equation, I stared at the ceiling and entertained regrets while Belinda Contague grew more attractive by the moment, any warts magically fading.

An incurable romantic. That's me.

was about to head out and see what Block had accomplished. Or had not, as was more probable—though the fact that he hadn't been back did seem promising. Belinda came bounding upstairs. "Can I go?"

"No."

"Hey!"

"There're people out there looking for you. I don't think your continued good health is uppermost in their minds. And the way you look, we'd be in trouble before we got two blocks."

"What's wrong with the way I look?"

"Not a damned thing. And that's the problem. Was I to walk out of here with you right now, my neighbors would hate me for life. Also, anybody Crask and Sadler might have watching the place would be sure to recognize you. It isn't like they trust me to dig my own grave unsupervised."

"Oh, hell!" She stamped a foot, a neat move you don't see that often. It felt rehearsed.

"If you were a redhead, nobody would pay any attention. I mean, the uglies wouldn't. My neighbors would hate me even more. And I don't know if I could stand it if you were everything you are now and a redhead besides."

Dean leaned out of the kitchen, behind Belinda, gave me a look that said he thought I was laying it on with a trowel.

Belinda said, 'You're laying it on with a trowel, Garrett. But I love it. I hate being cooped up. I'll see about becoming a redhead. Or maybe a blonde. Would you like that?" Breakfast was forgotten.

"Sure. Anything. I'm easy. Just don't put on a hundred pounds and grow a mustache."

She winked. My spine turned to water. But I wasn't a complete dummy. I wondered why she was getting so nice. I suggested, "You might change your look while you're at it. Especially if the black is like a trademark."

"Good idea." She blew me a kiss.

I looked at Dean, who looked back and shrugged, shook his head. I couldn't tell if he meant he didn't know or didn't want to be blamed.

I started toward the door again.

Garrett.

The story of my life. I can't go anywhere or do anything without everybody in range nibbling at my time.

I stalked into the Dead Man's room. "Yes?"

Tell Captain Block that, on consideration, I feel last night's abduction to have been that only. The Candy woman will not be murdered until tonight, at the necessary hour. If the captain has, as seems likely with him, given up searching and is waiting for a body to surface, then he is—

"I'm on my way."

I hit the street. I made the tail within a block. I took him for one of the outfit's boys, not chosen for his skill at remaining unobtrusive. Crask and Sadler wanted me to know they were watching. The really good tails would stay away till they thought I'd had time to do some serious searching.

I'd fool them. I wouldn't look at all.

Block wasn't hard to find.

I went to his headquarters hoping to get word where to look and, behold! There he was, right there in the shop. "What the hell you doing hanging out here?" I demanded.

"We didn't get anywhere last night. I had five hundred men on the street. They found squat. I called it off after midnight. Didn't seem there was much chance we'd do any good then. All the killings took place before midnight, near as we know."

"You're waiting for somebody to find the body for you. The Dead Man said you would be."

Block shrugged. "I'm open to suggestions. Unless you think you need another thousand marks just to open your mouth."

"On the house this time. The Dead Man said tell you the girl is alive. They won't do her till tonight. The killer never breaks his schedule. He just grabbed her last night because he knew we'd be watching later."

"Still alive?" Block grabbed his chin with his left hand and started kneading while he thought about that. "Still alive." More silence, more thought. "I've had all the men Winchell knew trying to guess where he'd go to hide, who he'd get to help him."

"Probably wouldn't need anyone but Ripley."

"Maybe not. Laudermill!"

A staff sort of sergeant materialized. A classic of the type, his butt was twice the width of his shoulders. "Sir?"

"Anything yet on Winchell or Ripley?"

"Winchell hasn't contacted any family or friends. They're still checking on Ripley, but he's a negative so far too."

I had a thought, which has been known to happen. "Maybe we could try looking on the inside." When this happens, it always startles people. This one surprised even me. "What was Winchell working on?"

"Huh?"

"Case-wise. Look, Block, I've been close enough to know you've been going a little further than you're telling anybody except maybe the Prince. Looking to make a splash when they cut you loose, I figure. Whatever. I don't care. But some of your guys have been making some serious efforts to do real police work lately. Was Winchell? What was he doing? Maybe—"

"I got you." Block held a debate with himself, showing expressions that suggested he was reluctant to let a cat get out of a bag. Finally, "Laudermill. Get me Relway and Spike. In here. Soon as you can."

Laudermill departed with astonishing quickness for one of his bulk. He was a twenty-year man for sure, growing anxious about his pension.

Block said, "These guys Relway and Spike were teamed with Winchell and Ripley on a decoy thing I wanted to test. They're irregulars. They're off shift now, so it might take a while to find them. I never thought to check the auxiliary operatives."

The irregular Watchmen appeared sooner than Block expected, and way too soon for me where peace of mind was concerned. Neither was human. Relway was some unlikely breed that was half dwarf and fractions of several other things. He was *ugly*. Also, to my surprise, he seemed to be decent and pleasant, less scarred by his ancestry and appearance than I'd have guessed. He was committed to the mission of the new Watch, an apparent fanatic.

Likewise Spike, who was a ratman. I don't like ratmen. My dislike verges on being a prejudice. I couldn't believe this ratman was for real. An honest ratman is a contradiction in terms, an oxymoron.

Block told me, "Relway and Spike are volunteer auxiliaries till I get my budget approved. I already have a verbal commitment for funds sufficient to add four hundred undercover operatives. These two will direct one of the companies, down where they'll be taking you."

Scary stuff, secret police. Great crimestoppers to begin, maybe, but how long before Block's ambitious Prince discovered that they could be employed to root out persons of doubtful political rectitude?

Sufficient unto the day . . . "So let's find out about our boys."

Block questioned Relway and Spike. They did know of a place where Winchell and Ripley might be hidden. It was a hole they'd scouted while scoping out their operation. They hadn't used it, but that wouldn't keep Winchell away now.

Block snapped, "Garrett, you go with these two. Cover the place. Scout it out. I'll be right behind you with reinforcements." Away he flew.

Relway and Spike eyed me expectantly, probably figuring me for a Watch officer. They were excited. They were going to be part of something big and real before they were even officially policemen.

I jerked my head toward the door. "Let's do it!"

lvis Winchell and his sidekick had guts. Relway and Spike told me about the scam they'd started before chance brought the corporal and Price Ripley up against something too big to handle.

Their target area was the waterfront around Ogre Town. Real badlands. Winchell would wander the worst parts pretending to be drunk. Ripley, Relway, and the ratman would blend into the derelict scenery, then would jump whoever jumped Winchell.

I admired Winchell's balls but had reservations about his methods. He'd made only two actual arrests, of two fairly inoffensive young muggers. But he'd sent a bunch of thugs home kneecapped, set to spend the rest of their lives on the victim side of the line. He felt that word would spread and the bad boys would take their business elsewhere.

"Maybe," I said. "But I think they'd have just killed you."

"Four of us?" Spike demanded. I was startled, not at all used to being addressed as an equal by a ratman. A second later I was amused by this discovery of my own flaw. Spike continued, "Muggers don't have a guild and they don't work in crowds. I lived in this area for years. The muggers never work in groups of more than four. Two is most common. We handled four-somes easily. Captain Block gave us the tools."

"Maybe I'd better not pursue this. I don't think I want to know."

"There's a New Order coming, Garrett," Relway said. "Lot of people have had all they can take. The pendulum is swinging. You're going to find people saying that if the Crown won't solve social problems, they'll take care of them themselves." The man went on, at great length, till I was ready to send him off to debate those women I'd sicced on the Dead Man that time. Relway, though he had no human blood, was determined to be a factor in TunFaire society.

I suggested, "Maybe you're overstepping, friend. Nonhumans are here only by treaty. They don't want to be subject to Karentine law, they better not claim its protection either."

"I hear you, Garrett. And you're right. There should be one law for everyone. You're born in this city and live in this city, you should help make this city a decent place to live. I done my part. I did my five in the Cantard and took my Karentine citizenship."

I got the message. Don't look down because he was a breed. He'd paid his dues same as me.

I edged away from Relway. He was a committed activist. Every third sentence included "the New Order," clearly capitalized.

Politicals make me nervous.

Translation: They scare the shit out of me. They're weird and they believe the weird shit they say without looking at the implications of their becoming successful. Luckily, politicals are few in TunFaire, and those few are despised, outcasts.

They ought to learn to be less threatening, like Barking Dog Amato.

Now I saw how Relway had sublimated the anger and hatred that should result from being an unusual breed and notably ugly besides. He would keep on smiling but would restructure the world so he'd become one of its shining lights.

Fine. Go for it, buddy. Just include me out of the revolution and its aftermath. I'm happy with my life the way it is.

Relway and Spike led me to a tenement that had burned recently but incompletely. Though abandoned, its cellars remained habitable—defining habitable by liberal standards.

I asked, "How do we find out if anybody's in there?" It was broad daylight. I was strutting around with two guys Winchell knew, two guys with no ability to cut any slack. They had black-and-white minds. An hour earlier Winchell and Ripley were their best buddies. Now those two were just names on the sleazeball list, scum in need of expungement.

Relway gave the ruins the fish eye. "Spike, you're better at getting around quietly. Check it out."

Ratmen are sneaky bastards. Spike went off like a ghost, not toward the place that interested us. Relway and I made ourselves invisible while we waited. Relway was a chatterbox with a nose a foot long. He wanted to know all about who I was and why I was interested in the case.

"None of your business," I told him.

In a huff, Relway said, "You could at least show some manners. You could be polite. I'll be important in the New Order."

"I'm not polite to Block. I wouldn't be polite to his boss. I'm not going to waste polite on you and the rat. I didn't particularly want to be here. Fate keeps messing me around."

"I hear what you're saying. Same shit happens to me. Maybe more, looking the way I do."

"Nothing wrong with the way you look," I lied. "There's the rat. What's he signaling?"

"I think he means they're in there. He wants to know what we do now."

"What we do now is wait for Block. I got a feeling this Winchell is nasty. I'd just hate it if he got away over my dead body."

"I know where you're coming from, Garrett." Relway waved and poked the air. So did Spike. "I'm not big on becoming a dead hero myself. I do want to see the New Order arrive. You wouldn't be the Garrett that's the investigator, would you?"

"Probably. Why? I didn't mess up any of your family or pals, did I?"

"No. Nope. What you're looking at is something you ain't going to believe exists. A real one in a trillion. A pervert. An honest breed who comes from a family that's never had even one member taken in for questioning." His tone was challenging, and deservedly so, because my attitude reflected the general prejudice. What was embarrassing was that it wasn't a prejudice I really felt.

"We're off on the wrong foot here and it's mostly my fault, Relway. It isn't personal. I've been in a foul mood since I got up. I usually save my venom for the ratmen."

"You're weird, Garrett. Here comes the man." He meant Block. Evidently Block was held in high esteem in some quarters.

48

Block still held me in high enough esteem that he sought approval before he moved. "The place is surrounded. Gonna take some doing for anybody to get out."

"Dead Man says take them alive if you can. The curse probably can't transfer while they're still alive."

"They?"

"Part must be touching Ripley somehow. Or Winchell, whichever isn't the primary carrier."

"Yeah. Got you. I guess there's no reason to stall anymore. Might as well do it."

A thought had wormed through my head several times lately. I'd pushed it out over and over. It came back again. I was going to be sorry, but, "I maybe ought to go with the first rush. The girl will recognize me. If I let her know it's a rescue, we can maybe keep the panic level down, maybe save ourselves some people getting hurt."

"That's up to you. You want to go, go. I'm giving Relway first shot. Tell him what you're doing, then don't give him no grief while he's doing his job. He's better than any of my regulars."

"Right." I joined Relway. "I'm going in with you. The girl knows me."

"You armed?"

"Not for blood." I showed him my head-knocker.

He shrugged. "Don't get in the way of the real cops."

What a straight line. It was all I could do to avoid temptation.

Relway's storm group were armed up to take a town from a Venageti Guards division. I hoped they'd had some experience along those lines. They hadn't had any training since.

"You figure to face that much trouble?"

"No," Relway said. "But this bunch will be ready for whatever trouble they do find."

"Good thinking. No way you can get chewed out for not being ready when you go in ready for everything."

Relway smiled. "There you go."

I looked across the street. Spike was restless. "Things always get more real at moments like this."

"You had it that way down there?"

"Worse. Lots worse. I was a scared kid then."

"Me too. You ready?"

"I won't get any readier."

"Follow me." He took off. Garrett the white knight pranced the cobblestones a step behind, followed by a half dozen uniformed champions of justice who had no idea how to accomplish what they'd been ordered to do. They hadn't joined the Watch to capture madmen or protect TunFaire from villains.

The ratman had a tiny basement window scouted. As we arrived, he dived through, wriggling, his hideous naked tail lashing behind him. I think that's what gets me about ratmen. The tails. They're really disgusting.

"After you," Relway said as that tail slithered inside.

"What?" That window was too small. It wasn't meant to pass a body. It was as big as it was only because some small-timers had worked on it so they could get inside and clean the place out. Of what, I can't imagine.

"You said you're the hero she knows."

"Shit." And I did volunteer for this.

I flopped on my belly and shoved my feet through the window. The ratman pulled. Relway shoved. I popped through, hit the floor, stumbled over a loose brick, muttered, "Where are they?"

"Back where you see the light," Spike whispered. That made him real hard to understand. Ratmen have trouble enough talking without whispering. Their throats aren't made for speech. "You cover while we get more men down." This ratman had spent a lifetime dealing with humans. He hadn't hidden himself away from the mainstream, content to live in society's cracks, taking only what no one else wanted. My respect for him rose.

I readied my head-knocker, advanced toward the light, which leaked around a poorly closed door. I wondered why Winchell and Ripley hadn't either attacked us or made a run for it. Seemed to me we were making an armageddon sort of racket.

All of a sudden I had three guys behind me and Relway telling them, "We've got the other way out covered. Let's do it. Garrett?"

I took a deep breath and hit the door. I hurled myself at it, expected to demolish my shoulder.

The door collapsed. I didn't know my own strength. I was a regular Saucerhead Tharpe. I tore it right off its hinges.

I collapsed after two staggering steps over a footing of broken bricks.

Elvis Winchell and Price Ripley were hard at work snoring on beds of sacks and rags. Evidently carrying a curse was exhausting work. The only open eyes around belonged to Candy. She responded to my entrance but not in any wild display of joy.

Hell. She didn't know why we were there. For all she knew, we were pals with Winchell and his sidekick. I stumbled to my feet. "We're the rescue crew." Winchell and Ripley had begun to respond, finally. Relway bopped Ripley over the head before the poor guy could get his eyes open. Relway wasn't having any trouble with the footing. He looked positively graceful.

Spike had less luck putting Winchell back to sleep. Winchell evaded his blows, scooted away, his eyes trying to sparkle green. Maybe he didn't quite have the hang of it yet.

Gods, he looked awful. Like he'd aged fifteen years in the time since he'd helped bring in the villain Downtown Byrd had given us. Ripley, too, looked bad, but not nearly as bad as Winchell.

"Rescue crew? You sure? You look more like a circus act."

Spike and two Watchmen were chasing Winchell. Winchell wasn't co-operating at all. Relway and the other man were stuffing Ripley into a big sack.

Block appeared at the other entrance to the cellar, was careful not to place himself in extreme danger. I called, "Hey, Captain. This one don't need rescuing. She's got it under control already."

Candy said, "You're the guy who's been hanging around Hullar's." I cut the cords binding her ankles. They were nice ankles. I hadn't noticed how nice before. I'd been entranced by all the nice stuff higher up. "Garrett?"

"That's me. Trusty knight-errant. Invariably refused and abused for try-ing to warn people that they're in danger."

"Watch the hands, boy. I've heard about you."

Ripley was headed for the street now, out of it, but Winchell was putting up a fight, even though Relway and Spike, working together, had a sack over his head and arms. Neither Relway nor Winchell was in uniform. Having been employed, both had been able to afford reasonably nice civilian clothing. Vaguely surprised, though, I noted that Winchell used a rather heavy-looking piece of rope for a belt.

"I've heard about me too. Sometimes I don't recognize myself. What did you hear? Obviously not that I'm a prize."

Spike, Relway, and the gang managed to get Winchell tipped over and all the way into the giant sack. Relway got busy tying it shut.

"Prize pig. You remember a Rose Tate?"

Relway kicked the flopping sack. "Better than a cell on wheels," he told nobody in particular.

"Ah, sweet Rosie again," I said. "Yes. Let me tell you about Rose. This is a true story that you'll believe if you know Rose and will call a fairy tale if you don't." I had time. The boys seemed to be getting along fine without me. Just to make sure I didn't lose my audience, I became totally inept at untangling and cutting. Relway and the boys started dragging Winchell toward the door. Winchell writhed and cussed all the way. He wasn't alone in that sack. In fact, green butterflies fluttered around the basement, confused, more worried about the single candle burning than anything else. Again I wondered what the butterflies had to do with anything, if they did. Maybe they were just something like a skunk's spray.

Then there was just Candy and me, and she didn't seem distressed by my lack of haste as I talked about Rose Tate. In fact, I started looking around for the knives I'd seen at the Hamilton place while I talked. In the back of my mind was a curiosity about how she knew Rose. When I finished my story I asked, "How'd you come to meet Rose?"

"You have a good idea what's going on with me? I know you've been asking around. Hullar told me."

"I was just trying to keep you from having a date with the guy they just hauled out of here. He likes to whittle on rich girls."

"I got that part. I guess maybe I should thank you for not letting him eat my liver."

"That would be nice." I finally found the knives under the mess Winchell had been using for a bed. I didn't want to touch them, but supposed they'd be harmless as long as Winchell was breathing.

"Thank you, Garrett. And I do mean it. I get real sarcastic when I'm scared." Notice how we weren't talking about how she'd met Rosie? I didn't.

"You must be scared shitless all the time when you're down to Hullar's, then." That was how she was known there. As a sarcastic bitch.

"You're going to ruin your chances, Garrett."

I made a sound like a steam whistle. "You're beautiful, but I'm losing interest fast. In fact, I'm beginning to wonder why I wasted my time here. Your personality is sabotaging the advantages nature gave you."

"Story of my life, Garrett. I make a point of shoving my foot into my mouth whenever things start going good. I'm predetermined to fail, that's what my mother says. All right. I promise. I'll try. Thank you. You saved my life. Other than the obvious, what can I do for you?"

Block appeared in the doorway and stuck his oar in. "What are you up to down here, Garrett?"

"Looking for stuff."

"Find anything?"

"Yeah. Those knives. The Dead Man said we should break them."

Block came a couple steps closer, looked at the four naked blades. "Is it safe to mess with them that way?"

"Winchell and Ripley still healthy?"

"Yeah."

"Then they're safe. Unless you go sticking yourself."

He made a rude sound, took the knives. "I'll bust them up right now." He left.

I told Candy, "Other than the obvious, which is less obvious than you think, you can come to my place and talk to my partner. He's the brains of the outfit. He wants to see you."

"He some kind of freak? Can't come see me?"

"He's handicapped." I hid my grin. Nobody is handicapped like the Dead Man is handicapped.

We climbed out of the cellar. Candy never stopped yammering. I did gestures of defeat, tried to introduce her to Block formally so she'd know who got official credit for her rescue. It didn't sink in. She was chattering at me. He was interested only in breaking the knives, which he accomplished thoroughly, cracking each into four pieces. "That ought to take care of that." Block was puffed up and happy.

Pride goeth before, I told myself. "Better make sure they don't have anything else off that bum. We don't *know* it's the knives carrying the curse."

"We burned the bum and everything he was wearing. Now we'll burn these. . . . Yeah. Right. Not before we can do something about the curse."

"Later." Candy was still after me. I said, "Woman, I'm not going to keep on. I don't do masochism. But do walk along with me, see my partner. My place is right on your way home."

I paused to stare at the captives. Both were lost inside burlap sacks. Winchell's seethed. Ripley's did nothing, but left me with an uncertain frown. A little bitty thing like a clothes moth fluttered away while I was looking.

Meantime, Candy demanded, "How do you know your house is on my way home?"

"I admit I haven't figured out who you really are yet. But I do know you come off the Hill. Rich girls are the only kind this killer liked. So if you're going to go home and hide out from the real world and tell yourself how lucky you were and forget all this and treat the lower—"

"You an Acmeist? Or an Anarchist?"

"Huh? You lost me." But I hadn't lost her. I was heading home and she was tagging right along. The Dead Man would be pleased.

"They're crackpot underground groups, Garrett. There are dozens of those. Pointillists. Deconstructionists. Calibrators. Avatars, Atheists, Realists, Post-Moderns. The way you were going on . . ."

"I don't have anything to do with politics, mainly in hopes that politics won't have anything to do with me. It's my considered, cynical opinion that, no matter how much we're overdue for a change, any human-directed change will be for the worse, to the benefit of a smaller and more corrupt ruling class." At that moment I saw the face of the next fad: revolution. "Meantime, do you have a name? A real name?"

All those *ists* would have as their troops poor little bored rich girls.

"Candace."

"Really? You're using your real name?"

"Might as well. Nobody ever used it but my brother. He died in the Cantard last year. He was a cavalry captain."

"I'm sorry."

"I'm sorry, Garrett."

"Huh?"

"You lost somebody there too."

I got it. "Yeah. Not like it's a unique experience, is it? So what do most people call you?"

"Mickey."

"Mickey? How did they get Mickey out of Candace?"

She laughed. She had a wonderful laugh when she was doing nothing but being happy. I could feel myself becoming distracted. "I don't know. From my nanny. She had pet names for all of us. What?"

I was chuckling. "You wakened a memory. My little brother. We called him Foobah."

"Foobah?"

"I don't know. My mom. She called me Wart."

"Wart? Yeah. I can see that." She danced away, pointed. "Wart! Wart!"

"Hey! Knock it off." People were staring.

She did a pirouette. "Wart. The famous investigator, Wart." She laughed, took off running.

She ran because I started after her. She could run pretty good. She had the legs. They were such nice legs, I didn't try too hard, just floated along enjoying the view.

That started when we weren't far from home. It swept into Macunado Street, so I caught up, said, "Couple blocks up that way. This is my neighborhood. People know me."

She laughed as she fought for breath. "Yes sir, Mr. Wart. I'll maintain your dignity, Mr. Wart." She was still laughing and giving me a hard time when Dean opened the front door.

elinda was in the hallway. She scowled at Candy. Candy scowled at Belinda. Wasn't any doubt they recognized one another. Candy gave me one last jab. "Did you know his nickname is Wart?"

"Dean," I growled, "bring refreshments to the Dead Man's room. Also smelling salts in case I bop this one over the head." I had a problem suddenly. I was caught between two gorgeous women, both interesting, each eyeing the other like a cat fixing to sharpen her claws. On me.

I was out of practice but remembered how my luck ran. When the fur started flying, most of it would be mine. They'd be happy to gang up on me.

I heard a noise from the small front room and suffered the inspiration of my life. I popped in there before Dean's latest stray made cover. It was a little fur ball so friendly that even I, if pressed, would've admitted it was cute. I darted back into the hall, where the ladies were exchanging killer stares. I got that kitten purring. "I guess you guys know each other." I told Candy, "She's hiding out here. From the killer." I told Belinda, "The killer snatched her last night. We just rescued her. I brought her by to talk to the Dead Man."

"I figured. I'd heard she'd been taken." She looked at the kitten without that sparkle kittens ignite in the eyes of their fans. Damn. Inspiration wasted.

"Aren't you sweet," Candy cooed.

Great. Halfway there, anyway. "Why don't you hold him while I check in with my partner?" She hadn't reacted to me calling him by name. I played pass the kitty, headed for the Dead Man's door. As I neared it, Candy jumped, frowned in that way people do when first they hear from His Nibs direct.

I stepped inside. "You see what I got out here? Any special way you want to handle her?"

Just bring her in. He was vastly amused by something. I could guess what. Two women. Me panting shamelessly, trying to conjure some way to have my Belinda and Candy too. *This will be a true test of your fabled charm. Especially as both women have been forewarned by your old friend Rose Tate.*

"Make fun of my misery."

Prepare her. She is under a great deal of stress still. My appearance may be too much for her as a surprise.

I thought she was handling her stress pretty well, taking it out on me.

The kitty thing did work. The women were together now, examining the cat but talking about Candy's adventure. I said, "He wants you to come in now. I need to warn you, he's not human. Don't be too startled when you see him."

Candy didn't seem surprised. "Is he real repulsive? Like an ogre?"

"No. He's just fat, mostly. And he's got a big nose."

"He's a sweetheart," Belinda said.

"Who is?" I demanded.

"Can I take Josh with me?" Candy meant the kitten. Named already. Belinda nodded, never consulting me.

"All right," I said, as though anyone cared what the owner thought in his own home. "Good idea." The cat could be a focus for some good feelings, good thoughts, when those might still be pretty hard to touch.

Candy went into the Dead Man's room. She didn't start screaming.

Belinda remarked, "I really do think you may be one of the good guys, Garrett."

"Huh?"

She waved a hand like she'd heard things about me she didn't want to repeat in my presence. I was baffled. How much could those two have said while I was with the Dead Man?

Women. Go figure them.

Belinda took my arm, cuddled up to my side. "It too early for you to take me to the kitchen and buy me a beer?"

We found Dean putting the final touches on a hot meal. "What's this?" I asked.

"You need to eat. And the young lady you brought home obviously hasn't had a decent meal for some time."

Food is serious stuff to Dean. If he had his way, every meal would be a production. He's appalled by my attitude, that food is just fuel—though I do enjoy good food when I eat it. I just won't go out of my way or spend any extra. Call me a savage.

I drew beer for Belinda. She said, "I've been thinking about my problem with Crask and Sadler."

"Good." *I* hadn't had time.

"Can you get the door, Mr. Garrett?" Dean asked. An impressive amount of racket had broken out there. "I can't interrupt this."

"Sorry," I told Belinda.

She just smiled and winked.

50

"**N**ow what?" I groaned as I stepped aside so Block could come in. "Don't tell me you screwed up again. I couldn't stand it if you told me you screwed up again."

"Winchell got away, Garrett."

"I *begged* you not to tell me you screwed up again."

"It wasn't my fault."

"The hell it wasn't. You were in charge. The guy was tied up in a gunnysack. How could he get away?"

"Some damned fool decided he wanted to take a look, so he opened the sack."

I nearly screamed. "And the butterflies got after him and Winchell just politely crawled out and waltzed away. Right?"

"Right."

"What I ought to do is take you and this other damned fool and tie you both up in a gunnysack and dump you in the river."

"This other damned fool is Prince Rupert. And he's been quite good about not trying to shift the blame."

"Well, good-ee. I'll cheer when he's crowned. So what? Why're you here bugging me?"

Block sneered. "I'm not. I want to see your partner. He's done well guessing what the killer will do."

"Because he has a diseased mind too. I'm sure he knows you're here. He has somebody with him right now. Just hang out in there." I indicated the small front room. "He'll call you. I'm having lunch." And you're not invited, you incompetent sonofabitch.

I sat down opposite Belinda. "Why don't we kiss off TunFaire? Why don't we get married and run off to the Carnival Islands and open a fortune-telling booth?"

"That's an interesting proposition. What brought it on?"

"The Watch let the killer get away. That madman is back on the street and he's got eight or ten hours to play his little prank."

"But if Candy and I are here—"

"He'll kill somebody else. He has to kill somebody."

Somehow, like it or not, my house became the tactical headquarters of the hunt for Elvis Winchell. By sunset Prince Rupert had made himself a guest. I couldn't keep him out, but I was a hardass about his yes-men. Jumped in there with a ferocious, confrontational smile and said, "Your lordship, I haven't the facilities to serve all those men." When he wasn't instantly offended enough to holler for the headsman, I went so far as to suggest, "Their numbers are attracting attention." It was way late, but the night people were out there and they were noticing the crowd.

We compromised. He didn't bring anybody inside.

This Prince Rupert was the first royal I'd met. What I saw didn't impress me either way, though later the Dead Man did blather on about the good intentions he'd found in the man's mind. At that time I wasn't in one of my better moods, so just remarked that the road to hell was paved, and so forth.

The sun hadn't yet risen when word came that they'd found Emma Setlow, AKA Dixie Starr, in the usual state. The troops had arrived while the ritual was winding down. Winchell had taken another successful powder but his helper had been captured. The knives had been recovered.

"Knives?" I asked. "What knives? We already broke the knives."

The knives in question turned out to be plain old kitchen knives, not the best for the job they had done.

The Dead Man observed, *I suspect we will find that the knives were not the vehicle for the curse.*

"Hell," I muttered, "I had that figured. Winchell wouldn't still be on the hoof if they were."

The knives are broken, shattered, but the red iron nights go on.

"Cute. What about the guy they caught?"

The helper was a retarded ratman (an oxymoron again) who admitted he'd been babysitting Dixie since her kidnapping, which had taken place well before the snatch on Candy. Meaning Winchell had decided to stock up on brunettes. After he had escaped from Block and the Prince he'd just run off to where he'd had Dixie stashed.

I muttered, "I don't like this. This Winchell sounds too damned smart."

"Winchell?" Block sneered. "Winchell needs help tying his shoes."

It is the curse, gentlemen. This time around—meaning this return to the world—it has reached some critical stage of growth. I suspect it would not be false to state that it has reached a point where it has begun to teach itself, not just to learn in the slow way a dog does, through numerous repetitions. It might behoove us to consider the horror of the possibility that it may develop an ability to reason.

"Wait a minute. Wait a minute. A curse makes your cow go dry or gives you shingles or makes your kid cross-eyed. It isn't something that—"

In the world of your village charm seller, you are correct. Probably no sorcerer alive today could cast this spell. But this spell comes down from a time when giants walked the earth.

Giants were walking the earth right outside. Well, within a mile, anyway. But I didn't argue. One of the earliest lessons I learned about dealing with Old Bones is: Don't get him going on the good old days. "Giants? Well, maybe. But we're here to develop a strategy."

Considering the Prince and Captain Block, that strategy would be as much political as it was aimed at removing a major villain from the streets.

The Dead Man agreed with me. *Winchell will keep as short a profile as possible but he will not be able to remain hidden. He may be able to do without a helper, but his need to kill is on a short and shortening cycle. Six nights from tonight he will have to kill again. Inasmuch as Miss . . . Altmontigo . . . has been rescued, he will have to develop his next victim from scratch—assuming we can keep our two houseguests isolated.* That he sent to me alone. Our guests didn't need to know we had anyone special squirreled away. *He will be hunting. If he manages to get his victim without help this time, he will still have to recruit helpers. He cannot stop killing and he cannot stop the circle of death growing smaller every time, so that he has to kill sooner.*

"Whoa! Whoa!" Block said. "There a point to all this yammer?"

Yes. Winchell's financial resources cannot be vast. Counter his recruiting efforts by offering a substantial reward for his capture.

"Who's Miss Altmontigo?" I asked, regretting it before I finished speaking. Yet I wondered why he'd hesitated that instant, before and after. Because of Block and the Prince?

Candy to you. Or Mickey.

One very unsettling point here. The Altmontigos are an ancient and honored family from the highest heights of the Hill. What was I getting into? I had a royal prince and as high-toned a young woman as could be found visiting at the same time? Not to mention I was giving shelter to a princess of the underworld.

All of that meant notice. I don't like being noticed by people with that kind of power.

The arguments went on and on. Dawn came and went. I said the hell with it. I wasn't contributing anything and wasn't hearing anything useful to me. What suggestions I did make were ignored. So let the great powers scope things out their own way. After they screwed up and looked like complete fools, I could lean back smugly and tell them they should've listened to me in the first place.

I stopped at the foot of the stairs. Belinda was up there. Candy was up there. Dean was on the daybed in the small front room again.

That damned kitten started rubbing up against my ankle, purring, trying to get in good. I picked him up. "Little buddy, first thing in the morning you get to learn a valuable lesson. You can't get by on cute and the kindness of strangers. You're going to hit the street."

The cat purred. And somebody pounded on the door.

didn't get in any hurry. I ambled toward the front door wondering if I couldn't booby-trap the front steps, putting in something where if you didn't trip the secret safety you got dumped into a bottomless pit.

Wonderful idea but, unfortunately, not really practical. The practical thing to do was ignore the door. Only most people who want to see me know I have that habit and know that I'll storm to the door eventually if they just raise hell long enough.

This little nightmare visitor was one neglected subject slash coconspirator name of Barking Dog Amato. Just what I needed in the middle of the night. Well, morning. It had turned morning when I wasn't looking.

"I didn't wake you up, did I?"

"No. Me? I haven't been to bed yet. I was just heading there. It's been a nasty day in a nasty week in a nasty month."

"The girl killer? I heard there was another one."

"That's on the street already?"

"Word gets around when people are interested."

"I guess. Come back to the kitchen." I jerked a thumb at the Dead Man's door. "Your old pal Block is in there cooking up something with His Nibs." I settled Amato at the kitchen table. "Beer?"

"Sure."

"What's up?" I asked as I drew two.

"Well . . . It's an imposition, I know. I got up, it was raining out, I was sick of doing signs and handbills. So I got out and started walking. My feet brought me here."

What the hell? I didn't need sleep. Who needs sleep when you lead a righteous life? "Some leftover apple pie here. Want some?"

"Sure. I don't get much decent food. What did you think the other day?"

"You made a hell of a start. I didn't get to see it all, though."

"I noticed you disappeared."

"Not by choice. Some of Chodo Contague's thugs came around, told me the man wanted to see me."

"I thought I saw some of those guys just before you disappeared."

"You know Chodo's people?"

"Not by direct experience, thank heaven. But I've watched the outfit for years, gathering information. They haven't tried to profit at my expense yet, but when they do, I'll be ready."

Which meant what? There was someone inside the outfit who suffered from mercy and tolerance? Not hardly.

Belinda walked in. Candy was right behind her. Neither was formally attired. Barking Dog immediately proved that he wasn't all crazy. His eyes bugged. He drooled. If the moon had been up, he would have howled at it. He squeaked, "Who are these lovely ladies, Garrett?"

"They're involved in the serial-killer thing. This one is Belinda and this one is Candy. Guys, this is Kropotkin Amato."

Belinda wasn't impressed but Candy practically jumped out of her underwear. She just *had* to ask: "Barking Dog Amato?" Looking me right in the eye, "Sas's father?"

In two blinks Amato was a changed man. "Sas? Like in a nickname for Lonie? You know Lonie Amato?"

Belinda caught on, grabbed Candy's hand. Candy was chalk pale but, apparently, Belinda's move wasn't fast enough to stifle her. She said, "Sure. We work with Sas. Don't we?" So, I thought. You girls have wasted the night away having a hen session upstairs. I hoped a guy named Garrett hadn't played too prominent a role.

Barking Dog said, "Lonie is my daughter. Not many people know. . . . I haven't seen her since she was five. My wife . . . She never believed in what I was doing. She thought I was crazy. Maybe I was. Maybe not. It didn't matter. She took off. With Lonie. You know Lonie? You really know Lonie?"

Even crackpots get to shed their tears.

The girls didn't know what to say. I waved them off. I said, "Old buddy, I guess I owe you a little confession. The reports we've been doing? They've been going to your daughter through Hullar. Yeah. He was a nominee but not a villain."

"Lonie? Really? You know my daughter, Garrett?"

"I've seen her, that's all. I don't know her."

"Is she all right? Tell me about her. Tell me everything."

"I'm going to break your heart, old buddy. I can't. We get along and we've worked some things together, but you aren't my client. Hullar is, for your daughter. I can't tell you anything unless they say it's all right. I will tell you that she's healthy. She ain't up in the world, but she's a long way from down. You want to know more, I'll see what Hullar says."

Belinda said, "I've changed my mind. You're a real shit, Garrett."

"What if I was working for you? Would you want me telling your business without permission?"

She grumbled. She made noises. She understood. Barking Dog might well be enthusiastic about news of his daughter, but would the daughter be eager to have him intrude upon *her* life?

Lonie's wishes had to be consulted.

Barking Dog reached that conclusion too. Maybe faster than I did. He said, "Garrett, you talk to her. See if she'll meet me. You work that out, where I can see her, I'll be your slave for life. Anything you want, it's yours. I loved that girl. And I haven't seen her since she was practically a baby."

Belinda and Candy looked at me like they expected pearls of wisdom to drip from my lips, as though with a wave of rusty knight's blade all could be made right between Barking Dog and his long-lost child. There was a lot of sentimental emotion floating around. If I was going to gain any ground with either of these beauties, I was going to have to play for the reunion.

I'm a cynic. I admit it. I had to do it to maintain my chances. No way was I going to waste my precious time on that out of sentiment. I'm one of the hard guys. You can't get me with that mush.

I hoped Amato's heart didn't break when he found out what his daughter did.

Hell, *I* didn't know what she did. Did I? She danced for Bishoff Hullar. That didn't make her a whore. Anyway, that wasn't any of my business.

I said, "I don't want to be impolite, guys, but I really am beat. I've been hustling all day. You ladies want to stay up, talk to Mr. Amato, that's fine with me. Make sure the front door is locked when you go to bed. What that means is, one of you has to stay up till Mr. Amato and those clowns in there with His Nibs leave."

The Dead Man proved that one of his brains had room left for me while he entertained royalty. *You need not concern yourself, Garrett. I suspect that I will not get rid of this prince short of being so rude he hauls us up on charges. I am confident Dean will be awake in ample time to see our last guest out. Do get some sleep.*

That didn't sound good at all. He isn't kind to me unless he has plans for me. If he wanted me rested, he meant to run me into the ground later.

I patted Amato's shoulder. "Talk to the girls. I'll see about your daughter."

Two minutes later I was between the sheets. I killed the lamp and was unconscious before my head hit the pillow.

●●●52

The Dead Man ran me into the ground for days. I got to do all the legwork Block's men were supposed to have done already.

Actually, they *had* gathered all the relevant records into one room
in the Chancery cellar. They just never got around to doing anything with
the documents. So I got to winnow and collate—where I could. I had to
bring in help with the older documents, which were recorded in the abandoned Odellic alphabet and wouldn't have been readable anyway because
the language has changed so much.

While I goofed off days and spent profligate evenings in the Tenderloin,
Block hunted Winchell and tried to avoid public notice. Word was out that
he was the man charged with ending the killings. It was also out that he
wasn't having much luck. The scale and scope of the mess were getting exaggerated. The precursors of hysteria filled the air—which made no sense because people get murdered every day, curse or no curse.

I think Block's mistake was offering a reward for Winchell, despite that
being the Dead Man's idea. That focused attention. Attention got the poor
fool working on an ulcer. His buddy Rupert couldn't shield him from all the
high-ranking dolts who just had to explain to him the best way of doing his
job. The Prince himself was guilty of forgetting they were after a killer who
was a bit out of the ordinary.

"Tell the man," Block grumbled. "He don't listen to me."

"Getting disenchanted?"

"Not yet. But close. I can still realize that he's got his own problems and that's why he can't give us more help. It's just a tad irritating when he shuts out whatever he doesn't want to hear, though."

I shrugged a cynic's shrug. I had no faith in his prince.

So Block made excuses for him. "He does have enemies, Garrett. Plenty of people think TunFaire is just dandy the way it is now. Mostly they're people whose fortunes would suffer from an outbreak of law and order."

"If it isn't law and order it'll be an outbreak of something." The signs were growing stronger. "I ran into some old ladies who want to demolish all the breweries, wineries, and distilleries."

"That's going too far."

"I tried to tell them. I said, 'There *is* no civilization without beer. Beer is the lifeblood in the veins of society.' They wouldn't listen."

That put a smile on his face. "Fanatics. What can you do? We get fifty complaints a day about these religious nuts, Mississans, whatever they are." His grin meant he thought I'd invented the old ladies. I hadn't. They were working the Chancery steps a few levels above Barking Dog, crowded into a spot nobody else wanted. I wasn't worried about them. In no rational society would theirs be an idea whose time could come.

I saw a lot of Amato, spending my days at the Chancery. He wasn't the same Barking Dog. The old fervor had gone. I made a point of catching him on his break. "What's happening, hey? Something gone wrong?"

"I'm scared." He didn't beat around it.

"Scared? You? Barking Dog Amato?"

"Yeah. Me. People haven't really noticed yet, but they will. You did. Then where'll I be?"

"What's the matter? What happened?" Maybe he had somebody persecuting him for real.

"My daughter. Suddenly I'm vulnerable. When I didn't know about her, nobody could get to me."

"You're safe. Hardly anybody knows about her now. We're not talking." I sniffed the air. What was that? Aha! Amato wasn't nearly as aromatic as once he'd been.

"Yeah. I guess. I keep telling myself them what knows is decent folk. Then I get scared *of* her."

I raised an eyebrow.

"I snuck down to the Tenderloin. I figured she had to hang out around that Hullar's place sometimes, else how would he know to hire you. Right?" Everybody thinks he's an investigator. "So I hang out and hang out and finally I get me a look at the gal they call Sas."

"And?"

"She looked all right."

"I told you that. She's got people to look out for her."

"Now I know about her, there's no way I can get around meeting her face-to-face. And that scares the shit out of me. What do you say to your kid you ain't seen since she was this high?"

It would terrify Sas too. When the time came. She didn't know that he was aware of her existence. I kept debating whether or not to tell Hullar. It would piss him off, but I guessed I'd better. "I understand. But don't let the stress get you. You may have a valuable mission ahead."

"Huh?"

"You should get out among the people. Hang around the taverns and sidewalk cafés." Plotting urban revolution isn't a poor boy's hobby. Poor folks stay too busy working to keep body and soul and family together.

Amato shook his head. "I wouldn't fit in."

"Sure you would. Get yourself some new clothes. Put in some time getting in touch with today's popular climate."

"How come?" Mild suspicion. He still didn't trust me completely.

"There's a new spirit afoot. It doesn't amount to much yet, but it could. You ought to be aware of it." I thought he could become a real force on the street if he addressed real fears and angers. Lots of people had heard of him. He was a folk hero. People did listen when he stopped talking about himself.

He spoke largely out of imagined pasts now, but there was no reason he couldn't apply his passion to futures as yet unimagined.

aptain Block caught me during my chat with Barking Dog. He looked less like a Watchman than ever, though he was well-dressed. His henchmen, too, were trading uniforms for street clothing. Apparel had become a statement. Those who shed the red and blue meant to take their work seriously. The rest would become unemployed if Prince Rupert gained control of the city's police powers.

"How's it going?" Block asked. He ignored Amato. Barking Dog pretended Block was invisible. It was a good working arrangement.

"I've got a story. Sort of. It's not as clear as I'd like. It won't be much use. The documentation is all of the we-did-this-and-that, this-woman-got-killed, so-did-that-one, we-caught-the-villain-and-hanged-him-and-buried-him-where-he-fell variety. Not a hint how to control the curse.

"Back then the curse didn't migrate from villain to villain the way it does now. It didn't get the chance. I think the people involved understood it better. And it wasn't as sophisticated as it is now. And the local wizards weren't always out of town. The job wasn't just up to the Watch.

"Before the second killing round ended, everybody knew they were dealing with an accursed man who'd opened the grave of the first killer." And we, as brilliant as our forebears, had gotten that far too. Hooray.

"They didn't do anything about it?"

"Sure. They hanged a man and buried him where they thought he wouldn't be found. They were wrong. I'm no expert on sorcery, but I'll bet this curse has some kind of summons built in that calls till somebody hears it and sets it free. Smarter and nastier than it's ever been before."

Block mused, "And today we can't do anything about it even if we want. We don't have anyone who can neutralize it. Because of the war."

Yep. All our real badass wizards were in the Cantard.

"What about your end?" I asked. You never know. He or his boys might have tripped over Winchell.

"Not a trace. We'll have to trap him. It's set. The girl goes back to work tonight. She skips tomorrow night, works the next two nights. The extra one is in case he can hold off for a day. Your partner says he wouldn't move two days early."

I didn't think Winchell would be dumb enough to go where he was expected at all.

Block continued, "The only people in the place not part of the cover team will be Hullar, the dwarf, and three girls Hullar trusts with his life. There won't be no way Winchell can get to her. If he *has* to do it, he'll *have* to take the bait."

If he had to have either Candy or Belinda. But I wasn't the least bit confident that Winchell wouldn't find other victims. Unless his girl luck was as bad as mine.

I didn't criticize. The Dead Man had scoped out this plan. He termed it his martial-arts approach. We would lay back and let the curse betray itself. I've already mentioned his plan's obvious weaknesses.

"Just suppose he gives it a skip and takes second best."

"The minute we find a body, we're on his trail. Spike's hired the best rat-man trackers in town. They're on call. In fact, he's got them wandering around in case they cross Winchell's track by chance."

When everything you can do isn't enough, you do whatever you can. Give Block that. This time he was giving a hundred percent.

He asked, "You identify the sorcerer responsible?"

"Only to a probability. It goes way back. Further than we thought. There's still some stuff I need translated before I can say for sure, though."

"God damn it, say something for unsure."

"Hey, temper. The oldest depositions, first time there were killings, mention a Drachir Nevets. I checked with a historian. He'd never heard of a Drachir Nevets but he did know about a Lopata Drachir of Nevetska, a real shadowy old-time superwizard who was always into it with a sorcerer named Lubbock Candide. Drachir's forte seems to have been writing curses so complicated that nobody could escape them."

Block grunted, thought a moment, amazed me by knowing the names. He was better educated than I'd suspected. "Why this particular curse? Any hints?"

"More shadowy stuff. Candide had a daughter."

"Arachne."

"Right. A major ass-kicker herself. Unless the translator was yanking my leg, both Drachir and Candide were out to win her favors and found a dynasty of witch-kings. Arachne decided she'd rather snuggle up with daddy, which pissed Drachir off mightily. Which, I'm guessing, led him to send a curse after her."

"All that would have been way, way before the first killings."

"Yeah. I'm thinking maybe that wasn't the real first time around, only the first that got recorded."

"Like maybe Arachne deflected the curse earlier and buried it and didn't tell anybody."

"Maybe." The man could think when he wanted. "It might be useful to find out if there are any extant portraits of Drachir and the Candides. Especially Arachne."

Block grunted. He wore a faraway look. "This just won't be settled the easy way, will it?"

"Not hardly." Heavens, the things I was going to have to talk over with the Dead Man. And him not in a charitable mood because the news from the Cantard had such a lull-before-the-storm feel. "Speaking of things not settling easily, without making a big to-do, catch a look at the guy watching us from up where the old ladies do their temperance thing."

Block looked. "Chodo's man Crask."

"Bingo. I'm going to trust you with something." Barking Dog had gone back to work early, not wanting to be close to a minion of his oppressors. No one would hear. "The other girl at my place. Belinda. Her full name is Belinda Contague. As in the daughter of Chodo Contague. She's hiding out with me because Crask and Sadler want to kill her."

"Huh? Why?"

"Because they did something to Chodo. Poisoned him or something. I've seen him." What the hell? Everybody lies to the police. "He's a vegetable. They just pretend he's giving the orders. Belinda knows that, which is why they want to get rid of her."

"I think I missed something, Garrett."

"Belinda can take them down. They have to cover their scam or lose control. I got into it because they wanted to hire me to find her for them."

"A girl who happens to be one of the main targets of our killer?"

That had been a problem for me, briefly. "I thought it was one damned long coincidence till I realized I was looking at it from the wrong end. From the end where we are, chasing Winchell. Look at it coming the other way. The thing between Belinda and Crask and them has been going on for months. The girl-killer thing is just something she stumbled into going somewhere else. She wouldn't have been involved at all if the other thing hadn't made her run away from home. Chance brought me into it at one point rather than another, sooner than later. The players had me chalked in for their game."

Block looked uncomfortable. "How come you're telling me? It ain't healthy knowing too much about Chodo's business."

"Because there's a very large and nasty man up there giving me very evil looks. He's unhappy because I haven't been busting my butt trying to find Belinda instead of noodling around with some who-cares serial-killing thing. As I recall, I'm supposed to call on the Watch if it can give me a hand. Not to mention that you might get a kick out of poking a stick into the eye of an evildoer of Crask's stature, knowing he doesn't really have Chodo behind him."

"Tell you the truth, Garrett, I think getting Crask off the street is a grand idea." He snarled it, setting off alarms. What had I done? "But I don't have much confidence in it being a healthy idea. What's he doing?"

"Glaring daggers. Probably thinking how nice it will be to drag me somewhere where he can do dental work on me."

"Why?"

"The girl. He doesn't know she's staying at my place. He hasn't seen me lift a finger to find her. Despite my having been told very plainly that it would be in my best interest to do so."

"You're sure Chodo's out of it?"

"Absolutely."

"Then maybe I'll have some fun with Crask. But don't expect a lot. These people always have friends in high places."

"How well I know," I muttered.

Block winked. "Have a nice day." He strolled away, looking thoughtful, leaving me beached and sputtering.

I did notice that he had friends in the crowd, mostly his auxiliaries. He'd begun to enjoy his role as honest Watchman. I wondered if he'd started turning all bribes away or only the most embarrassing ones.

I hoped the New Order thing didn't go to his head. Truly there can be such a thing as too much law and order—though I can't foresee TunFaire ever suffering from that.

I bade a soft farewell to Barking Dog. He was on a roll, did not have time to set his brass megaphone down. He indicated his latest report on himself. I snagged it and moved away, awaited Crask.

54

Crask was displeased with me. "What kind of creep are you, Garrett, hanging out with dogshit like Block?"

"He's not so bad. We're old pals. Didn't you know? Sort of in business together too. The new order, like that." I couldn't get the caps in like Block's creature Relway. "Got a problem with that?"

"I got a problem with you. You was hired to do something. You ain't doing it."

"You're mistaken. Despite having had money forced upon me, I didn't agree to anything. Not to say I refuse the job. But I do have a couple other things to wrap before I get to it. So flutter away."

"No. Chodo hires you, you're on the job now. It's the only job on your list."

"Aw, shucks. Here we go. How long you known me, Crask? Long enough. You know no matter how many ugly faces you pull, no matter how many muscles you flex, I'm going to do things my way. I told you, I have things to finish first. You wait in line just like you was real people."

"You're pissing me off, Garrett."

"Eek." That was the idea. "I have that effect on people. Especially the kind who jump lines or think they deserve special consideration." If he was going to do anything, I wanted him to do something stupid, in public. "Look here. Look real close. I want you should see my heartfelt pain at how I'm causing you distress."

"I come here just going to caution you gentle, Garrett. Just going to take a minute out to show you the error of your thinking, so to speak. But now I got a feeling we need to go someplace and talk."

"You aren't half as slick as you think, Crask." That was Block, materializing out of nowhere. "Why don't we all sit down on the steps here, like we was old buddies."

"Bug off, asshole," Crask said. "Ain't none of your business, what we're talking about."

"Maybe you're right. But maybe I'm not interested in that." Block backed up a couple steps, settled onto the stone wall at the edge of the Chancery steps. He waved. A man stepped out of the crowd. Even I was startled. He seemed to have come from nowhere. Block said, "Well, Blinky?"

Blinky replied, "We removed the coach. We arrested three men."

"Well. How about that?"

Crask didn't look at Block. He put it all on me. "What the hell's going on here, Garrett?"

"You know as much as I do."

Block said, "You could be going down."

"Shit. What're you pulling?"

Block smiled. "Times are changing, Crask. I been waiting for that to happen." He looked up at me, smile malicious. "Me and Crask go way back. Same neighborhood. Same outfit in the Cantard, to start. We share a lot of memories."

Crask stirred uneasily. The strain in Block's voice said this was old business coming to a head. Crask's confidence was less than complete. Things *did* seem to be changing. "You mess with me, Block, you'll think a shit avalanche fell on you."

"I doubt it. Like I said, times are changing. You're running out of friends. I been waiting. The day I made captain, I had a special cell fixed up in the Al-Khar. I'm looking for an excuse to put you in it, hoping you make me break all your bones putting you there. I don't know why it works out that way, but almost every prisoner who was on the Watch's top-fifty-assholes list seems to end up committing suicide. Maybe it's rough in there." He winked at me, said, "Thanks, Garrett. I'd almost forgotten what I owe this butthead."

At the same time, Crask put on his most menacing face. "You want to be dead, Garrett? You don't mess with me like this and get out alive."

"What do I have to lose? Weren't you going to do me and the kingpin's kid as soon as I found her?"

"Come on, Garrett!"

"You think I'm weak. By your standards. But do you really think I'm stupid?"

Crask was ready to skin people alive. My plan to drive him crazy had worked. Only . . .

One of Block's men stepped up and bopped Crask from behind, whaling on his head with a stick that was cousin to my own. Crask didn't go down first crack. The stick man stared at his tool for a moment, astonished. Then, before Crask regained his equilibrium, Block's man whacked him half a dozen times real fast, making sure he got the effect he wanted.

Traffic on the steps cleared back. Funny. Not one soul thought of hollering for the Watch.

Block asked, "What do you think? Shall I put him away? Let Sadler shit a few bricks trying to figure what happened to him?"

"You're not scared what they'll do?"

"Not anymore." Block smiled. Relway appeared. Though I had no solid reason to think so, I feared Relway was the most dangerous creature in this New Order Watch. "We'll lock him up for a few days. Just so he'll know what it can be like."

The show moved away from me then.

I worried for Block. This could cause him big trouble. He might have a cell fixed up for Crask, but I couldn't see Crask staying in it, no matter what Rupert planned. The kingpin had friends everywhere. Once Sadler learned about Crask's predicament, heavyweight wheels would start turning.

Still . . .

I watched Relway.

Block was creating his own personal secret police force. Fast. Possibly with the best of intentions, but if he pulled many stunts like snatching Crask, he'd find himself riding a tiger.

reported everything to the Dead Man. He was not pleased.

"You think I am, Chuckles?"

Captain Block has grown overconfident. His act is premature. His organization, however extensive, cannot challenge the syndicate even in transition. I cannot see his men remaining loyal through a crisis. Corruption has its own historical momentum.

"Historical momentum?" He starts using terms like that, it's time to batten down. There's about to be a big, sententious blow.

In the matter of Mr. Amato, his trepidation is understandable. Next time you see him, suggest he stop in and visit.

Just a down-home good old boy, my partner. I made a rude noise. I'd spent three days burrowing through centuries past, and he showed no interest whatsoever.

He could ignore with the best of them. *In the matter of the sorcerers Candide and Drachir, it appears that we should contact appropriate experts.*

"I consulted experts already, Smiley."

Linguists and generalists. Both names excite vague resonances but no special memories. Before my time, I fear. My opinion is that Block should have saved his special cell for our special villain.

He was racketing around all over the place. "Probably. It'll take a tough lockup to keep whoever's wearing the curse."

Till we get the appropriate wizards on the case.

Suddenly the Dead Man went shy. His tenor, tentative behind a display of confidence, baffled me, if only because I couldn't conceive of any situation in which he ought to be hiding something from his senior partner.

In the matter of Miss Altmontigo . . . Pause like he was fixing to feed me a line of bull so feeble he couldn't expect a moron to buy it. . . . *I had a visit from her stepfather. We enjoyed a turbulent session.*

"I'll bet." You know how fathers get.

He had to face facts.

"Meaning somebody who considers himself my partner outstubborned somebody who knew he was on this earth for only three score and ten and saw time slipping away?"

Meaning that relentless bombardment with fact forced him to assume a cooperative stance.

"You got to him by dropping the Prince's name." He's not so hard to figure.

Actually, the real clincher was my observation that he no longer has any legal hold on Miss Altmontigo's person, only on her property.

I frowned. Each time he mentioned "Miss Altmontigo" he sort of stumbled. But I turned to his point.

For reasons unclear to me, Karentine property law assumes women don't have the sense the gods gave a goose. The law gives husbands and fathers veto powers over all transfers—even where they have no other claim on money or property. I suppose that's meant to save those silly girls from giving everything to cults and/or con men. Only a widow can execute contracts in her own name. I guess good sense rubs off in bed.

I suggested she might get around him on the property, of which she has a great deal, inherited via his maternal grandmother, who was something of a feminist activist. He manages the property at a handsome profit to himself.

He'd hung a lantern on the loophole. A woman of legal age can marry without permission. She could marry a dying (or dead) man who had no other heirs, making herself a quick widow. This doesn't happen too often, but when it does and there is a fortune at stake, the cases become public entertainments. Witnesses sell their testimony to the highest bidder. You can guess about the lawyers. Everything not nailed down. It ain't nailed down if they can get it loose with a prybar.

"You're home." Belinda invited herself in, rolled her eyes skyward. "That woman. She may work at Hullar's, but she has no concept of the real world."

I frowned a question at the Dead Man.

A juvenile female rivalry. Ignore it.

Sensible advice, maybe. Though not taking sides can be dangerous too, if they're really wound up.

Belinda asked, "Did we make any headway today?"

I told her about my day. The Dead Man didn't grouse about hearing it all again. Was my report on Drachir all that intriguing?

Belinda became preoccupied after I mentioned Crask. Twice I had to ask, "What's with him?" before I got an explanation of the Dead Man's funk.

"That friend of yours, the big one, came by."

"Saucerhead?"

"Yes. He brought some news about the Cantard. I don't think it was welcome. Excuse me." Belinda didn't like military stuff.

"Bad news, Smiley?" I asked. "Something you didn't want to hear?"

Your Marines have recaptured Full Harbor.

"I told you it would be a different story." I felt me a big surge of pride. They really do get you.

That is the least of it. Karenta has launched a general offensive on a shoestring and a prayer. Supported by morCartha auxiliaries, Karentine forces are attacking Venageti and republicans everywhere.

"Going to be a lot of regrets going out to the mothers of a lot of Karentine heroes, then."

A great many more will go to Venageti and republican mothers. The mor-Cartha appear to be serving both loyally and with efficiency. If they persist, they will devour Glory Mooncalled's ability to gather superior intelligence, by harassing his scouts relentlessly. They are assuming all the traditional cavalry roles, including raiding and screening and holding. And they are doing it through the air, where neither Mooncalled nor the Venageti can touch them. They have wrested air supremacy from Mooncalled's flying allies already.

"So?"

Do not be thick. It may mean the war is all but over, with Karenta the winner. Assuming the morCartha remain steadfast, we will witness a slaughter. Karentine troops will be in the right place at the right time in superior numbers, supported vigorously from aloft, every time.

"And?"

The end of Mooncalled's dream may be the beginning of Karenta's nightmare. Victory may be defeat. Our wiser leaders may have realized that long ago. That may be why the war dragged on. When the cost of victory exceeds that of continued warfare—

"Huh?" I was in one of my sharper states.

You have, on occasion, commented on conditions that could arise should all the soldiers come home.

"Oh. Sure." After generations of warfare, the economy depends on continued conflict. Whole sectors are managed by nonhumans. Peace would bring on dislocations of vast magnitude, social stress, and strife. "Call it the war that's lost by winning."

Exactly.

"Have we done anything to steel ourselves?"

We are nonpolitical. Our services will be in demand always. Against fate, even the gods conspire in vain.

That sounded like a bowdlerized quote. I didn't mention my suspicions. It does no good to call him on a theft. He's shameless.

Belinda came back. "I've been thinking, Garrett. I need to see Captain Block."

A scheme worthy of your father, Miss Contague. But poorly timed. I do not think I can urge this strongly enough. This is not the moment to challenge Mr. Crask and Mr. Sadler. Their side of the ledger has all the pluses. And your few reliable friends are preoccupied with this traveling curse. Even so, let me suggest a few steps we might take when the time does come.

I groaned. When we take steps, I do the stepping.

They conversed. I waited, left out. Belinda was full of bounce when she left, having delivered a potent and promising thank-you kiss.

"What was she planning?"

Her scheme involved transporting me to Mr. Dotes's establishment. . . .

"Say what? The woman is *mad!*" I can't move him to sweep around him, let alone push him out of the house.

There was a certain elegant evil in her plan, he sent, rather wistfully. He did not explain. *We will explore elements of it in our free time these coming days. This will require visits from numerous outsiders. Apprise Dean.*

Right. And have Dean blame it all on me even when it was obvious the whole thing was one of the Dead Man's chuckleheaded schemes.

So there we were, fooling around closing out one of TunFaire's worst-ever serial-killer deals, up to our ears in Watch and informants, and the Dead Man was trying to set up some scam to get Crask and Sadler off Belinda's back. I got to play gofer. Grumbling gofer. When Block didn't have anything better for me to do.

I must admit, though, that Miss Belinda Contague's gratitude stretched the limits of imagination and, almost, those of endurance.

We had so many villains in and out, I lost count. Most weren't your basic thug type, they were magistrates and military men and entrepreneurs and, yes, even Watch officers. Men whose vision defects had made Chodo powerful and them wealthier than they should have been. They all knew Belinda. Her birthday parties had been Chodo's annual excuse for gathering them together.

They came. Belinda talked about Crask and Sadler and her dad while the Dead Man poked around inside their heads. Those who would line up against Belinda left with their thoughts scrambled so they'd forget having seen her.

Saucerhead and Morley and Morley's men Puddle and Sarge hung around being insurance.

• • •

The Dead Man was sure Winchell wouldn't go after Candy again even if we threw her out naked and gave him a big head start. Belinda offered to go dangle on the hook.

Came the night. This time I was determined to stick it out till it wrapped. Block and his all-thumbs boys weren't going to screw it up again.

I wanted out. I'd done work enough for three cases. The only upside was, I hadn't gotten pounded around, which happens too often in my line.

Hullar's place was stuffed with picked Watchmen, most of them auxiliaries. More of the same were scattered around the neighborhood. The Tenderloin was lousy with law. The outside crew came and went, buying beer. We insiders bought more.

Hullar leaned against the bar, told me, "This asshole with the knife is going to make me rich, all you guys in here sucking it down. You really got to catch him?"

"We could let him do his stuff right there on your dance floor, let the mess draw the ghoul trade."

"Touchy."

"Can't help it." The hour was late. Tension was rising. The troops worked harder and harder to pretend they were ordinary slobs. I should've told them to lean back and take it easy. They were plenty ordinary and they had slob down pat.

"We shouldn't be out here, Garrett."

Hullar was right. Winchell might recognize me. Maybe the Watch was rubbing off on me instead of the other way around.

Belinda came to the back room where Hullar and Crunch and I were killing time drinking. She needed reassurance.

So did Crunch. He was put out. Relway had ousted him from behind the bar. "I could handle any whippersnapper what went to bothering the girls, Hullar. No reason me being pushed off my job."

"I'm sure you could, Crunch. But I'm not in charge."

Crunch turned his glare on me. I said, "We're talking about a psycho killer, Crunch. A total crazy. You don't know him. The man behind the bar does." I hoped Relway's disguise would hold up. "If you were out there, he could walk in and cut your throat before you knew it was him. It's for your safety."

This had played before. I was tired of it. I gave Belinda a peck on the cheek, squeezed her hand. "Getting close. Hang in there. Break a leg. All that."

"He should've made some kind of move already, Garrett."

I was afraid she was right. Somebody should've come to check her out, maybe tried to pick her up. I was worried too.

An hour later the consensus had spread to the street. Something had gone wrong. Our fish hadn't bitten. Somewhere a woman was dying because . . .

But no one gave up playing his part.

I was in the shadows, looking into the dance hall, when Sadler walked in. He looked incredibly evil. His expression grew more wicked as he spotted Belinda.

She was dancing with a Watchman disguised as a sailor. She spotted Sadler. Momentary fire touched her eyes. Sadler headed toward her. Once he passed a certain point, everyone in sight moved. He realized he'd walked into something. Fur started flying. Steel lashed the air. I stepped out to remind the boys that we weren't killing people tonight.

Barking Dog Amato waltzed into the place.

There you go. We have us a rousing brawl going, everybody closing down a setup in which everybody had a specific role, including those of Hullar's girls who'd stuck around to make it look good. We have maybe twenty people screaming and yelling. We have bodies flying everywhere. And in walks Barking Dog Amato looking for his daughter. He spots me instead. He ignores the uproar. "Hey, Garrett! This's luck." A Watchman flew past him, thrown by Sadler, who was in a truly foul temper. I tried to get to Barking Dog so I could move him somewhere a little less violent. He demanded, "Where's my girl, Garrett? I come down here and come down here and hung out till I finally got me the nerve to talk to her, and when I do, I find out this Sas ain't my baby at all. Her name's Sasna Progel and all she knows about Lonie Amato is she's heard Hullar and his dwarf henchman mention the name." Another Watchman sailed by. "What're you trying to pull?"

"We're in the middle of something now. Could you maybe step over there out of the way and hang on a minute?"

Sadler roared my name like he'd decided I was the root of every evil he'd ever suffered. He charged.

"Better look out, Garrett," Amato said. He headed for a corner. "That fellow don't look too friendly."

That fellow didn't at that. He trampled Watchmen. Then he tripped over one. I planted a strong right on his temple. It put him on his knees but didn't put him out. I threw a little of everything I had while he was getting up. He got up anyway.

I bruised some knuckles on my left hand. Then Sadler hit me back. I flew off to visit Barking Dog. Sadler came after me, ignoring all those other people giving him hell. It was like he was holding me personally responsible for his pain. He bent down to pick me up.

Barking Dog let him have it. Which was like a bee stinging an elephant if the bee don't pick his spot. Barking Dog didn't. But he did irritate Sadler enough that he decided to hammer Amato one.

Bishoff Hullar, strongman, popped Sadler with something that looked like a fist but couldn't have been because Sadler folded right up. Hullar breathed on his knuckles, said, "We're supposed to be looking out for a girl, not having us a good time, Garrett." He pointed.

"I'll be go to hell."

Winchell had decided to drop in after all. There he was making his way to the bandstand, overlooked in all the excitement. "Hey, we got a party now." Belinda eyed him uncertainly, wondering if he was the one she was supposed to fear.

The whole place went silent.

Winchell started moving fast.

I yelled.

Everybody joined in.

It was the battle of Sadler all over again, only Winchell was tougher. The curse had made him a superman. He got to Belinda, hoisted her onto one shoulder, headed for the door. When I tried to talk him into changing his ways, he deposited me on the back of my lap under a table. Nobody slowed him down till Crunch decided to take matters into his own hands, brought up a pony keg, and politely tossed it across the room to meet Winchell's surprised face. The keg was full. Not bad for an old hairbag.

Winchell never got his eyes uncrossed. The boys from the street came in and helped close him down. They tied and gagged him, and most of the excitement was over. He looked small and old now, like the curse was turning him into the old green-eye who'd started it all at Morley's.

Then Belinda was all over me.

Past her I saw Barking Dog buttonhole Hullar.

It was a while before the excitement faded. Block arrived. He circled Winchell smugly. I told him, "You let him get away again, I'm personally going to drop you in the river with a reminder boulder tied to your toe."

"Relway. Get him sacked up and celled up. And don't let that gag slip." Winchell looked spooky enough with his eyes glowing. Grinning, Block bragged, "Won't be no mistakes this time, Garrett. This's our future here.

We're gonna be careful. We're gonna wall him up in the cell I let Crask stew in. Prince Rupert is gonna send for the wizard help we need soon as he knows we got him."

I grumbled, hinting that I might be less than confident about the competence of a certain prince and his Watch.

"You got any bright ideas?"

"Yeah. I got a real special one."

"So?"

"I go hit the sack. You want anything else, come bug the Dead Man. Tomorrow."

"Tomorrow afternoon," Belinda said. "Garrett's going to have to get some sleep too."

"Huh?" Us investigators have minds like steel traps. "Too?"

She winked. "I might let you catch a nap. If you're a good boy."

"Oh." Block had gotten it before I did. I was suitably chastened.

Meantime, Barking Dog was in full cry. He had Hullar and Crunch both confused and on the run.

was further chastened by fate's unrelenting efforts to keep me chaste.

Winchell had had a strong suspicion he was headed into a trap. The curse had compelled him to go anyway but had permitted him some latitude in preparation. It was smart enough to allow its steed its head when that was appropriate.

I hit Macunado Street with visions of a wild night dancing in my head—and found my front door shattered. Dean lay in the hall about halfway dead, his stray curled inside the curve of what looked like a broken arm, crying. Belinda said, "I'll look after Dean. You find out what happened."

I opened wide but sensed nothing from the Dead Man. That scared me. Only once before had the villains gotten in, and then they'd gotten only a few feet. The Dead Man turned would-be intruders into living statues—usually while they were still in the street. Here there was no evidence he'd been able to do anything. The invader (or invaders) had hiked straight from the entrance to the stairs.

Had the Dead Man finally taken that long last step across to the other shore? I got no sense of his presence.

"Go on!" Belinda snapped.

"Be careful." I edged forward, my heart in my throat. I'm not ashamed to admit I was scared. This had the same feel I recalled going into the worst raids we pulled back when I was one of Karenta's brave young Marines. I crept along the wall to the Dead Man's door, nudged it open.

I whirled inside, ready for anything.

Nobody there but my partner.

He looked unchanged, but there *was* a difference. I felt a tension unlike any I'd encountered before. I sensed that he was safe and awake but way too focused to spare me a thought.

Which meant the trouble was still in the house. And he was a nightmare.

Upstairs. He had to be upstairs. Candy was upstairs.

But we already had Winchell. . . .

I felt for the Dead Man, seeking confirmation. He did not respond. Of course.

"Whoever did it is still here," I told Belinda. "And he's so strong he's fought the Dead Man to a standstill. I think he's after Candy. I'm going after him. But I'm afraid if I go upstairs he won't be there. He'll grab you and take off."

"So check down here first." *She* was calm and practical. Maybe it was hereditary.

"I guess Old Bones can hold out a few minutes more."

"Nothing in here," Belinda said, having entered the kitchen boldly. "And the cellar door is locked from this side."

A shriek came from above, from Candy's room in Candy's voice. "Could be bait." Something thumped the floor. It sounded like a body falling. Belinda grabbed my arm. I asked, "You reckon it's a trap?"

"Garrett!"

"Right. This is no time to make light." Tell me a better time.

I told me to pretend I was Morley Dotes. This might be a job that called for Morley's legendary cool. If my honey didn't just have a guy up to play . . . Morley's cool. I was tempted to send out for it. Only . . .

Only what the hell was going on here? I did my part. I got Winchell sewn up and delivered. It was time to collect my reward and ride off into the sunset. What was all this mess?

My office was clean. I traded looks with Eleanor. That calmed me. It reminded me that I'd gotten through bad times before, that calm was my most potent weapon. "A little reason would help too, sweetheart."

The small front room contained nothing but an odor cat haters know well. "You little shit. You blew it."

I jammed my rain hat onto my head, set course for the kitchen. I banged around in there till I found the cheesecloth Dean bought the time he had a blue-sky idea about saving money by making his own cheese. I told him: Did I want to cut financial corners, I'd do without a housekeeper. Anyway, to date we were out the cost of cheesecloth without no cheese to show. I hacked off a few yards, folded the cloth over my rain hat, and tucked the edges under my collar, front and back.

"What in the world are you doing?"

"Beekeeper trick. You might want to try it yourself."

"You're insane, Garrett." But she followed my example. She even made herself crude mittens.

I dug through drawers and poked into closets till I found my sulfur candles. "Try not to breathe the fumes once I light these things. They'll knock you on your ass."

Belinda shook her head, muttered obscenities, but went along. "You're completely paranoid. You know that, don't you?"

"I have been ever since I found out they were out to get me. Anyway, I couldn't stand it if you was to get butchered now."

"You're a born romantic too."

"That's me. The man of a thousand faces." All this was punctuated by repeated thumps and yells from above. Then the yelling stopped. The silence seemed particularly ominous.

"I think you better get on your horse, Garrett."

"Yeah." I checked Dean. He was doing as well as could be hoped. He had his hair-ball buddy to look out for him. I wished we had time to send out for reinforcements, but the silence upstairs told me I was all out of time. "White knight to the rescue. Well, it was white back before the rust set in."

"Let's do it, Garrett."

No style, this one. But one hell of a set of legs.

58

"**I** knew it!" I moaned. "It had to be something impossible." There were butterflies on the second floor. They were big and green and unpleasantly carnivorous but blessedly few and stupid. "Watch those things. I got a feeling if they nip at you it could spread the curse the way mosquitoes spread yellow fever." People in TunFaire didn't generally know that, but in the islands you learned from the natives. If you were smart enough to listen when they told you something.

"So light some candles."

Belinda wasn't exactly supportive. Pushy, even. It wasn't time to light candles.

First I visited my goody closet, dug out a nasty knife, offered it to her. "Whoever he is comes near you, carve your initials on him with that." For myself I chose a knife with a blade nearly long enough to qualify it as a shortsword. I used it to point toward Candy's room.

I went first, macho clown that I am. And there was our interloper, a monster of a man, moving almost imperceptibly as he hoisted Candy toward the ceiling. He had rigged a block and tackle on a beam we'd exposed while rehabbing. He was ruled by the curse and he was going to do a girl on the spot.

"It really is multiplying," Belinda whispered.

I kept my mouth shut. My throat was too dry for chatter.

The man kept moving against all the Dead Man's power. What incredible strength the curse gave!

Why hadn't Candy run out on him? With the Dead Man slowing him down, he couldn't hardly keep up with her.

"Huh! Belinda. Don't look this clown in the eye. I have a feeling that if he lays the green eye on you you're a goner."

"Right." She wasn't nervous. Not my gal Belinda. She was as cold as her daddy. "You want to do some candles before the bugs carry me off?" They tended to leak from the corners of the villain's mouth.

I lighted a sulfur candle off the tallow candle Belinda had thought to bring, set it on the floor just inside the doorway to Candy's room. As I set out the second candle, the bad boy realized he had company.

Gods, he was huge! He looked like Saucerhead Tharpe's big brother. Where did Winchell find him? Nothing that big should have been running loose. He turned his head slowly.

"Why don't you stick him, Garrett? You want to make a career of farting around, don't you?"

I do. It's because I have this hyperactive conscience. In this case it was also because I was completely lost. This wasn't suppose to be happening. The girl-killer problem was supposed to have been solved at Hullar's place. I was supposed to be in bed now, if not asleep.

The big guy had Candy hoisted up till only her head was touching the floor. He let go the rope. It squealed through the block. Down she crashed. She started making noises behind her gag like she was trying out my name.

I really hoped she wasn't trying to relay a warning. I didn't have time to fish it out of her. The big guy had begun to get him a case of the green eye. He was barfing butterflies. Most of those were green too. Old Drachir had had a thing about green.

The big man was aging before my eyes. He'd put on a year or two in the past few minutes. He'd gotten shorter, too, though I wasn't ready to jump in for fifteen rounds.

He got a good look at Belinda.

He charged like he was headed into a hundred-mile-an-hour wind. He puffed and snorted. Moths leaked from his nostrils. They were pretty stupid moths—or the curse controlling them was pretty dumb. They mostly went after him.

I held a lighted sulfur candle in front of him. He roared out butterflies that couldn't get me because of the cheesecloth. He didn't seem to care, though. He had eyes only for Belinda.

"Don't look the bastard in the eyes," I reminded her, sliding to one side. I dropped to hands and knees, scooted forward while the villain continued his glacial charge. I cut the tendons behind his right knee and left ankle. It took a while for his brain to get the word, but he fell. Then he started to lift himself up again. I drove my knife through his right hand, pinning it to the floor.

Belinda did his other hand. "You might try to get a gag on him, Garrett." She did have the Contague flair.

The cumulative pain and damage shocked the man enough that the curse slipped control. The Dead Man jumped on that. The villain became as rigid as stone.

Like a far, far whisper on a contrary wind, came, *You took your sweet time.*

I got Candy loose. "How come you keep fooling around with these perverts?" I asked. "What's wrong with a nice straight guy like me?"

She threw her arms around me. She didn't say anything, even when Belinda cracked, "Maybe she figured you were taken." She just clung like she didn't plan to let go during this lifetime.

Butterflies zoomed around drunkenly. The sulfur fumes were getting to me too. The bugs discovered bare areas on Candy. They called their friends. I didn't know but what the curse could be carried by the little devils. "Let's get out of here. Lock them in with the candles." I considered sliding a few candles into the Dead Man's room while he was preoccupied, just for effect.

Belinda helped with Candy, though with poor grace.

I glanced at my unwanted guest. Butterflies still crawled out of his open mouth. Belinda said, "We can't leave him here."

"Why not?"

"He'll croak."

"Ask me if I care."

"Think, genius."

Indeed. Boggle us with a first.

"You keep out of this." I grunted, disgusted. If the villain died, I'd be the only place for the curse to migrate. I didn't think that was such a great idea. "We do need to keep him unconscious. He might commit suicide." I had a sudden conviction that the curse had driven Winchell into Hullar's place to provide a diversion from the attack here.

The Dead Man sent, *I can keep the man under control.*

"Like you were doing when I got here?"

Bind him if that makes you more comfortable.

"Right." I peeked inside Candy's room. The big guy's breath problem had improved. The floor was covered with fallen butterflies. Only a few showed any life. I said, "I've got an idea. Get the curse to jump to the Dead Man. Then it wouldn't—"

"Then it would be able to talk to you direct."

"Miss Practical." I rounded up a ball of linen cord and went to work on our villain. I used it all, then gagged him good. Then I saved him from the fumes. I gave Belinda my nightstick. "Bop him if he even twitches."

"Where are you going?"

"To get Block. To get this character out of here."

I didn't get that far. Not right away.

might have known. I should have expected it. Hell, I should have counted on it. It had to be in the stars. It started out being about Barking Dog Amato, and no matter how I wriggled, Amato kept getting in the way. So why on earth should I have been surprised to find Barking Dog camped out in my hallway with Sas and Dean, Sas looking mightily distressed while Amato fussed over Dean and Dean groggily insisted there was nothing wrong. Dean was so woozy he didn't know he was hurt.

"How do I get around this?" I muttered before anyone spotted me. At the moment I didn't much care about Barking Dog's troubles.

"Garrett!"

I'd been spotted. "Don't start. I've got problems of my own and it's going to be real hard to give a rat's ass about whatever is bugging you."

"Hey, yo, no problem. I kind of figured you'd be distracted when I saw this mess."

"The curse managed to split somehow. I've got another killer upstairs." Damn. That put a sparkle in his eye. What now? "I'm going to get Captain Block."

"That's all right. I understand. I'll hang out here, keep an eye on things."

"You don't need to. Go on home. Get some shut-eye. The Dead Man can be pretty handy when he wants."

I got a smug snicker from the other side of the wall and a denial from Amato. "I wouldn't feel right, Garrett. After everything you done for me. Anyway, I got to talk to you about my girl. This here Sas ain't my girl."

So I'd gathered earlier. I didn't stay around to find out anything more. I nurtured some small, vain hope that the Dead Man would pity me and run him off before I got back.

The only good thing about finding Block was I got to wake him up. Again. I never had a big case before where I got to wake other people up. It was always somebody coming around wanting me to be bright-eyed at some absurd hour of the morning.

"Yes!" I insisted, after getting through to his quarters. "You get off your fat political butt and come on over, you can see for yourself. The curse has spawned. You don't grab this guy, it keeps right on going like we never met anybody called Winchell. I guarantee. You think I'm running around at this hour because I'm nursing a grudge? You know me better."

Block grunted. "Unfortunately. You can't just bring him in tomorrow?"

"I'm going home. When I get there I'm handing this guy over to who-ever's around. If that's nobody, he walks. And I don't have nothing more to do with unraveling curses by old-time lunatic wizards. You really want to give me a thrill, come up with some excuse for arresting Barking Dog Amato. Material witness, maybe. He's set to drive me crazy."

Block observed me under his brows briefly, maybe wondering if he ought to jump on such a great straight line. A nasty smile crawled around on his lips. I said, "Don't go getting any ideas about doing something I'm going to regret."

"Me? Forsooth. Maybe even more sooth than that. Echavar!" A servile type materialized as though he'd been lurking outside, just hoping Block would holler. "Inform Relway that I need a squad to accompany me when I arrest another curse carrier. Or, failing that, a leading public nuisance."

I got the impression he wasn't talking about Barking Dog.

Block didn't recognize the man who'd invaded my place. Neither did his troops. After checking him over and taking statements from Candy and the Dead Man, Block grudgingly admitted, "It looks like you did the right thing, Garrett."

"I always do the right thing."

"Tell it to your smelly buddy downstairs."

Barking Dog hadn't gone home. The girl called Sas had, but only because Block's men had pried her loose from Amato. Block and Barking Dog still weren't wasting any love on one another.

Block and I observed while Relway and crew bagged my villain. Block asked, "You want me to vag him?"

"Say what?"

"Vag Amato. Oh. Sorry. You haven't been in on discussions of the tools we're getting to attack crime. Vagrancy laws. Relway's idea. Came out of the research on those old wizards. Had those kinds of laws in imperial times. You can't show you're gainfully employed or have money in your pocket, bam! You got a sudden choice of getting into a cell or getting out of town. Amato would be had if we went after him. He never has had a job."

"Don't do that." This was some scary shit. "Since when do you go around nailing people because one of your guys has an idea?"

"Since Rupert liked it so much he got it decreed as law. Applies to anybody inside the walls. Race don't matter. There's enough slack in the treaties to let us handle layabouts and social parasites as criminals—if we treat everybody the way we treat humans." Nasty smile.

We might have us some unpleasant times ahead. I hadn't a doubt that the law-and-order gang would deal with human undesirables more nastily than they would others.

"Meantime, my pals Crask and Sadler are out at the kingpin's place scheming up some special way to pay me back for whatever they think I did." That irked me. Block and his boys were panting with law and order, but Crask and Sadler had walked away because of their connections.

"Way it goes, Garrett. I could've let Relway deal with them, but you'da bitched about that too."

"Huh?"

"Crask coulda hanged hisself while he was inside. Out of remorse, maybe." He grinned. Remorse? That was a good one. "Somebody coulda stuck Sadler tonight. But if that'd happened, you'da pissed and moaned until we was all ready to help you swallow a chicken bone."

He was right. Morley was right. I really did have to hone me up a more practical set of ethics. It's a proved fact, fanatic adherence to ideals can be fatal in the real world. Especially in TunFaire, where ethics and ideals are mystic words in a tongue unknown to ninety-nine percent of the population.

I admitted he was right, possibly. "But pretend I'm your conscience sometimes. Don't get so eager taking back the streets that you forget why we have laws in the first place."

"Thanks, Garrett. Any day now I figure to see you in a long gray robe, howling on the steps of the Chancery."

I had to get away. He might brainwash me. I was that tired. He had me

halfway gone already. That was scary, agreeing with the Watch about anything.

Going home wasn't much improvement. I got rid of the worst of my uninvited guests, but then there was still Barking Dog. I wasn't especially kind.
"I've been awake more hours than I know how to count. During that time
three different people tried to kill me." Maybe I exaggerated. Who knows
what might have happened had certain parties had their way? "They tried
to kill friends of mine. The state I'm in, I'm not going to listen to much
complaining. You got a bitch, bring it around in a few days." I didn't remind
him that I wasn't on his payroll and he had no bitch coming.

So much for restraint. My remarks won me all kinds of points with the
ladies. Belinda opened her trick bag and discovered she had eleventeen varieties of hell she could give me for mistreating my elders. Candy got thoroughly huffy and completely forgot who'd just saved her delicate posterior.
She took Barking Dog home and didn't return.

She is his real daughter, the Dead Man told me.

"I figured that out. Didn't even have to count on my fingers."

It is a long story.

"Then don't waste your time telling it. I'm going to bed." I sped Belinda
a meaningful look. It didn't have any meaning for her. She fussed over Dean,
who had set up in the small front room again. Things she told him suggested
she wouldn't be following through on earlier threats.

*Her mother entered a liaison with a man Candy truly believed to be her
father till quite recently.*

"Must we? Now?" I eyed the front door. The door that wasn't anymore.
Could I trust the Dead Man to stay awake while I got some rest?

He indicated he could be trusted. Amidst his tearjerker story, in which
our beautiful young heroine overcame all obstacles to be reunited with her
real father.

"Right, Chuckles. We all saw how she was just foaming at the mouth to
be reunited."

I figured she'd be sick of him in about two days. In fact, she already knew
enough that she hadn't wanted anything direct to do with him till tonight.
Maybe never forever after once she got a look at the dump where he lived.

The Dead Man went on but I was stubborn. I shut him out. I shut out all
their demands and went up to bed. During the several seconds it took me
to fall asleep, I waxed nostalgic about the good old days when I lived alone
and sometimes got to do things the way *I* wanted.

ean let me in through the new door. His arm wasn't broken after all, and our disaster hit the spot for a busybody like him. He'd had work-men in, and was nagging them green, as soon as the sun rose. When I'd been able to sleep through the end-of-the-world racket no longer, I'd gotten up and gotten out, pursuing the Dead Man's suggestion that I double-check on Block and his boys.

"What they did," I told the Dead Man when I got back, "was stuff them in cells while they were unconscious. Then they bricked up the doors. The cells don't have windows. There's a slot in the door so food can be passed through."

That may be enough. Or a sewage chute. . . .

I jumped in smugly. "All taken care of, Smiley. Taken care of. I noticed the business about the rope belts."

The what?

"Rope belts. All our villains wore them. And then Winchell turned up at Hullar's with his belt partly unbraided. The guy that tore up our place had on what looked like it was what was missing from Winchell's rope. I knew what was happening, then. The rope carries the curse."

You failed to mention that.

I snickered. "So I cheated a little so I wouldn't get all the glory hogged away."

What glory? There will be none for you. The public is going to believe that the triumph over the curse is all Captain Block's fault. He will see to it.

Killjoy. "Block has the ropes locked up in a box stashed inside a sealed coffin in another bricked-up cell."

The Dead Man remained dubious, given the ineptitude of the Watch. I was worried too. I concealed it. "Got some final translations on my research. I was right. The whole thing started over a woman. They even found me a portrait of Drachir. . . ."

Who was a ringer for the old man in the coach, I presume.

"Yeah." You can't hold out on a determined mind reader. "And he wore butterfly earrings."

He had a strong interest in butterflies.

"Apparently."

And a stronger interest in outliving his rival.

He was stealing my thunder. Here I'd come home chock-full of news and he was stealing it out of my head or he'd figured it out already. "Yeah. He'd figured out how to become immortal the hard way. When he set up the curse thing, he put an extra twist on it so the Candide woman, who'd spurned him, would be sure to get got. Then he let himself get killed. Didn't matter to him. He would come back to life through his curse. Except his curse always gets stopped just before it finishes re-creating the man who created it."

You have to wonder about people like Drachir, who are willing to sacrifice hundreds on the off chance they might whip death for a while themselves. There are people out there, masquerading as human beings, who never see you and me as having any more value than a beetle. It's a pity they aren't content to devour each other.

I expected either prisoner to kill himself at the curse's behest. The Dead Man disagreed. *That would serve no purpose now. Suppose one of them did bite through the veins in his wrists? What then? Not even Block is stupid enough to enter the cell without a first-line wizard backing him up.*

"Assuming any ever shows up."

Indeed. They may never. They may never leave the Cantard.

"And meantime we got a corpse rotting. Someday somebody gets sick of the stink, opens the cell . . ." The Dead Man had stopped listening. Vaguely, he admitted there might be something to my concern. But I'd made the mistake of nudging his thoughts toward the Cantard. Suddenly he was preoccupied by the south.

There'd been a flood of news. I'd been picking it up all morning, but he'd gotten a big dose from Saucerhead already. That was my buddy Tharpe, rush right in with anything newsworthy—if it was going to make Garrett's life a little more miserable. I love the guy, but he doesn't know from consequences. If brains were glazier's putty, he couldn't weatherproof a windowless room.

Word out of the Cantard made it look like we were in for a Karentine triumph. We could look forward to endless parades and countless mind-numbing speeches.

Karentine losses were as heavy as I'd predicted, but the morCartha had rewritten the Cantard equation completely. The Venageti were done for. They'd collapsed. Quarache was their northernmost outpost now. That was so far to the south, even our long-range commandos hadn't reached it till recently.

And Glory Mooncalled's republican armies, while still motivated and courageous, couldn't overcome the combination of numbers, sorcery, and vastly superior intelligence now ranged against them. These days our commanders knew what the republicans planned before they started doing it.

Didn't take any military genius to see that they'd soon be on the run and the morCartha would be employed to hunt them down.

Hardly anyone believed the news. Many didn't want to believe it. But it was hard to deny evidence that said three generations of warfare would end within a year, that all-out peace might erupt at any time. And all because of some flying things that everybody considered vermin when they were visiting TunFaire.

Goes to show you, as Saucerhead says. You never know. A real philosopher of the street, Saucerhead Tharpe.

The future was becoming scary territory.

Belinda never got the Dead Man down to Morley's place. She did manage to see all the underworld heavyweights and most of her father's nominally legitimate associates. First thing I knew, she was headed home. Crask and Sadler had slipped away from Chodo's place. But they were still around somewhere, biding their time.

Candy faded from my life. She returned to the Hill, probably to escape Barking Dog, who was not welcome up there. Amato kept making a pest of himself, wanting things from me that were beyond my capacity to provide. I could not force open a door into a family that did not want to let him in. I could feel sorry for the guy, maybe, but not much more. I could continue delivering periodic reports to Hullar, without telling Barking Dog, so Candy could keep track. But I couldn't give him what he thought he wanted. I wouldn't give him Candy's adopted family name.

Belinda sent a letter inviting me out. I rented a buggy from Playmate and dragged my bones out to see her. She knew me better than I thought. She waitcd till after playtime to roll her dad out.

Same old Chodo. Frisky as a wedge, alert as a potato. She was using him exactly the way Crask and Sadler had. I was repelled. I left as soon as I could without leaving anyone angry.

I was disappointed. Belinda was no better than the men she'd ousted. She'd become the new kingpin by climbing over her father's still-warm flesh.

Must you? the Dead Man whined. *I was about to doze off. About to abandon this vale of sorrow for the land of sweet dreams.*

"Come on! That's really laying it on thick."

Report, then. Get it over. I need my sleep.

He couldn't have been too depressed, regardless of the war situation. He didn't threaten to close up shop for good.

I have suffered countless disappointments at the hands of your feckless race. One more will not nudge me over the edge. Get on with the report.

I described my visit to the Contague establishment. Most of it. Being a gentleman, I did employ some discretion.

Just to drive me crazy, he observed, *It might be interesting to have Mr. Contague visit sometime. I suspect that all may not be what it seems there.*

"What do you mean by . . . ? Hey!" He'd drifted off. At a very fast drift. And wasn't interested in awaking to explain himself.

Leaving me hanging was the root of his plan, of course.

No more Belinda, no more Candy, and Tinnie still hadn't come around to tell me I didn't need to apologize for what I hadn't done. "You and me again, lady," I told Eleanor. "Alone at last. Maybe. Fingers crossed?" The Dead Man was really working out on his napping, and there was a chance Dean would be getting back out of the house—for a while, anyway. One of his horde of ugly nieces had sold her soul or something and found a blind man to propose. Though I'm not religious, I was praying. No atheists on the battlefield. I wanted the engagement to take. I wanted Dean to travel to the wedding, which would take place out of town if it happened at all. I would get rid of the cat. I would burn a thousand sulfur candles. Or I might sell the place and contents and disappear before the one woke up and the other returned. Simplify my life. Move across town and change my name and get me an honest job.

I did learn that I have the second sight. My prophecy was correct. The next fad was revolution. It stumbled out of the cafés and failed abysmally.

Peopled by the very young, the revolution neither asked nor accepted any-thing from the old and experienced and wise. Westman Block and his secret police, directed by Relway Sencer, ate them alive. The rebellion collapsed without having stirred any dust. Afterward, Block bragged that five mem-bers of the seven-man Joint Revolutionary Direction had been Relway's agents.

Need any more convincing that those fools were fools of the first water? In the real world Block had to pay me to save his bacon when he ran into real troubles.

He hasn't been around lately. Happily. Word is, a whole cabal of wizards has agreed to research and unravel the Candide Curse (how come it isn't called the Drachir Curse?) and keep their eyes on one another so nobody gets any advantage from the spell. Just as soon as they catch Glory Moon-called.

Might be a while.

The Dead Man's hero hasn't given up. Neither the morCartha overhead nor the Venageti proposal of an armistice has daunted him.

Life was good. Life was normal. I could sit back and do some serious thinking and beer tasting.

Then Morley's nephew Spud showed up with the parrot. Supposedly a present from my leg-breaker friend. The parrot could talk. Morley figured I could use it to drive Dean crazy and get rid of his cat. The bird hated cats. It swooped on them, clawed at their ears and eyes.

Word of advice. Word to the wise. Voice of experience. Don't *ever* bring a talking parrot within thinking range of a dead Loghyr. Not *ever*.

Printed in the United States
by Baker & Taylor Publisher Services